DRED

A TALE OF THE
GREAT DISMAL SWAMP

DRED

A TALE OF THE
GREAT DISMAL SWAMP

Harriet Beecher Stowe

Edited with an Introduction and Notes by
Robert S. Levine

The University of North Carolina Press
Chapel Hill

Introduction and notes
© 2000 Robert S. Levine
All rights reserved
First published in the United States of America
by Phillips, Sampson and Company in 1856
Edition with an introduction and notes by Robert S. Levine
first published by Penguin Books in 2000
Published by The University of North Carolina Press in 2006

Manufactured in the United States of America
Set in Stempel Garamond

The paper in this book meets the guidelines for permanence
and durability of the Committee on Production Guidelines for
Book Longevity of the Council on Library Resources.

The Library of Congress has cataloged the original edition as follows:
Stowe, Harriet Beecher, 1811–1896
Dred: a tale of the Great Dismal Swamp / Harriet Beecher Stowe;
edited with an introduction and notes by Robert S. Levine.
p. cm.
Includes bibliographical references (p.)
1. Dismal Swamp (N.C. and Va.)—Fiction. 2. Slave insurrections—Fiction.
3. Fugitive slaves—Fiction. 4. Afro-Americans—Fiction.
I. Levine, Robert S. (Robert Steven), 1953– II. Title
PS2954. D7   2000
813'.3—dc21   00-028409

ISBN 978-0-8078-5685-7 (pbk.: alk. paper)
ISBN 0-8078-5685-1 (pbk.: alk. paper)

10 09 08 07 06   5 4 3 2 1

CONTENTS

Volume II

INTRODUCTION

As the great best seller of the 1850s, Harriet Beecher Stowe's *Uncle Tom's Cabin* (1852) had a marked impact on debates on race and slavery in the United States during that decade and beyond. Its impact was and remains controversial. Abraham Lincoln may have admiringly told Stowe during the Civil War that she was "the little woman who wrote the book that started this great war," but approximately one hundred years after the initial publication of her best-known antislavery novel, Stowe was castigated by the African American novelist and essayist James Baldwin for portraying black as the color of evil and for promoting easy sentimental solutions to racial conflict.[1] Praise and damnation have been the recurrent responses to Stowe's most influential and widely read novel, which has come to be regarded as her one statement on slavery and race, despite the fact that she wrote several antislavery sketches before publishing *Uncle Tom's Cabin* and went on to write a number of works after *Uncle Tom Cabin*—such as *A Key to Uncle Tom's Cabin* (1853) and *The Minister's Wooing* (1859)—that addressed slavery and race from considerably different perspectives.

Most notably, four years after the publication of *Uncle Tom's Cabin*, Stowe published a second antislavery novel, *Dred: A Tale of the Great Dismal Swamp*. This novel was hardly an obscure footnote to her masterwork. *Dred* quickly emerged as one of the most popular novels of the time, selling upwards of 200,000 copies during the nineteenth century and earning the praise of many reviewers, including the British novelist George Eliot, who proclaimed in the October 10, 1856, *Westminster Review* that the novel was "inspired by a rare genius—rare both in intensity and in range of power."[2] The enthusiastic assessments of Eliot and other contemporary reviewers notwithstanding, by the twentieth century the novel had gone out of favor. Since many critics have judged it racist, overly long, and incoherent, the overwhelming response to the novel has been simply to ignore it. There is considerable evidence, however, that Stowe remained not only highly responsive to debates on slavery and race after the publication of *Uncle Tom's Cabin*, but also surprisingly willing to rethink, modify, and revise her views. *Dred* can be read as Stowe's thoughtful novelistic response to the changing political and cultural climate of the mid-1850s, and as her own highly mediated "response" to *Uncle Tom's Cabin*.

It is time to restore *Dred* to a central place in Stowe's canon. Particularly attentive to what African American readers had to say about *Uncle Tom's Cabin*, Stowe in *Dred* revises her racialist representations, attempts new strategies of point of view that would allow for a fuller development of black revolutionary perspectives, and implicitly rejects African colonizationism—endorsed in *Uncle Tom's Cabin*—as a solution to the nation's racial problems. As interesting as Stowe's revised racial politics are in *Dred*, the novel, despite its length, is also a terrifically absorbing and compelling read, in part because the novel is *not* as neat and coherent as *Uncle Tom's Cabin*. *Dred* is a novel to be read next to Herman Melville's *Pierre* (1852) and Nathaniel Hawthorne's *The Marble Faun* (1860), two other fascinating works of the period that, in their length and "incoherence," open a window onto the authors' obsessions and anxieties—the very passions that inspired and informed their writings. In *Uncle Tom's Cabin*, Stowe appears to have a relatively clear sense of how to address the problem of slavery, how to represent race, and how to structure a novel in relation to a scriptural typology that unambiguously depicts good and bad characters and good and bad geographical locations. In *Dred*, on the other hand, Stowe tries out a number of different ways of addressing the problem of slavery, offers conflicting views on race, and shifts between romance and realism as if she were struggling to find the proper novelistic form that could tell the story both of the slave plantation mistress, Nina Gordon, and the black revolutionary, Dred. In many respects, *Dred* is Stowe's most honest and vulnerable fiction, revealing an antebellum novelist who is willing to take risks in an effort to better understand racial difference, and in doing so is not afraid to reveal her own fallibility and dread.

I

Stowe's antislavery writings of the 1850s were bold responses to immediate political and cultural pressures; they can also be read as the culmination of approximately two decades of wrestling with the politics of antislavery within a family context of liberal moderation on the issue. To review some of the familiar biographical facts: A daughter of the nationally prominent Protestant clergyman Lyman Beecher, Stowe was born in Litchfield, Connecticut, in 1811, and eventually moved with her family to Cincinnati in 1832 after her father accepted the presidency of Lane Theological Seminary. She became acutely aware of the controversy over slavery during that time, when a number of Lane students, including the soon-to-be-prominent abolitionist Theodore Dwight Weld, rebelled against Lyman Beecher's lukewarm antislavery position—he supported shipping American blacks to a colony in Africa—and withdrew from the seminary in 1834. Shortly thereafter, her sister Catharine Beecher, a prominent educator and domestic theorist, debated the South Carolina abolitionist Angelina Grimké in print on the role of women in the antislavery movement, with Grimké calling on women to take a public stance in speaking out against slavery (*Appeal to the Christian Women of the South* [1836], *Letters to Catharine Beecher* [1836]), while Catharine Beecher insisted that women could exert a more generalized moral influence on U.S. society from within the home (*Essay on Slavery and Abolition, with Reference to the Duty of American Females* [1837]). In 1836, a year that saw major anti-abolitionist riots in Cincinnati, Harriet Beecher married Calvin Stowe, a professor of theology at Lane. She had published sketches in newspapers and magazines during the 1830s, but perhaps because of her sympathy for her father's colonizationism and her sister's domestic politics of moral reform, it was not until 1845 that she published her first antislavery sketch, "Immediate Emancipation." After Calvin was appointed to a chair at Bowdoin College, she moved to Brunswick, Maine, in 1850. Outraged by the Fugitive Slave Law provision of the Compromise of 1850, which made all U.S. citizens legally obligated to return fugitive slaves to their masters, she began working on *Uncle Tom's Cabin*. The novel was serialized from June 5, 1851, to April 1, 1852, in the *National Era* and published as a book in the spring of 1852. It promptly sold out its first printing, selling 300,000 copies in its first year, and more than 1,000,000 copies by the end of the decade.

Influenced by her reading of slave narratives and abolitionist tracts, such as Weld's *American Slavery As It Is* (1839), and haunted by the death of her infant son Charley in 1849, Stowe depicted slavery as an iniquitous institution that separated mothers from children, husbands from wives, and generally wreaked havoc on both the black and white family. Through her use of direct address, she attempted to make her readers identify with the plight of the novel's embattled slaves. Sharing the domestic ideals of her sister Catharine Beecher, she depicted benevolent white women as having the potential to regenerate the United States by wielding moral influence from within the home. But in a world in which slaveholders like Simon Legree have unlimited power to torture, rape, and kill their slaves, slavery ultimately proves to be an insurmountable force of evil for most of the women of the novel. Clearly concerned about the plight of the black slaves, Stowe nonetheless follows the racialist thinking of the time in depicting blacks as essentially different from whites. Blacks are described as more passive and domestic than whites, and thus as having the potential, as evidenced by the martyrdom of Uncle Tom, to be better Christians than whites. The novel ends with the major black characters either dead or choosing to become missionaries in Africa. By depicting slavery as part of a national economy that benefits Northern investors and Southern masters alike, Stowe's novel can be read as an attack on capitalism and patriarchy. But overall what most concerns Stowe is the blasphemous nature of slavery, the way it encourages whites to assume godlike superiority over blacks. In the manner of a sermon, *Uncle Tom's Cabin* calls on the whites in power to diminish their potential for sinning by educating liberated blacks so that they can bring forth a redemptive black Christian republic in Africa.

The publication of *Uncle Tom's Cabin* made Stowe one of the best-known and respected antislavery voices of the period. Unsurprisingly, the novel was not her last word on slavery. In response to the complaints of some reviewers that she exaggerated the horrors of slavery, she collected supporting documentary evidence from newspapers, court cases, abolitionist tracts, slave narratives, and many other sources, and published *A Key to Uncle Tom's Cabin* in 1853. Shortly after the publication of *A Key* she set sail for England, arriving in Liverpool in April 1853 and commencing an approximately two-month antislavery lecture tour of Great Britain, where *Uncle Tom's Cabin* was even more popular than in the United States. As a sign of that popularity, she was presented in May with an antislavery proclamation, "An Affectionate and Christian Address of Many Thousands of Women of Great Britain and Ireland to Their Sisters the Women of the United States of America," signed by over half a million women of the British Isles. After touring France, Germany, and the Swiss Alps, Stowe, in September of that year, returned to Andover, Massachusetts, where her husband had assumed a new teaching position, and confronted an increasingly polarized political landscape.

Particularly worrisome to Stowe were the heated debates concerning the unsettled territories of Kansas and Nebraska. In January 1854, the Illinois senator Stephen A. Douglas proposed a bill calling for the repeal of the Missouri Compromise's ban on slavery in the territories north of latitude 36° 30', arguing that the settlers themselves should have the right to determine whether or not to legalize slavery in their new state constitutions. Attempting to marshal opposition to the bill, Stowe penned one of her most powerful antislavery statements, "An Appeal to the Women of the Free States of America, on the Present Crisis in Our Country," which was published in the New York *Independent* on February 23, 1854. In the "Appeal," Stowe urged women to fight the spread of slavery into the territories by undertaking petition drives and employing antislavery lecturers, and she offered the hope that "in the agitation of this question between the North and the South, the way of principle may not become a mere sectional conflict, degenerating into the encounter of physical force."[3] But violence was precisely what came about following the passage of the Kansas-Nebraska Bill on May 26, 1854, exacerbated in large part by Douglas's support for popular sovereignty. By late 1855, around the time Stowe began writing *Dred*, conflict between proslavery and antislavery forces in the Kansas and Nebraska territories had intensified. During May 1856, in what was dubbed "the sack of Lawrence," proslavery forces attacked Lawrence, Kansas, and destroyed the property and printing presses of the town's antislavery contingent. In response, the fiery abolitionist John Brown led an attack on proslavery groups at Pottawotomie Creek, killing five men. Just a few days earlier, at a time when Stowe was well into drafting *Dred*, the South Carolina congressman Preston Brooks struck and severely injured Massachusetts senator Charles Sumner with a gutta-percha cane two days after Sumner delivered an antislavery speech in Congress. Stunned by the attack, Stowe, who deeply admired Sumner, added a scene to her novel that describes a similar assault, not in the chambers of Congress but by the Dismal Swamp.

As a postscript to this sketch of the historical backgrounds of *Dred*, it should be noted that in March 1857, approximately six months after the publication of *Dred*, the Supreme Court issued its controversial ruling on *Dred Scott v. Sandford*, which asserted that African Americans had no legal rights in the United States and could never become citizens. The ruling also addressed the territorial issues raised by the Kansas-Nebraska Act, asserting in the broadest and most unambiguous terms that federal efforts to exclude slavery from the territories were unconstitutional. Though it seems unlikely that Stowe named her black revolutionary hero after Dred Scott (she claims Dred was named after one of Nat Turner's co-conspirators), the fact is that the case began to be heard in the Supreme Court in early 1856, and there is much in Stowe's prescient second novel that looks forward to these ominous developments of 1857.

The battles in "bleeding Kansas" led Stowe to write a novel that is less hopeful and arguably less naive than *Uncle Tom's Cabin*. White benevolence has relatively little impact on the events of *Dred*. Far more effective is black resistance and violence, and arguably the most eloquent antislavery voices in the novel belong to the black characters. Stowe's risky decision to try to develop those voices and perspectives was influenced not only by immediate social and political developments but also by critical responses to her first novel from white Southerners and black abolitionists. Because *Dred* can be read, in part, as a response to those responses, it would be useful briefly to review the reception of *Uncle Tom's Cabin* among these very different constituencies.

Not surprisingly, response to *Uncle Tom's Cabin* in the South was swift and furious, as numerous reviewers assailed Stowe for what they regarded as her libelous attacks on the South's cherished institutions. According to George F. Holmes, who reviewed the novel in the October 1852 *Southern Literary Messenger*, Stowe failed to see that it was precisely the institution of slavery that was responsible for producing such a perfect slave as Uncle Tom. In the July 1853 *Southern Quarterly Review*, the novelist William Gilmore Simms was even more vitriolic in his criticism of the novel, joining Holmes in arguing that Uncle Tom's saintliness testified to the positive value of slavery, and attacking Stowe personally as a depraved woman for having dared to write about sexual and political matters. Simms also argued that it was inappropriate to use the literary form of the novel to proffer social criticism. Nevertheless, Simms and other Southern writers quickly concluded that the most effective argument against what they regarded as the scurrilous representation of the South in *Uncle Tom's Cabin* would be to offer counter-representations. The period thus saw the publication of numerous anti–*Uncle Tom's Cabin* novels, notably Mary H. Eastman's *Aunt Phillis's Cabin* (1852), Maria J. McIntosh's *The Lofty and the Lowly* (1853), Simms's *Woodcraft* (1854), Caroline Lee Hentz's *The Planter's Northern Bride* (1854), and Thomas B. Thorpe's *The Master's House* (1854).[4] These works generally portrayed benign slave masters and contented slaves who thrived in the familial, paternalistic framework of the plantation. In Hentz's *The Planter's Northern Bride*, for example, a book Stowe probably read, since she and Hentz were on friendly terms in Cincinnati, the rebellious slaves of the plantation are depicted as the products of abolitionist meddling and are ultimately disdained by the contented black slaves. An attempt to restore agency to black characters in the setting of the plantation novel—and thus to offer her own response to Southern reaction to *Uncle Tom's Cabin*—may have been one of the large inspirations behind Stowe's decision to write a second antislavery novel.

An even more crucial inspiration was the response of African Americans to *Uncle Tom's Cabin*. Several black writers, including Martin R. Delany, criticized Stowe in the pages of *Frederick Douglass' Paper*, to which Stowe subscribed, for her apparent advocacy of Liberian colonization as a solution to the nation's racial problems—an idea advanced by the American Colonization Society. Founded in 1816 by antislavery moderates and subsequently championed by an odd mix of liberal clergy (such as Lyman Beecher) and Southern slaveholders, the society hoped to bring about the eventual end of slavery and racial conflict in the United States by shipping the nation's blacks to the African colony of Liberia. Stowe essentially supported that position in the final chapter of *Uncle Tom's Cabin*. In response to Delany's and other blacks' criticisms of Stowe's novel as colonizationist, Frederick Douglass, who championed Stowe because he thought *Uncle Tom's Cabin* had the potential to do more good than harm, asserted in his paper that Stowe may have become "more of an abolitionist now than when she wrote that chapter."[5] The evidence suggests that Stowe did change her mind on colonization, perhaps in response to black debate in *Frederick Douglass' Paper*, for she sent a letter to the May 1853 meeting of the American and Foreign Anti-Slavery Society declaring, in the paraphrased words of the proceedings, "that if she were to write 'Uncle Tom' again, she would not send George Harris to Liberia."[6] In *Dred*, she chooses to send no black characters to Liberia.

Stowe's change of mind on Liberia is not an isolated instance of her willingness to attend to black writings and views, and it is precisely her effort to comprehend such views that makes *Dred* more black-centered, revolutionary, and morally challenging than *Uncle Tom's Cabin*. Following the publication of *Uncle Tom's Cabin*, Stowe, as America's best-known white antislavery writer, had numerous encounters with African Americans. In 1852 she helped the former slave Milly Edmondson purchase her children from slavery and send two of her daughters to Oberlin College. That same year she corresponded with Harriet Jacobs about the possibility of helping Jacobs write her life history, and she entertained Sojourner Truth for several days at her home. One year later she entertained Frederick Douglass at her home. During her 1853 antislavery lecture tour of England, she had numerous firsthand encounters with black abolitionists, including William Wells Brown, William G. Allen, William and Ellen Craft, and Samuel Ward. In a remarkable shift from the racialism that informs *Uncle Tom's Cabin*, Stowe writes about Ward in her 1854 travel book, *Sunny Memories of Foreign Lands*: "All who converse with him are satisfied that there is no native difference between the African and other men."[7]

In the spirit of such egalitarianism, Stowe championed the careers of two black female performers, the singer Elizabeth Greenfield and the actress Mary Webb, for whom she wrote *The Christian Slave* (1855), a dramatic version of *Uncle Tom's Cabin*. She also wrote the introductions to three major African American texts of the 1850s: William C. Nell's *The Colored Patriots of the American Revolution* (1855), Frank J. Webb's *The Garies and Their Friends* (1857), and Josiah Henson's *Truth Stranger Than Fiction* (1858). In a review-essay of 1856 entitled "Anti-Slavery Literature," she spoke directly of the impact of black writers on her thinking, praising the autobiographies of Josiah Henson, Henry Bibb, Lewis Clarke, Frederick Douglass, and William Wells Brown for the ways in which they allowed readers "to know how a human heart like our own felt and thought and struggled, coming up in so strange a state as that of slavery."[8]

Stowe's effort to work her way into a black perspective on slavery is central to her achievement in *Dred*. In a passage from late in the novel that can be taken as a "key" to *Dred*, Stowe reflects on the importance of attempting to understand slavery from the point of view of the enslaved:

> There is no study in human nature more interesting than the aspects of the same subject seen in the points of view of different characters. One might almost imagine that there were no such thing as absolute truth, since a change of situation or temperament is capable of changing the whole force of an argument. We have been accustomed, even those of us who feel most, to look on the arguments for and against the system of slavery with the eyes of those who are at ease. We do not even know how fair is freedom, for we were always free. We shall never have all the materials for absolute truth on this subject, till we take into account, with our own views and reasonings, the views and reasonings of those who have bowed down to the yoke, and felt the iron enter into their souls. (445)[9]

This passage conveys the sorts of epistemological uncertainties and anxieties that we have come to regard as central to many of the canonical works of the "American Renaissance," texts that foreground interpretive dilemmas by emphasizing the shifts in meaning that come with shifts in interpretive perspective. Though Stowe's relatively firm belief in Christ's redemptive role in human history keeps her from reaching the sorts of interpretive abysses that one encounters, say, in *Moby-Dick*, *Dred* represents a brave departure from *Uncle Tom's Cabin* in the way it challenges her white readers' comfortable perspectives on the problem of slavery. Domesticity and sympathy go only so far in *Dred*, a novel that ultimately asks its readers to consider slavery from the point of view of black revolutionaries lurking in the recesses of the Dismal Swamp.

II

Despite its antislavery politics and avowed effort to comprehend black perspectives, *Dred* at first glance can seem oddly indebted to the plantation novel tradition inaugurated by John Pendleton Kennedy's *Swallow Barn* (1832) and reenergized by Southern novelists' responses to *Uncle Tom's Cabin*. The novel begins rather conventionally by focusing on the travails of the eighteen-year-old plantation belle, Nina Gordon, who has frivolously accepted marriage proposals from three different suitors but has rather quickly come to realize that she loves just one of them, Edward Clayton, who owns a slave plantation in South Carolina. Because her parents are dead and her younger brother Tom Gordon is an intemperate scamp, Nina is expected to play a central role in watching over the slaves of her North Carolina plantation. As in the typical plantation novel, the reader is introduced to such stock characters as the "mammy" Aunt Katy, the lazy stable-hand Old Hundred, and the pompous house-servant Uncle Pomp. But, unlike in the plantation novel, the reader is also introduced to a number of substantial and complex black characters. Supervising the plantation, for instance, is a light-complected slave named Harry who, unbeknownst to Nina, happens to be her older half-brother. As in William Wells Brown's *Clotel* (1853), Frederick Douglass's *My Bondage and My Freedom* (1855), Harriet Jacobs's *Incidents in the Life of a Slave Girl* (1861), and many other works by African American writers, Stowe's account of the genealogical background of the Gordon family exposes the licentiousness of the patriarchal master and the tragic consequences for the children. For much of the novel, Harry remains caught between his love for his wife, Lisette, and his love for Nina. But precisely because he loves his sister, he, too, can appear to be a loyal slave who hopes for the best for his slave mistress.

By focusing on the burgeoning romance between Nina and Clayton, Stowe, again in the manner of the plantation novel, initially situates her readers primarily with the white masters. Because of the centrality of the whites' point of view in the opening third or so of the novel, the racial politics of *Dred* can seem similar to the racial politics of *Uncle Tom's Cabin*, which depends on racialist notions of essential differences between "white" and "black" blood as a way of understanding character and action. The historian George M. Fredrickson has coined the term "Romantic Racialism" to describe Harriet Beecher Stowe's and other liberal whites' paternalistic views of blacks' supposed racial differences from whites. Influenced by Alexander Kinmont's *Twelve Lectures on the Natural History of Man* (1839), Stowe celebrated blacks in *Uncle Tom's Cabin* for what she believed were their more naturally Christian ways—domestic, noncompetitive, relatively passive.[10] *Dred* presents a far more complicated picture of race. To be sure, there are numerous suggestions in the novel that Stowe clings to racialist beliefs that blood differences produce differing behaviors—hence her insistence on emphasizing racial genealogies when introducing the various black characters. Harry's conflicted rebelliousness, for example, is initially linked to the blood mixture bequeathed by his hotheaded white father and "the soft and genial temperament of the beautiful Eboe mulatress who was his mother" (38). But in *Dred*, much more than in *Uncle Tom's Cabin*, Stowe also suggests the limits of racialism as a way of understanding character and action. In doing so, she takes her leave of the world of the Southern plantation novel and departs as well from the racial orthodoxies that had informed her first novel.

Stowe's most crucial revision of the color politics of *Uncle Tom's Cabin* is her challenge of the linkage of black skin (and blood) to a Christian domestic acquiescence—a linkage that had been central to her characterization of the black-skinned martyr Uncle Tom. In her portrayals of *Dred*'s major black-skinned characters (Aunt Milly, Old Tiff, and Dred), she takes pains to emphasize the central role played by the characters' evolving political consciousnesses. Tiff, for example, would appear to fit the bill of the loyal black slave, for he happily chooses to devote his life to serving the vulnerable white Cripps children after the death of their mother, in large part, it seems, because he is convinced that Fanny and Teddy are descendants of the "aristocratic" Peytons of Virginia. But even as he reveals what is clearly a compromised racial consciousness, he regularly demonstrates a shrewd awareness of the ways in which his performance of subordination allows him the freedom, say, to aid the rebellious slaves of the Dismal Swamp. Aunt Milly also appears to be the stereotypical loyal and religious slave, displaying a Christ-like capacity for suffering akin to Uncle Tom's. But when she describes to Nina (in a story drawn from the *Narrative of Sojourner Truth* [1850]) how her former mistress's betrayal led to the death of her youngest son, her rage at that mistress, as the increasingly distraught Nina senses, seems to focus on the white auditor at hand. Though Milly goes on to describe her subsequent Christian conversion, which leads her to affirm her love even for whites, Stowe's powerful account of Milly's storytelling to the unnerved white mistress makes it clear that proslavery idealizations of hierarchical relations on the plantation based on racialized notions of black submissiveness and dependency fail to address the deeper realities of black rage.

The black rebel Dred may be taken as the very embodiment of that rage; indeed, it is black rage that summons Dred into the novel. Angered by Tom Gordon's efforts to purchase Lisette as his sexual slave, Harry confronts his half-brother at the margins of the swamp only to receive a whipping in the face. Following Tom's departure, a mysterious black man emerges from the swamps, who is greeted by Harry with the offhand remark: "O, it is you, then, Dred!" (198). Harry's immediate recognition of Dred, who has not even been mentioned in the first seventeen chapters of the novel, enacts a point of rupture, as readers will initially find themselves disoriented by their own lack of knowledge of the existence and motives of this swamp-dwelling black man. Lacking Harry's casual knowledge of Dred's lurking presence, readers are linked with the plantation whites. This is a canny narrative strategy on Stowe's part, similar to Herman Melville's slyly implicating narrative strategies in his 1855 novella of black revolt, *Benito Cereno*. With the introduction of Dred (as with the revelation of the black plot in *Benito Cereno*), what we experience is a moment of revelation: that Stowe in a deliberately implicating fashion has to this point encouraged a reading of blacks and the plantation that is partial and misleading, for she has left out of the picture the presence of black revolutionaries. Her subsequent detailed account of Dred's background and activities significantly extends the reach of the plantation novel.

Initially described in terms of his black skin, muscular body, and African racial identity, Dred is an active revolutionary who uses violence to fight violence, traversing North Carolina and Virginia in an effort to recruit additional fugitive slaves to his community in the Dismal Swamp. In her most dramatic revision of the politics of color that had informed *Uncle Tom's Cabin*, Stowe thus soundly rejects the equation of black skin (and blood) to domestic passivity, focusing on the political (not just racial) genealogy of Dred's black political consciousness. Developing a perspective on black revolutionism similar to that informing Douglass's 1852 lecture "What To the Slave Is the Fourth of July?," Stowe legitimates black violence against the Southern slave power by depicting it as in the tradition of the violence deployed by the patriots of the American Revolution against the British "slave power."

Other key African American sources for Stowe's revisionary thinking on black revolutionary violence would have been Douglass's 1853 novella, *The Heroic Slave*, which celebrates the black-skinned leader of the 1841 rebellion aboard the *Creole*, and William Wells Brown's *Clotel*, which presents a powerful description of the black-skinned slave rebel Picquilo hiding out in the swamps. But perhaps the most crucial African American source for her revisionary thinking on the possibilities of black revolutionism was W. C. Nell's *The Colored Patriots of the American Revolution* (1855), for which Stowe wrote the introduction. Nell, in addition to supplying lengthy commentary on black participants in the Revolutionary War and the War of 1812, also provides discussions of black provocateurs and conspirators such as Denmark Vesey, David Walker, Nat Turner, and the Virginia maroons of the Great Dismal Swamp. In a chapter on the Virginia maroons, a term that refers to a community of runaway slaves, Nell writes: "The Great Dismal Swamp, which lies near the Eastern shore of Virginia, and, commencing near Norfolk, stretches quite into North Carolina, contains a large colony of negroes, who originally obtained their freedom by the grace of God and their own determined energy, instead of the consent of their owners, or by the help of the Colonization Society." A consecrated group of revolutionaries, the colony has "endured from generation to generation," Nell proclaims, "and is likely to continue until slavery is abolished throughout the land."[11]

These are precisely the terms in which Stowe represents Dred and his accomplices, the heirs of Denmark Vesey and Nat Turner, the two most famous (or notorious) black revolutionaries of the antebellum period. In *Dred*, Stowe provides one of the few accounts by an antebellum white of Denmark Vesey as a revolutionary hero. A literate free black carpenter in Charleston, South Carolina, Vesey in the early months of 1822 allegedly attempted to unite the city's free and enslaved blacks in a plot to kill the whites of the city and eventually escape to the Caribbean.[12] Betrayed by one or two house servants, Vesey was captured in June and executed along with more than thirty of his comrades. In the trial records of the time, Vesey was depicted as a bloodthirsty madman who was perverted by his reading of Northern antislavery speeches. By contrast, Stowe, in *Dred*, through selective use of the actual transcript of the 1822 trial, portrays Vesey and his accomplices as patriots who were inspired by their reading of the Declaration of Independence and the Bible to enact their own revolution against despotic authority. Unlike the Bible-reading Uncle Tom and Milly, Vesey deploys a typological reading of the Old Testament to legitimate uprisings against pharaonic oppressors, and he works in tandem with Gullah Jack, an African sorcerer who is regarded as diabolical by the white authorities. But what the white authorities of Charleston regarded as diabolical is represented by Stowe as central to the African American revolutionary consciousness that the historical Vesey and his compatriots bequeath to Stowe's fictional invention. Dred, as Vesey's son in the book, is a stand-in for another "son" or ideological descendent of Vesey, Nat Turner, who in 1831 led a bloody slave rebellion in Southampton, Virginia, that resulted in the deaths of approximately fifty whites. Vengeful whites subsequently killed more than twice that number of blacks.

In her account of the genealogical inheritance of Vesey's revolutionism by her Nat Turner–like hero Dred, Stowe explores the political, familial, and spiritual goals that guide Dred toward his own revolutionary action. At age ten a confidant of his father's conspiratorial plot, Dred, upon the capture of Vesey, pretends to dislike him so he can carry on his father's work. Sold from one plantation to the next, feared by overseers throughout the region because of his "desperate, unsubduable disposition" (209), Dred eventually kills an overseer (an act Stowe never condemns) and escapes to the swamps, where he begins the process of developing his ever-expanding swamp community of black revolutionaries. Experiencing moments of religious exaltation similar to those described by Nat Turner in Thomas Gray's 1831 *The Confessions of Nat Turner*, Dred regards Scripture as a living, unfolding text. Convinced that he has been chosen by God to be the prophetic avenger and liberator of his people, he spends much of his time in a dreamlike state in search of messages from God. While Stowe at times suggests the possibility that Dred may be mad or simply an inspired actor, the bulk of the descriptions present his revolutionism in relation to the political and spiritual consciousness bequeathed him by his father and his father's African sorcerer associate, Gullah Jack. In this way Stowe shows how the Bible can link syncretically with American political ideology and African spiritualism to encourage a rightful resistance to the authority of the slave masters.

Viewing Dred in this cultural context helps us to see that Stowe means to represent Dred's Afro-Christianity as a legitimate antislavery perspective that turns the world of the plantation novel upside down. Nowhere is this more apparent than in the great account of the camp meeting at the midpoint of the novel. Depicting the intemperate drinking and slave-trading that go on in the midst of the camp meeting, Stowe presents Dred as the true minister of the meeting when he interrupts the sermon of the corrupt slaveholder Father Bonnie to speak on judgment, wrath, and vengeance. As Dred preaches with an uncanny devotional energy, Stowe keeps the point of view fixed on the whites, who can barely make sense of what Dred is saying and cannot even see him. Yet the auditors are stirred by his impassioned declarations, fearing that they may have come under the judgment of a genuine prophet. After delivering his prophecies, Dred disappears into the thickets, but it remains difficult not to read all subsequent events of the novel in relation to our knowledge of Dred's lurking presence. That presence, which points to the limits of whites' perspectives on slavery and race, presses readers to assess unfolding events from the blacks' point of view and to remain suspicious of all explanatory narratives put forth by the novel's white characters.

(First-time readers of *Dred* should be forewarned that the remainder of the introduction discusses major plot developments of the novel.)

Stowe's creation of what could be termed a black counternarrative that, among other things, challenges and revises the racial politics of *Uncle Tom's Cabin*, is one of the great achievements of *Dred*. It becomes increasingly clear, for example, that Nina can no longer be viewed in an autonomous relationship to white Southern culture. To the very end, she remains ignorant of her genealogical connection to Harry (and presumably to some of the other slaves on her plantation); her religious growth as well has to be read in relation to the black culture that she sees but does not see. Undergoing a moral and spiritual growth that eventually leads her to want to free her slaves, Nina is guided as much by the spirituality of Tiff and Milly as by Clayton. When she succumbs to cholera several hundred pages before the end of the novel, there is every sense that her apparent salvation has come about through the spiritual ministering of the slaves she does not live to free.

Though Clayton, like Nina, turns out to be a "good" slave master who hopes to liberate his slaves, he can seem as blind as any of the other white characters to the black presence in the Dismal Swamp. Thus he repeatedly comments on blacks' need for paternalistic supervision. Consistent with Stowe's efforts to challenge whites to consider blacks' "views and reasonings," she eventually leads Clayton to the swamps, but not before he begins to see the limits of his own point of view through a series of painfully revelatory interactions with Harry, who joins Dred in the swamps, and his reenslaved sister Cora, who chooses to kill her own children rather than allow them to be taken into slavery. By the time the intemperate, power-driven Tom Gordon uses his gutta-percha cane to strike Clayton, as he had struck Harry, Clayton has proven his eligibility for the swamps. Rescued by Harry and Dred, Clayton is nursed within the maroon community, where he is surprised to find Tiff and the white children in his charge. A novel that begins with readers viewing the slave plantation from the perspective of Nina Gordon, the mistress of the plantation, now looks out at slave culture from the perspective of the revolutionary slaves of Dred's swamp community. Over the course of several interviews with Dred, Clayton begins to approach an understanding of African American revolutionism, coming close to concluding that there are compelling reasons for blacks to adopt the tactics of violent insurrectionism.

But is a slave rebellion moral and proper? That is one of the large questions debated in the novel, with whites clearly opposed (or blind to the possibility) and major black characters divided on the issue. As she does with *Dred*'s other thematic concerns, Stowe makes it clear that the issue of violence cannot be considered apart from blacks' points of view. Drawing on a widely reported confrontation between Sojourner Truth and Frederick Douglass at an 1852 antislavery meeting, Stowe reveals that blacks' attitudes toward violence are not necessarily monolithic. As Stowe described the confrontation in an 1863 *Atlantic* article, "Sojourner Truth, the Libyan Sibyl," Douglass and Truth took opposing positions on the question of slave violence, with Douglass calling for active resistance and Truth (the sympathetic figure in the article) responding that violence went against the spirit of God. Though Stowe positions Milly, the Truth character in *Dred*, in the camp of Christian patience and forgiveness, she is not all that firm in her alliance with Milly, and she allows Dred equal place and stature in articulating a rationale for a slave insurrection.

Milly and Dred had initiated their "debate" on black violence at the moment of Dred's introduction into the novel. When Dred attempts to lure Harry into his revolutionary community, Milly arrives on the scene to preach Christian forgiveness, and she seems to win out when Harry returns to the plantation. The debate between Milly and Dred resumes after Harry has joined Dred's maroon community.

When the news arrives that one of Dred's compatriots has been killed by Tom Gordon, Dred's response is to call for a "day of vengeance" (459) in which black rebels attempt to kill as many whites as possible. At this point Milly enters the scene, singing the praises of Christ as a peaceful, loving Lamb. There are indications that Stowe, again in a major revision of *Uncle Tom's Cabin*, sees the limits of Milly's position even as she respects and attempts to delineate *both* Milly's and Dred's perspectives on blacks' proper course of action. Milly's ability to love whites who enslave her may well suggest her transcendent religiosity, but even Clayton comes to see the limitations of her advice that blacks should await "de new covenant" (461). She certainly fails to persuade Dred to renounce his plans for a slave insurrection. What keeps him from taking violent action along the lines of a Nat Turner is that, when looking for a sign from God, he discerns only silence. Thus he continues to marshal his maroon community as a protective rather than aggressive force that attempts to check the state's brutal legal and policing authority. As a protector, liberator, and revolutionary, he remains to the very end the genuine hero of the novel.

Stowe makes Dred's heroism the cause of his fall, for it is precisely his brave decision to venture out on his own to spy on Tom Gordon's drunken, homicidal crew that leads to his death. Returning to the swamps bleeding from a wound in his breast, Dred, like Uncle Tom, is described in Christ-like spiritual terms, with the implication being that his imminent death has every promise of being as redemptive and sacred as Eva's and Tom's in *Uncle Tom's Cabin*. Even with respect to Nina's conversion and death, the two chapters on Dred's death would appear to constitute the sacred space of the novel. Stowe writes of Dred's compatriots' vigil: "It was evident to the little circle that He who is mightier than the kings of earth was there" (513). Stowe has not simply "killed off" or punished Dred for advocating self-protective violence over Milly's choice of love and patience. She has instead figured a glorious, redemptive death for him in the far reaches of the swamps, guiding the reader to share a moment of sacred community among the maroons and their allies: Harry, Tiff, and Clayton.

III

With the deaths of Nina and Dred, the question remains: "What is to be done?" This is the title of the concluding chapter of Stowe's *A Key to Uncle Tom's Cabin* (1853), and it is the paramount question begged by *Dred*'s increasingly bleak presentation of a Southern slave society presided over by Tom Gordon and his drunken minions. "What is to be done?" is also the question begged by the unfolding events of *Uncle Tom's Cabin*, and Stowe's suggested answers at the conclusion of her first antislavery novel have left a number of readers, both of her time and beyond, deeply unsatisfied. In that novel, Stowe appears to suggest two principal solutions to the problem of slavery in the United States: prayer and African colonization. We have already seen that African American leaders were angered by Stowe's apparent willingness to endorse African colonization, and that in response to their anger Stowe renounced colonizationism approximately a year after the publication of *Uncle Tom's Cabin*. Like Frederick Douglass and others who criticized her, she adopted the view that blacks have earned their rights to citizenship in the United States and should have a vital role in the nation's economic and spiritual future. In fact, there are hints of this perspective in the ending of *Uncle Tom's Cabin* when, after urging Northern whites to educate blacks so that they may journey to Africa "to put in practice the lessons they have learned in America," she describes a number of African Americans, including Frederick Douglass, who have successfully achieved "highly respectable stations" in U.S. society.[13] It is worth underscoring that in direct response to the question of "What is to be done?" in *Key*, she says nothing about African colonization and instead champions abolition and programs of education that would help to bring about black elevation in the United States. Sounding rather like Frederick Douglass and other African Americans working for black uplift, Stowe calls for an end to the segregationist practices that hinder blacks' efforts to rise in the culture, urging her white readers in particular: "As far as in you lies, endeavor to secure for them [free and enslaved blacks], in every walk of life, the ordinary privileges of American citizens."[14]

In *Dred*, Stowe is not quite as sanguine about the prospects for black elevation in the United States, though she certainly entertains that possibility as one answer to the question of what should be done. But, more importantly, the novel's complex ending points to the dangers of pigeonholing Stowe as an advocate of any particular "solution." For example, it appears for a long stretch of the novel that Stowe fundamentally supports the Claytons' reformist efforts to educate and emancipate the approximately four hundred slaves on their plantation.

Anne Clayton in particular, who teaches her slaves the importance of education, hygiene, industry, and Christianity, seems an especially sympathetic figure, perhaps a mouthpiece for Stowe's own views about how best to ensure that liberated blacks will have a central role to play in U.S. culture. But as Anne herself comes to realize, her goal of gradual emancipation through education is doomed to failure as long as most Southern whites remain hostile to the project. In chapters such as "The Legal Decision" and "The Clerical Conference," Stowe shows how those in power make use of legal and religious institutions to perpetuate their power. Acutely aware of what could be termed the *realpolitik* of social hegemony, she teaches those bleak lessons to the Claytons and her readers, particularly through her account of Judge Clayton's decision, based on Judge Thomas Ruffin's famous 1829 ruling in the North Carolina case of *State v. Mann,* that "THE POWER OF THE MASTER MUST BE ABSOLUTE, TO RENDER THE SUBMISSION OF THE SLAVE PERFECT" (353). It is only after Edward Clayton has spent some time in the swamps and returned to confront the social anarchy unleashed by Tom Gordon that he reaches Anne's conclusion that gradualist reform in the South is hopeless. Clayton's spineless friend Russel, who glibly capitulates to Southern slave culture in order to improve his chances of winning a state election, asserts that Anne and Edward have one of two options with their slaves: "You must either send them to Liberia, or to the Northern States" (537). Significantly, they choose to do neither.

Rather than arguing for Liberian colonization, Stowe, like Martin Delany, Mary Ann Shadd Cary, and many other black abolitionists, shows the advantages of black *emigration* to Canada. In Sarah J. Hale's colonizationist antislavery novel *Liberia; or, Mr. Peyton's Experiments* (1853), the noble white master Mr. Peyton, before taking his emancipated slaves to Liberia, tries out Canada, only to find that his former slaves hate the cold climate and are incapable of developing anything more than dilapidated tenements. Anne and Edward Clayton achieve quite different results when they lead their liberated slaves to Canada. Using funds secured from the sale of their plantation to purchase a tract of land in Canada, the Claytons help to establish a black township that, with its integrated schools and thriving farms, quickly becomes the envy of surrounding communities. Stowe informs her readers in a footnote that the community's success mirrors the success of the Elgin settlement founded in 1849 by the Presbyterian minister William King.

One of the most successful and admired of Canada's black communities, Elgin empowered its black participants by allowing them voting and property rights. Though Clayton, like King, retains a paternalistic relationship to the former slaves, whom he seeks to elevate with his money and reformist energies, the fact is that the blacks have a central place in Clayton's township. The intelligent and literate Harry and Hannibal emerge as the town's leaders, and Jim, Tom Gordon's former slave, becomes an industrious farmer. Moreover, because Clayton does not have an heir by the end of the novel, Stowe implicitly suggests that upon his death the community will become the responsibility of its black leaders and their children.

And yet it is crucial to note that Stowe presents the Claytons' emigration project as but one of several possibilities for the novel's black characters. Stowe also describes blacks who are not "sent" to the North, as Russel advises, but rather escape to New York on their own terms. Significantly, Dred's compatriots in the Dismal Swamp are not the only blacks who make their way North. Rejecting the role of martyr that she seems to have embraced and championed, Aunt Milly decides to escape with her grandchild Tomtit. By linking Milly to a grandchild whose odd name evokes the titular hero of her first antislavery novel, Stowe, in a departure from *Uncle Tom's Cabin*, has Milly rescue herself from what *Dred* increasingly suggests would have been a pointless Uncle Tom–like martyrdom at the hands of Southern enslavers. Through her subsequent account of Milly's social-reform work in New York City, Stowe provides a stateside rewriting of the African missionary work of the escaped slaves in *Uncle Tom's Cabin* and thus conveys her post-1852 conviction that the free blacks had an important role to play in the United States. After the passage of a number of years, Clayton visits New York to find that Milly lives "in a neat little tenement in one of the outer streets of New York, surrounded by about a dozen children, among whom were blacks, whites, and foreigners. These she had rescued from utter destitution in the streets, and was giving to them all the attention and affection of a mother." We learn that Milly has already "rescued" and raised a dozen other children and transformed the once frivolous Tomtit into an educated and religious young man who works for the abolitionist cause. Surprised by the inclusive nature of Milly's reformism, Clayton remarks, "I see you have black and white here." In response, Milly affirms the integrationist ideals central to the antislavery reformism of

William C. Nell, Frederick Douglass, and Sojourner Truth: "I don't make no distinctions of color,—I don't believe in them. White chil'en, when they 'haves themselves, is jest as good as black, and I loves 'em jest as well" (546). In a revisionary undercutting of the racist assumptions of white supremacist culture, Milly's black-centered rhetoric affirms the equality of the races by insisting (against the grain of the demonic portrait of Tom Gordon) that whites can one day be as good as blacks.

Milly's ability to love whites is shared by Old Tiff, who to the very end remains committed to the white children under his charge. Inspired by that love, he displays a revolutionary side to his character, first choosing to run off with Fanny and Teddy to Dred's refuge in the swamps, and eventually choosing to join Milly's group in its flight to New York. With her images of Tiff's and Milly's transracial love, Stowe concludes the novel with a fairly hopeful picture of blacks successfully finding a place in northeast culture and having an impact there. Strikingly, a novel that begins with whites in a paternalistic relationship to seemingly childlike black slaves concludes with images of self-reliant free blacks nurturing white children. As a social thinker, cultural critic, and race theorist, Stowe has come a long way from the ending of *Uncle Tom's Cabin*.

But the novel does not end with Milly and Tiff. *Dred* offers at least one more answer to the question "What is to be done?" Immediately after the depiction of Tiff comes a three-part appendix, the first section of which presents most of Thomas Gray's 1831 *The Confessions of Nat Turner*. A lawyer and reporter who was convinced that the slave rebel Nat Turner was insane, Gray interviewed Turner in his jail cell prior to his execution, and in *Confessions* offered Turner's supposed account of his bloody rebellion. Gray's *Confessions* sold around 50,000 copies and contributed to the Virginia legislature's decision to add greater protections for the slave masters. In her reprinting of the *Confessions*, Stowe chose to cut some of the more violent passages describing the black conspirators' murders of women and children, and also Gray's reassurances to his Southern readers that all of Nat Turner's accomplices had been captured. By leaving open the possibility that some of Turner's co-conspirators may still be at large, Stowe participates, as in *Dred* as a whole, in the political terror inspired by the prophetic tradition of the black heroic deliverer embodied by Denmark Vesey, Nat Turner, and her fictional creation Dred. And by noting in her prefatory comments to the *Confessions* that one of Turner's principal conspirators was named Dred, she presents violent rebellion as a logical, perhaps even sacred, response to slavery that, as with the novel's genealogical linkages from Vesey to Turner to Dred, will be embraced by blacks from generation to generation until slavery is abolished.

Stowe leads her readers into what she terms the "wild regions" (209) of the Dismal Swamp, and in doing so anticipates, promotes, and helps to supply the terms for understanding the bloodshed of the coming Civil War as a war of emancipation that enacts God's judgment on a sinful nation. As she writes in "The Chimney-Corner," an essay published in the *Atlantic* several months before Robert E. Lee's surrender at Appomattox: "The prophetic visions of Nat Turner, who saw the leaves drop blood and the land darkened, have been fulfilled. The work of justice which he predicted is being executed to the uttermost."[15] One of Stowe's signal accomplishments in *Dred* is to make it clear that the work of achieving racial justice in the United States is a collaborative effort requiring whites in power to "take account of the views and reasonings" of the marginalized and subordinated. With its racialism and evangelicism, the book was of its time, but with its call for a project of cross-racial conversation and social transformation that attends to multiple perspectives, the book continues to have much to say to readers of a new millennium.

Robert S. Levine
University of Maryland

Notes

1. See Joan D. Hedrick, *Harriet Beecher Stowe: A Life* (New York: Oxford University Press, 1994), vii, and James Baldwin, "Everybody's Protest Novel," *Partisan Review* 16 (1949): 578–85.

2. George Eliot, Review of *Dred*, *Westminster Review* 10 (1856): 571.

3. Harriet Beecher Stowe, "An Appeal to the Women of the Free States of America, on the Present Crisis in Our Country," *Independent* 6 (1854): 57.

4. On Southerners' responses to Stowe, see Thomas F. Gossett, *Uncle Tom's Cabin and American Culture* (Dallas: Southern Methodist University Press, 1985), chapter 11, and Cindy Weinstein, "*Uncle Tom's Cabin* and the South," in *The Cambridge Companion to Harriet Beecher Stowe* (New York and Cambridge: Cambridge University Press, 2004), 39–57.

5. Frederick Douglass, "The Letter of M. R. Delany," *Frederick Douglass' Paper*, 6 May 1853, p. 2. For documents pertaining to Delany's debate with Douglass on *Uncle Tom's Cabin*, see *Martin R. Delany: A Documentary Reader*, ed. Robert S. Levine (Chapel Hill: University of North Carolina Press, 2003), 224–37.

6. Quoted in Gossett, *Uncle Tom's Cabin and American Culture*, 294.

7. Stowe, *Sunny Memories of Foreign Lands* (Boston: Phillips, Sampson, 1854), 2:105.

8. Stowe, "Anti-Slavery Literature," *Independent* 8 (1856): 57.

9. All parenthetical page references are to this University of North Carolina Press edition of *Dred*.

10. See George M. Fredrickson, *The Black Image in the White Mind: The Debate on Afro-American Character and Destiny, 1817–1914* (New York: Harper Torchbooks, 1972), chapter 4, and Bruce Dain, *A Hideous Monster of the Mind: American Race Theory in the Early Republic* (Cambridge: Harvard University Press, 2002), chapter 8.

11. William C. Nell, *The Colored Patriots of the American Revolution* (Boston: Robert F. Wallcut, 1855), 227–28, 229.

12. In a controversial review essay, Michael P. Johnson argues that South Carolina authorities essentially invented the Vesey conspiracy as a way of killing blacks; see "Denmark Vesey and His Co-Conspirators," *William and Mary Quarterly*, 3rd Series, 58 (2001): 915–76. For a vigorous response that provides substantial evidence for the existence of the revolutionary conspiracy, see Robert L. Paquette, "From Rebellion to Revisionism: The Continuing Debate about the Denmark Vesey Affair," *Journal of the Historical Society* 4 (2004): 291–334. Stowe clearly took the Vesey conspiracy seriously as an expression of blacks' hatred of slavery.

13. Stowe, *Uncle Tom's Cabin*, ed. Elizabeth Ammons (New York: W. W. Norton and Company, 1994), 386, 388.

14. Stowe, *A Key to Uncle Tom's Cabin; Presenting the Original Facts and Documents upon which the Story is Founded. Together with Corroborative Statements Verifying the Truth of the Work* (Boston: J. P. Jewett, 1853), 252.

15. Stowe, "The Chimney-Corner," *Atlantic Monthly* 15 (1865): 115.

Selected Writings by Harriet Beecher Stowe on Slavery and Race

"Immediate Emancipation: A Sketch." *New-York Evangelist* 16 (1845): 1.

"The Freeman's Dream: A Parable." *National Era* 4 (1850): 121.

"The Two Altars; or, Two Pictures in One." *New-York Evangelist* 32 (1851): 93–94, 97–98.

Uncle Tom's Cabin; or, Life Among the Lowly. 2 vols. Boston: John P. Jewett and Co., 1852.

A Key to Uncle Tom's Cabin; Presenting the Original Facts and Documents upon which the Story is Founded. Together with Corroborative Statements Verifying the Truth of the Work. Boston: J. P. Jewett, 1853.

Uncle Sam's Emancipation; Earthly Care, A Heavenly Discipline; and Other Sketches. Philadelphia: Hazard, 1853.

"An Appeal to the Women of the Free States of America, on the Present Crisis in Our Country." *Independent* 6 (1854): 57.

The Christian Slave. A Drama, Founded on a Portion of Uncle Tom's Cabin. Dramatized by Harriet Beecher Stowe, Expressly for the Readings of Mrs. Mary E. Webb. Boston: Phillips, Sampson, 1855.

Introduction to *The Colored Patriots of the American Revolution*, by William C. Nell. Boston: Robert F. Wallcut, 1855.

Introduction to *Inside View of Slavery: or A Tour Among the Planters*, by C. G. Parsons. Boston: John P. Jewett and Company, 1855.

"Anti-Slavery Literature." *Independent* 8 (1856): 57.

The Edmondson Family and the Capture of the Schooner Pearl. Cincinnati: American Reform Tract and Book Society, 1856.

Preface to *The Garies and Their Friends*, by Frank J. Webb. London: G. Routledge & Co., 1857.

"A Brilliant Success." *Independent* 10 (1858): 1.

Preface to *Truth Stranger than Fiction: Father Henson's Story of His Own Life*, by Josiah Henson. Boston: John P. Jewett and Company, 1858.

The Minister's Wooing. New York: Derby and Jackson, 1859.

"What Is to Be Done With Them?" *Independent* 14 (1862): 1.

"Will You Take a Pilot?" *Independent* 14 (1862): 1.

"A Reply to 'The Affectionate and Christian Address of Many Thousands of Women of Great Britain and Ireland to Their Sisters the Women of the United States of America.'" *Atlantic Monthly* 11 (1863): 132–33.

"Sojourner Truth, the Libyan Sibyl." *Atlantic Monthly* 11 (1863): 473–81.

"The Chimney-Corner." *Atlantic Monthly* 15 (1865): 109–15.

"The Chimney-Corner of 1866. Being A Family Talk on Reconstruction." *Atlantic Monthly* 17 (1866): 88–100.

Men of Our Times; or Leading Patriots of the Day. Being Narratives of the Lives and Deeds of Statesmen, Generals, and Orators. Hartford, Connecticut: Hartford Publishing Co., 1868.

Palmetto-Leaves. Boston: James R. Osgood and Company, 1873.

Biographies of Stowe

Fields, Annie, ed. *Life and Letters of Harriet Beecher Stowe.* Boston: Houghton, Mifflin, 1897.

Hedrick, Joan D. *Harriet Beecher Stowe: A Life.* New York: Oxford University Press, 1994.

Rugoff, Milton. *The Beechers: An American Family in the Nineteenth Century.* New York: Harper and Row, 1981.

Stowe, Charles Edward. *Life of Harriet Beecher Stowe: Compiled from Her Letters and Journals.* Boston: Houghton, Mifflin, 1889.

Wilson, Forrest. *Crusader in Crinoline: The Life of Harriet Beecher Stowe.* Philadelphia: J. B. Lippincott, 1941.

Essays on Stowe

Baldwin, James. "Everybody's Protest Novel." *Partisan Review* 16 (1949): 578–85.

Boyd, Richard. "Models of Power in Harriet Beecher Stowe's *Dred.*" *Studies in American Fiction* 19 (1991): 15–30.

———. "Violence and Sacrificial Displacement in Harriet Beecher Stowe's *Dred.*" *Arizona Quarterly* 50 (1994): 51–72.

Brophy, Alfred L. "Humanity, Utility, and Logic in Southern Legal Thought: Harriet Beecher Stowe's *Dred: A Tale of the Great Dismal Swamp.*" *Boston University Law Review* 78 (1998): 1113–51.

Cox, James M. "Harriet Beecher Stowe: From Sectionalism to Regionalism." *Nineteenth-Century Fiction* 38 (1984): 444–66.

Crane, Gregg D. "Dangerous Sentiments: Sympathy, Rights and Revolution in Stowe's Antislavery Novels." *Nineteenth-Century Literature* 51 (1996): 176–204.

DeLombard, Jeannine Marie. "Representing the Slave: White Advocacy and Black Testimony in Harriet Beecher Stowe's *Dred*." *New England Quarterly* 75 (2002): 80–106.

Eliot, George. Review of *Dred*. *The Westminster Review* 10 (1856): 571–73.

Grant, David. "Stowe's *Dred* and the Narrative Logic of Slavery's Extension." *Studies in American Fiction* 28 (2000): 151–78.

Grüner, Mark Randall. "Stowe's *Dred*: Literary Domesticity and the Law of Slavery." *Prospects: An Annual of American Cultural Studies* 20 (1995): 1–37.

Hamilton, Cynthia S. "*Dred*: Intemperate Slavery." *Journal of American Studies* 34 (2000): 257–77.

Hill, Patricia R. "Writing out the War: Harriet Beecher Stowe's Averted Gaze." In *Divided Houses: Gender and the Civil War*. Ed. Catherine Clinton and Nina Silber. New York: Oxford University Press, 1992. 260–78.

Karafilis, Maria. "Spaces of Democracy in Harriet Beecher Stowe's *Dred*." *Arizona Quarterly* 55 (1999): 23–49.

Moers, Ellen. "Mrs. Stowe's Vengeance." *New York Review of Books*, 3 September 1970, 25–32.

Newman, Judie. Introduction to *Dred: A Tale of the Great Dismal Swamp*, by Harriet Beecher Stowe. Halifax, England: Ryburn Publishing, 1992.

———. "Was Tom White? Stowe's *Dred* and Twain's *Pudd'nhead Wilson*." *Slavery and Abolition* 20 (1999): 125–36.

Rowe, John Carlos. "Stowe's Rainbow Sign: Violence and Community in *Dred: A Tale of the Great Dismal Swamp*." *Arizona Quarterly* 58 (2002): 37–55.

Saje, Natasha. "Open Coffins and Sealed Books: The Death of the Coquette in Harriet Beecher Stowe's *Dred*." *Legacy: A Journal of American Women Writers* 15 (1998): 158–70.

Smith, Gail K. "Reading With the Other: Hermeneutics and the Politics of Difference in Stowe's *Dred*." *American Literature* 69 (1997): 289–313.

Stepto, Robert B. "Sharing the Thunder: The Literary Exchanges of Harriet Beecher Stowe, Henry Bibb, and Frederick Douglass." In *New Essays on Uncle Tom's Cabin*. Ed. Eric J. Sundquist. New York and Cambridge: Cambridge University Press, 1986. 135–53.

Wardley, Lynn. "Relic, Fetish, Femmage: The Aesthetics of Sentiment in the Work of Stowe." *Yale Journal of Criticism* 5 (1992): 165–91.

Whitney, Lisa. "In the Shadow of Uncle Tom's Cabin: Stowe's Vision of Slavery from the Great Dismal Swamp." *New England Quarterly* 66 (1993): 552–69.

Books on Stowe

Ammons, Elizabeth, ed. *Critical Essays on Harriet Beecher Stowe*. Boston: G. K. Hall, 1980.

Boydston, Jeanne, Mary Kelley, and Anne Margolis, eds. *The Limits of Sisterhood: The Beecher Sisters on Women's Rights and Woman's Sphere*. Chapel Hill: University of North Carolina Press, 1988.

Caskey, Marie. *Chariot of Fire: Religion and the Beecher Family*. New Haven: Yale University Press, 1978.

Crozier, Alice C. *The Novels of Harriet Beecher Stowe*. New York: Oxford University Press, 1969.

Gossett, Thomas F. *Uncle Tom's Cabin and American Culture*. Dallas: Southern Methodist University Press, 1985.

Hedrick, Joan D., ed. *The Oxford Harriet Beecher Stowe Reader*. New York: Oxford University Press, 1999.

Hovet, Theodore R. *The Master Narrative: Harriet Beecher Stowe's Subversive Story of Master and Slave in* Uncle Tom's Cabin *and* Dred. Lanham, Maryland: University Press of America, 1989.

Weinstein, Cindy, ed. *The Cambridge Companion to Harriet Beecher Stowe*. New York and Cambridge: Cambridge University Press, 2004.

White, Barbara A. *The Beecher Sisters*. New Haven: Yale University Press, 2003.

Historical and Cultural Criticism

Blassingame, John W. *The Slave Community: Plantation Life in the Antebellum South*. New York: Oxford University Press, 1979.

Brown, Gillian. *Domestic Individualism: Imagining Self in Nineteenth-Century America*. Berkeley: University of California Press, 1990.

Cassuto, Leonard. *The Inhuman Race: The Racial Grotesque in American Literature and Culture*. New York: Columbia University Press, 1997.

Clinton, Catherine. *The Plantation Mistress: Woman's World in the Old South*. New York: Pantheon Books, 1982.

Crane, Gregg D. *Race, Citizenship, and Law in American Literature*. New York and Cambridge: Cambridge University Press, 2002.

Dain, Bruce. *A Hideous Monster of the Mind: American Race Theory in the Early Republic*. Cambridge: Harvard University Press, 2002.

Davis, Mary Kemp. *Nat Turner Before the Bar of Judgment: Fictional Treatments of the Southampton Slave Insurrection*. Baton Rouge: Louisiana State University Press, 1999.

Egerton, Douglas R. *He Shall Go Out Free: The Lives of Denmark Vesey*. Madison, Wisconsin: Madison House, 1999.

Fredrickson, George M. *The Black Image in the White Mind: The Debate on Afro-American Character and Destiny, 1817–1914.* New York: Harper Torchbooks, 1972.

Genovese, Eugene. *From Rebellion to Revolution: Afro-American Slave Revolts in the Making of the New World.* Baton Rouge: Louisiana State University Press, 1979.

Glaude, Eddie S., Jr. *Exodus!: Religion, Race, and Nation in Early Nineteenth-Century Black America.* Chicago: University of Chicago Press, 2000.

Goddu, Teresa. *Gothic America: Narrative, History, and Nation.* New York: Columbia University Press, 1997.

Gossett, Thomas F. *Race: The History of An Idea in America.* 1963. New York: Oxford University Press, 1997.

Hendler, Glenn. *Public Sentiments: Structures of Feeling in Nineteenth-Century America.* Chapel Hill: University of North Carolina Press, 2001.

Levine, Robert S. *Martin Delany, Frederick Douglass, and the Politics of Representative Identity.* Chapel Hill: University of North Carolina Press, 1997.

Mabee, Carleton, with Susan Mabee Newhouse. *Sojourner Truth: Slave, Prophet, Legend.* New York: New York University Press, 1993.

Meer, Sarah. *Uncle Tom Mania: Slavery, Minstrelsy, and Transatlantic Culture in the 1850s.* Athens: University of Georgia Press, 2005.

Miller, David C. *Dark Eden: The Swamp in Nineteenth-Century American Culture.* New York and Cambridge University Press, 1989.

Moses, Wilson Jeremiah. *Black Messiahs and Uncle Toms: Social and Literary Manipulations of a Religious Myth.* University Park: Pennsylvania State University Press, 1993.

Noble, Marianne. *The Masochistic Pleasures of Sentimental Literature.* Princeton: Princeton University Press, 2000.

Powell, Timothy B. *Ruthless Democracy: A Multicultural Interpretation of the American Renaissance.* Princeton: Princeton University Press, 2000.

Price, Richard, ed. *Maroon Societies: Rebel Slave Communities in the Americas.* Baltimore: Johns Hopkins University Press, 1979.

Raboteau, Albert J. *Slave Religion: The "Invisible Institution" in the Antebellum South.* New York: Oxford University Press, 1978.

Romero, Lora. *Home Fronts: Domesticity and Its Critics in the Antebellum United States.* Durham, N.C.: Duke University Press, 1997.

Ryan, Susan M. *The Grammar of Good Intentions: Race and the Antebellum Culture of Benevolence.* Ithaca: Cornell University Press, 2003.

Sánchez-Eppler, Karen. *Touching Liberty: Abolition, Feminism, and the Politics of the Body*. Berkeley: University of California Press, 1993.

Sizer, Lyde Cullen. *The Political Work of Northern Women Writers and the Civil War, 1850- 1872*. Chapel Hill: University of North Carolina Press, 2000.

Sollers, Werner. *Neither Black Nor White Yet Both: Thematic Explorations of Interracial Literature*. New York: Oxford University Press, 1997.

Stuckey, Sterling. *Going through the Storm: The Influence of African American Art in History*. New York: Oxford University Press, 1994.

Sundquist, Eric J. *To Wake the Nations: Race in the Making of American Literature*. Cambridge: Harvard University Press, 1993.

Tompkins, Jane. *Sensational Designs: The Cultural Work of American Fiction, 1790–1860*. New York: Oxford University Press, 1985.

Weinstein, Cindy. *Family, Kinship, and Sympathy in Nineteenth-Century American Literature*. New York and Cambridge: Cambridge University Press, 2004.

Wonham, Henry B., ed. *Criticism and the Color Line: Desegregating American Literary Studies*. New Brunswick: Rutgers University Press, 1996.

Yellin, Jean Fagan. *The Intricate Knot: Black Figures in American Literature, 1776–1863*. New York: New York University Press, 1972.

———. *Women and Sisters: The Antislavery Feminists in American Culture*. New Haven: Yale University Press, 1989.

A NOTE ON THE TEXT

The text of this University of North Carolina Press edition is based on the first edition of *Dred: A Tale of the Great Dismal Swamp*, published in Boston in 1856 in two volumes by Phillips, Sampson and Company. The original spellings, usages, and punctuation have been retained, with two exceptions. This edition follows modern usage of employing a single set of quotation marks for each separate quotation (rather than printing open quotation marks at the beginning of each line containing quoted material), and this edition follows modern usage in closing the space in contractions so that they appear as single words.

The footnotes are Stowe's; the explanatory endnotes are the editor's.

DRED;

A

TALE OF THE GREAT DISMAL SWAMP.

BY

HARRIET BEECHER STOWE,

AUTHOR OF "UNCLE TOM'S CABIN."

"Away to the Dismal Swamp he speeds—
  His path was rugged and sore,
Through tangled juniper, beds of reeds,
Through many a fen, where the serpent feeds,
  And man never trod before.

And, when on the earth he sunk to sleep,
  If slumber his eyelids knew,
He lay where the deadly vine doth weep
Its venomous tears, that nightly steep
  The flesh with blistering dew."[1]

IN TWO VOLUMES.

VOL. I.

SIXTIETH THOUSAND.

BOSTON:

PHILLIPS, SAMPSON AND COMPANY.

1856.

Preface

THE WRITER OF THIS BOOK has chosen, once more, a subject from the scenes and incidents of the slaveholding states.

The reason for such a choice is two-fold. First, in a merely artistic point of view, there is no ground, ancient or modern, whose vivid lights, gloomy shadows, and grotesque groupings, afford to the novelist so wide a scope for the exercise of his powers. In the near vicinity of modern civilization of the most matter-of-fact kind, exist institutions which carry us back to the twilight of the feudal ages, with all their exciting possibilities of incident. Two nations, the types of two exactly opposite styles of existence, are here struggling; and from the intermingling of these two a third race has arisen, and the three are interlocked in wild and singular relations, that evolve every possible combination of romance.

Hence, if the writer's only object had been the production of a work of art, she would have felt justified in not turning aside from that mine whose inexhaustible stores have but begun to be developed.

But this object, however legitimate, was not the only nor the highest one. It is the moral bearings of the subject involved which have had the chief influence in its selection.

The issues presented by the great conflict between liberty and slavery do not grow less important from year to year. On the contrary, their interest increases with every step in the development of the national career. Never has there been a crisis in the history of this nation so momentous as the present. If ever a nation was raised up by Divine Providence, and led forth upon a conspicuous stage, as if for the express purpose of solving a great moral problem in the sight of all mankind, it is this nation. God in his providence is now asking the American people, Is the system of slavery, as set forth in the American slave code, *right?* Is it so desirable, that you will directly establish it over broad regions, where till now, you have

3

solemnly forbidden it to enter?[1] And this question the American people are about to answer. Under such circumstances the writer felt that no apology was needed for once more endeavoring to do something towards revealing to the people the true character of that system. If the people are to establish such a system, let them do it with their eyes open, with all the dreadful realities before them.

One liberty has been taken which demands acknowledgment in the outset. The writer has placed in the mouth of one of her leading characters a judicial decision of Judge Ruffin,[2] of North Carolina, the boldness, clearness, and solemn eloquence of which have excited admiration both in the Old World and the New. The author having no personal acquaintance with that gentleman, the character to whom she attributes it is to be considered as created merely on a principle of artistic fitness.

To maintain the unity of the story, some anachronisms with regard to the time of the session of courts have been allowed; for works of fiction must sometimes use some liberties in the grouping of incidents.

But as mere cold art, unquickened by sympathy with the spirit of the age, is nothing, the author hopes that those who now are called to struggle for all that is noble in our laws and institutions may find in this book the response of a sympathizing heart.

VOLUME I

D R E D

CHAPTER I

The Mistress of Canema

"BILLS, HARRY—Yes.—Dear me, where are they?—There!—No. Here?—O, look!—What do you think of this scarf? Isn't it lovely?"

"Yes, Miss Nina, beautiful—but—"

"O, those bills!—Yes—well, here goes—here—perhaps in this box. No—that's my opera-hat. By the by, what do you think of that? Isn't that bunch of silver wheat lovely? Stop a bit—you shall see it on me."

And, with these words, the slight little figure sprang up as if it had wings, and, humming a waltzing-tune, skimmed across the room to a looking-glass, and placed the jaunty little cap on the gay little head, and then, turning a pirouette on one toe, said, "There, now!"

"There, now!" Ah, Harry! ah, mankind generally! the wisest of you have been made fools of by just such dancing, glittering, fluttering little assortments of curls, pendants, streamers, eyes, cheeks, and dimples!

The little figure, scarce the height of the Venus,[1] rounded as that of an infant, was shown to advantage by a coquettish morning-dress of buff muslin, which fluttered open in front to display the embroidered skirt, and trim little mouse of a slipper. The face was one of those provoking ones which set criticism at defiance. The hair, waving, curling, dancing hither and thither, seemed to have a wild, laughing grace of its own; the brown eyes twinkled like the pendants of a chandelier; the little, wicked nose, which bore the forbidden upward curve, seemed to assert its right to do so, with a saucy freedom; and the pendants of multiplied brilliants that twinkled in her ears, and the nodding wreath of silver wheat that set off her opera-hat, seemed alive with mischief and motion.

"Well, what do you think?" said a lively, imperative voice,—just the kind of voice that you might have expected from the figure.

The young man to whom this question was addressed was a well-dressed, gentlemanly person of about thirty-five, with dark complexion and hair, and deep, full blue eyes. There was something marked and peculiar in the square, high forehead, and the finely-formed features, which indicated talent and ability; and the blue eyes had a depth and strength of color that might cause them at first glance to appear black. The face, with its strongly-marked expression of honesty and sense, had about it many care-worn and thoughtful lines. He looked at the little, defiant fay for a moment with an air of the most entire deference and admiration; then a heavy shadow crossed his face, and he answered, abstractedly, "Yes, Miss Nina, everything you wear becomes pretty—and that is perfectly charming."

"Isn't it, now, Harry? I thought you would think so. You see, it's my own idea. You ought to have seen what a thing it was when I first saw it in Mme. Le Blanche's window. There was a great hot-looking feather on it, and two or three horrid bows. I had them out in a twinkling, and got this wheat in—which shakes so, you know. It's perfectly lovely!—Well, do you believe, the very night I wore it to the opera, I got engaged?"

"Engaged, Miss Nina?"

"Engaged!—Yes, to be sure! Why not?"

"It seems to me that's a very serious thing, Miss Nina."

"Serious!—ha! ha! ha!" said the little beauty, seating herself on one arm of the sofa, and shaking the glittering hat back from her eyes. "Well, I fancy it was—to him, at least. I made him serious, I can tell you!"

"But, is this true, Miss Nina? *Are* you really engaged?"

"Yes, to be sure I am—to three gentlemen; and going to stay so till I find which I like best. May be you know I shan't like any of them."

"Engaged to three gentlemen, Miss Nina?"

"To be sure!—Can't you understand English, Harry? I *am* now—fact."

"Miss Nina, is that right?"

"Right?—why not? I don't know which to take—I positively don't; so I took them all on trial, you know."

"Pray, Miss Nina, tell us who they are."

"Well, there's Mr. Carson;—he's a rich old bachelor—horridly polite—one of those little, bobbing men, that always have such shiny dickies and collars, and such bright boots, and such tight straps. And he's rich—and perfectly wild about me. He wouldn't take no for an answer, you know; so I just said yes, to have a little quiet. Besides, he is very convenient about the opera and concerts, and such things."

"Well, and the next?"

"Well, the next is George Emmons. He's one of your pink-and-white men, you know, who look like cream-candy, as if they were good to eat. He's a lawyer, of a good family,—thought a good deal of, and all that. Well, really, they say he has talents—I'm no judge. I know he always bores me to death; asking me if I have read this or that—marking places in books that I never read. He's your sentimental sort—writes the most romantic notes on pink paper, and all that sort of thing."

"And the third?"

"Well, you see, I don't like *him* a bit—I'm sure I don't. He's a hateful creature! He isn't handsome; he's proud as Lucifer; and I'm sure I don't know how he got me to be engaged. It was a kind of an accident. He's real good, though—too good for me, that's a fact. But, then, I'm afraid of him a little."

"And his name?"

"Well, his name is Clayton—Mr. Edward Clayton, at your service. He's one of your high-and-mighty people—with such deep-set eyes—eyes that look as if they were in a cave—and such black hair! And his eyes have a desperate sort of sad look, sometimes—quite Byronic.[2] He's tall, and rather loose-jointed—has beautiful teeth; his mouth, too, is—well, when he smiles, sometimes it really is quite fascinating;—and then he's so different from other gentlemen! He's kind—but he don't care how he dresses; and wears the most horrid shoes. And, then, he isn't polite—he won't jump, you know, to pick up your thread or scissors; and sometimes he'll get into a brown study, and let you stand ten minutes before he thinks to give you a chair, and all such provoking things. He isn't a bit of a lady's man. Well, consequence is, as my lord won't court the girls, the girls all court my lord—that's the way, you know;—and they seem to think it's such a feather in their cap to get attention from him—because, you know, he's horrid sensible. So, you see, that just set me out to see what I could do with him. Well, you see, I

wouldn't court him;—and I plagued him, and laughed at him, and
spited him, and got him gloriously wroth; and he said some spiteful
things about me, and then I said some more about him, and we had
a real up-and-down quarrel;—and then I took a penitent turn, you
know, and just went gracefully down into the valley of humilia-
tion—as we witches can; and it took wonderfully—brought my
lord on to his knees before he knew what he was doing. Well, really, I don't know what was the matter, just then, but he spoke so
earnest and strong, that actually he got me to crying—hateful creature!—and I promised all sorts of things, you know—said altogether more than will bear thinking of."

"And are you corresponding with all these lovers, Miss Nina?"

"Yes—isn't it fun? Their letters, you know, can't speak. If they
could, when they come rustling together in the bag, wouldn't there
be a muss?"

"Miss Nina, I think you have given your heart to this last one."

"O, nonsense, Harry! Haven't got any heart!—don't care two
pins for any of them! All I want is to have a good time. As to love,
and all that, I don't believe I could love any of them; I should be
tired to death of any of them in six weeks. I never liked anything
that long."

"Miss Nina, you must excuse me, but I want to ask again, is it
right to trifle with the feelings of gentlemen in this way?"

"Why not?—Isn't all fair in war? Don't they trifle with us girls,
every chance they get—and sit up so pompous in their rooms, and
smoke cigars, and talk us over, as if they only had to put out their
finger and say, 'Come here,' to get any of us? I tell you, it's fun to
bring them down!—Now, there's that horrid George Emmons—I
tell you, if he didn't flirt all winter with Mary Stephens, and got
everybody to laughing about her!—it was so evident, you see, that
she liked him—she couldn't help showing it, poor little thing!—and
then my lord would settle his collar, and say he hadn't quite made
up his mind to take her, and all that. Well, I haven't made up my
mind to take him, either—and so poor Emma is avenged. As to the
old bach—that smooth-dicky man—you see, he can't be hurt; for
his heart is rubbed as smooth and hard as his dicky, with falling in
love and out again. He's been turned off by three girls, now; and his
shoes squeak as brisk as ever, and he's just as jolly. You see, he
didn't use to be so rich. Lately, he's come into a splendid property;

so, if I don't take him, poor man, there are enough that would be glad of him."

"Well, then, but as to that other one?"

"What! my lord Lofty? O, he wants humbling!—it wouldn't hurt him, in the least, to be put down a little. He's good, too, and afflictions always improve good people. I believe I was made for a means of grace to 'em all."

"Miss Nina, what if all three of them should come at once—or even two of them?"

"What a droll idea! Wouldn't it be funny? Just to think of it! What a commotion! What a scene! It would really be vastly entertaining."

"Now, Miss Nina, I want to speak as a friend."

"No, you shan't! it is just what people say when they are going to say something disagreeable. I told Clayton, once for all, that I wouldn't have him speak as a friend to me."

"Pray, how does he take all this?"

"Take it! Why, just as he must. He cares a great deal more for me than I do for him." Here a slight little sigh escaped the fair speaker. "And I think it fun to shock him. You know he is one of the fatherly sort, who is always advising young girls. Let it be understood that his standard of female character is wonderfully high, and all that. And, then, to think of his being tripped up before me!—it's *too* funny!" The little sprite here took off her opera-hat, and commenced waltzing a few steps, and, stopping midwhirl, exclaimed: "O, do you know we girls have been trying to learn the cachucha,[3] and I've got some castinets? Let me see—where are they?" And with this she proceeded to upset the trunk, from which flew a meteoric shower of bracelets, billets-doux,[4] French Grammars, drawing-pencils, interspersed with confectionary of various descriptions, and all the et-ceteras of a school-girl's depository. "There, upon my word, there are the bills you were asking for. There, take them!" throwing a package of papers at the young man. "Take them! Can you catch?"

"Miss Nina, these do not appear to be bills."

"O, bless me! those are love-letters, then. The bills are somewhere." And the little hands went pawing among the heap, making the fanciful collection fly in every direction over the carpet. "Ah! I believe now in this bonbon-box I did put them. Take care of your

head, Harry!" And, with the word, the gilded missile flew from the
little hand, and, opening on the way, showered Harry with a profu-
sion of crumpled papers. "Now you have got them all, except one,
that I used for curl-papers,[5] the other night. O, don't look so sober
about it! Indeed, I kept the pieces—here they are. And now don't
you say, Harry, don't you tell me that I never save my bills. You
don't know how particular I have been, and what trouble I have
taken. But, there—there's a letter Clayton wrote to me, one time
when we had a quarrel. Just a specimen of that creature!"

"Pray, tell us about it, Miss Nina," said the young man, with his
eyes fixed admiringly on the little person, while he was smoothing
and arranging the crumpled documents.

"Why, you see, it was just this way. You know, these men—how
provoking they are! They'll go and read all sorts of books—no matter what *they* read!—and then they are so dreadfully particular
about us girls. Do you know, Harry, this always made me angry?

"Well, so, you see, one evening, Sophy Elliot quoted some poetry from Don Juan,[6]—I never read it, but it seems folks call it a bad
book,—and my lord Clayton immediately fixed his eyes upon her
in such an appalling way, and says, 'Have you read Don Juan, Miss
Elliot?' Then, you know, as girls always do in such cases, she
blushed and stammered, and said her brother had read some extracts from it to her. I was vexed, and said, 'And, pray, what's the
harm if she did read it? *I* mean to read it, the very first chance I get!'

"O! everybody looked so shocked. Why, dear me! if I had said I
was going to commit murder, Clayton could not have looked more
concerned. So he put on that very edifying air of his, and said, 'Miss
Nina, I *trust*, as your friend, that you will not read that book. I
should lose all respect for a lady friend who had read that.'

" 'Have you read it, Mr. Clayton?' said I.

" 'Yes, Miss Nina,' said he, quite piously.

" 'What makes you read such bad books?' said I, very innocently.

"Then there followed a general fuss and talk; and the gentlemen,
you know, would not have their wives or their sisters read anything
naughty, for the world. They wanted us all to be like snow-flakes,
and all that. And they were quite high, telling they wouldn't marry
this, and they wouldn't marry that, till at last I made them a curtsey,
and said, 'Gentlemen, we ladies are infinitely obliged to you, but *we*

don't intend to marry people that read naughty books, either. Of course you know snow-flakes don't like smut!'

"Now, I really didn't mean anything by it, except to put down these men, and stand up for my sex. But Clayton took it in real earnest. He grew red and grew pale, and was just as angry as he could be. Well, the quarrel raged about three days. Then, do you know, I made him give up, and own that he was in the wrong. There, I think he was, too,—don't you? Don't you think men ought to be *as* good as we are, any way?"

"Miss Nina, I should think you would be afraid to express yourself so positively."

"O, if I cared a sou for any of them, perhaps I should. But there isn't one of the train that I would give *that* for!" said she, flirting a shower of peanut-shells into the air.

"Yes, but, Miss Nina, some time or other you must marry somebody. You need somebody to take care of the property and place."

"O, that's it, is it? You are tired of keeping accounts, are you, with me to spend the money? Well, I don't wonder. How I pity anybody that keeps accounts! Isn't it horrid, Harry? Those awful books! Do you know that Mme. Ardaine set out that 'we girls' should keep account of our expenses? I just tried it two weeks. I had a headache and weak eyes, and actually it nearly ruined my constitution. Some how or other, they gave it up, it gave them so much trouble. And what's the use? When money's spent, it's *spent;* and keeping accounts ever so strict won't get it back. I am very careful about my expenses. I never get anything that I can do without."

"For instance," said Harry, rather roguishly, "this bill of one hundred dollars for confectionary."

"Well, you know just how it is, Harry. It's so horrid to have to study! Girls must have something. And you know I didn't get it all for myself; I gave it round to all the girls. Then they used to ask me for it, and I couldn't refuse—and so it went."

"I didn't presume to comment, Miss Nina. What have we here?—Mme. Les Cartes, $450?"

"O, Harry, that horrid Mme. Les Cartes! You never saw anything like her! Positively it is not my fault. She puts down things I never got, I know she does. Nothing in the world but because she is from Paris. Everybody is complaining of her. But, then, nobody gets anything anywhere else. So what can one do, you know? I assure you, Harry, I am economical."

The young man, who had been summing up the accounts, now burst out into such a hearty laugh as somewhat disconcerted the fair rhetorician.

She colored to her temples.

"Harry, now, for shame! Positively, you aren't respectful!"

"O, Miss Nina, on my knees I beg pardon!" still continuing to laugh; "but, indeed, you must excuse me. I am positively delighted to hear of your economy, Miss Nina."

"Well, now, Harry, you may look at the bills and see. Haven't I ripped up all my silk dresses and had them colored over, just to economize? You can see the dyer's bill, there; and Mme. Carteau told me she always expected to turn my dresses twice, at least. O, yes, I have been very economical."

"I have heard of old dresses turned costing more than new ones, Miss Nina."

"O, nonsense, Harry! What should you know of girls' things? But I'll tell you one thing I've got, Harry, and that is a gold watch for you. There it is," throwing a case carelessly towards him; "and there's a silk dress for your wife," throwing him a little parcel. "I have sense enough to know what a good fellow you are, at any rate. I couldn't go on as I do, if you didn't rack your poor head fifty ways to keep things going straight here at home, for me."

A host of conflicting emotions seemed to cross the young man's face, like a shadow of clouds over a field, as he silently undid the packages. His hands trembled, his lips quivered, but he said nothing.

"Come, Harry, don't this suit you? I thought it would."

"Miss Nina, you are too kind."

"No, I'm not, Harry; I am a selfish little concern, that's a fact," said she, turning away, and pretending not to see the feeling which agitated him.

"But, Harry, wasn't it droll, this morning, when all our people came up to get their presents! There was Aunt Sue, and Aunt Tike, and Aunt Kate, each one got a new sack pattern,[7] in which they are going to make up the prints I brought them. In about two days our place will be flaming with aprons and sacks. And *did* you see Aunt Rose in that pink bonnet, with the flowers? You could see every tooth in her head! Of course, now they'll be taken with a very pious streak, to go to some camp-meeting or other, to show their finery. Why don't you laugh, Harry?"

"I do, don't I, Miss Nina?"

"You only laugh on your face. You don't laugh deep down. What's the matter? I don't believe it's good for you to read and study so much. Papa used to say that he didn't think it was good for—"

She stopped, checked by the expression on the face of her listener.

"For *servants*, Miss Nina, your papa said, I suppose."

With the quick tact of her sex, Nina perceived that she had struck some disagreeable chord in the mind of her faithful attendant, and she hastened to change the subject, in her careless, rattling way.

"Why, yes, Harry, study is horrid for you, or me either, or anybody else, except musty old people, who don't know how to do anything else. Did ever anybody look out of doors, such a pleasant day as this, and want to study? Think of a bird's studying, now, or a bee! They don't study—they live. Now, I don't want to study—I want to live. So, now, Harry, if you'll just get the ponies and go in the woods, I want to get some jessamines, and spring beauties, and wild honeysuckles, and all the rest of the flowers that I used to get before I went to school."

CHAPTER II

Clayton

THE CURTAIN RISES on our next scene, and discovers a tranquil library, illuminated by the slant rays of the afternoon's sun. On one side the room opened by long glass windows on to a garden, from whence the air came in perfumed with the breath of roses and honeysuckles. The floor covered with white matting, the couches and sofas robed in smooth glazed linen, gave an air of freshness and coolness to the apartment. The walls were hung with prints of the great master-pieces of European art, while bronzes and plaster-casts, distributed with taste and skill, gave evidence of artistic culture in the general arrangement. Two young men were sitting together near the opened window at a small table, which displayed an antique coffee-set of silver, and a silver tray of ices and fruits. One of these has already been introduced to the notice of our readers, in the description of our heroine in the last chapter.

Edward Clayton, the only son of Judge Clayton, and representative of one of the oldest and most distinguished families of North Carolina, was in personal appearance much what our lively young friend had sketched—tall, slender, with a sort of loose-jointedness and carelessness of dress, which might have produced an impression of clownishness, had it not been relieved by a refined and intellectual expression on the head and face. The upper part of the face gave the impression of thoughtfulness and strength, with a shadowing of melancholy earnestness; and there was about the eye, in conversation, that occasional gleam of troubled wildness which betrays the hypochondriac temperament. The mouth was even feminine in the delicacy and beauty of its lines, and the smile which sometimes played around it had a peculiar fascination. It seemed to be a smile of but half the man's nature; for it never rose as high as the eyes, or seemed to disturb the dark stillness of their thoughtfulness.

The other speaker was in many respects a contrast; and we will introduce him to our readers by the name of Frank Russel. Furthermore, for their benefit, we will premise that he was the only son of a once distinguished and wealthy, but now almost decayed family, of Virginia.

It is supposed by many that friendship is best founded upon similarity of nature; but observation teaches that it is more common by a union of opposites, in which each party is attracted by something wanting in itself. In Clayton, the great preponderance of those faculties which draw a man inward, and impair the efficiency of the outward life, inclined him to over-value the active and practical faculties, because he saw them constantly attended with a kind of success which he fully appreciated, but was unable to attain. Perfect ease of manner, ready presence of mind under all social exigencies, adroitness in making the most of passing occurrences, are qualities which are seldom the gift of sensitive and deeply-thoughtful natures, and which for this very reason they are often disposed to over-value. Russel was one of those men who have just enough of all the higher faculties to appreciate their existence in others, and not enough of any one to disturb the perfect availability of his own mind. Everything in his mental furnishing was always completely under his own control, and on hand for use at a moment's notice. From infancy he was noted for quick tact and ready reply. At school he was the universal factotum, the "good fellow" of the ring, heading all the mischief among the boys, and yet walking with exemplary gravity on the blind side of the master. Many a scrape had he rescued Clayton from, into which he had fallen from a more fastidious moral sense, a more scrupulous honor, than is for worldly profit either in the boy's or man's sphere; and Clayton, superior as he was, could not help loving and depending on him.

The diviner part of man is often shame-faced and self-distrustful, ill at home in this world, and standing in awe of nothing so much as what is called common sense; and yet common sense very often, by its own keenness, is able to see that these unavailable currencies of another's mind are of more worth, if the world only knew it, than the ready coin of its own; and so the practical and the ideal nature are drawn together.

So Clayton and Russel had been friends from boyhood; had roomed together their four years in college; and, tho' instruments of a vastly different quality, had hitherto played the concerts of life with scarce a discord.

In person, Russel was of about the medium size, with a well-knit, elastic frame, all whose movements were characterized by sprightliness and energy. He had a frank, open countenance, clear blue eyes, a high forehead shaded by clusters of curling brown hair; his flexible lips wore a good-natured yet half-sarcastic smile. His feelings, though not inconveniently deep, were easily touched; he could be moved to tears or to smiles, with the varying humor of a friend; but never so far as to lose his equipoise—or, as he phrased it, forget what he was about.

But we linger too long in description. We had better let the reader hear the *dramatis personæ*,[1] and judge for himself.

"Well, now, Clayton," said Russel, as he leaned back in a stuffed leather chair, with a cigar between his fingers, "how considerate of them to go off on that marooning party,[2] and leave us to ourselves, here! I say, old boy, how goes the world now?—Reading law, hey?—booked to be Judge Clayton the second! Now, my dear fellow, if *I* had the opportunities that you have—only to step into my father's shoes—I should be a lucky fellow."

"Well, you are welcome to all my chances," said Clayton, throwing himself on one of the lounges; "for I begin to see that I shall make very little of them."

"Why, what's the matter?—Don't you like the study?"

"The study, perhaps, well enough—but not the practice. Reading the theory is always magnificent and grand. 'Law hath her seat in the bosom of God; her voice is the harmony of the world.'[3] You remember we used to declaim that. But, then, come to the practice of it, and what do you find? Are legal examinations anything like searching after truth? Does not an advocate commit himself to one-sided views of his subject, and habitually ignore all the truth on the other side? Why, if I practised law according to my conscience, I should be chased out of court in a week."

"There you are, again, Clayton, with your everlasting conscience, which has been my plague ever since you were a boy, and I have never been able to convince you what a humbug it is! It's what I call a *crotchety* conscience—always in the way of your doing anything like anybody else. I suppose, then, of course, you won't go into political life.—Great pity, too. You'd make a very imposing figure as senator. You have exactly the cut for a conscript father— one of the old Viri Romæ."[4]

"And what do you think the old Viri Romæ would do in Washington? What sort of a figure do you think Regulus, or Quintus Curtius, or Mucius Scævola,[5] would make, there?"

"Well, to be sure, the style of political action has altered somewhat since those days. If political duties were what they were then,—if a gulf would open in Washington, for example,—you would be the fellow to plunge in, horse and all, for the good of the republic; or, if anything was to be done by putting your right hand in the fire and burning it off—or, if there were any Carthaginians who would cut off your eyelids, or roll you down hill in a barrel of nails, for truth and your country's sake,—you would be on hand for any such matter. That's the sort of foreign embassy that you would be after. All these old-fashioned goings on would suit you to a T; but as to figuring in purple and fine linen, in Paris or London, as American minister, you would make a dismal business of it. But, still, I thought you might practise law in a wholesome, sensible way,—take fees, make pleas with abundance of classical allusions, show off your scholarship, marry a rich wife, and make your children princes in the gates—all without treading on the toes of your too sensitive moral what-d'-ye-call-ems. But you've done one thing like other folks, at least, if all's true that I've heard."

"And what is that, pray?"

"What's that? Hear the fellow, now! How innocent we are! I suppose you think I haven't heard of your campaign in New York—carrying off that princess of little flirts, Miss Gordon."

Clayton responded to the charge only with a slight shrug and a smile, in which not only his lips but his eyes took part, while the color mounted to his forehead.

"Now, do you know, Clayton," continued Russel, "I *like* that. Do you know I always thought I should detest the woman that you should fall in love with? It seemed to me that such a portentous combination of all the virtues as you were planning for would be something like a comet—an alarming spectacle. Do you remember (I should like to know, if you do) just what that woman was to be?—was to have all the learning of a man, all the graces of a woman (I think I have it by heart); she was to be practical, poetical, pious, and everything else that begins with a *p;* she was to be elegant and earnest; take deep and extensive views of life; and there was to be a certain air about her, half Madonna, half Venus, made of every creature's best. Ah, bless us! what poor creatures we are! Here comes along our little coquette, flirting, tossing her fan; picks you up like a great, solid chip, as you are, and throws you into her chip-basket of beaux, and goes on dancing and flirting as before. Aren't you ashamed of it, now?"

"No. I am really much like the minister in our town, where we fitted for college, who married a pretty Polly Peters in his sixtieth year, and, when the elders came to inquire if she had the requisite qualifications for a pastor's lady, he told them that he didn't think she had. 'But the fact is, brethren,' said he, 'though I don't pretend she is a saint, she is a very pretty little sinner, *and I love her.*' That's just my case."

"Very sensibly said; and, do you know, as I told you before, I'm perfectly delighted with it, because it is acting like other folks. But, then, my dear fellow, do you think you have come to anything really solid with this little Venus of the sea-foam? Isn't it much the same as being engaged to a cloud, or a butterfly? One wants a little *streak* of reality about a person that one must take for better or for worse. You have a deep nature, Clayton. You really want a wife who will have some glimmering perception of the difference between you and the other things that walk and wear coats, and are called men."

"Well, then, really," said Clayton, rousing himself, and speaking with energy, "I'll tell you just what it is: Nina Gordon is a flirt and a coquette—a spoiled child, if you will. She is not at all the person I ever expected would obtain any power over me. She has no culture, no reading, no habits of reflection; but she has, after all, a certain tone and quality to her, a certain '*timbre,*' as the French say of voices, which suits me. There is about her a mixture of energy, individuality, and shrewdness, which makes her, all uninformed as she is, more piquant and attractive than any woman I ever fell in with. She never reads; it is almost impossible to get her to read; but, if you can catch her ear for five minutes, her literary judgments have a peculiar freshness and truth. And so with her judgment on all other subjects, if you can stop her long enough to give you an opinion. As to heart, I think she has yet a wholly unawakened nature. She has lived only in the world of sensation, and that is so abundant and so buoyant in her that the deeper part still sleeps. It is only two or three times that I have seen a flash of this under nature look from her eyes, and color her voice and intonation. And I believe—I'm quite sure—that I am the only person in the world that ever touched it at all. I'm not at all sure that she loves me *now;* but I'm almost equally sure that she will."

"They say," said Russel, carelessly, "that she is generally engaged to two or three at a time."

"That may be also," said Clayton, indolently. "I rather suspect it to be the case now, but it gives me no concern. I've seen all the men by whom she is surrounded, and I know perfectly well there's not one of them that she cares a rush for."

"Well, but, my dear fellow, how can your extra fastidious moral notions stand the idea of her practising this system of deception?"

"Why, of course, it isn't a thing to my taste; but, then, like the old parson, if I love the 'little sinner,' what am I to do? I suppose you think it a lover's paradox; yet I assure you, though she deceives, she is not deceitful; though she acts selfishly, she is not selfish. The fact is, the child has grown up, *motherless* and an heiress, among servants. She has, I believe, a sort of an aunt, or some such relative, who nominally represents the head of the family to the eye of the world. But I fancy little madam has had full sway. Then she has been to a fashionable New York boarding-school, and that has developed the talent of shirking lessons, and evading rules, with a taste for side-walk flirtation. These are all the attainments that I ever heard of being got at a fashionable boarding-school, unless it be a hatred of books, and a general dread of literary culture."

"And her estates are—"

"Nothing very considerable. Managed nominally by an old uncle of hers; really by a very clever quadroon[6] servant, who was left her by her father, and who has received an education, and has talents very superior to what are common to those in his class. He is, in fact, the overseer of her plantation, and I believe the most loyal, devoted creature breathing."

"Clayton," said his companion, "this affair might not be much to one who takes the world as I do, but for you it may be a little too serious. Don't get in beyond your depth."

"You are too late, Russel, for that—I *am* in."

"Well, then, good luck to you, my dear fellow! And now, as we are about it, I may as well tell you that I'm *in* for it, too. I suppose you have heard of Miss Benoir, of Baltimore. Well, she is my fate."

"And are you really engaged?"

"All signed and sealed, and to be delivered next Christmas."

"Let's hear about her."

"Well, she is of a good height (I always said I shouldn't marry a short woman),—not handsome, but reasonably well-looking—very fine manners—knows the world—plays and sings handsomely—has a snug little fortune. Now, you know I never held to marrying for money and nothing else; but, then, as I'm situated, I could not have fallen in love without that requisite. Some people call this heartless. I don't think it is. If I had met Mary Benoir, and had known that she hadn't anything, why, I should have known that it wouldn't do for me at all to cultivate any particular intimacy; but, knowing she had fortune, I looked a little further, and found she had other things, too. Now, if that's marrying for money, so be it. Yours, Clayton, is a genuine case of falling in love. But, as for me, I walked in with my eyes wide open."

"And what are *you* going to do with yourself in the world, Russel?"

"I must get into practice, and get some foothold there, you know; and then, hey for Washington!—I'm to be president, like every other adventurer in these United States. Why not I, as well as another man?"

"I don't know, certainly," said Clayton, "if you want it, and are willing to work hard enough and long enough and pay all the price. I would as soon spend my life walking the drawn sword which they say is the bridge to Mahomet's paradise."[7]

"Ah! ah! I fancy I see you doing it! What a figure you'd make, my dear fellow, balancing and posturing on the sword-blade, and making horrid wry faces! Yet I know you'd be as comfortable there as you would in political life. And yet, after all, you are greatly superior to me in every respect. It would be a thousand pities if such a man as you couldn't have the management of things. But our national ship has to be navigated by second-rate fellows, Jerry-go-nimbles, like me, simply because we are good in dodging and turning. But that's the way. Sharp's the word, and the sharpest wins."

"For my part," said Clayton, "I shall never be what the *world* calls a *successful* man. There seems to be one inscription written over every passage of success in life, as far as I've seen,—'What shall it profit a man if he gain the whole world, and lose his own soul?' "[8]

"I don't understand you, Clayton."

"Why, it seems to me just this. As matters are going on now in our country, I must either lower my standard of right and honor, and sear my soul in all its nobler sensibilities, or I must be what the world calls an unsuccessful man. There is no path in life, that I know of, where humbuggery and fraud and deceit are not essential to success—none where a man can make the purity of his moral nature the first object. I see Satan standing in every avenue, saying, 'All these things will I give thee, if thou wilt fall down and worship me.' "[9]

"Why don't you take the ministry, then, Clayton, at once, and put up a pulpit-cushion and big Bible between you and the fiery darts of the devil?"

"I'm afraid I should meet him there, too. I could not gain a right to speak in any pulpit without some profession or pledge to speak this or that, that would be a snare to my conscience, by and by. At the door of every pulpit I must swear always to find truth in a certain formula; and living, prosperity, success, reputation, will all be pledged on my finding it there. I tell you I should, if I followed my own conscience, preach myself out of pulpits quicker than I should plead out at the bar."

"Lord help you, Clayton! What *will* you do? Will you settle down on your plantation, and raise cotton and sell niggers? I'm expecting to hear, every minute, that you've subscribed for the *Liberator*,[10] and are going to turn Abolitionist."

"I do mean to settle down on my plantation, but not to *raise* cotton or negroes as a chief end of man. I do take the *Liberator*, because I'm a free man, and have a right to take what I have a mind to. I don't agree with Garrison, because I think I know more about the matter, where I stand, than he does, or can, where he stands. But it's his *right*, as an honest man, to say what he thinks; and I should use it in his place. If I saw things as he does, I *should* be an Abolitionist. But I don't."

"That's a mercy, at least," said Russel, "to a man with your taste for martyrdom. But what are you going to do?"

"What any Christian man should do who finds four hundred odd of his fellow men and women placed in a state of absolute dependence on him. I'm going to educate and fit them for freedom. There isn't a sublimer power on earth than God has given to us masters. The law gives us absolute and unlimited control. A plantation such as a plantation might be would be 'a light to lighten the gentiles.'[11] There is a wonderful and beautiful development locked up in this Ethiopian race, and it is worth being a life-object to unlock it. The raising of cotton is to be the least of the thing. I regard my plantation as a sphere for raising *men and women,* and demonstrating the capabilities of a race."

"Selah!"[12] said Russel.

Clayton looked angry.

"I beg your pardon, Clayton. This is all superb, sublime! There is just one objection to it—it is wholly impossible."

"Every good and great thing has been called impossible before it is done."

"Well, let me tell you, Clayton, just how it will be. You will be a mark for arrows, both sides. You will offend all your neighbors by doing better than they do. You will bring your negroes up to a point in which they will meet the current of the whole community against them, and meanwhile you will get no credit with the Abolitionists. They will call you a cut-throat, pirate, sheep-stealer, and all the rest of their elegant little list of embellishments, all the same. You'll get a state of things that nobody can manage but yourself, and you by the hardest; and then you'll die, and it'll all run to the devil faster than you run it up. Now, if you would do the thing by halves, it wouldn't be so bad; but I know you of old. You won't be satisfied with teaching a catechism and a few hymns, parrot-wise, which I think is a respectable religious amusement for our women. You'll teach 'em all to read, and write, and think, and speak. I shouldn't wonder to hear of an importation of black-boards and spelling-books. You'll want a lyceum and debating society. Pray, what does sister Anne say to all this? Anne is a sensible girl now, but I'll warrant you've got her to go in for it."

"Anne is as much interested as I, but her practical tact is greater than mine, and she is of use in detecting difficulties that I do not see. I have an excellent man, who enters fully into my views, who takes charge of the business interests of the plantation, instead of one of these scoundrel overseers. There is to be a graduated system of work and wages introduced—a system that shall teach the nature and rights of property, and train to habits of industry and frugality, by making every man's acquirements equal to his industry and good conduct."

"And what sort of a support do *you* expect to make out of all this? Are you going to live for them, or they for you?"

"I shall set them the example of living for *them,* and trust to awaken the good that is in them, in return. The strong ought to live for the weak—the cultivated for the ignorant."

"Well, Clayton, the Lord help you! I'm in earnest now—fact! Though I know you won't do it, yet I wish you could. It's a pity, Clayton, you were born in this world. It isn't you, but our planet and planetary ways, that are in fault. Your mind is a splendid store-house—gold and gems of Ophir[13]—but they are all up in the fifth story, and no staircase to get 'em down into common life. Now, I've just enough appreciation of the sort of thing that's in you, not to laugh at you. Nine out of ten would. To tell you the truth, if I were already set up in life, and had as definite a position as you have,—family, friends, influence, and means,—why, perhaps I might afford to cultivate this style of thing. But, I tell you what it is, Clayton, such a conscience as yours is cursedly expensive to keep. It's like a carriage—a fellow mustn't set it up unless he can afford it. It's one of the luxuries."

"It's a *necessary* of life, with me," said Clayton, dryly.

"Well, that's your nature. I can't afford it. I've got my way to make. *I must succeed,* and with your ultra notions I couldn't suc-ceed. So there it is. After all, I can be as religious as dozens of your most respectable men, who have taken their seats in the night-train for Paradise, and keep the daylight for their own business."

"I dare say you can."

"Yes, and I shall get all I aim at; and you, Clayton, will be always an unhappy, dissatisfied aspirant after something too high for mor-tality. There's just the difference between us."

The conversation was here interrupted by the return of the fam-ily party.

CHAPTER III

The Clayton Family and Sister Anne

THE FAMILY PARTY which was now ushered in, consisted of Clayton's father, mother, and sister. Judge Clayton was a tall, dignified, elderly personage, in whom one recognized, at a glance, the gentleman of the old school. His hair, snowy white, formed a singular contrast with the brightness of his blue eyes, whose peculiar acuteness of glance might remind one of a falcon. There was something stately in the position of the head and the carriage of the figure, and a punctilious exactness in the whole air and manner, that gave one a slight impression of sternness. The clear, sharp blue of his eye seemed to be that of a calm and decided intellect, of a logical severity of thought; and contrasted with the silvery hair with that same expression of cold beauty that is given by the contrast of snow mountains cutting into the keen, metallic blue of an Alpine sky. One should apprehend much to fear from such a man's reason— little to hope from any outburst of his emotional nature. Yet, as a man, perhaps injustice was done to Judge Clayton by this first impression; for there was, deep beneath this external coldness, a severely-repressed nature, of the most fiery and passionate vehemence. His family affections were strong and tender, seldom manifested in words, but always by the most exact appreciation and consideration for all who came within his sphere. He was strictly and impartially just in all the little minutiæ of social and domestic life, never hesitating to speak a truth, or acknowledge an error.

Mrs. Clayton was a high-bred, elderly lady, whose well-preserved delicacy of complexion, brilliant dark eyes, and fine figure, spoke of a youth of beauty. Of a nature imaginative, impulsive, and ardent, inclining constantly to generous extremes, she had thrown herself with passionate devotion round her clear-judging husband, as the Alpine rose girdles with beauty the breast of the bright, pure glacier.

Between Clayton and his father there existed an affection deep and entire; yet, as the son developed to manhood, it became increasingly evident that they could never move harmoniously in the same practical orbit. The nature of the son was so veined and crossed with that of the mother, that the father, in attempting the age-long and often-tried experiment of making his child an exact copy of himself, found himself extremely puzzled and confused in the operation. Clayton was ideal to an excess; ideality colored every faculty of his mind, and swayed all his reasonings, as an unseen magnet will swerve the needle. Ideality pervaded his conscientiousness, urging him always to rise above the commonly-received and so-called practical in morals. Hence, while he worshipped the theory of law, the practice filled him with disgust; and his father was obliged constantly to point out deficiencies in reasonings, founded more on a keen appreciation of what things ought to be, than on a practical regard to what they are. Nevertheless, Clayton partook enough of his father's strong and steady nature to be his mother's idol, who, perhaps, loved this second rendering of the parental nature with even more doting tenderness than the first.

Anne Clayton was the eldest of three sisters, and the special companion and confidant of the brother; and, as she stands there untying her bonnet-strings, we must also present her to the reader. She is a little above the medium height, with that breadth and full development of chest which one admires in English women. She carries her well-formed head on her graceful shoulders with a positive, decided air, only a little on this side of haughtiness. Her clear brown complexion reddens into a fine glow in the cheek, giving one the impression of sound, perfect health. The positive outline of the small aquiline nose, the large, frank, well-formed mouth, with its clear rows of shining teeth, the brown eyes, which have caught something of the falcon keenness of the father, are points in the picture by no means to be overlooked. Taking her air altogether, there was an honest frankness about her which encouraged conversation, and put one instantly at ease. Yet no man in his senses could ever venture to take the slightest liberty with Anne Clayton. With all her frankness, there was ever in her manner a perfectly-defined "thus far shalt thou come, and no further." Beaux, suitors, lovers in abundance, had stood, knelt, and sighed protesting, at her shrine. Yet Anne Clayton was twenty-seven, and unmarried. Everybody wondered why; and as to that, we can only wonder with the rest. Her own account of the matter was simple and positive. She did not wish to marry—was happy enough without.

The intimacy between the brother and sister had been more than usually strong, notwithstanding marked differences of character; for Anne had not a particle of ideality. Sense she had, shrewdness, and a pleasant dash of humor, withal; but she was eminently what people call a practical girl. She admired highly the contrary of all this in her brother; she delighted in the poetic-heroic element in him, for much the same reason that young ladies used to admire Thaddeus of Warsaw, and William Wallace[1]—because it was something quite out of her line. In the whole world of ideas she had an almost idolatrous veneration for her brother; in the sphere of practical operations she felt free to assert, with a certain good-natured positiveness, her own superiority. There was no one in the world, perhaps, of whose judgment in this respect Clayton stood more in awe.

At the present juncture of affairs Clayton felt himself rather awkwardly embarrassed in communicating to her an event which she would immediately feel she had a right to know before. A sister of Anne Clayton's positive character does not usually live twenty-seven years in constant intimacy with a brother like Clayton, without such an attachment as renders the first announcement of a contemplated marriage somewhat painful. Why, then, had Clayton, who always unreservedly corresponded with his sister, not kept her apprised of his gradual attachment to Nina? The secret of the matter was, that he had had an instinctive consciousness that he could not present Nina to the practical, clear-judging mind of his sister, as she appeared through the mist and spray of his imaginative nature. The hard facts of her case would be sure to tell against her in any communication he might make; and sensitive people never like the fatigue of justifying their instincts. Nothing, in fact, is less capable of being justified by technical reasons than those fine insights into character whereupon affection is built. We have all had experience of preferences which would not follow the most exactly ascertained catalogue of virtues, and would be made captive where there was very little to be said in justification of the captivity.

But, meanwhile, rumor, always busy, had not failed to convey to Anne Clayton some suspicions of what was passing; and, though her delicacy and pride forbade any allusion to it, she keenly felt the want of confidence, and of course was not any more charitably disposed towards the little rival for this reason. But now the matter had attained such a shape in Clayton's mind that he felt the necessity of apprising his family and friends. With his mother the task was made easier by the abundant hopefulness of her nature, which enabled her in a moment to throw herself into the sympathies of those she loved. To her had been deputed the office of first breaking the tidings to Anne, and she had accomplished it during the pleasure-party of the morning.

The first glance that passed between Clayton and his sister, as she entered the room, on her return from the party, showed him that she was discomposed and unhappy. She did not remain long in the apartment, or seem disposed to join in conversation; and, after a few abstracted moments, she passed through the open door into the garden, and began to busy herself apparently among her plants. Clayton followed her. He came and stood silently beside her for some time, watching her as she picked the dead leaves off her geranium.

"Mother has told you," he said, at length.

"Yes," said Anne.

There was a long pause, and Anne picked off dry leaves and green promiscuously, threatening to demolish the bush.

"Anne," said Clayton, "how I wish you could see her!"

"I've *heard* of her," replied Anne, dryly, "through the Livingstons."

"And what have you heard?" said Clayton, eagerly.

"Not such things as I could wish, Edward; not such as I expected to hear of the lady that you would choose."

"And, pray, what *have* you heard? Out with it," said Clayton,—"let's know what the world says of her."

"Well, the world says," said Anne, "that she is a coquette, a flirt, a jilt. From all I've heard, I should think she must be an unprincipled girl."

"That is hard language, Anne."

"Truth is generally hard," replied Anne.

"My dear sister," said Clayton, taking her hand, and seating her on the seat in the garden, "have you lost all faith in me?"

"I think it would be nearer truth," replied Anne, "to say that *you* had lost all faith in *me*. Why am I the last one to know all this? Why am I to hear it first from reports, and every way but from you?

Would I have treated you so? Did I ever have anything that I did not tell you? Down to my very soul I've always told you everything!"

"This is true, I own, dear Anne; but what if you had loved some man that you felt sure I should not like? Now, you are a positive person, Anne, and this might happen. Would you want to tell me at once? Would you not, perhaps, wait, and hesitate, and put off, for one reason or another, from day to day, and find it grow more and more difficult, the longer you waited?"

"I can't tell," said Anne, bitterly. "I never did love any one better than you,—that's the trouble."

"Neither do I love anybody *better* than you, Anne. The love I have for you is a whole, perfect thing, just as it was. See if you do not find me every way as devoted. My heart was only opened to take in another love, another wholly different; and which, because it is so wholly different, never can infringe on the love I bear to you. And, Anne, my dear sister, if you could love her as a part of me—"

"I wish I could," said Anne, somewhat softened; "but what I've heard has been so unfavorable! She is not, in the least, the person I should have expected you to fancy, Edward. Of all things I despise a woman who trifles with the affections of gentlemen."

"Well, but, my dear, Nina isn't a woman; she is a *child*—a gay, beautiful, unformed child; and I'm sure you may apply to her what Pope says:

'If to her share some female errors fall,
Look in her face, and you forget them all.' "[2]

"Yes, indeed," said Anne, "I believe all you men are alike—a pretty face bewitches any of you. I thought you were an exception, Edward; but there you are."

"But, Anne, is this the way to encourage my confidence? Suppose I am bewitched and enchanted, you cannot disentangle me without indulgence. Say what you will about it, the *fact* is just this—it is my fate to love this child. I've tried to love many women before. I have seen many whom I knew no sort of reason why I shouldn't love,—handsomer far, more cultivated, more accomplished,—and yet I've seen them without a movement or a flutter of the pulse. But this girl has awakened all there is to me. I do not see in her what the world sees. I see the ideal image of what she can be, what I'm sure she *will* be, when her nature is fully awakened and developed."

"Just there, Edward—just that," said Anne. "You never see anything; that is, you see a glorified image—a something that might, could, would, or should be—that is your difficulty. You glorify an ordinary boarding-school coquette into something symbolic, sublime; you clothe her with all your own ideas, and then fall down to worship her."

"Well, my dear Anne, suppose it were so, what then? I am, as you say, ideal,—you, real. Well, be it so; I must act according to what is in me. I have a right to my nature, you to yours. But it is not every person whom I *can* idealize; and I suspect this is the great reason why I never could love some very fine women, with whom I have associated on intimate terms; they had no capacity of being idealized; they could receive no color from my fancy; they wanted, in short, just what Nina has. She is just like one of those little whisking, chattering cascades in the White Mountains,[3] and the atmosphere round her is favorable to rainbows."

"And you always see her through them."

"Even so, sister; but some people I cannot. Why should you find fault with me? It's a pleasant thing to look through a rainbow. Why should you seek to disenchant, if I *can* be enchanted?"

"Why," replied Anne, "you remember the man who took his pay of the fairies in gold and diamonds, and, after he had passed a certain brook, found it all turned to slate-stones. Now, marriage is like that brook; many a poor fellow finds his diamonds turned to slate on the other side; and this is why I put in my plain, hard common sense, against your visions. I see the plain facts about this young girl; that she is an acknowledged flirt, a noted coquette and jilt; and a woman who is so is necessarily heartless; and you are too good, Edward, too noble, I have loved you too long, to be willing to give you up to *such* a woman."

"There, my dear Anne, there are at least a dozen points in that sentence to which I don't agree. In the first place, as to coquetry, it isn't the unpardonable sin in my eyes—that is, under some circumstances."

"That is, you mean, when Nina Gordon is the coquette?"

"No, I don't mean that. But the fact is, Anne, there is so little of true sincerity, so little real benevolence and charity, in the common intercourse of young gentlemen and ladies in society, and our sex, who ought to set the example, are so selfish and unprincipled in their ways of treating women, that I do not wonder that, now and then, a lively girl, who has the power, avenges her sex by playing off *our* weak points. Now, I don't think Nina capable of trifling with a real, deep, unselfish attachment—a love which sought her good, and was willing to sacrifice itself for her; but I don't believe any such has ever been put at her disposal. There's a great difference between a man's wanting a woman to *love him,* and loving her. Wanting to appropriate a woman as a wife, does not, of course, imply that a man loves her, or that he is capable of loving anything. All these things girls *feel,* because their instincts are quick; and they are often accused of trifling with a man's heart, when they only see through him, and know he hasn't any. Besides, love of power has always been considered a respectable sin in us men; and why should we denounce a woman for loving her kind of power?"

"O, well, Edward, there isn't anything in the world that you cannot theorize into beauty. But I don't like coquettes, for all that; and, then, I'm told Nina Gordon is so very odd, and says and does such very extraordinary things, sometimes."

"Well, perhaps that charms me the more. In this conventional world, where women are all rubbed into one uniform surface, like coins in one's pocket, it's a pleasure now and then to find one who can't be made to do and think like all the rest. You have a little dash of this merit, yourself, Anne; but you must consider that you have been brought up with mamma, under her influence, trained and guided every hour, even more than you knew. Nina has grown up an heiress among servants, a boarding-school girl in New York; and, furthermore, you are twenty-seven and she is eighteen, and a great deal may be learned between eighteen and twenty-seven."

"But, brother, you remember Miss Hannah More[4] says,—or some of those good women, I forget who: at any rate it's a sensible saying,—'that a man who chooses his wife as he would a picture in a public exhibition-room, should remember that there is this difference, that the picture cannot go back to the exhibition, but the woman may.' You have chosen her from seeing her brilliancy in society; but, after all, can you make her happy in the dull routine of a commonplace life? Is she not one of the sort that must have a constant round of company and excitement to keep her in spirits?"

"I think not," said Clayton. "I think she is one of those whose vitality is in herself, and one whose freshness and originality will keep life anywhere from being commonplace; and that, living with us, she will sympathize, naturally, in all our pursuits."

"Well, now, don't flatter yourself, brother, that you can make this girl over, and bring her to any of your standards."

"Who—I? Did you think I meditated such an impertinence? The last thing I should try, to marry a wife to educate her! It's generally one of the most selfish tricks of our sex. Besides, I don't want a wife who will be a mere mirror of my opinions and sentiments. I don't want an innocent sheet of blotting-paper, meekly sucking up all I say, and giving a little fainter impression of my ideas. I want a wife for an alternative; all the vivacities of life lie in differences."

"Why, surely," said Anne, "one wants one's friends to be congenial, I should think."

"So we do; and there is nothing in the world so congenial as differences. To be sure, the differences must be harmonious. In music, now, for instance, one doesn't want a repetition of the same notes, but differing notes that chord. Nay, even discords are indispensable to complete harmony. Now, Nina has just that difference from me which chords with me; and all our little quarrels—for we have had a good many, and I dare say shall have more—are only a sort of chromatic passages,—discords of the seventh, leading into harmony. My life is inward, theorizing, self-absorbed. I am hypochondriac—often morbid. The vivacity and acuteness of her outer life makes her just what I need. She wakens, she rouses, and keeps me in play; and her quick instincts are often more than a match for my reason. I reverence the child, then, in spite of her faults. She has taught me many things."

"Well," said Anne, laughing, "I give you up, if it comes to that. If you come to talk about reverencing Nina Gordon, I see it's all over with you, Edward, and I'll be good-natured, and make the best of it. I hope it may all be true that you think, and a great deal more. At all events, no effort of mine shall be wanting to make you as happy in your new relation as you ought to be."

"There, now, that's Anne Clayton! It's just like *you*, sister, and I couldn't say anything better than that. You have unburdened your conscience, you have done all you can for me, and now very properly yield to the inevitable. Nina, I know, will love you; and, if you never *try* to advise her and influence her, you will influence her very much. Good people are a long while learning *that*, Anne. They think to do good to others, by interfering and advising. They don't know that all they have to do is to live. When I first knew Nina, I was silly enough to try my hand that way, myself; but I've learned better. Now, when Nina comes to us, all that you and mamma have got to do is just to be kind to her, and *live* as you always have lived; and whatever needs to be altered in her, she will alter herself."

"Well," said Anne, "I wish, as it is so, that I could see her."

"Suppose you write a few lines to her in this letter that I am going to write; and then that will lead in due time to a visit."

"Anything in the world, Edward, that you say."

CHAPTER IV

The Gordon Family

A WEEK OR TWO had passed over the head of Nina Gordon since she was first introduced to our readers, and during this time she had become familiar with the details of her home life. Nominally, she stood at the head of her plantation, as mistress and queen in her own right of all, both in doors and out; but, really, she found herself, by her own youth and inexperience, her ignorance of practical details, very much in the hands of those she professed to govern.

The duties of a southern housekeeper, on a plantation, are onerous beyond any amount of northern conception. Every article wanted for daily consumption must be kept under lock and key, and doled out as need arises. For the most part, the servants are only grown-up children, without consideration, forethought, or self-control, quarrelling with each other, and divided into parties and factions, hopeless of any reasonable control. Every article of wear, for some hundreds of people, must be thought of, purchased, cut and made, under the direction of the mistress; and add to this the care of young children, whose childish mothers are totally unfit to govern or care for them, and we have some slight idea of what devolves on southern housekeepers.

Our reader has seen what Nina was on her return from New York, and can easily imagine that she had no idea of embracing, in good earnest, the hard duties of such a life.

In fact, since the death of Nina's mother, the situation of the mistress of the family had been only nominally filled by her aunt, Mrs. Nesbit. The real housekeeper, in fact, was an old mulatto woman, named Katy, who had been trained by Nina's mother. Notwithstanding the general inefficiency and childishness of negro servants, there often are to be found among them those of great practical ability. Whenever owners, through necessity or from tact, select such servants, and subject them to the kind of training and responsibility which belongs to a state of freedom, the same qualities are developed which exist in free society. Nina's mother, being always in delicate health, had, from necessity, been obliged to commit much responsibility to "Aunt Katy," as she was called; and she had grown up under the discipline into a very efficient housekeeper. With her tall red turban, her jingling bunch of keys, and an abundant sense of the importance of her office, she was a dignitary not lightly to be disregarded.

It is true that she professed the utmost deference for her young mistress, and very generally passed the compliment of inquiring what she would have done; but it was pretty generally understood that her assent to Aunt Katy's propositions was considered as much a matter of course as the queen's to a ministerial recommendation. Indeed, had Nina chosen to demur, her prime minister had the power, without departing in the slightest degree from a respectful bearing, to involve her in labyrinths of perplexity without end. And, as Nina hated trouble, and wanted, above all things, to have her time to herself for her own amusement, she wisely concluded not to interfere with Aunt Katy's reign, and to get by persuasion and coaxing, what the old body would have been far too consequential and opinionated to give to authority.

In like manner, at the head of all out-door affairs was the young quadroon, Harry, whom we introduced in the first chapter. In order to come fully at the relation in which he stood to the estate, we must, after the fashion of historians generally, go back a hundred years or so, in order to give our readers a fair start. Behold us, therefore, assuming historic dignity, as follows.

Among the first emigrants to Virginia, in its colonial days, was one Thomas Gordon, Knight, a distant offshoot of the noble Gordon family, renowned in Scottish history. Being a gentleman of some considerable energy, and impatient of the narrow limits of the Old World, where he found little opportunity to obtain that wealth which was necessary to meet the demands of his family pride, he struck off for himself into Virginia. Naturally of an adventurous turn, he was one of the first to propose the enterprise which afterwards resulted in a settlement on the banks of the Chowan River, in North Carolina. Here he took up for himself a large tract of the finest alluvial land, and set himself to the business of planting, with the energy and skill characteristic of his nation; and, as the soil was new and fertile, he soon received a very munificent return for his enterprise. Inspired with remembrances of old ancestral renown, the Gordon family transmitted in their descent all the traditions, feelings, and habits, which were the growth of the aristocratic caste from which they sprung. The name of Canema, given to the estate, came from an Indian guide and interpreter, who accompanied the first Col. Gordon as confidential servant.

The estate, being entailed, passed down through the colonial times unbroken in the family, whose wealth, for some years, seemed to increase with every generation.

The family mansion was one of those fond reproductions of the architectural style of the landed gentry in England, in which, as far as their means could compass it, the planters were fond of indulging.

Carpenters and carvers had been brought over, at great expense, from the old country, to give the fruits of their skill in its erection; and it was a fancy of the ancestor who built it, to display, in its wood-work, that exuberance of new and rare woods with which the American continent was supposed to abound. He had made an adventurous voyage into South America, and brought from thence specimens of those materials more brilliant than rose-wood, and hard as ebony, which grow so profusely on the banks of the Amazon that the natives use them for timber. The floor of the central hall of the house was a curiously-inlaid parquet of these brilliant materials, arranged in fine block-work, highly polished.

The outside of the house was built in the old Virginian fashion, with two tiers of balconies running completely round, as being much better suited to the American climate than any of European mode. The inside, however, was decorated with sculpture and carvings, copied, many of them, from ancestral residences in Scotland, giving to the mansion an air of premature antiquity.

Here, for two or three generations, the Gordon family had lived in opulence. During the time, however, of Nina's father, and still more after his death, there appeared evidently on the place signs of that gradual decay which has conducted many an old Virginian family to poverty and ruin. Slave labor, of all others the most worthless and profitless, had exhausted the first vigor of the soil, and the proprietors gradually degenerated from those habits of energy which were called forth by the necessities of the first settlers, and everything proceeded with that free-and-easy abandon, in which both master and slave appeared to have one common object,—that of proving who should waste with most freedom.

At Colonel Gordon's death, he had bequeathed, as we have already shown, the whole family estate to his daughter, under the care of a servant, of whose uncommon intelligence and thorough devotion of heart he had the most ample proof. When it is reflected that the overseers are generally taken from a class of whites who are often lower in ignorance and barbarism than even the slaves, and that their wastefulness and rapacity are a by-word among the planters, it is no wonder that Colonel Gordon thought that, in leaving his plantation under the care of one so energetic, competent, and faithful, as Harry, he had made the best possible provision for his daughter.

Harry was the son of his master, and inherited much of the temper and constitution of his father, tempered by the soft and genial temperament of the beautiful Eboe[1] mulattress who was his mother. From this circumstance Harry had received advantages of education very superior to what commonly fell to the lot of his class. He had also accompanied his master as valet during the tour of Europe, and thus his opportunities of general observation had been still further enlarged, and that tact by which those of the mixed blood seem so peculiarly fitted to appreciate all the finer aspects of conventional life, had been called out and exercised; so that it would be difficult in any circle to meet with a more agreeable and gentlemanly person. In leaving a man of this character, and his own son, still in the bonds of slavery, Colonel Gordon was influenced by that passionate devotion to his daughter which with him overpowered every consideration. A man so cultivated, he argued to himself, might find many avenues opened to him in freedom; might be tempted to leave the estate to other hands, and seek his own fortune. He therefore resolved to leave him bound by an indissoluble tie for a term of years, trusting to his attachment to Nina to make this service tolerable.

Possessed of very uncommon judgment, firmness, and knowledge of human nature, Harry had found means to acquire great ascendency over the hands of the plantation; and, either through fear or through friendship, there was a universal subordination to him. The executors of the estate scarcely made even a feint of overseeing him; and he proceeded, to all intents and purposes, with the perfect ease of a free man. Everybody, for miles around, knew and respected him; and, had he not been possessed of a good share of the thoughtful, forecasting temperament derived from his Scottish parentage, he might have been completely happy, and forgotten even the existence of the chains whose weight he never felt.

It was only in the presence of Tom Gordon—Colonel Gordon's lawful son—that he ever realized that he was a slave. From childhood, there had been a rooted enmity between the brothers, which deepened as years passed on; and, as he found himself, on every return of the young man to the place, subjected to taunts and ill-usage, to which his defenceless position left him no power to reply, he had resolved never to marry, and lay the foundation for a family, until such time as he should be able to have the command of his own destiny, and that of his household. But the charms of a pretty French quadroom overcame the dictates of prudence.

The history of Tom Gordon is the history of many a young man grown up under the institutions and in the state of society which formed him. Nature had endowed him with no mean share of talent, and with that perilous quickness of nervous organization, which, like fire, is a good servant, but a bad master. Out of those elements, with due training, might have been formed an efficient and eloquent public man; but, brought up from childhood among servants to whom his infant will was law, indulged during the period of infantile beauty and grace in the full expression of every whim, growing into boyhood among slaves with but the average amount of plantation morality, his passions developed at a fearfully early time of life; and, before his father thought of seizing the reins of authority, they had gone out of his hands forever. Tutor after tutor was employed on the plantation to instruct him, and left, terrified by his temper. The secluded nature of the plantation left him without that healthful stimulus of society which is often a help in enabling a boy to come to the knowledge and control of himself. His associates were either the slaves, or the overseers, who are generally unprincipled and artful, or the surrounding whites, who lay in a yet lower deep of degradation. For one reason or another, it was for the interest of all these to flatter his vices, and covertly to assist him in opposing and deceiving his parents. Thus an early age saw him an adept in every low form of vice. In despair, he was at length sent to an academy at the North, where he commenced his career on the first day by striking the teacher in the face, and was consequently expelled. Thence he went to another, where, learning caution from experience, he was enabled to maintain his foot-hold. There he was a successful colporteur[2] and missionary in the way of introducing a knowledge of bowie-knives, revolvers, and vicious literature. Artful, bold, and daring, his residence for a year at a school was sufficient to initiate in the way of ruin perhaps one fourth of the boys. He was handsome, and, when not provoked, good-natured, and had that off-hand way of spending money which passes among boys for generosity. The simple sons of hard-working farmers, bred in habits of industry and frugality, were dazzled and astonished by the freedom with which he talked, and drank, and spit, and swore. He was a hero in their eye, and they began to wonder at the number of things, to them unknown before, which went to make up the necessaries of life. From school he was transferred to college, and there placed under the care of a professor, who was paid an exorbitant sum for overlooking his affairs. The consequence was, that while many a northern boy, whose father could not afford to pay for similar patronage, was disciplined, rusticated,[3] or expelled, as the case might be, Tom Gordon exploited gloriously through college, getting drunk every week or two, breaking windows, smoking freshmen, heading various sprees in different parts of the country, and at last graduating nobody knew how, except the patron professor, who received an extra sum for the extra difficulties of the case. Returned home, he went into a lawyer's office in Raleigh, where, by a pleasant fiction, he was said to be reading law, because he was occasionally seen at the office during the intervals of his more serious avocations of gambling, and horse-racing, and drinking. His father, an affectionate but passionate man, was wholly unable to control him, and the conflicts between them often shook the whole domestic fabric. Nevertheless, to the last Colonel Gordon indulged the old hope for such cases made and provided, that Tom would get through sowing his wild oats, some time, and settle down and be a respectable man; in which hope he left him the half of his property. Since that time, Tom seemed to have studied on no subject except how to accelerate the growth of those wings which riches are said to be inclined to take, under the most favorable circumstances.

As often happens in such cases of utter ruin, Tom Gordon was a much worse character for all the elements of good which he possessed. He had sufficient perception of right, and sufficient conscience remaining, to make him bitter and uncomfortable. In proportion as he knew himself unworthy of his father's affection and trust, he became jealous and angry at any indications of the want of it. He had contracted a settled ill-will to his sister, for no other apparent reason except that the father took a comfort in her which he did not in him. From childhood, it was his habit to vex and annoy her in every possible way; and it was for this reason, among many others, that Harry had persuaded Mr. John Gordon, Nina's uncle and guardian, to place her at the New York boarding-school, where she acquired what is termed an education. After finishing her school career, she had been spending a few months in a family of a cousin of her mother's, and running with loose rein the career of fashionable gayety.

Luckily, she brought home with her unspoiled a genuine love of nature, which made the rural habits of plantation life agreeable to her. Neighbors there were few. Her uncle's plantation, five miles distant, was the nearest. Other families with whom the Gordons were in the habit of exchanging occasional visits were some ten or fifteen miles distant. It was Nina's delight, however, in her muslin wrapper, and straw hat, to patter about over the plantation, to chat with the negroes among their cabins, amusing herself with the various drolleries and peculiarities to which long absence had given the zest of novelty. Then she would call for her pony, and, attended by Harry, or some of her servants, would career through the woods, gathering the wild-flowers with which they abound; perhaps stop for a day at her uncle's, have a chat and a romp with him, and return the next morning.

In the comparative solitude of her present life her mind began to clear itself of some former follies, as water when at rest deposits the sediment which clouded it. Apart from the crowd, and the world of gayeties which had dizzied her, she could not help admitting to herself the folly of much she had been doing. Something, doubtless, was added to this by the letters of Clayton. The tone of them, so manly and sincere, so respectful and kind, so removed either from adulation or sentimentalism, had an effect upon her greater than she was herself aware of. So Nina, in her positive and off-hand way, sat down, one day, and wrote farewell letters to both her other lovers, and felt herself quite relieved by the process.

A young person could scarce stand more entirely alone, as to sympathetic intercourse with relations, than Nina. It is true that the presence of her mother's sister in the family caused it to be said that she was residing under the care of an aunt.

Mrs. Nesbit, however, was simply one of those well-bred, well-dressed lay-figures, whose only office in life seems to be to occupy a certain room in a house, to sit in certain chairs at proper hours, to make certain remarks at suitable intervals of conversation. In her youth this lady had run quite a career as a belle and beauty. Nature had endowed her with a handsome face and figure, and youth and the pleasure of admiration for some years supplied a sufficient flow of animal spirits to make the beauty effective. Early married, she became the mother of several children, who were one by one swept into the grave. The death of her husband, last of all, left her with a very small fortune alone in the world; and, like many in similar circumstances, she was content to sink into an appendage to another's family.

Mrs. Nesbit considered herself very religious; and, as there is a great deal that passes for religion, ordinarily, of which she may be fairly considered a representative, we will present our readers with a philosophical analysis of the article. When young, she had thought only of self in the form of admiration, and the indulgence of her animal spirits. When married, she had thought of self only in her husband and children, whom she loved because they were *hers,* and for no other reason.

When death swept away her domestic circle, and time stole the beauty and freshness of animal spirits, her self-love took another form; and, perceiving that this world was becoming to her somewhat passé, she determined to make the best of her chance for another.

Religion she looked upon in the light of a ticket, which, being once purchased, and snugly laid away in a pocket-book, is to be produced at the celestial gate, and thus secure admission to heaven.

At a certain period of her life, while she deemed this ticket unpurchased, she was extremely low-spirited and gloomy, and went through a quantity of theological reading enough to have astonished herself, had she foreseen it in the days of her belle-ship. As the result of all, she at last presented herself as a candidate for admission to a Presbyterian church in the vicinity, there professing her determination to run the Christian race. By the Christian race, she understood going at certain stated times to religious meetings, reading the Bible and hymn-book at certain hours in the day, giving at regular intervals stipulated sums to religious charities, and preserving a general state of leaden indifference to everybody and everything in the world.

She thus fondly imagined that she had renounced the world, because she looked back with disgust on gayeties for which she had no longer strength or spirits. Nor did she dream that the intensity with which her mind travelled the narrow world of self, dwelling on the plaits of her caps, the cut of her stone-colored satin gowns, the making of her tea and her bed, and the saving of her narrow income, was exactly the same in kind, though far less agreeable in development, as that which once expended itself in dressing and dancing. Like many other apparently negative characters, she had a pertinacious intensity of an extremely narrow and aimless self-will. Her plans of life, small as they were, had a thousand crimps and plaits, to every one of which she adhered with invincible pertinacity. The poor lady little imagined, when she sat, with such punctilious satisfaction, while the Rev. Mr. Orthodoxy demonstrated that selfishness is the essence of all moral evil, that the sentiment had the slightest application to her; nor dreamed that the little, quiet, muddy current of self-will, which ran without noise or indecorum under the whole structure of her being, might be found, in a future day, to have undermined all her hopes of heaven. Of course, Mrs. Nesbit regarded Nina, and all other lively young people, with a kind of melancholy endurance—as shocking spectacles of worldliness. There was but little sympathy, to be sure, between the dashing, and out-spoken, and almost defiant little Nina, and the sombre silver-gray apparition which glided quietly about the wide halls of her paternal mansion. In fact, it seemed to afford the latter a mischievous pleasure to shock her respectable relative on all convenient occasions. Mrs. Nesbit felt it occasionally her duty, as she remarked, to call her lively niece into her apartment, and endeavor to persuade her to read some such volume as Law's Serious Call,[4] or Owen on the One Hundred and Nineteenth Psalm;[5] and to give her a general and solemn warning against all the vanities of the world, in which were generally included dressing in any color but black and drab, dancing, flirting, writing love-letters, and all other enormities, down to the eating of pea-nut candy. One of these scenes is just now enacting in this good lady's apartment, upon which we will raise the curtain.

Mrs. Nesbit, a diminutive, blue-eyed, fair-complexioned little woman, of some five feet high, sat gently swaying in that respectable asylum for American old age, commonly called a rocking-chair. Every rustle of her silvery silk gown, every fold of the snowy kerchief on her neck, every plait of her immaculate cap, spoke a soul long retired from this world and its cares. The bed, arranged with extremest precision, however, was covered with a melange of French finery, flounces, laces among which Nina kept up a continual agitation like that produced by a breeze in a flower-bed, as she unfolded, turned, and fluttered them, before the eyes of her relative.

"I have been through all this, Nina," said the latter, with a melancholy shake of her head, "and I know the vanity of it."

"Well, aunty, I *haven't* been through it, so *I* don't know."

"Yes, my dear, when I was of your age, I used to go to balls and parties, and could think of nothing but of dress and admiration. I have been through it all, and seen the vanity of it."

"Well, aunt, I want to go through it, and see the vanity of it, too. That's just what I'm after. I'm on the way to be as sombre and solemn as you are, but I'm bound to have a good time first. Now, look at this pink brocade!"

Had the brocade been a pall, it could scarcely have been regarded with a more lugubrious aspect.

"Ah, child! such a dying world as this! To spend so much time and thought on dress!"

"Why, Aunt Nesbit, yesterday you spent just two whole hours in thinking whether you should turn the breadths of your black silk dress upside down, or down side up; and this was a dying world all the time. Now, I don't see that it is any better to think of black silk than it is of pink."

This was a view of the subject which seemed never to have occurred to the good lady.

"But, now, aunt, do cheer up, and look at this box of artificial flowers. You know I thought I'd bring a stock on from New York. Now, aren't these perfectly lovely? I like flowers that *mean* something. Now, these are all imitations of natural flowers, so perfect that you'd scarcely know them from the real. See—there, that's a moss-rose; and now look at these sweet peas, you'd think they had just been picked; and, there—that heliotrope, and these jessamines, and those orange-blossoms, and that wax camelia—"

"Turn off my eyes from beholding vanity!" said Mrs. Nesbit, shutting her eyes, and shaking her head:

" 'What if we wear the richest vest,—
Peacocks and flies are better drest;
This flesh, with all its glorious forms,
Must drop to earth, and feed the worms.' "

"Aunt, I do think you have the most horrid, disgusting set of hymns, all about worms, and dust, and such things!"

"It's my duty, child, when I see you so much taken up with such sinful finery."

"Why, aunt, do you think artificial flowers are sinful?"

"Yes, dear; they are a sinful waste of time and money, and take off our mind from more important things."

"Well, aunt, then what did the Lord make sweet peas, and roses, and orange-blossoms for? I'm sure it's only doing as he does, to make flowers. He don't make everything gray, or stone-color. Now, if you only would come out in the garden, this morning, and see the oleanders, and the crape myrtle, and the pinks, the roses, and the tulips, and the hyacinths, I'm sure it would do you good."

"O, I should certainly catch cold, child, if I went out doors. Milly left a crack opened in the window, last night, and I've sneezed three or four times since. It will never do for me to go out in the garden; the feeling of the ground striking up through my shoes is very unhealthy."

"Well, at any rate, aunt, I should think, if the Lord didn't wish us to wear roses and jessamines, he would not have made them. And it is the most natural thing in the world to want to wear flowers."

"It only feeds vanity and a love of display, my dear."

"I don't think it's vanity, or a love of display. I should want to dress prettily, if I were the only person in the world. I love pretty things because they *are* pretty. I like to wear them because they make me look pretty."

"There it is, child; you want to dress up your poor perishing body to look pretty—that's the thing!"

"To be sure I do. Why shouldn't I? I mean to look as pretty as I can, as long as I live."

"You seem to have quite a conceit of your beauty!" said Aunt Nesbit.

"Well, I know I am pretty. I'm not going to pretend I don't. I like my own looks, now, that's a fact. I'm not like one of your Greek statues, I know. I'm not wonderfully handsome, nor likely to set the world on fire with my beauty. I'm just a pretty little thing; and I like flowers and laces, and all of those things; and I mean to like them, and I don't think there'll be a bit of religion in my not liking them; and as for all that disagreeable stuff about the worms, that you are always telling me, I don't think it does me a particle of good. And, if religion is going to make me so *poky,* I shall put it off as long as I can."

"I used to feel just as you do, dear, but I've seen the folly of it!"

"If I've got to lose my love for everything that is bright, everything that is lively, and everything that is pretty, and like to read such horrid stupid books, why, I'd rather be buried, and done with it!"

"That's the opposition of the natural heart, my dear."

The conversation was here interrupted by the entrance of a bright, curly-headed mulatto boy, bearing Mrs. Nesbit's daily luncheon.

"O, here comes Tomtit," said Nina; "now for a scene! Let's see what he has forgotten, now."

Tomtit was, in his way, a great character in the mansion. He and his grandmother were the property of Mrs. Nesbit. His true name was no less respectable and methodical than that of Thomas; but, as he was one of those restless and effervescent sprites, who seem to be born for the confusion of quiet people, Nina had rechristened him Tomtit, which sobriquet was immediately recognized by the whole household as being eminently descriptive and appropriate. A constant ripple and eddy of drollery seemed to pervade his whole being; his large, saucy black eyes had always a laughing fire in them, that it was impossible to meet without a smile in return. Slave and property though he was, yet the first sentiment of reverence for any created thing seemed yet wholly unawakened in his curly pate. Breezy, idle, careless, flighty, as his woodland namesake, life to him seemed only a repressed and pent-up ebullition of animal enjoyment; and almost the only excitement of Mrs. Nesbit's quiet life was her chronic controversy with Tomtit. Forty or fifty times a day did the old body assure him "that she was astonished at his conduct;" and as many times would he reply by showing the whole set of his handsome teeth, on the broad grin, wholly inconsiderate of the state of despair into which he thus reduced her.

On the present occasion, as he entered the room, his eye was caught by the great display of finery on the bed; and, hastily dumping the waiter on the first chair that occurred, with a flirt and a spring as lithe as that of a squirrel, he was seated in a moment astride the foot-board, indulging in a burst of merriment.

"Good law, Miss Nina, whar on earth dese yer come from? Good law, some on 'em for me, isn't 'er?"

"You see that child!" now said Mrs. Nesbit, rocking back in her chair with the air of a martyr. "After all my talkings to him! Nina, you ought not to allow that; it just encourages him!"

"Tom, get down, you naughty creature you, and get the stand and put the waiter on it. Mind yourself, now!" said Nina, laughing.

Tomtit cut a somerset[6] from the foot-board to the floor, and, striking up, on a very high key, "I'll bet my money on a bob-tail nag," he danced out a small table, as if it had been a partner, and deposited it, with a jerk, at the side of Mrs. Nesbit, who aimed a cuff at his ears; but, as he adroitly ducked his head, the intended blow came down upon the table with more force than was comfortable to the inflictor.

"I believe that child is made of air!—I never can hit him!" said the good lady, waxing red in the face. "He is enough to provoke a saint!"

"So he is, aunt; enough to provoke two saints like you and me. Tomtit, you rogue," said she, giving a gentle pull to a handful of his curly hair, "be good, now, and I'll show you the pretty things, by and by. Come, put the waiter on the table, now; see if you can't walk, for once!"

Casting down his eyes with an irresistible look of mock solemnity, Tomtit marched with the waiter, and placed it by his mistress.

The good lady, after drawing off her gloves and making sundry little decorous preparations, said a short grace over her meal, during which time Tomtit seemed to be holding his sides with repressed merriment; then, gravely laying hold of the handle of the teapot, she stopped short, gave an exclamation, and flirted her fingers, as she felt it almost scalding hot.

"Tomtit, I do believe you intend to burn me to death, some day!"

"Laws, missus, dat are hot? O, sure I was tickler to set the nose round to the fire."

"No, you didn't! you stuck the handle right into the fire, as you're always doing!"

"Laws, now, wonder if I did," said Tomtit, assuming an abstracted appearance. " 'Pears as if never can 'member which dem dare is nose, and which handle. Now, I's a studdin on dat dare most all de morning—was so," said he, gathering confidence, as he saw, by Nina's dancing eyes, how greatly she was amused.

"You need a sound whipping, sir—that's what you need!" said Mrs. Nesbit, kindling up in sudden wrath.

"O, I knows it," said Tomtit. "We's unprofitable servants, all on us. Lord's mercy that we an't 'sumed, all on us!"[7]

Nina was so completely overcome by this novel application of the text which she had heard her aunt laboriously drumming into Tomtit, the Sabbath before, that she laughed aloud, with rather uproarious merriment.

"O, aunt, there's no use! He don't know anything! He's nothing but an incarnate joke, a walking hoax!"

"No, I doesn't know nothing, Miss Nina," said Tomtit, at the same time looking out from under his long eyelashes. "Don't know nothing at all—never can."

"Well, now, Tomtit," said Mrs. Nesbit, drawing out a little blue cowhide from under her chair, and looking at him resolutely, "you see, if this teapot handle is hot again, I'll give it to you! Do you hear?"

"Yes, missis," said Tomtit, with that indescribable sing-song of indifference, which is so common and so provoking in his class.

"And, now, Tomtit, you go down stairs and clean the knives for dinner."

"Yes, missis," said he, pirouetting towards the door. And once in the passage, he struck up a vigorous "O, I'm going to glory, won't you go along with me;" accompanying himself, by slapping his own sides, as he went down two stairs at a time.

"Going to glory!" said Mrs. Nesbit, rather shortly; "he looks like it, I think! It's the third or fourth time that that child has blistered my fingers with this teapot, and I know he does it on purpose! So ungrateful, when I spend my time, teaching him, hour after hour, laboring with him so! I declare, I don't believe these children have got any souls!"

"Well, aunt, I declare, I should think you'd get out of all patience with him; yet he's so funny, I cannot, for the life of me, help laughing."

Here a distant whoop on the staircase, and a tempestuous chorus to a Methodist hymn, with the words, "O come, my loving brethren," announced that Tomtit was on the return; and very soon, throwing open the door, he marched in, with an air of the greatest importance.

"Tomtit, didn't I tell you to go and clean the knives?"

"Law, missis, come up here to bring Miss Nina's love-letters," said he, producing two or three letters. "Good law, though," said he, checking himself, "forgot to put them on a waity!" and, before a word could be said, he was out of the room and down stairs, and at the height of furious contest with the girl who was cleaning the silver, for a waiter to put Miss Nina's letters on.

"Dar, Miss Nina," appealing to her when she appeared, "Rosa won't let me have no waity!"

"I could pull your hair for you, you little image!" said Nina, seizing the letters from his hands, and laughing while she cuffed his ears.

"Well," said Tomtit, looking after her with great solemnity, "missis in de right on 't. An't no kind of order in this here house, 'pite of all I can do. One says put letters on waity. Another one won't let you have waity to put letters on. And, finally, Miss Nina, she pull them all away. Just the way things going on in dis yer house, all the time! I can't help it; done all I can. Just the way missis says!"

There was one member of Nina's establishment of a character so marked that we cannot refrain from giving her a separate place in our picture of her surroundings,—and this was Milly, the waiting-woman of Aunt Nesbit.

Aunt Milly, as she was commonly called, was a tall, broad-shouldered, deep-chested African woman, with a fulness of figure approaching to corpulence. Her habit of standing and of motion was peculiar and majestic, reminding one of the Scripture expression "upright as the palm-tree."[8] Her skin was of a peculiar blackness and softness, not unlike black velvet. Her eyes were large, full, and dark, and had about them that expression of wishfulness and longing which one may sometimes have remarked in dark eyes. Her mouth was large, and the lips, though partaking of the African fulness, had, nevertheless, something decided and energetic in their outline, which was still further seconded by the heavy moulding of the chin. A frank smile, which was common with her, disclosed a row of most splendid and perfect teeth. Her hair, without approaching to the character of the Anglo-Saxon, was still different from the ordinary woolly coat of the negro, and seemed more like an infinite number of close-knotted curls, of brilliant, glossy blackness.

The parents of Milly were prisoners taken in African wars; and she was a fine specimen of one of those warlike and splendid races, of whom, as they have seldom been reduced to slavery, there are but few and rare specimens among the slaves of the south.

Her usual head-dress was a high turban, of those brilliant colored Madras[9] handkerchiefs in which the instinctive taste of the dark races leads them to delight. Milly's was always put on and worn with a regal air, as if it were the coronet of the queen. For the rest, her dress consisted of a well-fitted gown of dark stuff, of a quality somewhat finer than the usual household apparel. A neatly-starched white muslin handkerchief folded across her bosom, and a clean white apron, completed her usual costume.

No one could regard her, as a whole, and not feel their prejudice in favor of the exclusive comeliness of white races somewhat shaken. Placed among the gorgeous surroundings of African landscape and scenery, it might be doubted whether any one's taste could have desired, as a completion to her appearance, to have blanched the glossy skin whose depth of coloring harmonizes so well with the intense and fiery glories of a tropical landscape.

In character, Milly was worthy of her remarkable external appearance. Heaven had endowed her with a soul as broad and generous as her ample frame. Her passions rolled and burned in her bosom with a tropical fervor; a shrewd and abundant mother wit, united with a vein of occasional drollery, gave to her habits of speech a quaint vivacity.

A native adroitness gave an unwonted command over all the functions of her fine body; so that she was endowed with that much-coveted property which the New Englander denominates "faculty," which means the intuitive ability to seize at once on the right and best way of doing everything which is to be done. At the same time, she was possessed of that high degree of self-respect which led her to be incorruptibly faithful and thorough in all she undertook; less, as it often seemed, from any fealty or deference to those whom she served, than from a kind of native pride in well-doing, which led her to deem it beneath herself to slight or pass over the least thing which she had undertaken. Her promises were inviolable. Her owners always knew that what she once said would be done, if it were within the bounds of possibility.

The value of an individual thus endowed in person and character may be easily conceived by those who understand how rare, either among slaves or freemen, is such a combination. Milly was, therefore, always considered in the family as a most valuable piece of property, and treated with more than common consideration.

As a mind, even when uncultivated, will ever find its level, it often happened that Milly's amount of being and force of character gave her ascendency even over those who were nominally her superiors. As her ways were commonly found to be the best ways, she was left, in most cases, to pursue them without opposition or control. But, favorite as she was, her life had been one of deep sorrows. She had been suffered, it is true, to contract a marriage with a very finely-endowed mulatto man, on a plantation adjoining her owner's, by whom she had a numerous family of children, who inherited all her fine physical and mental endowments. With more than usual sensibility and power of reflection, the idea that the children so dear to her were from their birth not her own,—that they were, from the first hour of their existence, merchantable articles, having a fixed market value in proportion to every excellence, and liable to all the reverses of merchantable goods,—sank with deep weight into her mind. Unfortunately, the family to which she belonged being reduced to poverty, there remained, often, no other means of making up the deficiency of income than the annual sale of one or two negroes. Milly's children, from their fine developments, were much-coveted articles. Their owner was often tempted by extravagant offers for them; and therefore, to meet one crisis or another of family difficulties, they had been successively sold from her. At first, she had met this doom with almost the ferocity of a lioness; but the blow, oftentimes repeated, had brought with it a dull endurance, and Christianity had entered, as it often does with the slave, through the rents and fissures of a broken heart. Those instances of piety which are sometimes, though rarely, found among slaves, and which transcend the ordinary development of the best-instructed, are generally the results of calamities and afflictions so utterly desolating as to force the soul to depend on God alone. But, where one soul is thus raised to higher piety, thousands are crushed in hopeless imbecility.

CHAPTER V

Harry and His Wife

SEVERAL MILES from the Gordon estate, on an old and somewhat decayed plantation, stood a neat log cabin, whose external aspect showed both taste and care. It was almost enveloped in luxuriant wreaths of yellow jessamine, and garlanded with a magnificent lamarque rose, whose cream-colored buds and flowers contrasted beautifully with the dark, polished green of the finely-cut leaves.

The house stood in an enclosure formed by a high hedge of the American holly, whose evergreen foliage and scarlet berries made it, at all times of the year, a beautiful object. Within the enclosure was a garden, carefully tended, and devoted to the finest fruits and flowers.

This little dwelling, so different in its air of fanciful neatness from ordinary southern cabins, was the abode of Harry's little wife. *Lisette,* which was her name, was the slave of a French creole woman, to whom a plantation had recently fallen by inheritance.

She was a delicate, airy little creature, formed by a mixture of the African and French blood, producing one of those fanciful, exotic combinations, that give one the same impression of brilliancy and richness that one receives from tropical insects and flowers. From both parent races she was endowed with a sensuous being exquisitely quick and fine,—a nature of everlasting childhood, with all its freshness of present life, all its thoughtless, unreasoning fearlessness of the future.

She stands there at her ironing-table, just outside her cottage door, singing gayly at her work. Her round, plump, childish form is shown to advantage by the trim blue basque,[1] laced in front, over a chemisette of white linen. Her head is wreathed with a gay turban, from which escapes, now and then, a wandering curl of her silky black hair. Her eyes, as she raises them, have the hazy, dreamy languor, which is so characteristic of the mixed races. Her little,

52

childish hands are busy, with nimble fingers adroitly plaiting and arranging various articles of feminine toilet, too delicate and expensive to have belonged to those in humble circumstances. She ironed, plaited, and sung, with busy care. Occasionally, however, she would suspend her work, and, running between the flower-borders to the hedge, look wistfully along the road, shading her eyes with her hand. At last, as she saw a man on horseback approaching, she flew lightly out, and ran to meet him.

"Harry, Harry! You've come, at last. I'm so glad! And what have you got in that paper? Is it anything for me?"

He held it up, and shook it at her, while she leaped after it.

"No, no, little curiosity!" he said, gayly.

"I know it's something for me," said she, with a pretty, half-pouting air.

"And why do you know it's for you? Is everything to be for you in the world, you little good-for-nothing?"

"Good-for-nothing!" with a toss of the gayly-turbaned little head. "You may well say that, sir! Just look at the two dozen shirts I've ironed, since morning! Come, now, take me up; I want to ride."

Harry put out the toe of his boot and his hand, and, with an adroit spring, she was in a moment before him, on his horse's neck, and, with a quick turn, snatched the paper parcel from his hand.

"Woman's curiosity!" said he.

"Well, I want to see what it is. Dear me, what a tight string! O, I can't break it! Well, here it goes; I'll tear a hole in it, anyhow. O, silk, as I live! Aha! tell me now this isn't for me, you bad thing, you!"

"Why, how do you know it isn't to make me a summer coat?"

"Summer coat!—likely story! Aha! I've found you out, mister! But, come, do make the horse canter: I want to go fast. Make him canter, do!"

Harry gave a sudden jerk to the reins, and in a minute the two were flying off as if on the wings of the wind. On and on they went, through a small coppice of pines, while the light-hearted laugh rang on the breeze behind them. Now they are lost to view. In a few minutes, emerging from the pine woods in another direction, they come sweeping, gay and laughing, up to the gate. To fasten the horse, to snatch the little wife on his shoulder, and run into the cottage with her, seemed the work only of a moment; and, as he set her down, still laughing, he exclaimed,

"There, go, now, for a pretty little picture, as you are! I have helped them get up les tableaux vivans,[2] at their great houses; but you are my tableau. You aren't good for much. You are nothing but a humming-bird, made to live on honey!"

"That's what I am!" said the little one. "It takes a great deal of honey to keep me. I want to be praised, flattered, and loved, all the time. It isn't enough to have you love me. I want to hear you tell me so every day, and hour, and minute. And I want you always to admire me, and praise everything that I do. Now—"

"Particularly when you tear holes in packages!" said Harry.

"O, my silk—my new silk dress!" said Lisette, thus reminded of the package which she held in her hand. "This hateful string! How it cuts my fingers! I *will* break it! I'll bite it in two. Harry, Harry, don't you see how it hurts my fingers? Why don't you cut it?"

And the little sprite danced about the cottage floor, tearing the paper, and tugging at the string, like an enraged humming-bird. Harry came laughing behind her, and, taking hold of her two hands, held them quite still, while he cut the string of the parcel, and unfolded a gorgeous plaid silk, crimson, green, and orange.

"There, now, what do you think of that? Miss Nina brought it, when she came home, last week."

"O, how lovely! Isn't she a beauty? Isn't she good? How beautiful it is! Dear me, dear me! how happy I am! How happy *we* are!— an't we, Harry?"

A shadow came over Harry's forehead as he answered, with a half-sigh,

"Yes."

"I was up at three o'clock, this morning, on purpose to get all my ironing done to-day, because I thought you were to come home to-night. Ah! ah! you don't know what a supper I've got ready! You'll see, by and by. I'm going to do something uncommon. You mustn't look in that other room, Harry—you mustn't!"

"Mustn't I?" said Harry, getting up, and going to the door.

"There, now! who's curiosity now, I wonder!" said she, springing nimbly between him and the door. "No, you shan't go in, though. There, now; don't, don't! *Be* good now, Harry!"

"Well, I may as well give up first as last. This is your house, not mine, I suppose," said Harry.

"Mr. Submission, how meek we are, all of a sudden! Well, while the fit lasts, you go to the spring and get me some water to fill this tea-kettle. Off with you, now, this minute! Mind you don't stop to play by the way!"

And, while Harry is gone to the spring, we will follow the wife into the forbidden room. Very cool and pleasant it is, with its white window-curtains, its matted floor, and displaying in the corner that draped feather-bed, with its ruffled pillows and fringed curtains, which it is the great ambition of the southern cabin to attain and maintain.

The door, which opened on to a show of most brilliant flowers, was overlaid completely by the lamarque rose we have before referred to; and large clusters of its creamy blossoms, and wreaths of its dark-green leaves, had been enticed in and tied to sundry nails and pegs by the small hands of the little mistress, to form an arch of flowers and roses. A little table stood in the door, draped with a spotless damasked table-cloth, fine enough for the use of a princess, and only produced by the little mistress on festive occasions. On it were arranged dishes curiously trimmed with moss and vine-leaves, which displayed strawberries and peaches, with a pitcher of cream and one of whey, small dishes of curd, delicate cakes and biscuit, and fresh golden butter.

After patting and arranging the table-cloth, Lisette tripped gayly around, and altered here and there the arrangement of a dish, occasionally stepping back, and cocking her little head on one side, much like a bird, singing gayly as she did so; then she would pick a bit of moss from this, and a flower from that, and retreat again, and watch the effect.

"How surprised he will be!" she said to herself. Still humming a tune in a low, gurgling undertone, she danced hither and thither, round the apartment. First she gave the curtains a little shake, and, unlooping one of them, looped it up again, so as to throw the beams of the evening sun on the table.

"There, there, there! how pretty the light falls through those nasturtions! I wonder if the room smells of the mignonette. I gathered it when the dew was on it, and they say that will make it smell all day. Now, here's Harry's book-case. Dear me! these flies! How they do get on to everything! Shoo, shoo! now, now!" and, catching a gay bandana handkerchief from the drawer, she perfectly exhausted herself in flying about the room in pursuit of the buzzing intruders, who soared, and dived, and careered, after the manner of flies in general, seeming determined to go anywhere but out of the door, and finally were seen brushing their wings and licking their feet, with great alertness, on the very topmost height of the sacred bed-curtains; and as just this moment a glimpse was caught of Harry returning from the spring, Lisette was obliged to abandon the chase, and rush into the other room, to prevent a premature development of her little tea-tableau. Then a small, pug-nosed, black tea-kettle came on to the stage of action, from some unknown cupboard; and Harry had to fill it with water, and of course spilt the water on to the ironing-table, which made another little breezy, chattering commotion; and then the flat-irons were cleared away, and the pug-nosed kettle reigned in their stead on the charcoal brazier.

"Now, Harry, was ever such a smart wife as I am? Only think, besides all the rest that I've done, I've ironed your white linen suit, complete! Now, go put it on. Not in there! not in there!" she said, pushing him away from the door. "You can't go there, yet. You'll do well enough out here."

And away she went, singing through the garden walks; and the song, floating back behind her, seemed like an odor brushed from the flowers. The refrain came rippling in at the door—

"Me think not what to-morrow bring;
Me happy, so me sing!"

"Poor little thing!" said Harry to himself; "why should I try to teach her anything?"

In a few minutes she was back again, her white apron thrown over her arm, and blossoms of yellow jessamine, spikes of blue lavender, and buds of moss-roses, peeping out from it. She skipped gayly along, and deposited her treasure on the ironing-table; then, with a zealous, bustling earnestness, which characterized everything she did, she began sorting them into two bouquets, alternately talking and singing, as she did so,

"Come on, ye rosy hours,
All joy and gladness bring!"

"You see, Harry, you're going to have a bouquet to put into the button-hole of that coat. It will make you look so handsome! There, now—there, now,

"We'll strew the way with flowers,
And merrily, merrily sing."

Suddenly stopping, she looked at him archly, and said, "You can't tell, now, what I'm doing all this for!"

"There's never any telling what you women do anything for."

"Do hear him talk—so pompous! Well, sir, it's for your birthday, now. Aha! you thought, because I can't keep the day of the month, that I didn't know anything about it; but I did. And I have put down now a chalk-mark every day, for four weeks, right under where I keep my ironing-account, so as to be sure of it. And I've been busy about it ever since two o'clock this morning. And now—there, the tea-kettle is boiling!"—and away she flew to the door.

"O, dear me!—dear me, now!—I've killed myself, now, I have!" she cried, holding up one of her hands, and flirting it up in the air. "Dear me! who knew it was so hot?"

"I should think a little woman that is so used to the holder *might* have known it," said Harry, as he caressed the little burnt hand.

"Come, now, let me carry it for you," said Harry, "and I'll make the tea, if you'll let me go into that mysterious room."

"Indeed, no, Harry—I'm going to do everything myself;" and, forgetting the burnt finger, Lisette was off in a moment, and back in a moment with a shining teapot in her hand, and the tea was made. And at last the mysterious door opened, and Lisette stood with her eyes fixed upon Harry, to watch the effect.

"Superb!—magnificent!—splendid! Why, this is good enough for a king! And where *did* you get all these things?" said Harry.

"O, out of our garden—all but the peaches. Those old Mist gave me—they come from Florida. There, now, you laughed at me, last summer, when I set those strawberry-vines, and made all sorts of fun of me. And what do you think now?"

"Think! I think you're a wonderful little thing—a perfect witch."

"Come, now, let's sit down, then—you there, and I here." And, opening the door of the bird-cage, which hung in the lamarque rose-bush, "Little Button shall come, too."

Button, a bright yellow canary, with a smart black tuft upon his head, seemed to understand his part in the little domestic scene perfectly; for he stepped obediently upon the finger which was extended to him, and was soon sitting quite at his ease on the mossy edge of one of the dishes, pecking at the strawberries.

"And, now, do tell me," said Lisette, "all about Miss Nina. How does she look?"

"Pretty and smart as ever," said Harry. "Just the same witchy, wilful ways with her."

"And did she show you her dresses?"

"O, yes; the whole."

"O, do tell me about them, Harry—do!"

"Well, there's a lovely pink gauze, covered with spangles, to be worn over white satin."

"With flounces?" said Lisette, earnestly.

"With flounces."

"How many?"

"Really, I don't remember."

"Don't remember how many flounces? Why, Harry, how stupid! Say, Harry, don't you suppose she will let me come and look at her things?"

"O, yes, dear, I don't doubt she will; and that will save my making a gazette of myself."

"O, when will you take me there, Harry?"

"Perhaps to-morrow, dear. And now," said Harry, "that you have accomplished your surprise upon me, I have a surprise, in return, for you. You can't guess, now, what Miss Nina brought for me."

"No, indeed! What?" said Lisette, springing up; "do tell me—quick."

"Patience—patience!" said Harry, deliberately fumbling in his pocket, amusing himself with her excited air. But who should speak the astonishment and rapture which widened Lisette's dark eyes, when the watch was produced? She clapped her hands, and danced for joy, to the imminent risk of upsetting the table, and all the things on it.

"I do think we are the most fortunate people—you and I, Harry! Everything goes just as we want it to—doesn't it, now?"

Harry's assent to this comprehensive proposition was much less fervent than suited his little wife.

"Now, what's the matter with you? What goes wrong? Why don't you rejoice as I do?" said she, coming and seating herself down upon his knee. "Come, now, you've been working too hard,

I know. I'm going to sing to you, now; you want something to cheer you up." And Lisette took down her banjo, and sat down in the doorway under the arch of lamarque roses, and began thrumming gayly.

"This is the nicest little thing, this banjo!" she said; "I wouldn't change it for all the guitars in the world. Now, Harry, I'm going to sing something specially for you." And Lisette sung:

> *"What are the joys of white man, here,*
> *What are his pleasures, say?*
> *He great, he proud, he haughty fine,*
> *While I my banjo play:*
> *He sleep all day, he wake all night;*
> *He full of care, his heart no light;*
> *He great deal want, he little get;*
> *He sorry, so he fret.*

> *"Me envy not the white man here.*
> *Though he so proud and gay;*
> *He great, he proud, he haughty fine,*
> *While I my banjo play:*
> *Me work all day, me sleep all night;*
> *Me have no care, me heart is light;*
> *Me think not what to-morrow bring;*
> *Me happy, so me sing."*

Lisette rattled the strings of the banjo, and sang with such a hearty abandon of enjoyment that it was a comfort to look at her. One would have thought that a bird's soul put into a woman's body would have sung just so.

"There," she said, throwing down her banjo, and seating herself on her husband's knee, "do you know I think you are like white man in the song? I should like to know what is the matter with you. I can see plain enough when you are not happy; but I don't see why."

"O, Lisette, I have very perplexing business to manage," said Harry. "Miss Nina is a dear, good little mistress, but she doesn't know anything about accounts, or money; and here she has brought me home a set of bills to settle, and I'm sure I don't know where the money is to be got from. It's hard work to make the old place profitable in our days. The ground is pretty much worked up; it doesn't bear the crops it used to. And, then, our people are so childish, they don't, a soul of them, care how much they spend, or how carelessly they work. It's very expensive keeping up such an establishment. You know the Gordons must be Gordons. Things can't be done now as some other families would do them; and, then, those bills which Miss Nina brings from New York are perfectly frightful."

"Well, Harry, what are you going to do?" said Lisette, nestling down close on his shoulder. "You always know how to do something."

"Why, Lisette, I shall have to do what I've done two or three times before—take the money that I have saved, to pay these bills— our freedom-money, Lisette."

"O, well, then, don't worry! We can get it again, you know. Why, you know, Harry, you can make a good deal with your trade, and one thing and another that you do; and, then, as for me, why, you know, my ironing, and my muslins, how celebrated they are. Come, don't worry one bit; we shall get on nicely."

"Ah! But, Lisette, all this pretty house of ours, garden, and everything, is only built on air, after all, till we are free. Any accident can take it from us. Now, there's Miss Nina; she is engaged, she tells me, to two or three lovers, as usual."

"Engaged, is she?" said Lisette, eagerly, female curiosity getting the better of every other consideration; "she always did have lovers, just, you know, as I used to."

"Yes; but, Lisette, she will marry, some time, and what a thing that would be for you and me! On her husband will depend all my happiness for all my life. He may set her against me; he may not like me. O, Lisette! I've seen trouble enough coming of marriages; and I was hoping, you see, that before that time came the money for my freedom would all be paid in, and I should be my own man. But, now, here it is. Just as the sum is almost made up, I must pay out five hundred dollars of it, and that throws us back two or three years longer. And what makes me feel the most anxious is, that I'm pretty sure Miss Nina will marry one of these lovers before long."

"Why, what makes you think so, Harry?"

"O, I've seen girls before now, Lisette, and I know the signs."

"What does she do? What does she say? Tell me, now, Harry."

"O, well, she runs on abusing the man, after her sort; and she's so very earnest and positive in telling me she don't like him."

"Just the way I used to do about you, Harry, isn't it?"

"Besides," said Harry, "I know, by the kind of character she gives of him, that she thinks of him very differently from what she ever did of any man before. Miss Nina little knows, when she is rattling about her beaux, what I'm thinking of. I'm saying, all the while, to myself, 'Is that man going to be my master?' and this Clayton, I'm very sure, is going to be my master."

"Well, isn't he a good man?"

"She *says* he is; but there's never any saying what good men will do, never. Good men think it right sometimes to do the strangest things. This man may alter the whole agreement between us,—he will have a right to do it, if he is her husband; he may refuse to let me buy myself; and, then, all the money that I've paid will go for nothing."

"But, certainly, Harry, Miss Nina will never consent to such a thing."

"Lisette, Miss Nina is one thing, but Mrs. Clayton may be quite another thing. I've seen all *that,* over and over again. I tell you, Lisette, that we who live on other people's looks and words, we watch and think a great deal! Ah! we come to be very sharp, I can tell you. The more Miss Nina has liked me, the less her husband may like me; don't you know that?"

"No; Harry, you don't dislike people I like."

"Child, child, that's quite another thing."

"Well, then, Harry, if you feel so bad about it, what makes you pay this money for Miss Nina? She don't know anything about it; she don't ask you to. I don't believe she would want you to, if she did know it. Just go and pay it in, and have your freedom-papers made out. Why don't you tell her all about it?"

"No, I can't, Lisette. I've had the care of her all her life, and I've made it as smooth as I could for her, and I won't begin to trouble her now. Do you know, too, that I'm afraid that, perhaps, if she knew all about it, she wouldn't do the right thing. There's never any knowing, Lisette. *Now,* you see, I say to myself, 'Poor little thing! she doesn't know anything about accounts, and she don't know how I feel.' But, if I should *tell* her; and she shouldn't care, and act as I've seen women act, why, then, you know, I couldn't think so any more. I don't *believe* she would, mind you; but, then, I don't like to try."

"Harry, what does make you love her so much?"

"Don't you know, Lisette, that Master Tom was a dreadful bad boy, always wilful and wayward, almost broke his father's heart; and he was always ugly and contrary to her? I'm sure I don't know why; for she was a sweet little thing, and she loves him now, ugly as he is, and he is the most selfish creature I ever saw. And, as for Miss Nina, she isn't selfish—she is only inconsiderate. But I've known her do for him, over and over, just what I do for her, giving him her money and her jewels to help him out of a scrape. But, then, to be sure, it all comes upon me, at last, which makes it all the more aggravating. Now, Lisette, I'm going to tell you something, but you mustn't tell anybody. Nina Gordon is my sister!"

"Harry!"

"Yes, Lisette, you may well open your eyes," said Harry, rising involuntarily; "I'm Colonel Gordon's oldest son! Let me have the comfort of saying it once, if I never do again."

"Harry, who told you?"

"*He* told me, Lisette—he, himself, told me, when he was dying, and charged me always to watch over her; and I have done it! I never told Miss Nina; I wouldn't have her told for the world. It wouldn't make her love me; more likely it would turn her against me. I've seen many a man sold for nothing else but looking too much like his father, or his brothers and sisters. I was given to her, and my sister and my mother went out to Mississippi with Miss Nina's aunt."

"I never heard you speak of this sister, Harry. Was she pretty?"

"Lisette, she was beautiful, she was graceful, and she had real genius. I've heard many singers on the stage that could not sing, with all their learning, as she did by nature."

"Well, what became of her?"

"O, what becomes of such women always, among us! Nursed, and petted, and caressed; taught everything elegant, nothing solid. Why, the woman meant well enough that had the care of her,—Mrs. Stewart, Colonel Gordon's sister,—but she couldn't prevent her son's wanting her, and taking her, for his mistress; and when she died there she was."

"Well."

"When George Stewart had lived with her two or three years, he was taken with small-pox. You know what perfect horror that always creates. None of his white acquaintances and friends would come near his plantation; the negroes were all frightened to death, as usual; overseer ran off. Well, then Cora Gordon's blood came up; she nursed him all through that sickness. What's more, she had influence to keep order on the place; got the people to getting the cotton crops themselves, so that when the overseer came sneaking back, things hadn't all gone to ruin, as they might have done. Well, the young fellow had more in him than some of them do; for when he got well he left his plantation, took her up to Ohio, and married her, and lived with her there."

"Why didn't he live with her on his plantation?" said Lisette.

"He couldn't have freed her there; it's against the laws. But, lately, I've got a letter from her, saying that he had died and left to her and her son all his property on the Mississippi."

"Why, she will be rich, won't she?"

"Yes, if she gets it. But there's no knowing how that will be; there are fifty ways of cheating her out of it, I suppose. But, now, as to Miss Nina's estate, you don't know how I feel about it. I was trusted with it, and trusted with her. She never has known, more than a child, where the money came from, or went to; and it shan't be said that I've brought the estate in debt, for the sake of getting my own liberty. If I have one pride in life, it is to give it up to Miss Nina's husband in good order. But, then, the *trouble* of it, Lisette! The trouble of getting anything like decent work from these creatures; the ways that I have to turn and twist to get round them, and manage them, to get anything done. They hate me; they are jealous of me. Lisette, I'm just like the bat in the fable; I'm neither bird nor beast. How often I've wished that I was a good, honest, black nigger, like Uncle Pomp! Then I should know what I was; but, now, I'm neither one thing nor another. I come just near enough to the condition of the white to look into it, to enjoy it, and want everything that I see. Then, the way I've been educated makes it worse. The fact is, that when the fathers of such as we feel any love for us, it isn't like the love they have for their white children. They are half-ashamed of us; they are ashamed to show their love, if they have it; and, then, there's a kind of remorse and pity about it, which they make up to themselves by petting us. They load us with presents and indulgences. They amuse themselves with us while we are children, and play off all our passions as if we were instruments to be played on. If we show talent and smartness, we hear some one say, aside, 'It's rather a pity, isn't it?' or, 'He is too smart for his place.' Then, we have all the family blood and the family pride; and what to do with it? I feel that I am a Gordon. I feel in my very heart that I'm like Colonel Gordon—I know I am; and, sometimes, I know I look like him, and that's one reason why Tom Gordon always hated me; and, then, there's another thing, the hardest of all, to have a sister like Miss Nina, to feel she *is* my sister, and never dare to say a word of it! She little thinks, when she plays and jokes with me, sometimes, how I feel. I have eyes and senses; I can compare myself with Tom Gordon. I know he *never would* learn anything at any of the schools he was put to; and I know that when his tutors used to teach me, how much faster I got along than he did. And yet he must have all the position, and all the respect; and, then, Miss Nina so often says to me, by way of apology, when she puts up with his ugliness, 'Ah! well, you know, Harry, he is the only brother I have got in the world!' Isn't it too bad? Col. Gordon gave me every advantage of education, because I think he meant me for just this place which I fill. Miss Nina was his pet. He was wholly absorbed in her, and he was frightened at Tom's wickedness; and so he left me bound to the estate in this way, only stipulating that I should buy myself on favorable terms before Miss Nina's marriage. She has always been willing enough. I might have taken any and every advantage of her inconsiderateness. And Mr. John Gordon has been willing, too, and has been very kind about it, and has signed an agreement as guardian, and Miss Nina has signed it too, that, in case of her death, or whatever happened, I'm to have my freedom on paying a certain sum, and I have got his receipts for what I have paid. So that's tolerably safe. Lisette, I had meant never to have been married till I was a free man; but, somehow, you bewitched me into it. I did very wrong."

"O, pshaw! pshaw!" interrupted Lisette. "I an't going to hear another word of this talk! What's the use? We shall do well enough. Everything will come out right,—you see if it don't, now. I was always lucky, and I always shall be."

The conversation was here interrupted by a loud whooping, and a clatter of horse's heels.

"What's that?" said Harry, starting to the window. "As I live, now, if there isn't that wretch of a Tomtit, going off with that horse! How came he here? He will ruin him! Stop there! hallo!" he exclaimed, running out of doors after Tomtit.

Tomtit, however, only gave a triumphant whoop, and disappeared among the pine-trees.

"Well, I should like to know what sent him here!" said Harry, walking up and down, much disturbed.

"O, he is only going round through the grove; he will be back again," said Lisette; "never fear. Isn't he a handsome little rogue?"

"Lisette, you never can see trouble anywhere!" said Harry, almost angrily.

"Ah! yes, I do," said Lisette, "when you speak in that tone! Please don't, Harry! What should you want me to see trouble for?"

"I don't know, you little thing," said Harry, stroking her head fondly.

"Ah, there comes the little rascal, just as I knew he would!" said Lisette. "He only wanted to take a little race; he hasn't hurt the horse;" and, tripping lightly out, she caught the reins, just as Tomtit drove up to the gate; and it seemed but a moment before he was over in the garden, with his hands full of flowers.

"Stop, there, you young rascal, and tell me what sent you here!" said Harry, seizing him, and shaking him by the shoulder.

"Laws, Massa Harry, I wants to get peaches, like other folks," said the boy, peeping roguishly in at the window, at the tea-table.

"And he shall have a peach, too," said Lisette, "and some flowers, if he'll be a good boy, and not tread on my borders."

Tomtit seized greedily at the peach she gave him, and, sitting flat down where he stood, and throwing the flowers on the ground beside him, began eating it with an earnestness of devotion as if his whole being were concentrated in the act. The color was heightened in his brown cheek by the exercise, and, with his long, drooping curls and eyelashes, he looked a very pretty centre to the flowerpiece which he had so promptly improvised.

"Ah, how pretty he is!" said Lisette, touching Harry's elbow. "I wish he was mine!"

"You'd have your hands full, if he was," said Harry, eying the intruder discontentedly, while Lisette stood picking the hulls from a fine bunch of strawberries which she was ready to give him when he had finished the peach.

"Beauty makes fools of all you girls," said Harry, cynically.

"Is that the reason I married you?" said Lisette, archly. "Well, I know I could make him good, if I had the care of him. Nothing like coaxing; is there, Tom?"

"I'll boun' there an't!" said Tom, opening his mouth for the strawberries with much the air of a handsome, saucy robin.

"Well," said Harry, "I should like to know what brought him over here. Speak, now, Tom! Weren't you sent with some message?"

"O laws, yes!" said Tom, getting up, and scratching his curly head. "Miss Nina sent me. She wants you to get on dat ar horse, and make tracks for home like split foot. She done got letters from two or three of her beaux, and she is dancing and tearing round there real awful. She done got scared, spects; feard they'd all come together."

"And she sent you on a message, and you haven't told me, all this time!" said Harry, making a motion as though he was going to box the child's ears; but the boy glided out of his hands as if he had been water, and was gone, vanishing among the shrubbery of the garden; and while Harry was mounting his horse, he reappeared on the roof of the little cabin, caricoling and dancing, shouting at the topmost of his voice.

"Away down old Virginny,
Dere I bought a yellow girl for a guinea."

"I'll give it to you, some time!" said Harry, shaking his fist at him.

"No, he won't, either," cried Lisette, laughing. "Come down here, Tomtit, and I'll make a good boy of you."

CHAPTER VI

The Dilemma

IN ORDER TO UNDERSTAND the occasion which hurried Harry home, we must go back to Canema. Nina, after taking her letters from the hands of Tomtit, as we have related, ran back with them into Mrs. Nesbit's room, and sat herself down to read them. As she read, she evidently became quite excited and discomposed, crumpling a paper with her little hand, and tapping her foot impatiently on the carpet.

"There, now, I'm sure I don't know what I shall do, Aunt Nesbit!" addressing her aunt, because it was her outspoken habit to talk to any body or thing which happened to be sitting next to her. "I've got myself into a pretty scrape now!"

"I told you you'd get into trouble, one of these days!"

"O, you *told* me so! If there's anything I hate, it is to have anybody tell me 'I told you so!' But, now, aunt, really, I know I've been foolish, but I don't know what to do. Here are two gentlemen coming together, that I wouldn't have meet each other here for the world; and I don't know really what I had better do."

"You'd better do just as you please, as you always do, and always would, ever since I knew you," said Aunt Nesbit, in a calm, indifferent tone.

"But, really, aunt, I don't know what's proper to do in such a case."

"Your and my notions of propriety, Nina, are so different, that I don't know how to advise you. You see the consequences, now, of not attending to the advice of your friends. I always knew these flirtations of yours would bring you into trouble." And Aunt Nesbit said this with that quiet, satisfied air with which precise elderly people so often edify their thoughtless young friends under difficulties.

"Well, I didn't want a sermon, now, Aunt Nesbit; but, as you've seen a great deal more of the world than I have, I thought you might help me a little, just to tell me whether it wouldn't be proper for me to write and put one of these gentlemen off; or make some excuse for me, or something. I'm sure *I* never kept house before. I don't want to do anything that don't seem hospitable; and yet I don't want them to come together. Now, there, that's flat!"

There was a long pause, in which Nina sat vexed and coloring, biting her lips, and nestling uneasily in her seat.

Mrs. Nesbit looked calm and considerate, and Nina began to hope that she was taking the case a little to heart.

At last the good old lady looked up, and said, very quietly, "I wonder what time it is."

Nina thought she was debating the expediency of sending some message; and therefore she crossed the room with great alacrity, to look at the old clock in the entry.

"It's half-past two, aunt!" and she stood, with her lips apart, looking at Mrs. Nesbit for some suggestion.

"I was going to tell Rosa," said she, abstractedly, "that that onion in the stuffing does not agree with me. It rose on my stomach all yesterday morning; but it's too late now."

Nina actually stamped with anger.

"Aunt Nesbit, you are the most selfish person I ever saw in my life!"

"Nina, child, you astonish me!" said Aunt Nesbit, with her wonted placidity. "What's the matter?"

"I don't care!" said Nina, "I don't care a bit! I don't see how people can be so! If a dog should come to me and tell me he was in trouble, I think I should listen to him, and show some kind of interest to help him! I don't care how foolish anybody has been; if they are in trouble, I'd help them, if I could; and I think you might think enough of it to give me some little advice!"

"O, you are talking about that affair, yet?" said her aunt. "Why, I believe I told you I didn't know what to advise, didn't I? Shouldn't give way to this temper, Nina; it's very unladylike, besides being sinful. But, then, I don't suppose it's any use for me to talk!" And Aunt Nesbit, with an abused air, got up, walked quietly to the looking-glass, took off her morning cap, unlocked her drawer, and laid it in; took out another, which Nina could not see differed a particle from the last, held it up thoughtfully on her hand, and appeared absorbed in the contemplation of it,—while Nina, swelling with a mixture of anger and mortification, stood regarding her as she leisurely picked out each bow, and finally, with a decorous air of solemnity, arranged it upon her head, patting it tenderly down.

"Aunt Nesbit," she said, suddenly, as if the words hurt her, "I think I spoke improperly, and I'm very sorry for it. I beg your pardon."

"O, it's no matter, child; I didn't care about it. I'm pretty well used to your temper."

Bang went the door, and in a moment Nina stood in the entry, shaking her fist at it with impotent wrath.

"You stony, stiff, disagreeable old creature! how came you ever to be my mother's sister?" And, with the word mother, she burst into a tempest of tears, and rushed violently to her own chamber. The first object that she saw was Milly, arranging some clothes in her drawer; and, to her astonishment, Nina rushed up to her, and, throwing her arms round her neck, sobbed and wept, in such tumultuous excitement, that the good creature was alarmed.

"Laws bless my soul, my dear little lamb! what's the matter? Why, don't! Don't, honey! Why, bless the dear little soul! bless the dear precious lamb! who's been a hurting of it?" And, at each word of endearment, Nina's distress broke out afresh, and she sobbed so bitterly that the faithful creature really began to be frightened.

"Laws, Miss Nina, I hope there an't nothing happened to you now!"

"No, no, nothing, Milly, only I am lonesome, and I want my mother! I haven't got any mother! Dear me!" she said, with a fresh burst.

"Ah, the poor thing!" said Milly, compassionately, sitting down, and fondling Nina in her arms, as if she had been a babe. "Poor chile! Laws, yes; I 'member your ma was a beautiful woman!"

"Yes," said Nina, speaking between her sobs, "the girls at school had mothers. And there was Mary Brooks, she used to read to me her mother's letters, and I used to feel so, all the while, to think nobody wrote such letters to me! And there's Aunt Nesbit—I don't care what they say about her being religious, she is the most selfish, hateful creature I ever did see! I do believe, if I was lying dead and laid out in the next room to her, she would be thinking what she'd get next for dinner!"

"O, don't, my poor lamb, don't!" said Milly, compassionately.

"Yes, I will, too! She's always taking it for granted that I'm the greatest sinner on the face of the earth! She don't scold me—she don't care enough about me to scold! She only takes it for granted, in her hateful, quiet way, that I'm going to destruction, and that she can't help it, and don't care! Supposing I'm not good!—what's to make me good? Is it going to make me good for people to sit up so stiff, and tell me they always knew I was a fool, and a flirt, and all that? Milly, I've had dreadful turns of wanting to be good, and I've laid awake nights and cried because I wasn't good. And what makes it worse is, that I think, if Ma was alive, she could help me. She wasn't like Aunt Nesbit, was she, Milly?"

"No, honey, she wasn't. I'll tell you about your ma, some time, honey."

"The worst of it is," said Nina, "when Aunt Nesbit speaks to me in her hateful way, I get angry; then I speak in a way that isn't proper, I know. O, if she only would get angry with me back again! or if she'd do anything in the world but stand still, in her still way, telling me she is astonished at me! That's a lie, too; for she never was astonished at anything in her life! She hasn't life enough to be!"

"Ah, Miss Nina, we mustn't spect more of folks than there is in them."

"Expect? I don't expect!"

"Well, bless you, honey, when you knows what folks *is,* don't let's worry. Ye can't fill a quart-cup out of a thimble, honey, no way you can fix it. There's just whar 't is. I knowed your ma, and I's knowed Miss Loo, ever since she was a girl. 'Pears like they wan't no more alike than snow is like sugar. Miss Loo, when she was a girl, she was that pretty, that everybody was wondering after her; but to de love, dat ar went arter your ma. Couldn't tell why it was, honey. 'Peared like Miss Loo wan't techy, nor she wan't one of your bursting-out sort, scolding round. 'Peared like she'd never hurt nobody; and yet our people, they couldn't none of dem bar her. 'Peared like nobody did nothing for her with a will."

"Well, good reason!" said Nina; "she never did anything for anybody else with a will! She never cared for anybody! Now, I'm selfish; I always knew it. I do a great many selfish things; but it's a different kind from hers. Do you know, Milly, she don't seem to know she is selfish? There she sits, rocking in her old chair, so sure she's going straight to heaven, and don't care whether anybody else gets there or not!"

"O laws, now, Miss Nina, you's too hard on her. Why, look

how patient she sits with Tomtit, teaching him his hymns and varses."

"And you think that's because she cares anything about him? Do you know she thinks he isn't fit to go to heaven, and that if he dies he'll go to the bad place. And yet, if he was to die to-morrow, she'd talk to you about clear-starching her caps! No wonder the child don't love her! She talks to him just as she does to me; tells him she don't expect anything of him—she knows he'll never come to any good; and the little wretch has got it by heart, now. Do you know that, though I get in a passion with Tom, sometimes, and though I'm sure I should perish sitting boring with him over those old books, yet I really believe I care more for him than she does? And he knows it, too. He sees through her as plain as I do. You'll never make me believe that Aunt Nesbit has got religion. I know there is such a thing as religion; but she hasn't got it. It isn't all being sober, and crackling old stiff religious newspapers, and boring with texts and hymns, that makes people religious. She is just as wordly-minded as I am, only it's in another way. There, now, I wanted her to advise me about something, to-day. Why, Milly, all girls want somebody to talk with; and if she'd only showed the least interest in what I said, she might scold me and lecture me as much as she'd a mind to. But, to have her not even hear me! And when she must have seen that I was troubled and perplexed, and wanted somebody to advise me, she turned round so cool, and began to talk about the onions and the stuffing! Got me so angry! I suppose she is in her room, now, rocking, and thinking what a sinner I am!"

"Well, now, Miss Nina, 'pears though you've talked enough about dat ar; 'pears like it won't make you feel no better."

"Yes it *does* make me feel better! I had to speak to somebody, Milly, or else I should have burst; and now I wonder where Harry is. He always could find a way for me out of anything."

"He is gone over to see his wife, I think, Miss Nina."

"O, too bad! Do send Tomtit after him, right away. Tell him that I want him to come right home, this very minute—something very particular. And, Milly, you just go and tell Old Hundred to get out the carriage and horses, and I'll go over and drop a note in the post-office, myself. I won't trust it to Tomtit; for I know he'll lose it."

"Miss Nina," said Milly, looking hesitatingly, "I 'spect you don't know how things go about round here; but the fact is, Old Hundred has got so kind of cur'ous, lately, there can't nobody do noth-

ing with him, except Harry. Don't 'tend to do nothing Miss Loo
tells him to. I's feared he'll make up some story or other about the
horses; but he won't get 'em out—now, mind, I tell you, chile!"

"He won't! I should like to know if he won't, when I tell him to!
A pretty story that would be! I'll soon teach him that he has a live
mistress—somebody quite different from Aunt Loo!"

"Well, well, chile, perhaps you'd better go. He wouldn't mind
me, I know. Maybe he'll do it for you."

"O, yes; I'll just run down to his house, and hurry him up." And
Nina, quite restored to her usual good-humor, tripped gayly across
to the cabin of Old Hundred, that stood the other side of the house.

Old Hundred's true name was, in fact, John. But he had derived
the appellation by which he was always known, from the extreme
moderation of all his movements. Old Hundred had a double share
of that profound sense of the dignity of his office which is an attribute of the tribe of coachmen in general. He seemed to consider
the horses and carriage as a sort of family ark, of which he was the
high priest, and which it was his business to save from desecration.
According to his own showing, all the people on the plantation, and
indeed the whole world in general, were in a state of habitual conspiracy against the family carriage and horses, and he was standing
for them, single-handed, at the risk of his life. It was as much part of
his duty, in virtue of his office, to show cause, on every occasion,
why the carriage should *not* be used, as it is for state attorneys to
undertake prosecutions. And it was also a part of the accomplish-
ment of his situation to conduct his refusal in the most decorous
manner; always showing that it was only the utter impossibility of
the case which prevented. The available grounds of refusal Old
Hundred had made a life-study, and had always a store of them cut
and dried for use, all ready at a moment's notice. In the first place,
there were always a number of impossibilities with regard to the
carriage. Either "it was muddy, and he was laying out to wash it;"
or else "he had washed it, and couldn't have it splashed;" or "he had
taken out the back curtain, and had laid out to put a stitch in it, one
of dese yer days;" or there was something the matter with the irons.
"He reckoned they was a little bit sprung." He " 'lowed he'd ask the
blacksmith about it, some of these yer times." And, then, as to the
horses the possibilities were rich and abundant. What with strains,
and loose shoes, and stones getting in at the hoofs, dangers of all
sorts of complaints, for which he had his own vocabulary of names,

it was next to an impossibility, according to any ordinary rule of computing chances, that the two should be in complete order together.

Utterly ignorant, however, of the magnitude of the undertaking which she was attempting, and buoyant with the consciousness of authority, Nina tripped singing along, and found Old Hundred tranquilly reclining in his tent-door, watching through his half-shut eyes, while the afternoon sunbeam irradiated the smoke which rose from the old pipe between his teeth. A large, black, one-eyed crow sat perching, with a quizzical air, upon his knee; and when he heard Nina's footsteps approaching, cocked his remaining eye towards her, with a smart, observing attitude, as if he had been deputed to look out for applications while his master dozed. Between this crow, who had received the sobriquet of Uncle Jeff, and his master, there existed a most particular bond of friendship and amity. This was further strengthened by the fact that they were both equally disliked by all the inhabitants of the place. Like many people who are called to stand in responsible positions, Old Hundred had rather failed in the humble virtues, and become dogmatical and dictatorial to that degree that nobody but his own wife could do anything with him. And as to Jeff, if the principle of thievery could be incarnate, he might have won a temple among the Lacedemonians.[1] In various skirmishes and battles consequent on his misdeeds, Jeff had lost an eye, and had a considerable portion of the feathers scalded off on one side of his head; while the remaining ones, discomposed by the incident, ever after stood up in a protesting attitude, imparting something still more sinister to his goblin appearance. In another rencounter he had received a permanent twist in the neck, which gave him always the appearance of looking over his shoulder, and added not a little to the oddity of the general effect. Uncle Jeff thieved with an assiduity and skill which were worthy of a better cause; and, when not upon any serious enterprise of this kind, employed his time in pulling up corn, scratching up newly-planted flower-seeds, tangling yarn, pulling out knitting-needles, pecking the eyes of sleeping people, scratching and biting children, and any other little miscellaneous mischief which occurred to him. He was invaluable to Old Hundred, because he was a standing apology for any and all discoveries made on his premises of things which ought not to have been there. No matter what was brought to light,—whether spoons from the great house, or a pair of sleeve-buttons, or a handkerchief, or a pipe from a neighboring cabin,—Jeff was always called up to answer. Old Hundred regularly scolded, on these occasions, and declared he was enough to "spile the character of any man's house." And Jeff would look at him comically over the shoulder, and wink his remaining eye, as much as to say that the scolding was a settled thing between them, and that he wasn't going to take it at all in ill part.

"Uncle John," said Nina, "I want you to get the carriage out for me, right away. I want to take a ride over the cross run."

"Laws bless you sweet face, honey, chile, I's dreadful sorry; but you can't do it dis yer day."

"Can't do it! why not?"

"Why, bless you, chile, it an't possible, no way. Can't have the carriage and hosses dis yer arternoon."

"But I *must* go over to cross run to the post-office. I must go this minute!"

"Law, chile, you can't do it! fur you can't walk, and it's sartain you can't ride, because dese yer hosses, nor dis yer carriage, can't stir out dis yer arternoon, no way you can fix it. Mout go, perhaps, to-morrow, or next week."

"O, Uncle John, I don't believe a word of it! I want them this afternoon, and I say I *must* have them!"

"No, you can't, chile," said Old Hundred, in a tender, condescending tone, as if he was speaking to a baby. "I tell you dat ar is impossible. Why, bless your soul, Miss Nina, de curtains is all off de carriage!"

"Well, put them on again, then!"

"Ah, Miss Nina, dat ar an't all. Pete was desperate sick, last night; took with de thumps, powerful bad. Why, Miss Nina, he was dat sick I had to be up with him most all night!" And, while Old Hundred thus adroitly issued this little work of fiction, the raven nodded waggishly at Nina, as much as to say, "You hear that fellow, now!"

Nina stood quite perplexed, biting her lips, and Old Hundred seemed to go into a profound slumber.

"I don't believe but what the horses can go to-day! I mean to go and look."

"Laws, honey, chile, ye can't, now; de do's is all locked, and I've got de key in my pocket. Every one of dem critturs would have been killed forty times over 'fore now. I think everybody in dis yer world is arter dem dar critturs. Miss Loo, she's wanting 'em to go one way, and Harry's allers usin' de critturs. Got one out, dis yer arternoon, riding over to see his wife. Don't see no use in his riding round so grand, noway! Laws, Miss Nina, your pa used to say to me, says he, 'Uncle John, you knows more about dem critturs dan I do; and, now I tell you what it is, Uncle John—you take care of dem critturs; don't you let nobody kill 'em for nothing.' Now, Miss Nina, I's always a walking in the steps of the colonel's 'rections. Now, good, clar, bright weather, over good roads, I likes to trot the critturs out. Dat ar is reasonable. But, den, what roads is over the cross run, I want to know? Dem dere roads is de most mis'ablest things you ever did see. Mud! Hi! Ought for to see de mud down dar by de creek! Why, de bridge all tared off! Man drowned in dat dar creek once! Was so! It an't no sort of road for young ladies to go over. Tell you, Miss Nina; why don' you let Harry carry your letter over? If he must be ridin' round de country, don't see why he couldn't do some good wid his ridin'. Why, de carriage wouldn't get over before ten o'clock, dis yer night! Now, mine, I tell you. Besides, it's gwine fur to rain. I's been feeling dat ar in my corns, all dis yer morning; and Jeff, he's been acting like the berry debil his-self—de way he always does 'fore it rains. Never knowed dat ar sign to fail."

"The short of the matter is, Uncle John, you are determined not to go," said Nina. "But I tell you you *shall* go!—there, now! Now, do you get up immediately, and get out those horses!"

Old Hundred still sat quiet, smoking; and Nina, after reiterating her orders till she got thoroughly angry, began, at last, to ask herself the question, how she was going to carry them into execution. Old Hundred appeared to have descended into himself in a profound revery, and betrayed not the smallest sign of hearing anything she said.

"I wish Harry would come back quick," she said to herself, as she pensively retraced her steps through the garden; but Tomtit had taken the commission to go for him in his usual leisurely way, spending the greater part of the afternoon on the road.

"Now, an't you ashamed of yourself, you mean old nigger!" said Aunt Rose, the wife of Old Hundred, who had been listening to the conversation; "talking 'bout de creek, and de mud, and de critturs, and lor knows what all, when we all knows it's nothing but your laziness!"

"Well," said Old Hundred, "and what would come o' the critturs if I wasn't lazy, I want to know? Laziness! it's the berry best thing for the critturs can be. Where'd dem horses a been now, if I had been one of your highfelutin sort, always driving round? Where'd dey a been, and what would dey a been, hey? Who wants to see hosses all skin and bone? Lord! if I had been like some o' de coachmen, de buzzards would have had the picking of dem critturs, long ago!"

"I rally believe that you've told dem dar lies till you begin to believe them yourself!" said Rose. "Telling our dear, sweet young lady about your being up with Pete all night, when de Lord knows you laid here snoring fit to tar de roof off!"

"Well, must say something! Folks must be 'spectful to de ladies. Course I couldn't tell her I *wouldn't* take de critturs out; so I just trots out scuse. Ah! lots of dem scuses I keeps! I tell you, now, scuses is excellent things. Why, scuses is like dis yer grease that keeps de wheels from screaking. Lord bless you, de whole world turns round on scuses. Whar de world be if everybody was such fools to tell the raal reason for everything they are gwine for to do, or an't gwine fur to!"

CHAPTER VII

Consultation

"O, HARRY, I'm so glad to see you back! In such trouble as I've been to-day! Don't you think, this very morning, as I was sitting in Aunt Nesbit's room, Tomtit brought up these two letters; and one of them is from Clayton, and the other from Mr. Carson; and, now, see here what Clayton says: 'I shall have business that will take me in your vicinity next week; and it is quite possible, unless I hear from you to the contrary, that you may see me at Canema next Friday or Saturday.' Well, then, see here; there's another from Mr. Carson,—that hateful Carson! Now, you see, he hasn't got my letter; says he is coming. What impudence! I'm tired to death of that creature, and he'll be here just as certain! Disagreeable people always do keep their promises! He'll certainly be here!"

"Well, Miss Nina, you recollect you said you thought it would be good fun."

"O, Harry, don't bring that up, I beg of you! The fact is, Harry, I've altered my mind about that. You know I've put a stop to all those foolish things at once, and am done with them. You know I wrote to Carson and Emmons, both, that my sentiments had changed, and all that sort of thing, that the girls always say. I'm going to dismiss all of 'em at once, and have no more fooling."

"What, all? Mr. Clayton and all?"

"Well, I don't know, exactly,—no. Do you know, Harry, I think his letters are rather improving?—at least, they are different letters from any I've got before; and, though I don't think I shall break my heart after him, yet I like to get them. But the other two I'm sick to death of; and, as for having that creature boring round here, I won't! At any rate, I don't want him and Clayton here together. I wouldn't have them together for the world; and I wrote a letter to keep Carson off, this morning, and I've been in trouble all day. Everybody has plagued me. Aunt Nesbit only gave me one of her mopy lectures about flirting, and wouldn't help me in the least.

And, then, Old Hundred: I wanted him to get out the carriage and horses for me to go over and put this letter in the office, and I never saw such a creature in my life! I can't make him do anything! I should like to know what the use is of having servants, if you can't get anything done!"

"O, as to Old Hundred, I understand him, and he understands me," said Harry. "I never find any trouble with him; but he is a provoking old creature. He stands very much on the dignity of his office. But, if you want your letter carried to-night, I can contrive a safer way than that, if you'll trust it to me."

"Ah! well, do take it!"

"Yes," said Harry, "I'll send a messenger across on horseback, and I have means to make him faithful."

"Well, Harry, Harry!" said Nina, catching at his sleeve as he was going out, "come back again, won't you? I want to talk to you."

During Harry's absence, our heroine drew a letter from her bosom, and read it over.

"How well he writes!" she said to herself. "So different from the rest of them! I wish he'd keep away from here,—that's what I do! It's a pretty thing to get his letters, but I don't think I want to see *him*. O, dear! I wish I had somebody to talk to about it—Aunt Nesbit is *so* cross! I can't—no, I won't care about him! Harry is a kind soul."

"Ah, Harry, have you sent the letter?" said she eagerly, as he entered.

"I have, Miss Nina; but I can't flatter you too much. I'm afraid it's too late for the mail—though there's never any saying when the mail goes out, within two or three hours."

"Well, I hope it will stay for me, once. If that stupid creature comes, why, I don't know what I shall do! He's so presuming! and he'll squeak about with those horrid shoes of his; and then, I suppose, it will all come out, one way or another; and I don't know what Clayton will think."

"But I thought you didn't care *what* he thought."

"Well, you know, he's been writing to me all about his family. There's his father, is a very distinguished man, of a very old family; and he's been writing to me about his sister, the most dreadfully sensible sister, he has got—good, lovely, accomplished, and pious! O, dear me! I don't know what in the world he ever thought of *me* for! And, do you think, there's a postscript from his sister, written elegantly as can be!"

"As to family, Miss Nina," said Harry, "I think the Gordons can hold up their heads with anybody; and, then, I rather think you'll like Miss Clayton."

"Ah! but, then, Harry, this talking about fathers and sisters, it's bringing the thing awfully *near!* It looks so much, you know, as if I really were caught. Do you know, Harry, I think I'm just like my pony? You know, she likes to have you come and offer her corn, and stroke her neck; and she likes to *make you believe* she's going to let you catch her; but when it comes to putting a bridle on her, she's off in a minute. Now, that's the way with me. It's rather exciting, you know, these beaux, and love-letters, and talking sentiment, going to the opera, and taking rides on horseback, and all that. But, when men get to talking about their fathers, and their sisters, and to act as if they were sure of me, I'm just like Sylfine—I want to be off. You know, Harry, I think it's a very serious thing, this being married. It's dreadful! I don't want to be a woman grown. I wish I could always be a girl, and live just as I have lived, and have plenty more girls come and see me, and have fun. I haven't been a bit happy lately, not a bit; and I never was unhappy before in my life."

"Well, why don't you write to Mr. Clayton, and break it all off, if you feel so about it?"

"Well, why don't I? I don't know. I've had a great mind to do it; but I'm afraid I should feel worse than I do now. He's coming just like a great dark shadow over my life, and everything is beginning to feel so real to me! I don't want to take up life in earnest. I read a story, once, about Undine;[1] and, do you know, Harry, I think I feel just as Undine did, when she felt her soul coming in her?"

"And is Clayton Knight Heldebound?"[2] said Harry, smiling.

"I don't know. What if he should be? Now, Harry, you see the fact is that sensible men get their heads turned by such kind of girls as I am; and they pet us, and humor us. But, then, I'm afraid they're thinking, all the while, that their turn to rule is coming, by and by. They marry us because they think they are going to make us over; and what I'm afraid of is, I never *can* be made over. Don't think I was cut out right in the first place; and there never will be much more of me than there is now. And he'll be comparing me with his pattern sister; and I shan't be any the more amiable for that. Now, his sister is what folks call highly-educated, you know, Harry. She understands all about literature, and everything. As for me, I've just cultivation enough to appreciate a fine horse—that's the extent. And yet I'm proud. I wouldn't wish to stand second, in his opinion, even to his sister. So, there it is. That's the way with us girls! We are always wanting what we know we ought not to have, and are not willing to take the trouble to get."

"Miss Nina, if you'll let me speak my mind out frankly, now, I want to offer one piece of advice. Just be perfectly true and open with Mr. Clayton; and, if he and Mr. Carson should come together, just tell him frankly how the matter stands. You are a Gordon, and they say truth always runs in the Gordon blood; and now, Miss Nina, you are no longer a school-girl, but a young lady at the head of the estate."

He stopped, and hesitated.

"Well, Harry, you needn't stop. I understand you—got a few grains of sense left, I hope, and haven't got so many friends that I can afford to get angry with you for nothing."

"I suppose," said Harry, thoughtfully, "that your aunt will be well enough to be down to the table. Have you told her how matters stand?"

"Who? Aunt Loo? Catch me telling her anything! No, Harry, I've got to stand all alone. I haven't any mother, and I haven't any sister; and Aunt Loo is worse than nobody, because it's provoking to have somebody round that you feel might take an interest, and ought to, and don't care a red cent for you. Well, I declare, if I'm not much,—if I'm not such a model as Miss Clayton, there,—how could any one expect it, when I have just come up by myself, first at the plantation, here, and then at that French boarding-school? I tell you what, Harry, boarding-schools are not what they're cried up to be. It's good fun, no doubt, but we never learnt anything there. That is to say, we never learnt it internally, but had it just rubbed on to us outside. A girl can't help, of course, learning something; and I've learnt just what I happened to like and couldn't help, and a deal that isn't of the most edifying nature besides."

Well! we shall see what will come!

CHAPTER VIII

Old Tiff

"I SAY, TIFF, *do* you think he will come, to-night?"

"Laws, laws, Missis, how can Tiff tell? I's been a gazin' out de do'. Don't see nor hear nothin'."

"It's so lonesome!—*so* lonesome!—and the nights so long!"

And the speaker, an emaciated, feeble little woman, turned herself uneasily on the ragged pallet where she was lying, and, twirling her slender fingers nervously, gazed up at the rough, unplastered beams above.

The room was of the coarsest and rudest cast. The hut was framed of rough pine logs, filled between the crevices with mud and straw; the floor made of rough-split planks, unevenly jointed together; the window was formed by some single panes arranged in a row where a gap had been made in one of the logs. At one end was a rude chimney of sticks, where smouldered a fire of pine-cones and brush-wood, covered over with a light coat of white ashes. On the mantle over it was a shelf, which displayed sundry vials, a cracked teapot and tumbler, some medicinal-looking packages, a turkey's wing, much abridged and defaced by frequent usage, some bundles of dry herbs, and lastly a gayly-painted mug of coarse crockery-ware, containing a bunch of wild-flowers. On pegs, driven into the logs, were arranged different articles of female attire, and divers little coats and dresses, which belonged to smaller wearers, with now and then soiled and coarse articles of man's apparel.

The woman, who lay upon a coarse chaff pallet in the corner, was one who once might have been pretty. Her skin was fair, her hair soft and curling, her eyes of a beautiful blue, her hands thin and transparent as pearl. But the deep, dark circles under the eyes, the thin, white lips, the attenuated limbs, the hurried breathing, and the burning spots in the cheek, told that, whatever she might have been, she was now not long for this world.

Beside her bed was sitting an old negro, in whose close-curling wool age had begun to sprinkle flecks of white. His countenance presented, physically, one of the most uncomely specimens of negro features; and would have been positively frightful, had it not been redeemed by an expression of cheerful kindliness which beamed from it. His face was of ebony blackness, with a wide, upturned nose, a mouth of portentous size, guarded by clumsy lips, revealing teeth which a shark might have envied. The only fine feature was his large, black eyes, which, at the present, were concealed by a huge pair of plated spectacles, placed very low upon his nose, and through which he was directing his sight upon a child's stocking, that he was busily darning. At his foot was a rude cradle, made of a gum-tree log, hollowed out into a trough, and wadded by various old fragments of flannel, in which slept a very young infant. Another child, of about three years of age, was sitting on the negro's knee, busily playing with some pine-cones and mosses.

The figure of the old negro was low and stooping; and he wore, pinned round his shoulders, a half-handkerchief or shawl of red flannel, arranged much as an old woman would have arranged it. One or two needles, with coarse, black thread dangling to them, were stuck in on his shoulder; and, as he busily darned on the little stocking, he kept up a kind of droning intermixture of chanting and talking to the child on his knee.

"So, ho, Teddy!—bub dar!—my man!—sit still!—'cause yer ma's sick, and sister's gone for medicine. Dar, Tiff'll sing to his little man.

> 'Christ was born in Bethlehem,
> Christ was born in Bethlehem,
>   And in a manger laid.'

Take car, dar!—dat ar needle scratch yer little fingers!—poor little fingers! Ah, be still, now!—play wid yer pretty tings, and see what yer pa'll bring ye!"

"O, dear me!—well!" said the woman on the bed, "I shall give up!"

"Bress de Lord, no, missis!" said Tiff, laying down the stocking, and holding the child to him with one hand, while the other was busy in patting and arranging the bed-clothes. "No use in givin' up! Why, Lord bress you, missis, we'll be all up right agin in a few days. Work has been kinder pressin', lately, and chil'ns clothes an't quite so 'speckable; but den I's doin' heaps o' mendin'. See dat ar!" said he, holding up a slip of red flannel, resplendent with a black patch, "dat ar hole won't go no furder—and it does well enough for Teddy to wear rollin' round de do', and such like times, to save his bettermost. And de way I's put de yarn in dese yer stockings an't slow. Den I's laid out to take a stitch in Teddy's shoes; and dat ar hole in de kiverlet, dat ar'll be stopped 'fore morning. O, let me alone!— he! he! he!—Ye didn't keep Tiff for nothing, missis—ho, ho, ho!" And the black face seemed really to become unctuous with the oil of gladness, as Tiff proceeded in his work of consolation.

"O, Tiff, Tiff! you're a good creature! But you don't know. Here I've been lying alone day after day, and he off nobody knows where! And when he comes, it'll be only a day, and he's off; and all he does don't amount to anything—all miserable rubbish brought home and traded off for other rubbish. O, what a fool I was for being married! O, dear! girls little know what marriage is! I thought it was so dreadful to be an old maid, and a pretty thing to get married! But, O, the pain, and worry, and sickness, and suffering, I've gone through!—always wandering from place to place, never settled; one thing going after another, worrying, watching, weary,—and all for nothing, for I am worn out, and I shall die!"

"O, Lord, no!" said Tiff, earnestly. "Lor, Tiff'll make ye some tea, and give it to ye, ye poor lamb! It's dreful hard, so 't is; but times'll mend, and massa'll come round and be more settled, like, and Teddy will grow up and help his ma; and I'm sure dere isn't a peartier young un dan dis yer puppet!" said he, turning fondly to the trough where the little fat, red mass of incipient humanity was beginning to throw up two small fists, and to utter sundry small squeaks, to intimate his desire to come into notice.

"Lor, now," said he, adroitly depositing Teddy on the floor, and taking up the baby, whom he regarded fondly through his great spectacles; "stretch away, my pretty! stretch away! ho-e-ho! Lor, if he hasn't got his mammy's eye, for all dis worl! Ah, brave! See him, missis!" said he, laying the little bundle on the bed by her. "Did ye ever see a peartier young un? He, he, he! Dar, now, his mammy should take him, so she should! and Tiff'll make mammy some tea, so he will!" And Tiff, in a moment, was on his knees, carefully laying together the ends of the burned sticks, and, blowing a cloud of white ashes, which powdered his woolly head and red shawl like snow-flakes, while Teddy was busy in pulling the needles out of some knitting-work which hung in a bag by the fire.

Tiff, having started the fire by blowing, proceeded very carefully to adjust upon it a small, black porringer of water, singing, as he did so,

> *"My way is dark and cloudy,*
> > *So it is, so it is;*
> *My way is dark and cloudy,*
> > *All de day."*

Then, rising from his work, he saw that the poor, weak mother had clasped the baby to her bosom, and was sobbing very quietly. Tiff, as he stood there, with his short, square, ungainly figure, his long arms hanging out from his side like bows, his back covered by the red shawl, looked much like a compassionate tortoise standing on its hind legs. He looked pitifully at the sight, took off his glasses and wiped his eyes, and lifted up his voice in another stave:

> *"But we'll join de forty tousand, by and by,*
> > *So we will, so we will.*
> *We'll join de forty tousand, upon de golden shore,*
> *And our sorrows will be gone forevermore, more, more."*

"Bress my soul, Mas'r Teddy! now us been haulin' out de needles from Miss Fanny's work! dat ar an't purty, now! Tiff'll be 'shamed of ye, and ye do like dat when yer ma's sick! Don't ye know ye must be good, else Tiff won't tell ye no stories! Dar, now, sit down on dis yer log; dat ar's just the nicest log! plenty o' moss on it yer can be a pickin' out! Now, yer sit still dar, and don't be interruptin' yer ma."

The urchin opened a wide, round pair of blue eyes upon Tiff, looking as if he were mesmerized, and sat, with a quiet, subdued air, upon his log, while Tiff went fumbling about in a box in the corner. After some rattling, he produced a pine-knot, as the daylight was fading fast in the room, and, driving it into a crack in another log which stood by the chimney corner, he proceeded busily to light it, muttering, as he did so,

"Want to make it more cheerful like."

Then he knelt down and blew the coals under the little porringer, which, like pine-coals in general, always sulked and looked black when somebody was not blowing them. He blew vigorously, regardless of the clouds of ashes which encircled him, and which settled even on the tips of his eyelashes, and balanced themselves on the end of his nose.

"Bress de Lord, I's dreadful strong in my breff! Lord, dey might have used me in blacksmissin! I's kep dis yer chimney a gwine dis many a day. I wonder, now, what keeps Miss Fanny out so long."

And Tiff rose up with the greatest precaution, and, glancing every moment towards the bed, and almost tipping himself over in his anxiety to walk softly, advanced to the rude door, which opened with a wooden latch and string, opened it carefully, and looked out. Looking out with him, we perceive that the little hut stands alone, in the heart of a dense pine forest, which shuts it in on every side.

Tiff held the door open a few moments to listen. No sound was heard but the shivering wind, swaying and surging in melancholy cadences through the long pine-leaves,—a lonesome, wailing, uncertain sound.

"Ah! dese yer pine-trees! dey always a talkin'!" said Tiff to himself, in a sort of soliloquy. "Whisper, whisper, whisper! De Lord knows what it's all about! dey never tells folks what dey wants to know. Hark! da is Foxy, as sure as I'm a livin sinner! Ah! dar she is!" as a quick, loud bark reverberated. "Ah, ha! Foxy! you'll bring her along!" caressing a wolfish-looking, lean cur, who came bounding through the trees.

"Ah, yer good-for-nothing! what makes yer run so fast, and leave yer missus behind ye? Hark! what's dat!"

The clear voice came carolling gayly from out the pine-trees,

"If you get there before I do—
I'm bound for the land of Canaan."

Whereupon Tiff, kindling with enthusiasm, responded,

"Look out for me—I'm coming too—
I'm bound for the land of Canaan."

The response was followed by a gay laugh, as a childish voice shouted, from the woods,

"Ha! Tiff, you there?"

And immediately a bold, bright, blue-eyed girl, of about eight years old, came rushing forward.

"Lors, Miss Fannie, so grad you's come! Yer ma's powerful weak dis yer arternoon!" And then, sinking his voice to a whisper,

"Why, now, yer'd better b'leve her sperits isn't the best! Why, she's that bad, Miss Fannie, she actually been a cryin' when I put the baby in her arms. Railly, I'm consarned, and I wish yer pa 'ud come home. Did yer bring de medicine?"

"Ah, yes; here 't is."

"Ah! so good! I was a makin' of her some tea, to set her up, like, and I'll put a little drop of dis yer in 't. You gwin, now, and speak to yer ma, and I'll pick up a little light wood round here, and make up de fire. Massa Teddy'll be powerful glad to see yer. Hope you's got him something, too!"

The girl glided softly into the room, and stood over the bed where her mother was lying.

"Mother, I've come home," said she, gently.

The poor, frail creature in the bed seemed to be in one of those helpless hours of life's voyage, when all its waves and billows are breaking over the soul; and while the little new-comer was blindly rooting and striving at her breast, she had gathered the worn counterpane over her face, and the bed was shaken by her sobbings.

"Mother! mother! mother!" said the child, softly touching her.

"Go away! go away, child! O, I wish I had never been born! I wish you had never been born, nor Teddy, nor the baby! It's all nothing but trouble and sorrow! Fanny, don't you ever marry! Mind what I tell you!"

The child stood frightened by the bedside, while Tiff had softly deposited a handful of pine-wood near the fireplace, had taken off the porringer, and was busily stirring and concocting something in an old cracked china mug. As he stirred, a strain of indignation seemed to cross his generally tranquil mind, for he often gave short sniffs and grunts, indicative of extreme disgust, and muttered to himself,

"Dis yer comes of quality marrying these yer poor white folks! Never had no 'pinion on it, no way! Ah! do hear the poor lamb now! 'nough to break one's heart!"

By this time, the stirring and flavoring being finished to his taste, he came to the side of the bed, and began, in a coaxing tone,

"Come, now, Miss Sue, come! You's all worn out! No wonder! dat ar great fellow tugging at you! Bless his dear little soul, he's gaining half a pound a week! Nough to pull down his ma entirely! Come, now; take a little sup of this—just a little sup! Warm you up, and put a bit of life in you; and den I 'spects to fry you a morsel of der chicken, 'cause a boy like dis yer can't be nursed on slops, dat I knows! Dere, dere, honey!" said he, gently removing the babe, and passing his arm under the pillow. "I's drefful strong in the back. My arm is long and strong, and I'll raise you up just as easy! Take a good sup on it, now, and wash dese troubles down. I reckon the good man above is looking down on us all, and bring us all round right, some time."

The invalid, who seemed exhausted by the burst of feeling to which she had been giving way, mechanically obeyed a voice to which she had always been accustomed, and drank eagerly, as if with feverish thirst; and when she had done, she suddenly threw her arms around the neck of her strange attendant.

"O, Tiff, Tiff! poor old black, faithful Tiff! What should I have done without you? So sick as I've been, and so weak, and so lonesome! But, Tiff, it's coming to an end pretty soon. I've seen, to-night, that I an't going to live long, and I've been crying to think the children have got to live. If I could only take them all into my arms, and all lie down in the grave together, I should be so glad! I never knew what God made me for! I've never been fit for anything, nor done anything!"

Tiff seemed so utterly overcome by this appeal, his great spectacles were fairly washed down in a flood of tears, and his broad, awkward frame shook with sobs.

"Law bless you, Miss Sue, don't be talking dat ar way! Why, if de Lord *should* call you, Miss Sue, I can take care of the children. I can bring them up powerful, I tell ye! But you *won't* be a-going; you'll get better! It's just the sperits is low; and, laws, why shouldn't dey be?"

Just at this moment a loud barking was heard outside the house, together with the rattle of wheels and the tramp of horses' feet.

"Dar's massa, sure as I'm alive!" said he, hastily laying down the invalid, and arranging her pillows.

A rough voice called, "Hallo, Tiff! here with a light!"

Tiff caught the pine-knot, and ran to open the door. A strange-looking vehicle, of a most unexampled composite order, was standing before the door, drawn by a lean, one-eyed horse.

"Here, Tiff, help me out. I've got a lot of goods here. How's Sue?"

"Missis is powerful bad; been wanting to see you dis long time."

"Well, away, Tiff! take this out," indicating a long, rusty piece of stove-pipe.

"Lay this in the house; and here!" handing a cast-iron stove-door, with the latch broken.

"Law, Massa, what on earth is the use of dis yer?"

"Don't ask questions, Tiff; work away. Help me out with these boxes."

"What on arth now?" said Tiff to himself, as one rough case after another was disgorged from the vehicle, and landed in the small cabin. This being done, and orders being given to Tiff to look after the horse and equipage, the man walked into the house, with a jolly, slashing air.

"Hallo, bub!" said he, lifting the two-year-old above his head. "Hallo, Fan!" imprinting a kiss on the cheek of his girl. "Hallo, Sis!" coming up to the bed where the invalid lay, and stooping down over her. Her weak, wasted arms were thrown around his neck, and she said, with sudden animation,

"O, you've come at last! I thought I should die without seeing you!"

"O, you an't a-going to die, Sis! Why, what talk!" said he, chucking her under the chin. "Why, your cheeks are as red as roses!"

"Pa, see the baby!" said little Teddy, who, having climbed over the bed, opened the flannel bundle.

"Ah! Sis, I call that ar a tolerable fair stroke of business! Well, I tell *you* what, I've done up a trade now that will set us up, and no mistake. Besides which, I've got something now in my coat-pocket that would raise a dead cat to life, if she was lying at the bottom of a pond, with a stone round her neck! See here! 'Dr. Puffer's Elixir of the Water of Life!' warranted to cure janders, tooth-ache, ear-ache, scrofula, speptia, 'sumption, and everything else that ever I hearn of! A teaspoonful of that ar, morn and night, and in a week you'll be round agin, as pert as a cricket!"

It was astonishing to see the change which the entrance of this man had wrought on the invalid. All her apprehensions seemed to have vanished. She sat up on the bed, following his every movement with her eyes, and apparently placing full confidence in the new medicine, as if it were the first time that ever a universal remedy had been proposed to her. It must be noticed, however, that Tiff, who

had returned, and was building the fire, indulged himself, now and
then, when the back of the speaker was turned, by snuffing at him
in a particularly contemptuous manner. The man was a thick-set
and not ill-looking personage, who might have been forty or forty-
five years of age. His eyes, of a clear, lively brown, his close-curling
hair, his high forehead, and a certain devil-may-care frankness of
expression, were traits not disagreeable, and which went some way
to account for the partial eagerness with which the eye of the wife
followed him.

The history of the pair is briefly told. He was the son of a small
farmer of North Carolina. His father having been so unfortunate as
to obtain possession of a few negroes, the whole family became ever
after inspired with an intense disgust for all kinds of labor; and
John, the oldest son, adopted for himself the ancient and honorable
profession of a loafer. To lie idle in the sun in front of some small
grog-shop, to attend horse-races, cock-fights, and gander-pullings,[1]
to flout out occasionally in a new waistcoat, bought with money
which came nobody knew how, were pleasures to him all-
satisfactory. He was as guiltless of all knowledge of common-
school learning as Governor Berkley[2] could desire, and far more
clear of religious training than a Mahometan or a Hindoo.

In one of his rambling excursions through the country, he
stopped a night at a worn-out and broken-down old plantation,
where everything had run down, through many years of misman-
agement and waste. There he staid certain days, playing cards with
the equally hopeful son of the place, and ended his performances by
running away one night with the soft-hearted daughter, only fifteen
years of age, and who was full as idle, careless, and untaught, as he.

The family, whom poverty could not teach to forget their pride,
were greatly scandalized at the marriage; and, had there been anything left in the worn-out estate wherewith to portion her, the
bride, nevertheless, would have been portionless. The sole piece of
property that went out with her from the paternal mansion was
one, who, having a mind and will of his own, could not be kept
from following her. The girl's mother had come from a distant
branch of one of the most celebrated families in Virginia, and Tiff
had been her servant; and, with a heart forever swelling with the remembrances of the ancestral greatness of the Peytons, he followed
his young mistress in her mésalliance with long-suffering devotion.
He even bowed his neck so far as to acknowledge for his master a

man whom he considered by position infinitely his inferior; for Tiff, though crooked and black, never seemed to cherish the slightest doubt that the whole force of the Peyton blood coursed through his veins, and that the Peyton honor was intrusted to his keeping. His mistress was a Peyton, her children were Peyton children, and even the little bundle of flannel in the gum-tree cradle was a Peyton; and as for him, he was Tiff Peyton, and this thought warmed and consoled him as he followed his poor mistress during all the steps of her downward course in the world. On her husband he looked with patronizing, civil contempt. He wished him well; he thought it proper to put the best face on all his actions; but, in a confidential hour, Tiff would sometimes raise his spectacles emphatically, and give it out, as his own private opinion, "that dere could not be much 'spected from dat ar 'scription of people!"

In fact, the roving and unsettled nature of John Cripps's avocations and locations might have justified the old fellow's contempt. His industrial career might be defined as comprising a little of everything, and a great deal of nothing. He had begun, successively, to learn two or three trades; had half made a horse-shoe, and spoiled one or two carpenter's planes; had tried his hand at stage-driving; had raised fighting-cocks, and kept dogs for hunting negroes. But he invariably retreated from every one of his avocations, in his own opinion a much-abused man. The last device that had entered his head was suggested by the success of a shrewd Yankee pedler, who, having a lot of damaged and unsalable material to dispose of, talked him into the belief that he possessed yet an undeveloped talent for trade; and poor John Cripps, guiltless of multiplication or addition table, and who kept his cock-fighting accounts on his fingers and by making chalk-marks behind the doors, actually was made to believe that he had at last received his true vocation.

In fact, there was something in the constant restlessness of this mode of life that suited his roving turn; and, though he was constantly buying what he could not sell, and losing on all that he did sell, yet somehow he kept up an illusion that he was doing something, because stray coins now and then passed through his pockets, and because the circle of small taverns in which he could drink and loaf was considerably larger. There was one resource which never failed him when all other streams went dry; and that was the unceasing ingenuity and fidelity of the bondman Tiff.

Tiff, in fact, appeared to be one of those comfortable old creatures, who retain such a good understanding with all created nature
that food never is denied them. Fish would always bite on Tiff's
hook when they wouldn't on anybody's else; so that he was wont
confidently to call the nearest stream "Tiff's pork-barrel." Hens always laid eggs for Tiff, and cackled to him confidentially where
they were deposited. Turkeys gobbled and strutted for him, and led
forth for him broods of downy little ones. All sorts of wild game,
squirrels, rabbits, coons, and possums, appeared to come with pleasure and put themselves into his traps and springes; so that, where
another man might starve, Tiff would look round him with unctuous satisfaction, contemplating all nature as his larder, where his
provisions were wearing fur coats, and walking about on four legs,
only for safe keeping till he got ready to eat them. So that Cripps
never came home without anticipation of something savory, even
although he had drank up his last quarter of a dollar at the tavern.
This suited Cripps. He thought Tiff was doing his duty, and occasionally brought him home some unsalable bit of rubbish, by way
of testimonial of the sense he entertained of his worth. The spectacles in which Tiff gloried came to him in this manner; and, although
it might have been made to appear that the glasses were only plain
window-glass, Tiff was happily ignorant that they were not the best
of convex lenses, and still happier in the fact that his strong, unim-
paired eyesight made any glasses at all entirely unnecessary. It was
only an aristocratic weakness in Tiff. Spectacles he somehow considered the mark of a gentleman, and an appropriate symbol for one
who had "been fetched up in the very fustest families of Old Virginny."

He deemed them more particularly appropriate, as, in addition
to his manifold outward duties, he likewise assumed, as the reader
has seen, some feminine accomplishments. Tiff could darn a stocking with anybody in the country; he could cut out children's
dresses and aprons; he could patch, and he could seam; all which he
did with infinite self-satisfaction.

Notwithstanding the many crooks and crosses in his lot, Tiff
was, on the whole, a cheery fellow. He had an oily, rollicking fulness of nature, an exuberance of physical satisfaction in existence,
that the greatest weight of adversity could only tone down to becoming sobriety. He was on the happiest terms of fellowship with
himself; he *liked* himself, he believed in himself; and, when nobody

else would do it, he would pat himself on his own shoulder, and say, "Tiff, you're a jolly dog, a fine fellow, and I like you!" He was seldom without a running strain of soliloquy with himself, intermingled with joyous bursts of song, and quiet intervals of laughter. On pleasant days Tiff laughed a great deal. He laughed when his beans came up, he laughed when the sun came out after a storm, he laughed for fifty things that you never think of laughing at; and it agreed with him—he throve upon it. In times of trouble and perplexity, Tiff talked to himself, and found a counsellor who always kept secrets. On the present occasion it was not without some inward discontent that he took a survey of the remains of one of his best-fatted chickens, which he had been intending to serve up, piecemeal, for his mistress. So he relieved his mind by a little confidential colloquy with himself.

"Dis yer," he said to himself, with a contemptuous inclination towards the newly-arrived, "will be for eating like a judgment, I 'pose. Wish, now, I had killed de old gobbler! Good enough for him—raal tough, he is. Dis yer, now, was my primest chicken, and dar she'll just sit and see him eat it! Laws, dese yer women! Why, dey does get so sot on husbands! Pity they couldn't have something like to be sot on! It jist riles me to see him gobbling down everything, and she a-looking on! Well, here goes," said he, depositing the frying-pan over the coals, in which the chicken was soon fizzling. Drawing out the table, Tiff prepared it for supper. Soon coffee was steaming over the fire, and corn-dodgers baking in the ashes. Meanwhile, John Cripps was busy explaining to his wife the celebrated wares that had so much raised his spirits.

"Well, now, you see, Sue, this yer time I've been up to Raleigh; and I met a fellow there, coming from New York or New Orleans, or some of them northern states."

"New Orleans isn't a northern state," humbly interposed his wife, "is it?"

"Well, New something! Who the devil cares? Don't you be interrupting me, you Suse!"

Could Cripps have seen the vengeful look which Tiff gave him over the spectacles at this moment, he might have trembled for his supper. But, innocent of this, he proceeded with his story.

"You see, this yer fellow had a case of bonnets just the height of the fashion. They come from Paris, the capital of Europe; and he sold them to me for a mere song. Ah, you ought to see 'em! I'm go-

ing to get 'em out. Tiff, hold the candle, here." And Tiff held the
burning torch with an air of grim scepticism and disgust, while
Cripps hammered and wrenched the top boards off, and displayed
to view a portentous array of bonnets, apparently of every obsolete
style and fashion of the last fifty years.

"Dem's fust rate for scare-crows, anyhow!" muttered Tiff.

"Now, what," said Cripps,—"Sue, what do you think I gave for
these?"

"I don't know," said she, faintly.

"Well, I gave fifteen dollars for the whole box! And there an't
one of these," said he, displaying the most singular specimen on his
hand, "that isn't worth from two to five dollars. I shall clear, at
least, fifty dollars on that box."

Tiff, at this moment, turned to his frying-pan, and bent over it,
soliloquizing as he did so.

"Any way, I's found out one ting—where de women gets dem
roosts of bonnets dey wars at camp-meetings. Laws, dey's enough
to spile a work of grace, dem ar! If I was to meet one of dem ar of a
dark night in a grave-yard, I should tink I was sent for—not the
pleasantest way of sending, neither. Poor missis!—looking mighty
faint!—Don't wonder!—'Nough to scarr a weakly woman into
fits!"

"Here, Tiff, help me to open this box. Hold the light, here.
Durned if it don't come off hard! Here's a lot of shoes and boots I
got of the same man. Some on 'em's mates, and some an't; but, then,
I took the lot cheap. Folks don't always warr both shoes alike.
Might like to warr an odd one, sometimes, ef it's cheap. Now, this
yer parr of boots is lady's gaiters, all complete, 'cept there's a hole
in the lining down by the toe; body ought to be careful about
putting it on, else the foot will slip between the outside and the lining. Anybody that bears that in mind—just as nice a pair of gaiters
as they'd want! Bargain, there, for somebody—complete one, too.
Then I've got two or three old bureau-drawers that I got cheap at
auction; and I reckon some on 'em will fit the old frame that I got
last year. Got 'em for a mere song."

"Bless you, massa, dat ar old bureau I took for de chicken-coop!
Turkeys, chickens hops in lively."

"O, well, scrub it up—'t will answer just as well. Fit the drawers
in. And now, old woman, we will sit down to supper," said he,
planting himself at the table, and beginning a vigorous onslaught on

the fried chicken, without invitation to any other person present to assist him.

"Missis can't sit up at the table," said Tiff. "She's done been sick ever since de baby was born." And Tiff approached the bed with a nice morsel of chicken which he had providently preserved on a plate, and which he now reverently presented on a board, as a waiter, covered with newspaper.

"Now, do eat, missis; you can't live on looking, no ways you can fix it. Do eat, while Tiff gets on de baby's night-gown."

To please her old friend, the woman made a feint of eating, but, while Tiff's back was turned to the fire, busied herself with distributing it to the children, who had stood hungrily regarding her, as children will regard what is put on to a sick mother's plate.

"It does me good to see them eat," she said, apologetically once, when Tiff, turning round, detected her in the act.

"Ah, missis, may be! but *you've* got to eat for *two,* now. What dey eat an't going to dis yer little man, here. Mind dat ar."

Cripps apparently bestowed very small attention on anything except the important business before him, which he prosecuted with such devotion that very soon coffee, chicken, and dodgers, had all disappeared. Even the bones were sucked dry, and the gravy wiped from the dish.

"Ah, that's what I call comfortable!" said he, lying back in his chair. "Tiff, pull my boots off! and hand out that ar demijohn. Sue, I hope you've made a comfortable meal," he said, incidentally, standing with his back to her, compounding his potation of whiskey and water; which having drank, he called up Teddy, and offered him the sugar at the bottom of the glass. But Teddy, being forewarned by a meaning glance through Tiff's spectacles, responded, very politely,

"No, I thank you, pa. I don't love it."

"Come here, then, and take it off like a man. It's good for you," said John Cripps.

The mother's eyes followed the child wishfully; and she said, faintly, "Don't, John!—don't!" And Tiff ended the controversy by taking the glass unceremoniously out of his master's hand.

"Laws bless you, massa, can't be bodered with dese yer young ones dis yer time of night! Time dey's all in bed, and dishes washed up. Here, Tedd," seizing the child, and loosening the buttons of his slip behind, and drawing out a rough trundle-bed, "you crawl in dere, and curl up in your nest; and don't you forget your prars, honey, else maybe you'll never wake up again."

Cripps had now filled a pipe with tobacco of the most villainous character, with which incense he was perfuming the little apartment.

"Laws, massa, dat are smoke an't good for missis," said Tiff. "She done been sick to her stomach all day."

"O, let him smoke! I like to have him enjoy himself," said the indulgent wife. "But, Fanny, you had better go to bed, dear. Come here and kiss me, child; good-night,—good-night!"

The mother held on to her long, and looked at her wishfully; and when she had turned to go, she drew her back, and kissed her again, and said, "Good-night, dear child, good-night!"

Fanny climbed up a ladder in one corner of the room, through a square hole, to the loft above.

"I say," said Cripps, taking his pipe out of his mouth, and looking at Tiff, who was busy washing the dishes, "I say it's kind of peculiar that gal keeps sick so. Seemed to have good constitution when I married her. I'm thinking," said he, without noticing the gathering wrath in Tiff's face, "I'm a thinking whether steamin' wouldn't do her good. Now, I got a most dreadful cold when I was up at Raleigh—thought I should have given up; and there was a steam-doctor there. Had a little kind of machine, with kettle and pipes, and he put me in a bed, put in the pipes, and set it a-going. I thought, my soul, I should have been floated off; but it carried off the cold, complete. I'm thinking if something of that kind wouldn't be good for Miss Cripps."

"Laws, massa, don't go for to trying it on her! She is never no better for dese yer things you do for her."

"Now," said Cripps, not appearing to notice the interruption, "these yer stove-pipes, and the tea-kettle,—I shouldn't wonder if we could get up a steam with them!"

"It's my private 'pinion, if you do, she'll be sailing out of the world," said Tiff. "What's one man's meat is another one's pisin, my old mis's used to say. Very best thing you can do for her is to let her alone. Dat ar is my 'pinion."

"John," said the little woman, after a few minutes, "I wish you'd come here, and sit on the bed."

There was something positive, and almost authoritative, in the manner in which this was said, which struck John as so unusual, that he came with a bewildered air, sat down, and gazed at her with his mouth wide open.

"I'm so glad you've come home, because I have had things that I've wanted to say to you! I've been lying here thinking about it, and I have been turning it over in my mind. I'm going to die soon, I know."

"Ah! bah! Don't be bothering a fellow with any of your hysterics!"

"John, John! it isn't hysterics! Look at me! Look at my hand! look at my face! I'm so weak, and sometimes I have such coughing spells, and every time it seems to me as if I should die. But it an't to trouble you that I talk. I don't care about myself, but I don't want the children to grow up and be like what we've been. You have a great many contrivances; do, pray, contrive to have them taught to read, and make something of them in the world."

"Bah! what's the use? I never learnt to read, and I'm as good a fellow as I want. Why, there's plenty of men round here making their money, every year, that can't read or write a word. Old Hubell, there, up on the Shad plantation, has hauled in money, hand over hand, and he always signs his mark. Got nine sons—can't a soul of them read or write, more than I. I tell you there's nothing ever comes of this yer larning. It's all a sell—a regular Yankee hoax! I've always got cheated by them damn reading, writing Yankees, whenever I've traded with 'em. What's the good, I want to know! You was teached how to read when you was young—much good it's ever done you!"

"Sure enough! Sick day and night, moving about from place to place, sick baby crying, and not knowing what to do for it no more than a child! O, I hope Fanny will learn something! It seems to me, if there was some school for my children to go to, or some church, or something—now, *if there is* any such place as heaven, I should like to have them get to it."

"Ah! bah! Don't bother about that! When we get keeled up, that will be the last of us! Come, come, don't plague a fellow any more with such talk! I'm tired, and I'm going to sleep." And the man, divesting himself of his overcoat, threw himself on the bed, and was soon snoring heavily in profound slumber.

Tiff, who had been trotting the baby by the fire, now came softly to the bedside, and sat down.

"Miss Sue," he said, "it's no 'count talking to him! I don't mean

nothing dis'pectful, Miss Sue, but de fac is, dem dat isn't *born* gentlemen can't be 'spected fur to see through dese yer things like us of
de old families. Law, missis, don't you worry! Now, jest leave dis
yer matter to old Tiff! Dere never wasn't anything Tiff couldn't do,
if he tried. He! he! he! Miss Fanny, she done got de letters right
smart; and I know I'll come it round mas'r, and make him buy de
books for her. I'll tell you what's come into my head, to-day.
There's a young lady come to de big plantation, up dere, who's
been to New York getting edicated, and I's going for to ask her
about dese yer things. And, about de chil'en's going to church, and
dese yer things, why, preaching, you know, is mazin' unsartin
round here; but I'll keep on de look-out, and do de best I can. Why,
Lord, Miss Sue, I's bound for the land of Canaan, myself, the best
way I ken; and I'm sartain I shan't go without taking the chil'en
along with me. Ho! ho! ho! Dat's what I shan't! De chil'en will
have to be with Tiff, and Tiff will have to be with the chil'en, wherever dey is! Dat's it! He! he! he!"

"Tiff," said the young woman, her large blue eyes looking at
him, "I have heard of the Bible. Have you ever seen one, Tiff?"

"O, yes, honey, dar was a big Bible that your ma brought in the
family when she married; but dat ar was tore up to make wadding
for de guns, one thing or another, and dey never got no more. But
I's been very 'serving, and kept my ears open in a camp-meeting,
and such places, and I's learnt right smart of de things that's in it."

"Now, Tiff, can you say anything?" said she, fixing her large,
troubled eyes on him.

"Well, honey, dere's one thing the man said at de last camp-
meeting. He preached 'bout it, and I couldn't make out a word he
said, 'cause I an't smart about preaching like I be about most things.
But he said dis yer so often that I couldn't help 'member it. Says he,
it was dish yer way: 'Come unto me, all ye labor and are heavy
laden, and I will give you rest.' "[3]

"Rest, rest, rest!" said the woman, thoughtfully, and drawing a
long sigh. "O, how much I want it! Did he say *that* was in the
Bible?"

"Yes, he said so; and I spects, by all he said, it's de good man
above dat says it. It always makes me feel better to think on it. It
'peared like it was jist what I was wanting to hear."

"And I, too!" she said, turning her head wearily, and closing her
eyes. "Tiff," she said, opening them, "where I'm going, may be I

shall meet the one who said that, and I'll ask him about it. Don't talk to me more, now. I'm getting sleepy. I thought I was better a little while after he came home, but I'm more tired yet. Put the baby in my arms—I like the feeling of it. There, there; now give me rest—*please* do!" and she sank into a deep and quiet slumber.

Tiff softly covered the fire, and sat down by the bed, watching the flickering shadows as they danced upward on the wall, listening to the heavy sighs of the pine-trees, and the hard breathing of the sleeping man. Sometimes he nodded sleepily, and then, recovering, rose, and took a turn to awaken himself. A shadowy sense of fear fell upon him; not that he apprehended anything, for he regarded the words of his mistress only as the forebodings of a wearied invalid. The idea that she could actually die, and go anywhere, without him to take care of her, seemed never to have occurred to him. About midnight, as if a spirit had laid its hand upon him, his eyes flew wide open with a sudden start. Her thin, cold hand was lying on his; her eyes, large and blue, shone with a singular and spiritual radiance.

"Tiff," she gasped, speaking with difficulty, "I've seen the one that said *that,* and it's all true, too! and I've seen all why I've suffered so much. He—He—He is going to take me! Tell the children about Him!" There was a fluttering sigh, a slight shiver, and the lids fell over the eyes forever.

CHAPTER IX

The Death

DEATH IS ALWAYS SUDDEN. However gradual may be its approaches, it is, in its effects upon the survivor, always sudden at last. Tiff thought, at first, that his mistress was in a fainting-fit, and tried every means to restore her. It was affecting to see him chafing the thin, white, pearly hands, in his large, rough, black paws; raising the head upon his arm, and calling in a thousand tones of fond endearment, pouring out a perfect torrent of loving devotion on the cold, unheeding ear. But, then, spite of all he could do, the face settled itself, and the hands would not be warmed; the thought of death struck him suddenly, and, throwing himself on the floor by the bed, he wept with an exceeding loud and bitter cry. Something in his heart revolted against awakening that man who lay heavily breathing by her side. He would not admit to himself, at this moment, that this man had any right in her, or that the sorrow was any part of his sorrow. But the cry awoke Cripps, who sat up bewildered in bed, clearing the hair from his eyes with the back of his hand.

"Tiff, what the durned are you howling about?"

Tiff got up in a moment, and, swallowing down his grief and his tears, pointed indignantly to the still figure on the bed.

"Dar! dar! Wouldn't b'lieve her last night! Now what you think of dat ar? See how you look now! Good Shepherd hearn you abusing de poor lamb, and he's done took her whar you'll never see her again!"

Cripps had, like coarse, animal men generally, a stupid and senseless horror of death;—he recoiled from the lifeless form, and sprang from the bed with an expression of horror.

"Well, now, who would have thought it?" he said. "That I should be in bed with a corpse! I hadn't the least idea!"

"No, dat's plain enough, you didn't! You'll believe it now, won't you? Poor little lamb, lying here suffering all alone! I tell you, when

99

folks have been sick so long, dey *has* to die to make folks believe anything ails 'em!"

"Well, really," said Cripps, "this is really—why, it an't comfortable! darned if it is! Why, I'm sorry about the gal! I meant to steam her up, or done something with her. What's we to do now?"

"Pretty likely you don't know! Folks like you, dat never tends to nothing good, is always flustered when de Master knocks at de do'! *I* knows what to do, though. I's boun' to get up de crittur, and go up to de old plantation, and bring down a woman and do something for her, kind of decent. You mind the chil'en till I come back."

Tiff took down and drew on over his outer garment a coarse, light, woollen coat, with very long skirts and large buttons, in which he always arrayed himself in cases of special solemnity. Stopping at the door before he went out, he looked over Cripps from head to foot, with an air of patronizing and half-pitiful contempt, and delivered himself as follows:

"Now, mas'r, I's gwine up, and will be back quick as possible; and now do pray be decent, and let dat ar whiskey alone for one day in your life, and 'member death, judgment, and 'ternity. Just act, now, as if you'd got a *streak* of something in you, such as a man ought for to have who is married to one of de very fustest families in old Virginny. 'Flect, now, on your latter end; may be will do your poor old soul some good; and don't you go for to waking up the chil'en before I gets back. They'll learn de trouble soon enough."

Cripps listened to this oration with a stupid, bewildered stare, gazing first at the bed, and then at the old man, who was soon making all the speed he could towards Canema.

Nina was not habitually an early riser, but on this morning she had awaked with the first peep of dawn, and, finding herself unable to go to sleep again, she had dressed herself, and gone down to the garden.

She was walking up and down in one of the alleys, thinking over the perplexities of her own affairs, when her ear was caught by the wild and singular notes of one of those tunes commonly used among the slaves as dirges. The words "She ar dead and gone to heaven" seemed to come floating down upon her; and, though the voice was cracked and strained, there was a sort of wildness and pathos in it, which made a singular impression in the perfect stillness of everything around her. She soon observed a singular-looking vehicle appearing in the avenue.

This wagon, which was no other than the establishment of Cripps, drew Nina's attention, and she went to the hedge to look at it. Tiff's watchful eye immediately fell upon her, and, driving up to where she was standing, he climbed out upon the ground, and, lifting his hat, made her a profound obeisance, and "hoped de young lady was bery well, dis morning."

"Yes, quite well, thank you, Uncle," said Nina, regarding him curiously.

"We's in 'fliction to our house!" said Tiff, solemnly. "Dere's been a midnight cry dere, and poor Miss Sue (dat's my young missis), she's done gone home."

"Who is your mistress?"

"Well, her name *was* Seymour 'fore she married, and her ma come from de Virginny Peytons,—great family, dem Peytons! She was so misfortunate as to get married, as gals will, sometimes," said Tiff, speaking in a confidential tone. "The man wan't no 'count, and she's had a dreful hard way to travel, poor thing! and dere she's a lying at last stretched out dead, and not a woman nor nobody to do de least thing; and please, missis, Tiff comed for to see if de young lady wouldn't send a woman for to do for her—getting her ready for a funeral."

"And who are you, pray?"

"Please, missis, I's Tiff Peyton, I is. I's raised in Virginny, on de great Peyton place, and I's gin to Miss Sue's mother; and when Miss Sue married dis yer man, dey was all 'fended, and wouldn't speak to her; but I tuck up for her, 'cause what's de use of makin' a bad thing worse? I's a 'pinion, and told 'em, dat he oughter be 'couraged to behave hisself, seein' the thing was done, and couldn't be helped. But no, dey wouldn't; so I jest tells 'em, says I, 'You may do jis you please, but old Tiff's a gwine with her,' says I. 'I'll follow Miss Sue to de grave's mouth,' says I; and ye see I has done it."

"Well done of you! I like you better for it," said Nina. "You just drive up to the kitchen, there, and tell Rose to give you some breakfast, while I go up to Aunt Nesbit."

"No, thank you, Miss Nina, I's noways hungry. 'Pears like, when a body's like as I be, swallerin' down, and all de old times risin' in der throat all de time, dey can't eat; dey gets filled all up to der eyes with feelin's. Lord, Miss Nina, I hope ye won't never know what 't is to stand outside de gate, when de best friend you've got's gone in; it's hard, dat ar is!" And Tiff pulled out a decayed-looking handkerchief, and applied it under his spectacles.

"Well, wait a minute, Tiff." And Nina ran into the house, while Tiff gazed mournfully after her.

"Well, Lor; just de way Miss Sue used to run—trip, trip, trip!—little feet like mice! Lord's will be done!"

"O, Milly!" said Nina, meeting Milly in the entry, "here you are. Here's a poor fellow waiting out by the hedge, his mistress dead all alone in the house, with children—no woman to do for them. Can't you go down? you could do so well! You know how better than any one else in the house."

"Why, that must be poor old Tiff!" said Milly; "faithful old creature! So that poor woman's gone, at last? the better for her, poor soul! Well, I'll ask Miss Loo if I may go—or you ask her, Miss Nina."

A quick, imperative tap on her door startled Aunt Nesbit, who was standing at her toilet, finishing her morning's dressing operations.

Mrs. Nesbit was a particularly systematic, early riser. Nobody knew why; only folks who have nothing to do are often the most particular to have the longest possible time to do it in.

"Aunt," said Nina, "there's a poor fellow, out here, whose mistress is just dead, all alone in the house, and wants to get some woman to go there to help. Can't you spare Milly?"

"Milly was going to clear-starch my caps, this morning," said Aunt Nesbit. "I have arranged everything with reference to it, for a week past."

"Well, aunt, can't she do it to-morrow, or next day, just as well?"

"To-morrow she is going to rip up that black dress, and wash it. I am always systematic, and have everything arranged beforehand. Should like very much to do anything I could, if it wasn't for that. Why can't you send Aunt Katy?"

"Why, aunt, you know we are to have company to dinner, and Aunt Katy is the only one who knows where anything is, or how to serve things out to the cook. Besides, she's so hard and cross to poor people, I don't think she would go. I don't see, I'm sure, in such a case as this, why you couldn't put your starching off. Milly

is such a kind, motherly, experienced person, and they are in affliction."

"O, these low families don't mind such things much," said Aunt
Nesbit, fitting on her cap, quietly; "they never have much feeling.
There's no use doing for them—they are miserable poor creatures."

"Aunt Nesbit, do, now, as a favor to me! I don't often ask favors," said Nina. "*Do* let Milly go! she's just the one wanted. Do,
now, say yes!" And Nina pressed nearer, and actually seemed to
overpower her slow-feeling, torpid relative, with the vehemence
that sparkled in her eyes.

"Well, I don't care, if—"

"There, Milly, she says yes!" said she, springing out the door.
"She says you may. Now, hurry; get things ready. I'll run and have
Aunt Katy put up biscuits and things for the children; and you get
all that you know you will want, and be off quick, and I'll have the
pony got up, and come on behind you."

CHAPTER X

The Preparation

THE EXCITEMENT produced by the arrival of Tiff, and the fitting out of Milly to the cottage, had produced a most favorable diversion in Nina's mind from her own especial perplexities.

Active and buoyant, she threw herself at once into whatever happened to come uppermost on the tide of events. So, having seen the wagon despatched, she sat down to breakfast in high spirits.

"Aunt Nesbit, I declare I was so interested in that old man! I intend to have the pony, after breakfast, and ride over there."

"I thought you were expecting company."

"Well, that's one reason, now, why I'd like to be off. Do I want to sit all primmed up, smiling and smirking, and running to the window to see if my gracious lord is coming? No, I won't do that, to please any of them. If I happen to fancy to be out riding, I *will* be out riding."

"I think," said Aunt Nesbit, "that the hovels of these miserable creatures are no proper place for a young lady of your position in life."

"My position in life! I don't see what that has to do with it. My position in life enables me to do anything I please—a liberty which I take pretty generally. And, then, really, I couldn't help feeling rather sadly about it, because that Old Tiff, there (I believe that's his name), told me that the woman had been of a good Virginia family. Very likely she may have been just such another wild girl as I am, and thought as little about bad times, and of dying, as I do. So I couldn't help feeling sad for her. It really came over me when I was walking in the garden. Such a beautiful morning as it was—the birds all singing, and the dew all glittering and shining on the flowers! Why, aunt, the flowers really seemed alive; it seemed as though I could hear them breathing, and hear their hearts beating like mine. And, all of a sudden, I heard the most wild, mournful singing, over in the woods. It wasn't anything very beautiful, you know, but it was so wild, and strange! 'She is dead and gone to heaven!—she is dead and gone to heaven!' And pretty soon I saw the funniest old wagon—I don't know what to call it—and this queer old black man in it, with an old white hat and surtout on, and a pair of great, funny-looking spectacles on his nose. I went to the fence to see who he was; and he came up and spoke to me, made the most respectful bow—you ought to have seen it! And then, poor fellow, he told me how his mistress was lying dead, with the children around her, and nobody in the house! The poor old creature, he actually cried, and I felt so for him! He seemed to be proud of his dead mistress, in spite of her poverty."

"Where do they live?" said Mrs. Nesbit.

"Why, he told me over in the pine woods, near the swamp."

"O," said Mrs. Nesbit, "I dare say it's that Cripps family, that's squatted in the pine woods. A most miserable set—all of them liars and thieves! If I had known who it was, I'm sure I shouldn't have let Milly go over. Such families oughtn't to be encouraged; there oughtn't a thing to be done for them; we shouldn't encourage them to stay in the neighborhood. They always will steal from off the plantations, and corrupt the negroes, and get drunk, and everything else that's bad. There's never a woman of decent character among them, that ever I heard of; and, if you were my daughter, I shouldn't let you go near them."

"Well, I'm not your daughter, thank fortune!" said Nina, whose graces always rapidly declined in controversies with her aunt, "and so I shall do as I please. And I don't know what you pious people talk so for; for Christ went with publicans and sinners, I'm sure."

"Well," said Aunt Nesbit, "the Bible says we mustn't cast pearls before swine; and, when you've lived to be as old as I am, you'll know more than you do now. Everybody knows that you can't do anything with these people. You can't give them Bibles, nor tracts; for they can't read. I've tried it, sometimes, visiting them, and talking to them; but it didn't do them any good. I always thought there ought to be a law passed to make 'em all slaves, and then there would be somebody to take care of them."

"Well, I can't see," said Nina, "how it's their fault. There isn't any school where they could send their children, if they wanted to learn; and, then, if they want to work, there's nobody who wants to hire them. So, what can they do?"

"I'm sure I don't know," said Aunt Nesbit, in that tone which generally means I don't care. "All I know is, that I want them to get away from the neighborhood. Giving to them is just like putting into a bag with holes. I'm sure I put myself to a great inconvenience on their account to-day; for, if there's anything I do hate, it is having things irregular. And to-day is the day for clear-starching the caps—and such a good, bright, sunny day!—and to-morrow, or any other day of the week, it may rain. Always puts me all out to have things that I've laid out to do put out of their regular order. I'd been willing enough to have sent over some old things; but why they must needs take Milly's time, just as if the funeral couldn't have got ready without her! These funerals are always miserable drunken times with them! And, then, who knows, she may catch the small-pox, or something or other. There's never any knowing what these people die of."

"They die of just such things as we do," said Nina. "They have that in common with us, at any rate."

"Yes; but there's no reason for risking our lives, as I know of—especially for such people—when it don't do any good."

"Why, aunt, what do you know against these folks? Have you ever known of their doing anything wicked?"

"O, I don't know that I know anything against this family in particular; but I know the whole race. These squatters—I've known them ever since I was a girl in Virginia. Everybody that knows anything knows exactly what they are. There isn't any help for them, unless, as I said before, they were made slaves; and then they could be kept decent. You may go to see them, if you like, but *I* don't want *my* arrangements to be interfered with on their account."

Mrs. Nesbit was one of those quietly-persisting people, whose yielding is like the stretching of an India-rubber band, giving way only to a violent pull, and going back to the same place when the force is withdrawn. She seldom refused favors that were urged with any degree of importunity; not because her heart was touched, but simply because she seemed not to have force enough to refuse; and whatever she granted was always followed by a series of subdued lamentations over the necessity which had wrung them from her.

Nina's nature was so vehement and imperious, when excited, that it was a disagreeable fatigue to cross her. Mrs. Nesbit, therefore, made amends by bemoaning herself as we have seen. Nina started up, hastily, on seeing her pony brought round to the door; and, soon arrayed in her riding-dress, she was cantering through the pine woods in high spirits. The day was clear and beautiful. The floor of the woodland path was paved with a thick and cleanly carpet of the fallen pine-leaves. And Harry was in attendance with her, mounted on another horse, and riding but a very little behind; not so much so but that his mistress could, if she would, keep up a conversation with him.

"You know this Old Tiff, Harry?"

"O, yes, very well. A very good, excellent creature, and very much the superior of his master, in most respects."

"Well, he says his mistress came of a good family."

"I shouldn't wonder," said Harry. "She always had a delicate appearance, very different from people in their circumstances generally. The children, too, are remarkably pretty, well-behaved children; and it's a pity they couldn't be taught something, and not grow up and go on these miserable ways of these poor whites!"

"Why don't anybody ever teach them?" said Nina.

"Well, Miss Nina, you know how it is: everybody has his own work and business to attend to—there are no schools for them to go to—there's no work for them to do. In fact, there don't seem to be any place for them in society. Boys generally grow up to drink and swear. And, as for girls, they are of not much account. So it goes on from generation to generation."

"This is so strange, and so different from what it is in the northern states! Why, all the children go to school there—the very poorest people's children! Why, a great many of the first men, there, were poor children! Why can't there be some such thing here?"

"O, because people are settled in such a scattering way, they can't have schools. All the land that's good for anything is taken up for large estates. And, then, these poor folks that are scattered up and down in between, it's nobody's business to attend to them, and they can't attend to themselves; and so they grow up, and nobody knows how they live, and everybody seems to think it a pity they are in the world. I've seen those sometimes that would be glad to do something, if they could find anything to do. Planters don't want them on their places—they'd rather have their own servants. If one of them wants to be a blacksmith, or a carpenter, there's no encouragement. Most of the large estates have their own carpenters and blacksmiths. And there's nothing for them to do, unless it is keeping dogs to hunt negroes; or these little low stores where they sell whiskey, and take what's stolen from the plantations. Sometimes a smart one gets a place as overseer on a plantation. Why, I've heard of their coming so low as actually to sell their children to traders, to get a bit of bread."

"What miserable creatures! But do you suppose it can be possible that a woman of any respectable family can have married a man of this sort?"

"Well, I don't know, Miss Nina; that might be. You see, good families sometimes degenerate; and when they get too poor to send their children off to school, or keep any teachers for them, they run down very fast. This man is not bad-looking, and he really is a person who, if he had had any way opened to him, might have been a smart man, and made something of himself and family; and when he was young and better-looking, I shouldn't wonder if an uneducated girl, who had never been off a plantation, might have liked him; he was fully equal, I dare say, to her brothers. You see, Miss Nina, when *money* goes, in this part of the country, everything goes with it; and when a family is not rich enough to have everything in itself, it goes down very soon."

"At any rate, I pity the poor things," said Nina. "I don't despise them, as Aunt Nesbit does."

Here Nina, observing the path clear and uninterrupted for some distance under the arching pines, struck her horse into a canter, and they rode on for some distance without speaking. Soon the horses' feet splashed and pattered on the cool, pebbly bottom of a small, shallow stream, which flowed through the woods. This stream went meandering among the pines like a spangled ribbon, sometimes tying itself into loops, leaving open spots—almost islands of green— graced by its waters. Such a little spot now opened to the view of the two travellers. It was something less than a quarter of an acre in extent, entirely surrounded by the stream, save only a small neck of about four feet, which connected it to the main land.

Here a place had been cleared and laid off into a garden, which, it was evident, was carefully tended. The log-cabin which stood in the middle was far from having the appearance of wretchedness which Nina had expected. It was almost entirely a dense mass of foliage, being covered with the intermingled drapery of the Virginia creeper and the yellow jessamine. Two little borders, each side of the house, were blooming with flowers. Around the little island the pine-trees closed in unbroken semi-circle, and the brook meandered away through them, to lose itself eventually in that vast forest of swampy land which girdles the whole Carolina shore. The whole air of the place was so unexpectedly inviting, in its sylvan stillness and beauty, that Nina could not help checking her horse, and exclaiming,

"I'm sure, it's a pretty place. They can't be such very forsaken people, after all."

"O, that's all Tiff's work," said Harry. "He takes care of everything outside and in, while the man is off after nobody knows what. You'd be perfectly astonished to see how that old creature manages. He sews, and he knits, and works the garden, does the house-work, and teaches the children. It's a fact! You'll notice that they haven't the pronunciation or the manners of these wild white children; and I take it to be all Tiff's watchfulness, for that creature hasn't one particle of selfishness in him. He just identifies himself with his mistress and her children."

By this time Tiff had perceived their approach, and came out to assist them in dismounting.

"De Lord above bless you, Miss Gordon, for coming to see my poor missis! Ah! she is lying dere just as beautiful, just as she was the very day she was married! All her young looks come back to her; and Milly, she done laid her out beautiful! Lord, I's wanting somebody to come and look at her, because she has got good blood, if she be poor. She is none of your common sort of poor whites, Miss Nina. Just come in; come in, and look at her."

Nina stepped into the open door of the hut. The bed was covered with a clean white sheet, and the body, arrayed in a long white night-dress brought by Milly, lay there so very still, quiet, and life-like, that one could scarcely realize the presence of death. The expression of exhaustion, fatigue, and anxiety, which the face had latterly worn, had given place to one of tender rest, shaded by a sort of mysterious awe, as if the closed eyes were looking on unutterable things. The soul, though sunk below the horizon of existence, had thrown back a twilight upon the face radiant as that of the evening heavens.

By the head of the bed the little girl was sitting, dressed carefully, and her curling hair parted in front, apparently fresh from the brush; and the little boy was sitting beside her, his round blue eyes bearing an expression of subdued wonder.

Cripps was sitting at the foot of the bed, evidently much the worse for liquor; for, spite of the exhortation of Tiff, he had applied to the whiskey-jug immediately on his departure. Why not? He was uncomfortable—gloomy; and every one, under such circumstances, naturally inclines towards *some* source of consolation. He who is intellectual reads and studies; he who is industrious flies to business; he who is affectionate seeks friends; he who is pious, religion; but he who is none of these—what has he but his whiskey? Cripps made a stupid, staring inclination toward Nina and Harry, as they entered, and sat still, twirling his thumbs and muttering to himself.

The sunshine fell through the panes on the floor, and there came floating in from without the odor of flowers and the song of birds. All the Father's gentle messengers spoke of comfort; but he as a deaf man heard not—as a blind man did not regard. For the rest, an air of neatness had been imparted to the extreme poverty of the room, by the joint efforts of Milly and Tiff.

Tiff entered softly, and stood by Nina, as she gazed. He had in his hand several sprays of white jessamine, and he laid one on the bosom of the dead.

"She had a hard walk of it," he said, "but she's got home! Don't she look peaceful?—poor lamb!"

The little, thoughtless, gay coquette had never looked on a sight like this before. She stood with a fixed, tender thoughtfulness, unlike her usual gayety, her riding-hat hanging carelessly by its strings from her hands, her loose hair drooping over her face.

She heard some one entering the cottage, but she did not look up. She was conscious of some one looking over her shoulder, and thought it was Harry.

"Poor thing! how young she looks," she said, "to have had so much trouble!" Her voice trembled, and a tear stood in her eye. There was a sudden movement; she looked up, and Clayton was standing by her.

She looked surprised, and the color deepened in her cheek, but was too ingenuously and really in sympathy with the scene before her even to smile. She retained his hand a moment, and turned to the dead, saying, in an under-tone, "See here!"

"I see," he said. "Can I be of service?"

"The poor thing died last night," said Nina. "I suppose some one might help about a funeral. Harry," she said, walking softly towards the door, and speaking low, "you provide a coffin; have it made neatly."

"Uncle," she said, motioning Tiff towards her, "where would they have her buried?"

"Buried?" said Tiff. "O, Lord! buried!" And he covered his face with his hard hands, and the tears ran through his fingers. "Lord, Lord! Well, it must come, I know, but 'pears like I couldn't! Laws, she's so beautiful! Don't, to-day! don't!"

"Indeed, Uncle," said Nina, tenderly, "I'm sorry I grieved you; but you know, poor fellow, that must come."

"I's known her ever since she's dat high!" said Tiff. "Her har was curly, and she used to war such pretty red shoes, and come running after me in de garden. 'Tiff, Tiff,' she used to say—and dar she is now, and stroubles brought her dar! Lord, what a pretty gal she was! pretty as you be, Miss Nina. But since she married *dat ar*," pointing with his thumb over his shoulder, and speaking confidentially, "everything went wrong. I's held her up—did all I could; and now here she is!"

"Perhaps," said Nina, laying her hand on his, "perhaps she's in a better place than this."

"O, Lord, dat she is! She told me dat when she died. She saw de Lord at last,—she did so! Dem's her last words. 'Tiff,' she says, 'I see Him, and He will give me rest. Tiff,' she says,—I'd been asleep, you know, and I kinder felt something cold on my hand, and I woke up right sudden, and dar she was, her eyes so bright, looking at me and breathing so hard; and all she says was, 'Tiff, I've seen Him, and I know now why I've suffered so; He's gwine to take me, and give me rest!' "

"Then, my poor fellow, you ought to rejoice that she is safe."

" 'Deed I does," said Tiff; "yet I's selfish. I wants to be dere too, I does—only I has de chil'en to care for."

"Well, my good fellow," said Nina, "we must leave you now. Harry will see about a coffin for your poor mistress; and whenever the funeral is to be, our carriage will come over, and we will all attend."

"Lord bless you, Miss Gordon! Dat ar *too* good on ye! My heart's been most broke, tinking nobody cared for my poor young mistress! you's too good, dat you is!"

Then, drawing near to her, and sinking his voice, he said: " 'Bout de mourning, Miss Nina. *He* an't no 'count, you know—body can see how 't is with him very plain. But missis was a Peyton, you know; and I's a Peyton, too. I naturally feels a 'sponsibility he couldn't be 'spected fur to. I's took de ribbons off of Miss Fanny's bonnet, and done de best I could trimming it up with black crape what Milly gave me; and I's got a band of black crape on Master Teddy's hat; and I 'lowed to put one on mine, but there wasn't quite enough. You know, missis, old family servants always wars mourning. If missis just be pleased to look over my work! Now, dis yer is Miss Fanny's bonnet. You know I can't be 'spected for to make it like a milliner."

"They are very well indeed, Uncle Tiff."

"Perhaps, Miss Nina, you can kind of touch it over."

"O, if you like, Uncle Tiff, I'll take them all home, and do them for you."

"The Lord bless *you*, Miss Gordon! Dat ar was just what I wanted, but was most 'fraid to ask you. Some gay young ladies doesn't like to handle black."

"Ah! Uncle Tiff, I've no fears of that sort; so put it in the wagon, and let Milly take it home."

So saying, she turned and passed out of the door where Harry was standing, holding the horses. A third party might have seen, by the keen, rapid glance with which his eye rested upon Clayton, that he was measuring the future probability which might make him the arbiter of his own destiny—the disposer of all that was dear to him in life. As for Nina, although the day before a thousand fancies and coquetries would have colored the manner of her meeting Clayton, yet now she was so impressed by what she had witnessed, that she scarcely appeared to know that she had met him. She placed her pretty foot on his hand, and let him lift her on to the saddle, scarcely noticing the act, except by a serious, graceful inclination of her head.

One great reason of the ascendency which Clayton had thus far gained over her, was that his nature, so quiet, speculative, and undemonstrative, always left her such perfect liberty to follow the more varying moods of her own. A man of a different mould would have sought to awake her out of the trance—would have remarked on her abstracted manner, or rallied her on her silence. Clayton merely mounted his horse and rode quietly by her side, while Harry, passing on before them, was soon out of sight.

CHAPTER XI

The Lovers

THEY RODE ON IN SILENCE, till their horses' feet again clattered in the clear, pebbly water of the stream. Here Nina checked her horse; and, pointing round the circle of pine forests, and up the stream, overhung with bending trees and branches, said:

"Hush!—listen!" Both stopped, and heard the swaying of the pine-trees, the babble of the waters, the cawing of distant crows, and the tapping of the woodpecker.

"How beautiful everything is!" she said. "It seems to me so sad that people must die! I never saw anybody dead before, and you don't know how it makes me feel! To think that that poor woman was just such a girl as I am, and used to be just so full of life, and never thought any more than I do that she should lie there all cold and dead! Why is it things are made so beautiful, if we must die?"

"Remember what you said to the old man, Miss Nina. Perhaps she sees more beautiful things, now."

"In heaven? Yes; I wish we knew more about heaven, so that it would seem natural and home-like to us, as this world does. As for me, I can't feel that I ever want to leave this world—I enjoy living so much! I can't forget how cold her hand was! I never felt anything like that cold!"

In all the varying moods of Nina, Clayton had never seen anything that resembled this. But he understood the peculiar singleness and earnestness of nature which made any one idea, or impression, for a time absolute in her mind. They turned their horses into the wood-path, and rode on in silence.

"Do you know," said she, "it's such a change coming from New York to live here? Everything is so unformed, so wild, and so lonely! I never saw anything so lonesome as these woods are. Here you can ride miles and miles, hours and hours, and hear nothing but the swaying of the pine-trees, just as you hear it now. Our place (you never were there, were you?) stands all by itself, miles from

113

any other; and I've been for so many years used to a thickly-settled country, that it seems very strange to me. I can't help thinking things look rather deserted and desolate, here. It makes me rather sober and sad. I don't know as you'll like the appearance of our place. A great many things are going to decay about it; and yet there are some things that can't decay; for papa was very fond of trees and shrubbery, and we have a good deal more of them than usual. Are you fond of trees?"

"Yes; I'm almost a tree-worshipper. I have no respect for a man who can't appreciate a tree. The only good thing I ever heard of Xerxes[1] was, that he was so transported with the beauty of a plane-tree, that he hung it with chains of gold. This is a little poetical is-land in the barbarism of those days."

"Xerxes!" said Nina. "I believe I studied something about him in that dismal, tedious history, at Madame Ardaine's; but nothing so interesting as that, I'm sure. But what should he hang gold chains on a tree for?"

" 'T was the best way he knew of expressing his good opinion."

"Do you know," said Nina, half checking her horse, suddenly, "that I never had the least idea that these men were alive that we read about in these histories, or that they had any feelings like ours? We always studied the lessons, and learnt the hard names, and how forty thousand were killed on one side, and fifty thousand on the other; and we don't know any more about it than if we never had. That's the way we girls studied at school, except a few 'poky' ones, who wanted to be learned, or meant to be teachers."

"An interesting résumé, certainly," said Clayton, laughing.

"But, how strange it is," said Nina, "to think that all those folks we read about are alive now, doing something somewhere; and I get to wondering where they are—Xerxes, and Alexander,[2] and the rest of them. Why, they were so full of life they kept everything in commotion while in this world; and I wonder if they have been keeping a going ever since. Perhaps Xerxes has been looking round at our trees—nobody knows. But here we are coming now to the beginning of our grounds. There, you see that holly-hedge! Mamma had that set out. She travelled in England, and liked the hedges there so much that she thought she would see what could be done with our American holly. So she had these brought from the woods, and planted. You see it all grows wild, now, because it hasn't been cut for many years. And this live-oak avenue my grandfather set out. It's my pride and delight."

As she spoke, a pair of broad gates swung open, and they cantered in beneath the twilight arches of the oaks. Long wreaths of pearly moss hung swinging from the branches, and, although the sun now was at high noon, a dewy, dreamy coolness seemed to rustle through all the leaves. As Clayton passed in, he took off his hat, as he had often done in foreign countries in cathedrals.

"Welcome to Canema!" said she, riding up to him, and looking up frankly into his face.

The air, half queenly, half childish, with which this was said, was acknowledged by Clayton with a grave smile, as he replied, bowing, "Thank you, madam."

"Perhaps," she added, in a grave tone, "you'll be sorry that you ever came here."

"What do you mean by that?" he replied.

"I don't know; it just came into my head to say it. We none of us ever know what's going to come of what we do."

At this instant, a violent clamor, like the cawing of a crow, rose on one side of the avenue; and the moment after, Tomtit appeared, caricoling,[3] and cutting a somerset; his curls flying, his cheeks glowing.

"Why, Tomtit, what upon earth is this for?" said Nina.

"Laws, missis, deres been a gen'elman waiting for you at the house these two hours. And missis, she's done got on her best cap, and gone down in the parlor for him."

Nina felt herself blush to the roots of her hair, and was vexed and provoked to think she did so. Involuntarily her eyes met Clayton's. But he expressed neither curiosity nor concern.

"What a pretty drapery this light moss makes!" said he. "I wasn't aware that it grew so high up in the state."

"Yes; it is very pretty," said Nina, abstractedly.

Clayton, however, had noticed both the message and the blush, and was not so ill-informed as Nina supposed as to the whole affair, having heard from a New York correspondent of the probability that an arrival might appear upon the field about this time. He was rather curious to watch the development produced by this event. They paced up the avenue, conversing in disconnected intervals, till they came out on the lawn which fronted the mansion—a large, gray, three-story building, surrounded on the four sides by wide balconies of wood. Access was had to the lower of these by a broad flight of steps. And there Nina saw, plain enough, her Aunt Nesbit in all the proprieties of cap and silk gown, sitting, making the agreeable to Mr. Carson.

Mr. Frederic Augustus Carson was one of those nice little epitomes of conventional society, which appear to such advantage in factitious life, and are so out of place in the undress, sincere surroundings of country life. Nina had liked his society extremely well in the drawing-rooms and opera-houses of New York. But, in the train of thought inspired by the lonely and secluded life she was now leading, it seemed to her an absolute impossibility that she could, even in coquetry and in sport, have allowed such an one to set up pretensions to her hand and heart. She was vexed with herself that she had done so, and therefore not in the most amiable mood for a meeting. Therefore, when, on ascending the steps, he rushed precipitately forward, and, offering his hand, called her Nina, she was ready to die with vexation. She observed, too, a peculiar swelling and rustling of Aunt Nesbit's plumage,—an indescribable air of tender satisfaction, peculiar to elderly ladies who are taking an interest in an affair of the heart, which led her to apprehend that the bachelor had commenced operations by declaring his position to her. 'T was with some embarrassment that Nina introduced Mr. Clayton, whom Aunt Nesbit received with a most stately curtsey, and Mr. Carson with a patronizing bow.

"Mr. Carson has been waiting for you these two hours," said Aunt Nesbit.

"Very warm riding, Nina," said Mr. Carson, observing her red cheeks. "You've been riding too fast, I fear. You must be careful of yourself. I've known people bring on very grave illnesses by overheating the blood!"

Clayton seated himself near the door, and seemed to be intent on the scene without. And Carson, drawing his chair close to Nina, asked, in a confidential under-tone,

"Who is that gentleman?"

"Mr. Clayton, of Claytonville," said Nina, with as much hauteur as she could assume.

"Ah, yes!—Hem!—hem! I've heard of the family—a very nice family—a very worthy young man—extremely, I'm told. Shall be happy to make his acquaintance."

"I beg," said Nina, rising, "the gentlemen will excuse me a moment or two."

Clayton replied by a grave bow, while Mr. Carson, with great empressement, handed Nina to the door. The moment it was closed, she stamped, with anger, in the entry.

"The provoking fool! to take these airs with me! And I, too—I deserve it! What on earth could make me think I could tolerate that man?"

As if Nina's cup were not yet full, Aunt Nesbit followed her to her chamber with an air of unusual graciousness.

"Nina, my dear, he has told me all about it! and I assure you I'm very much pleased with him!"

"Told you all about *what?*" said Nina.

"Why, your engagement, to be sure! I'm delighted to think you've done so well! I think your Aunt Maria, and all of them, will be delighted! Takes a weight of care off my mind!"

"I wish you wouldn't trouble yourself about me, or my affairs, Aunt Nesbit!" said Nina. "And, as for this old pussy-cat, with his squeaking boots, I won't have him purring round *me*, that's certain! *So* provoking, to take that way towards me! Call me Nina, and talk as though he were lord paramount of me, and everything here! I'll let him know!"

"Why, Nina! Seems to me this is very strange conduct! I am very much astonished at you!"

"I dare say you are, aunt! I never knew the time I didn't astonish you! But this man I detest!"

"Well, then, my dear, what were you engaged to him for?"

"*Engaged!* Aunt, for pity's sake, do hush! Engaged! I should like to know what a New York engagement amounts to! Engaged at the opera!—Engaged for a joke! Why, he was my bouquet-holder! The man is just an opera libretto! He was very useful in his time. But who wants him afterwards?"

"But, my dear Nina, this trifling with gentlemen's hearts!"

"I'll warrant his heart! It's neither sugar nor salt, I'll assure you. I'll tell you what, aunt, he loves good eating, good drinking, nice clothes, nice houses, and good times generally; and he wants a pretty wife as a part of a whole; and he thinks he'll take me. But he is mistaken! Calling me 'Nina,' indeed! Just let me have a chance of seeing him alone! I'll teach him to call me 'Nina'! I'll let him know how things stand!"

"But, Nina, you must confess you've given him occasion for all this."

"Well, supposing I have? I'll give him occasion for something else, then!"

"Why, my dear," said Aunt Nesbit, "he came on to know when you'll fix the day to be married!"

"Married! O, my gracious! Just think of the creature's talking about it! Well, it *is* my fault, as you say; but I'll do the best I can to mend it."

"Well, I'm really sorry for him," said Aunt Nesbit.

"You are, aunt? Why don't you *take* him yourself, then? You are as young and good-looking as he is."

"Nina, how you talk!" said Aunt Nesbit, coloring and bridling. "There *was* a time when I wasn't bad-looking, to be sure; but that's long since past."

"O, that's because you always dress in stone-color and drab," said Nina, as she stood brushing and arranging her curls. "Come, now, and go down, aunt, and do the best you can till I make my appearance. After all, as you say, I'm the most to blame. There's no use in being vexed with the old soul. So, aunt, do be as fascinating as you can; see if you can't console him. Only remember how *you* used to turn off lovers, when you were of my age."

"And who is this other gentleman, Nina?"

"O, nothing, only he is a friend of mine. A very good man— good enough for a minister, any day, aunt, and not so stupid as good people generally are, either."

"Well, perhaps you are engaged to *him?*"

"No, I am not; that is to say, I won't be to anybody. This is an insufferable business! I *like* Mr. Clayton, because he can let me alone, don't look at me in that abominably delighted way all the time, and dance about, calling me *Nina!* He and I are very good friends, that's all. I'm not going to have any engagements *anywhere.*"

"Well, Nina, I'll go down, and you make haste."

While the gentlemen and Aunt Nesbit were waiting in the saloon, Carson made himself extremely happy and at home. It was a large, cool apartment, passing, like a hall, completely through the centre of the house. Long French windows, at either end, opened on to balconies. The pillars of the balconies were draped and garlanded with wreaths of roses now in full bloom. The floor of the room was the polished mosaic of different colors to which we have formerly alluded. Over the mantel-piece was sculptured in oak the Gordon arms. The room was wainscoted with dark wood, and hung with several fine paintings, by Copley and Stuart,[4] of different members of the family. A grand piano, lately arrived from New York, was the most modern-looking article in the room. Most of the furniture was of the heavy dark mahogany, of an antique pattern. Clayton sat by the door, still admiring the avenue of oaks which were to be seen across the waving green of the lawn.

In about half an hour Nina reäppeared in a flossy cloud of muslin, lace, and gauzy ribbons. Dress was one of those accomplishments for which the little gypsy had a natural instinct; and, without any apparent thought, she always fell into that kind of color and material which harmonized with her style of appearance and character. There was always something floating and buoyant about the arrangement of her garments and drapery; so that to see her move across the floor gave one an airy kind of sensation, like the gambols of thistle-down. Her brown eyes had a peculiar resemblance to a bird's; and this effect was increased by a twinkling motion of the head, and a fluttering habit of movement peculiar to herself; so that when she swept by in rosy gauzes, and laid one ungloved hand lightly on the piano, she seemed to Clayton much like some saucy bird—very good indeed if let alone, but ready to fly on the slightest approach.

Clayton had the rare faculty of taking in every available point of observation, without appearing to stare.

" 'Pon my word, Nina," said Mr. Carson, coming towards her with a most delighted air, "you look as if you had fallen out of a rainbow!"

Nina turned away very coolly, and began arranging her music.

"O, that's right!" said Carson; "give us one of your songs. Sing something from the Favorita.[5] You know it's my favorite opera," said he, assuming a most sentimental expression.

"O, I'm entirely out of practice—I don't sing at all. I'm sick of all those opera-songs!" And Nina skimmed across the floor, and out of the open door by which Clayton was lounging, and began busying herself amid the flowers that wreathed the porch. In a moment Carson was at her heels; for he was one of those persons who seem to think it a duty never to allow any one to be quiet, if they can possibly prevent it.

"Have you ever studied the language of flowers, Nina?" said he.

"No, I don't like to study languages."

"You know the signification of a full-blown rose?" said he, tenderly presenting her with one.

Nina took the rose, coloring with vexation, and then, plucking from the bush a rose of two or three days' bloom, whose leaves were falling out, she handed it to him, and said,

"Do you understand the signification of this?"

"O, you have made an unfortunate selection! This rose is all falling to pieces!" said Mr. Carson, innocently.

"So I observed," said Nina, turning away quickly; then, making one of her darting movements, she was in the middle of the saloon again, just as the waiter announced dinner.

Clayton rose gravely, and offered his arm to Aunt Nesbit; and Nina found herself obliged to accept the delighted escort of Mr. Carson, who, entirely unperceiving, was in the briskest possible spirits, and established himself comfortably between Aunt Nesbit and Nina.

"You must find it very dull here—very barren country, shockingly so! What do you find to interest yourself in?" said he.

"Will you take some of this gumbo?" replied Nina.

"I always thought," said Aunt Nesbit, "it was a good plan for girls to have a course of reading marked out to them when they left school."

"O, certainly," said Carson. "I shall be happy to mark out one for her. I've done it for several young ladies."

At this moment Nina accidentally happened to catch Clayton's eye, which was fixed upon Mr. Carson with an air of quiet amusement greatly disconcerting to her.

"Now," said Mr. Carson, "I have no opinion of making *blues* of young ladies; but still, I think, Mrs. Nesbit, that a little useful information adds greatly to their charms. Don't you?"

"Yes," said Mrs. Nesbit. "I've been reading Gibbon's Decline and Fall of the Roman Empire,[6] lately."

"Yes," said Nina, "aunt's been busy about that ever since I can remember."

"That's a very nice book," said Mr. Carson, looking solemnly at Nina; "only, Mrs. Nesbit, an't you afraid of the infidel principle? I think, in forming the minds of the young, you know, one cannot be too careful."

"Why, he struck me as a very pious writer!" said Aunt Nesbit, innocently. "I'm sure, he makes the most religious reflections, all along. I liked him particularly on that account."

It seemed to Nina that, without looking at Clayton, she was forced to meet his eye. No matter whether she directed her attention to the asparagus or the potatoes, it was her fatality always to end by a rencounter with his eye; and she saw, for some reason or other, the conversation was extremely amusing to him.

"For my part," said Nina, "I don't know what sort of principles Aunt Nesbit's history, there, has; but one thing I'm pretty certain of,—that I'm not in any danger from any such thick, close-printed, old, stupid-looking books as that. I hate reading, and I don't intend to have my mind formed; so that nobody need trouble themselves to mark out courses for me! What is it to me what all these old empires have been, a hundred years ago? It is as much as I can do to attend to what is going on now."

"For my part," said Aunt Nesbit, "I've always regretted that I neglected the cultivation of my mind when I was young. I was like Nina, here, immersed in vanity and folly."

"People always talk," said Nina, reddening, "as if there was but one kind of vanity and folly in the world. I think there can be as much learned vanity and folly as we girls have!" And she looked at Clayton indignantly, as she saw him laughing.

"I agree with Miss Gordon, entirely. There is a great deal of very stupid respectable trifling, which people pursue under the head of courses of reading," he said. "And I don't wonder that most compends[7] of history which are studied in schools should inspire any lively young lady with a life-long horror, not only of history, but of reading."

"Do you think so?" said Nina, with a look of inexpressible relief.

"I do, indeed," said Clayton. "And it would have been a very good thing for many of our historians, if they had been obliged to have shaped their histories so that they would interest a lively school-girl. We literary men, then, would have found less sleepy reading. There is no reason why a young lady, who would sit up all night reading a novel, should not be made to sit up all night with a history. I'll venture to say there's no romance can come up to the gorgeousness and splendor, and the dramatic power, of things that really have happened. All that's wanting is to have it set before us with an air of reality."

"But, then," said Nina, "you'd have to make the history into a romance."

"Well, a good historical romance is generally truer than a dull history; because it gives some sort of conception of the truth; whereas, the dull history gives none."

"Well, then," said Nina, "I'll confess, now, that about all the history I do know has been got from Walter Scott's novels.[8] *I* always told our history-teacher so; but she insisted upon it that it was very dangerous reading."

"For my part," said Mrs. Nesbit, "I've a great horror of novel-reading, particularly for young ladies. It did me a great deal of harm when I was young. It dissipates the mind; it gives false views of life."

"O, law!" said Nina. "We used to write compositions about that, and I've got it all by heart—how it raises false expectations, and leads people to pursue phantoms, rainbows, and meteors, and all that sort of thing!"

"And yet," said Clayton, "all these objections would lie against *perfectly* true history, and the more so just in proportion to its truth. If the history of Napoleon Bonaparte[9] were graphically and minutely given, it would lie open to the very same objections. It would produce the very same cravings for something out of the commonplace course of life. There would be the same dazzling mixture of bad and good qualities in the hero, and the same lassitude and exhaustion after the story was finished. And common history does not do this, simply because it is not true—does not produce a vivid impression of the reality as it happened."

Aunt Nesbit only got an indefinite impression, from this harangue, that Clayton was defending novel-reading, and felt herself called to employ her own peculiar line of reasoning to meet it, which consisted in saying the same thing over and over, at regular intervals, without appearing to hear or notice anything said in reply. Accordingly, she now drew herself up, with a slightly virtuous air, and said to Mr. Clayton,

"I must say, after all, that I don't approve of novel-reading. It gives false views of life, and disgusts young people with their duties."

"I was only showing, madam, that the same objection would apply to the best-written history," said Clayton.

"I think novel-reading does a great deal of harm," rejoined Aunt

Nesbit. "I never allow myself to read any work of fiction. I'm principled against it."

"For my part," said Nina, "I wish I could find that kind of history you are speaking of; I believe I could read that."

" 'T would be very interesting history, certainly," said Mr. Carson. "I should think it would prove a very charming mode of writing. I wonder somebody don't produce one."

"For my part," said Aunt Nesbit, "I confine myself entirely to what is practically useful. Useful information is all I desire."

"Well, I suppose, then, I'm very wicked," said Nina; "but I don't like anything useful. Why, I've sometimes thought, when I've been in the garden, that the summer-savory, sage, and sweet-majoram, were just as pretty as many other flowers; and I couldn't see any reason why I shouldn't like a sprig of one of them for a bouquet, except that I've seen them used so much for stuffing turkeys. Well, now, that seems very bad of me, don't it?"

"That reminds me," said Aunt Nesbit, "that Rose has been putting sage into this turkey again, after all that I said to her. I believe she does it on purpose."

At this moment Harry appeared at the door, and requested to speak to Nina.

After a few moments' whispered conversation, she came back to the table, apparently disconcerted.

"I'm so sorry—so very sorry!" she said. "Harry has been riding all round the country to find a minister to attend the funeral, this evening. It will be such a disappointment to that poor fellow! You know the negroes think so much of having prayers at the grave!"

"If no one else can be found to read prayers, I will," said Clayton.

"O, thank you! will you, indeed?" said Nina. "I'm glad of it, now, for poor Tiff's sake. The coach will be out at five o'clock, and we'll ride over together, and make as much of a party as we can."

"Why, child," said Aunt Nesbit to Nina, after they returned to the parlor, "I did not know that Mr. Clayton was an Episcopalian."

"He isn't," said Nina. "He and his family all attend the Presbyterian church."[10]

"How strange that he should offer to read prayers!" said Aunt Nesbit. "I don't approve of such things, for my part."

"Such things as what?"

"Countenancing Episcopal errors. If we are right, they are wrong, and we ought not to countenance them."

"But, aunt, the burial-service is beautiful."

"Don't approve of it!" said Aunt Nesbit.

"Why, you know, as Clayton isn't a minister, he would not feel like making an extempore prayer."

"Shows great looseness of religious principle," said Aunt Nesbit. "Don't approve of it!"

CHAPTER XII

Explanations

THE GOLDEN ARROWS of the setting sun were shooting hither and thither through the pine woods, glorifying whatever they touched with a life not its own. A chorus of birds were pouring out an evening melody, when a little company stood around an open grave. With instinctive care for the feeling of the scene, Nina had arrayed herself in a black silk dress, and plain straw bonnet with black ribbon—a mark of respect to the deceased remembered and narrated by Tiff for many a year after.

Cripps stood by the head of the grave, with that hopeless, imbecile expression with which a nature wholly gross and animal often contemplates the symbols of the close of mortal existence. Tiff stood by the side of the grave, his white hat conspicuously draped with black crape, and a deep weed of black upon his arm. The baby, wrapped in an old black shawl, was closely fondled in his bosom, while the two children stood weeping bitterly at his side. The other side of the grave stood Mr. Carson and Mr. Clayton, while Milly, Harry, and several plantation slaves, were in a group behind.

The coffin had been opened, that all might take that last look, so coveted, yet so hopeless, which the human heart will claim on the very verge of the grave. It was but a moment since the coffin had been closed; and the burst of grief which shook the children was caused by that last farewell. As Clayton, in a musical voice, pronounced the words "I am the resurrection and the life," Nina wept and sobbed as if the grief had been her own; nor did she cease to weep during the whole touching service. It was the same impulsive nature which made her so gay in other scenes that made her so sympathetic here. When the whole was over, she kissed the children, and, shaking hands with old Tiff, promised to come and see them on the morrow. After which, Clayton led her to the carriage, into which he and Carson followed her.

"Upon my word," said Carson, briskly, "this has been quite

solemn! Really, a very interesting funeral, indeed! I was delighted with the effect of our church service; in such a romantic place, too! 'T was really very interesting. It pleases me, also, to see young ladies in your station, Nina, interest themselves in the humble concerns of the poor. If young ladies knew how much more attractive it made them to show a charitable spirit, they would cultivate it more. Singular-looking person, that old negro! Seems to be a good creature. Interesting children, too! I should think the woman must have been pretty when she was young. Seen a great deal of trouble, no doubt, poor thing! It's a comfort to hope she is better off now."

Nina was filled with indignation at this monologue; not considering that the man was giving the very best he had in him, and laboring assiduously at what he considered his vocation, the prevention of half an hour of silence in any spot of earth where he could possibly make himself heard. The same excitement which made Nina cry made him talk. But he was not content with talking, but insisted upon asking Nina, every moment, if she didn't think it an interesting occasion, and if she had not been much impressed.

"I don't feel like talking, Mr. Carson," said Nina.

"O—ah—yes, indeed! You've been so deeply affected—yes. Naturally *does* incline one to silence. Understand your feelings perfectly. Very gratifying to me to see you take such a deep interest in your fellow-creatures."

Nina could have pushed him out of the carriage.

"For my part," continued Carson, "I think we don't reflect enough about this kind of things—I positively don't. It really is useful sometimes to have one's thoughts turned in this direction. It does us good."

Thus glibly did Carson proceed to talk away the impression of the whole scene they had witnessed. Long before the carriage reached home, Nina had forgotten all her sympathy in a tumult of vexation. She discovered an increasing difficulty in making Carson understand, by any degree of coolness, that he was not acceptable; and saw nothing before her but explanations in the very plainest terms, mortifying and humiliating as that might be. His perfect self-complacent ease, and the air with which he constantly seemed to appropriate her as something which of right belonged to himself, filled her with vexation. But yet her conscience told her that she had brought it upon herself.

"I won't bear this another hour!" she said to herself, as she ascended the steps toward the parlor. "All this before Clayton, too! What must he think of me?" But they found tea upon the table, and Aunt Nesbit waiting.

"It's a pity, madam, you were not with us. Such an interesting time!" said Mr. Carson, launching, with great volubility, into the tide of discourse.

"It wouldn't have done for me at all," said Mrs. Nesbit. "Being out when the dew falls, always brings on hoarseness. I have been troubled in that way these two or three years. Now I have to be very careful. Then I'm timid about riding in a carriage with John's driving."

"I was amused enough," said Nina, "with Old Hundred's indignation at having to get out the carriage and horses to go over to what he called a 'cracker funeral.'[1] I really believe, if he could have upset us without hurting himself, he would have done it."

"For my part," said Aunt Nesbit, "I hope that family will move off before long. It's very disagreeable having such people round."

"The children look very pretty and bright," said Nina.

"O, there's no hope for them! They'll grow up and be just like their parents. I've seen that sort of people all through and through. I don't wish them any evil; only I don't want to have anything to do with them!"

"For my part," said Nina, "I'm sorry for them. I wonder why the legislature, or somebody, don't have schools, as they do up in New York State? There isn't anywhere there where children can't go to school, if they wish to. Besides, aunt, these children really came from an old family in Virginia. Their old servant-man says that their mother was a Peyton."

"I don't believe a word of it! They'll lie—all of them. They always do."

"Well," said Nina, "I shall do something for these children, at any rate."

"I quite agree with you, Nina. It shows a very excellent spirit in you," said Mr. Carson. "You'll always find me ready to encourage everything of that sort."

Nina frowned, and looked indignant. But to no purpose. Mr. Carson went on remorselessly with his really good-hearted rattle, till Nina, at last, could bear it no longer.

"How dreadfully warm this room is!" said she, springing up. "Come, let's go back into the parlor."

Nina was as much annoyed at Clayton's silence, and his quiet, observant reserve, as with Carson's forth-putting. Rising from table, she passed on before the company, with a half-flying trip, into the hall, which lay now cool, calm, and breezy, in the twilight, with the odor of the pillar-roses floating in at the window. The pale white moon, set in the rosy belt of the evening sky, looked in at the open door. Nina would have given all the world to be still; but, well aware that stillness was out of the question, she determined to select her own noise; and, sitting down at the piano, began playing very fast, in a rapid, restless, disconnected manner. Clayton threw himself on a lounge by the open door; while Carson busied himself fluttering the music, opening and shutting music-books, and interspersing running commentaries and notes of admiration on the playing.

At last, as if she could bear it no longer, she rose, with a very decided air, from the piano, and, facing about towards Mr. Carson, said:

"It looks very beautifully out doors. Don't you want to come out? There's a point of view at the end of one of the paths, where the moon looks on the water, that I should like to show you."

"Won't you catch cold, Nina?" said Aunt Nesbit.

"No, indeed! I never catch cold," said Nina, springing into the porch, and taking the delighted Mr. Carson's arm. And away she went with him, with almost a skip and a jump, leaving Clayton tête-à-tête with Aunt Nesbit.

Nina went so fast that her attendant was almost out of breath. They reached a little knoll, and there Nina stopped suddenly, and said, "Look here, Mr. Carson; I have something to say to you."

"I should be delighted, my dear Nina! I'm perfectly charmed!"

"No—no—if you please—*don't!*" said Nina, putting up her hand to stop him. "Just wait till you hear what I have to say. I believe you did not get a letter which I wrote you a few days ago, did you?"

"A letter! no, indeed. How unfortunate!"

"Very unfortunate for me!" said Nina; "and for you, too. Because, if you had, it would have saved you and me the trouble of this interview. I wrote that letter to tell you, Mr. Carson, that I cannot *think* of such a thing as an engagement with you! That I've acted very wrong and very foolishly; but that I cannot do it. In New York, where everybody and everything seemed to be trifling, and where the girls all trifled with these things, I was engaged—just for a frolic—nothing more. I had no idea what it would amount to; no idea what I was saying, nor how I should feel afterwards. But, every hour since I've been home, here, since I've been so much alone, has made me feel how wrong it is. Now, I'm very sorry, I'm sure. But I must speak the truth, this time. But it is—I can't tell you how—disagreeable to me to have you treat me as you have since you've been here!"

"Miss Gordon!" said Mr. Carson, "I am positively astonished! I—I don't know what to think!"

"Well, I only want you to think that I am in earnest; and that, though I can *like* you very well as an acquaintance, and shall always wish you well, yet anything else is just as far out of the question as that moon there is from us. I can't tell you how sorry I am that I've made you all this trouble. I really am," said she, good-naturedly; "but please now to understand how we stand." She turned, and tripped away.

"There!" said she, to herself, "at any rate, I've done *one* thing!"

Mr. Carson stood still, gradually recovering from the stupor into which this communication had thrown him. He stretched himself, rubbed his eyes, took out his watch and looked at it, and then began walking off with a very sober pace in the opposite direction from Nina. Happily-constituted mortal that he was, nothing ever could be subtracted from his sum of complacence that could not be easily balanced by about a quarter of an hour's consideration. The walk through the shrubbery in which he was engaged was an extremely pretty one, and wound along on the banks of the river through many picturesque points of view, and finally led again to the house by another approach. During the course of this walk Mr. Carson had settled the whole question for himself. In the first place, he repeated the comfortable old proverb, that there were as good fish in the sea as ever were caught. In the second place, as Mr. Carson was a shrewd business-man, it occurred to him, in this connection, that the plantation was rather run down, and not a profitable acquisition. And, in the third place, contemplating Nina as the fox of old did his bunch of sour grapes, he began to remember that, after all, she was dressy, expensive, and extravagant. Then, as he did not want in that imperturbable good-nature which belongs to a very shallow capability of feeling, he said to himself that he shouldn't like the girl a bit the less. In fact, when he thought of his own fine fortune, his house in New York, and all the accessories which went to make up himself, he considered her, on the whole, as an object of pity; and, by the time that he ascended the balcony steps again, he was in as charitable and Christian a frame as any rejected suitor could desire.

He entered the drawing-room. Aunt Nesbit had ordered candles, and was sitting up with her gloves on, alone. What had transpired during his walk, he did not know; but we will take our readers into confidence.

Nina returned to the house with the same decided air with which she went out, and awakened Mr. Clayton from a revery with a brisk little tap of her fan on his shoulder.

"Come up here with me," she said, "and look out of the library window, and see this moonlight."

And up she went, over the old oaken staircase, stopping on each landing; and, beckoning to Clayton, with a whimsically authoritative gesture, threw open the door of a large, black-wainscoted room, and ushered him in. The room lay just above the one where they had been sitting, and, like that, opened on to the veranda by long-sashed windows, through which, at the present moment, a flood of moonlight was pouring. A large mahogany writing-table, covered with papers, stood in the middle of the room, and the moon shone in so brightly that the pattern of the bronze inkstand, and the color of the wafers and sealing-wax, were plainly revealed. The window commanded a splendid view of the river over the distant tree-tops, as it lay shimmering and glittering in the moonlight.

"Isn't that a beautiful sight?" said Nina, in a hurried voice.

"Very beautiful!" said Clayton, sitting down in the large lounging-chair before the window, and looking out with the abstracted air which was habitual with him.

After a moment's thought, Nina added, with a sudden effort,

"But, after all, that was not what I wanted to speak to you about. I wanted to see you somewhere, and say a few words which it seems to me it is due to you that I should say. I got your last letter, and I'm sure I am very much obliged to your sister for all the kind things she says; but I think you must have been astonished at what you have seen since you have been here."

"Astonished at what?" said Clayton, quietly.

"At Mr. Carson's manners towards me."

"I have not been astonished at all," replied Clayton, quietly.

"I think, at all events," said Nina, "I think it is no more than honorable that I should tell you exactly how things have stood. Mr. Carson has thought that he had a right to me and mine; and I was so foolish as to give him reason to think so. The fact is, that I have been making a game of life, and saying and doing anything and everything that came into my head, just for frolic. It don't seem to me that there has been anything serious or real about me, until very lately. Somehow, my acquaintance with you has made things seem more real to me than they ever did before; and it seems to me now perfectly incredible, the way we girls used to play and trifle with everything in the world. Just for sport, I was engaged to that man; just for sport, too, I have been engaged to another one."

"And," said Clayton, breaking the silence, "just for sport, have you been engaged to me?"

"No," said Nina, after a few moments' silence, "not in sport, certainly; but, yet, not enough in earnest. I think I am about half waked up. I don't know myself. I don't know where or what I am, and I want to go back into that thoughtless dream. I do really think it's too hard to take up the responsibility of living in good earnest. Now, it seems to me just this,—that I cannot be bound to anybody. I want to be free. I have positively broken all connection with Mr. Carson; I have broken with another one, and I wish—"

"To break with me?" said Clayton.

"I don't really know as I can say what I do wish. It is a very different thing from any of the others, but there's a feeling of dread, and responsibility, and constraint, about it; and, though I think I should feel very lonesome now without you, and though I like to get your letters, yet it seems to me that I cannot be engaged,—that is a most dreadful feeling to me."

"My dear friend," said Clayton, "if that is all, make yourself easy. There's no occasion for our being engaged. If you can enjoy being with me and writing to me, why, do it in the freest way, and tomorrow shall take care for the things of itself. You shall say what you please, do what you please, write when you please, and not write when you please, and have as many or as few letters as you like. There can be no true love without liberty."

"O, I'm sure I'm much obliged to you!" said Nina, with a sigh of relief. "And, now, do you know, I like your sister's postscript very much, but I can't tell what it is in it; for the language is as kind as can be, that would give me the impression that she is one of those very proper kind of people, that would be dreadfully shocked if she knew of all my goings on in New York."

Clayton could hardly help laughing at the instinctive sagacity of this remark.

"I'm sure I don't know," said he, "where you could have seen that,—in so short a postscript, too."

"Do you know, I never take anybody's hand-writing into my hand, that I don't feel an idea of them come over me, just as you have when you see people? And that idea came over me when I read your sister's letter."

"Well, Nina, to tell you the truth, sister Anne is a little bit conventional—a little set in her ways; but, after all, a large-hearted, warm-hearted woman. You would like each other, I know."

"I don't know about that," said Nina. "I am very apt to shock proper people. Somehow or other, they have a faculty of making me contrary."

"Well, but, you see, Anne isn't merely a conventional person; there's only the slightest crust of conventionality, and a real warm heart under it."

"Whereas," said Nina, "most conventional people are like a shallow river, frozen to the bottom. But, now, really, I should like very much to have your sister come and visit us, if I could think that she would come as any other friend; but, you know, it isn't very agreeable to have anybody come to look one over to see if one will do."

Clayton laughed at the naïve, undisguised frankness of this speech.

"You see," said Nina, "though I'm nothing but an ignorant school-girl, I'm as proud as if I had everything to be proud of. Now, do you know, I don't much like writing to your sister, because I don't think I write very good letters! I never could sit still long enough to write."

"Write exactly as you talk," said Clayton. "Say just what comes into your head, just as you would talk it. I hope you will do that much, for it will be very dull writing all on one side."

"Well," said Nina, rising, with animation, "now, Mr. Edward Clayton, if we have settled about this moonlight, we may as well go down into the parlor, where Aunt Nesbit and Mr. Carson are tête-à-tête."

"Poor Carson!" said Clayton.

"O, don't pity him! Good soul! he's a man that one night's rest would bring round from anything in creation. He's so thoroughly good-natured! Besides, I shall like him better, now. He did not use to seem to me so intrusive and disagreeable. We girls used to like him very well, he was such a comfortable, easy-tempered, agreeable creature, always brisk and in spirits, and knowing everything that went on. But he is one of those men that I think would be really insufferable, if anything serious were the matter with one. Now, you heard how he talked, coming from that funeral! Do you know, that if he had been coming from *my* funeral, it would have been just so?"

"O, no, not quite so bad," said Clayton.

"Indeed he is," said Nina. "That man! why, he just puts me in mind of one of these brisk blue-flies, whirring and whisking about, marching over pages of books, and alighting on all sorts of things. When he puts on that grave look, and begins to talk about serious things, he actually looks to me just as a fly does when he stands brushing his wings on a Bible! But, come, let's go down to the good soul."

Down they went, and Nina seemed like a person enfranchised. Never had she seemed more universally gracious. She was chatty and conversable with Carson, and sang over for him all her old opera-songs, with the better grace that she saw that Clayton was listening intently.

As they were sitting and conversing together, the sound of horse's heels was heard coming up the avenue.

"Who can that be, this time of night?" said Nina, springing to the door, and looking out.

She saw Harry hastening in advance to meet her, and ran down the veranda steps to speak to him.

"Harry, who is coming?"

"Miss Nina, it's Master Tom," said Harry, in a low voice.

"Tom! O, mercy!" said Nina, in a voice of apprehension. "What sent him here, now?"

"What sends him anywhere?" said Harry.

Nina reäscended the steps, and stood looking apprehensively towards the horseman, who approached every moment nearer. Harry came up on the veranda, and stood a little behind her. In a few moments the horse was up before the steps.

"Hallo, there!" said the rider. "Come, take my horse, you rascal!"

Harry remained perfectly still, put his arms by his side, and stood with a frowning expression on his forehead.

"Don't you hear?" said the horseman, throwing himself off, with an oath. "Come here, boy, and take my horse!"

"For pity's sake," said Nina, turning and looking in Harry's face, "don't have a scene here! Do take his horse, quick! *Anything* to keep him quiet!"

With a sudden start, Harry went down the steps, and took the bridle from the hand of the newly-arrived in silence.

The horseman sprang up the steps.

"Hallo, Nin, is this you?" And Nina felt herself roughly seized in the arms of a shaggy great-coat, and kissed by lips smelling of brandy and tobacco. She faintly said, as she disengaged herself,

"Tom, is it you?"

"Yes, to be sure! Who did you think it was? Devilish glad to see me, an't you? Suppose you was in hopes I wouldn't come!"

"Hush, Tom, do! I *am* glad to see you. There are gentlemen in there; don't speak so loud!"

"Some of your beaux, hey? Well, I am as good a fellow as any of 'em! Free country, I hope! No, I an't going to whisper, for any of them. So now, Nin— If there isn't old Starchy, to be sure!" said he, as Aunt Nesbit came to the door. "Hallo, old girl, how are you?"

"Thomas!" said Mrs. Nesbit, softly, "Thomas!"

"None of your Thomasing me, you old pussy-cat! Don't you be telling me, neither, to hush! I won't hush, neither! I know what I am about, I guess! It's my house, as much as it is Nin's, and I'm going to do as I have a mind to here! I an't going to have my mouth shut on account of her beaux! So, clear out, I tell you, and let me come in!" and Aunt Nesbit gave back. He pushed his way into the apartment.

He was a young man, about twenty-five years old, who evidently had once possessed advantages of face and figure; but every outline in the face was bloated and rendered unmeaning by habits of constant intemperance. His dark eyes had that muddy and troubled expression which in a young man too surely indicates the habitual consciousness of inward impurity. His broad, high forehead was flushed and pimpled, his lips swollen and tumid, and his whole air and manner gave painful evidence that he was at present too far under the influence of stimulus justly to apprehend what he was about.

Nina followed him, and Clayton was absolutely shocked at the ghastly paleness of her face. She made an uncertain motion towards him, as if she would have gone to him for protection. Clayton rose; Carson, also; and all stood for a moment in silent embarrassment.

"Well, this is a pretty business, to be sure! Nina," said he, turning to her, with a tremendous oath, "why don't you introduce me? Pretty way to meet a brother you haven't seen for three or four years! You act as if you were ashamed of me! Confound it all! introduce me, I say!"

"Tom, don't speak so!" said Nina, laying her hand on his arm, in a soothing tone. "This gentleman is Mr. Clayton; and, Mr. Clayton," she said, lifting her eyes to him, and speaking in a trembling voice, "this is my brother."

Mr. Clayton offered his hand, with the ordinary expressions of civility.

"Mr. Carson," said Nina, "my brother."

There was something inexpressibly touching and affecting in the manner in which this was said. One other person noticed it. Harry, who had given the horses to the servants, stood leaning against the doorway, looking on. A fiery gleam, like that of a steel blade, seemed to shoot from his blue eyes; and each time that Nina said "my brother," he drew in his breath, as one who seeks to restrain himself in some violent inward emotion.

"I suppose you don't any of you want to see me much," said the new-comer, taking a chair, and sitting down doggedly in the centre of the group, with his hat on his head. "Well, I have as good a right as anybody to be here!" he continued, spitting a quid of tobacco at Aunt Nesbit's feet. "For my part, I think relations ought to have natural affection, and be glad to see one another. Well, now, you can see, gentlemen, with your own eyes, just how it is here! There's my sister, there. You better believe me, she hasn't seen me for three years! Instead of appearing glad, or anything, there she sits, all curled up in a corner! Won't come near me, more than if I had the plague! Come here, now, you little kit, and sit in my lap!"

He made a movement to pull Nina towards him, which she resisted with an air of terror, looking at her aunt, who, more terrified still, sat with her feet drawn up on the sofa, as if he had been a mad dog. There was reason enough for the terror which seemed to possess them both. Both had too vivid recollections of furious domestic hurricanes that had swept over the family when Tom Gordon came home. Nina remembered the storms of oaths and curses that had terrified her when a child; the times that she had seen her father looking like death, leaning his head on his hand, and sighing as only those sigh who have an only son worse than dead.

It is no wonder, therefore, that Nina, generally courageous and fearless as she was, should have become fearful and embarrassed at his sudden return.

"Tom," she said, softly, coming up to him, "you haven't been to supper. Hadn't you better come out?"

"No you don't!" said he, catching her round the waist, and drawing her on his knee. "You won't get me out of the room, now! I know what I am about! Tell me," continued he, still holding her on his knee, "which of them is it, Nin?—which is the favored one?"

Clayton rose and went out on the veranda, and Mr. Carson asked Harry to show him into his room.

"Hallo! shelling out there, are they? Well, Nin, to tell the truth, I am deuced hungry. For my part, I don't see what the thunder keeps my Jim out so long. I sent him across to the post-office. He ought to have been back certainly as soon as I was. O, here he comes! Hallo! you dog, there!" said he, going to the door, where a very black negro was dismounting. "Any letters?"

"No, mas'r. I spect de mails have gin up. Der an't been no letters dere, for no one, for a month. It is some 'quatic disorganization of dese yer creeks, I s'pose. So de letter-bags goes anywhere 'cept der right place."

"Confound it all! I say, you Nin," turning round, "why don't you offer a fellow some supper? Coming home, here, in my own father's house, everybody acts as if they were scared to death! No supper!"

"Why, Tom, I've been asking you, these three or four times."

"Bless us!" said Jim, whispering to Harry. "De mischief is, he an't more than half-primed! Tell her to give him a little more brandy, and after a little we will get him into bed as easy as can be!"

And the event proved so; for, on sitting down to supper, Tom Gordon passed regularly through all the stages of drunkenness; became as outrageously affectionate as he had been before surly, kissed Nina and Aunt Nesbit, cried over his sins and confessed his iniquities, laughed and cried feebly, till at last he sank in his chair asleep.

"Dar, he is done for, now!" said Jim, who had been watching the gradual process. "Now, just you and I, let's tote him off," said he to Harry.

Nina, on her part, retired to a troubled pillow. She foresaw nothing before her but mortification and embarrassment, and realized more than ever the peculiar loneliness of her situation.

For all purposes of consultation and aid, Aunt Nesbit was nobody in her esteem, and Nina was always excited and vexed by every new attempt that she made to confide in her.

"Now, to-morrow," she said to herself, as she lay down, "no one knows what will turn up. He will go round as usual, interfering with everything—threatening and frightening my servants, and getting up some difficulty or other with Harry. Dear me! it seems to me life is coming over me hard enough, and all at once, too!"

As Nina said this, she saw some one standing by her bed. It was Milly, who stooped tenderly over her, smoothing and arranging the bed-clothes in a motherly way.

"Is that you, Milly? O, sit down here a minute! I am so troubled! It seems to me I've had so much trouble to-day! Do you know Tom came home to-night *so* drunk! O, dear Milly, it was horrid! Do you know he took me in his arms and kissed me; and, though he is my only brother, it's perfectly dreadful to me! And I feel so worried, and so anxious!"

"Yes, lamb, I knows all about dese yer things," said Milly. "I's seen him many and many times."

"The worst of it is," said Nina, "that I don't know what he will do to-morrow—and before Mr. Clayton, too! It makes me feel so helpless, ashamed, and mortifies me so!"

"Yes, yes, chile," said Milly, gently stroking her head.

"I stand so much alone!" said Nina. "Other girls have some friend or relation to lean on; but I have nobody!"

"Why don't you ask your *Father* to help you?" said Milly to Nina, in a gentle tone.

"Ask *who?*" said Nina, lifting up her head from the pillow.

"Your Father!" said Milly, with a voice of solemnity. "Don't you know 'Our Father who art in Heaven'?[2] You haven't forgot your prayers, I hope, honey."

Nina looked at her with surprise. And Milly continued, "Now, if I was you, lamb, I would tell my Father all about it. Why, chile, He loves you! He wouldn't like nothing better, now, than to have you just come to Him and tell Him all about your troubles, and He'll make 'em all straight. That's the way I does; and I's found it come out right, many and many a time."

"Why, Milly, you wouldn't have me go to God about *my* little foolish affairs?"

"Laws, chile, what should you go to Him 'bout, den? Sure dese are all de 'fairs you's got."

"Well, but, Milly," said Nina, apprehensively, "you know I've been a very bad girl about religion. It's years and years since I've said any prayers. At school, the girls used to laugh at anybody who said prayers; and so I never did. And, since I've neglected my heavenly Father when things went well with me, it wouldn't be fair to call on Him now, just because I've got into trouble. I don't think it would be honorable."

"De Lord bless dis yer chile! Do hear her talk! Just as if de heavenly Father didn't know all about you, and hadn't been a loving and watching you de whole time! Why, chile, He knows what poor foolish creatures we be; and He an't noways surprised, nor put out. Why, laws, don't you know He's de good shepherd? And what you suppose dey has shepherds fur, 'cept de sheeps are all de time running away, and getting into trouble? Why, honey, *dat's what dey's fur.*"

"Well, but it is so long since I prayed, that I don't know anything how to pray, Milly."

"Bless you, chile, who wanted you to pray? I never prays myself. Used to try, but I made such drefful poor work on it that I gin it up. Now, I just goes and *talks* to de Father, and tells Him anything and everything; and I think He likes it a great deal better. Why, He is just as willing to hear me now, as if I was the greatest lady in the land. And He takes such an interest in all my poor 'fairs! Why, sometimes I go to Him when my heart is *so* heavy; and, when I tells Him all about it, I comes away as light as a feather!"

"Well, but, after I've forgotten Him so many years!"

"Why, honey, now just look yere! I 'member once, when you was a little weety thing, that you toddles down dem steps dere, and you slips away from dem dat was watching you, and you toddles away off into de grove, yonder, and dere you got picking flowers, and one thing and another, mighty tickled and peart. You was down dere 'joying yourself, till, by and by, your pa missed you; and den such another hunt as dere was! Dere was a hurrying here, and a looking dere; and finally your pa run down in the woods, and dere you'd got stuck fast in de mud! both your shoes off, and well scratched with briers; and dere you stood a crying, and calling your pa. I tell you he said dat ar was de sweetest music he ever heard in his life. I 'member he picked you up, and came up to de house kissing you. Now, dere 't was, honey! You didn't call on your pa till you got into trouble. And laws, laws, chile, dat's de way with us all. We never does call on de Father till we gets into trouble; and it takes heaps and heaps of trouble, sometimes, to bring us round. Some time, chile, I'll tell you my sperence. I's got a sperence on this point. But, now, honey, don't trouble yourself no more; but just ask your Father to take care of your 'fairs, and turn over and go to sleep. And He'll do it. Now you mind."

So saying, Milly smoothed the pillow with anxious care, and, kissing Nina on the forehead, departed.

CHAPTER XIII

Tom Gordon

"I SAY, NINA," said her brother, coming in, a day or two after, from a survey that he had been taking round the premises, "you want *me* here to manage this place. Everything going at sixes and sevens;[1] and that nigger of a Harry riding round with his boots shining. That fellow cheats you, and feathers his own nest well. I know! These white niggers are all deceitful."

"Come, Tom, you know the estate is managed just as father left word to have it; and Uncle John says that Harry is an excellent manager. I'm sure nobody could have been more faithful to me; and I am very well satisfied."

"Yes, I dare say. All left to you and the executors, as you call them; as if *I* were not the natural guardian of my sister! Then I come here to put up with that fellow's impudence!"

"Whose?—Harry's? He is never impudent. He is always gentlemanly. Everybody remarks it."

"Gentlemanly! There it is, Nin! What a fool you are to encourage the use of that word in connection with any of your niggers! Gentleman, forsooth! And while he plays gentleman, who takes care? I tell you what, you'll find, one of these days, how things are going on. But that's just the way! You never would listen to me, or pay the least attention to my advice."

"O, Tom, don't talk about that—don't! I never interfere about your affairs. Please leave me the right to manage mine in my own way."

"And who is this Clayton that's hanging about here? Are you going to have him, or he you—hey?"

"I don't know," said Nina.

"Because *I*, for one, don't like him; and I shan't give my consent to let him have you. That other one is worth twice as much. He has one of the largest properties in New York. Joe Snider has told me about him. You shall have him."

"I shall *not* have him, say what you please; and I *shall* have Mr. Clayton, if I choose!" said Nina, with a heightened color. "You have no right to dictate to me of my own affairs; and I shan't submit to it, I tell you frankly."

"Highty-tighty! We are coming up, to be sure!" said Tom.

"Moreover," said Nina, "I wish you to let everything on this place entirely alone; and remember that my servants are not your servants, and that you have no control over them, whatever."

"Well, we will see how you'll help yourself! I am not going to go skulking about on my father's own place as if I had no right or title there; and if your niggers don't look sharp, they'll find out whether I am the master here or not, especially that Harry. If the dog dare so much as to lift his fingers to countermand any one of my orders, I'd put a bullet through his head as soon as I would through a buck's. I give you warning!"

"O, Tom, pray don't talk so!" said Nina, who really began to be alarmed. "What do you want to make me such trouble, for?"

The conversation was here suspended by the entrance of Milly.

"If you please, Miss Nina, come and show me which of your muslins you wish to be done up, as I's starching for Miss Loo."

Glad of an opportunity to turn the conversation, Nina ran up to her room, whither she was followed by Milly, who shut the door, and spoke to her in mysterious tones.

"Miss Nina, can't you make some errand to get Harry off the place for two or three days, while Mas'r Tom's round?"

"But what right," said Nina, with heightened color, "has he to dictate to my servants, or me? or to interfere with any of our arrangements here?"

"O, dere's no use talking about *rights*, honey. We must all do jest what we *ken*. Don't make much odds whether our rights is one way or t' other. You see, chile, it's just here. Harry's your right hand. But you see he an't learnt to *bend* 'fore the wind, like the rest of us. He is spirity; he is just as full now as a powder-box; and Mas'r Tom is bent on aggravating him. And, laws, chile, dere may be bloody work—dere may so!"

"Why, do you think he'd *dare*—"

"Chile, don't talk to me! Dare!—yes; sure 'nough he will dare! Besides, dere's fifty ways young gentlemen may take to aggravate and provoke. And, when flesh and blood can't bear it no longer, if Harry raises his hand, why, den shoot him down! Nothing said—

nothing done. You can't help yourself. You won't want to have a law-suit with your own brother; and, if you did, 't wouldn't bring Harry to life! Laws, chile, ef I could tell you what I've seen—you don't know nothing 'bout it. Now, I tell you, get up some message to your uncle's plantation; send him off for anything or nothing; only have him gone! And then speak your brother fair, and then may be he will go off. But don't you quarrel! don't you cross him, come what may! Dere an't a soul on the place that can bar de sight on him. But, then, you see the rest dey *all bends!* But, chile, you must be quick about it! Let me go right off and find him. Just you come in the little back room, and I'll call him in."

Pale and trembling, Nina descended into the room; and, in a few moments after, Milly appeared, followed by Harry.

"Harry!" said Nina, in a trembling voice, "I want you to take your horse and go over to Uncle John's plantation, and carry a note for me."

Harry stood with his arms folded, and his eyes fixed upon the ground, and Nina continued,

"And, Harry, I think you had better make some business or errand to keep you away two or three days, or a week."

"Miss Nina," said Harry, "the affairs of the place are very pressing now, and need overlooking. A few days' neglect now may produce a great loss, and then it will be said that I neglected my business to idle and ride round the country."

"Well, but, if I send you, I take the responsibility, and I'll bear the loss. The fact is, Harry, I'm afraid that you won't have patience to be here, now Tom is at home. In fact, Harry, I'm afraid for your life! And now, if you have any regard for me, make the best arrangement with the work you can, and be off. I'll tell him that I sent you on business of my own, and I am going to write a letter for you to carry. It's the only safe way. He has so many ways in which he can provoke and insult you, that, at last, you may say or do something that will give him occasion against you; and I think he is determined to drive you to this."

"Isn't this provoking, now? isn't this outrageous?" said Harry, between his teeth, looking down, "that everything must be left, and all because I haven't the right to stand up like a man, and protect you and yours!"

"It is a pity! it is a shame!" said Nina. "But, Harry, don't stop to think upon it; do go!" She laid her hand softly on his. "For my sake, now, be good—be good!"

The room where they were standing had long windows, which opened, like those of the parlor, on the veranda, and commanded a view of a gravel-walk bordered with shrubbery. As Harry stood, hesitating, he started at seeing Lisette come tripping up the walk, balancing on her head a basket of newly-ironed muslins and linens. Her trim little figure was displayed in a close-fitting gown of blue, a snowy handkerchief crossed upon her bust, and one rounded arm raised to steady the basket upon her head. She came tripping forward, with her usual airy motion, humming a portion of a song; and attracted, at the same moment, the attention of Tom Gordon and of her husband.

" 'Pon my word, if that isn't the prettiest concern!" said Tom, as he started up and ran down the walk to meet her.

"Good-morning, my pretty girl!" he said.

"Good-morning, sir," returned Lisette, in her usual tone of gay cheerfulness.

"Pray, who do you belong to, my pretty little puss? I think I've never seen you on this place."

"Please, sir, I'm Harry's wife."

"Indeed! you are, hey? Devilish good taste he has!" said he, laying his hand familiarly on her shoulder.

The shoulder was pulled away, and Lisette moved rapidly on to the other side of the path, with an air of vexation which made her look rather prettier.

"What, my dear, don't you know that I am your husband's young master? Come, come!" he said, following her, and endeavoring to take hold of her arm.

"Please let me alone!" said Lisette, coloring, and in a petted, vexed tone.

"Let you alone? No, that I shan't, not while you ask it in such a pretty way as that!" And again the hand was laid upon her shoulder.

It must be understood that Harry had witnessed so far, in pantomime, this scene. He had stood with compressed lips, and eyes slowly dilating, looking at it. Nina, who was standing with her back to the window, wondered at the expression of his countenance.

"Look there, Miss Nina!" he said. "Do you see my wife and your brother?"

Nina turned, and in an instant the color mounted to her cheeks; her little form seemed to dilate, and her eyes flashed fire; and before Harry could see what she was doing, she was down in the gravel-walk, and had taken Lisette's hand.

"Tom Gordon," she said, "I'm ashamed of you! Hush! hush!" she continued, fixing her eyes on him, and stamping her foot. "*Dare* to come to my place, and take such liberties here! You shall not be allowed to while *I* am mistress; and *I am* mistress! *Dare* to lay a finger on this girl while she is here under my protection! Come, Lisette!" And she seized the trembling girl by the hand, and drew her along towards the house.

Tom Gordon was so utterly confused at this sudden burst of passion in his sister, that he let them go off without opposition. In a few moments he looked after her, and gave a long, low whistle.

"Ah! Pretty well up for her! But she'll find it's easier said than done, I fancy!" And he sauntered up to the veranda, where Harry stood with his arms folded, and the veins in his forehead swelling with repressed emotion.

"Go in, Lisette," said Nina; "take the things into my room, and I'll come to you."

" 'Pon my word, Harry," said Tom, coming up, and addressing Harry in the most insulting tone, "we are all under the greatest obligations to you for bringing such a pretty little fancy article here!"

"My wife does not belong to this place," said Harry, forcing himself to speak calmly. "She belongs to a Mrs. Le Clere, who has come into Belleville plantation."

"Ah! thank you for the information! I may take a fancy to buy her, and I'd like to know who she belongs to. I've been wanting a pretty little concern of that sort. She's a good housekeeper, isn't she, Harry? Does up shirts well? What do you suppose she could be got for? I must go and see her mistress."

During this cruel harangue Harry's hands twitched and quivered, and he started every now and then, looking first at Nina, and then at his tormentor. He turned deadly pale; even his lips were of ashy whiteness; and, with his arms still folded, and making no reply, he fixed his large blue eyes upon Tom, and, as it sometimes happened in moments of excitement and elevation, there appeared on the rigid lines of his face, at that moment, so strong a resemblance to Col. Gordon, that Nina noticed and was startled by it. Tom Gordon noticed it also. It added fuel to the bitterness of his wrath; and there glared from his eyes a malignancy of hatred that was perfectly appalling. The two brothers seemed like thunderclouds opposing each other, and ready to dart lightning. Nina hastened to interfere.

"Hurry, hurry, Harry! I want that message carried. Do, pray, go directly!"

"Let me see," said Tom, "I must call Jim, and have my horse. Which is the way to that Belleville plantation? I think I'll ride over there." And he turned and walked indolently down the steps.

"For shame, Tom! you won't! you can't! How can you want to trouble me so?" said Nina.

He turned and looked upon her with an evil smile, turned again, and was gone.

"Harry, Harry, go quick! Don't you worry; there's no danger!" she added, in a lower voice. "Madam Le Clere never would consent."

"There's no knowing!" said Harry, "never any knowing! People act about money as they do about nothing else."

"Then—then I'll send and buy her myself!" said Nina.

"You don't know how our affairs stand, Miss Nina," said Harry, hurriedly. "The money couldn't be raised now for it, especially if I have to go off this week. It will make a great difference, my being here or not being here; and very likely Master Tom may have a thousand dollars to pay down on the spot. I never knew him to want money when his will was up. Great God! haven't I borne this yoke long enough?"

"Well, Harry," said Nina, "I'll sell everything I've got—my jewels—everything! I'll mortgage the plantation, before Tom Gordon shall do this thing! I'm not *quite* so selfish as I've always seemed to be. I know you've made the sacrifice of body and soul to my interest; and I've always taken it, because I loved my ease, and was a spoiled child. But, after all, I know I've as much energy as Tom has, when I am roused, and I'll go over this very morning and make an offer for her. Only you be off. You can't stand such provocation as you get here; and if you yield, as any man will do, at last, then everything and everybody will go against you, and I can't protect you. Trust to *me*. I'm not so much of a child as I have seemed to be! You'll find I can act for myself, and you too! There comes Mr. Clayton through the shrubbery—that's right! Order two horses round to the door immediately, and we'll go over there this morning."

Nina gave her orders with a dignity as if she had been a princess, and in all his agitation Harry could not help marvelling at the sudden air of womanliness which had come over her.

"I could serve *you*," he said, in a low voice, "to the last drop of my blood! But," he added, in a tone which made Nina tremble, "I hate everybody else! I hate your country! I hate your laws!"

"Harry," said Nina, "you do wrong—you forget yourself!"

"O, I do wrong, do I? We are the people that are *never* to do wrong! People may stick pins in us, and stick knives in us, wipe their shoes on us, spit in our face—*we* must be amiable! we must be models of Christian patience! I tell you, your father should rather have put me into quarters and made me work like a field-negro, than to have given me the education he did, and leave me under the foot of every white man that dares tread on me!"

Nina remembered to have seen her father in transports of passion, and was again shocked and startled to see the resemblance between his face and the convulsed face before her.

"Harry," she said, in a pitying, half-admonitory tone, "do think what you are saying! If you love me, be quiet!"

"Love you? You have always held my heart in your hand! That has been the clasp upon my chain! If it hadn't been for you, I should have fought my way to the north before now, or I would have found a grave on the road!"

"Well, Harry," said Nina, after a moment's thought, "my love shall not be a clasp upon *any* chain; for, as there is a God in heaven, I will set you free! I'll have a bill introduced at the very next legislature, and I know what friend will see to it. So go, now, Harry, go!"

Harry stood a moment, then suddenly raised the hand of his little mistress to his lips, turned, and was gone.

Clayton, who had been passing through the shrubbery, and who had remarked that Nina was engaged in a very exciting conversation, had drawn off, and stood waiting for her at the foot of the veranda steps. As soon as Nina saw him, she reached out her hand frankly, saying,

"O, there, Mr. Clayton, you are just the person! Wouldn't you like to take a ride with me?"

"Of course I should," said he.

"Wait here a moment," said she, "till I get ready. The horses will be here immediately." And, running up the steps, she passed quickly by him, and went into the house.

Clayton had felt himself in circumstances of considerable embarrassment ever since the arrival of Tom Gordon, the evening before. He had perceived that the young man had conceived an instinctive dislike of himself, which he was at no particular pains to conceal; and he had found it difficult to preserve the appearance of one who does not notice. He did not wish to intrude upon Nina any embarrassing recognition of her situation, even under the guise of sympathy and assistance; and waited, therefore, till some word from her should authorize him to speak. He held himself, therefore, ready to meet any confidence which she might feel disposed to place in him; not doubting, from the frankness of her nature, that she would soon find it impossible not to speak of what was so deeply interesting to her.

Nina soon reäppeared, and, mounting their horses, they found themselves riding through the same forest-road that led to the cottage of Tiff, from which a divergent path went to the Belleville plantation.

"I'm glad to see you alone this morning, for many reasons," said Nina; "for I think I never needed a friend's help more. I'm mortified that you should have seen what you did last night; but, since you have, I may as well speak of it. The fact is, that my brother, though he is the only one I have, never did treat me as if he loved me. I can't tell what the reason is: whether he was jealous of my poor father's love for me, or whether it was because I was a wilful, spoiled girl, and so gave him reason to be set against me, or whatever the reason might be,—he never has been kind to me long at a time. Perhaps he would be, if I would always do exactly as he says; but I am made as positive and wilful as he is. I never have been controlled, and I can't recognize the right which he seems to assume to control me, and to dictate as to my own private affairs. He was not left my guardian; and, though I do love him, I shan't certainly take him as one. Now, you see, he has a bitter hatred, and a most unreasonable one, towards my Harry; and I had no idea, when I came home, in how many ways he had the power to annoy me. It does seem as if an evil spirit possessed them both when they get together; they seem as full of electricity as they can be, and I am every instant afraid of an explosion. Unfortunately for Harry, he has had a much superior education to the generality of his class and station, and the situation of trust in which he has been placed has given him more the feelings of a free man and a gentleman than is usual; for, except Tom, there isn't one of our family circle that hasn't always treated him with kindness, and even with deference—and I think this very thing angers Tom the more, and makes him take every possible occasion of provoking and vexing. I believe it is his intention to push Harry up to some desperate action; and, when I see how frightfully they look at each other, I tremble for the consequences. Harry has lately married a very pretty wife, with whom he lives in a little cottage on the extremity of the Belleville estate; and this morning Tom happened to spy her, and it seemed to inspire him with a most ingenious plan to trouble Harry. He threatened to come over and buy her of Madam Le Clere; and so, to quiet Harry, I promised to come over here before him, and make an offer for her."

"Why," said Clayton, "do you think her mistress would sell her?"

"I can't say," said Nina. "She is a person I am acquainted with only by report. She is a New Orleans creole,[2] who has lately bought the place. Lisette, I believe, hires her time of her. Lisette is an ingenious, active creature, and contrives, by many little arts and accomplishments, to pay a handsome sum, monthly, to her mistress. Whether the offer of a large sum at once would tempt her to sell her, is more than I know until it's tried. I should like to have Lisette, for Harry's sake."

"And do you suppose your brother was really serious?"

"I shouldn't be at all surprised if he were. But, serious or not serious, I intend to make the matter sure."

"If it be necessary to make an immediate payment," said Clayton, "I have a sum of money which is lying idle in the bank, and it's but drawing a check which will be honored at sight. I mention this, because the ability to make an immediate payment may make the negotiation easier. You ought to allow me the pleasure of joining you in a good work."

"Thank you," said Nina, frankly. "It may not be necessary; but, if it should be, I will take it in the same spirit in which it is offered."

After a ride of about an hour, they arrived in the boundaries of Belleville plantation.

In former days, Nina had known this as the residence of an ancient rich family, with whom her father was on visiting terms. She was therefore uncomfortably struck with the air of poverty, waste, and decay, everywhere conspicuous through the grounds.

Nothing is more depressing and disheartening than the sight of a gradual decay of what has been arranged and constructed with great care; and when Nina saw the dilapidated gateway, the crushed and broken shrubbery, the gaps in the fine avenue where trees had been improvidently cut down for fire-wood, she could not help a feeling of depression.

"How different this place used to be when I came here as a child!" said she. "This madam, whatever her name is, can't be much of a manager."

As she said this, their horses came up the front of the house, in which the same marks of slovenly neglect were apparent. Blinds were hanging by one hinge; the door had sunk down into the rotten sill; the wooden pillars that supported it were decayed at the bottom; and the twining roses which once climbed upon them laid trailing, dishonored, upon the ground. The veranda was littered with all kinds of rubbish,—rough boxes, saddles, bridles, overcoats; and various nondescript articles formed convenient hiding-places and retreats, in which a troop of negro children and three or four dogs were playing at hide-and-go-seek with great relish and noise. On the alighting of Nina and Clayton at the door, they all left their sports, and arranged themselves in a grinning row, to see the new comers descend. Nothing seemed to be further from the minds of the little troop than affording the slightest assistance in the way of holding horses or answering questions. All they did was alternately to look at each other and the travellers, and grin.

A tattered servant-man, with half a straw hat on his head, was at length raised by a call of Clayton, who took their horses—having first distributed a salutation of kicks and cuffs among the children, asking where their manners were that they didn't show the gentleman and lady in. And Nina and Clayton were now marshalled by the whole seven of them into an apartment on the right of the great hall. Everything in the room appeared in an unfinished state. The curtains were half put up at the windows, and part lying in a confused heap on the chairs. The damp, mouldy paper, which hung loosely from the wall, had been torn away in some places, as if to prepare for repapering; and certain half-opened rolls of costly wall-paper lay on the table, on which appeared the fragment of some ancient luncheon; to wit, plates, and pieces of bread and cheese, dirty tumblers, and an empty bottle. It was difficult to find a chair sufficiently free from dust to sit down on. Nina sent up her card by one of the small fry, who, having got half-way up the staircase, was suddenly taken with the desire to slide down the banisters with it in his hand. Of course he dropped the card in the operation; and the whole group precipitated themselves briskly on to it, all in a heap, and fought, tooth and nail, for the honor of carrying it up stairs. They were aroused, however, by the entrance of the man with half a hat; who, on Nina's earnest suggestion, plunged into the troop, which ran, chattering and screaming like so many crows, to different parts of the hall, while he picked up the card, and with infinite good-will beaming on his shining black face, went up with it, leaving Nina and Clayton waiting below. In a few moments he returned.

"Missis will see de young lady up stairs."

Nina tripped promptly after him, and left Clayton the sole tenant of the parlor for an hour. At length she returned, skipping down the stairs, and opening the door with great animation.

"The thing is done!" she said. "The bill of sale will be signed as soon as we can send it over."

"I had better bring it over myself," said Clayton, "and make the arrangement."

"So be it!" said Nina. "But pray let us be delivered from this place! Did you ever see such a desolate-looking house? I remember when I've seen it a perfect paradise—full of the most agreeable people."

"And pray what sort of a person did you find?" said Clayton, as they were riding homeward.

"Well," said Nina, "she's one of the tow-string order of women.[3] Very slack-twisted, too, I fancy—tall, snuffy, and sallow. Clothes looked rough-dry, as if they had been pulled out of a bag. She had a bright-colored Madras handkerchief tied round her head, and spoke French a little more through her nose than French people usually do. Flourished a yellow silk pocket-handkerchief. Poor soul! She said she had been sick for a week with tooth-ache, and kept awake all night! So, one mustn't be critical! One comfort about these

French people is, that they are always 'ravis de vous voir,'[4] let what will turn up. The good soul was really polite, and insisted on clearing all the things off from a dusty old chair for me to sit down in. The room was as much at sixes and sevens as the rest of the house. She apologized for the whole state of things by saying that they could not get workmen out there to do anything for her; and so everything is left in the second future tense; and the darkeys, I imagine, have a general glorification in the chaos. She is one of the indulgent sort, and I suspect she'll be eaten up by them like the locusts. Poor thing! she is shockingly home-sick, and longing for Louisiana, again. For, notwithstanding her snuffy appearance, and yellow pocket-handkerchief, she really has a genuine taste for beauty; and spoke most feelingly of the oleanders, crape myrtles, and cape jessamines, of her native state."

"Well, how did you introduce your business?" said Clayton, laughing at this description.

"Me?—Why, I flourished out the little French I have at command, and she flourished her little English; and I think I rather prepossessed the good soul, to begin with. Then I made a sentimental story about Lisette and Harry's amours; because I know French people always have a taste for the sentimental. The old thing was really quite affected—wiped her little black eyes, pulled her hooked nose as a tribute to my eloquence, called Lisette her 'enfant mignon,'[5] and gave me a little lecture on the tender passion, which I am going to lay up for future use."

"Indeed!" said Clayton. "I should be charmed to have you repeat it. Can't you give us a synopsis?"

"I don't know what synopsis means. But, if you want me to tell you what she said, I shan't do it. Well, now do you know I am in the best spirits in the world, now that I've got this thing off my mind, and out of that desolate house? Did you ever see such a direful place? What is the reason, when we get down south, here, everything seems to be going to destruction, so? I noticed it all the way down through Virginia. It seems as if everything had stopped growing, and was going backwards. Well, now, it's so different at the north! I went up, one vacation, into New Hampshire. It's a dreadfully poor, barren country; nothing but stony hills, and poor soil. And yet the people there seem to be so well off! They live in such nice, tight, clean-looking white houses! Everything around them looks so careful and comfortable; and yet their land isn't half so good as ours, down here. Why, actually, some of those places seem as if there were nothing but rock! And, then, they have winter about nine months in the year, I do believe! But these Yankees turn everything to account. If a man's field is covered with rock, he'll find some way to sell it, and make money out of it; and if they freeze up all winter, they sell the ice, and make money out of that. They just live by selling their disadvantages!"

"And we grow poor by wasting our advantages," said Clayton.

"Do you know," said Nina, "people think it's a dreadful thing to be an abolitionist? But, for my part, I've a great inclination to be one. Perhaps because I have a contrary turn, and always have a little spite against what everybody else believes. But, if you won't tell anybody, I'll tell you—I don't believe in slavery!"

"Nor I, either!" said Clayton.

"You don't! Well, really, I thought I was saying something original. Now, the other day, Aunt Nesbit's minister was at our house, and they sat crooning together, as they always do; and, among other things, they said, 'What a blessed institution it was to bring these poor Africans over here to get them Christianized!' So, by way of saying something to give them a start, I told them I thought they came nearer to making heathen of us than we to making Christians of them."

"That's very true," said Clayton. "There's no doubt that the kind of society which is built up in this way constantly tends to run back towards barbarism. It prevents general education of the whites, and keeps the poorer classes down to the lowest point, while it enriches a few."

"Well, what do we have it for?" said Nina. "Why don't we blow it up, right off?"

"That's a question easier asked than answered. The laws against emancipation are very stringent. But I think it is every owner's business to contemplate this as a future resort, and to educate his servants in reference to it. That is what I am trying to do on my plantation."

"Indeed!" said Nina, looking at him with a good deal of interest. "Well, now, that reminds me of what I was going to say to you. Generally speaking, my conscience don't trouble me much about my servants, because I think they are doing about as well with me as they would be likely to do anywhere else. But, now, there's

Harry! He is well-educated, and I know that he could do for him-self, anywhere, better than he does here. I have always had a kind of sense of this; but I've thought of it more lately, and I'm going to try to have him set free at the next legislature. And I shall want you to help me about all the what-do-you-call-'ems."

"Of course, I shall be quite at your service," said Clayton.

"There used to be some people, when I was up at the north, who talked as if all of us were no better than a pack of robbers and thieves. And, of course, when I was there I was strong for our insti-tutions, and would not give them an inch of ground. It set me to thinking, though; and the result of my thinking is, that we have no right to hold those to work for us who clearly can do better. Now, there's Aunt Nesbit's Milly—there's Harry and Lisette. Why, it's clear enough, if they can support themselves and us too, they cer-tainly can support themselves alone. Lisette has paid eight dollars a month to her mistress, and supported herself besides. I'm sure it's *we* that are the helpless ones!"

"Well, do you think your Aunt Nesbit is going to follow your example?"

"No! catch her at it! Aunt Nesbit is doubly fortified in her reli-gion. She is so satisfied with something or other about 'cursed be Canaan,' that she'd let Milly earn ten dollars a month for her, all the year round, and never trouble her head about taking every bit of it. Some folks, you know, have a way of calling everything they want to do a dispensation of providence! Now, Aunt Nesbit is one of 'em. She always calls it a dispensation that the negroes were brought over here, and a dispensation that we are the mistresses. Ah! Milly will not get free while Aunt Nesbit is alive! And do you know, though it does not seem very generous in me, yet I'm re-signed to it, because Milly is such a good soul, and such a comfort to me?—do you know she seems a great deal more like a mother to me than Aunt Nesbit? Why, I really think, if Milly had been edu-cated as we are, she would have made a most splendid woman— been a perfect Candace queen of Ethiopia.[6] There's a vast deal that is curious and interesting in some of these old Africans. I always did love to be with them; some of them are so shrewd and original! But, I wonder, now, what Tom will think of my cutting him out so neatly? 'T will make him angry, I suppose."

"O, perhaps, after all, he had no real intention of doing anything of the kind," said Clayton. "He may have said it merely for bravado."

"I should have thought so, if I hadn't known that he always had a grudge against Harry."

At this moment the galloping of a horse was heard in the woodland path before them; and very soon Tom Gordon appeared in sight, accompanied by another man, on horseback, with whom he was in earnest conversation. There was something about the face of this man which, at the first glance, Nina felt to be very repulsive. He was low, thick-set, and yet lean; his features were thin and sharp; his hair and eyebrows bushy and black, and a pair of glassy, pale-blue eyes formed a peculiar contrast to their darkness. There was something in the expression of the eye which struck Nina as hard and cold. Though the man was habited externally as a gentleman, there was still about him an under-bred appearance, which could be detected at the first glance, as the coarseness of some woods will reveal themselves through every varnish.

"Good-morrow, Nina," said her brother, drawing his horse up to meet hers, and signing to his companion to arrest his, also. "Allow me to present to you my friend Mr. Jekyl. We are going out to visit the Belleville plantation."

"I wish you a pleasant ride!" said Nina. And, touching her horse, she passed them in a moment.

Looking back almost fiercely, a moment, she turned and said to Clayton:

"I hate that man!"

"Who is it?" said Clayton.

"I don't know!" said Nina. "I never saw him before. But I hate him! He is a bad man! I'd as soon have a serpent come near me, as that man!"

"Well, the poor fellow's face isn't prepossessing," said Clayton. "But I should not be prepared for such an anathema."

"Tom's badness," continued Nina, speaking as if she were following out a train of thought without regarding her companion's remark, "is good turned to bad. It's wine turned to vinegar. But this man don't even know what good is!"

"How can you be so positive about a person that you've only seen once?" said Clayton.

"O," said Nina, resuming her usual gay tones, "don't you know that girls and dogs, and other inferior creatures, have the gift of seeing what's in people? It doesn't belong to highly-cultivated folks, like you, but to us poor creatures, who have to trust to our instincts. So, beware!" And, as she spoke, she turned to him with a fascinating air of half-saucy defiance.

"Well," said Clayton, "have you seen, then, what is in me?"

"Yes, to be sure!" said Nina, with energy; "I knew what you were the very first time I saw you. And that's the reason why—"

Clayton made an eager gesture, and his eye met hers with a sudden flash of earnestness. She stopped, and blushed, and then laughed.

"What, Nina?"

"O, well, I always thought you were a grandfatherly body, and that you wouldn't take advantage of 'us girls,' as some of the men do. And so I've treated you with confidence, as you know. I had just the same feeling that you could be trusted, as I have that that other fellow cannot!"

"Well," said Clayton, "that deduction suits me so well that I should be sorry to undermine your faith. Nevertheless, I must say such a way of judging isn't always safe. Instinct may be a greater matter than we think; yet it isn't infallible, any more than our senses. We try the testimony even of our eyesight by reason. It will deceive us, if we don't. Much more we ought to try this more subtle kind of sight."

"May be so," said Nina; "yet, I don't think I shall like that man, after all. But I'll give him a chance to alter my feeling, by treating him civilly if Tom brings him back to dinner. That's the best I can do."

CHAPTER XIV

Aunt Nesbit's Loss

ON ENTERING THE HOUSE, Nina was met at the door by Milly, with a countenance of some anxiety.

"Miss Nina," she said, "your aunt has heard bad news, this morning."

"Bad news!" said Nina, quickly,—"what?"

"Well, honey, ye see dere has been a lawyer here," said Milly, following Nina as she was going up stairs; "and she has been shut up with him all de mornin'; and when he come out I found her taking on quite dreadful! And she says she has lost all her property."

"O! is that all?" said Nina. "I didn't know what dreadful thing might have happened. Why, Milly, this isn't so very bad. She hadn't much to lose."

"O, bless you, chile! nobody wants to lose all they got, much or little!"

"Yes; but," said Nina, "you know she can always live here with us; and what little money she wants to fuss with, to buy new caps, and paregoric for her cough, and all such little matters, we can give her, easily enough."

"Ah, Miss Nina, your heart is free enough; you'd give away both ends of the rainbow, if you had 'em to give. But the trouble is, chile, you *haven't got 'em.* Why, chile, dis yer great place, and so many mouths opened to eat and eat, chile, I tell you it takes heaps to keep it a going. And Harry, I tell you, finds it hard work to bring it even all the year round, though he never says nothing to you about his troubles,—wants you always to walk on flowers, with both hands full, and never think where they come from. I tell you what, chile, we's boun' to think for you a little; and I tell you what, I's jist a going to hire out."[1]

"Why, Milly, how ridiculous!"

"It an't ridiculous, now. Why, just look on it, Miss Nina. Here's Miss Loo, dat's one; here's me, dat's two; here's Polly,—great

156

grown girl,—three; dere's Tomtit, four; all on us, eating your bread, and not bringing in a cent to you, 'cause all on us together an't done much more than wait on Miss Loo. Why, you's got servants enough of your own to do every turn that wants doing in dis yer house. I know, Miss Nina, young ladies don't like to hear about dese things; but the fac' is, victuals cost something, and dere must be some on us to bring in something. Now, dat ar gentleman what talked with your aunt, he said he could find me a right good place up dar to the town, and I was just a going. Sally, she is big enough now to do everything that I have been used to doing for Miss Loo, and I am jest a going; besides, to tell you the truth, I think Miss Loo has kind o' set her heart upon it. You know she is a weakly kind of thing,—don't know how to do much 'cept sit in her chair and groan. She has always been so used to having me make a way for her; and when I told her about dis yer, she kind o' brightened up."

"But, Milly, what shall I do? I can't spare you at all," said Nina.

"Law bless *you*, chile! don't you suppose I's got eyes? I tell you, Miss Nina, I looked that gen'leman over pretty well for you, and my opinion is he'll *do*."

"O, come, you hush!" said Nina.

"You see, chile, it wouldn't be everybody that our people would be willing to have come on to the place, here; but there an't one of 'em that wouldn't go in for dis yer, now I tell you. Dere's Old Hundred, as you calls him, told me 't was just as good as a meeting to hear him reading the prayers dat ar day at de funeral. Now, you see, I's seen gen'lemen handsome, and rich, and right pleasant, too, dat de people wouldn't want at all; 'cause why? dey has dere frolics and drinks, and de money flies one way for dis ting and one way for dat, till by and by it's all gone. Den comes de sheriff, and de people is all sold, some one way and some another way. Now, Mr. Clayton, he an't none of dem."

"But, Milly, all this may be very well; but if I couldn't love him?"

"Law sakes, Miss Nina! You look me in the face and tell me dat ar? Why, chile, it's plain enough to see through *you*. 'T is so! The people's all pretty sure, by this time. Sakes alive, we's used to looking out for the weather; and we knows pretty well what's coming. And now, Miss Nina, you go right along and give him a good word, 'cause you see, dear lamb, you *need* a good husband to take care of you,—dat's what you want, chile. Girls like you has a hard life being at the head of a place, especially your brother being just what he is. Now, if you had a husband here, Mas'r Tom 'ud be quiet, 'cause he knows he couldn't do nothing. But just as long as you's alone he'll plague you. But, now, chile, it's time for you to be getting ready for dinner."

"O, but, do you know, Milly," said Nina, "I've something to tell you, which I had liked to have forgotten! I have been out to the Belleville plantation, and bought Harry's wife."

"You has, Miss Nina! Why, de Lord bless *you!* Why, Harry was dreadful worked, dis yer morning, 'bout what Mas'r Tom said. 'Peared like he was most crazy."

"Well," said Nina, "I've done it. I've got the receipt here."

"Why, but, chile, where alive did you get all the money to pay down right sudden so?"

"Mr. Clayton lent it to me," said Nina.

"Mr. Clayton! Now, chile, didn't I tell you so? Do you suppose, now, you'd a let him lend you dat ar money if you hadn't liked him? But, come, chile, hurry! Dere's Mas'r Tom and dat other gen'leman coming back, and you must be down to dinner."

The company assembled at the dinner-table was not particularly enlivening. Tom Gordon, who, in the course of his morning ride, had discovered the march which his sister had stolen upon him, was more sulky and irritable than usual, though too proud to make any allusion to the subject. Nina was annoyed by the presence of Mr. Jekyl, whom her brother insisted should remain to dinner. Aunt Nesbit was uncommonly doleful, of course. Clayton, who, in mixed society, generally took the part of a listener rather than a talker, said very little; and had it not been for Carson, there's no saying whether any of the company could have spoken. Every kind of creature has its uses, and there are times when a lively, unthinking chatterbox is a perfect godsend. Those unperceiving people, who never notice the embarrassment of others, and who walk with the greatest facility into the gaps of conversation, simply because they have no perception of any difficulty there, have their hour; and Nina felt positively grateful to Mr. Carson for the continuous and cheerful rattle which had so annoyed her the day before. Carson drove a brisk talk with the lawyer about the value of property, percentage, etc.; he sympathized with Aunt Nesbit on her last-caught cold; rallied Tom on his preöccupation; complimented Nina on her

improved color from her ride; and seemed on such excellent terms
both with himself and everybody else, that the thing was really in-
fectious.

"What do you call your best investments, down here,—land,
eh?" he said to Mr. Jekyl.

Mr. Jekyl shook his head.

"Land deteriorates too fast. Besides, there's all the trouble and
risk of overseers, and all that. I've looked this thing over pretty
well, and I always invest in niggers."

"Ah!" said Mr. Carson, "you do?"

"Yes, sir, I invest in niggers; that's what I do; and I hire them
out, sir,—hire them out. Why, sir, if a man has a knowledge of human nature, knows where to buy and when to buy, and watches his
opportunity, he gets a better percentage on his money that way
than any other. Now, that was what I was telling Mrs. Nesbit, this
morning. Say, now, that you give one thousand dollars for a man,—
and I always buy the best sort, that's economy,—well, and he
gets—put it at the lowest figure—ten dollars a month wages, and
his living. Well, you see there, that gives you a pretty handsome
sum for your money. I have a good talent of buying. I generally
prefer mechanics. I have got now working for me three bricklayers.
I own two first-rate carpenters, and last month I bought a perfect
jewel of a blacksmith. He is an uncommonly ingenious man; a fellow that will make, easy, his fifteen dollars a month; and he is the
more valuable because he has been religiously brought up. Why,
some of them, now, will cheat you, if they can; but this fellow has
been brought up in a district where they have a missionary, and a
great deal of pains has been taken to form his religious principles.
Now, this fellow would no more think of touching a cent of his
earnings than he would of stealing right out of my pocket. I tell
people about him, sometimes, when I find them opposed to religious instruction. I tell them, 'See there, now—you see how godli-
ness is profitable to the life that now is.'[2] You know the Scriptures,
Mrs. Nesbit?"

"Yes," said Aunt Nesbit, "I always believed in religious education."

"Confound it all!" said Tom, "I *don't!* I don't see the use of
making a set of hypocritical sneaks of them! I'd make niggers bring
me my money; but, hang it all, if he came snuffling to me, pretend-

ing 't was his duty, I'd choke him! They never think so,—they don't, and they can't,—and it's all hypocrisy, this religious instruction, as you call it!"

"No, it isn't," said the undiscouraged Mr. Jekyl, "not when you found it on right principles. Take them early enough, and work them right, you'll get it ground into them. Now, when they begun religious instruction, there was a great prejudice against it in our part of the country. You see they were afraid that the niggers would get *uppish*. Ah, but you see the missionaries are pretty careful; they put it in strong in the catechisms about the rights of the master. You see the instruction is just grounded on this, that the master stands in God's place to them."

"D——d bosh!" said Tom Gordon.

Aunt Nesbit looked across the table as if she were going to faint. But Mr. Jekyl's composure was not in the slightest degree interrupted.

"I can tell you," he said, "that, in a business, practical view,—for I am used to investments,—that, since the publishing of those catechisms, and the missionaries' work among the niggers, the value of that kind of property has risen ten per cent. They are better contented. They don't run away, as they used to. Just that simple idea that their master stands in God's place to them. Why, you see, it cuts its way."

"I have a radical objection to all that kind of instruction," said Clayton.

Aunt Nesbit opened her eyes, as if she could hardly believe her hearing.

"And pray what is your objection?" said Mr. Jekyl, with an unmoved countenance.

"My objection is that it is all a lie," said Clayton, in such a positive tone that everybody looked at him with a start.

Clayton was one of those silent men who are seldom roused to talk, but who go with a rush when they are. Not seeming to notice the startled looks of the company, he went on: "It's a worse lie, because it's told to bewilder a simple, ignorant, confiding creature. I never could conceive how a decent man could ever look another man in the face and say such things. I remember reading, in one of the missionary reports, that when this doctrine was first propounded in an assembly of negroes somewhere, all the most intelligent of them got up and walked deliberately out of the house; and I honor them for it."

"Good for them!" said Tom Gordon. "I can keep my niggers down without any such stuff as that!"

"I have no doubt," said Clayton, "that these missionaries are well-intending, good men, and that they actually think the only way to get access to the negroes at all is, to be very positive in what will please the masters. But I think they fall into the same error that the Jesuits did when they adulterated Christianity with idolatry in order to get admission in Japan.[3] A lie never works well in religion, nor in morals."

"That's what I believe," said Nina, warmly.

"But, then, if you can't teach them this, what can you teach them?" said Mr. Jekyl.

"Confound it all!" said Tom Gordon, "teach them that you've *got the power!*—teach them the weight of your fist! That's enough for them. I am bad enough, I know; but I can't bear hypocrisy. I show a fellow my pistol. I say to him, You see that, sir! I tell him, You do so and so, and you shall have a good time with me. But, you do that, and I'll thrash you within an inch of your life! That's my short method with niggers, and poor whites, too. When one of these canting fellows comes round to my plantation, let him see what he'll get, that's all!"

Mr. Jekyl appeared properly shocked at this declaration. Aunt Nesbit looked as if it was just what she had expected, and went on eating her potato with a mournful air, as if nothing could surprise her. Nina looked excessively annoyed, and turned a sort of appealing glance upon Clayton.

"For my part," said Clayton, "I base my religious instruction to my people on the ground that every man and every woman must give an account of themselves *to God alone;* and that God is to be obeyed first, and before me."

"Why," said Mr. Jekyl, "that would be destructive of all discipline. If you are going to allow every fellow to judge for himself, among a parcel of ignorant, selfish wretches, what the will of God is, one will think it's one thing, another will think it's another; and there will be an end of all order. It would be absolutely impossible to govern a place in that way."

"They must not be left an ignorant set," said Clayton. "They must be taught to read the Scriptures for themselves, and be able to see that my authority accords with it. If I command anything contrary to it, they ought to oppose it!"

"Ah! I should like to see a plantation managed in that way!" said Tom Gordon, scornfully.

"Please God, you shall see such an one, if you'll come to mine," said Clayton, "where I should be very happy to see you, sir."

The tone in which this was said was so frank and sincere, that Tom was silenced, and could not help a rather sullen acknowledgment.

"I think," said Mr. Jekyl, "that you'll find such a course, however well it may work at first, will fail at last. You begin to let people think, and they won't stop where you want them to; they'll go too far; it's human nature. The more you give, the more you may give. You once get your fellows to thinking, and asking all sorts of questions, and they get discontented at once. I've seen that thing tried in one or two instances, and it didn't turn out well. Fellows got restless and discontented. The more was given to them, the more dissatisfied they grew, till finally they put for the free states."

"Very well," said Clayton; "if that's to be the result, they may all 'put' as soon as they can get ready. If my title to them won't bear an intelligent investigation, I don't wish to keep them. But I never will consent to keep them by making false statements to them in the name of religion, and presuming to put myself as an object of obedience before my Maker."

"I think," said Mr. Carson, "Mr. Clayton shows an excellent spirit—excellent spirit! On my word, I think so. I wish some of our northern agitators, who make such a fuss on the subject, could hear him. I'm always disgusted with these abolitionists producing such an unpleasantness between the north and the south, interrupting trade, and friendship, and all that sort of thing."

"He shows an excellent spirit," said Mr. Jekyl; "but I must think he is mistaken, if he thinks that he can bring up people in that way, under our institutions, and not do them more harm than good. It's a notorious fact that the worst insurrections have arisen from the reading of the Bible by these ignorant fellows. That was the case with Nat Turner,[4] in Virginia. That was the case with Denmark Vesey,[5] and his crew, in South Carolina. I tell you, sir, it will never do, this turning out a set of ignorant people to pasture in the Bible! That blessed book is a savor of life unto life when it's used right;

but it's a savor of death unto death when ignorant people take hold of it. The proper way is this: administer such portions only as these creatures are capable of understanding. This admirable system of religious instruction keeps the matter in our own hands, by allowing us to select for them such portions of the word as are best fitted to keep them quiet, dutiful, and obedient; and I venture to predict that whoever undertakes to manage a plantation on any other system will soon find it getting out of his hands."

"So you are afraid to trust the Lord's word without holding the bridle!" said Tom, with a sneer. "That's pretty well for you!"

"*I* am not!" said Clayton. "I'm willing to resign any rights to any one that I am not able to defend in God's word—any that I cannot make apparent to any man's cultivated reason. I scorn the idea that I must dwarf a man's mind, and keep him ignorant and childish, in order to make him believe any lie I choose to tell him about my rights over him! I intend to have an educated, intelligent people, who shall submit to me because they think it clearly for their best interests to do so; because they shall feel that what I command is right in the sight of God."

"It's my opinion," said Tom, "that both these ways of managing are humbugs. One way makes hypocrites, and the other makes rebels. The best way of educating is, to show folks that they can't help themselves. All the fussing and arguing in the world isn't worth one dose of certainty on that point. Just let them know that there are no two ways about it, and you'll have all still enough."

From this point the conversation was pursued with considerable warmth, till Nina and Aunt Nesbit rose and retired to the drawing-room. Perhaps it did not materially discourage Clayton, in the position he had taken, that Nina, with the frankness usual to her, expressed the most eager and undisguised admiration of all that he said.

"Didn't he talk beautifully? Wasn't it noble?" she said to Aunt Nesbit, as she came in the drawing-room. "And that hateful Jekyl! isn't he mean?"

"Child!" said Aunt Nesbit, "I'm surprised to hear you speak so! Mr. Jekyl is a very respectable lawyer, an elder in the church, and a very pious man. He has given me some most excellent advice about my affairs; and he is going to take Milly with him, and find her a good place. He's been making some investigations, Nina, and he's going to talk to you about them, after dinner. He's discovered that there's an estate in Mississippi worth a hundred thousand dollars, that ought properly to come to you!"

"I don't believe a word of it!" said Nina. "Don't like the man!—think he is hateful!—don't want to hear anything he has to say!—don't believe in him!"

"Nina, how often I have warned you against such sudden prejudices—against such a good man, too!"

"You won't make me believe he is good, not if he were elder in twenty churches!"

"Well, but, child, at any rate you must listen to what he has got to say. Your brother will be very angry if you don't; and it's really very important. At any rate, you ought not to offend Tom, when you can help it."

"That's true enough," said Nina; "and I'll hear, and try and behave as well as I can. I hope the man will go, some time or other! I don't know why, but his talk makes me feel worse than Tom's swearing! That's certain."

Aunt Nesbit looked at Nina as if she considered her in a most hopeless condition.

CHAPTER XV

Mr. Jekyl's Opinions

AFTER THE RETURN of the gentlemen to the drawing-room, Nina, at the request of Tom, followed him and Mr. Jekyl into the library.

"Mr. Jekyl is going to make some statements to us, Nina, about our property in Mississippi, which, if they turn out as he expects, will set us up in the world," said Tom.

Nina threw herself carelessly into the leathern arm-chair by the window, and looked out of it.

"You see," said Mr. Jekyl, also seating himself, and pulling out the stiff points of his collar, "having done law business for your father, and known, in that way, a good deal about the family property, I have naturally always felt a good deal of interest in it; and you remember your father's sister, Mrs. Stewart, inherited, on the death of her husband, a fine estate in Mississippi."

"I remember," said Tom,—"well, go on."

"Well, she died, and left it all to her son. Well, he, it seems, like some other young men, lived in a very reprehensible union with a handsome quadroon girl, who was his mother's maid; and she, being an artful creature, I suppose, as a great many of them are, got such an ascendency over him, that he took her up to Ohio, and married her, and lived there with her some years, and had two children by her. Well, you see, he had a deed of emancipation recorded for her in Mississippi, and, just taking her into Ohio, set her free by the laws of that state. Well, you see, he thought he'd fixed it so that the thing couldn't be undone, and she thought so too; and I understand she's a pretty shrewd woman—has a considerable share of character, or else she wouldn't have done just what she has; for, you see, he died about six months ago, and left the plantation and all the property to her and her children, and she has been so secure that she has actually gone and taken possession. You see, she is so near white, you must know that there isn't one in twenty would think what she was,—and the people round there, actually, some of them, had forgotten all about it, and didn't know but what she was a white woman from Ohio; and so, you see, the thing never would have been looked into at all, if I hadn't happened to have been down there. But, you see, she turned off an overseer that had managed the place, because the people complained of him; and I happened to fall in with the man, and he began telling me his story, and, after a little inquiry, I found who these people were. Well, sir, I just went to one of the first lawyers, for I suspected there was false play; and we looked over the emancipation laws together, and we found out that, as the law stood, the deed of emancipation was no more than so much waste paper. And so, you see, she and her children are just as much slaves as any on her plantation; and the whole property, which is worth a hundred thousand dollars, belongs to your family. I rode out with him, and looked over the place, and got introduced to her and her children, and looked them over. Considered as property, I should call them a valuable lot. She is past forty, but she don't look older than twenty-seven or twenty-eight, I should say. She is a very good-looking woman, and then, I'm told, a very capable woman. Well, her price in the market might range between one thousand and fifteen hundred dollars. Smalley said he had seen no better article sold for two thousand dollars; but, then, he said, they had to give a false certificate as to the age,—and that I couldn't hear of, for I never countenance anything like untruth. Then, the woman's children: she has got two fine-looking children as I have ever seen—almost white. The boy is about ten years old; the little girl, about four. You may be sure I was pretty careful not to let on, because I consider the woman and children are an important part of the property, and, of course, nothing had better be said about it, lest she should be off before we are ready to come down on them. Now, you see, you Gordons are the proper owners of this whole property; there isn't the slightest doubt in my mind that you ought to put in your claim immediately. The act of emancipation was contrary to law, and, though the man meant well, yet it amounted to a robbery of the heirs. I declare, it rather raised my indignation to see that creature so easy in the possession of property which of right belongs to you. Now, if I have only the consent of the heirs, I can go on and commence operations immediately."

Nina had been sitting regarding Mr. Jekyl with a fixed and determined expression of countenance. When he had finished, she said to him,

"Mr. Jekyl, I understand you are an elder in the church; is that true?"

"Yes, Miss Gordon, I have that privilege," said Mr. Jekyl, his sharp, business tone subsiding into a sigh.

"Because," said Nina, "I am a wild young girl, and don't profess to know much about religion; but I want you to tell me, as a Christian, if you think it would be *right* to take this woman and children, and her property."

"Why, certainly, my dear Miss Gordon; isn't it right that every one should have his own property? I view things simply with the eye of the law; and, in the eye of the law, that woman and her children are as much your property as the shoe on your foot; there is no manner of doubt of it."

"I should think," said Nina, "that you might see with the eye of the Gospel, sometimes! Do you think, Mr. Jekyl, that doing this is doing as I should wish to be done by, if I were in the place of this woman?"

"My dear Miss Gordon, young ladies of fine feeling, at your time of life, are often confused on this subject by a wrong application of the Scripture language. Suppose I were a robber, and had possession of your property? Of course, I shouldn't wish to be made to give it up. But would it follow that the golden rule obliged the lawful possessor not to take it from me? This woman is your property; this estate is your property, and she is holding it as unlawfully as a robber. Of course, she won't want to give it up; but right is right, notwithstanding."

Like many other young persons, Nina could *feel* her way out of a sophistry much sooner than she could think it out; and she answered to all this reasoning,

"After all, I can't think it would be right."

"O, confound the humbug!" said Tom, "who cares whether it is right or not? The fact is, Nin, to speak plain sense to you, you and I both are deuced hard up for money, and want all we can get; and what's the use of being more religious than the very saints themselves at our time of day? Mr. Jekyl is a pious man—one of the tallest kind! He thinks this is all right, and why need we set ourselves all up? He has talked with Uncle John, and he goes in for it.

As for my part, I am free to own I don't care whether it's right or not! I'll do it if I can. Might makes right,—that's my doctrine!"

"Why," said Mr. Jekyl, "I have examined the subject, and I haven't the slightest doubt that slavery is a divinely-appointed institution, and that the rights of the masters are sanctioned by God; so, however much I may naturally feel for this woman, whose position is, I must say, an unfortunate one, still it is my duty to see that the law is properly administered in the case."

"All I have to say, Mr. Jekyl," said Nina, "is just this: that I won't have anything to do with this matter; for, if I can't prove it's wrong, I shall always feel it is."

"Nina, how ridiculous!" said Tom.

"I have said my say," said Nina, as she rose and left the room.

"Very natural,—fine feelings, but uninstructed," said Mr. Jekyl.

"Certainly, we pious folks know a trick worth two of that, don't we?" said Tom. "I say, Jekyl, this sister of mine is a pretty rapid little case, I can tell you, as you saw by the way she circumvented us, this morning. She is quite capable of upsetting the whole dish, unless we go about it immediately. You see, her pet nigger, this Harry, is this woman's brother; and if she gave him the word, he'd write at once, and put her on the alarm. You and I had better start off tomorrow, before this Harry comes back. I believe he is to be gone a few days. It's no matter whether she consents to the suit or not. She don't need to know anything about it."

"Well," said Jekyl, "I advise you to go right on, and have the woman and children secured. It's a perfectly fair, legal proceeding. There has been an evident evasion of the law of the state, by means of which your family are defrauded of an immense sum. At all events, it will be tried in an open court of justice, and she will be allowed to appear by her counsel. It's a perfectly plain, above-board proceeding; and, as the young lady has shown such fine feelings, there's the best reason to suppose that the fate of this woman would be as good in her hands as in her own."

Mr. Jekyl was not now talking to convince Tom Gordon, but himself; for, spite of himself, Nina's questions had awakened in his mind a sufficient degree of misgiving to make it necessary for him to pass in review the arguments by which he generally satisfied himself. Mr. Jekyl was a theologian, and a man of principle. His metaphysical talent, indeed, made him a point of reference among his Christian brethren; and he spent much of his leisure time in reading theological treatises. His favorite subject of all was the nature of true virtue; and this, he had fixed in his mind, consisted in a love of the greatest good. According to his theology, right consisted in creating the greatest amount of happiness; and every creature had rights to be happy in proportion to his capacity of enjoyment or being. He whose capacity was ten pounds had a right to place his own happiness before that of him who had five, because, in that way, five pounds more of happiness would exist in the general whole. He considered the right of the Creator to consist in the fact that he had a greater amount of capacity than all creatures put together, and, therefore, was bound to promote his own happiness before all of them put together. He believed that the Creator made himself his first object in all that he did; and, descending from him, all creatures were to follow the same rule, in proportion to their amount of being; the greater capacity of happiness always taking precedence of the less. Thus, Mr. Jekyl considered that the Creator brought into the world yearly myriads of human beings with no other intention than to make them everlastingly miserable; and that this was right, because, his capacity of enjoyment being greater than all theirs put together, he had a right to gratify himself in this way.

Mr. Jekyl's belief in slavery was founded on his theology. He assumed that the white race had the largest amount of being; therefore, it had a right to take precedence of the black. On this point he held long and severe arguments with his partner, Mr. Israel McFogg, who, belonging to a different school of theology, referred the whole matter to no natural fitness, but to a Divine decree, by which it pleased the Creator in the time of Noah to pronounce a curse upon Canaan.[1] The fact that the African race did *not* descend from Canaan was, it is true, a slight difficulty in the chain of the argument; but theologians are daily in the habit of surmounting much greater ones. Either way, whether by metaphysical fitness or Divine decree, the two partners attained the same practical result.

Mr. Jekyl, though a coarse-grained man, had started from the hands of nature no more hard-hearted or unfeeling than many others; but his mind, having for years been immersed in the waters of law and theology, had slowly petrified into such a steady consideration of the greatest general good, that he was wholly inaccessible to any emotion of particular humanity. The trembling, eager tone of pity, in which Nina had spoken of the woman and children who were about to be made victims of a legal process, had excited but a moment's pause. What considerations of temporal loss and misery can shake the constancy of the theologian who has accustomed himself to contemplate and discuss, as a cool intellectual exercise, the eternal misery of generations?—who worships a God that creates myriads only to glorify himself in their eternal torments?

CHAPTER XVI

Milly's Story

NINA SPENT THE EVENING in the drawing-room; and her brother, in the animation of a new pursuit, forgetful of the difference of the morning, exerted himself to be agreeable, and treated her with more consideration and kindness than he had done any time since his arrival. He even made some off-hand advances towards Clayton, which the latter received with good-humor, and which went further than she supposed to raise the spirits of Nina; and so, on the whole, she passed a more than usually agreeable evening. On retiring to her room, she found Milly, who had been for some time patiently waiting for her, having despatched her mistress to bed some time since.

"Well, Miss Nina, I am going on my travels in the morning. Thought I must have a little time to see you, lamb, 'fore I goes."

"I can't bear to have you go, Milly! I don't like that man you are going with."

"I 'spects he's a nice man," said Milly. "Of course he'll look me out a nice place, because he has always took good care of Miss Loo's affairs. So you never trouble yourself 'bout me! I tell you, chile, I never gets where I can't find de Lord; and when I finds Him, I gets along. 'De Lord is my shepherd, I shall not want.' "[1]

"But you have never been used to living except in our family," said Nina, "and, somehow, I feel afraid. If they don't treat you well, come back, Milly; will you?"

"Laws, chile, I isn't much feared but what I'll get along well enough. When people keep about dere business, doing the best dey ken, folks doesn't often trouble dem. I never yet seed de folks I couldn't suit," she added, with a glow of honest pride. "No, chile, it isn't for myself I's fearing; it's just for you, chile. Chile, you don't know what it is to live in dis yer world, and I wants you to get de Best Friend to go with you. Why, dear lamb, you wants somebody to go to and open your heart; somebody dat'll love you, and always stand by you; somebody dat'll always lead you right, you know.

171

You has more cares than such a young thing ought for to have; great many looking to you, and 'pending on you. Now, if your ma was alive, it would be different; but, just now, I see how 't is; dere'll be a hundred things you'll be thinking and feeling, and nobody to say 'em to. And now, chile, you must learn to go to de Lord. Why, chile, he loves you! Chile, he loves you *just as you be;* if you only saw how much, it would melt your heart right down. I told you I was going some time fur to tell you my sperience—how I first found Jesus. O Lord, Lord! but it is a long story."

Nina, whose quick sympathies were touched by the earnestness of her old friend, and still more aroused by the allusion to her mother, answered,

"O, yes, come, tell me about it!" And, drawing a low ottoman, she sat down, and laid her head on the lap of her humble friend.

"Well, well, you see, chile," said Milly, her large, dark eyes fixing themselves on vacancy, and speaking in a slow and dreamy voice, "a body's life, in dis yer world, is a mighty strange thing! You see, chile, my mother—well, dey brought her from Africa; my father, too. Heaps and heaps my mother has told me about dat ar. Dat ar was a mighty fine country, where dey had gold in the rivers, and such great, big, tall trees, with de strangest beautiful flowers on them you ever did see! Laws, laws! well, dey brought my mother and my father into Charleston, and dere Mr. Campbell,—dat was your ma's father, honey,—he bought dem right out of de ship; but dey had five children, and dey was all sold, and dey never knowed where they went to. Father and mother couldn't speak a word of English when dey come ashore; and she told me often how she couldn't speak a word to nobody, to tell 'em how it hurt her.

"Laws, when I was a chile, I 'member how often, when de day's work was done, she used to come out and sit and look up at de stars, and groan, groan, and groan! I was a little thing, playing round; and I used to come up to her, dancing, and saying,

" 'Mammy, what makes you groan so? what's de matter of you?'

" 'Matter enough, chile!' she used to say. 'I's a thinking of my poor children. I likes to look at the stars, because dey sees the same stars dat I do. 'Pears like we was in one room; but I don't know where dey is! Dey don't know where I be!'

"Den she'd say to me,

" 'Now, chile, you may be sold away from your mammy. Der's

no knowing what may happen to you, chile; but, if you gets into any trouble, as I does, you mind, chile, you ask God to help you.'

" 'Who is God, mammy,' says I, 'any how?'

" 'Why, chile,' says she, 'he made dese yer stars.'

"And den I wanted mammy to tell me more about it; only she says,

" 'He can do anything he likes; and, if ye are in any kind of trouble, he can help you.'

"Well, to be sure, I didn't mind much about it—all dancing round, because pretty well don't need much help. But she said dat ar to me so many times, I couldn't help 'member it. Chile, troubles will come; and, when dey does come, you ask God, and he will help you.

"Well, sure enough, I wasn't sold from her, but she was took from me, because Mr. Campbell's brother went off to live in Orleans, and parted de hands. My father and mother was took to Orleans, and I was took to Virginny. Well, you see, I growed up along with de young ladies,—your ma, Miss Harrit, Miss Loo, and de rest on 'em,—and I had heaps of fun. Dey all like Milly. Dey couldn't nobody run, nor jump, nor ride a horse, nor row a boat, like Milly; and so it was Milly here, and Milly dere, and whatever de young ladies wanted, it was Milly made de way for it.

"Well, dere was a great difference among dem young ladies. Dere was Miss Loo—she was de prettiest, and she had a great many beaux; but, den, dere was your ma—everybody loved her; and den dere was Miss Harrit—she had right smart of life in her, and was always for *doing* something—always right busy 'tending to something or other, and she liked me because I'd always go in with her. Well, well! dem dar was pleasant times enough; but when I got to be about fourteen or fifteen, I began to feel kind o' bad—sort of strange and heavy. I really didn't know why, but 'peared like's when I got older, I felt I was in bondage.

" 'Member one day your ma came in, and seed me looking out of window, and she says to me,

" 'Milly, what makes you so dull lately?'

" 'O,' says I, 'I, somehow, I don't have good times.'

" 'Why?' says she; 'why not? Don't everybody make much of you, and don't you have everything that you want?'

" 'O, well,' says I, 'missis, I's a poor slave-girl, for all dat.'

"Chile, your ma was a weety thing, like you. I 'member just how she looked dat minute. I felt sorry, 'cause I thought I'd hurt her feelings. But says she,

" 'Milly, I don't wonder you feel so. I know I should feel so, myself, if I was in your place.'

"Afterwards, she told Miss Loo and Miss Harrit; but dey laughed, and said dey guessed der wasn't many girls who were as well off as Milly. Well, den, Miss Harrit, she was married de first. She married Mr. Charles Blair; and when she was married, nothing was to do but she must have me to go with her. I liked Miss Harrit; but, den, honey, I'd liked it much better if it had been your ma. I'd always counted that I wanted to belong to your ma, and I think your ma wanted me; but, den, she was still, and Miss Harrit she was one of the sort dat never lost nothing by not asking for it. She was one of de sort dat always *got things*, by hook or by crook. She always had more clothes, and more money, and more everything, dan the rest of them, 'cause she was always wide awake, and looking out for herself.

"Well, Mr. Blair's place was away off in another part of Virginny, and I went dere with her. Well, she wan't very happy, no ways, she wan't; because Mr. Blair, he was a high fellow. Laws, Miss Nina, when I tells you dis yere one you've got here is a good one, and I 'vise you to take him, it's because I knows what comes o' girls marrying high fellows. Don't care how good-looking dey is, nor what dere manners is,—it's just the ruin of girls that has them. Law, when he was a courting Miss Harrit, it was all nobody but her. She was going to be his angel, and he was going to give up all sorts of bad ways, and live *such* a good life! Ah! she married him; it all went to smoke! 'Fore de month was well over, he got a going in his old ways; and den it was go, go, all de time, carousing and drinking,—parties at home, parties abroad,—money flying like de water.

"Well, dis made a great change in Miss Harrit. She didn't laugh no more; she got sharp and cross, and she wan't good to me like what she used to be. She took to be jealous of me and her husband. She might have saved herself de trouble. I shouldn't have touched him with a pair of tongs. But he was always running after everything that came in his way; so no wonder. But, 'tween them both, I led a bad life of it.

"Well, things dragged kind along in this way. She had three children, and, at last, he was killed, one day, falling off his horse when he was too drunk to hold the bridle. Good riddance, too, I thought. And den, after he's dead, Miss Harrit, she seemed to grow more quiet like, and setting herself picking up what pieces and crumbs was left for her and de children. And I 'member she had one of her uncles dere a good many days helping her in counting up de debts. Well, dey was talking one day in missis' room, and dere was a little light closet on one side, where I got set down to do some fine stitching; but dey was too busy in their 'counts to think anything 'bout me. It seemed dat de place and de people was all to be sold off to pay de debts,—all 'cept a few of us, who were to go off with missis, and begin again on a small place,—and I heard him telling her about it.

" 'While your children are small,' he says, 'you can live small, and keep things close, and raise enough on the place for ye all; and den you can be making the most of your property. Niggers is rising in de market. Since Missouri came in,[2] they's worth double; and so you can just sell de increase of 'em for a good sum. Now, there's that black girl Milly, of yourn.'—You may be sure, now, I pricked up my ears, Miss Nina.—'You don't often see a girl of finer breed than she is,' says he, just as if I'd been a cow, you know. 'Have you got her a husband?'

" 'No,' said Miss Harrit; and then says she, 'I believe Milly is something of a coquette among the young men. She's never settled on anybody yet,' says she.

" 'Well,' says he, 'that must be attended to, 'cause that girl's children will be an estate of themselves. Why, I've known women to have twenty! and her children wouldn't any of 'em be worth less than eight hundred dollars. There's a fortune at once. If dey's like her, dey'll be as good as cash in the market, any day. You can send out and sell one, if you happen to be in any straits, just as soon as you can draw a note on the bank.'

"O, laws, Miss Nina, I tell you dis yer fell on me like so much lead. 'Cause, you see, I'd been keeping company with a very nice young man, and I was going to ask Miss Harrit about it dat very day; but, dere—I laid down my work dat minute, and thinks, says I, 'True as de Lord's in heaven I won't never be married in dis world!' And I cried 'bout it, off and on, all day, and at night I told Paul 'bout it. He was de one, you know. But Paul, he tried to make it all smooth. He guessed it wouldn't happen; he guessed missis would think better on 't. At any rate, we loved each other, and why shouldn't we take as much comfort as we could? Well, I went to Miss Harrit, and told her just what I thought 'bout it. Allers had spoke my mind to Miss Harrit 'bout everything, and I wan't going to stop den. And she laughed at me, and told me not to cry 'fore I's hurt. Well, things went on so two or three weeks, and finally Paul he persuaded me. And so we was married. When our first child was born, Paul was so pleased, he thought strange that I wan't.

" 'Paul,' said I, 'dis yer child an't ourn; it may be took from us, and sold, any day.'

" 'Well, well,' says he, 'Milly, it may be God's child, any way, even if it an't ourn.'

" 'Cause, you see, Miss Nina, Paul, he was a Christian. Ah, well, honey, I can't tell you; after dat I had a great many chil'en, girls and boys, growing up round me. Well, I's had fourteen chil'en, dear, and dey's all been sold from me, every single one of 'em. Lord, it's a heavy cross! heavy, heavy! None knows but dem dat bears it!"

"What a shame!" said Nina. "How could Aunt Harriet be such a wicked woman?—an aunt of mine do so!"

"Chile, chile," said Milly, "we doesn't none of us know what's in us. When Miss Harrit and I was gals together, hunting hens' eggs and rowing de boat in de river,—well, I wouldn't have thought it would have been so, and she wouldn't have thought so, neither. But, den, what little's bad in girls when dey's young and handsome, and all de world smiling on 'em—O, honey, it gets dreffful strong when dey gets grown women, and de wrinkles comes in der faces! Always, when she was a girl,—whether it was eggs, or berries, or chincapins,³ or what,—it was Miss Harrit's nature to *get* and to *keep;* and when she got old, dat all turned to money."

"O! but," said Nina, "it does seem impossible that a woman—a lady born, too, and my aunt—could do such a thing!"

"Ah, ah, honey! ladies-born have some bad stuff in dem, sometimes, like de rest of us. But, den, honey, it was de most natural thing in de world, come to look on 't; for now, see here, honey, dere was your aunt—she was poor, and she was pestered for money. Dere was Mas'r George's bills and Peter's bills to pay, and Miss Susy's; and every one of 'em must have everything, and dey was all calling for money, money; and dere has been times she didn't know which way to turn. Now, you see, when a woman is pestered to pay two hundred here and tree hundred dere, and when she has got more niggers on her place dan she can keep, and den a man calls in and lays down eight hundred dollars in gold and bills before her, and says, 'I want dat ar Lucy or George of yourn,' why, don't you see? Dese yer soul-drivers is always round, tempting folks dey know is poor; and dey always have der money as handy as de devil has his. But, den, I oughtn't fur to be hard upon dem poor soul-drivers, neither, 'cause dey an't taught no better. It's dese yer Christians, dat profess Christ, dat makes great talks 'bout religion, dat has der Bibles, and turns der backs upon swearing soul-drivers, and tinks dey an't fit to speak to—it's *dem,* honey, dat's de root of de whole business. Now, dere was dat uncle of hern,—mighty great Christian he was, with his prayer-meetings, and all dat!—he was always a putting her up to it. O, dere's been times—dere was times 'long first, Miss Nina, when my first chil'en was sold—dat, I tell you, I poured out my soul to Miss Harrit, and I've seen dat ar woman cry so dat I was sorry for her. And she said to me, 'Milly, I'll never do it again.' But, Lord! I didn't trust her,—not a word on 't,—'cause I knowed she would. I knowed dere was dat in her heart dat de devil wouldn't let go of. I knowed he'd no kind of objection to her 'musing herself with meetin's, and prayers, and all dat; but he'd no notion to let go his grip on her heart.

"But, Lord! she wasn't *quite* a bad woman,—poor Miss Harrit wasn't,—and she wouldn't have done so bad, if it hadn't been for *him.* But he'd come and have prayers, and exhort, and den come prowling round my place like a wolf, looking at my chil'en.

" 'And, Milly,' he'd say, 'how do you do now? Lucy is getting to be a right smart girl, Milly. How old is she? Dere's a lady in Washington has advertised for a maid,—a nice woman, a pious lady. I suppose you wouldn't object, Milly? Your poor mistress is in great trouble for money.'

"I never said nothing to that man. Only once, when he asked me what I thought my Lucy would be worth, when she was fifteen years old, says I to him:

" 'Sir, she is worth to me just what your daughter is worth to you.'

"Den I went in and shut de door. I didn't stay to see how he took it. Den he'd go up to de house, and talk to Miss Harrit. 'T was her duty, he'd tell her, to take proper care of her goods. And dat ar meant selling my chil'en! I 'member, when Miss Susy came home from boarding-school, she was a pretty girl; but I didn't look on her very kind, I tell you, 'cause three of my chil'en had been sold to keep her at school. My Lucy,—ah, honey!—she went for a lady's maid. I knowed what dat ar meant, well enough. De lady had a son grown, and he took Lucy with him to Orleans, and dere was an end of dat. Dere don't no letters go 'tween us. Once gone, we can't write, and it is good as being dead. Ah, no, chile, not so good! Paul used to teach Lucy little hymns, nights, 'fore she went to sleep. And if she'd a died right off after one of dem, it would have been better for her. O, honey, 'long dem times, I used to rave and toss like a bull in a net—I did so!

"Well, honey, I wasn't what I was. I got cross and ugly. Miss Harrit, she grew a great Christian, and joined de church, and used to have heaps of ministers and elders at her house; and some on 'em used to try and talk to me. I told 'em I'd seen enough of der old religion, and I didn't want to hear no more. But Paul, he was a Christian; and when he talked to me, I was quiet, like, though I couldn't be like what he was. Well, last, my missis promised me one. She'd give me my youngest child, sure and certain. His name was Alfred. Well, dat boy!—I loved dat child better dan any of de rest of 'em. He was all I'd got left to love; for, when he was a year old, Paul's master moved away down to Louisiana, and took him off, and I never heard no more of him. So it 'peared as if dis yer child was all I had left. Well, he *was* a bright boy. O, he was most uncommon! He was so handy to anything, and saved me so many steps! O, honey, he had such ways with him—dat boy!—would always make me laugh. He took after larnin' mighty, and he larned himself to read; and he'd read de Bible to me, sometimes. I just brought him up and teached him de best way I could. All dat made me 'fraid for him was, dat he was so spirity. I's 'fraid 't would get him into trouble.

"He wan't no more spirity dan white folks would like der chil'en fur to be. When white children holds up der heads, and answers back, den de parents laugh, and say, 'He's got it in him! He's a bright one!' But, if one of ourn does so, it's a drefful thing. I was allers talking to Alfred 'bout it, and told him to keep humble. It 'peared like there was so much in him, you couldn't keep it down. Laws, Miss Nina, folks may say what dey like about de black folks, dey'll never beat it out of my head;—dere's some on 'em can be as smart as any white folks, if dey could have de same chance. How many white boys did you ever see would take de trouble for to

teach theirselves to read? And dat's what my Alfred did. Laws, I
had a mighty heap of comfort in him, 'cause I was thinkin' to get
my missis to let me hire my time; den I was going to work over
hours, and get money, and buy him; because, you see, chile, I
knowed he was too spirity for a slave. You see he couldn't *learn to
stoop;* he wouldn't let nobody impose on him; and he always had a
word back again to give anybody as good as dey sent. Yet, for all
dat, he was a dear, good boy to me; and when I used to talk to him,
and tell him dese things was dangerous, he'd always promise fur to
be kerful. Well, things went on pretty well while he was little, and I
kept him with me till he got to be about twelve or thirteen years
old. He used to wipe de dishes, and scour de knives, and black de
shoes, and such-like work. But, by and by, dey said it was time dat
he should go to de reg'lar work; an dat ar was de time I felt feared.
Missis had an overseer, and he was real aggravating, and I felt feared
dere'd be trouble; and sure enough dere was, too. Dere was always
somethin' brewing 'tween him and Alfred; and he was always running to missis with tales, and I was talking to Alfred. But 'peared
like he aggravated de boy so, dat he couldn't do right. Well, one
day, when I had been up to town for an errand, I come home at
night, and I wondered Alfred didn't come home to his supper. I
thought something was wrong; and I went to de house, and dere sat
Miss Harrit by a table covered with rolls of money, and dere she
was a counting it.

" 'Miss Harrit,' says I, 'I can't find Alfred. An't you seen him?'
says I.

"At first she didn't answer, but went on counting—fifty-one,
fifty-two, fifty-three. Finally I spoke again.

" 'I hope dere an't nothing happened to Alfred, Miss Harrit?'

"She looked up, and says she to me,

" 'Milly,' says she, 'de fact is, Alfred has got too much for me
to manage, and I had a great deal of money offered for him; and I
sold him.'

"I felt something strong coming up in my throat, and I just went
up and took hold of her shoulders, and said I,

" 'Miss Harrit, you took de money for thirteen of my chil'en,
and you promised me, sure enough, I should have dis yer one. You
call dat being·a Christian?' says I.

" 'Why,' says she, 'Milly, he an't a great way off; you can see him
about as much. It's only over to Mr. Jones's plantation. You can go

and see him, and he can come and see you. And you know you didn't like the man who had the care of him here, and thought he was always getting him into trouble.'

" 'Miss Harrit,' says I, 'you may cheat yourself saying dem things; but you don't cheat me, nor de Lord neither. You folks have de say all on your side, with your ministers preaching us down out of de Bible; you won't teach us to read. But I'm going straight to de Lord with dis yer case. I tell you, if de Lord is to be found, I'll find him; and I'll ask him to look on 't,—de way you've been treating me,—selling *my* chil'en, all the way 'long, to pay for *your* chil'en, and now breaking your word to me, and taking dis yer boy, de last drop of blood in my heart! I'll pray de Lord to curse every cent of dat ar money to you and your chil'en!'

"Dat ar was de way I spoke to her, child. I was poor, ignorant cretur, and didn't know God, and my heart was like a red-hot coal. I turned and walked right straight out from her. I didn't speak no more to her, and she didn't speak no more to me. And when I went to bed at night, dar, sure 'nough, was Alfred's bed in de corner, and his Sunday coat hanging up over it, and his Sunday shoes I had bought for him with my own money; 'cause he was a handsome boy, and I wanted him always to look nice. Well, so, come Sunday morning, I took his coat and his shoes, and made a bundle of 'em, and I took my stick, and says I, 'I'll just go over to Jones's place and see what has 'come of Alfred.' All de time, I hadn't said a word to missis, nor she to me. Well, I got about half-way over to de place, and dere I stopped under a big hickory-tree to rest me a bit, and I looked along and seed some one a coming; and pretty soon I knowed it was Huldah. She was one that married Paul's cousin, and she lived on Jones's place. And so I got up and went to meet her, and told her I was going over to see 'bout Alfred.

" 'Lord!' says she, 'Milly, haven't you heard dat Alfred's dead?'

"Well, Miss Nina, it seemed as if my heart and everything in it stopped still. And said I, 'Huldah, has dey killed him?'

"And said she, 'Yes.' And she told me it was dis yer way: Dat Stiles—he dat was Jones's overseer—had heard dat Alfred was dreadful spirity; and when boys is so, sometimes dey aggravates 'em to get 'em riled, and den dey whips 'em to break 'em in. So Stiles, when he was laying off Alfred's task, was real aggravating to him; and dat boy—well, he answered back, just as he allers would be doing, 'cause he was smart, and it 'peared like he couldn't keep it in.

And den dey all laughed round dere, and den Stiles was mad, and swore he'd whip him; and den Alfred, he cut and run. And den Stiles he swore awful at him, and he told him to 'come here, and he'd give him hell, and pay him de cash.' Dem is de very words he said to my boy. And Alfred said he wouldn't come back; he wasn't going to be whipped. And just den young Master Bill come along, and wanted to know what was de matter. So Stiles told him, and he took out his pistol, and said, 'Here, young dog, if you don't come back before I count five, I'll fire!'

" 'Fire ahead!' says Alfred; 'cause, you see, dat boy never knowed what fear was. And so he fired. And Huldah said he just jumped up and give one scream, and fell flat. And dey run up to him, and he was dead; 'cause, you see, de bullet went right through his heart. Well, dey took off his jacket and looked, but it wan't of no use; his face settled down still. And Huldah said dat dey just dug a hole and put him in. Nothing on him—nothing round him—no coffin; like he'd been a dog. Huldah showed me de jacket. Dere was de hole, cut right round in it, like it was stamped, and his blood running out on it. I didn't say a word. I took up de jacket, and wrapped it up with his Sunday clothes, and I walked straight—straight home. I walked up into missis' room, and she was dressed for church, sure enough, and sat dere reading her Bible. I laid it right down under her face, dat jacket. 'You see dat *hole!*' said I; 'you see dat blood! Alfred's killed! *You* killed him; his blood be on you and your chil'en! O, Lord God in heaven, hear me, and *render unto her double!*' "[4]

Nina drew in her breath hard, with an instinctive shudder. Milly had drawn herself up, in the vehemence of her narration, and sat leaning forward, her black eyes dilated, her strong arms clenched before her, and her powerful frame expanding and working with the violence of her emotion. She might have looked, to one with mythological associations, like the figure of a black marble Nemesis[5] in a trance of wrath. She sat so for a few minutes, and then her muscles relaxed, her eyes gradually softened; she looked tenderly, but solemnly, down on Nina. "Dem was awful words, chile; but I was in Egypt den. I was wandering in de wilderness of Sinai.[6] I had heard de sound of de trumpet, and de voice of words; but, chile, I hadn't seen de Lord. Well—I went out, and I didn't speak no more to Miss Harrit. Dere was a great gulf fixed 'tween us; and dere didn't no words pass over it. I did my work—I scorned not to do it;

but I didn't speak to her. Den it was, chile, dat I thought of what
my mother told me, years ago; it came to me, all fresh—'Chile,
when trouble comes, you ask de Lord to help you;' and I saw dat I
hadn't asked de Lord to help me; and now, says I to myself, de
Lord can't help me; 'cause he couldn't bring back Alfred, no way
you could fix it; and yet I wanted to find de Lord, 'cause I was so
tossed up and down. I wanted just to go and say, 'Lord, you see
what dis woman has done.' I wanted to put it to him, if he'd stand
up for such a thing as that. Lord, how de world, and everything,
looked to me in dem times! Everything goin' on in de way it did;
and dese yer Christians, dat said dat dey was going into de kingdom, doing as dey did! I tell you, I sought de Lord early and late.
Many nights I have been out in de woods and laid on de ground till
morning, calling and crying, and 'peared like nobody heerd me. O,
how strange it used to look, when I looked up to de stars! winking
at me, so kind of still and solemn, but never saying a word! Sometimes I got dat wild, it seemed as if I could tear a hole through de
sky, 'cause I must find God; I had an errand to him, and I must find
him.

"Den I heard 'em read out de Bible, 'bout how de Lord met
a man on a threshing-floor,[7] and I thought maybe if I had a
threshing-floor he would come to me. So I threshed down a place
just as hard as I could under de trees; and den I prayed dere—but he
didn't come. Den dere was coming a great camp-meeting; and I
thought I'd go and see if I could find de Lord dere; because, you
see, missis, she let her people go Sunday to de camp-meeting. Well,
I went into de tents and heerd dem sing; and I went afore de altar,
and I heerd preaching; but it 'peared like it was no good. It didn't
touch me nowhere; and I couldn't see nothing to it. I heerd 'em
read out of de Bible, 'O, dat I knew where I might find him. I
would come even to his seat. I would order my cause before him. I
would fill my mouth with arguments;'[8] and I thought, sure enough,
dat ar's just what I want. Well, came on dark night, and dey had all
de camp-fires lighted up, and dey was singing de hymns round and
round, and I went for to hear de preaching. And dere was a man—
pale, lean man he was, with black eyes and black hair. Well, dat ar
man, he preached a sermon, to be sure, I never shall forget. His text
was, 'He that spared not his own Son, but freely delivered him up
for us all, how shall he not with him freely give us all things?'[9] Well,
you see, the first sound of dis took me, because I'd lost my son.

And the man, he told us who de Son of God was,—Jesus,—O, how sweet and beautiful he was! How he went round doing for folks. O, Lord, what a story dat ar was! And, den, how dey took him, and put de crown of thorns on his head, and hung him up bleeding, bleeding, and bleeding! God so loved us dat he let his own dear Son suffer all dat for us. Chile, I got up, and I went to de altar, and I kneeled down with de mourners; and I fell flat on my face, and dey said I was in a trance. Maybe I was. Where I was, I don't know; but I saw de Lord! Chile, it seemed as if my very heart was still. I saw him, suffering, bearing with us, year in and year out—bearing—bearing—bearing so patient! 'Peared like, it wan't just on de cross; but bearing always, everywhar! O, chile, I saw how he loved us!—us *all*—all—every one on us!—we dat hated each other so! 'Peared like he was using his heart up for us, all de time—bleedin' for us like he did on Calvary,[10] and willin' to bleed! O, chile, I saw what it was for me to be hatin', like I'd hated. 'O, Lord,' says I, 'I give up! O, Lord, I never see you afore! I didn't know. Lord, I's a poor sinner! I won't hate no more!' And O, chile, den dere come such a rush of love in my soul! Says I, 'Lord, I ken love even de white folks!' And den came another rush; and says I, 'Yes, Lord, I love poor Miss Harrit, dat's sole all my chil'en, and been de death of my poor Alfred! I loves her.' Chile, I overcome—I did so—I overcome by de blood of de *Lamb*[11]—de Lamb!—Yes, de Lamb, chile!—'cause if he'd been a lion I could a kept in; 't was de *Lamb* dat overcome.

"When I come to, I felt like a chile. I went home to Miss Harrit; and I hadn't spoke peaceable to her since Alfred died. I went in to her. She'd been sick, and she was in her room, looking kinder pale and yaller, poor thing; 'cause her son, honey, he got drunk and 'bused her awful. I went in, and says I, 'O, Miss Harrit, I's seen de Lord! Miss Harrit, I an't got no more hard feelin's; I forgive ye, and loves ye with all my heart, just as de Lord does.' Honey, ye ought to see how dat woman cried! Says she, 'Milly, I's a great sinner.' Says I, 'Miss Harrit, we's sinners, both on us, but de Lord gives hisself for us both; and if he loves us poor sinners, we mustn't be hard on each other. Ye was tempted, honey,' says I (for you see I felt like makin' scuses for her); 'but de Lord Jesus has got a pardon for both on us.'

"After dat, I didn't have no more trouble with Miss Harrit. Chile, we was sisters in Jesus. I bore her burdens, and she bore mine. And, dear, de burdens was heavy; for her son he was brought home a corpse; he shot hisself right through de heart, trying to load a gun when he was drunk. O, chile, I thought den how I'd prayed de Lord to render unto her double; but I had a better mind den. Ef I could have brought poor Mas'r George to life, I'd a done it; and I held de poor woman's head on my arm all dat ar night, and she a screamin' every hour. Well, dat ar took her down to de grave. She didn't live much longer; but she was ready to die. She sent and bought my daughter Lucy's son, dis here Tom, and gin him to me. Poor thing! she did all she could.

"I watched with her de night she died. O, Miss Nina, if ever ye're tempted to hate anybody, think how 't 'll be with 'em when dey comes to die.

"She died hard, poor thing! and she was cast down 'bout her sins. 'O, Milly,' says she, 'the Lord and you may forgive me, but I *can't* forgive myself.'

"And, says I to her, 'O, missis, don't think of it no more; *de Lord's hid it in his own heart!*' O, but she struggled long, honey; she was all night dyin', and 't was 'Milly! Milly!' all the time; 'O, Milly, stay with me!'

"And, chile, I felt I loved her like my own soul; and when de day broke de Lord set her free, and I laid her down like she'd been one o' my babies. I tóok up her poor hand. It was warm, but the strength was all gone out on 't; and, 'O,' I thought, 'ye poor thing, how could I ever have hated ye so?' Ah, chile, we mustn't hate nobody; we's all poor creaturs, and de dear Lord he loves us all."

CHAPTER XVII

Uncle John

ABOUT FOUR MILES EAST of Canema lay the plantation of Nina's uncle, whither Harry had been sent on the morning which we have mentioned. The young man went upon his errand in no very enviable mood of mind. Uncle Jack, as Nina always called him, was the nominal guardian of the estate, and a more friendly and indulgent one Harry could not have desired. He was one of those joyous, easy souls, whose leading desire seemed to be that everybody in the world should make himself as happy as possible, without fatiguing him with consultations as to particulars. His confidence in Harry was unbounded; and he esteemed it a good fortune that it was so, as he was wont to say, laughingly, that his own place was more than he could manage. Like all gentlemen who make the study of their own ease a primary consideration, Uncle Jack found the whole course of nature dead-set against him. For, as all creation is evidently organized with a view to making people work, it follows that no one has so much care as the man who resolves not to take any. Uncle Jack was systematically, and as a matter of course, cheated and fleeced, by his overseers, by his negroes, and the poor whites of his vicinity; and, worst of all, continually hectored and lectured by his wife therefor. Nature, or destiny, or whoever the lady may be that deals the matrimonial cards, with her usual thoughtfulness in balancing opposites, had arranged that jovial, easy, care-hating Uncle John should have been united to a most undaunted and ever-active spirit of enterprise and resolution, who never left anything quiet in his vicinity. She it was who continually disturbed his repose, by constantly ferreting out, and bringing before his view, all the plots, treasons, and conspiracies, with which plantation-life is ever abounding; bringing down on his devoted head the necessity of discriminations, decisions, and settlements, most abhorrent to an easy man.

The fact was, that responsibility, aggravated by her husband's

negligence, had transformed the worthy woman into a sort of domestic dragon of the Hesperides;[1] and her good helpmeet declared
that he believed she never slept, nor meant anybody else should. It
was all very well, he would observe. He wouldn't quarrel with her
for walking the whole night long, or sleeping with her head out of
the window, watching the smoke-house; for stealing out after
one o'clock to convict Pompey, or circumvent Cuff, if she only
wouldn't bother him with it. Suppose the half of the hams were carried off, between two and three, and sold to Abijah Skinflint for
rum?—He must have his sleep; and, if he had to pay for it in ham,
why, he'd pay for it in ham; but sleep he must, and would. And,
supposing he really believed, in his own soul, that Cuffy, who came
in the morning, with a long face, to announce the theft, and to propose measures of discovery, was in fact the main conspirator—what
then? He couldn't prove it on him. Cuff had gone astray from the
womb, speaking lies ever since he was born; and what would be the
use of his fretting and sweating himself to death to get truth out of
Cuff? No, no! Mrs. G., as he commonly called his helpmeet, might
do that sort of thing, but she mustn't bother him about it. Not that
Uncle Jack was invariable in his temper; human nature has its limits,
and a personage who finds "mischief still for idle hands to do" often
seems to take a malicious pleasure in upsetting the temper of idle
gentlemen. So, Uncle Jack, though confessedly the best fellow in
the world, was occasionally subject to a tropical whirlwind of passion, in which he would stamp, tear, and swear, with most astound-
ing energy; and in those ignited moments all the pent-up sorrows of
his soul would fly about him, like red-hot shot, in every direction.
And then he would curse the negroes, curse the overseers, curse the
plantation, curse Cuff and Pomp and Dinah, curse the poor white
folks round, curse Mr. Abijah Skinflint, and declare that he would
send them and the niggers all severally to a department which politeness forbids us to mention. He would pour out awful threats of
cutting up, skinning alive, and selling to Georgia. To all which commotion and bluster the negroes would listen, rolling the whites of
their eyes, and sticking their tongues in their cheeks, with an air of
great satisfaction and amusement; because experience had sufficiently proved to them that nobody had ever been cut up, skinned
alive, or sent to Georgia; as the result of any of these outpourings.
So, when Uncle Jack had one of these fits, they treated it as hens do

an approaching thunder-storm,—ran under cover, and waited for it to blow over.

As to Madam Gordon, her wrath was another affair. And her threats they had learned to know generally meant something; though it very often happened that, in the dispensation of most needed justice, Uncle Jack, if in an extra good humor, would rush between the culprit and his mistress, and bear him off in triumph, at the risk of most serious consequences to himself afterwards. Our readers are not to infer from this that Madam Gordon was really and naturally an ill-natured woman. She was only one of that denomination of vehement housekeepers who are to be found the world over—women to whom is appointed the hard mission of combating, single-handed, for the principles of order and exactness, against a whole world in arms. Had she had the good fortune to have been born in Vermont or Massachusetts, she would have been known through the whole village as a woman who couldn't be cheated half a cent on a pound in meat, and had an instinctive knowledge whether a cord of wood was too short, or a pound of butter too light. Put such a woman at the head of the disorderly rabble of a plantation, with a cheating overseer, surrounded by thieving poor whites, to whom the very organization of society leaves no resource but thieving, with a never-mind husband, with land that has seen its best days, and is fast running to barrenness, and you must not too severely question her temper, if it should not be at all times in perfect subjection. In fact, Madam Gordon's cap habitually bristled with horror, and she was rarely known to sit down. Occasionally, it is true, she alighted upon a chair; but was in a moment up again, to pursue some of her household train, or shout, at the top of her lungs, some caution toward the kitchen.

When Harry reined up his horse before the plantation, the gate was thrown open for him by old Pomp, a superannuated negro, who reserved this function as his peculiar sinecure.

"Lord bress you, Harry, dat you? Bress you, you ought fur to see mas'r! Such a gale up to de house!"

"What's the matter, Pomp?"

"Why, mas'r, he done got one of he fits! Tarin' round dar, fit to split!—stompin' up and down de 'randy, swarin' like mad! Lord, if he an't! He done got Jake tied up, dar!—swars he's goin' to cut him to pieces! He! he! he! Has so! Got Jake tied up dar! Ho! ho! ho!

Real curus! And he's blowin' hisself out dere mighty hard, I tell
you! So, if you want to get word wid him, you can't do it till he
done got through with dis yer!" And the old man ducked his
pepper-and-salt-colored head, and chuckled with a lively satisfaction.

As Harry rode slowly up the avenue to the house, he caught
sight of the portly figure of its master, stamping up and down the
veranda, vociferating and gesticulating in the most violent manner.
He was a corpulent man, of middle age, with a round, high forehead, set off with grizzled hair. His blue eyes, fair, rosy, fat face, his
mouth adorned with brilliant teeth, gave him, when in good-
humor, the air of a handsome and agreeable man. At present his
countenance was flushed almost to purple, as he stood storming,
from his rostrum, at a saucy, ragged negro, who, tied to the horse-
post, stood the picture of unconcern; while a crowd of negro men,
women, and children, were looking on.

"I'll teach you!" he vociferated, shaking his fist. "I won't—won't
bear it of you, you dog, you! You won't take my orders, won't
you? I'll *kill* you—that I will! I'll cut you up into inch-pieces!"

"No, you won't, and you know you won't!" interposed Mrs.
Gordon, who sat at the window behind him. "You won't, and you
know you won't! and *they* know you won't, too! It will all end in
smoke, as it always does. I only wish you wouldn't talk and
threaten, because it makes you ridiculous!"

"Hold your tongue, too! I'll be master in my own house, I say!
Infernal dog!—I say, Cuff, cut him up!—Why don't you go at
him?—Give it to him!—What you waiting for?"

"If mas'r pleases!" said Cuff, rolling up his eyes, and making a
deprecating gesture.

"If I please! Well, blast you, I *do* please! Go at him!—thrash
away! Stay, I'll come myself." And, seizing a cowhide, which lay
near him, he turned up his cuffs, and ran down the steps; but, missing his footing in his zeal, came head-first against the very post
where the criminal was tied.

"There! I hope, now, you are satisfied! You have killed me!—
you have broke my head, you have! I shall be laid up a month, all
for you, you ungrateful dog!"

Cuffy and Sambo came to the rescue, raised him up carefully,
and began brushing the dust off his clothes, smothering the laughter
with which they seemed ready to explode, while the culprit at the

post seemed to consider this an excellent opportunity to put in his submission.

"Please, mas'r, do forgive me! I tole 'em to go out, and dey said dey wouldn't. I didn't mean no harm when I said 'Mas'r had better go hisself;' 'cause I thinks so now. Mas'r *had* better go! Dem folks is curus, and dey won't go for none of us. Dey just acts ridiculous, dey does! And I didn't mean fur to be sarcy, nor nothin'. I say 'gin, if mas'r'll take his horse and go over dar, mas'r drive dose folks out; and nobody else can't do it! We done can't do it—dey jest sarce us. Now, for my Heavenly Master, all dis yere is de truth I've been telling. De Lord, de Master, knows it is; and, if mas'r 'll take his horse, and ride down dere, he'd see so; so dere, just as I've been telling mas'r. I didn't mean no harm at all, I didn't!"

The quarrel, it must be told, related to the ejecting of a poor white family, which had *squatted*, as the phrase is, in a deserted cabin, on a distant part of the Gordon plantation. Mrs. Gordon's untiring assiduity having discovered this fact, she had left her husband no peace till something was undertaken in the way of ejectment. He accordingly commissioned Jake, a stout negro, on the morning of the present day, to go over and turn them off. Now, Jake, who inherited to the full the lofty contempt with which the plantation negro regards the poor white folks, started upon his errand, nothing loth, and whistled his way in high feather, with two large dogs at his heels. But, when he found a miserable, poor, sick woman, surrounded by four starving children, Jake's mother's milk came back to him; and, instead of turning them out, he actually pitched a dish of cold potatoes in among them, which he picked up in a neighboring cabin, with about the same air of contemptuous pity with which one throws scraps to a dog. And then, meandering his way back to the house, informed his master that "He couldn't turn de white trash out; and, if he wanted them turned out, he would have to go hisself."

Now, we all know that a fit of temper has very often nothing to do with the thing which appears to give rise to it. When a cloud is full charged with electricity, it makes no difference which bit of wire is put in. The flash and the thunder come one way as well as another. Mr. Gordon had received troublesome letters on business, a troublesome lecture from his wife, his corn-cake had been overdone at breakfast, and his coffee burned bitter; besides which, he had a cold in his head coming on, and there was a settlement brew-

ing with the overseer. In consequence of all which things, though
Jake's mode of delivering himself wasn't a whit more saucy than ordinary, the storm broke upon him then and there, and raged as we
have described. The heaviest part of it, however, being now spent,
Mr. Gordon consented to pardon the culprit on condition that he
would bring him up his horse immediately, when he would ride
over and see if he couldn't turn out the offending party. He pressed
Harry, who was rather a favorite of his, into the service; and, in the
course of a quarter of an hour, they were riding off in the direction
of the squatter's cabin.

"It's perfectly insufferable, what we proprietors have to bear
from this tribe of creatures!" he said. "There ought to be hunting-
parties got up to chase them down, and exterminate 'em, just as we
do rats. It would be a kindness to them; the only thing you can do
for them is to kill them. As for charity, or that kind of thing, you
might as well throw victuals into the hollow logs as to try to feed
'em. The government ought to pass laws,—we will have laws, somehow or other,—and get them out of the state."

And, so discoursing, the good man at length arrived before the
door of a miserable, decaying log-cabin, out of whose glassless windows dark emptiness looked, as out of the eye-holes of a skull. Two
scared, cowering children disappeared round the corner as he approached. He kicked open the door, and entered. Crouched on a
pile of dirty straw, sat a miserable, haggard woman, with large, wild
eyes, sunken cheeks, dishevelled, matted hair, and long, lean hands,
like bird's-claws. At her skinny breast an emaciated infant was
hanging, pushing, with its little skeleton hands, as if to force the
nourishment which nature no longer gave; and two scared-looking
children, with features wasted and pinched blue with famine, were
clinging to her gown. The whole group huddled together, drawing
as far as possible away from the new comer, looked up with large,
frightened eyes, like hunted wild animals.

"What you here for?" was the first question of Mr. Gordon, put
in no very decided tone; for, if the truth must be told, his combat-
iveness was oozing out.

The woman did not answer, and, after a pause, the youngest
child piped up, in a shrill voice,

"An't got nowhere else to be!"

"Yes," said the woman, "we camped on Mr. Durant's place, and

Bobfield—him is the overseer—pulled down the cabin right over our head. 'Pears like we couldn't get nowhere."

"Where is your husband?"

"Gone looking for work. 'Pears like he couldn't get none nowhere. 'Pears like nobody wants us. But we have got to be somewhere, though!" said the woman, in a melancholy, apologetic tone. "We can't die, as I see!—wish we could!"

Mr. Gordon's eye fell upon two or three cold potatoes in a piece of broken crock, over which the woman appeared keeping jealous guard.

"What you doing with those potatoes?"

"Saving them for the children's dinner."

"And is that all you've got to eat, I want to know?" said Mr. Gordon, in a high, sharp tone, as if he were getting angry very fast.

"Yes," said the woman.

"What did you have to eat yesterday?"

"Nothing!" said the woman.

"And what did you eat the day before?"

"Found some old bones round the nigger houses; and some on 'em give us some corn-cake."

"Why the devil didn't you send up to *my* house, and get some bacon? Picking up bones, slop, and swill, round the nigger huts? Why didn't you send up for some ham, and some meal? Lord bless you, you don't think Madam Gordon is a dog, to bite you, do you? Wait here till I send you down something fit to eat. Just end in my having to take care of you, I see! And, if you are going to stay here, there will be something to be done to keep the rain out!"

"There, now," he said to Harry, as he was mounting his horse, "just see what 't is to be made with hooks in one's back, like me! Everybody hangs on to me, of course! Now, there's Durant turns off these folks; there's Peters turns them off! Well, what's the consequence? They come and litter down on me, just because I am an easy, soft-hearted old fool! It's too devilish bad! They breed like rabbits! What God Almighty makes such people for, I don't know! I suppose He does. But there's these poor, miserable trash have children like sixty; and there's folks living in splendid houses, dying for children, and can't have any. If they manage one or two, the scarlet-fever or whooping-cough makes off with 'em. Lord bless me, things go on in a terrible mixed-up way in this world! And, then, what upon earth I'm to say to Mrs. G.! I know what she'll say to me. She'll tell me she told me so—that's what she always says. I wish she'd go and see them herself—I do so! Mrs. G. is the nicest kind of a woman—no mistake about that; but she has an awful deal of energy, that woman! It's dreadful fatiguing to a quiet man, like me—dreadful! But I'm sure I don't know what I should do without her. She'll be down upon me about this woman; but the woman must have some ham, that's flat! Cold potatoes and old bones! Pretty story! Such people have no business to live at all; but, if they will live, they ought to eat Christian things! There goes Jake. Why couldn't he turn 'em off before I saw 'em? It would have saved me all this plague! Dog knew what he was about, when he got me down here! Jake! O, Jake, Jake! come here!"

Jake came shambling along up to his master, with an external appearance of the deepest humility, under which was too plainly seen to lurk a facetious air of waggish satisfaction.

"Here, you, Jake; you get a basket—"

"Yes, mas'r!" said Jake, with an air of provoking intelligence.

"Be still saying 'Yes, mas'r,' and hear what I've got to say! Mind yourself!"

Jake gave a side glance of inexpressible drollery at Harry, and then stood like an ebony statue of submission.

"You go to your missis, and ask her for the key of the smoke-house, and bring it to me."

"Yes, sir."

"And you tell your missis to send me a peck of meal. Stay—a loaf of bread, or some biscuit, or corn-cake, or anything else which may happen to be baked up. Tell her I want them sent out right away."

Jake bowed and disappeared.

"Now we may as well ride down this path, while he is gone for the things. Mrs. G. will blow off on him first, so that rather less of it will come upon me. I wish I could get her to see them herself. Lord bless her, she is a kind-hearted woman enough! but she thinks there's no use doing,—and there an't. She is right enough about it. But, then, as the woman says, there must be some place for them to *be* in the world. The world is wide enough, I'm sure! Plague take it! why can't we pass a law to take them all in with our niggers, and then they'd have some one to take care of them! Then we'd do something for them, and there'd be some hope of keeping 'em comfortable."

Harry felt in no wise inclined to reply to any of this conversation, because he knew that, though nominally addressed to him, the good gentleman was talking merely for the sake of easing his mind, and that he would have opened his heart just as freely to the next hickory-bush, if he had not happened to be present. So he let him expend himself, waiting for an opportunity to introduce subjects which lay nearer his heart.

In a convenient pause, he found opportunity to say,

"Miss Nina sent me over here, this morning."

"Ah, Nin! my pretty little Nin! Bless the child! She did? Why couldn't she come over herself, and comfort an old fellow's heart? Nin is the prettiest girl in the county! I tell you that, Harry!"

"Miss Nina is in a good deal of trouble. Master Tom came home last night drunk, and to-day he is so cross and contrary she can't do anything with him."

"Drunk? O, what a sad dog! Tom gets drunk too often! Carries that too far, altogether! Told him that, the last time I talked to him. Says I, 'Tom, it does very well for a young man to have a spree once in one or two months. I did it myself, when I was young. But,' says I, 'Tom, to spree *all* the time, won't do, Tom!' says I. 'Nobody minds a fellow being drunk *occasionally;* but he ought to be moderate about it, and know where to stop,' says I; 'because, when it comes to that, that he is drunk every day, or every other day, why, it's my opinion that he may consider the devil's got him!' I talked to Tom just so, right out square; because, you see, I'm in a father's place to him. But, Lord, it don't seem to have done him a bit of good! Good Lord! they tell me he is drunk one half his time, and acts like a crazy creature! Goes too far, Tom does, altogether. Mrs. G. an't got any patience with him. She blasts at him every time he comes here, and he blasts at her; so it an't very comfortable having him here. Good woman at heart, Mrs. Gordon, but a little strong in her ways, you know; and Tom is strong, too. So it's fire fight fire, when they get together. It's no ways comfortable to a man wanting to have everybody happy around him. Lord bless me! I wish Nin were my daughter! Why can't she come over here, and live with me? She hasn't got any more spirit in her than just what I like. Just

enough fizz in her to keep one from flatting out. What about those
beaux of hers? Is she going to be married? Hey?"

"There's two gentlemen there, attending upon Miss Nina. One is
Mr. Carson, of New York—"

"Hang it all! she isn't going to marry a d——d Yankee! Why,
brother would turn over in his grave!"

"I don't think it will be necessary to put himself to that trouble,"
said Harry, "for I rather think it's Mr. Clayton who is to be the favored one."

"Clayton! good blood!—like that! Seems to be a gentlemanly,
good fellow, doesn't he?"

"Yes, sir. He owns a plantation, I'm told, in South Carolina."

"Ah! ah! that's well! But I hate to spare Nin! I never half liked
sending her off to New York. Don't believe in boarding-schools. I've
seen as fine girls grown on plantations as any man need want. What
do we want to send our girls there, to get fipenny-bit ideas? I thank
the Lord, I never was in New York, and I never mean to be! Carolina
born and raised, I am; and my wife is Virginia—pure breed! No
boarding-school about her! And, when I stood up to be married to
her, there wasn't a girl in Virginia could stand up with her. Her
cheeks were like damask roses! A tall, straight, lively girl, she was!
Knew her own mind, and had a good notion of speaking it, too. And
there isn't a woman, now, that can get through the business she can,
and have her eyes always on everything. If it does make me uncomfortable, every now and then, I ought to take it, and thank the Lord
for it. For, if it wan't for her, what with the overseer, and the niggers,
and the poor white trash, we should all go to the devil in a heap!"

"Miss Nina sent me over here to be out of Master Tom's way,"
said Harry, after a pause. "He is bent upon hectoring me, as usual.
You know, sir, that he always had a spite against me, and it seems to
grow more and more bitter. He quarrels with her about the management of everything on the place; and you know, sir, that I try to
do my very best, and you and Mrs. Gordon have always been
pleased to say that I did well."

"So we did, Harry, my boy! So we did! Stay here as long as you
like. Just suit yourself about that. Maybe you'd like to go out
shooting with me."

"I'm worried," said Harry, "to be obliged to be away just at the
time of putting in the seed. Everything depends upon my overseeing."

"Why don't you go back, then? Tom's ugliness is nothing but because he is drunk. There's where it is! I see through it! You see, when a fellow has had a drunken spree, why, the day after it he is all at loose ends and cross—nerves all ravelled out, like an old stocking. Then fellows are sulky and surly like. I've heard of their having temperance societies up in those northern states, and I think something of that sort would be good for our young men. They get drunk too often. Full a third of them, I should reckon, get the delirium tremens[2] before they are fifty. If we could have a society like them, and that sort of thing, and agree to be moderate! Nobody expects young men to be old before their time; but, if they'd agree not to blow out more than once a month, or something in that way!"

"I'm afraid," said Harry, "Master Tom's too far gone for that."

"O, ay! yes! Pity, pity! Suppose it is so. Why, when a fellow gets so far, he's like a nigger's old patched coat—you can't tell where the real cloth is. Now, Tom; I suppose he never is himself—always up on a wave, or down in the trough! Heigho! I'm sorry!"

"It's very hard on Miss Nina," said Harry. "He interferes, and I have no power to stand for her. And, yesterday, he began talking to my wife in a way I can't bear, nor won't! He *must* let her alone!"

"Sho! sho!" said Mr. Gordon. "See what a boy that is, now! That an't in the least worth while—that an't! I shall tell Tom so. And, Harry, mind your temper! Remember, young men will be young; and, if a fellow will treat himself to a pretty wife, he must expect trials. But Tom ought not to do so. I shall tell him. High! there comes Jake, with the basket and the smoke-house key. Now for something to send down to those poor hobgoblins. If people are going to starve, they mustn't come on to my place to do it. I don't mind what I don't see—I wouldn't mind if the whole litter of 'em was drowned to-morrow; but, hang it, I can't stand it if I know it! So, here, Jake, take this ham and bread, and look 'em up an old skillet, and see if you can't tinker up the house a bit. I'd set the fellow to work, when he comes back; only we have two hands to every turn, now, and the niggers always plague 'em. Harry, you go home, and tell Nin Mrs. G. and I will be over to dinner."

CHAPTER XVIII

Dred

HARRY SPENT THE NIGHT at the place of Mr. John Gordon, and arose the next morning in a very discontented mood of mind. Nothing is more vexatious to an active and enterprising person than to be thrown into a state of entire idleness; and Harry, after lounging about for a short time in the morning, found his indignation increased by every moment of enforced absence from the scene of his daily labors and interests. Having always enjoyed substantially the privileges of a freeman in the ability to regulate his time according to his own ideas, to come and go, to buy and sell, and transact business unfettered by any felt control, he was the more keenly alive to the degradation implied in his present position.

"Here I must skulk around," said he to himself, "like a partridge in the bushes, allowing everything to run at loose ends, preparing the way for my being found fault with for a lazy fellow, by and by; and all for what? Because my younger brother chooses to come, without right or reason, to domineer over me, to insult my wife; and because the laws will protect him in it, if he does it! Ah! ah! that's it. They are all leagued together! No matter how right I am—no matter how bad he is! Everybody will stand up for him, and put me down; all because my grandmother was born in Africa, and his grandmother was born in America. Confound it all, I won't stand it! Who knows what he'll be saying and doing to Lisette while I am gone? I'll go back and face him, like a man! I'll keep straight about my business, and, if he crosses me, let him take care! He hasn't got but one life, any more than I have. Let him look out!"

And Harry jumped upon his horse, and turned his head homeward. He struck into a circuitous path, which led along that immense belt of swampy land, to which the name of Dismal[1] has been given. As he was riding along, immersed in thought, the clatter of horses' feet was heard in front of him. A sudden turn of the road

brought him directly facing to Tom Gordon and Mr. Jekyl, who
had risen early and started off on horseback, in order to reach a certain stage-dépôt before the heat of the day. There was a momentary
pause on both sides; when Tom Gordon, like one who knows his
power, and is determined to use it to the utmost, broke out, scornfully:

"Stop, you damned nigger, and tell your master where you are
going!"

"You are not my master!" said Harry, in words whose concentrated calmness conveyed more bitterness and wrath than could
have been given by the most violent outburst.

"You d——d whelp!" said Tom Gordon, striking him across the
face twice with his whip, "take *that,* and *that!* We'll see if I'm not
your master! There, now, help yourself, won't you? Isn't that a
master's mark?"

It had been the life-long habit of Harry's position to repress
every emotion of anger within himself. But, at this moment, his face
wore a deadly and frightful expression. Still, there was something
majestic and almost commanding in the attitude with which he
reined back his horse, and slowly lifted his hand to heaven. He tried
to speak, but his voice was choked with repressed passion. At last
he said:

"You may be sure, Mr. Gordon, this mark will *never* be forgotten!"

There are moments of high excitement, when all that is in a human being seems to be roused, and to concentrate itself in the eye
and the voice. And, in such moments, *any* man, apparently by
virtue of his mere humanity, by the mere awfulness of the human
soul that is in him, gains power to over-awe those who in other
hours scorn him. There was a minute's pause, in which neither
spoke; and Mr. Jekyl, who was a man of peace, took occasion to
touch Tom's elbow, and say:

"It seems to me this isn't worth while—we shall miss the stage."
And, as Harry had already turned his horse and was riding away,
Tom Gordon turned his, shouting after him, with a scornful laugh:

"I called on your wife before I came away, this morning, and I
liked her rather better the second time than I did the first!"

This last taunt flew like a Parthian[2] arrow backward, and struck
into the soul of the bondman with even a keener power than the de-

grading blow. The sting of it seemed to rankle more bitterly as he rode along, till at last he dropped the reins on his horse's neck, and burst into a transport of bitter cursing.

"Aha! aha! it has come nigh *thee*, has it? It toucheth *thee*, and thou faintest!" said a deep voice from the swampy thicket beside him.

Harry stopped his horse and his imprecations. There was a crackling in the swamp, and a movement among the copse of briers; and at last the speaker emerged, and stood before Harry. He was a tall black man, of magnificent stature and proportions. His skin was intensely black, and polished like marble. A loose shirt of red flannel, which opened very wide at the breast, gave a display of a neck and chest of herculean strength. The sleeves of the shirt, rolled up nearly to the shoulders, showed the muscles of a gladiator. The head, which rose with an imperial air from the broad shoulders, was large and massive, and developed with equal force both in the reflective and perceptive department. The perceptive organs jutted like dark ridges over the eyes, while that part of the head which phrenologists[3] attribute to the moral and intellectual sentiments, rose like an ample dome above them. The large eyes had that peculiar and solemn effect of unfathomable blackness and darkness which is often a striking characteristic of the African eye. But there burned in them, like tongues of flame in a black pool of naphtha,[4] a subtle and restless fire, that betokened habitual excitement to the verge of insanity. If any organs were predominant in the head, they were those of ideality, wonder, veneration, and firmness, and the whole combination was such as might have formed one of the wild old warrior prophets of the heroic ages. He wore a fantastic sort of turban, apparently of an old scarlet shawl, which added to the outlandish effect of his appearance. His nether garments, of coarse negro-cloth, were girded round the waist by a strip of scarlet flannel, in which was thrust a bowie-knife and hatchet. Over one shoulder he carried a rifle, and a shot-pouch was suspended to his belt. A rude game-bag hung upon his arm. Wild and startling as the apparition might have been, it appeared to be no stranger to Harry; for, after the first movement of surprise, he said, in a tone of familiar recognition, in which there was blended somewhat of awe and respect:

"O, it is you, then, Dred! I didn't know that you were hearing me!"

"Have I not heard?" said the speaker, raising his arm, and his eyes gleaming with wild excitement. "How long wilt thou halt between two opinions? Did not Moses refuse to be called the son of Pharaoh's daughter? How long wilt thou cast in thy lot with the oppressors of Israel, who say unto thee, 'Bow down that we may walk over thee'? Shall not the Red Sea be divided? 'Yea,' saith the Lord, 'it shall.' "[5]

"Dred! I know what you mean!" said Harry, trembling with excitement.

"Yea, thou dost!" said the figure. "Yea, thou dost! Hast thou not eaten the fat and drunk the sweet with the oppressor, and hid thine eyes from the oppression of thy people? Have not *our* wives been for a prey, and thou hast not regarded? Hath not our cheek been given to the smiter? Have we not been counted as sheep for the slaughter? But thou saidst, Lo! I knew it not, and didst hide thine eyes! Therefore, the curse of Meroz[6] is upon thee, saith the Lord. And *thou* shalt bow down to the oppressor, and his rod shall be upon thee; and *thy* wife shall be for a prey!"[7]

"Don't talk in that way!—don't!" said Harry, striking out his hands with a frantic gesture, as if to push back the words. "You are raising the very devil in me!"

"Look here, Harry," said the other, dropping from the high tone he at first used to that of common conversation, and speaking in bitter irony, "did your master strike you? It's sweet to kiss the rod,[8] isn't it? Bend your neck and ask to be struck again!—won't you? Be meek and lowly; that's the religion for you! You are a *slave,* and you wear broadcloth, and sleep soft. By and by he will give you a fip[9] to buy salve for those cuts! Don't fret about your wife! Women always like the master better than the slave! Why shouldn't they? When a man licks his master's foot, his wife scorns him,—serves him right. Take it meekly, my boy! 'Servants, obey your masters.'[10] Take your master's old coats—take your wife when he's done with her—and bless God that brought you under the light of the Gospel! Go! *you* are a slave! But, as for me," he said, drawing up his head, and throwing back his shoulders with a deep inspiration, "*I* am a free man! Free by this," holding out his rifle. "Free by the Lord of hosts, that numbereth the stars, and calleth them forth by their names. Go home—that's all I have to say to you! You sleep in a curtained bed.—I sleep on the ground, in the swamps! You eat the fat of the land. I have what the ravens bring me! But no man whips me!—no man touches *my* wife!—no man says to me, 'Why do ye so?' Go! *you* are a slave!—I am free!" And, with one athletic bound, he sprang into the thicket, and was gone.

The effect of this address on the already excited mind of the bondman may be better conceived than described. He ground his teeth, and clenched his hands.

"Stop!" he cried, "Dred, I will—I will—I'll do as you tell me—I will not be a slave!"

A scornful laugh was the only reply, and the sound of crackling footsteps retreated rapidly. He who retreated struck up, in a clear, loud voice, one of those peculiar melodies in which vigor and spirit are blended with a wild, inexpressible mournfulness. The voice was one of a singular and indescribable quality of tone; it was heavy as the sub-bass of an organ, and of a velvety softness, and yet it seemed to pierce the air with a keen dividing force which is generally characteristic of voices of much less volume. The words were the commencement of a wild camp-meeting hymn, much in vogue in those parts:

> *"Brethren, don't you hear the sound?*
> *The martial trumpet now is blowing;*
> *Men in order listing round,*
> *And soldiers to the standard flowing."*

There was a wild, exultant fulness of liberty that rolled in the note; and, to Harry's excited ear, there seemed in it a fierce challenge of contempt to his imbecility, and his soul at that moment seemed to be rent asunder with a pang such as only those can know who have felt what it is to be a slave. There was an uprising within him, vague, tumultuous, overpowering; dim instincts, heroic aspirations; the will to do, the soul to dare; and then, in a moment, there followed the picture of all society leagued against him, the hopeless impossibility of any outlet to what was burning within him. The waters of a nature naturally noble, pent up, and without outlet, rolled back upon his heart with a suffocating force; and, in his hasty anguish, he cursed the day of his birth. The spasm of his emotion was interrupted by the sudden appearance of Milly coming along the path.

"Why, bless you, Milly," said Harry, in sudden surprise, "where are you going?"

"O, bless you, honey, chile, I's gwine on to take de stage. Dey wanted to get up de wagon for me; but, bless you, says I, what you s'pose de Lord gin us legs for? I never wants no critturs to tug me round, when I can walk myself. And, den, honey, it's so pleasant like, to be a walking along in de bush here, in de morning; 'pears like de voice of de Lord is walking among de trees. But, bless you, chile, honey, what's de matter o' yer face?"

"It's Tom Gordon, d——n him!" said Harry.

"Don't talk dat ar way, chile!" said Milly; using the freedom with Harry which her years and weight of character had gradually secured for her among the members of the plantation.

"I *will* talk that way! Why shouldn't I? I am not going to be good any longer."

"Why, 't won't help de matter to be *bad,* will it, Harry? 'Cause you hate Tom Gordon, does you want to act just like him?"

"No!" said Harry, "I won't be like him, but I'll have my revenge! Old Dred has been talking to me again, this morning. He always did stir me up so that I could hardly live; and I won't stand it any longer!"

"Chile," said Milly, "you take care! Keep clear on him! He's in de wilderness of Sinai; he is with de blackness, and darkness, and tempest. He han't come to de heavenly Jerusalem. O! O! honey! dere's a blood of sprinkling dat speaketh better things dan dat of Abel.[11] Jerusalem above is *free*—is *free,* honey; so, don't you mind, now, what happens in *dis* yer time."

"Ah, ah, Aunt Milly! this may do well enough for old women like you; but, stand opposite to a young fellow like me, with good strong arms, and a pair of doubled fists, and a body and soul just as full of fight as they can be; it don't answer to go to telling about a heavenly Jerusalem! We want something here. We'll have it too! How do you know there is any heaven, any how?"

"Know it?" said Milly, her eye kindling, and striking her staff on the ground. "Know it? I knows it by de *hankering arter it* I got in here;" giving her broad chest a blow which made it resound like a barrel. "De Lord knowed what he was 'bout when he made us. When he made babies rooting round, with der poor little mouths open, he made milk, and de mammies for 'em too. Chile, we's nothing but great babies, dat an't got our eyes opened—rooting round and round; but de Father'll feed us yet—he will so."

"He's a long time about it," said Harry, sullenly.

"Well, chile, an't it a long time 'fore your corn sprouts—a long time 'fore it gets into de ears?—but you plants, for all dat. What's dat to me what I is here?—Shan't I reign with de Lord Jesus?"

"I don't know," said Harry.

"Well, honey, *I does!* Jest so sure as I's standing on dis yer ground, I knows in a few years I shall be reigning with de Lord Jesus, and a casting my crown at his feet. Dat's what I knows. Flesh and blood didn't reveal it unto me, but de Spirit of de Father. It's no odds to me what I does here; every road leads straight to glory, and de glory an't got no end to it!" And Milly uplifted her voice in a favorite stave—

> *"When we've been dere ten thousand years,*
> *Bright shining like de sun,*
> *We've no less days to sing God's praise*
> *Than when we first begun."*

"Chile," said she to him, solemnly, "I an't a fool. Does ye s'pose dat I thinks folks has any business to be sitting on der cheers all der life long, and working me, and living on my money? Why, I knows dey han't! An't it all wrong, from fust to last, de way dey makes merchandise o' us! Why, I knows it is; but I's still about it, for de Lord's sake. I don't work for Miss Loo—I works for de Lord Jesus; and he is good pay—no mistake, now I tell you."

"Well," said Harry, a little shaken, but not convinced, "after all, there isn't much use in trying to do any other way. But you're lucky in feeling so, Aunt Milly; but I can't."

"Well, chile, any way, don't you do nothing rash, and don't you hear *him.* Dat ar way out is through seas of blood. Why, chile, would you turn against Miss Nina? Chile, if they get a going, they won't spare nobody. Don't you start up dat ar tiger; 'cause, I tell ye, ye can't chain him, if ye do!"

"Yes," said Harry, "I see it's all madness, perfect madness; there's no use thinking, no use talking. Well, good-morning, Aunt Milly. Peace go with you!" And the young man started his horse, and was soon out of sight.

CHAPTER XIX

The Conspirators

WE OWE OUR READERS NOW some words of explanation respecting the new personage who has been introduced into our history; therefore we must go back somewhat, and allude to certain historical events of painful significance.

It has been a problem to many, how the system of slavery in America should unite the two apparent inconsistencies of a code of slave-laws more severe than that of any other civilized nation, with an average practice at least as indulgent as any other; for, bad as slavery is at the best, it may yet be admitted that the practice, as a whole, has been less cruel in this country than in many. An examination into history will show us that the cruelty of the laws resulted from the effects of indulgent practice. During the first years of importation of slaves into South Carolina, they enjoyed many privileges. Those who lived in intelligent families, and had any desire to learn, were instructed in reading and writing. Liberty was given them to meet in assemblies of worship, in class-meetings, and otherwise, without the presence of white witnesses; and many were raised to situations of trust and consequence. The result of this was the development of a good degree of intelligence and manliness among the slaves. There arose among them grave, thoughtful, energetic men, with their ears and eyes open, and their minds constantly awake to compare and reason.

When minds come into this state, in a government professing to be founded on principles of universal equality, it follows that almost every public speech, document, or newspaper, becomes an incendiary publication.

Of this fact the southern slave states have ever exhibited the most singular unconsciousness. Documents containing sentiments most dangerous for slaves to hear have been publicly read and applauded among them. The slave has heard, amid shouts, on the Fourth of

July, that his masters held the truth to be self-evident, that all men were born equal, and had an *inalienable right* to life, liberty, and the pursuit of happiness; and that all governments derive their just power from the consent of the governed. Even the mottoes of newspapers have embodied sentiments of the most insurrectionary character.

Such inscriptions as "Resistance to tyrants is obedience to God"[1] stand, to this day, in large letters, at the head of southern newspapers; while speeches of senators and public men, in which the principles of universal democracy are asserted, are constant matters of discussion. Under such circumstances, it is difficult to induce the servant, who feels that he is a man, to draw those lines which seem so obvious to masters, by whom this fact has been forgotten. Accordingly we find that when the discussions for the admission of Missouri as a slave state produced a wave whose waters undulated in every part of the Union, there were found among the slaves men of unusual thought and vigor, who were no inattentive witnesses and listeners. The discussions were printed in the newspapers; and what was printed in the newspapers was further discussed at the post-office door, in the tavern, in the bar-room, at the dinner-party, where black servants were listening behind the chairs. A free colored man in the city of Charleston, named Denmark Vesey, was the one who had the hardihood to seek to use the electric fluid in the cloud thus accumulated. He conceived the hopeless project of imitating the example set by the American race, and achieving independence for the blacks.

Our knowledge of this man is derived entirely from the printed reports of the magistrates who gave an account of the insurrection,[2] of which he was the instigator, and who will not, of course, be supposed to be unduly prejudiced in his favor. They state that he was first brought to the country by one Captain Vesey, a young lad, distinguished for personal beauty and great intelligence, and that he proved, for twenty years, a most faithful slave; but, on drawing a prize of fifteen hundred dollars in the lottery, he purchased his freedom of his master, and worked as a carpenter in the city of Charleston. He was distinguished for strength and activity, and, as the accounts state, maintained such an irreproachable character, and enjoyed so much the confidence of the whites, that when he was accused, the charge was not only discredited, but he was not even arrested for several days after, and not till the proof of his guilt had become too strong to be doubted. His historians go on, with considerable naïveté, to remark:

"It is difficult to conceive *what motive he had to enter into such a plot,* unless it was the one mentioned by one of the witnesses, who said that Vesey had *several children who were slaves,* and that he said, on one occasion, *he wished he could see them free,* as he himself artfully remarked in his defense on his trial."

It appears that the project of rousing and animating the blacks to this enterprise occupied the mind of Vesey for more than four years, during which time he was continually taking opportunities to animate and inspire the spirits of his countrymen. The account states that the speeches in Congress of those opposed to the admission of Missouri into the Union, perhaps garbled and misrepresented, furnished him with ample means for inflaming the minds of the colored population.

"Even while walking in the street," the account goes on to say, "he was not idle; for, if his companion bowed to a white person, as slaves universally do, he would rebuke him, and observe, 'that all men were born equal, and that he was surprised that any one would degrade himself by such conduct; that he would never cringe to the whites; nor ought any one to, who had the feelings of a man.'* When answered, 'We are slaves,' he would say, sarcastically and indignantly, 'You deserve to remain slaves!' And, if he were further asked, 'What can we do?' he would remark, 'Go and buy a spelling-book, and read the fable of "Hercules and the Wagoner." '[3] He also sought every opportunity of entering into conversation with white persons, during which conversation he would artfully introduce some bold remark on slavery; and sometimes, when, from the character he was conversing with, he found he might be still bolder, he would go so far that, had not his declarations been clearly proved, they would scarcely have been credited."

But his great instrument of influence was a book that has always been prolific of insurrectionary movements, under all systems of despotism.

"He rendered himself perfectly familiar with all those parts of Scripture which he thought he could pervert to his purpose, and would readily quote them to prove that slavery was contrary to the laws of God, and that slaves were bound to attempt their emancipa-

---

*These extracts are taken from the official report.

tion, however shocking and bloody might be the consequences; that such efforts would not only be pleasing to the Almighty, but were absolutely enjoined."

Vesey, in the course of time, associated with himself five slave-men of marked character—Rolla, Ned, Peter, Monday, and Gullah Jack. Of these, the account goes on to say:

"In the selection of his leaders, Vesey showed great penetration and sound judgment. Rolla was plausible, and possessed uncommon self-possession; bold and ardent, he was not to be deterred from his purpose by danger. Ned's appearance indicated that he was a man of firm nerves and desperate courage. Peter was intrepid and resolute, true to his engagements, and cautious in observing secrecy where it was necessary; he was not to be daunted nor impeded by difficulties, and, though confident of success, was careful in providing against any obstacles or casualties which might arise, and intent upon discovering every means which might be in their power, if thought of beforehand. Gullah Jack was regarded as a sorcerer, and, as such, feared by the natives of Africa, who believe in witchcraft. He was not only considered invulnerable, but that he could make others so by his charms, and that he could, and certainly would, provide all his followers with arms. He was artful, cruel, bloody; his disposition, in short, was diabolical. His influence among the Africans was inconceivable. Monday was firm, resolute, discreet, and intelligent.

"It is a melancholy truth that the general good conduct of all the leaders, except Gullah Jack, was such as rendered them objects least liable to suspicion. Their conduct had secured them not only the unlimited confidence of their owners, but they had been indulged in every comfort, and allowed every privilege compatible with their situation in the community; and, though Gullah Jack was not remarkable for the correctness of his deportment, he by no means sustained a bad character. But," adds the report, "not only were the leaders of good character, and very much indulged by their owners, but this was very generally the case with all who were convicted, many of them possessing the highest confidence of their owners, *and not one a bad character.*

"The conduct and behavior of Vesey and his five leaders during their trial and imprisonment may be interesting to many. When Vesey was tried, he folded his arms, and seemed to pay great attention to the testimony given against him, but with his eyes fixed on the floor. In this situation he remained immovable until the witnesses had been examined by the court, and cross-examined by his counsel, when he requested to be allowed to examine the witnesses himself, which he did. The evidence being closed, he addressed the court at considerable length. When he received his sentence, tears trickled down his cheeks.

"Rolla, when arraigned, affected not to understand the charge against him; and when, at his request, it was explained to him, assumed, with wonderful adroitness, astonishment and surprise. He was remarkable throughout his trial for composure and great presence of mind. When he was informed that he was convicted, and was advised to prepare for death, he appeared perfectly confounded, but exhibited no signs of fear.

"In Ned's behavior there was nothing remarkable. His countenance was stern and immovable, even while he was receiving sentence of death. From his looks it was impossible to discover or conjecture what were his feelings. Not so with Peter Poyes. In his countenance were strongly marked disappointed ambition, revenge, indignation, and an anxiety to know how far the discoveries had extended. He did not appear to fear personal consequences, for his whole behavior indicated the reverse, but exhibited an evident anxiety for the success of their plan, in which his whole soul was embarked. His countenance and behavior were the same when he received his sentence, and his only words were, on retiring, 'I suppose you'll let me see my wife and family before I die,' and that in no supplicating tone. When he was asked, a day or two after, 'If it was possible that he could see his master and family murdered, who had treated him so kindly?' he replied to the question only by a smile. In their prison, the convicts resolutely refused to make any confessions or communications which might implicate others; and Peter Poyes sternly enjoined it upon them to maintain this silence— *Do not open your lips; die silent, as you will see me do!* and in this resolute silence they met their fate. Twenty-two of the conspirators were executed upon one gallows."

The account says, "That Peter Poyes was one of the most active of the recruiting agents. All the principal conspirators kept a list of those who had consented to join them, and Peter was said, by one of the witnesses, to have had six hundred names on his list; but, so resolutely to the last did he observe his pledge of secrecy to his associates, that, of the whole number arrested and tried, not one of them belonged to his company. In fact, in an insurrection in which thousands of persons were supposed to have been implicated, only thirty-six were convicted."

Among the children of Denmark Vesey was a boy by a Mandingo[4] slave-woman, who was his father's particular favorite. The Mandingos are one of the finest of African tribes, distinguished for intelligence, beauty of form, and an indomitable pride and energy of nature. As slaves, they are considered particularly valuable by those who have tact enough to govern them, because of their great capability and their proud faithfulness; but they resent a government of brute force, and under such are always fractious and dangerous.

This boy received from his mother the name of Dred; a name not unusual among the slaves, and generally given to those of great physical force.

The development of this child's mind was so uncommon as to excite astonishment among the negroes. He early acquired the power of reading, by an apparent instinctive faculty, and would often astonish those around him with things which he had discovered in books. Like other children of a deep and fervent nature, he developed great religious ardor, and often surprised the older negroes by his questions and replies on this subject. A son so endowed could not but be an object of great pride and interest to a father like Denmark Vesey. The impression seemed to prevail universally among the negroes that this child was born for extraordinary things; and perhaps it was the yearning to acquire liberty for the development of such a mind which first led Denmark Vesey to reflect on the nature of slavery, and the terrible weights which it lays on the human intellect, and to conceive the project of liberating a race.

The Bible, of which Vesey was an incessant reader, stimulated this desire. He likened his own position of comparative education, competence, and general esteem among the whites, to that of Moses among the Egyptians; and nourished the idea that, like Moses, he was sent as a deliverer. During the process of the conspiracy, this son, though but ten years of age, was his father's confidant; and he often charged him, though he should fail in the attempt, never to be discouraged. He impressed it upon his mind that he should never submit tamely to the yoke of slavery; and nourished the idea already impressed, that some more than ordinary destiny was reserved for him. After the discovery of the plot, and the execution of its leaders, those more immediately connected with them were sold from the state, even though not proved to have participated. With the most guarded caution, Vesey had exempted this son from suspicion. It had been an agreed policy with them both, that in the presence of others they should counterfeit alienation and dislike. Their confidential meetings with each other had been stolen and secret. At the time of his father's execution, Dred was a lad of fourteen. He could not be admitted to his father's prison, but he was a witness of the undaunted aspect with which he and the other conspirators met their doom. The memory dropped into the depths of his soul, as a stone drops into the desolate depths of a dark mountain lake.

Sold to a distant plantation, he became noted for his desperate, unsubduable disposition. He joined in none of the social recreations and amusements of the slaves, labored with proud and silent assiduity, but, on the slightest rebuke or threat, flashed up with a savage fierceness, which, supported by his immense bodily strength, made him an object of dread among overseers. He was one of those of whom they gladly rid themselves; and, like a fractious horse, was sold from master to master. Finally, an overseer, hardier than the rest, determined on the task of subduing him. In the scuffle that ensued Dred struck him to the earth, a dead man, made his escape to the swamps, and was never afterwards heard of in civilized life.

The reader who consults the map will discover that the whole eastern shore of the Southern States, with slight interruptions, is belted by an immense chain of swamps, regions of hopeless disorder, where the abundant growth and vegetation of nature, sucking up its forces from the humid soil, seems to rejoice in a savage exuberance, and bid defiance to all human efforts either to penetrate or subdue. These wild regions are the homes of the alligator, the moccassin, and the rattle-snake. Evergreen trees, mingling freely with the deciduous children of the forest, form here dense jungles, verdant all the year round, and which afford shelter to numberless birds, with whose warbling the leafy desolation perpetually resounds. Climbing vines, and parasitic plants, of untold splendor and boundless exuberance of growth, twine and interlace, and hang from the heights of the highest trees pennons of gold and purple,— triumphant banners, which attest the solitary majesty of nature. A species of parasitic moss wreaths its abundant draperies from tree to tree, and hangs in pearly festoons, through which shine the scarlet berry and green leaves of the American holly.

What the mountains of Switzerland were to the persecuted Vaudois,[5] this swampy belt has been to the American slave. The constant effort to recover from thence fugitives has led to the adoption, in these states, of a separate profession, unknown at this time in any other Christian land—hunters, who train and keep dogs for the hunting of men, women, and children. And yet, with all the convenience of this profession, the reclaiming of the fugitives from these fastnesses of nature has been a work of such expense and difficulty, that the near proximity of the swamp has always been a considerable check on the otherwise absolute power of the overseer. Dred carried with him to the swamp but one solitary companion—the Bible of his father. To him it was not the messenger of peace and good-will, but the herald of woe and wrath!

As the mind, looking on the great volume of nature, sees there a reflection of its own internal passions, and seizes on that in it which sympathizes with itself,—as the fierce and savage soul delights in the roar of torrents, the thunder of avalanches, and the whirl of ocean-storms,—so is it in the great answering volume of revelation. There is something there for every phase of man's nature; and hence its endless vitality and stimulating force. Dred had heard read, in the secret meetings of conspirators, the wrathful denunciations of ancient prophets against oppression and injustice. He had read of kingdoms convulsed by plagues; of tempest, and pestilence, and locusts; of the sea cleft in twain, that an army of slaves might pass through, and of their pursuers whelmed in the returning waters. He had heard of prophets and deliverers, armed with supernatural powers, raised up for oppressed people; had pondered on the nail of Jael, the goad of Shamgar, the pitcher and lamp of Gideon; and thrilled with fierce joy as he read how Samson, with his two strong arms, pulled down the pillars of the festive temple, and whelmed his triumphant persecutors in one grave with himself.[6]

In the vast solitudes which he daily traversed, these things entered deep into his soul. Cut off from all human companionship, often going weeks without seeing a human face, there was no recurrence of every-day and prosaic ideas to check the current of the enthusiasm thus kindled. Even in the soil of the cool Saxon heart the Bible has thrown out its roots with an all-pervading energy, so that the whole frame-work of society may be said to rest on soil held together by its fibres. Even in cold and misty England, armies have been made defiant and invincible by the incomparable force and deliberate valor which it breathes into men. But, when this oriental seed, an exotic among us, is planted back in the fiery soil of a tropical heart, it bursts forth with an incalculable ardor of growth.

A stranger cannot fail to remark the fact that, though the slaves of the South are unable to read the Bible for themselves, yet most completely have its language and sentiment penetrated among them, giving a Hebraistic coloring to their habitual mode of expression. How much greater, then, must have been the force of the solitary perusal of this volume on so impassioned a nature!—a nature, too, kindled by memories of the self-sacrificing ardor with which a father and his associates had met death at the call of freedom; for none of us may deny that, wild and hopeless as this scheme was, it was still the same in kind with the more successful one which purchased for our fathers a national existence.

A mind of the most passionate energy and vehemence, thus awakened, for years made the wild solitudes of the swamp its home. That book, so full of startling symbols and vague images, had for him no interpreter but the silent courses of nature. His life passed in a kind of dream. Sometimes, traversing for weeks these desolate regions, he would compare himself to Elijah traversing for forty days and nights the solitudes of Horeb; or to John the Baptist in the wilderness, girding himself with camel's hair, and eating locusts and wild honey.[7] Sometimes he would fast and pray for days; and then voices would seem to speak to him, and strange hieroglyphics would be written upon the leaves.[8] In less elevated moods of mind, he would pursue, with great judgment and vigor, those enterprises necessary to preserve existence. The negroes lying out in the swamps are not so wholly cut off from society as might at first be imagined. The slaves of all the adjoining plantations, whatever they may pretend, to secure the good-will of their owners, are at heart secretly disposed, from motives both of compassion and policy, to favor the fugitives. They very readily perceive that, in the event of any difficulty occurring to themselves, it might be quite necessary to have a friend and protector in the swamp; and therefore they do not hesitate to supply these fugitives, so far as they are able, with anything which they may desire. The poor whites, also, who keep small shops in the neighborhood of plantations, are never particularly scrupulous, provided they can turn a penny to their own advantage; and willingly supply necessary wares in exchange for game, with which the swamp abounds.

Dred, therefore, came in possession of an excellent rifle, and never wanted for ammunition, which supplied him with an abundance of food. Besides this, there are here and there elevated spots in the swampy land, which, by judicious culture, are capable of great productiveness. And many such spots Dred had brought under cultivation, either with his own hands, or from those of other fugitives, whom he had received and protected. From the restlessness of his nature, he had not confined himself to any particular region, but had traversed the whole swampy belt of both the Carolinas, as well as that of Southern Virginia; residing a few months in one place, and a few months in another. Wherever he stopped, he formed a sort of retreat, where he received and harbored fugitives. On one occasion, he rescued a trembling and bleeding mulatto woman from the dogs of the hunters, who had pursued her into the swamp. This woman he made his wife, and appeared to entertain a very deep affection for her. He made a retreat for her, with more than common ingenuity, in the swamp adjoining the Gordon plantation; and, after that, he was more especially known in that locality. He had fixed his eye upon Harry, as a person whose ability, address, and strength of character, might make him at some day a leader in a conspiracy against the whites. Harry, in common with many of the slaves on the Gordon plantation, knew perfectly well of the presence of Dred in the neighborhood, and had often seen and conversed with him. But neither he nor any of the rest of them ever betrayed before any white person the slightest knowledge of the fact.

This ability of profound secrecy is one of the invariable attendants of a life of slavery. Harry was acute enough to know that his position was by no means so secure that he could afford to dispense with anything which might prove an assistance in some future emergency. The low white traders in the neighborhood also knew Dred well; but, as long as they could drive an advantageous trade with him, he was secure from their intervention. So secure had he been, that he had been even known to mingle in the motley throng of a camp-meeting unmolested. Thus much with regard to one who is to appear often on the stage before our history is done.

CHAPTER XX

Summer Talk at Canema

IN THE COURSE of a few days the family circle at Canema was enlarged by the arrival of Clayton's sister; and Carson, in excellent spirits, had started for a Northern watering-place. In answer to Nina's letter of invitation, Anne had come with her father, who was called to that vicinity by the duties of his profession. Nina received her with her usual gay frankness of manner; and Anne, like many others, soon found herself liking her future sister much better than she had expected. Perhaps, had Nina been in any other situation than that of hostess, her pride might have led her to decline making the agreeable to Anne, whom, notwithstanding, she very much wished to please. But she was mistress of the mansion, and had an Arab's idea of the privileges of a guest; and so she chatted, sang, and played, for her; she took her about, showed her the walks, the arbors, the flower-garden; waited on her in her own apartment, with a thousand little attentions, all the more fascinating from the kind of careless independence with which they were rendered. Besides, Nina had vowed a wicked little vow in her heart that she would ride rough-shod over Anne's dignity; that she wouldn't let her be grave or sensible, but that she should laugh and frolic with her. And Clayton could scarce help smiling at the success that soon crowned her exertions. Nina's gayety, when in full tide, had a breezy infectiousness in it, that seemed to stir up every one about her, and carry them on the tide of her own spirits; and Anne, in her company, soon found herself laughing at everything and nothing, simply because she felt gay.

To crown all, Uncle John Gordon arrived, with his cheery, jovial face; and he was one of those fearless, hit-or-miss talkers, that are invaluable in social dilemmas, because they keep something or other all the while in motion.

With him came Madam Gordon, or, as Nina commonly called her, Aunt Maria. She was a portly, finely-formed, middle-aged woman, who might have been handsome, had not the lines of care and nervous anxiety ploughed themselves so deeply in her face. Her bright, keen, hazel eyes, fine teeth, and the breadth of her ample form, attested the vitality of the old Virginia stock from whence she sprung.

"There," said Nina, to Anne Clayton, as they sat in the shady side of the veranda, "I've marshalled Aunt Maria up into Aunt Nesbit's room, and there they will have a comfortable dish of lamentation over me."

"Over you?" said Anne.

"Yes—over me, to be sure!—that's the usual order of exercises. Such a setting down as I shall get! They'll count up on their fingers all the things I ought to know and don't, and ought to do and can't. I believe that's the way relatives always show their affection—aunts in particular—by mourning over you."

"And what sort of a list will they make out?" said Anne.

"O, bless me, that's easy enough. Why, there's Aunt Maria, is a perfectly virulent housekeeper—really insane, I believe, on that subject. Why, she chases up every rat and mouse and cockroach, every particle of dust, every scrap of litter. She divides her hours, and is as punctual as a clock. She rules her household with a rod of iron, and makes everybody stand round; and tells each one how many times a day they may wink. She keeps accounts like a very dragon, and always is sure to pounce on anybody that is in the least out of the way. She cuts out clothes by the bale; she sews, and she knits, and she jingles keys. And all this kind of bustle she calls housekeeping! Now, what do you suppose she must think of me, who just put on my hat in the morning, and go sailing down the walks, looking at the flowers, till Aunt Katy calls me back, to know what my orders are for the day?"

"Pray, who is Aunt Katy?" said Anne.

"O, she is my female prime minister; and she is very much like some prime ministers I have studied about in history, who always contrive to have their own way, let what will come. Now, when Aunt Katy comes and wants to know, so respectfully, 'What Miss Nina is going to have for dinner,' do you suppose she has the least expectation of getting anything that I order? She always has fifty objections to anything that I propose. For sometimes the fit comes over me to try to be *housekeepy,* like Aunt Maria; but it's no go, I can tell you. So, when she has proved that everything that I propose is the height of absurdity, and shown conclusively that there's nothing fit to be eaten in the neighborhood, by that time I am reduced to a proper state of mind. And, when I humbly say, 'Aunt Katy, what *shall* we do?' then she gives a little cough, and out comes the whole program, just as she had arranged it the night before. And so it goes. As to accounts, why, Harry has to look after them. I detest everything about money, except the spending of it—I have rather a talent for that. Now, just think how awfully all this must impress poor Aunt Maria! What sighings, and rollings up of eyes, and shakings of heads, there are over me! And, then, Aunt Nesbit is always dinging at me about improving my mind! And improving my mind means reading some horrid, stupid, boring old book, just as she does! Now, I like the idea of improving my mind. I am sure it wants improving, bad enough; but, then, I can't help thinking that racing through the garden, and cantering through the woods, improves it faster than getting asleep over books. It seems to me that books are just like dry hay—very good when there isn't any fresh grass to be had. But I'd rather be out and eat what's growing. Now, what people call nature never bores me; but almost every book I ever saw does. Don't you think people are made differently? Some like books, and some like things; don't you think so?"

"I can give you a good fact on your side of the argument," said Clayton, who had come up behind them during the conversation.

"I didn't know I was arguing; but I shall be glad to have anything on my side," said Nina, "of course."

"Well, then," said Clayton, "I'll say that the books that have influenced the world the longest, the widest, and deepest, have been written by men who attended to *things* more than to books; who, as you say, eat what was growing, instead of dry hay. Homer couldn't have had much to read in his time, nor the poets of the Bible; and they have been fountains for all ages. I don't believe Shakspeare was much of a reader."

"Well, but," said Anne, "don't you think that, for us common folks, who are not going to be either Homers or Shakspeares, that it's best to have two strings to our bow, and to gain instruction both from books and things?"

"To be sure," said Clayton, "if we only use books aright. With many people, reading is only a form of mental indolence, by which they escape the labor of thinking for themselves. Some persons are like Pharaoh's lean kine;[1] they swallow book upon book, but remain as lean as ever."

"My grandfather used to say," said Anne, "that the Bible and Shakspeare were enough for a woman's library."

"Well," said Nina, "I don't like Shakspeare, there! I'm coming out flat with it. In the first place, I don't understand half he says; and, then, they talk about his being so very natural! I'm sure I never heard people talk as he makes them. Now, did you ever hear people talk in blank verse, with every now and then one or two lines of rhyme, as his characters do when they go off in long speeches? Now, did you?"

"As to that," said Clayton, "it's about half and half. His conversations have just about the same resemblance to real life that acting at the opera has. It is not natural for Norma[2] to burst into a song when she discovers the treachery of her husband. You make that concession to the nature of the opera, in the first place; and then, with that reserve, all the rest strikes you as natural, and the music gives an added charm to it. So, in Shakspeare, you concede that the plays are to be poems, and that the people are to talk in rhythm, and with all the exaltation of poetic sentiment; and, that being admitted, their conversations may seem natural."

"But I can't *understand* a great deal that Shakspeare says," said Nina.

"Because so many words and usages are altered since he wrote," said Clayton. "Because there are so many allusions to incidents that have passed, and customs that have perished, that you have, as it were, to acquire his language before you can understand him. Suppose a poem were written in a foreign tongue; you couldn't say whether you liked it or disliked it till you could read the language. Now, my opinion is, that there is a liking for Shakspeare hidden in your nature, like a seed that has not sprouted."

"What makes you think so?"

"O, I see it in you, just as a sculptor sees a statue in a block of marble."

"And are you going to chisel it out?" said Nina.

"With your leave," said Clayton. "After all, I like your sincerity in saying what you do think. I have often heard ladies profess an admiration for Shakspeare that I knew couldn't be real. I knew that they had neither the experience of life, nor the insight into human nature, really to appreciate what is in him; and that their liking for him was all a worked-up affair, because they felt it would be very shocking not to like him."

"Well," said Nina, "I'm much obliged to you for all the sense you find in my nonsense. I believe I shall keep you to translate my fooleries into good English."

"You know I'm quite at your disposal," said Clayton, "for that or anything else."

At this moment the attention of Nina was attracted by loud exclamations from that side of the house where the negro cottages were situated.

"Get along off! don't want none o' yo old trash here! No, no, Miss Nina don't want none o' yo old fish! She's got plenty of niggers to ketch her own fish."

"Somebody taking my name in vain in those regions," said Nina, running to the other end of the veranda. "Tomtit," she said to that young worthy, who lay flat on his back, kicking up his heels in the sun, waiting for his knives to clean themselves, "pray tell me what's going on there!"

"Laws, missis," said Tom, "it's just one of dese yer poor white trash, coming round here trying to sell one thing o' nother. Miss Loo says it won't do 'courage 'em, and I's de same 'pinion."

"Send him round here to me," said Nina, who, partly from humanity, and partly from a spirit of contradiction, had determined to take up for the poor white folks, on all occasions. Tomtit ran accordingly, and soon brought to the veranda a man whose wretchedly tattered clothing scarcely formed a decent covering. His cheeks were sunken and hollow, and he stood before Nina with a cringing, half-ashamed attitude; and yet one might see that, with better dress and better keeping, he might be made to assume the appearance of a handsome, intelligent man. "What do you ask for your fish?" she said to him.

"Anything ye pleases!"

"Where do you live?" said Nina, drawing out her purse.

"My folks 's staying on Mr. Gordon's place."

"Why don't you get a place of your own to stay on?" said Nina. There was an impatient glance flashed from the man's eye, but it gave place immediately to his habitual cowed expression, as he said,

"Can't get work—can't get money—can't get nothing."

"Dear me," said her Uncle John, who had been standing for a

moment listening to the conversation. "This must be husband of that poor hobgoblin that has lighted down on my place lately. Well, you may as well pay him a good price for his fish. Keep them from starving one day longer, may be." And Nina paid the man a liberal sum, and dismissed him.

"I suppose, now, all my eloquence wouldn't make Rose cook those fish for dinner," said Nina.

"Why not, if you told her to?" said Aunt Maria, who had also descended to the veranda.

"Why not?—Just because, as she would say, she hadn't *laid out* to do it."

"That's not the way *my* servants are taught to do!" said Aunt Maria.

"I'll warrant not," said Nina. "But yours and mine are quite different affairs, aunt. They all do as they have a mind to, in my '*diggings.*'³ All I stipulate for is a little of the same privilege."

"That man's wife and children have come and '*squatted*' down on my place," said Mr. Gordon, laughing; "and so, Nin, all you paid for his fish is just so much saving to me."

"Yes, to be sure! Mr. Gordon is just one of those men that will have a tribe of shiftless hangers on at his heels!" said Mrs. Gordon.

"Well, bless my soul! what's a fellow to do? Can't see the poor heathen starve, can we? If society could only be organized over, now, there would be hope for them. The brain ought to control the hands; but among us the hands try to set up for themselves;—and see what comes of it!"

"Who do you mean by brain?" said Nina.

"Who?—Why, *we* upper crust, to be sure! We educated people! We ought to have an absolute sway over the working classes, just as the brain rules the hand. It must come to that, at last—no other arrangement is possible. The white working classes can't take care of themselves, and must be put into a condition for us to take care of them. What is liberty to them?—Only a name—liberty to be hungry and naked, that's all. It's the strangest thing in the world, how people stick to names! I suppose that fellow, up there, would flare up terribly at being put in with my niggers; and yet he and his children are glad of the crumbs that fall from their table! It's astonishing to me how, with such examples before them, any decent man can be so stone blind as to run a tilt against slavery. Just compare the free working classes with our slaves! Dear me! the blindness of people in this world! It's too much for my patience, particularly in hot weather!" said Mr. John, wiping his face with a white pocket-handkerchief.

"Well, but, Uncle John," said Nina, "my dear old gentleman, you haven't travelled, as I have."

"No, child! I thank the Lord I never stepped my foot out of a slave state, and I never mean to," said Uncle John.

"But you ought to see the *northern* working people," said Nina. "Why, the Governors of the States are farmers, sometimes, and work with their own men. The brain and the hand go together, in each one—not one great brain to fifty pair of hands. And, I tell you, work is *done* up there very differently from what's done here! Just look at our ploughs and our hoes!—the most ridiculous things that I ever saw. I should think one of them would weigh ten pounds!"

"Well, if you don't have 'em heavy enough to go into the ground by their own weight, these cussed lazy nigs won't do anything with them. They'd break a dozen Yankee hoes in a forenoon," said Uncle John.

"Now," said Nina, "Uncle John, you dear old heathen, you! do let me tell you a little how it is there. I went up into New Hampshire, once, with Livy Ray, to spend a vacation. Livy's father is a farmer; works part of every day with his own men; hoes, digs, plants; but he is Governor of the State. He has a splendid farm—all in first-rate order; and his sons, with two or three hired men, keep it in better condition than our places ever saw. Mr. Ray is a man who reads a great deal; has a fine library, and he's as much of a gentleman as you'll often see. There are no high and low *classes* there. Everybody works; and everybody seems to have a good time. Livy's mother has a beautiful dairy, spring house, and two strong women to help her; and everything in the house looks beautifully; and, for the greater part of the day, the house seems so neat and still, you wouldn't know anything had been done in it. Seems to me this is better than making slaves of all the working classes, or having any working classes at all."

"How wise young ladies always are!" said Uncle John. "Undoubtedly the millennium is begun in New Hampshire! But, pray, my dear, what part do *young* ladies take in all this? Seems to me, Nin, *you* haven't picked up much of this improvement in person."

"O, as to that, I labor in my vocation," said Nina; "that is, of enlightening dull, sleepy old gentlemen, who never travelled out of the state they were born in, and don't know what can be done. I come as a missionary to them; I'm sure that's work enough for one."

"Well," said Aunt Maria, "I know I am as great a slave as any of the poor whites, or negroes either. There isn't a soul in my whole troop that pretends to take any care, except me, either about themselves or their children, or anything else."

"I hope that isn't a slant at me!" said Uncle John, shrugging his shoulders.

"I must say you are as bad as any of them," said Aunt Maria.

"There it goes!—now I'm getting it!" said Uncle John. "I declare, the next time we get a preacher out here, I'm going to make him hold forth on the duties of wives!"

"And husbands, too!" said Aunt Maria.

"Do," said Nina; "I should like a little prospective information."

Nina, as often, spoke before she thought. Uncle John gave a malicious look at Clayton. Nina could not recall the words. She colored deeply, and went on hastily to change the subject.

"At any rate, I know that aunt, here, has a much harder time than housekeepers do in the free states. Just the shoes she wears out chasing up her negroes would hire help enough to do all her work. They used to have an idea up there, that all the southern ladies did was to lie on the sofa. I used to tell them it was as much as they knew about it."

"*Your* cares don't seem to have worn you much!" said Uncle John.

"Well, they will, Uncle John, if you don't behave better. It's enough to break anybody down to keep you in order."

"I wish," said Uncle John, shrugging up his shoulders, and looking quizzically at Clayton, "somebody would take warning!"

"For my part," said Aunt Maria, "I know one thing; I'd be glad to get rid of my negroes. Sometimes I think life is such a burden that I don't think it's worth having."

"O, no, you don't, mother!" said Uncle John; "not with such a charming husband as you've got, who relieves you from all care so perfectly!"

"I declare," said Nina, looking along the avenue, "what's that? Why, if there isn't old Tiff, coming along with his children!"

"Who is he?" said Aunt Maria.

"O, he belongs to one of these miserable families," said Aunt Nesbit, "that have squatted in the pine-woods somewhere about here—a poor, worthless set! but Nina has a great idea of patronizing them."

"Clear Gordon, every inch of her!" said Aunt Maria, as Nina ran down to meet Tiff. "Just like her uncle!"

"Come, now, old lady, I'll tell of *you,* if you don't take care!" said Mr. Gordon. "Didn't I find you putting up a basket of provisions for those folks you scolded me so for taking in?"

"Scold, Mr. Gordon? I never scold!"

"I beg pardon—that you reproved me for!"

Ladies generally are not displeased for being reproached for their charities; and Aunt Maria, whose bark, to use a vulgar proverb, was infinitely worse than her bite, sat fanning herself, with an air of self-complacency. Meanwhile, Nina had run down the avenue, and was busy in a confidential communication with Tiff. On her return, she came skipping up the steps, apparently in high glee.

"O, Uncle John! there's the greatest fun getting up! You must all go, certainly! What do you think? Tiff says there's to be a camp-meeting[4] in the neighborhood, only about five miles off from his place. Let's make up a party, and all go!"

"That's the time of day!" said Uncle John. "I enrol myself under your banner, at once. I am open to improvement! Anybody wants to convert me, here I am!"

"The trouble with you, Uncle John," said Nina, "is that you don't *stay* converted. You are just like one of these heavy fishes—you bite very sharp, but, before anybody can get you fairly on to the bank, you are flapping and floundering back into the water, and down you go into your sins again. I know at least three ministers who thought they had hooked you out; but they were mistaken."

"For my part," said Aunt Maria, "I think these camp-meetings do more harm than good. They collect all the scum and the riff-raff of the community, and I believe there's more drinking done at camp-meetings in one week than is done in six anywhere else. Then, of course, all the hands will want to be off; and Mr. Gordon has brought them up so that they feel dreadfully abused if they are not in with everything that's going on. I shall set down *my* foot, this year, that they shan't go any day except Sunday."

"My wife knows that she was always celebrated for having the handsomest foot in the county, and so she is always setting it down at *me!*" said Mr. Gordon; "for she knows that a pretty foot is irresistible with me."

"Mr. Gordon, how can you talk so? I should think that you'd got old enough not to make such silly speeches!" said Aunt Maria.

"Silly speeches! It's a solemn fact, and you won't hear anything truer at the camp-meeting!" said Uncle John. "But come, Clayton, will you go? My dear fellow, your grave face will be an appropriate ornament to the scene, I can assure you; and, as to Miss Anne, it won't do for an old fellow like me, in this presence, to say what a happiness it would be."

"I suspect," said Anne, "Edward is afraid he may be called on for some of the services. People are always taking him for a clergyman, and asking him to say grace at meals, and to conduct family prayers, when he is travelling among strangers."

"It's a comment on our religion, that these should be thought peculiar offices of clergymen," said Clayton. "Every Christian man ought to be ready and willing to take them."

"I honor that sentiment!" said Uncle John. "A man ought not to be ashamed of his religion anywhere, no more than a soldier of his colors. I believe there's more religion hid in the hearts of honest laymen, now, than is plastered up behind the white cravats of clergymen; and they ought to come out with it. Not that I have any disrespect for the clergy, either," said Uncle John. "Fine men—a little stiffish, and don't call things by good English names. Always talking about dispensation, and sanctification, and edification, and so forth; but I like them. They are sincere. I suppose they wouldn't any of them give me a chance for heaven, because I rip out with an oath, every now and then. But, the fact is, what with niggers, and overseers, and white trash, my chances of salvation are dreadfully limited. I can't help swearing, now and then, if I was to die for it. They say it's dreadfully wicked; but I feel more Christian when I let out than when I keep in!"

"Mr. Gordon," said Aunt Maria, reprovingly, "do consider what you're saying!"

"My dear, I *am* considering. I am considering all the time! I never do anything else but consider—except, as I said before, every now and then, when what's-his-name gets the advantage over me. And, hark you, Mrs. G., let's have things ready at our house, if any of the clergy would like to spend a week or so with us; and we could get them up some meetings, or any little thing in their line. I always like to show respect for them."

"Our beds are *always* prepared for company, Mr. Gordon," said Aunt Maria, with a stately air.

"O, yes, yes, I don't doubt that! I only meant some special preparation—some little fatted-calf killing, and so on."

"Now," said Nina, "shall we set off to-morrow morning?"

"Agreed!" said Uncle John.

CHAPTER XXI

Tiff's Preparations

THE ANNOUNCEMENT of the expected camp-meeting produced a vast sensation at Canema, in other circles beside the hall. In the servants' department, everybody was full of the matter, from Aunt Katy down to Tomtit. The women were thinking over their available finery; for these gatherings furnish the negroes with the same opportunity of display that Grace Church[1] does to the Broadway belles. And so, before Old Tiff, who had brought the first intelligence to the plantation, had time to depart, Tomtit had trumpeted the news through all the cluster of negro-houses that skirted the right side of the mansion, proclaiming that "dere was gwine to be a camp-meeting, and tip-top work of grace, and Miss Nina was going to let all de niggers go." Old Tiff, therefore, found himself in a prominent position in a group of negro-women, among whom Rose, the cook, was conspicuous.

"Law, Tiff, ye gwine? and gwine to take your chil'en? ha! ha! ha!" said she. "Why, Miss Fanny, dey'll tink Tiff's yer mammy! Ho! ho! ho!"

"Yah! yah! Ho! ho! ho!" roared in a chorus of laughter on all sides, doing honor to Aunt Rosy's wit; and Tomtit, who hung upon the skirts of the crowd, threw up the fragment of a hat in the air, and kicked it in an abandon of joy, regardless of the neglected dinner-knives. Old Tiff, mindful of dignities, never failed to propitiate Rose, on his advents to the plantation, with the gift which the "wise man saith maketh friends;" and, on the present occasion, he had enriched her own peculiar stock of domestic fowl by the present of a pair of young partridge-chicks, a nest of which he had just captured, intending to bring them up by hand, as he did his children. By this discreet course, Tiff stood high where it was of most vital consequence that he should so stand; and many a choice morsel did Rose cook for him in secret, besides imparting to him most invaluable recipes on the culture and raising of sucking babies. Old Hundred, like many other persons, felt that general attention lavished on any other celebrity was so much taken from his own merits, and, therefore, on the present occasion, sat regarding Tiff's evident popularity with a cynical eye. At last, coming up, like a wicked fellow as he was, he launched his javelin at Old Tiff, by observing to his wife,

"I's 'stonished at you, Rose! *You*, cook to de Gordons, and making youself so cheap—so familiar with de poor white folks' niggers!"

Had the slant fallen upon himself, personally, Old Tiff would probably have given a jolly crow, and laughed as heartily as he generally did if he happened to be caught out in a rain-storm; but the reflection on his family connection fired him up like a torch, and his eyes flashed through his big spectacles like fire-light through windows.

"You go 'long, talking 'bout what you don' know nothing 'bout! I like to know what you knows 'bout de old Virginny fam'lies? *Dem's* de real old stock! You Car'lina folks come from *dem*, stick and stock, every blest one of you! De Gordons is a nice family— an't nothing to say agin de Gordons—but whar was you raised, dat ye didn't hear 'bout de Peytons? Why, old Gen'al Peyton, didn't he use to ride with six black horses afore him, as if he'd been a king? Dere wan't one of dem horses dat hadn't a tail as long as my arm. *You* never see no such critters in *your* life!"

"I han't, han't I?" said Old Hundred, now, in his turn, touched in a vital point. "Bless me, if I han't seen de Gordons riding out with der eight horses, any time o' day!"

"Come, come, now, dere wasn't so many!" said Rose, who had her own reasons for staying on Tiff's side. "Nobody never rode with eight horses!"

"Did too! You say much more, I'll make sixteen on 'em! 'Fore my blessed master, how dese yer old niggers will lie! Dey's always zaggerating der families. Makes de very har rise on my head, to hear dese yer old niggers talk, dey lie so!" said Old Hundred.

"You tink folks dat take to lying is using up your business, don't ye?" said Tiff. "But, I tell you, any one dat says a word agin de Peytons got me to set in with!"

"Laws, dem chil'en an't Peytons!" said Old Hundred; "dey's

Crippses; and I like to know who ever hearn of de Crippses? Go
way! don't tell me nothing about dem Crippses! Dey's poor white
folks! A body may see *dat* sticking out all over 'em!"

"You shut up!" said Tiff. "I don't b'lieve you was born on de
Gordon place, 'cause you an't got no manners. I spects you some
old, second-hand nigger, Colonel Gordon must a took for debt,
some time, from some of dese yer mean Tennessee families, dat
don' know how to keep der money when dey gets it. Der niggers is
allers de meanest kind. 'Cause all de real Gordon niggers is ladies
and gen'lemen—every one of 'em! " said Old Tiff, like a true orator,
bent on carrying his audience along with him.

A general shout chorused this compliment; and Tiff, under cover
of the applause, shook up his reins, and rode off in triumph.

"Dar, now, you aggravating old nigger," said Rose, turning to
her bosom lord, "I hope yer got it now! De plaguest old nigger dat
ever I see! And you, Tom, go 'long and clean your knives, if yer
don't mean to be cracked over!"

Meanwhile Tiff, restored to his usual tranquillity, ambled along
homeward behind his one-eyed horse, singing "I'm bound for the
land of Canaan," with some surprising variations.

At last Miss Fanny, as he constantly called her, interposed with a
very pregnant question.

"Uncle Tiff, where is the land of Canaan?"[2]

"De Lord-a-mercy, chile, dat ar's what I'd like to know, myself."

"Is it heaven?" said Fanny.

"Well, I reckon so," said Tiff, dubiously.

"Is it where ma is gone?" said Fanny.

"Chile, I reckon it is," said Tiff.

"Is it down under ground?" said Fanny.

"Why, no! ho! ho! honey!" said Tiff, laughing heartily. "What
put dat ar in your head, Miss Fanny?"

"Didn't ma go that way?" said Fanny; "down through the
ground?"

"Lordy, no, chile! Heaven's up!" said Tiff, pointing up to the intense blue sky which appeared through the fringy hollows of the
pine-trees above them.

"Is there any stairs anywhere? or any ladder to get up by?" said
Fanny. "Or do they walk to where the sky touches the ground, and
get up? Perhaps they climb up on the rainbow."

"I don' know, chile, how dey works it," said Uncle Tiff. "Dey gets dar somehow. I's studdin' upon dat ar. I's gwine to camp-meeting to find out. I's been to plenty of dem ar, and I never could quite see clar. 'Pears like dey talks about everything else more 'n dey does about dat. Dere's de Methodists,[3] dey cuts up de Presbyter'ans; and de Presbyter'ans pitches into de Methodists; and den both on 'em's down on de 'Piscopals. My ole mist' was 'Piscopal, and I never seed no harm in 't. And de Baptists[4] think dey an't none on 'em right; and, while dey's all a blowing out at each other, dat ar way, I's a wondering whar's de way to Canaan. It takes a mighty heap o' larning to know about dese yer things, and I an't got no larning. I don' know nothing, only de Lord, he 'peared to your ma, and he knows de way, and he took her. But, now, chile, I's gwine to fix you up right smart, and take you, Teddy, and de baby, to dis yer camp-meeting, so you can seek de Lord in yer youth."

"Tiff, if you please, I'd rather not go!" said Fanny, in an apprehensive tone.

"O, bress de Lord, Miss Fanny, why not? Fust-rate times dere."

"There'll be too many people. I don't want them to see us."

The fact was, that Rose's slant speech about Tiff's maternal relationship, united with the sneers of Old Hundred, had their effect upon Fanny's mind. Naturally proud, and fearful of ridicule, she shrank from the public display which would thus be made of their family condition; yet she would not for the world have betrayed to her kind old friend the real reason of her hesitation. But Old Tiff's keen eye had noticed the expression of the child's countenance at the time. If anybody supposes that the faithful old creature's heart was at all wounded by the perception, they are greatly mistaken.

To Tiff it appeared a joke of the very richest quality; and, as he rode along in silence for some time, he indulged himself in one of his quiet, long laughs, actually shaking his old sides till the tears streamed down his cheeks.

"What's the matter with you, Tiff?" said Fanny.

"O, Miss Fanny, Tiff knows!—Tiff knows de reason ye don't want to go to camp-meeting. Tiff's seen it in yer face—ye ho! ho! ho! Miss Fanny, is you 'fraid dey'll take Old Tiff for yer mammy?—ye ho! ho! ho!—for yer mammy?—and Teddy's, and de baby's?—bless his little soul!" And the amphibious old creature rollicked over the idea with infinite merriment. "Don't I look like it, Miss Fanny? Lord, ye por dear lamb, can't folks see ye's a born lady, with yer white, little hands? Don't ye be 'feared, Miss Fanny!"

"I know it's silly," said Fanny; "but, beside, I don't like to be called *poor white folksy!*"

"O, chile, it's only dem mean niggers! Miss Nina's allers good to ye, an't she? Speaks to ye so handsome! Ye must memorize dat ar, Miss Fanny, and talk like Miss Nina. I's 'feard, now yer ma's dead, ye'll fall into some o' my nigger ways of talking. 'Member you mustn't talk like Old Tiff, 'cause young ladies and gen'lemen mustn't talk like niggers. Now, I says 'dis and dat, dis yer and dat ar.' Dat ar is nigger talk, and por white folksy, too. Only de por white folks, dey's mis'able, 'cause niggers *knows* what's good talk, but dey doesn't. Lord, chile, Old Tiff *knows* what good talk is. An't he heard de greatest ladies and gen'lemen in de land talk? But he don't want de trouble to talk dat ar way, 'cause he's a nigger! Tiff likes his own talk—it's good enough for Tiff. Tiff's talk serves him mighty well, I tell yer. But, den, white children mustn't talk so. Now, you see, Miss Nina has got de prettiest way of saying her words. Dey drops out one after another, one after another, so pretty! Now, you mind, 'cause she's coming to see us off and on—she promised so. And den you keep a good lookout how she walks, and how she holds her pocket-handkerchief. And when she sits down she kind o' gives a little flirt to her clothes, so dey all set out round her like ruffles. Dese yer little ways ladies have! Why, dese yer por white folks, did yer ever mind der settin' down? Why, dey jist slaps down into a chair like a spoonful o' mush, and der clothes all stick tight about 'em. I don't want nothing *poor white folksy* 'bout you. Den, if you don't understand what people's a saying to you, any time, you mustn't star, like por white chil'en, and say, 'what?' but you must say 'I beg pardon, sir,' or, 'I beg pardon, ma'am.' Dat ar's de way. And, Miss Fanny, you and Teddy, you must study yer book; 'cause, if you can't read, den dey'll be sure to say yer por white folks. And, den, Miss Fanny, you see dat ladies don't demean demselves with sweeping and scrubbing, and dem tings; and yet *dey does work,* honey! Dey sews, and dey knits; and it would be good for you to larn how to sew and knit; 'cause, you know, I can't allers make up all de clothes; 'cause, you see, young ladies haves ways wid 'em dat niggers can't get. Now, you see, Miss Fanny, all dese yer tings I was telling you, you must 'bserve. Now, you see, if you was one of dese yer por white folks, dere be no use of your trying; 'cause dat ar 'scription o' people couldn't never be ladies, if dey was waring themselves out a trying. But, you see, you's got it in you; you was born to it, honey. It's in de blood; and what's in de blood must come out—ho! ho! ho!" And, with this final laugh, Tiff drew up to his dwelling.

A busy day was before Old Tiff; for he was to set his house in order for a week's campaign. There was his corn to be hoed, his parsley to be weeded, there was his orphan family of young partridges to be cared for. And Tiff, after some considerable consideration, resolved to take them along with him in a basket; thinking, in the intervals of devotion, he should have an abundant opportunity to minister to their wants, and superintend their education. Then he went to one of his favorite springes, and brought from thence, not a fatted calf,[5] to be sure, but a fatted coon, which he intended to take with him, to serve as the basis of a savory stew on the campground. Tiff had a thriving company of pot-herbs, and a flourishing young colony of onions; so that, whatever might be true of the sermons, it was evident that the stew would lack no savor. Teddy's clothes, also, were to be passed in review; washing and ironing to be done; the baby fitted up to do honor to his name, or rather to the name of his grandfather. With all these cares upon his mind, the old creature was even more than usually alert. The day was warm, and he resolved, therefore, to perform his washing operations in the magnificent kitchen of nature. He accordingly kindled a splendid bonfire, which was soon crackling at a short distance from the house, slung over it his kettle, and proceeded to some other necessary avocations. The pine-wood, which had been imperfectly seasoned, served him the ungracious trick that pine-wood is apt to do: it crackled and roared merrily while he was present, but while he was down examining his traps in the woods went entirely out, leaving only the blackened sticks.

"Uncle Tiff," said Teddy, "the fire is all gone out!"

"Ho! ho! ho!—Has it?" said Tiff, coming up. "Curus enough! Well, bress de Lord, got all de wood left, any way; had a real bright fire, beside," said Tiff, intent on upholding the sunniest side of things. "Lord, it's de sun dat puts de fire out o' countenance. Did you ever see fire dat wouldn't go out when de sun's shining right in its face? Dat ar is a curus fact. I's minded it heaps o' times. Well, I'll jist have to come out wid my light-wood kindlings, dat's all. Bress de Lord, ho! ho! ho!" said Tiff, laughing to himself, "if dese yer an't the very sp'rit of de camp-meeting professors! Dey blazes away at de camp-meeting, and den dey's black all de year round! See 'em at de camp-meetings, you'd say dey war gwine right into de kingdom, sure enough! Well, Lord have marcy on us all! Our 'ligion's drefful poor stuff! We don' know but a despert leetle, and what we does know we don' do. De good Mas'r above must have his hands full, with us!"

CHAPTER XXII

The Worshippers

THE CAMP-MEETING is one leading feature in the American development of religion, peculiarly suited to the wide extent of country, and to the primitive habits which generally accompany a sparse population. Undoubtedly its general effects have been salutary. Its evils have been only those incident to any large gatherings, in which the whole population of a country are brought promiscuously together. As in many other large assemblies of worship, there are those who go for all sorts of reasons; some from curiosity, some from love of excitement, some to turn a penny in a small way of trade, some to scoff, and a few to pray. And, so long as the heavenly way remains straight and narrow, so long the sincere and humble worshippers will ever be the minority in all assemblies. We can give no better idea of the difference of motive which impelled the various worshippers, than by taking our readers from scene to scene, on the morning when different attendants of the meeting were making preparations to start.

Between the grounds of Mr. John Gordon and the plantation of Canema stood a log cabin, which was the trading establishment of Abijah Skinflint. The establishment was a nuisance in the eyes of the neighboring planters, from the general apprehension entertained that Abijah drove a brisk underhand trade with the negroes, and that the various articles which he disposed for sale were many of them surreptitiously conveyed to him in nightly instalments from off their own plantations. But of this nothing could be proved.

Abijah was a shrewd fellow, long, dry, lean, leathery, with a sharp nose, sharp, little gray eyes, a sharp chin, and fingers as long as bird's-claws. His skin was so dry that one would have expected that his cheeks would crackle whenever he smiled, or spoke; and he rolled in them a never-failing quid of tobacco.

Abijah was one of those over-shrewd Yankees, who leave their country for their country's good, and who exhibit, wherever they

231

settle, such a caricature of the thrifty virtue of their native land as to justify the aversion which the native-born Southerner entertains for the Yankee. Abijah drank his own whiskey,—*prudently*, however,—or, as he said, "never so as not to know what he was about."

He had taken a wife from the daughters of the land; who also drank whiskey, but less prudently than her husband, so that sometimes she did *not* know what she was about. Sons and daughters were born unto this promising couple, white-headed, forward, dirty, and ill-mannered. But, amid all domestic and social trials, Abijah maintained a constant and steady devotion to the main chance—the acquisition of money. For money he would do anything; for money he would have sold his wife, his children, even his own soul, if he had happened to have one. But that article, had it ever existed, was now so small and dry, that one might have fancied it to rattle in his lean frame like a shrivelled pea in a last year's peascod. Abijah was going to the camp-meeting for two reasons. One, of course, was to make money; and the other was to know whether his favorite preacher, Elder Stringfellow, handled the doctrine of election according to his views; for Abijah had a turn for theology, and could number off the five points of Calvinism[1] on his five long fingers, with unfailing accuracy.

It is stated in the Scriptures that the devils believe and tremble. The principal difference between their belief and Abijah's was, that he believed and did *not* tremble. Truths awful enough to have shaken the earth, and veiled the sun, he could finger over with as much unconcern as a practised anatomist the dry bones of a skeleton.

"You, Sam!" said Abijah to his only negro helot,[2] "you mind, you steady that ar bar'l, so that it don't roll out, and pour a pailful of water in at the bung. It won't do to give it to 'em too strong. Miss Skinflint, you make haste! If you don't, I shan't wait for you; 'cause, whatever the rest may do, it's important I should be on the ground early. Many a dollar lost for not being in time, in this world. Hurry, woman!"

"I am ready, but Polly an't!" said Mrs. Skinflint. "She's busy a plastering down her hair."

"Can't wait for her!" said Abijah, as he sallied out of the house to get into the wagon, which stood before the door, into which he had packed a copious supply of hams, eggs, dressed chickens, cornmeal, and green summer vegetables, to say nothing of the barrel of whiskey aforesaid.

"I say, Dad, you stop!" called Polly, from the window. "If you don't, I'll make work for you 'fore you come home; you see if I don't! Durned if I won't!"

"Come along, then, can't you? Next time we go anywhere, I'll shut you up over night to begin to dress!"

Polly hastily squeezed her fat form into a red calico dress, and, seizing a gay summer shawl, with her bonnet in her hand, rushed to the wagon and mounted, the hooks of her dress successively exploding, and flying off, as she stooped to get in.

"Durned if I knows what to do!" said she; "this yer old durned gear coat's all off my back!"

"Gals is always fools!" said Abijah, consolingly.

"Stick in a pin, Polly," said her mother, in an easy, sing-song drawl.

"Durn you, old woman, every hook is off!" said the promising young lady.

"Stick in more pins, then," said the mamma; and the vehicle of Abijah passed onward.

On the verge of the swamp, a little beyond Tiff's cabin, lived Ben Dakin.

Ben was a mighty hunter; he had the best pack of dogs within thirty miles round; and his advertisements, still to be seen standing in the papers of his native state, detailed with great accuracy the precise terms on which he would hunt down and capture any man, woman, or child, escaping from service and labor in that country. Our readers must not necessarily suppose Ben to have been a monster for all this, when they recollect that, within a few years, both the great political parties of our Union solemnly pledged themselves, as far as in them lay, to accept a similar vocation;[3] and, as many of them were in good and regular standing in churches, and had ministers to preach sermons to the same effect, we trust they'll entertain no unreasonable prejudice against Ben on this account.

In fact, Ben was a tall, broad-shouldered, bluff, hearty-looking fellow, who would do a kind turn for a neighbor with as much good-will as anybody; and, except that he now and then took a little too much whiskey, as he himself admitted, he considered himself quite as promising a candidate for the kingdom as any of the company who were going up to camp-meeting. Had any one ventured to remonstrate with Ben against the nature of his profession, he would probably have defended it by pretty much the same arguments by which modern theologians defend the institution of which it is a branch.

Ben was just one of those jovial fellows who never could bear to be left behind in anything that was going on in the community, and was always one of the foremost in a camp-meeting. He had a big, loud voice, and could roll out the chorus of hymns with astonishing effect. He was generally converted at every gathering of this kind; though, through the melancholy proclivity to whiskey, before alluded to, he usually fell from grace before the year was out. Like many other big and hearty men, he had a little, pale, withered, moonshiny wisp of a wife, who hung on his elbow much like an empty work-bag; and Ben, to do him justice, was kind to the wilted little mortal, as if he almost suspected that he had absorbed her vitality into his own exuberant growth. She was greatly given to eating clay, cleaning her teeth with snuff, and singing Methodist hymns, and had a very sincere concern for Ben's salvation. The little woman sat resignedly on the morning we speak of, while a long-limbed, broad-shouldered child, of two years, with bristly white hair, was pulling her by her ears and hair, and otherwise maltreating her, to make her get up to give him a piece of bread and molasses; and she, without seeming to attend to the child, was giving earnest heed to her husband.

"There's a despit press of business now!" said Ben. "There's James's niggers, and Smith's Polly, and we ought to be on the trail, right away!"

"O, Ben, you ought to 'tend to your salvation afore anything else!" said his wife.

"That's true enough!" said Ben; "meetings don't come every day."

"But what are we to do with dis yer 'un?" pointing to the door of an inner room.

"Dis yer 'un" was no other than a negro-woman, named Nance, who had been brought in by the dogs, the day before.

"Laws!" said his wife, "we can set her something to eat, and leave the dogs in front of the door. She can't get out."

Ben threw open the door, and displayed to view a low kind of hutch, without any other light than that between the crevices of the logs. On the floor, which was of hard-trodden earth, sat a sinewy, lean negro-woman, drawing up her knees with her long arms, and resting her chin upon them.

"Hollo, Nance, how are you?" said Ben, rather cheerily.

"Por'ly, mas'r," said the other, in a sullen tone.

"Nance, you think your old man will whale you, when he gets you?" said Ben.

"I reckons he will," said Nance; "he allers does."

"Well, Nance, the old woman and I want to go to a camp-meeting; and I'll just tell you what it is,—you stay here quiet, while we are gone, and I'll make the old fellow promise not to wallop you. I wouldn't mind taking off something of the price—that's fair, an't it?"

"Yes, mas'r!" said the woman, in the same subdued tone.

"Does your foot hurt you much?" said Ben.

"Yes, mas'r!" said the woman.

"Let me look at it," said Ben.

The woman put out one foot, which had been loosely bound up in old rags, now saturated in blood.

"I declar, if that ar dog an't a pealer!" said Ben. "Nance, you ought ter have stood still; then he wouldn't have hurt you so."

"Lord, he hurt me so I couldn't stand still!" said the woman. "It an't natur to stand still with a critter's teeth in yer foot."

"Well, I don't know as it is," said Ben, good-naturedly. "Here, Miss Dakin, you bind up this here gal's foot. Stop your noise, sir-ee!" he added, to the young aspirant for bread and molasses, who, having despatched one piece, was clamoring vigorously for another.

"I'll tell you what!" said Ben, to his wife, "I am going to talk to that ar old Elder Settle. I runs more niggers for him than any man in the county, and I know there's some reason for it. Niggers don't run into swamps when they's treated well. Folks that professes religion, I think, oughtn't to starve their niggers, no way!"

Soon the vehicle of Ben was also on the road. He gathered up the reins vigorously, threw back his head to get the full benefit of his lungs, and commenced a vehement camp-meeting melody, to the tune of

"*Am I a soldier of the cross,*
A follower of the Lamb?"[4]

A hymn, by the by, which was one of Ben's particular favorites.

We come next to Tiff's cottage, of which the inmates were astir, in the coolness of the morning, bright and early. Tiff's wagon was a singular composite article, principally of his own construction. The body of it consisted of a long packing-box. The wheels were all odd ones, that had been brought home at different times by Cripps. The shafts were hickory-poles, thinned at one end, and fastened to the wagon by nails. Some barrel-hoops bent over the top, covered by coarse white cotton cloth, formed the curtains, and a quantity of loose straw dispersed inside was the only seat. The lean, one-eyed horse was secured to this vehicle by a harness made of old ropes; but no millionnaire, however, ever enjoyed his luxuriantly-cushioned coach with half the relish with which Tiff enjoyed his equipage. It was the work of his hands, the darling of his heart, the delight of his eyes. To be sure, like other mortal darlings, it was to be admitted that it had its weak points and failings. The wheels would now and then come off, the shafts get loose, or the harness break; but Tiff was always prepared, and, on occasion of any such mishaps, would jump out and attend to them with such cheerful alacrity, that, if anything, he rather seemed to love it better for the accident. There it stands now, before the enclosure of the little cabin; and Tiff, and Fanny, and Teddy, with bustling assiduity, are packing and arranging it. The gum-tree cradle-trough took precedence of all other articles. Tiff, by the private advice of Aunt Rose, had just added to this an improvement, which placed it, in his view, tip-top among cradles. He had nailed to one end of it a long splint of elastic hickory, which drooped just over the baby's face. From this was suspended a morsel of salt pork, which this young scion of a noble race sucked with a considerable relish, while his large, round eyes opened and shut with sleepy satisfaction. This arrangement Rose had recommended, in mysterious tones, as all powerful in making sucking babies forget their mammies, whom otherwise they might pine for in a manner prejudicial to their health.

Although the day was sultry, Tiff was arrayed in his long-skirted white great-coat, as his nether garments were in too dilapidated a state to consist with the honor of the family. His white felt hat still bore the band of black crape.

"It's a 'mazin' good day, bless de Lord!" said Tiff. " 'Pears like dese yer birds would split der troats, praising de Lord! It's a mighty good zample to us, any way. You see, Miss Fanny, you never see birds put out, nor snarly like, rain or shine. Dey's allers a praising de Lord. Lord, it seems as if critters is better dan we be!" And, as Tiff spoke, he shouldered into the wagon a mighty bag of corn; but, failing in what he meant to do, the bag slid over the side, and tumbled back into the road. Being somewhat of the oldest, the fall burst it asunder, and the corn rolled into the sand, with that provoking alacrity which things always have when they go the wrong way. Fanny and Teddy both uttered an exclamation of lamentation; but Tiff held on to his sides and laughed till the tears rolled down his cheeks.

"He! he! he! ho! ho! ho! Why, dat ar is de last bag we's got, and dar's all de corn a running out in de sand! Ho! ho! ho! Lord, it's so curus!"

"Why, what are you going to do?" said Fanny.

"O, bress you, Miss Fanny," said Tiff, "I's bound to do something, any how. 'Clare for it, now, if I han't got a box!" And Tiff soon returned with the article in question, which proved too large for the wagon. The corn, however, was emptied into it *pro tem.*, and Tiff, producing his darning-needle and thimble, sat down seriously to the task of stitching up the hole.

"De Lord's things an't never in a hurry," said Tiff. "Corn and 'tatoes will have der time, and why shouldn't I? Dar," he said, after having mended the bag and replaced the corn, "dat ar's better now nor 't was before."

Besides his own store of provisions, Tiff prudently laid into his wagon enough of garden stuff to turn a penny for Miss Fanny and the children, on the camp-ground. His commissariat department, in fact, might have provoked appetite, even among the fastidious. There were dressed chickens and rabbits, the coon aforesaid, bundles of savory herbs, crisp, dewy lettuce, bunches of onions, radishes, and green peas.

"Tell ye what, chil'en," said Tiff, "we'll live like princes! And, you mind, order me round *well.* Let folks har ye; 'cause what's de use of having a nigger, and nobody knowing it?"

And, everything being arranged, Tiff got in, and jogged comfortably along. At the turn of the cross-road, Tiff, looking a little behind, saw, on the other road, the Gordon carriage coming, driven by Old Hundred, arrayed in his very best ruffled shirt, white gloves, and gold hat-band.

If ever Tiff came near having a pang in his heart, it was at that

moment; but he retreated stoutly upon the idea that, however appearances might be against them, his family was no less ancient and
honorable for that; and, therefore, putting on all his dignity, he gave
his beast an extra cut, as who should say, "I don't care."

But, as ill-luck would have it, the horse, at this instant, giving a
jerk, wrenched out the nails that fastened the shaft on one side, and
it fell, trailing dishonored on the ground. The rope harness pulled
all awry, and just at this moment the Gordon carriage swept up.

" 'Fore I'd drive sich old trash!" said Old Hundred, scornfully;
"pulls all to pieces every step! If dat ar an't a poor white folksy
'stablishment, I never seed one!"

"What's the matter?" said Nina, putting her head out. "O, Tiff!
good-morning, my good fellow. Can we help you, there? John, get
down and help him."

"Please, Miss Nina, de hosses is so full o' tickle, dis yer mornin',
I couldn't let go, no ways!" said Old Hundred.

"O, laws bless you, Miss Nina," said Tiff, restored to his usual
spirits, " 't an't nothin'. Broke in a strordinary good place dis yer
time. I ken hammer it up in a minute."

And Tiff was as good as his word; for a round stone and big nail
made all straight.

"Pray," said Nina, "how are little Miss Fanny, and the children?"

Miss Fanny! If Nina had heaped Tiff with presents, she could
not have conferred the inexpressible obligation conveyed in these
words. He bowed low to the ground, with the weight of satisfaction, and answered that "Miss Fanny and the chil'en were well."

"There," said Nina, "John, you may drive on. Do you know,
friends, I've set Tiff up for six weeks, by one word? Just saying *Miss*
Fanny has done more for him than if I'd sent him six bushels of
potatoes."

*   *   *   *

We have yet to take our readers to one more scene before we finish the review of those who were going to the camp-meeting. The
reader must follow us far beyond the abodes of man, into the recesses of that wild desolation known as the "Dismal Swamp." We
pass over vast tracts where the forest seems growing out of the water. Cypress, red cedar, sweet gum, tulip, poplar, beech, and holly,
form a goodly fellowship, waving their rustling boughs above. The

trees shoot up in vast columns, fifty, seventy-five, and a hundred feet in height; and below are clusters of evergreen gall-bushes, with their thick and glossy foliage, mingled in with swamp honeysuckles, grape-vines, twining brier, and laurels, and other shrubs, forming an impenetrable thicket. The creeping plants sometimes climb seventy or eighty feet up the largest trees, and hang in heavy festoons from their branches. It would seem impossible that human foot could penetrate the wild, impervious jungle; but we must take our readers through it, to a cleared spot, where trunks of fallen trees, long decayed, have formed an island of vegetable mould, which the art of some human hand has extended and improved. The clearing is some sixty yards long by thirty broad, and is surrounded with a natural rampart, which might well bid defiance to man or beast. Huge trees have been felled, with all their branches lying thickly one over another, in a circuit around; and nature, seconding the efforts of the fugitives who sought refuge here, has interlaced the frame-work thus made with thorny cat-briers, cables of grape-vine, and thickets of Virginia creeper, which, running wild in their exuberance, climb on to the neighboring trees, and, swinging down, again lose themselves in the mazes from which they spring, so as often to form a verdurous wall fifty feet in height. In some places the laurel, with its glossy green leaves, and its masses of pink-tipped snowy blossoms, presents to the eye, rank above rank, a wilderness of beauty. The pendants of the yellow jessamine swing to and fro in the air like censers, casting forth clouds of perfume. A thousand twining vines, with flowers of untold name, perhaps unknown as yet to the botanist, help to fill up the mosaic. The leafy ramparts sweep round on all the sides of the clearing, for the utmost care has been taken to make it impenetrable; and, in that region of heat and moisture, nature, in the course of a few weeks, admirably seconds every human effort. The only egress from it is a winding path cut through with a hatchet, which can be entered by only one person at a time; and the water which surrounds this island entirely cuts off the trail from the scent of dogs. It is to be remarked that the climate, in the interior of the swamp, is far from being unhealthy. Lumbermen, who spend great portions of the year in it, cutting shingles and staves, testify to the general salubrity of the air and water. The opinion prevails among them that the quantity of pine and other resinous trees that grow there, impart a balsamic property to the water, and impregnate the air with a healthy resinous fragrance,

which causes it to be an exception to the usual rule of the unhealth-
iness of swampy land. The soil also, when drained sufficiently for
purposes of culture, is profusely fertile. Two small cabins stood
around the border of the clearing, but the centre was occupied with
patches of corn and sweet potatoes, planted there to secure as much
as possible the advantage of sun and air.

At the time we take our readers there, the afternoon sun of a sultry June day is casting its long shadows over the place, and a whole
choir of birds is echoing in the branches. On the ground, in front of
one of the cabins, lies a negro-man, covered with blood; two
women, with some little children, are grouped beside him; and a
wild figure, whom we at once recognize as Dred, is kneeling by
him, busy in efforts to stanch a desperate wound in the neck. In
vain! The red blood spurts out at every pulsation of the heart, with
a fearful regularity, telling too plainly that it is a great life-artery
which has been laid open. The negro-woman, kneeling on the other
side, is anxiously holding some bandages, which she has stripped
from a portion of her raiment.

"O, put these on, quick—do!"

"It's no use," said Dred; "he is going!"

"O, do!—don't, don't let him go! *Can't* you save him?" said the
woman, in tones of agony.

The wounded man's eyes opened, and first fixed themselves,
with a vacant stare, on the blue sky above; then, turning on the
woman, he seemed to try to speak. He had had a strong arm; he
tries to raise it, but the blood wells up with the effort, the eye
glazes, the large frame shivers for a few moments, and then all is
still. The blood stops flowing now, for the heart has stopped beating, and an immortal soul has gone back to Him who gave it.

The man was a fugitive from a neighboring plantation—a simple-
hearted, honest fellow, who had fled, with his wife and children, to
save her from the licentious persecution of the overseer. Dred had
received and sheltered him; had built him a cabin, and protected
him for months.

A provision of the Revised Statutes of North Carolina[5] enacts
that slaves thus secreted in the swamps, not returning within a given
time, shall be considered outlawed; and that "it shall be lawful for
any person or persons whatsoever to kill and destroy such slaves,
by such ways and means as they shall think it, without any accusation or impeachment of crime for the same." It also provides that,

when any slave shall be killed in consequence of such outlawry, the value of such slave shall be ascertained by a jury, and the owner entitled to receive two thirds of the valuation from the sheriff of the county wherein the slave was killed.

In olden times, the statute provided that the proclamation of outlawry should be published on a Sabbath day, at the door of any church or chapel, or place where divine service should be performed, immediately after divine service, by the parish clerk or reader.

In the spirit of this permission, a party of negro-hunters, with dogs and guns, had chased this man, who, on this day, had unfortunately ventured out of his concealment.

He succeeded in outrunning all but one dog, which sprang up, and, fastening his fangs in his throat, laid him prostrate within a few paces of his retreat. Dred came up in time to kill the dog, but the wound, as appeared, had proved a mortal one.

As soon as the wife perceived that her husband was really dead, she broke into a loud wail.

"O, dear, he's gone! and 't was all for me he did it! O, he was so good, such a good man! O, do tell me, *is* he dead, is he?"

Dred lifted the yet warm hand in his a moment, and then dropped it heavily.

"Dead!" he said, in a deep undertone of suppressed emotion. Suddenly kneeling down beside him, he lifted his hands, and broke forth with wild vehemence:

"O, Lord God, to whom vengeance belongeth, show thyself! Lift up thyself, thou Judge of the earth, render a reward to the proud! Doubtless thou art our Father, though Abraham be ignorant of us, and Israel acknowledge us not. Thou, O Lord, art our Father, our Redeemer: thy ways are everlasting;—where is thy zeal and thy strength, and the sounding of thy bowels towards us? Are they restrained?" Then, tossing his hands to heaven, with a yet wilder gesture, he almost screamed, "O, Lord! O, Lord! how long? O, that thou wouldst rend the heavens and come down! O, let the sighings of the prisoner come before thee! Our bones are scattered at the grave's mouth, as when one cutteth and cleaveth wood! We are given as sheep to the slaughter! We are killed all the day long! O, Lord, avenge us of our adversaries!"

These words were spoken with a vehement earnestness of gesture and voice, that hushed the lamentation of the mourners. Rising up from his knees, he stood a moment looking down at the lifeless form before him. "See here," he said, "what harm had this man done? Was he not peaceable? Did he not live here in quietness, tilling the ground in the sweat of his brow? Why have they sent the hunters upon him? Because he wanted to raise his corn for himself, and not for another. Because he wanted his wife for himself, and not for another. Was not the world wide enough? Isn't there room enough under the sky? Because this man wished to eat the fruit of his own labor, the decree went forth against him, even the curse of Cain,[6] so that whosoever findeth him shall kill him. Will not the Lord be avenged on such a people as this? To-night they will hold their solemn assembly, and blow the trumpet in their new moon, and the prophets will prophesy falsely, and the priests will speak wickedly concerning oppression. The word of the Lord saith unto me, 'Go unto this people, and break before them the staff beauty and the staff bands, and be a sign unto this people of the terror of the Lord. Behold, saith the Lord, therefore have I raised thee up and led thee through the wilderness, through the desolate places of the land not sown.' "

As Dred spoke, his great black eye seemed to enlarge itself and roll with a glassy fulness, like that of a sleep-walker in a somnambulic dream. His wife, seeing him prepare to depart, threw herself upon him.

"O, don't, don't leave us! You'll be killed, some of these times, just as they killed him!"

"Woman! the burden of the Lord is upon me. The word of the Lord is as a fire shut up in my bones. The Lord saith unto me, 'Go show unto this people their iniquity, and be a sign unto this evil nation!' "

Breaking away from his wife, he precipitated himself through an opening into the thicket, and was gone.

CHAPTER XXIII

The Camp-Meeting

THE PLACE SELECTED for the camp-meeting was in one of the most picturesque portions of the neighborhood. It was a small, partially-cleared spot, in the midst of a dense forest, which stretched away in every direction, in cool, green aisles of checkered light and shade.

In the central clearing, a sort of rude amphitheatre of seats was formed of rough-pine slabs. Around on the edges of the forest the tents of the various worshippers were pitched; for the spending of three or four days and nights upon the ground is deemed an essential part of the service. The same clear stream which wound round the dwelling of Tiff prattled its way, with a modest gurgle, through this forest, and furnished the assembly with water.

The Gordons, having come merely for the purposes of curiosity, and having a residence in the neighborhood, did not provide themselves with a tent. The servants, however, were less easily satisfied. Aunt Rose shook her head, and declared, oracularly, that "De blessing was sure to come down in de night, and dem dat wanted to get a part of it would have to be dar!"

Consequently, Nina was beset to allow her people to have a tent, in which they were to take turns in staying all night, as candidates for the blessing. In compliance with that law of good-humored indulgence which had been the traditionary usage of her family, Nina acceded; and the Gordon tent spread its snowy sails, to the rejoicing of their hearts. Aunt Rose predominated about the door, alternately slapping the children and joining the chorus of hymns which she heard from every part of the camp-ground. On the outskirts were various rude booths, in which whiskey and water, and sundry articles of provision, and fodder for horses, were dispensed for a consideration. Abijah Skinflint here figured among the money-changers, while his wife and daughter were gossiping through the tents of the women. In front of the seats, under a dense cluster of pines, was the preachers' stand: a rude stage of rough boards, with a railing around it, and a desk of small slabs, supporting a Bible and a hymn-book.

The preachers were already assembling; and no small curiosity was expressed with regard to them by the people, who were walking up and down among the tents. Nina, leaning on the arm of Clayton, walked about the area with the rest. Anne Clayton leaned on the arm of Uncle John. Aunt Nesbit and Aunt Maria came behind. To Nina the scene was quite new, for a long residence in the Northern States had placed her out of the way of such things; and her shrewd insight into character, and her love of drollery, found an abundant satisfaction in the various little points and oddities of the scene. They walked to the Gordon tent, in which a preliminary meeting was already in full course. A circle of men and women, interspersed with children, were sitting, with their eyes shut, and their heads thrown back, singing at the top of their voices. Occasionally, one or other would vary the exercises by clapping of hands, jumping up straight into the air, falling flat on the ground, screaming, dancing, and laughing.

"O, set me up on a rock!" screamed one.

"I's sot up!" screamed another.

"Glory!" cried the third, and a tempest of "amens" poured in between.

"I's got a sperience!" cried one, and forthwith began piping it out in a high key, while others kept on singing.

"I's got a sperience!" shouted Tomtit, whom Aunt Rose, with maternal care, had taken with her.

"No, you an't, neither! Sit down!" said Aunt Rose, kneading him down as if he had been a batch of biscuits, and going on at the same time with her hymn.

"I's on the Rock of Ages!" screamed a neighbor.

"I want to get on a rock edgeways!" screamed Tomtit, struggling desperately with Aunt Rose's great fat hands.

"Mind yourself!—I'll crack you over!" said Aunt Rose. And Tomtit, still continuing rebellious, *was* cracked over accordingly, with such force as to send him head-foremost on the straw at the bottom of the tent; an indignity which he resented with loud howls of impotent wrath, which, however, made no impression in the general whirlwind of screaming, shouting, and praying.

Nina and Uncle John stood at the tent-door laughing heartily.

Clayton looked on with his usual thoughtful gravity of aspect.
Anne turned her head away with an air of disgust.

"Why don't you laugh?" said Nina, looking round at her.

"It doesn't make me feel like it," said Anne. "It makes me feel
melancholy."

"Why so?"

"Because religion is a sacred thing with me, and I don't like to
see it travestied," said she.

"O," said Nina, "I don't respect religion any the less for a good
laugh at its oddities. I believe I was born without any organ of reverence, and so don't feel the incongruity of the thing as you do. The
distance between laughing and praying isn't so very wide in my
mind as it is in some people's."

"We must have charity," said Clayton, "for every religious man-
ifestation. Barbarous and half-civilized people always find the
necessity for outward and bodily demonstration in worship; I suppose because the nervous excitement wakes up and animates their
spiritual natures, and gets them into a receptive state, just as you
have to shake up sleeping persons and shout in their ears to put
them in a condition to understand you. I have known real conversions to take place under just these excitements."

"But," said Anne, "I think we might teach them to be decent.
These things ought not to be allowed!"

"I believe," said Clayton, "intolerance is a rooted vice in our nature. The world is as full of different minds and bodies as the woods
are of leaves, and each one has its own habit of growth. And yet our
first impulse is to forbid everything that would not be proper for
us. No, let the African scream, dance, and shout, and fall in trances.
It suits his tropical lineage and blood, as much as our thoughtful inward ways do us."

"I wonder who that is!" said Nina, as a general movement on the
ground proclaimed the arrival of some one who appeared to be exciting general interest. The stranger was an unusually tall, portly
man, apparently somewhat past the middle of life, whose erect carriage, full figure, and red cheeks, and a certain dashing frankness of
manner, might have indicated him as belonging rather to the military than the clerical profession. He carried a rifle on his shoulder,
which he set down carefully against the corner of the preachers'
stand, and went around shaking hands among the company with a

free and jovial air that might almost be described by the term rollicking.

"Why," said Uncle John, "that's father Bonnie! How are you,
my fine fellow?"

"What! *you*, Mr. Gordon?—How do you do?" said father Bonnie, grasping his hand in his, and shaking it heartily. "Why, they tell
me," he said, looking at him with a jovial smile, "that you have
fallen from grace!"

"Even so!" said Uncle John. "I am a sad dog, I dare say."

"O, I tell *you* what," said father Bonnie, "but it takes a strong
hook and a long line to pull in you *rich* sinners! Your money-bags
and your niggers hang round you like mill-stones! You are too
tough for the Gospel! Ah!" said he, shaking his fist at him, play-
fully, "but I'm going to come down upon you, to-day, with the law,
I can tell you! You want the thunders of Sinai![1] You must have a
dose of the law!"

"Well," said Uncle John, "thunder away! I suppose we need it,
all of us. But, now, father Bonnie, you ministers are always preaching to us poor dogs on the evils of riches; but, somehow, I don't see
any of you that are much afraid of owning horses, or niggers, or
any other good thing that you can get your hands on. Now, I hear
that you've got a pretty snug little place, and a likely drove to work
it. You'll have to look out for your own soul, father Bonnie!"

A general laugh echoed this retort; for father Bonnie had the reputation of being a shrewder hand at a bargain, and of having more
expertness in swapping a horse or trading a negro, than any other
man for six counties round.

"He's into you, now, old man!" said several of the bystanders,
laughingly.

"O, as to that," said father Bonnie, laughing, also, "I go in with
Paul,—they that preach the Gospel must live of the Gospel. Now,
Paul was a man that stood up for his rights to live as other folks do.
'Isn't it right,' says he, 'that those that plant a vineyard should first
eat of the fruit?[2] Haven't we power to lead about a sister, a wife?'
says he. And if Paul had lived in our time he would have said
a drove of niggers, too! No danger about us ministers being hurt
by riches, while you laymen are so slow about supporting the
Gospel!"

At the elbow of father Bonnie stood a brother minister, who was in many respects his contrast. He was tall, thin, and stooping, with earnest black eyes, and a serene sweetness of expression. A thread-bare suit of rusty black, evidently carefully worn, showed the poverty of his worldly estate. He carried in his hand a small port-manteau, probably containing a change of linen, his Bible, and a few sermons. Father Dickson was a man extensively known through all that region. He was one of those men among the ministers of America, who keep alive our faith in Christianity, and renew on earth the portrait of the old apostle: "In journeyings often, in weari-ness and painfulness, in watchings often, in hunger and thirst, in fastings often, in cold and nakedness. Besides those things that are without, that which cometh upon them daily, the care of all the churches. Who is weak, and they are not weak? who is offended, and they burn not?"[3]

Every one in the state knew and respected father Dickson; and, like the generality of the world, people were very well pleased, and thought it extremely proper and meritorious for him to bear weari-ness and painfulness, hunger and cold, in their spiritual service, leaving to them the right of attending or not attending to him, ac-cording to their own convenience. Father Dickson was one of those who had never yielded to the common customs and habits of the country in regard to the holding of slaves. A few, who had been left him by a relation, he had at great trouble and expense transported to a free state, and settled there comfortably. The world need not trouble itself with seeking to know or reward such men; for the world cannot know and has no power to reward them. Their citi-zenship is in heaven, and all that can be given them in this life is like a morsel which a peasant gives in his cottage to him who to-morrow will reign over a kingdom.

He had stood listening to the conversation thus far with the grave yet indulgent air with which he generally listened to the sal-lies of his ministerial brothers. Father Bonnie, though not as much respected or confided in as father Dickson, had, from the frankness of his manners, and a certain rude but effective style of eloquence, a more general and apparent popularity. He produced more sensation on the camp-ground; could sing louder and longer, and would often rise into flights of eloquence both original and impressive. Many were offended by the freedom of his manner out of the pulpit; and the stricter sort were known to have said of him, "that when out he never ought to be in, and when in never out." As the laugh that rose at his last sally died away, he turned to father Dickson, and said:

"What do you think?"

"I don't think," said father Dickson, mildly, "that you would ever have found Paul leading a drove of negroes."

"Why not, as well as Abraham, the father of the faithful? Didn't he have three hundred trained servants?"

"Servants, perhaps; but not slaves!" said father Dickson, "for they all bore arms. For my part, I think that the buying, selling, and trading, of human beings for purposes of gain, is a sin in the sight of God."

"Well, now, father Dickson, I wouldn't have thought you had read your Bible to so little purpose as that! I wouldn't believe it! What do you say to Moses?"

"He led out a whole army of fugitive slaves through the Red Sea," said father Dickson.

"Well, I tell you, now," said father Bonnie, "if the buying, selling, or holding, of a slave for the sake of gain, is, as you say, a sin, then three fourths of all the Episcopalians, Methodists, Baptists, and Presbyterians, in the slave states of the Union, are of the devil!"

"I think it is a sin, notwithstanding," said father Dickson, quietly.

"Well, but doesn't Moses say expressly, 'Ye shall buy of the heathen round about you'?"[4]

"There's into him!" said a Georgia trader, who, having camped with a coffle of negroes in the neighborhood, had come up to camp-meeting.

"All those things," said father Dickson, "belong to the old covenant, which Paul says was annulled for the weakness and unprofitableness thereof, and have nothing to do with us, who have risen with Christ. We have got past Mount Sinai and the wilderness, and have come unto Mount Zion;[5] and ought to seek the things that are above, where Christ sitteth."

"I say, brother," said another of the ministers, tapping him on the shoulder, "it's time for the preaching to begin. You can finish your discussion some other time. Come, father Bonnie, come forward, here, and strike up the hymn."

Father Bonnie accordingly stepped to the front of the stand, and with him another minister, of equal height and breadth of frame, and, standing with their hats on, they uplifted, in stentorian voices, the following hymn:

> *"Brethren, don't you hear the sound?*
> *The martial trumpet now is blowing;*
> *Men in order 'listing round,*
> *And soldiers to the standard flowing."*

As the sound of the hymn rolled through the aisles and arches of the wood, the heads of different groups, who had been engaged in conversation, were observed turning toward the stand, and voices from every part of the camp-ground took up the air, as, suiting the action to the words, they began flowing to the place of preaching. The hymn went on, keeping up the same martial images:

> *"Bounty offered, life and peace;*
> *To every soldier this is given,*
> *When the toils of life shall cease,*
> *A mansion bright, prepared in heaven."*

As the throng pressed up, and came crowding from the distant aisles of the wood, the singers seemed to exert themselves to throw a wilder vehemence into the song, stretching out their arms and beckoning eagerly. They went on singing:

> *"You need not fear; the cause is good,*
> *Let who will to the crown aspire:*
> *In this cause the martyrs bled,*
> *And shouted victory in the fire.*

> *"In this cause let's follow on,*
> *And soon we'll tell the pleasing story,*
> *How by faith we won the crown,*
> *And fought our way to life and glory.*

> *"O, ye rebels, come and 'list!*
> *The officers are now recruiting:*
> *Why will you in sin persist,*
> *Or waste your time in vain disputing?*

> *"All excuses now are vain;*
> *For, if you do not sue for favor,*
> *Down you'll sink to endless pain,*
> *And bear the wrath of God forever."*

There is always something awful in the voice of the multitude. It would seem as if the breath that a crowd breathed out together, in moments of enthusiasm, carried with it a portion of the dread and mystery of their own immortal natures. The whole area before the pulpit, and in the distant aisles of the forest, became one vast, surging sea of sound, as negroes and whites, slaves and freemen, saints and sinners, slave-holders, slave-hunters, slave-traders, ministers, elders, and laymen, alike joined in the pulses of that mighty song. A flood of electrical excitement seemed to rise with it, as, with a voice of many waters, the rude chant went on:

> "*Hark! the victors singing loud!*
> *Emanuel's chariot-wheels[6] are rumbling;*
> *Mourners weeping through the crowd,*
> *And Satan's kingdom down is tumbling!*"

Our friend, Ben Dakin, pressed to the stand, and, with tears streaming down his cheeks, exceeded all others in the energy of his vociferations. Ben had just come from almost a fight with another slave-hunter, who had boasted a better-trained pack of dogs than his own; and had broken away to hurry to the camp-ground, with the assurance that he'd "give him fits when the preachin' was over;" and now he stood there, tears rolling down his cheeks, singing with the heartiest earnestness and devotion. What shall we make of it? Poor heathen Ben! is it any more out of the way for him to think of being a Christian in this manner, than for some of his more decent brethren, who take Sunday passage for eternity in the cushioned New York or Boston pews, and solemnly drowse through very sleepy tunes, under a dim, hazy impression that they are going to heaven? Of the two, we think Ben's chance is the best; for, in some blind way, he does think himself a sinner, and in need of something he calls salvation; and, doubtless, while the tears stream down his face, the poor fellow makes a new resolve against the whiskey-bottle, while his more respectable sleepy brethren never think of making one against the cotton-bale.

Then there was his rival, also, Jim Stokes,—a surly, foul-mouthed, swearing fellow,—he joins in the chorus of the hymn, and feels a troublous, vague yearning, deep down within him, which makes him for the moment doubt whether he had better knock down Ben at the end of the meeting.

As to Harry, who stood also among the crowd, the words and

tune recalled but too vividly the incidents of his morning's interview with Dred, and with it the tumultuous boiling of his bitter
controversy with the laws of the society in which he found himself.
In hours of such high excitement, a man seems to have an intuitive
perception of the whole extent and strength of what is within himself; and, if there be anything unnatural or false in his position, he
realizes it with double intensity.

Mr. John Gordon, likewise, gave himself up, without resistance,
to be swayed by the feeling of the hour. He sung with enthusiasm,
and wished he was a soldier of somebody, going somewhere, or a
martyr shouting victory in the fire; and if the conflict described had
been with any other foe than his own laziness and self-indulgence—
had there been any outward, tangible enemy, at the moment—he
would doubtless have enlisted, without loss of time.

When the hymn was finished, however, there was a general wiping of eyes, and they all sat down to listen to the sermon. Father
Bonnie led off in an animated strain. His discourse was like the
tropical swamp, bursting out with a lush abundance of every kind
of growth—grave, gay, grotesque, solemn, fanciful, and even coarse
caricature, provoking the broadest laughter. The audience were
swayed by him like trees before the wind. There were not wanting
touches of rude pathos, as well as earnest appeals. The meeting was
a union one of Presbyterians and Methodists, in which the ministers
of both denominations took equal part; and it was an understood
agreement among them, of course, that they were not to venture
upon polemic ground, or attack each other's peculiarities of doctrine. But Abijah's favorite preacher could not get through a sermon without some quite pointed exposition of scripture bearing on
his favorite doctrine of election, which caused the next minister to
run a vehement tilt on the correlative doctrines of free grace,[7] with a
eulogy on John Wesley.[8] The auditors, meanwhile, according to
their respective sentiments, encouraged each preacher with a cry of
"Amen!" "Glory be to God!" "Go on, brother!" and other similar
exclamations.

About noon the services terminated, *pro tem.,*[9] and the audience
dispersed themselves to their respective tents through the grove,
where there was an abundance of chatting, visiting, eating, and
drinking, as if the vehement denunciations and passionate appeals
of the morning had been things of another state of existence. Uncle
John, in the most cheery possible frame of mind, escorted his party

into the woods, and assisted them in unpacking a hamper containing wine, cold fowls, cakes, pies, and other delicacies which Aunt Katy had packed for the occasion.

Old Tiff had set up his tent in a snug little nook on the banks of the stream, where he informed passers by that it was his young mas'r and missis's establishment, and that he, Tiff, had come to wait on them. With a good-natured view of doing him a pleasure, Nina selected a spot for their nooning at no great distance, and spoke in the most gracious and encouraging manner to them, from time to time.

"See, now, can't you, how real quality behaves demselves!" he said, grimly, to Old Hundred, who came up bringing the carriage-cushions for the party to sit down upon. "Real quality sees into things! I tell ye what, blood sees into blood. Miss Nina sees dese yer chil'en an't de common sort—dat's what she does!"

"Umph!" said Old Hundred, "such a muss as ye keep up about yer chil'en! Tell you what, dey an't no better dan oder white trash!"

"Now, you talk dat ar way, I'll knock you down!" said Old Tiff, who, though a peaceable and law-abiding creature, in general, was driven, in desperation, to the last resort of force.

"John, what are you saying to Tiff?" said Nina, who had overheard some of the last words. "Go back to your own tent, and don't you trouble him! I have taken him under my protection."

The party enjoyed their dinner with infinite relish, and Nina amused herself in watching Tiff's cooking preparations. Before departing to the preaching-ground, he had arranged a slow fire, on which a savory stew had been all the morning simmering, and which, on the taking off of the pot-lid, diffused an agreeable odor through the place.

"I say, Tiff, how delightfully that smells!" said Nina, getting up, and looking into the pot. "Wouldn't Miss Fanny be so kind as to favor us with a taste of it?"

Fanny, to whom Tiff punctiliously referred the question, gave a bashful consent. But who shall describe the pride and glory that swelled the heart of Tiff as he saw a bowl of his stew smoking among the Gordon viands, praised and patronized by the party? And, when Nina placed on their simple board—literally a board, and nothing more—a small loaf of frosted cake, in exchange, it certainly required all the grace of the morning exercises to keep Tiff within due bounds of humility. He really seemed to dilate with satisfaction.

"Tiff, how did you like the sermon?" said Nina.

"Dey's pretty far, Miss Nina. Der's a good deal o' quality preaching."

"What do you mean by quality preaching, Tiff?"

"Why, dat ar kind dat's good for quality—full of long words, you know. I spects it's very good; but poor nigger like me can't see his way through it. You see, Miss Nina, what I's studdin' on, lately, is, how to get dese yer chil'en to Canaan; and I hars fus with one ear, and den with t' oder, but 'pears like an't clar 'bout it, yet. Dere's a heap about mose everything else, and it's all very good; but 'pears like I an't clar, arter all, about dat ar. Dey says, 'Come to Christ;' and I says, 'Whar is he, any how?' Bress you, I *want* to come! Dey talks 'bout going in de gate, and knocking at de do', and 'bout marching on de road, and 'bout fighting and being soldiers of de cross; and de Lord knows, now, I'd be glad to get de chil'en through any gate; and I could take 'em on my back and travel all day, if dere was any road; and if dere was a do', bless me, if dey wouldn't hear Old Tiff a rapping! I spects de Lord would have fur to open it—would so. But, arter all, when de preaching is done, dere don't 'pear to be nothing to it. Dere an't no gate, dere an't no do', nor no way; and dere an't no fighting, 'cept when Ben Dakin and Jim Stokes get jawing about der dogs; and everybody comes back eating der dinner quite comf'table, and 'pears like dere wan't no such ting dey's been preaching 'bout. Dat ar troubles me—does so—'cause I wants fur to get dese yer chil'en in de kingdom, some way or oder. I didn't know but some of de quality would know more 'bout it."

"Hang me, if I haven't felt just so!" said Uncle John. "When they were singing that hymn about enlisting and being a soldier, if there had been any fighting doing anywhere, I should have certainly gone right into it; and the preaching always stirs me up terribly. But, then, as Tiff says, after it's all over, why, there's dinner to be eaten, and I can't see anything better than to eat it; and then, by the time I have drank two or three glasses of wine, it's all gone. Now, that's just the way with me!"

"Dey says," said Tiff, "dat we must wait for de blessing to come down upon us, and Aunt Rose says it's dem dat shouts dat gets de blessing; and I's been shouting till I's most beat out, but I hasn't got it. Den, one of dem said none of dem could get it but de 'lect; but, den, t' oder one, he seemed to tink different; and in de meeting dey tells about de scales falling from der eyes,—and I wished dey fall from mine—I do so! Perhaps, Miss Nina, now, you could tell me someting."

"O, don't ask me!" said Nina; "I don't know anything about these things. I think I feel a little like Uncle John," she said, turning to Clayton. "There are two kinds of sermons and hymns; one gets me to sleep, and the other excites and stirs me up in a general kind of way; but they don't either seem to do me real good."

"For my part, I am such an enemy to stagnation," said Clayton, "that I think there is advantage in everything that stirs up the soul, even though we see no immediate results. I listen to music, see pictures, as far as I can, uncritically. I say, 'Here I am; see what you can do with me.' So I present myself to almost all religious exercises. It is the most mysterious part of our nature. I do not pretend to understand it, therefore never criticize."

"For *my* part," said Anne, "there is so much in the wild freedom of these meetings that shocks my taste and sense of propriety, that I am annoyed more than I am benefited."

"There spoke the true, well-trained conventionalist," said Clayton. "But look around you. See, in this wood, among these flowers, and festoons of vine, and arches of green, how many shocking, unsightly growths! *You* would not have had all this underbrush, these dead limbs, these briers running riot over trees, and sometimes choking and killing them. You would have well-trimmed trees and velvet turf. But I love briers, dead limbs, and all, for their very savage freedom. Every once in a while you see in a wood a jessamine, or a sweet-brier, or grape-vine, that throws itself into a gracefulness of growth which a landscape gardener would go down on his knees for, but cannot get. Nature resolutely denies it to him. She says, 'No! I keep this for *my own*. You won't have my wildness—my freedom; very well, then you shall not have the graces that spring from it.' Just so it is with men. Unite any assembly of common men in a great enthusiasm,—work them up into an abandon, and let every one 'let go,' and speak as nature prompts,—and you will have brush, underwood, briers, and all grotesque growths; but, now and then, some thought or sentiment will be struck out with a freedom or power such as you cannot get in any other way. You cultivated people are much mistaken when you despise the enthusiasms of the masses. There is more truth than you think in the old 'vox populi, vox Dei.' "

"What's that?" said Nina.

" 'The voice of the people is the voice of God.' There is truth in it. I never repent my share in a popular excitement, provided it be of the higher sentiments; and I do not ask too strictly whether it has produced any tangible results. I reverence the people, as I do the woods, for the wild, grand freedom with which their humanity develops itself."

"I'm afraid, Nina," said Aunt Nesbit, in a low tone, to the latter, "I'm afraid he isn't orthodox."

"What makes you think so, aunt?"

"O, I don't know; his talk hasn't the real sound."

"You want something that ends in 'ation,' don't you, aunt?—justification, sanctification, or something of that kind."

*   *   *   *   *   *   *

Meanwhile, the department of Abijah Skinflint exhibited a decided activity. This was a long, low booth, made of poles, and roofed with newly-cut green boughs. Here the whiskey-barrel was continually pouring forth its supplies to customers who crowded around it. Abijah sat on the middle of a sort of rude counter, dangling his legs, and chewing a straw, while his negro was busy in helping his various customers. Abijah, as we said, being a particularly high Calvinist, was recreating himself by carrying on a discussion with a fat, little, turnipy brother, of the Methodist persuasion.

"I say," he said, "Stringfellow put it into you Methodists, this morning! Hit the nail on the head, I thought!"

"Not a bit of it!" said the other, contemptuously. "Why, elder Baskum chawed him up completely! There wan't nothin' left of him!"

"Well," said Abijah, "strange how folks will see things! Why, it's just as clar to me that all things is decreed! Why, that ar nails everything up tight and handsome. It gives a fellow a kind of comfort to think on it. Things is just as they have got to be. All this free-grace stuff is dreful loose talk. If things is been decreed 'fore the world was made, well, there seems to be some sense in their coming to pass. But, if everything kind of turns up whenever folks think on 't, it's a kind of shaky business."

"I don't like this tying up things so tight," said the other, who evidently was one of the free, jovial order. "I go in for the freedom of the will. Free Gospel, and free grace."

"For my part," said Abijah, rather grimly, "if things was managed my way, I shouldn't commune with nobody that didn't believe in election, up to the hub."

"You strong electioners think you's among the elect!" said one of the bystanders. "You wouldn't be so crank about it, if you didn't! Now, see here: if everything is decreed, how am I going to help myself?"

"That ar is none of *my* look-out," said Abijah. "But there's a pint my mind rests upon—everything is fixed as it can be, and it makes a man mighty easy."

                    *   *   *   *   *

In another part of the camp-ground, Ben Dakin was sitting in his tent door, caressing one of his favorite dogs, and partaking his noontide repast with his wife and child.

"I declar," said Ben, wiping his mouth, "wife, I intend to go into it, and sarve the Lord, now, full chisel! If I catch the next lot of niggers, I intend to give half the money towards keeping up preaching somewhere round here. I'm going to enlist, now, and be a soldier."

"And," said his wife, "Ben, just keep clear of Abijah Skinflint's counter, won't you?"

"Well, I will, durned if I won't!" said Ben. "I'll be moderate. A fellow wants a glass or two, to strike up the hymn on, you know; but I'll be moderate."

The Georgia trader, who had encamped in the neighborhood, now came up.

"Do you believe, stranger," said he, "one of them durned niggers of mine broke loose and got in the swamps, while I was at meeting this morning! Couldn't you take your dog, here, and give 'em a run? I just gave nine hundred dollars for that fellow, cash down."

"Ho! what you going to *him* for?" said Jim Stokes, a short, pursy, vulgar-looking individual, dressed in a hunting-shirt of blue Kentucky jean, who just then came up. "Why, darn ye, his dogs an't no breed 't all! Mine's the true grit, I can tell you; they's the true Florida blood-hounds! I's seen one of them ar dogs shake a nigger in his mouth like he'd been a sponge."

Poor Ben's new-found religion could not withstand this sudden attack of his spiritual enemy; and, rousing himself, notwithstanding the appealing glances of his wife, he stripped up his sleeves, and, squaring off, challenged his rival to a fight.

A crowd gathered round, laughing and betting, and cheering on the combatants with slang oaths and expressions, such as we will not repeat, when the concourse was routed by the approach of father Bonnie on the outside of the ring.

"Look here, boys, what works of the devil have you got round here? None of this on the camp-ground! This is the Lord's ground, here; so shut up your swearing, and don't fight."

A confused murmur of voices now began to explain to father Bonnie the cause of the trouble.

"Ho, ho!" said he, "let the nigger run; you can catch him fast enough when the meetings are over. You come here to 'tend to your salvation. Ah, don't you be swearing and blustering round! Come, boys, join in a hymn with me." So saying, he struck up a well-known air:

"When Israel went to Jericho,
O, good Lord, in my soul!"

in which one after another joined, and the rising tumult was soon assuaged.

"I say," said father Bonnie to the trader, in an under tone, as he was walking away, "you got a good cook in your lot, hey?"

"Got a prime one," said the trader; "an A number one cook, and no mistake! Picked her up real cheap, and I'll let you have her for eight hundred dollars, being as you are a minister."

"You must think the Gospel a better trade than it is," said father Bonnie, "if you think a minister can afford to pay at that figure!"

"Why," said the trader, "you haven't seen her; it's dirt cheap for her, I can tell you! A sound, strong, hearty woman; a prudent, careful housekeeper; a real pious Methodist, a member of a class-meeting! Why, eight hundred dollars an't anything! I ought to get a thousand for her; but I don't hear preaching for nothing,—always think right to make a discount to ministers!"

"Why couldn't you bring her in?" said father Bonnie. "Maybe I'll give you seven hundred and fifty for her."

"Couldn't do that, no way!" said the trader. "Couldn't, indeed!"

"Well, after the meetings are over I'll talk about it."

"She's got a child, four years old," said the trader, with a little cough; "healthy, likely child; I suppose I shall want a hundred dollars for him!"

"O, that won't do!" said father Bonnie. "I don't want any more children round my place than I've got now!"

"But, I tell you," said the trader, "it's a likely boy. Why, the keeping of him won't cost you anything, and before you think of it you'll have a thousand-dollar hand grown on your own place."

"Well," said father Bonnie, "I'll think of it!"

In the evening the scene on the camp-ground was still more picturesque and impressive. Those who conduct camp-meetings are generally men who, without much reasoning upon the subject, fall into a sort of tact, in influencing masses of mind, and pressing into the service all the great life forces and influences of nature. A kind of rude poetry pervades their minds, colors their dialect, and influences their arrangements. The solemn and harmonious grandeur of night, with all its mysterious power of exalting the passions and intensifying the emotions, has ever been appreciated, and used by them with even poetic skill. The day had been a glorious one in June; the sky of that firm, clear blue, the atmosphere of that crystalline clearness, which often gives to the American landscape such a sharply defined outline, and to the human system such an intense consciousness of life. The evening sun went down in a broad sea of light, and even after it had sunk below the purple horizon, flashed back a flood of tremulous rose-colored radiance, which, taken up by a thousand filmy clouds, made the whole sky above like a glowing tent of the most ethereal brightness. The shadows of the forest aisles were pierced by the rose-colored rays; and, as they gradually faded, star after star twinkled out, and a broad moon, ample and round, rose in the purple zone of the sky. When she had risen above the horizon but a short space, her light was so resplendent, and so profuse, that it was decided to conduct the evening service by that alone; and when, at the sound of the hymn, the assembly poured in and arranged themselves before the preaching-stand, it is probable that the rudest heart present was somewhat impressed with the silent magnificence by which God was speaking to them through his works. As the hymn closed, father Bonnie, advancing to the front of the stage, lifted his hands, and pointing to the purple sky, and in a deep and not unmelodious voice, repeated the words of the Psalmist:

"The heavens declare the glory of God, and the firmament showeth his handy-work; day unto day uttereth speech, and night unto night showeth knowledge."[10]

"O, ye sinners!" he exclaimed, "look up at the moon, there, walking in her brightness, and think over your oaths, and your cursings, and your drinkings! Think over your backbitings, and your cheatings! think over your quarrellings and your fightings! How do they look to you now, with that blessed moon shining down upon you? Don't you see the beauty of our Lord God upon her? Don't you see how the saints walk in white with the Lord, like her? I dare say some of you, now, have had a pious mother, or a pious wife, or a pious sister, that's gone to glory; and there they are walking with the Lord!—walking with the Lord, through the sky, and looking down on you, sinners, just as that moon looks down! And what does she see you doing, your wife, or your mother, or sister, that's in glory? Does she see all your swearings, and your drinkings, and your fightings, and your hankerings after money, and your horse-racings, and your cock-fightings? O, sinners, but you are a bad set! I tell you the Lord is looking now down on you, out of that moon! He is looking down in mercy! But, I tell you, he'll look down quite another way, one of these days! O, there'll be a time of wrath, by and by, if you don't repent! O, what a time there was at Sinai, years ago, when the voice of the trumpet waxed louder and louder, and the mountain was all of a smoke, and there were thunderings and lightnings, and the Lord descended on Sinai! That's nothing to what you'll see, by and by! No more moon looking down on you! No more stars, but the heavens shall pass away with a great noise, and the elements shall melt with fervent heat! Ah! did you ever see a fire in the woods? I have; and I've seen the fire on the prairies, and it rolled like a tempest, and men and horses, and everything, had to run before it. I have seen it roaring and crackling through the woods, and great trees shrivelled in a minute like tinder! I have seen it flash over trees seventy-five and a hundred feet high, and in a minute they'd be standing pillars of fire, and the heavens were all a blaze, and the crackling and roaring was like the sea in a storm. There's a judgment-day for you! O, sinner, what will become of you in that day? Never cry, Lord, Lord! Too late—too late, man! You wouldn't take mercy when it was offered, and now you shall have wrath! No place to hide! The heavens and earth are passing away, and there shall be no more sea! There's no place for you now in God's universe."

By this time there were tumultuous responses from the audience, of groans, cries, clapping of hands, and mingled shouts of glory and amen!

The electric shout of the multitude acted on the preacher again, as he went on, with a yet fiercer energy. "Now is your time, sinners! Now is your time! Come unto the altar, and God's people will pray for you! Now is the day of grace! Come up! Come up, you that have got pious fathers and mothers in glory! Come up, father! come up, mother! come up, brother! Come, young man! we want you to come! Ah, there's a hardened sinner, off there! I see his lofty looks! Come up, come up! Come up, you rich sinners! You'll be poor enough in the day of the Lord, I can tell you! Come up, you young women! You daughters of Jerusalem, with your tinkling ornaments! Come, saints of the Lord, and labor with me in prayer. Strike up a hymn, brethren, strike up the hymn!" And a thousand voices commenced the hymn,

"Stop, poor sinner, stop and think,
Before you further go!"

And, meanwhile, ministers and elders moved around the throng, entreating and urging one and another to come and kneel before the stand. Multitudes rushed forward, groans and sobs were heard, as the speaker continued, with redoubled vehemence.

"I don't care," said Mr. John Gordon, "who sees me; I'm going up! I am a poor old sinner, and I ought to be prayed for, if anybody."

Nina shrank back, and clung to Clayton's arm. So vehement was the surging feeling of the throng around her, that she wept with a wild, tremulous excitement.

"Do take me out,—it's dreadful!" she said.

Clayton passed his arm round her, and, opening a way through the crowd, carried her out beyond the limits, where they stood together alone, under the tree.

"I know I am not good as I ought to be," she said, "but I don't know how to be any better. Do you think it would do me any good to go up there? Do you believe in these things?"

"I sympathize with every effort that man makes to approach his Maker," said Clayton; "these ways do not suit me, but I dare not judge them. I cannot despise them. I must not make myself a rule for others."

"But, don't you think," said Nina, "that these things do harm sometimes?"

"Alas, child, what form of religion does not? It is our fatality that everything that does good must do harm. It's the condition of our poor, imperfect life here."

"I do not like these terrible threats," said Nina. "Can fear of fire make me love? Besides, I have a kind of courage in me that always rises up against a threat. It isn't my nature to fear."

"If we may judge our Father by his voice in nature," said Clayton, "he deems severity a necessary part of our training. How inflexibly and terribly regular are all his laws! Fire and hail, snow and vapor, stormy wind, fulfilling his word—all these have a crushing regularity in their movements, which show that he is to be feared as well as loved."

"But I want to be religious," said Nina, "entirely apart from such considerations. Not driven by fear, but drawn by love. You can guide me about these things, for you are religious."

"I fear I should not be accepted as such in any church," said Clayton. "It is my misfortune that I cannot receive any common form of faith, though I respect and sympathize with all. Generally speaking, preaching only weakens my faith; and I have to forget the sermon in order to recover my faith. I do not *believe*—I *know* that our moral nature needs a thorough regeneration; and I believe this must come through Christ. This is all I am certain of."

"I wish I were like Milly," said Nina. "She is a Christian, I know; but she has come to it by dreadful sorrows. Sometimes I'm afraid to ask my heavenly Father to make me good, because I think it will come by dreadful trials, if he does."

"And I," said Clayton, speaking with great earnestness, "would be willing to suffer anything conceivable, if I could only overcome all evil, and come up to my highest ideas of good." And, as he spoke, he turned his face up to the moonlight with an earnest fervor of expression, that struck Nina deeply.

"I almost shudder to hear you say so! You don't know what it may bring on you!"

He looked at her with a beautiful smile, which was a peculiar expression of his face in moments of high excitement.

"I say it again!" he said. "Whatever it involves, let it come!"

      *   *   *   *   *   *   *

The exercises of the evening went on with a succession of addresses, varied by singing of hymns and prayers. In the latter part of the time many declared themselves converts, and were shouting loudly. Father Bonnie came forward.

"Brethren," he shouted, "we are seeing a day from the Lord! We've got a glorious time! O, brethren, let us sing glory to the Lord! The Lord is coming among us!"

The excitement now became general. There was a confused sound of exhortation, prayers, and hymns, all mixed together, from different parts of the ground. But, all of a sudden, every one was startled by a sound which seemed to come pealing down directly from the thick canopy of pines over the heads of the ministers.

"Woe unto you that desire the day of the Lord! To what end shall it be for *you?* The day of the Lord shall be darkness, and not light! Blow ye the trumpet in Zion! Sound an alarm in my holy mountain! Let all the inhabitants of the land tremble! for the day of the Lord cometh!"

There was deep, sonorous power in the voice that spoke, and the words fell pealing down through the air like the vibrations of some mighty bell. Men looked confusedly on each other; but, in the universal license of the hour, the obscurity of the night, and the multitude of the speakers, no one knew exactly whence it came. After a moment's pause, the singers were recommencing, when again the same deep voice was heard.

"Take away from me the noise of thy songs, and the melody of thy viols; for I will not hear them, saith the Lord. I hate and despise your feast-days! I will not smell in your solemn assemblies; for your hands are defiled with blood, and your fingers are greedy for violence! Will ye kill, and steal, and commit adultery, and swear falsely, and come and stand before *me,* saith the Lord? Ye oppress the poor and needy, and hunt the stranger; also in thy skirts is found the blood of poor innocents! and yet ye say, Because I am clean shall his anger pass from me! Hear this, ye that swallow up the needy, and make the poor of the land to fail, saying, When will the new moon be gone, that we may sell corn? that we may buy the poor for silver, and the needy for a pair of shoes? The Lord hath sworn, saying, I will never forget their works. I will surely visit you!"[11]

The audience, thus taken, in the obscurity of the evening, by an unknown speaker, whose words seemed to fall apparently from the clouds, in a voice of such strange and singular quality, began to feel a creeping awe stealing over them. The high state of electrical excitement under which they had been going on, predisposed them to a sort of revulsion of terror; and a vague, mysterious panic crept upon them, as the boding, mournful voice continued to peal from the trees.

"Hear, O ye rebellious people! The Lord is against this nation! The Lord shall stretch out upon it the line of confusion, and the stones of emptiness! For thou saidst, I will ascend into the stars; I will be as God! But thou shalt be cast out as an abominable branch, and the wild beasts shall tread thee down! Howl, fir-tree, for thou art spoiled! Open thy doors, O Lebanon, that the fire may devour thy cedars! for the Lord cometh out of his place to punish the inhabitants of the land! The Lord shall utter his voice before his army, for his camp is very great! Multitudes! multitudes! in the valley of decision! For the day of the Lord is near in the valley of decision! The sun and the moon shall be dark, and the stars withdraw their shining; for the Lord shall utter his voice from Jerusalem, and the heavens and earth shall shake! In that day I will cause the sun to go down at noon, and darken the whole earth! And I will turn your feasts into mourning, and your songs into lamentation! Woe to the bloody city! It is full of lies and robbery! The noise of a whip!—the noise of the rattling of wheels!—of the prancing horses, and the jumping chariot! The horseman lifteth up the sword and glittering spear! and there is a multitude of slain! There is no end of their corpses!—They are stumbling upon the corpses! For, Behold, I am against thee, saith the Lord, and I will make thee utterly desolate!"[12]

There was a fierce, wailing earnestness in the sound of these dreadful words, as if they were uttered in a paroxysm of affright and horror, by one who stood face to face with some tremendous form. And, when the sound ceased, men drew in their breath, and looked on each other, and the crowd began slowly to disperse, whispering in low voices to each other.

So extremely piercing and so wildly earnest had the voice been, that it actually seemed, in the expressive words of Scripture, to make every ear to tingle. And, as people of rude and primitive habits are always predisposed to superstition, there crept through the different groups wild legends of prophets strangely commissioned to announce coming misfortunes. Some spoke of the predic-

tions of the judgment-day; some talked of comets, and strange signs
that had preceded wars and pestilences. The ministers wondered,
and searched around the stand in vain. One auditor alone could,
had he desired it, make an explanation. Harry, who stood near the
stand, had recognized the voice. But, though he searched, also,
around, he could find no one.

He who spoke was one whose savage familiarity with nature
gave him the agility and stealthy adroitness of a wild animal. And,
during the stir and commotion of the dispersing audience, he had
silently made his way from tree to tree, over the very head of those
who were yet wondering at his strange, boding words, till at last he
descended in a distant part of the forest.

After the service, as father Dickson was preparing to retire to his
tent, a man pulled him by the sleeve. It was the Georgia trader.

"We have had an awful time, to-night!" said he, looking actually pale with terror. "Do you think the judgment-day really is
coming?"

"My friend," said father Dickson, "it surely is! Every step we
take in life is leading us directly to the judgment-seat of Christ!"

"Well," said the trader, "but do you think that was from the
Lord, the last one that spoke? Durned if he didn't say awful
things!—'nough to make the hair rise! I tell you what, I've often
had doubts about my trade. The ministers may prove it's all right
out of the Old Testament; but I'm durned if I think they know all
the things that we do! But, then, I an't so bad as some of 'em. But,
now, I've got a gal out in my gang that's dreadful sick, and I partly
promised her I'd bring a minister to see her."

"I'll go with you, friend," said father Dickson; and forthwith he
began following the trader to the racks where their horses were tied.
Selecting, out of some hundred who were tied there, their own
beasts, the two midnight travellers soon found themselves trotting
along under the shadow of the forest's boughs.

"My friend," said father Dickson, "I feel bound in conscience to
tell you that I think your trade a ruinous one to your soul. I hope
you'll lay to heart the solemn warning you've heard to-night. Why,
your own sense can show you that a trade can't be right that you'd
be afraid to be found in if the great judgment-day were at hand."

"Well, I rather spect you speak the truth; but, then, what makes
father Bonnie stand up for 't?"

"My friend, I must say that I think father Bonnie upholds a soul-destroying error. I must say that, as conscience-bound. I pray the Lord for him and you both. I put it right to your conscience, my friend, whether you think you could keep to your trade, and live a Christian life."

"No; the fact is, it's a d——d bad business, that's just where 't is. We an't fit to be trusted with such things that come to us—gals and women. Well, I feel pretty bad, I tell you, to-night; 'cause I know I haven't done right by this yer gal. I ought fur to have let her alone; but, then, the devil or something possessed me. And now she has got a fever, and screeches awfully. I declar, some things she says go right through me!"

Father Dickson groaned in spirit over this account, and felt himself almost guilty for belonging ostensibly and outwardly to a church which tolerated such evils. He rode along by the side of his companion, breaking forth into occasional ejaculations and snatches of hymns. After a ride of about an hour, they arrived at the encampment. A large fire had been made in a cleared spot, and smouldering fragments and brands were lying among the white ashes. One or two horses were tied to a neighboring tree, and wagons were drawn up by them. Around the fire, in different groups, lay about fifteen men and women, with heavy iron shackles on their feet, asleep in the moonlight. At a little distance from the group, and near to one of the wagons, a blanket was spread down on the ground under a tree, on which lay a young girl of seventeen, tossing and moaning in a disturbed stupor. A respectable-looking mulatto-woman was sitting beside her, with a gourd full of water, with which from time to time she moistened her forehead. The woman rose as the trader came up.

"Well, Nance, how does she do now?" said the trader.

"Mis'able enough!" said Nance. "She done been tossing, a throwing round, and crying for her mammy, ever since you went away!"

"Well, I've brought the minister," said he. "Try, Nance, to wake her up; she'll be glad to see him."

The woman knelt down, and took the hand of the sleeper. "Emily! Emily!" she said, "wake up!"

The girl threw herself over with a sudden, restless toss. "O, how my head burns!—O, dear!—O, my mother! Mother!—mother!—mother!—why don't you come to me?"

Father Dickson approached and knelt the other side of her. The mulatto-woman made another effort to bring her to consciousness.

"Emily, here's the minister you was wanting so much! Emily, wake up!"

The girl slowly opened her eyes—large, tremulous, dark eyes. She drew her hand across them, as if to clear her sight, and looked wistfully at the woman.

"Minister!—minister!" she said.

"Yes, minister! You said you wanted to see one."

"O, yes, I did!" she said, heavily.

"My daughter!" said father Dickson, "you are very sick!"

"Yes!" she said, "very! And I'm glad of it! I'm going to die!— I'm glad of that, too! That's all I've got left to be glad of! But I wanted to ask you to write to my mother. She is a free woman; she lives in New York. I want you to give my love to her, and tell her not to worry any more. Tell her I tried all I could to get to her; but they took us, and mistress was so angry she sold me! I forgive her, too. I don't bear her any malice, 'cause it's all over, now! She used to say I was a wild girl, and laughed too loud. I shan't trouble any one that way any more! So that's no matter!"

The girl spoke these sentences at long intervals, occasionally opening her eyes and closing them again in a languid manner. Father Dickson, however, who had some knowledge of medicine, placed his finger on her pulse, which was rapidly sinking. It is the usual instinct, in all such cases, to think of means of prolonging life. Father Dickson rose, and said to the trader:

"Unless some stimulus be given her, she will be gone very soon!"

The trader produced from his pocket a flask of brandy, which he mixed with a little water in a cup, and placed it in father Dickson's hand. He kneeled down again, and, calling her by name, tried to make her take some.

"What is it?" said she, opening her wild, glittering eyes.

"It's something to make you feel better."

"I don't want to feel better! I want to die!" she said, throwing herself over. "What should I want to live for?"

What should she? The words struck father Dickson so much that he sat for a while in silence. He meditated in his mind how he could reach, with any words, that dying ear, or enter with her into that land of trance and mist, into whose cloudy circle the soul seemed already to have passed. Guided by a subtle instinct, he seated himself by the dying girl, and began singing, in a subdued, plaintive air, the following well-known hymn:

"Hark, my soul! it is the Lord,
'Tis thy Saviour, hear his word;
Jesus speaks—he speaks to thee!
Say, poor sinner, lov'st thou me?"

The melody is one often sung among the negroes; and one which, from its tenderness and pathos, is a favorite among them. As oil will find its way into crevices where water cannot penetrate, so song will find its way where speech can no longer enter. The moon shone full on the face of the dying girl, only interrupted by flickering shadows of leaves; and, as father Dickson sung, he fancied he saw a slight, tremulous movement of the face, as if the soul, so worn and weary, were upborne on the tender pinions of the song. He went on singing:

"Can a mother's tender care
Cease toward the child she bare?
Yes, she may forgetful be:
Still will I remember thee."

By the light of the moon, he saw a tear steal from under the long lashes, and course slowly down her cheek. He continued his song:

"Mine is an eternal love,
Higher than the heights above,
Deeper than the depths beneath,
True and faithful—strong as death.

"Thou shalt see my glory soon,
When the work of faith is done;
Partner of my throne shalt be!
Say, poor sinner, lov'st thou me?"[13]

O, love of Christ! which no sin can weary, which no lapse of time can change; from which tribulation, persecution, and distress, cannot separate—all-redeeming, all-glorifying, changing even death and despair to the gate of heaven! Thou hast one more triumph here in the wilderness, in the slave-coffle, and thou comest to bind up the broken-hearted.

As the song ceased, she opened her eyes.

"Mother used to sing that!" she said.

"And can you believe in it, daughter?"

"Yes," she said, "I see Him now! *He* loves me! Let me go!"

There followed a few moments of those strugglings and shiverings which are the birth-pangs of another life, and Emily lay at rest.

Father Dickson, kneeling by her side, poured out the fulness of his heart in an earnest prayer. Rising, he went up to the trader, and, taking his hand, said to him,

"My friend, this may be the turning-point with your soul for eternity. It has pleased the Lord to show you the evil of your ways; and now my advice to you is, break off your sins at once, and do works meet for repentance. Take off the shackles of these poor creatures, and tell them they are at liberty to go."

"Why, bless your soul, sir, this yer lot's worth ten thousand dollars!" said the trader, who was not prepared for so close a practical application.

Do not be too sure, friend, that the trader is peculiar in this. The very same argument, though less frankly stated, holds in the bonds of Satan many extremely well-bred, refined, respectable men, who would gladly save their souls, if they could afford the luxury.

"My friend," said father Dickson, using the words of a very close and uncompromising preacher of old, "what shall it profit a man if he should gain the whole world, and lose his own soul?"[14]

"I know that," said the trader, doubtfully; "but it's a very hard case, this. I'll think about it, though. But there's father Bonnie wants to buy Nance. It would be a pity to disappoint him. But I'll think it over."

Father Dickson returned to the camp-ground between one and two o'clock at night, and, putting away his horse, took his way to the ministers' tent. Here he found father Bonnie standing out in the moonlight. He had been asleep within the tent; but it is to be confessed that the interior of a crowded tent on a camp-ground is anything but favorable to repose. He therefore came out into the fresh air, and was there when father Dickson came back to enter the tent.

"Well, brother, where have you been so late?" said father Bonnie.

"I have been looking for a few sheep in the wilderness, whom everybody neglects," said father Dickson. And then, in a tone tremulous from agitation, he related to him the scene he had just witnessed.

"Do you see," he said, "brother, what iniquities you are countenancing? Now, here, right next to our camp, a slave-coffle[15] encamped! Men and women, guilty of no crime, driven in fetters through our land, shaming us in the sight of every Christian nation! What horrible, abominable iniquities are these poor traders tempted to commit! What perfect hells are the great trading-houses, where men, women, and children, are made merchandise of, and where no light of the Gospel ever enters! And, when this poor trader is convicted of sin, and wants to enter into the kingdom, you stand there to apologize for his sins! Brother Bonnie, I much fear you are the stumbling-block over which souls will stumble into hell. I don't think you believe your argument from the Old Testament, yourself. You must see that it has no kind of relation to such kind of slavery as we have in this country. There's an awful scripture which saith: 'He feedeth on ashes; a deceived heart hath turned him aside, so that he cannot deliver his soul, nor say, Is there not a lie in my right hand?' "[16]

The earnestness with which father Dickson spoke, combined with the reverence commonly entertained for his piety, gave great force to his words. The reader will not therefore wonder to hear that father Bonnie, impulsive and easily moved as he was, wept at the account, and was moved by the exhortation. Nor will he be surprised to learn that, two weeks after, father Bonnie drove a brisk bargain with the same trader for three new hands.

The trader had discovered that the judgment-day was not coming yet a while; and father Bonnie satisfied himself that Noah, when he awoke from his wine, said, "Cursed be Canaan."[17]

＊　　＊　　＊　　＊　　＊　　＊　　＊

We have one scene more to draw before we dismiss the auditors of the camp-meeting.

At a late hour the Gordon carriage was winding its way under the silent, checkered, woodland path. Harry, who came slowly on a horse behind, felt a hand laid on his bridle. With a sudden start, he stopped.

"O, Dred, is it you? How dared you—how *could* you be so imprudent? How dared you come here, when you know you risk your life?"

"Life!" said the other, "what is life? He that loveth his life shall lose it.[18] Besides, the Lord said unto me, Go! The Lord is with me as a mighty and terrible one! Harry, did you mark those men? Hunters of men, their hands red with the blood of the poor, all seeking unto the Lord! Ministers who buy and sell us! Is this a people prepared for the Lord? I left a man dead in the swamps, whom their dogs have torn! His wife is a widow—his children, orphans! They eat and wipe their mouth, and say, 'What have I done?' The temple of the Lord, the temple of the Lord, are we!"[19]

"I know it," said Harry, gloomily.

"And you join yourself unto them?"

"Don't speak to me any more about that! I won't betray you, but I won't consent to have blood shed. My mistress is my sister."

"O, yes, to be sure! They read Scripture, don't they? Cast out the children of the bond-woman! That's Scripture for them!"

"Dred," said Harry, "I love her better than I love myself. I will fight for her to the last, but never against her, nor hers!"

"And you will serve Tom Gordon?" said Dred.

"Never!" said Harry.

Dred stood still a moment. Through an opening among the branches the moonbeams streamed down on his wild, dark figure. Harry remarked his eye fixed before him on vacancy, the pupil swelling out in glassy fulness, with a fixed, somnambulic stare. After a moment, he spoke, in a hollow, altered voice, like that of a sleep-walker:

"Then shall the silver cord be loosed, and the golden bowl be broken.[20] Yes, cover up the grave—cover it up! Now, hurry! come to me, or he will take thy wife for a prey!"

"Dred, what do you mean?" said Harry. "What's the matter?" He shook him by the shoulder.

Dred rubbed his eyes, and stared on Harry.

"I must go back," he said, "to my den. 'Foxes have holes, the birds of the air have nests,' and in the habitation of dragons the Lord hath opened a way for his outcasts!"[21]

He plunged into the thickets, and was gone.

DRED;

A

TALE OF THE GREAT DISMAL SWAMP.

VOL. II.

CHAPTER I

Life in the Swamps

OUR READERS will perhaps feel an interest to turn back with us, and follow the singular wanderings of the mysterious personage, whose wild denunciations had so disturbed the minds of the worshippers at the camp-meeting.

There is a twilight-ground between the boundaries of the sane and insane, which the old Greeks and Romans regarded with a peculiar veneration. They held a person whose faculties were thus darkened as walking under the awful shadow of a supernatural presence; and, as the mysterious secrets of the stars only become visible in the night, so in these eclipses of the more material faculties they held there was often an awakening of supernatural perceptions.

The hot and positive light of our modern materialism, which exhales from the growth of our existence every dew-drop, which searches out and dries every rivulet of romance, which sends an unsparing beam into every cool grotto of poetic possibility, withering the moss, and turning the dropping cave to a dusty den—this spirit, so remorseless, allows us no such indefinite land. There are but two words in the whole department of modern anthropology—the sane and the insane; the latter dismissed from human reckoning almost with contempt. We should find it difficult to give a suitable name to the strange and abnormal condition in which this singular being, of whom we are speaking, passed the most of his time.

It was a state of exaltation and trance, which yet appeared not at all to impede the exercise of his outward and physical faculties, but rather to give them a preternatural keenness and intensity, such as sometimes attends the more completely-developed phenomena of somnambulism.

In regard to his physical system there was also much that was peculiar. Our readers may imagine a human body of the largest and keenest vitality, to grow up so completely under the nursing influ-

273

ences of nature, that it may seem to be as perfectly *en rapport*[1] with them as a tree; so that the rain, the wind, and the thunder, all those forces from which human beings generally seek shelter, seem to hold with it a kind of fellowship, and to be familiar companions of existence.

Such was the case with Dred. So completely had he come into sympathy and communion with nature, and with those forms of it which more particularly surrounded him in the swamps, that he moved about among them with as much ease as a lady treads her Turkey carpet. What would seem to us in recital to be incredible hardship, was to him but an ordinary condition of existence. To walk knee-deep in the spongy soil of the swamp, to force his way through thickets, to lie all night sinking in the porous soil, or to crouch, like the alligator, among reeds and rushes, were to him situations of as much comfort as well-curtained beds and pillows are to us.

It is not to be denied, that there is in this savage perfection of the natural organs a keen and almost fierce delight, which must excel the softest seductions of luxury. Anybody who has ever watched the eager zest with which the hunting-dog plunges through the woods, darts through the thicket, or dives into water, in an ecstasy of enjoyment, sees something of what such vital force must be.

Dred was under the inspiring belief that he was the subject of visions and supernatural communications. The African race are said by mesmerists[2] to possess, in the fullest degree, that peculiar temperament which fits them for the evolution of mesmeric phenomena; and hence the existence among them, to this day, of men and women who are supposed to have peculiar magical powers. The grandfather of Dred, on his mother's side, had been one of these reputed African sorcerers; and he had early discovered in the boy this peculiar species of temperament. He had taught him the secret of snake-charming, and had possessed his mind from childhood with expectations of prophetic and supernatural impulses. That mysterious and singular gift, whatever it may be, which Highland seers[3] denominate second sight, is a very common tradition among the negroes; and there are not wanting thousands of reputed instances among them to confirm belief in it. What this faculty may be, we shall not pretend to say. Whether there be in the soul a yet undeveloped attribute, which is to be to the future what memory is to the past, or whether in some individuals an extremely high and perfect condition of the sensuous organization endows them with something of that certainty of instinctive discrimination which belongs to animals, are things which we shall not venture to decide upon.

It was, however, an absolute fact with regard to Dred, that he had often escaped danger by means of a peculiarity of this kind. He had been warned from particular places where the hunters had lain in wait for him; had foreseen in times of want where game might be ensnared, and received intimations where persons were to be found in whom he might safely confide; and his predictions with regard to persons and things had often chanced to be so strikingly true, as to invest his sayings with a singular awe and importance among his associates.

It was a remarkable fact, but one not peculiar to this case alone, that the mysterious exaltation of mind in this individual seemed to run parallel with the current of shrewd, practical sense; and, like a man who converses alternately in two languages, he would speak now the language of exaltation, and now that of common life, interchangeably. This peculiarity imparted a singular and grotesque effect to his whole personality.

On the night of the camp-meeting, he was, as we have already seen, in a state of the highest ecstasy. The wanton murder of his associate seemed to flood his soul with an awful tide of emotion, as a thunder-cloud is filled and shaken by slow-gathering electricity. And, although the distance from his retreat to the camp-ground was nearly fifteen miles, most of it through what seemed to be impassable swamps, yet he performed it with as little consciousness of fatigue as if he had been a spirit. Even had he been perceived at that time, it is probable that he could no more have been taken, or bound, than the demoniac of Gadara.[4]

After he parted from Harry, he pursued his way to the interior of the swamp, as was his usual habit, repeating to himself, in a chanting voice, such words of prophetic writ as were familiar to him.

The day had been sultry, and it was now an hour or two past midnight, when a thunder-storm, which had long been gathering and muttering in the distant sky, began to develop its forces.

A low, shivering sigh crept through the woods, and swayed in weird whistlings the tops of the pines; and sharp arrows of lightning came glittering down among the darkness of the branches, as if sent from the bow of some warlike angel. An army of heavy clouds swept in a moment across the moon; then came a broad, dazzling, blinding sheet of flame, concentrating itself on the top of a tall pine near where Dred was standing, and in a moment shivered all its branches to the ground, as a child strips the leaves from a twig. Dred clapped his hands with a fierce delight; and, while the rain and wind were howling and hissing around him, he shouted aloud:

"Wake, O, arm of the Lord! Awake, put on thy strength! The voice of the Lord breaketh the cedars—yea, the cedars of Lebanon! The voice of the Lord divideth the flames of fire! The voice of the Lord shaketh the wilderness of Kadesh! Hail-stones and coals of fire!"[5]

The storm, which howled around him, bent the forest like a reed, and large trees, uprooted from the spongy and tremulous soil, fell crashing with a tremendous noise; but, as if he had been a dark spirit of the tempest, he shouted and exulted.

The perception of such awful power seemed to animate him, and yet to excite in his soul an impatience that He whose power was so infinite did not awake to judgment.

"Rend the heavens," he cried, "and come down! Avenge the innocent blood! Cast forth thine arrows, and slay them! Shoot out thy lightnings, and destroy them!"[6]

His soul seemed to kindle with almost a fierce impatience, at the toleration of that Almighty Being, who, having the power to blast and to burn, so silently endures. Could Dred have possessed himself of those lightnings, what would have stood before him? But his cry, like the cry of thousands, only went up to stand in waiting till an awful coming day!

Gradually the storm passed by; the big drops dashed less and less frequently; a softer breeze passed through the forest, with a patter like the clapping of a thousand little wings; and the moon occasionally looked over the silvery battlements of the great clouds.

As Dred was starting to go forward, one of these clear revealings showed him the cowering form of a man, crouched at the root of a tree, a few paces in front of him. He was evidently a fugitive, and, in fact, was the one of whose escape to the swamps the Georgia trader had complained on the day of the meeting.

"Who is here, at this time of night?" said Dred, coming up to him.

"I have lost my way," said the other. "I don't know where I am!"

"A runaway?" inquired Dred.

"Don't betray me!" said the other, apprehensively.

"Betray you! Would *I* do that?" said Dred. "How did you get into the swamp?"

"I got away from a soul-driver's camp, that was taking us on through the states."

"O, O!" said Dred. "Camp-meeting and driver's camp right alongside of each other! Shepherds that sell the flock, and pick the bones! Well, come, old man; I'll take you home with me."

"I'm pretty much beat out," said the man. "It's been up over my knees every step; and I didn't know but they'd set the dogs after me. If they do, I'll let 'em kill me, and done with it, for I'm 'bout ready to have it over with. I got free once, and got clear up to New York, and got me a little bit of a house, and a wife and two children, with a little money beforehand; and then they nabbed me, and sent me back again, and mas'r sold me to the drivers,—and I believe I's 'bout as good 's die. There's no use in trying to live—everything going agin a body so!"

"Die! No, indeed, you won't," said Dred; "not if I've got hold of you! Take heart, man, take heart! Before morning I'll put you where the dogs can't find you, nor anything else. Come, up with you!"

The man rose up, and made an effort to follow; but, wearied, and unused as he was to the choked and perplexed way, he stumbled and fell almost every minute.

"How now, brother?" said Dred. "This won't do! I must put you over my shoulder as I have many a buck before now!" And, suiting the action to the word, he put the man on his back, and, bidding him hold fast to him, went on, picking his way as if he scarcely perceived his weight.

It was now between two and three o'clock, and the clouds, gradually dispersing, allowed the full light of the moon to slide down here and there through the wet and shivering foliage. No sound was heard, save the humming of insects and the crackling plunges by which Dred made his way forward.

"You must be pretty strong!" said his companion. "Have you been in the swamps long?"

"Yes," said the other, "I have been a wild man—every man's hand against me—a companion of the dragons and the owls, this many a year. I have made my bed with the leviathan, among the

reeds and the rushes. I have found the alligators and the snakes better neighbors than Christians. They let those alone that let them
alone; but Christians will hunt for the precious life."

After about an hour of steady travelling, Dred arrived at the outskirts of the island which we have described. For about twenty
paces before he reached it, he waded waist-deep in water. Creeping
out, at last, and telling the other one to follow him, he began carefully coursing along on his hands and knees, giving, at the same
time, a long, shrill, peculiar whistle. It was responded to by a similar sound, which seemed to proceed through the bushes. After a
while, a crackling noise was heard, as of some animal, which gradually seemed to come nearer and nearer to them, till finally a large
water-dog emerged from the underbrush, and began testifying his
joy at the arrival of the new comer, by most extravagant gambols.

"So, ho! Buck! quiet, my boy!" said Dred. "Show us the way
in!"

The dog, as if understanding the words, immediately turned into
the thicket, and Dred and his companion followed him, on their
hands and knees. The path wound up and down the brushwood,
through many sharp turnings, till at last it ceased altogether, at the
roots of a tree; and, while the dog disappeared among the brush-
wood, Dred climbed the tree, and directed his companion to follow
him, and, proceeding out on to one of the longest limbs, he sprang
nimbly on to the ground in the cleared space which we have before
described.

His wife was standing waiting for him, and threw herself upon
him with a cry of joy.

"O, you've come back! I thought, sure enough, dey'd got you
dis time!"

"Not yet! I must continue till the opening of the seals[7]—till the
vision cometh! Have ye buried him?"

"No; there's a grave dug down yonder, and he's been carried
there."

"Come, then!" said Dred.

At a distant part of the clearing was a blasted cedar-tree, all
whose natural foliage had perished. But it was veiled from head to
foot in long wreaths of the tillandsia, the parasitic moss of these regions, and, in the dim light of the approaching dawn, might have
formed no unapt resemblance to a gigantic spectre dressed in
mourning weeds.

Beneath this tree Dred had interred, from time to time, the bodies of fugitives which he found dead in the swamps, attaching to this disposition of them some peculiar superstitious idea.

The widow of the dead, the wife of Dred, and the new comer, were now gathered around the shallow grave; for the soil was such as scarcely gave room to make a place deep enough for a grave without its becoming filled with water.

The dawn was just commencing a dim foreshadowing in the sky. The moon and stars were still shining.

Dred stood and looked up, and spoke, in a solemn voice.

"Seek him that maketh Arcturus and Orion[8]—that turneth the shadow of death into morning! Behold those lights in the sky—the lights in his hands pierced for the sins of the world, and spread forth as on a cross! But the day shall come that he shall lay down the yoke, and he will bear the sin of the world no longer. Then shall come the great judgment. He will lay righteousness to the line and judgment to the plummet, and the hail shall sweep away the refuges of lies."[9]

He stooped, and, lifting the body, laid him in the grave, and at this moment the wife broke into a loud lament.

"Hush, woman!" said Dred, raising his hand. "Weep ye not for the dead, neither bewail him; but weep ye sore for the living! He must rest till the rest of his brethren be killed; for the vision is sealed up for an appointed time. If it tarry, wait for it. It shall surely come, and shall not tarry!"

CHAPTER II

More Summer Talk

A GLORIOUS MORNING, washed by the tears of last night's shower, rose like a bride upon Canema. The rain-drops sparkled and winked from leaf to leaf, or fell in showery diamonds in the breeze. The breath of numberless roses, now in full bloom, rose in clouds to the windows.

The breakfast-table, with its clean damask, glittering silver, and fragrant coffee, received the last evening's participants of the camp-meeting in fresh morning spirits, ready to discuss, as an every-day affair, what, the evening before, they had felt too deeply, perhaps, to discuss.

On the way home, they had spoken of the scenes of the day, and wondered and speculated on the singular incident which closed it. But, of all the dark circle of woe and crime,—of all that valley of vision which was present to the mind of him who spoke,—they were as practically ignorant as the dwellers of the curtained boudoirs of New York are of the fearful mysteries of the Five Points.[1]

The aristocratic nature of society at the South so completely segregates people of a certain position in life from any acquaintance with the movements of human nature in circles below them, that the most fearful things may be transacting in their vicinity unknown or unnoticed. The horrors and sorrows of the slave-coffle were a sealed book to Nina and Anne Clayton. They had scarcely dreamed of them; and Uncle John, if he knew their existence, took very good care to keep out of their way, as he would turn from any other painful and disagreeable scene.

All of them had heard something of negro-hunters, and regarded them as low, vulgar people, but troubled their heads little further on the subject; so that they would have been quite at a loss for the discovery of any national sins that could have appropriately drawn down the denunciations of Heaven.

The serious thoughts and aspirations which might have risen in any of the company, the evening before, assumed, with everything else, quite another light under the rays of morning.

All of us must have had experience, in our own histories, of the great difference between the night and the morning view of the same subject.

What we have thought and said in the august presence of witnessing stars, or beneath the holy shadows of moonlight, seems with the hot, dry light of next day's sun to take wings, and rise to heaven with the night's clear drops. If all the prayers and good resolutions which are laid down on sleeping pillows could be found there on awaking, the world would be better than it is.

Of this Uncle John Gordon had experience, as he sat himself down at the breakfast-table. The night before, he realized, in some dim wise, that he, Mr. John Gordon, was not merely a fat, elderly gentleman, in blue coat and white vest, whose great object in existence was to eat well, drink well, sleep well, wear clean linen, and keep out of the way of trouble. He had within him a tumult of yearnings and aspirings,—uprisings of that great, life-long sleeper, which we call *soul*, and which, when it wakes, is an awfully clamorous, craving, exacting, troublesome inmate, and which is therefore generally put asleep again in the shortest time, by whatever opiates may come to hand. Last night, urged on by this troublesome guest, stimulated by the vague power of such awful words as judgment and eternity, he had gone out and knelt down as a mourner for sin and a seeker for salvation, both words standing for very real and awful facts; and, this morning, although it was probably a more sensible and appropriate thing than most of the things he was in the habit of doing, he was almost ashamed of it. The question arose, at table, whether another excursion should be made to the camp-ground.

"For my part," said Aunt Maria, "I hope you'll not go again, Mr. Gordon. I think you had better keep out of the way of such things. I really was vexed to see you in that rabble of such very common people!"

"You'll observe," said Uncle John, "that, when Mrs. G. goes to heaven, she'll notify the Lord, forthwith, that she has only been accustomed to the most select circles, and requests to be admitted at the front door."

"It isn't because I object to being with common people," said Anne Clayton, "that I dislike this custom of going to the altar; but

it seems to me an invasion of that privacy and reserve which belong
to our most sacred feelings. Besides, there are in a crowd coarse,
rude, disagreeable people, with whom it isn't pleasant to come in
contact."

"For my part," said Mrs. John Gordon, "I don't believe in it at
all! It's a mere temporary excitement. People go and get wonderfully wrought up, come away, and are just what they were before."

"Well," said Clayton, "isn't it better to be wrought up once in a
while, than *never* to have any religious feelings? Isn't it better to
have a vivid impression of the vastness and worth of the soul,—of
the power of an endless life,—for a few hours once a year, than
never to feel it at all? The multitudes of those people, there, never
hear or think a word of these things at any other time in their lives.
For my part," he added, "I don't see why it's a thing to be ashamed
of, if Mr. Gordon or I should have knelt at the altar last night, even
if we do not feel like it this morning. We are too often ashamed of
our better moments;—I believe Protestant Christians are the only
people on earth who are ashamed of the outward recognition of
their religion. The Mahometan will prostrate himself in the street,
or wherever he happens to be when his hour for prayer comes. The
Roman Catholic sailor, or soldier, kneels down at the sound of the
vesper bell. But we rather take pride in having it understood that we
take our religion moderately and coolly, and that we are not going
to put ourselves much out about it."

"Well, but, brother," said Anne, "I will maintain, still, that there
is a reserve about these things which belongs to the best Christians.
And did not our Saviour tell us that our prayers and alms should be
in secret?"

"I do not deny at all what you say, Anne," said Clayton; "but I
think what I said is true, notwithstanding; and, both being true, of
course, in some way they must be consistent with each other."

"I think," said Nina, "the sound of the singing at these camp-
meetings is really quite spirit-stirring and exciting."

"Yes," said Clayton, "these wild tunes, and the hymns with
which they are associated, form a kind of forest liturgy, in which
the feelings of thousands of hearts have been embodied. Some of
the tunes seem to me to have been caught from the song of birds, or
from the rushing of wind among the branches. They possess a peculiar rhythmical energy, well suited to express the vehement emo-

tions of the masses. Did camp-meetings do no other good than to scatter among the people these hymns and tunes, I should consider them to be of inestimable value."

"I must say," said Anne, "I always had a prejudice against that class both of hymns and tunes."

"You misjudge them," said Clayton, "as you refined, cultivated women always do, who are brought up in the kid-slipper and carpet view of human life. But just imagine only the old Greek or Roman peasantry elevated to the level of one of these hymns. Take, for example, a verse of one I heard them sing last night:

> 'The earth shall be dissolved like snow,
>   The sun shall cease to shine,
> But God, who called me here below,
>   Shall be forever mine.'[2]

What faith is there! What confidence in immortality! How could a man feel it, and not be ennobled? Then, what a rough, hearty heroism was in that first hymn! It was right manly!"

"Ah, but," said Anne, "half the time they sing them without the slightest perception of their meaning, or the least idea of being influenced by them."

"And so do the worshippers in the sleepiest and most aristocratic churches," said Clayton. "That's nothing peculiar to the campground. But, if it is true, what a certain statesman once said, 'Let me make the ballads of the people, and I care not who makes their laws,'[3] it is certainly a great gain to have such noble sentiments as many of these hymns contain, circulating freely among the people."

"What upon earth," said Uncle John, "do you suppose that last fellow was about, up in the clouds, there? Nobody seemed to know where he was, or *who* he was; and I thought his discourse seemed to be rather an unexpected addition. He put it into us pretty strong, I thought! Declare, such a bundle of woes and curses I never heard distributed! Seemed to have done up all the old prophets into one bundle, and tumbled it down upon our heads! Some of them were quite superstitious about it, and began talking about warnings, and all that."

"Pooh!" said Aunt Maria, "the likelihood is that some itinerant poor preacher has fallen upon this trick for producing a sensation. There is no end to the trickeries and the got-up scenes in these camp-meetings, just to produce effect. If I had had a pistol, I should like to have fired into the tree, and see whether I couldn't have changed his tune."

"It seemed to me," said Clayton, "from the little that I did hear, that there was some method in his madness. It was one of the most singular and impressive voices I ever heard; and, really, the enunciation of some of those latter things was tremendous. But, then, in the universal license and general confusion of the scene, the thing was not so much to be wondered at. It would be the most natural thing in the world, that some crazy fanatic should be heated almost to the point of insanity by the scene, and take this way of unburthening himself. Such excitements most generally assume the form of denunciation."

"Well, now," said Nina, "to tell the truth, I should like to go out again to-day. It's a lovely ride, and I like to be in the woods. And, then, I like to walk around among the tents, and hear the people talk, and see all the different specimens of human nature that are there. I never saw such a gathering together in my life."

"Agreed!" said Uncle John. "I'll go with you. After all, Clayton, here, has got the right of it, when he says a fellow oughtn't to be ashamed of his religion, such as it is."

"Such as it is, to be sure!" said Aunt Maria, sarcastically.

"Yes, I say again, such as it is!" said Uncle John, bracing himself. "I don't pretend it's much. We'll all of us bear to be a good deal better, without danger of being translated. Now, as to this being converted, hang me if I know how to get at it! I suppose that it is something like an electric shock,—if a fellow is going to get it, he must go up to the machine!"

"Well," said Nina, "you do hear some queer things there. Don't you remember that jolly, slashing-looking fellow, whom they called Bill Dakin, that came up there with his two dogs? In the afternoon, after the regular services, we went to one of the tents where there was a very noisy prayer-meeting going on, and there was Bill Dakin, on his knees, with his hands clasped, and the tears rolling down his cheeks; and father Bonnie was praying over him with all his might. And what do you think he said? He said, 'O, Lord, here's Bill Dakin; he is converted; now take him right to heaven, now he is ready, or he'll be drunk again in two weeks!' "

"Well," said Anne Clayton, tossing her head, indignantly, "that's blasphemy, in my opinion."

"O, perhaps not," said Clayton, "any more than the clownish talk of any of our servants is intentional rudeness."

"Well," said Anne, "don't you think it shows a great want of perception?"

"Certainly, it does," said Clayton. "It shows great rudeness and coarseness of fibre, and is not at all to be commended. But still we are not to judge of it by the rules of cultivated society. In well-trained minds every faculty keeps its due boundaries; but, in this kind of wild-forest growth, mirthfulness will sometimes overgrow reverence, just as the yellow jessamine will completely smother a tree. A great many of the ordinances of the old Mosaic dispensation were intended to counteract this very tendency."

"Well," said Nina, "did you notice poor Old Tiff, so intent upon getting his children converted? He didn't seem to have the least thought or reference to getting into heaven himself. The only thing with him was to get those children in. Tiff seems to me just like those mistletoes that we see on the trees in the swamps. He don't seem to have any root of his own; he seems to grow out of something else."

"Those children are very pretty-looking, genteel children," said Anne; "and how well they were dressed!"

"My dear," said Nina, "Tiff prostrates himself at my shrine, every time he meets me, to implore my favorable supervision as to that point; and it really is diverting to hear him talk. The old Caliban[4] has an eye for color, and a sense of what is suitable, equal to any French milliner. I assure you, my dear, I always was reputed for having a talent for dress; and Tiff *appreciates* me. Isn't it charming of him? I declare, when I see the old creature lugging about those children, I always think of an ugly old cactus with its blossoms. I believe he verily thinks they belong to him just as much. Their father is entirely dismissed from Tiff's calculations. Evidently all he wants of him is to keep out of the way, and let him work. The whole burden of their education lies on his shoulders."

"For my part," said Aunt Nesbit, "I'm glad you've faith to believe in those children. I haven't; they'll be sure to turn out badly—you see if they don't."

"And I think," said Aunt Maria, "we have enough to do with our own servants, without taking all these miserable whites on our hands, too."

"I'm not going to take all the whites," said Nina. "I'm going to take these children."

"I wish you joy!" said Aunt Maria.

"I wonder," said Aunt Nesbit, "if Harry is under concern of mind. He seems to be dreadfully down, this morning."

"Is he?" said Nina. "I hadn't noticed it."

"Well," said Uncle John, "perhaps he'll get set up, to-day—who knows? In fact, I hope I shall myself. I tell you what it is, parson," said he, laying his hand on Clayton's shoulder, "you should take the gig, to-day, and drive this little sinner, and let me go with the ladies. Of course you know Mrs. G. engrosses my whole soul; but, then, there's a kind of insensible improvement that comes from such celestial bodies as Miss Anne, here, that oughtn't to be denied to me. The clergy ought to enumerate female influence among the means of grace. I'm sure there's nothing builds me up like it."

Clayton, of course, assented very readily to this arrangement; and the party was adjusted on this basis.

"Look ye here, now, Clayton," said Uncle John, tipping him a sly wink, after he had handed Nina in, "you must confess that little penitent! She wants a spiritual director, my boy! I tell you what, Clayton, there isn't a girl like that in North Carolina. There's blood, sir, there. You must humor her on the bit, and give her her head a while. Ah, but she'll draw well at last! I always like a creature that kicks to pieces harness, wagon, and all, to begin with. They do the best when they are broken in."

With which profound remarks Uncle John turned to hand Anne Clayton to the carriage.

Clayton understood too well what he was about to make any such use of the interview as Uncle John had suggested. He knew perfectly that his best chance, with a nature so restless as Nina's, was to keep up a sense of perfect freedom in all their intercourse; and, therefore, no grandfather could have been more collected and easy in a tête-à-tête drive than he. The last conversation at the camp-meeting he knew had brought them much nearer to each other than they had ever stood before, because both had spoken in deep earnestness of feeling of what lay deepest in their hearts; and one such moment he well knew was of more binding force than a hundred nominal betrothals.

The morning was one of those perfect ones which succeed a thunder-shower in the night; when the air, cleared of every gross vapor, and impregnated with moist exhalations from the woods, is both balmy and stimulating. The steaming air developed to the full the balsamic properties of the pine-groves through which they rode; and, where the road skirted the swampy land, the light fell slanting on the leaves of the deciduous trees, rustling and dripping with the last night's shower. The heavens were full of those brilliant, island-like clouds, which are said to be a peculiarity of American skies, in their distinct relief above the intense blue. At a long distance they caught the sound of camp-meeting hymns. But, before they reached the ground, they saw, in more than one riotous group, the result of too frequent an application to Abijah Skinflint's department, and others of a similar character. They visited the quarters of Old Tiff, whom they found busy ironing some clothes for the baby, which he had washed and hung out the night before. The preaching had not yet commenced, and the party walked about among the tents. Women were busy cooking and washing dishes under the trees; and there was a great deal of good-natured gossiping.

One of the most remarkable features of the day was a sermon from father Dickson, on the sins of the church. It concluded with a most forcible and solemn appeal to all on the subject of slavery. He reminded both the Methodists and Presbyterians that their books of discipline had most pointedly and unequivocally condemned it; that John Wesley had denounced it as the sum of all villainies, and that the general assemblies of the Presbyterian church had condemned it as wholly inconsistent with the religion of Christ, with the great law which requires us to love others as ourselves. He related the scene which he had lately witnessed in the slave-coffle. He spoke of the horrors of the inter-state slave-trade, and drew a touching picture of the separation of families, and the rending of all domestic and social ties, which resulted from it; and, alluding to the unknown speaker of the evening before, told his audience that he had discerned a deep significance in his words, and that he feared, if there was not immediate repentance and reformation, the land would yet be given up to the visitations of divine wrath. As he spoke with feeling, he awakened feeling in return. Many were affected even to tears; but, when the sermon was over, it seemed to melt away, as a wave flows back again into the sea. It was far easier to join in a temporary whirlwind of excitement, than to take into consideration troublesome, difficult, and expensive reforms.

Yet, still, it is due to the degenerate Christianity of the slave states to say, that, during the long period in which the church there has been corrupting itself, and lowering its standard of right to meet a depraved institution, there have not been wanting, from time to time, noble confessors, who have spoken for God and humanity. For many years they were listened to with that kind of pensive tolerance which men give when they acknowledge their fault without any intention of mending. Of late years, however, the lines have been drawn more sharply, and such witnesses have spoken in peril of their lives; so that now seldom a voice arises except in approbation of oppression.

The sermon was fruitful of much discussion in different parts of the camp-ground; and none, perhaps, was louder in the approbation of it than the Georgia trader, who, seated on Abijah Skinflint's counter, declared: "That was a *parson* as *was* a parson, and that he liked his *pluck;* and, for his part, when ministers and church-members would give over buying, he should take up some other trade."

"That was a very good sermon," said Nina, "and I believe every word of it. But, then, what do you suppose *we* ought to do?"

"Why," said Clayton, "we ought to contemplate emancipation as a future certainty, and prepare our people in the shortest possible time."

This conversation took place as the party were seated at their nooning under the trees, around an unpacked hamper of cold provisions, which they were leisurely discussing.

"Why, bless my soul, Clayton," said Uncle John, "I don't see the sense of such an anathema maranatha⁵ as we got to-day. Good Lord, what earthly harm are we doing? As to our niggers, they are better off than we are! I say it coolly—that is, as coolly as a man can say anything between one and two o'clock, in such weather as this. Why, look at my niggers! Do *I* ever have any chickens, or eggs, or cucumbers? No, to be sure. All *my* chickens die, and the cut-worm plays the devil with *my* cucumbers; but the niggers have enough. *Theirs* flourish like a green bay tree; and of course I have to buy of *them. They* raise chickens. *I* buy 'em, and cook 'em, and then *they* eat 'em! That's the way it goes. As to the slave-coffles, and slave-prisons, and the trade, why, that's abominable, to be sure. But,

Lord bless you, *I* don't want it done! I'd kick a trader off my door-steps forthwith, though I'm all eaten up with woolly-heads, like locusts. I don't like such sermons, for my part."

"Well," said Aunt Nesbit, "our Mr. Titmarsh preached quite an-other way when I attended church in E——. He proved that slavery was a scriptural institution, and established by God."

"I should think anybody's common sense would show that a thing which works so poorly for both sides couldn't be from God," said Nina.

"Who is Mr. Titmarsh?" said Clayton to her, aside.

"O, one of Aunt Nesbit's favorites, and one of my aversions! He isn't a *man*—he's nothing but a theological dictionary with a cravat on! I can't bear him!"

"Now, people may talk as much as they please of the educated democracy of the north," said Uncle John. "*I* don't like 'em. What do working-men want of education?—Ruins 'em! I've heard of their learned blacksmiths bothering around, neglecting their work, to make speeches. I don't like such things. It raises them above their sphere. And there's nothing going on up in those Northern States but a constant confusion and hubbub. All sorts of heresies come from the North, and infidelity, and the Lord knows what! We have peace, down here. To be sure, our poor whites are in a devil of a fix; but we haven't got 'em under yet. We shall get 'em in, one of these days, with our niggers, and then all will be contentment."

"Yes," said Nina, "there's Uncle John's view of the millennium!"

"To be sure," said Uncle John, "the lower classes want *govern-ing*—they want care; that's what they want. And all they need to know is, what the Episcopal church catechism says, 'to learn and la-bor truly to get their own living in the state wherein it has pleased God to call them.' That makes a well-behaved lower class, and a handsome, gentlemanly, orderly state of society. The upper classes ought to be considerate and condescending, and all that. That's my view of society."

"Then you are no republican," said Clayton.

"Bless you, yes, I am! I believe in the equality of *gentlemen*, and the equal rights of well-bred people. That's my idea of a republic."

Clayton, Nina, and Anne, laughed.

"Now," said Nina, "to see uncle so jovial and free, and 'Hail fel-low well met,' with everybody, you'd think he was the greatest democrat that ever walked. But, you see, it's only because he's so immeasurably certain of his superior position—that's all. He isn't afraid to kneel at the altar with Bill Dakin, or Jim Sykes, because he's so sure that his position can't be compromised."

"Besides that, chick," said Uncle John, "I *have* the sense to know that, in my Maker's presence, all human differences are child's play." And Uncle John spoke with a momentary solemnity which was heartfelt.

It was agreed by the party that they would not stay to attend the evening exercises. The novelty of the effect was over, and Aunt Nesbit spoke of the bad effects of falling dew and night air. Accordingly, as soon as the air was sufficiently cooled to make riding practicable, the party were again on their way home.

The woodland path was streaked with green and golden bands of light thrown between the tree-trunks across the way, and the trees reverberated with the evening song of birds. Nina and Clayton naturally fell into a quiet and subdued train of conversation.

"It is strange," said Nina, "these talkings and searchings about religion. Now, there are people who have something they call religion, which I don't think does them any good. It isn't of any use— it doesn't make them better—and it makes them very disagreeable. I would rather be as I am, than to have what they call religion. But, then, there are others that have something which I know *is* religion; something that I know I have not; something that I'd give all the world to have, and don't know how to get. Now, there was Livy Ray—you ought to have seen Livy Ray—there was something so superior about her; and, what was extraordinary is, that she was *good* without being *stupid*. What do you suppose the reason is that good people are generally so stupid?"

"A great deal," said Clayton, "is called goodness, which is nothing but want of force. A person is said to have self-government simply because he has nothing to govern. They talk about self-denial, when their desires are so weak that one course is about as easy to them as another. Such people easily fall into a religious routine, get by heart a set of phrases, and make, as you say, very stupid, good people."

"Now, Livy," said Nina, "was remarkable. She had that kind of education that they give girls in New England, stronger and more like a man's than ours. She could read Greek and Latin as easily as she could French and Italian. She was keen, shrewd, and witty, and had a kind of wild grace about her, like these grape-vines; yet she was so *strong!* Well, do you know, I almost worship Livy? And I think, the little while she was in our school, she did me more good than all the teachers and studying put together. Why, it does one good to know that such people are possible. Don't you think it does?"

"Yes," said Clayton; "all the good in the world is done by the personality of people. Now, in books, it isn't so much what you learn from them, as the contact it gives you with the personality of the writer, that improves you. A real book always makes you feel that there is more in the writer than anything that he has said."

"That," said Nina, eagerly, "is just the way I feel toward Livy. She seems to me like a mine. When I was with her the longest, I always felt as if I hadn't half seen her. She always made me hungry to know her more. I mean to read you some of her letters, some time. She writes beautiful letters; and I appreciate that very much, because I can't do it. I can talk better than I can write. Somehow my ideas will not take a course down through my arms; they always will run up to my mouth. But you ought to see Livy; such people always make me very discontented with myself. I don't know what the reason is that I like to see superior people, and things, when they always make me realize what a poor concern I am. Now, the first time I heard Jenny Lind[6] sing, it spoiled all my music and all my songs for me,—turned them all to trash at one stroke,—and yet I liked it. But I don't seem to have got any further in goodness than just dissatisfaction with myself."

"Well," said Clayton, "there's where the foundation-stone of all excellence is laid. The very first blessing that Christ pronounced was on those who were poor in spirit. The indispensable condition to all progress in art, science, or religion, is to feel that we have nothing."

"Do you know," said Nina, after something of a pause, "that I can't help wondering what you took up with me for? I have thought very often that you ought to have Livy Ray."

"Well, I'm much obliged to you," said Clayton, "for your consideration in providing for me. But, supposing I should prefer my own choice, after all? We men are a little wilful, sometimes, like you of the gentler sex."

"Well," said Nina, "if you *will* have the bad taste, then, to insist on liking me, let me warn you that you don't know what you are about. I'm a very unformed, unpractical person. I don't keep accounts. I'm nothing at all of a housekeeper. I shall leave open drawers, and scatter papers, and forget the day of the month, and tear the newspaper, and do everything else that is wicked; and then, one of these days, it will be, 'Nina, why haven't you done this? and why haven't you done that? and why don't you do the other? and why *do* you do something else?' Ah, I've heard you men talk before! And, then, you see, I shan't like it, and I shan't behave well. Haven't the least hope of it; won't ever engage to!—So, now, won't you take warning?"

"No," said Clayton, looking at her with a curious kind of smile, "I don't think I shall."

"How dreadfully positive and self-willed men are!" said Nina, drawing a long breath, and pretending to laugh.

"There's so little of that in you ladies," said Clayton, "we have to do it for both."

"So, then," said Nina, looking round with a half-laugh and half-blush, "you *will* persist?"

"Yes, you wicked little witch!" said Clayton, "since you challenge me, I *will.*" And, as he spoke, he passed his arm round Nina firmly, and fixed his eyes on hers. "Come, now, my little Baltimore oriole, have I caught you?" And — But we are making our chapter too long.

CHAPTER III

Milly's Return

THE VISIT OF CLAYTON and his sister, like all other pleasant things, had its end. Clayton was called back to his law-office and books, and Anne went to make some summer visits previous to her going to Clayton's plantation of Magnolia Grove, where she was to superintend his various schemes for the improvement of his negroes.

Although it was gravely insisted to the last that there was no *engagement* between Nina and Clayton, it became evident enough to all parties that only the name was wanting. The warmest possible friendship existed between Nina and Anne; and, notwithstanding that Nina almost every day said something which crossed Anne's nicely-adjusted views, and notwithstanding Anne had a gentle infusion of that disposition to sermonize which often exists in very excellent young ladies, still the two got on excellently well together.

It is to be confessed that, the week after they left, Nina was rather restless and lonesome, and troubled to pass her time. An incident, which we shall relate, however, gave her something to think of, and opens a new page in our story.

While sitting on the veranda, after breakfast, her attention was called by various exclamations from the negro department, on the right side of the mansion; and, looking out, to her great surprise, she saw Milly standing amid a group, who were surrounding her with eager demonstrations. Immediately she ran down the steps to inquire what it might mean. Approaching nearer, she was somewhat startled to see that her old friend had her head bound up and her arm in a sling; and, as she came towards her, she observed that she seemed to walk with difficulty, with a gait quite different from her usual firm, hilarious tread.

"Why, Milly!" she said, running towards her with eagerness, "what is the matter?"

"Not much, chile, I reckon, now I's got home!" said Milly.

"Well, but what's the matter with your arm?"

293

"No great! Dat ar man shot me; but, praise de Lord, he didn't kill me! I don't owe him no grudge; but I thought it wan't right and fit that I should be treated so; and so I just *put!*"

"Why, come in the house this minute!" said Nina, laying hold of her friend, and drawing her towards the steps. "It's a shame! Come in, Milly, come in! That man! I *knew* he wasn't to be trusted. So, this is the good place he found for you, is it?"

"Jes so," said Tomtit, who, at the head of a dark stream of young juveniles, came after, with a towel hanging over one arm, and a knife half cleaned in his hand, while Rose and Old Hundred, and several others, followed to the veranda.

"Laws-a-me!" said Aunt Rose, "just to think on 't! Dat's what 't is for old fam'lies to hire der niggers out to common people!"

"Well," said Old Hundred, "Milly was allers too high feelin'; held her head up too much. An't no ways surprised at it!"

"O, go 'long, you old hominy-beetle!" said Aunt Rose "Don't know nobody dat holds up der head higher nor you does!"

Nina, after having dismissed the special train of the juveniles and servants, began to examine into the condition of her friend. The arm had evidently been grazed by a bullet, producing somewhat of a deep flesh-wound, which had been aggravated by the heat of the weather and the fatigue which she had undergone. On removing the bandage around her head, a number of deep and severe flesh-cuts were perceived.

"What's all this?" said Nina.

"It's whar he hit me over de head! He was in drink, chile; he didn't well know what he was 'bout!"

"What an abominable shame!" said Nina. "Look here," turning round to Aunt Nesbit, "see what comes of hiring Milly out!"

"I am sure I don't know what's to be done!" said Aunt Nesbit, pitifully.

"Done! why, of course, these are to be bandaged and put up, in the first place," said Nina, bustling about with great promptness, tearing off bandages, and ringing for warm water. "Aunt Milly, I'll do them up for you myself. I'm a pretty good nurse, when I set about it."

"Bless *you,* chile, but it seems good to get home 'mong friends!"

"Yes; and you won't go away again in a hurry!" said Nina, as she proceeded rapidly with her undertaking, washing and bandaging the wound. "There, now," she said, "you look something like; and now you shall lie down in my room, and take a little rest!"

"Thank ye, honey, chile, but I'll go to my own room; 'pears like it's more home like," said Milly. And Nina, with her usual energy, waited on her there, closed the blinds, and spread a shawl over her after she had lain down, and, after charging her two or three times to go to sleep and be quiet, she left her. She could hardly wait to have her get through her nap, so full was she of the matter, and so interested to learn the particulars of her story.

"A pretty business, indeed!" she said to Aunt Nesbit. "We'll prosecute those people, and make them pay dear for it."

"That will be a great expense," said Aunt Nesbit, apprehensively, "besides the loss of her time."

"Well," said Nina, "I shall write to Clayton about it directly. I know he'll feel just as I do. He understands the law, and all about those things, and he'll know how to manage it."

"Everything will make expense!" said Aunt Nesbit, in a deplorable voice. "I'm sure misfortunes never come single! Now, if she don't go back, I shall lose her wages! And here's all the expenses of a law-suit, besides! I think she ought to have been more careful."

"Why, aunt, for pity's sake, you don't pretend that you wish Milly to go back?"

"O, no, of course I don't; but, then, it's a pity. It will be a great loss, every way."

"Why, aunt, you really talk as if you didn't think of anything but your loss. You don't seem to think anything about what *Milly* has had to suffer!"

"Why, of course, I feel sorry for that," said Aunt Nesbit. "I wonder if she is going to be laid up long. I wish, on the whole, I had hired out one that wasn't quite so useful to me."

"Now, if that isn't just like her!" said Nina, in an indignant tone, as she flung out of the room, and went to look softly in at Milly's door. "Never can see, hear, or think, of anything but herself, no matter what happens! I wonder why Milly couldn't have belonged to me!"

After two or three hours' sleep, Milly came out of her room, seeming much better. A perfectly vigorous physical system, and vital powers all moving in the finest order, enabled her to endure much more than ordinary; and Nina soon became satisfied that no

material injury had been sustained, and that in a few days she would
be quite recovered.

"And now, Milly, do pray tell me where you have been," said
Nina, "and what this is all about."

"Why, you see, honey, I was hired to Mr. Barker, and dey said
'he was a mighty nice man;' and so he was, honey, most times; but,
den, you see, honey, dere's some folks dere's *two* men in 'em,—one
is a good one, and t' oder is very bad. Well, dis yer was just dat sort.
You see, honey, I wouldn't go for to say dat he got drunk; but he
was dat sort dat if he took ever so little, it made him kind o' ugly
and cross, and so dere wan't no suiting him. Well, his wife, she was
pretty far; and so he was, too, 'cept in spots. He was one of dese yer
streaked men, dat has drefful ugly streaks; and, some of dem times,
de Lord only knows what he won't do! Well, you see, honey, I
thought I was getting along right well, at first, and I was mighty
pleased. But dere was one day he came home, and 'peared like dere
couldn't nobody suit him. Well, you see, dey had a gal dere, and she
had a chile, and dis yer chile was a little thing. It got playing with a
little burnt stick, and it blacked one of his clean shirts, I had just
hung up,—for I'd been ironing, you see. Just den he came along,
and you never heard a man go on so! I's heerd bad talk afore, but I
never heerd no sich! He swore he'd kill de chile; and I thought my
soul he would! De por little thing run behind me, and I just kep him
off on it, 'cause I knowed he wan't fit to touch it; and den he turned
on me, and he got a cow-hide, and he beat me over de head. I
thought my soul he'd kill me! But I got to de door, and shut de
chile out, and Hannah, she took it and run with it. But, bless you, it
'peared like he was a tiger,—screeching, and foaming, and beating
me! I broke away from him, and run. He just caught de rifle,—he
always kep one loaded,—and shot at me, and de ball just struck my
arm, and glanced off again. Bless de Lord, it didn't break it. Dat ar
was a mighty close run, I can tell you! But I did run, 'cause, thinks
I, dere an't no safety for me in dat ar house; and, you see, I run till I
got to de bush, and den I got to whar dere was some free colored
folks, and dey did it up, and kep me a day or two. Den I started and
came home, just as you told me to."

"Well," said Nina, "you did well to come home; and I tell you
what, I'm going to have that man prosecuted!"

"O, laws, no, Miss Nina! don't you goes doing nothing to him!

His wife is a mighty nice woman, and 'peared like he didn't rightly know what he was 'bout."

"Yes, but, Milly, you ought to be willing, because it may make him more careful with other people."

"Laws, Miss Nina, why, dere is some sense in dat; but I wouldn't do it as bearing malice."

"Not at all," said Nina. "I shall write to Mr. Clayton, and take his advice about it."

"He's a good man," said Milly. "He won't say nothing dat an't right. I spect dat will do very well, dat ar way."

"Yes," said Nina, "such people must be taught that the law will take hold of them. That will bring them to their bearings!"

Nina went immediately to her room, and despatched a long letter to Clayton, full of all the particulars, and begging his immediate assistance.

Our readers, those who have been in similar circumstances, will not wonder that Clayton saw in this letter an immediate call of duty to go to Canema. In fact, as soon as the letter could go to him, and he could perform a rapid horseback journey, he was once more a member of the domestic circle.

He entered upon the case with great confidence and enthusiasm.

"It is a debt which we owe," he said, "to the character of our state, and to the purity of our institutions, to prove the efficiency of the law in behalf of that class of our population whose helplessness places them more particularly under our protection. They are to us in the condition of children under age; and any violation of their rights should be more particularly attended to."

He went immediately to the neighboring town, where Milly had been employed, and found, fortunately, that the principal facts had been subject to the inspection of white witnesses.

A woman, who had been hired to do some sewing, had been in the next room during the whole time; and Milly's flight from the house, and the man's firing after her, had been observed by some workmen in the neighborhood. Everything, therefore, promised well, and the suit was entered forthwith.

CHAPTER IV

The Trial

"WELL, NOW," said Frank Russel, to one or two lawyers with whom he was sitting, in a side-room of the courthouse at E., "look out for breakers! Clayton has mounted his war-horse, and is coming upon us, now, like leviathan from the rushes."

"Clayton is a good fellow," said one of them. "I like him, though he doesn't talk much."

"Good?" said Russel, taking his cigar from his mouth; "why, as the backwoodsmen say, he an't nothing else! He is a great seventy-four pounder, charged to the muzzle with goodness! But, if he should be once fired off, I'm afraid he'll carry everything out of the world with him. Because, you see, abstract goodness doesn't suit our present mortal condition. But it is a perfect godsend that he has such a case as this to manage for his maiden plea, because it just falls in with his heroic turn. Why, when I heard of it, I assure you I bestirred myself. I went about, and got Smithers, and Jones, and Peters, to put off suits, so as to give him fair field and full play. For, if he succeeds in this, it may give him so good a conceit of the law, that he will keep on with it."

"Why," said the other, "don't he like the law? What's the matter with the law?"

"O, nothing, only Clayton has got one of those ethereal stomachs that rise against almost everything in this world. Now, there isn't more than one case in a dozen that he'll undertake. He sticks and catches just like an old bureau drawer. Some conscientious crick in his back is always taking him at a critical moment, and so he is knocked up for actual work. But this defending a slave-woman will suit him to a T."

"She is a nice creature, isn't she?" said one of them.

"And belongs to a good old family," said another.

"Yes," said the third, "and I understand his lady-love has something to do with the case."

"Yes," said Russel, "to be sure she has. The woman belongs to a family connection of hers, I'm told. Miss Gordon is a spicy little puss—one that would be apt to resent anything of that sort; and the Gordons are a very influential family. He is sure to get the case, though I'm not clear that the law is on his side, by any means."

"Not?" said the other barrister, who went by the name of Will Jones.

"No," said Russel. "In fact, I'm pretty clear it isn't. But that will make no odds. When Clayton is thoroughly waked up, he is a whole team, I can tell you. He'll take jury and judge along with him, fast enough."

"I wonder," said one, "that Barker didn't compound the matter."

"O, Barker is one of the stubbed sort. You know these middling kind of people always have a spite against old families. He makes fight because it is the Gordons, that's all. And there comes in his republicanism. He isn't going to be whipped in by the Gordons. Barker has got Scotch blood in him, and he'll hang on to the case like death."

"Clayton will make a good speech," said Jones.

"Speech? that he will!" said Russel. "Bless me, I could lay off a good speech on it, myself. Because, you see, it really was quite an outrage; and the woman is a presentable creature. And, then, there's the humane dodge; that can be taken, beside all the chivalry part of defending the helpless, and all that sort of thing. I wouldn't ask for a better thing to work up into a speech. But Clayton will do it better yet, because he is actually sincere in it. And, after all's said and done, there's a good deal in that. When a fellow speaks in solemn earnest, he gives a kind of weight that you can't easily get at any other way."

"Well, but," said one, "I don't understand you, Russel, why you think the law isn't on Clayton's side. I'm sure it's a very clear case of terrible abuse."

"O, certainly it is," said Russel, "and the man is a dolt, and a brute beast, and ought to be shot, and so forth; but, then, he hasn't really exceeded his legal limits, because, you see, the law gives to the hirer all the rights of the master. There's no getting away from that, in my opinion. Now, any *master* might have done all that, and nobody could have done anything about it. They *do* do it, for that matter, if they're bad enough, and nobody thinks of touching them."

"Well, I say," said Jones, "Russel, don't you think that's too bad?"

"Laws, yes, man; but the world is full of things that are too bad. It's a bad kind of a place," said Russel, as he lit another cigar.

"Well, how do you think Clayton is going to succeed," said Jones, "if the law is so clearly against him?"

"O, bless you, you don't know Clayton. He is a glorious mystifier. In the first place, he mystifies himself. And, now, you mark me. When a powerful fellow mystifies *himself,* so that he really gets himself thoroughly on to his own side, there's nobody he *can't* mystify. I speak it in sober sadness, Jones, that the want of this faculty is a great hindrance to me in a certain class of cases. You see I can put on the pathetic and heroic, after a sort; but I don't take myself along with me—I don't really believe myself. There's the trouble. It's this power of self-mystification that makes what you call earnest men. If men saw the real bread and butter and green cheese of life, as I see it,—the hard, dry, primitive facts,—they couldn't raise such commotions as they do."

"Russel, it always makes me uncomfortable to hear you talk. It seems as if you didn't believe in anything!"

"O, yes, I do," said Russel; "I believe in the multiplication table, and several other things of that nature at the beginning of the arithmetic; and, also, that the wicked will do wickedly. But, as to Clayton's splendid abstractions, I only wish him joy of them. But, then, I shall believe him while I hear him talk; so will you; so will all the rest of us. That's the fun of it. But the thing will be just where it was before, and I shall find it so when I wake up to-morrow morning. It's a pity such fellows as Clayton couldn't be used as we use big guns. He is death on anything he fires at; and if he only would let me load and point him, he and I together would make a firm that would sweep the land. But here he comes, upon my word."

"Hallo, Clayton, all ready."

"Yes," said Clayton, "I believe so. When will the case be called?"

"To-day, I'm pretty sure," said Russel.

Clayton was destined to have something of an audience in his first plea; for, the Gordons being an influential and a largely-connected family, there was quite an interest excited among them in the affair. Clayton also had many warm personal friends, and his father, mother, and sister, were to be present; for, though residing in a different part of the state, they were at this time on a visit in the vicinity of the town of E.

There is something in the first essay of a young man, in any profession, like the first launching of a ship, which has a never-ceasing hold on human sympathies. Clayton's father, mother, and sister, with Nina, at the time of the dialogue we have given, were sitting together in the parlor of a friend's house in E., discussing the same event.

"I am sure that he will get the case," said Anne Clayton, with the confidence of a generous woman and warm-hearted sister. "He has been showing me the course of his argument, and it is perfectly irresistible. Has he said anything to you about it, father?"

Judge Clayton had been walking up and down the room, with his hands behind him, with his usual air of considerate gravity. Stopping short at Anne's question, he said,

"Edward's mind and mine work so differently, that I have not thought best to embarrass him by any conference on the subject. I consider the case an unfortunate one, and would rather he could have had some other."

"Why," said Anne, eagerly, "don't you think he'll gain it?"

"Not if the case goes according to law," said Judge Clayton. "But, then, Edward has a great deal of power of eloquence, and a good deal of skill in making a diversion from the main point; so that perhaps he may get the case."

"Why," said Nina, "I thought cases were always decided according to law! What else do they make laws for?"

"You are very innocent, my child," said Judge Clayton.

"But, father, the proof of the outrage is most abundant. Nobody could pretend to justify it."

"Nobody will, child. But that's nothing to the case. The simple point is, *did* the man exceed his legal power? It's my impression he did not."

"Father, what a horrible doctrine!" said Anne.

"I simply speak of what is," said Judge Clayton. "I don't pretend to justify it. But Edward has great power of exciting the feelings, and under the influence of his eloquence the case may go the other way, and humanity triumph at the expense of law."

Clayton's plea came on in the afternoon, and justified the expectations of his friends. His personal presence was good, his voice melodious, and his elocution fine. But what impressed his auditors, perhaps, more than these, was a certain elevation and clearness in the moral atmosphere around him,—a gravity and earnestness of conviction, which gave a secret power to all he said. He took up the doctrine of the dependent relations of life, and of those rules by which they should be guided and restrained; and showed that while absolute power seems to be a necessary condition of many relations of life, both reason and common sense dictate certain limits to it. "The law guarantees to the parent, the guardian, and the master, the right of enforcing obedience by chastisement; and the reason for it is, that the subject being supposed to be imperfectly developed, his good will, on the whole, be better consulted by allowing to his lawful guardian this power."

"*The good of the subject,*" he said, "is understood to be the foundation of the right; but, when chastisement is inflicted without just cause, and in a manner so inconsiderate and brutal as to endanger the safety and well-being of the subject, the great foundation principle of the law is violated. The act becomes perfectly lawless, and as incapable of legal defence as it is abhorrent to every sentiment of humanity and justice."

"He should endeavor to show," he said, "by full testimony, that the case in question was one of this sort."

In examining witnesses Clayton showed great dignity and acuteness, and as the feeling of the court was already prepossessed in his favor, the cause evidently gathered strength as it went on. The testimony showed, in the most conclusive manner, the general excellence of Milly's character, and the utter brutality of the outrage which had been committed upon her. In his concluding remarks, Clayton addressed the jury in a tone of great elevation and solemnity, on the duty of those to whom is intrusted the guardianship of the helpless.

"No obligation," he said, "can be stronger to an honorable mind, than the obligation of *entire dependence*. The fact that a human being has no refuge from our power, no appeal from our decisions, so far from leading to careless security, is one of the strongest possible motives to caution, and to most exact care. The African race," he said, "had been bitter sufferers. Their history had been one of wrong and cruelty, painful to every honorable mind. We of the present day, who sustain the relation of slaveholder," he said, "receive from the hands of our fathers an awful trust. Irresponsible power is the greatest trial of humanity, and if we do not strictly guard our own moral purity in the use of it, we shall degenerate into despots and tyrants. No consideration can justify us in holding this people in slavery an hour, unless we make this slavery a guardian relation, in which our superior strength and intelligence is made the protector and educator of their simplicity and weakness.

"The eyes of the world are fastened upon us," he said. "Our continuing in this position at all is, in many quarters, matter of severe animadversion. Let us therefore show, by the spirit in which we administer our laws, by the impartiality with which we protect their rights, that the master of the helpless African is his best and truest friend."

It was evident, as Clayton spoke, that he carried the whole of his audience with him. The counsel on the other side felt himself much straitened. There is very little possibility of eloquence in defending a manifest act of tyranny and cruelty; and a man speaks, also, at great disadvantage, who not only is faint-hearted in his own cause, but feels the force of the whole surrounding atmosphere against him.

In fact, the result was, that the judge charged the jury, if they found the chastisement to have been disproportionate and cruel, to give verdict for the plaintiff. The jury, with little discussion, gave it unanimously accordingly, and so Clayton's first cause was won.

If ever a woman feels proud of her lover, it is when she sees him as a successful public speaker; and Nina, when the case was over, stood half-laughing, half-blushing, in a circle of ladies, who alternately congratulated and rallied her on Clayton's triumph.

"Ah," said Frank Russel, "we understand the magic! The knight always fights well when his lady-love looks down! Miss Gordon must have the credit of this. She took all the strength out of the other side,—like the mountain of loadstone, that used to draw all the nails out of the ship."

"I am glad," said Judge Clayton, as he walked home with his wife, "I am very glad that Edward has met with such success. His nature is so fastidious that I have had my fears that he would not adhere to the law. There are many things in it, I grant, which would naturally offend a fastidious mind, and one which, like his, is always idealizing life."

"He has established a noble principle," said Mrs. Clayton.

"I wish he had," said the judge. "It would be a very ungrateful task, but I could have shattered his argument all to pieces."

"Don't tell him so!" said Mrs. Clayton, apprehensively; "let him have the comfort of it."

"Certainly I shall. Edward is a good fellow, and I hope, after a while, he'll draw well in the harness."

Meanwhile, Frank Russel and Will Jones were walking along in another direction.

"Didn't I tell you so?" said Russel. "You see, Clayton run Bedford down, horse and foot, and made us all as solemn as a preparatory lecture."

"But he had a good argument," said Jones.

"To be sure he had—I never knew him to want that. He builds up splendid arguments, always, and the only thing to be said of him, after it's all over, is, it isn't so; it's no such thing. Barker is terribly wroth, I can assure you. He swears he'll appeal the case. But that's no matter. Clayton has had his day all the same. He is evidently waked up. O, he has no more objection to a little popularity than you and I have, now; and if we could humor him along, as we would a trout, we should have him a first-rate lawyer, one of these days. Did you see Miss Gordon while he was pleading? By George! she looked so handsome, I was sorry I hadn't taken her myself!"

"Is she that dashing little flirting Miss Gordon that I heard of in New York?"

"The very same."

"How came she to take a fancy to him?"

"She? How do I know? She's as full of streaks as a tulip; and her liking for him is one of them. Did you notice her, Will?—scarf flying one way, and little curls, and pennants, and streamers, and veil, the other! And, then, those eyes! She's alive, every inch of her! She puts me in mind of a sweet-brier bush, winking and blinking, full of dew-drops, full of roses, and brisk little thorns, beside! Ah, she'll keep him awake!"

CHAPTER V

Magnolia Grove

JUDGE CLAYTON was not mistaken in supposing that his son would contemplate the issue of the case he had defended with satisfaction. As we have already intimated, Clayton was somewhat averse to the practice of the law. Regard for the feelings of his father had led him to resolve that he would at least give it a fair trial. His own turn of mind would have led him to some work of more immediate and practical philanthropy. He would much preferred to have retired to his own estate, and devoted himself, with his sister, to the education of his servants. But he felt that he could not, with due regard to his father's feelings, do this until he had given professional life a fair trial.

After the scene of the trial which we have described, he returned to his business, and Anne solicited Nina to accompany her for a few weeks to their plantation at Magnolia Grove, whither, as in duty bound, we may follow her.

Our readers will therefore be pleased to find themselves transported to the shady side of a veranda belonging to Clayton's establishment at Magnolia Grove.

The place derived its name from a group of these beautiful trees, in the centre of which the house was situated. It was a long, low cottage, surrounded by deep verandas, festooned with an exuberance of those climbing plants which are so splendid in the southern latitude.

The range of apartments which opened on the veranda where Anne and Nina were sitting were darkened to exclude the flies; but the doors, standing open, gave picture-like gleams of the interior. The white, matted floors, light bamboo furniture, couches covered with glazed white linen, and the large vases of roses disposed here and there, where the light would fall upon them, presented a background of inviting coolness.

It was early in the morning, and the two ladies were enjoying the luxury of a tête-à-tête breakfast before the sun had yet dried the heavy dews which give such freshness to the morning air. A small table which stood between them was spread with choice fruits, arranged on dishes in green leaves; a pitcher of iced milk, and a delicate little tête-à-tête coffee-service, dispensing the perfume of the most fragrant coffee. Nor were they wanting those small, delicate biscuits, and some of those curious forms of corn-bread, of the manufacture of which every southern cook is so justly proud. Nor should we omit the central vase of monthly roses, of every shade of color, the daily arrangement of which was the special delight of Anne's brown little waiting-maid, Lettice.

Anne Clayton, in a fresh white morning-wrapper, with her pure, healthy complexion, fine teeth, and frank, beaming smile, looked like a queenly damask rose. A queen she really was on her own plantation, reigning by the strongest of all powers, that of love.

The African race have large ideality and veneration; and in no drawing-room could Anne's beauty and grace, her fine manners and carriage, secure a more appreciating and unlimited admiration and devotion. The negro race, with many of the faults of children, unite many of their most amiable qualities, in the simplicity and confidingness with which they yield themselves up in admiration of a superior friend.

Nina had been there but a day, yet could not fail to read in the eyes of all how absolute was the reign which Anne held over their affections.

"How delightful the smell of this magnolia blossom!" said Nina. "O, I'm glad that you waked me so early, Anne!"

"Yes," said Anne, "in this climate early rising becomes a necessary of life to those who mean to have any real, positive pleasure in it; and I'm one of the sort that must have *positive* pleasures. Merely negative rest, lassitude, and dreaming, are not enough for me. I want to feel that I'm alive, and that I accomplish something."

"Yes, I see," said Nina, "you are not nominally like me, but really housekeeper. What wonderful skill you seem to have! Is it possible that you keep nothing locked up here?"

"No," said Anne, "nothing. I am released from the power of the keys, thank fortune! When I first came here, everybody told me it was sheer madness to try such a thing. But I told them that I was determined to do it, and Edward upheld me in it; and you can see how well I've succeeded."

"Indeed," said Nina, "you must have magic power, for I never saw a household move on so harmoniously. All your servants seem to think, and contrive, and take an interest in what they are doing. How did you begin? What did you do?"

"Well," said Anne, "I'll tell you the history of the plantation. In the first place, it belonged to mamma's uncle; and, not to spoil a story for relation's sake, I must say he was a dissipated, unprincipled man. He lived a perfectly heathen life here, in the most shocking way you can imagine; and so the poor creatures who were under him were worse heathen than he. He lived with a quadroon woman, who was violent tempered, and when angry ferociously cruel; and so the servants were constantly passing from the extreme of indulgence to the extreme of cruelty. You can scarce have an idea of the state we found them in. My heart almost failed me; but Edward said, 'Don't give it up, Anne; try the good that is in them.' Well, I confess, it seemed very much as it seemed to me when I was once at a water-cure[1] establishment,—patients would be brought in languid, pale, cold, half dead, and it appeared as if it would kill them to apply cold water; but, somehow or other, there was a vital power in them that reacted under it. Well, just so it was with my servants. I called them all together, and I said to them, 'Now, people have always said that you are the greatest thieves in the world; that there is no managing you except by locking up everything from you. But, I think differently. I have an idea that you can be trusted. I have been telling people that they don't know how much good there is in you; and now, just to show them what you can do, I'm going to begin and leave the closets and doors, and everything, unlocked, and I shall not watch you. You can take my things, if you choose; and if, after a time, I find that you can't be trusted, I shall go back to the old way.' Well, my dear, I wouldn't have believed myself that the thing would have answered so well. In the first place, approbativeness is a stronger principle with the African race than almost any other; they like to be thought well of. Immediately there was the greatest spirit in the house, for the poor creatures, having suddenly made the discovery that somebody thought they were to be trusted, were very anxious to keep up the reputation. The elder ones watched the younger; and, in fact, my dear, I had very little trouble. The children at first troubled me going into my store-closet and getting the cake, notwithstanding very spirited government on the part of the mammies. So, I called my family in session again, and said that their conduct had confirmed my good opinion; that I always knew they could be trusted, and that my friends were astonished to hear how well they did; but that I had observed that some of the children probably had taken my cake. 'Now, you know,' said I, 'that I have no objection to your having some. If any of you would enjoy a piece of cake, I shall be happy to give it to them, but it is not agreeable to have things in my closet fingered over—I shall therefore set a plate of cake out every day, and anybody that wishes to take some I hope will take that.' Well, my dear, my plate of cake stood there and dried. You won't believe me, but in fact it wasn't touched."

"Well," said Nina, "I shouldn't think you could have had our Tomtit here! Why, really, this goes beyond the virtue of white children."

"My dear, it isn't such a luxury to white children to be thought well of, and have a character. You must take that into account. It was a taste of a new kind of pleasure, made attractive by its novelty."

"Yes," said Nina, "I have something in me which makes me feel this would be the right way. I know it would be with me. There's nothing like confidence. If a person trusts me, I'm bound."

"Yet," said Anne, "I can't get the ladies of my acquaintance to believe in it. They see how I get along, but they insist upon it that it's some secret magic, or art, of mine."

"Well, it is so," said Nina. "Such things are just like the divining-rod; they won't work in every hand; it takes a real, generous, warm-hearted woman, like you, Anne. But, could you carry your system through your plantation, as well as your house?"

"The field-hands were more difficult to manage, on some accounts," said Anne, "but the same principle prevailed with them. Edward tried all he could to awaken self-respect. Now, I counselled that we should endeavor to form some decent habits before we built the cabins over. I told him they could not appreciate cleanliness and order. 'Very likely they cannot,' he said, 'but we are not to suppose it;' and he gave orders immediately for that pretty row of cottages you saw down at the quarters. He put up a large bathing establishment. Yet he did not enforce at first personal cleanliness by strict rules. Those who began to improve first were encouraged and noticed; and, as they found this a passport to favor, the thing took rapidly. It required a great while to teach them how to be consis-

tently orderly and cleanly even after the first desire had been awakened, because it isn't every one that likes neatness and order, who
has the forethought and skill to secure it. But there has been a
steady progress in these respects. One curious peculiarity of Edward's management gives rise to a good many droll scenes. He has
instituted a sort of jury trial among them. There are certain rules for
the order and well-being of the plantation, which all agree to abide
by; and, in all offences, the man is tried by a jury of his peers. Mr.
Smith, our agent, says that these scenes are sometimes very diverting, but on the whole there's a good deal of shrewdness and sense
manifested; but he says that, in general, they incline much more to
severity than he would. You see the poor creatures have been so
barbarized by the way they have been treated in past times, that it
has made them hard and harsh. I assure you, Nina, I never appreciated the wisdom of God, in the laws which he made for the Jews in
the wilderness, as I have since I've tried the experiment myself of
trying to bring a set of slaves out of barbarism. Now, this that I'm
telling you is the fairest side of the story. I can't begin to tell you
the thousand difficulties and trials which we have encountered in it.
Sometimes I've been almost worn out and discouraged. But, then, I
think, if there is a missionary work in this world, it is this."

"And what do your neighbors think about it?" said Nina.

"Well," said Anne, "they are all very polite, well-bred people,
the families with whom we associate; and such people, of course,
would never think of interfering, or expressing a difference of opinion, in any very open way; but I have the impression that they regard it with suspicion. They sometimes let fall words which make
me think they do. It's a way of proceeding which very few would
adopt, because it is not a money-making operation, by any means.
The plantation barely pays for itself, because Edward makes that
quite a secondary consideration. The thing which excites the most
murmuring is our teaching them to read. I teach the children myself
two hours every day, because I think this would be less likely to be
an offence than if I should hire a teacher. Mr. Smith teaches any of
the grown men who are willing to take the trouble to learn. Any
man who performs a certain amount of labor can secure to himself
two or three hours a day to spend as he chooses; and many do
choose to learn. Some of the men and the women have become
quite good readers, and Clayton is constantly sending books for
them. This, I'm afraid, gives great offence. It is against the law to do

it;[2] but, as unjust laws are sometimes lived down, we thought we would test the practicability of doing this. There was some complaint made of our servants, because they have not the servile, subdued air which commonly marks the slave, but look, speak, and act, as if they respected themselves. I'm sometimes afraid that we shall have trouble; but, then, I hope for the best."

"What does Mr. Clayton expect to be the end of all this?" said Nina.

"Why," said Anne, "I think Edward has an idea that one of these days they may be emancipated on the soil, just as the serfs were in England.[3] It looks to me rather hopeless, I must say; but he says the best way is for someone to begin and set an example of what ought to be done, and he hopes that in time it will be generally followed. It would, if all men were like him; but there lies my doubt. The number of those who would pursue such a disinterested course is very small. But who comes there? Upon my word, if there isn't my particular admirer, Mr. Bradshaw!"

As Anne said this, a very gentlemanly middle-aged man came up on horseback, on the carriage-drive which passed in front of the veranda. He bore in his hand a large bunch of different-colored roses; and, alighting, and delivering his horse to his servant, came up the steps, and presented it to Anne.

"There," said he, "are the first fruits of my roses, in the garden that I started in Rosedale."

"Beautiful," said Anne, taking them. "Allow me to present to you Miss Gordon."

"Miss Gordon, your most obedient," said Mr. Bradshaw, bowing obsequiously.

"You are just in season, Mr. Bradshaw," said Anne, "for I'm sure you couldn't have had your breakfast before you started; so sit down and help us with ours."

"Thank you, Miss Anne," said Mr. Bradshaw, "the offer is too tempting to be refused." And he soon established himself as a third at the little table, and made himself very sociable.

"Well, Miss Anne, how do all your plans proceed—all your benevolences and cares? I hope your angel ministrations don't exhaust you."

"Not at all, Mr. Bradshaw; do I look like it?"

"No, indeed! but such energy is perfectly astonishing to us all."

Nina's practised eye observed that Mr. Bradshaw had that particular nervous, restless air, which belongs to a man who is charged with a particular message, and finds himself unexpectedly blockaded by the presence of a third person. So, after breakfast, exclaiming that she had left her crochet-needle in her apartment, and resisting Anne's offer to send a servant for it, by declaring that nobody could find it but herself, she left the veranda. Mr. Bradshaw had been an old family friend for many years, and stood with Anne almost on the easy footing of a relation, which gave him the liberty of speaking with freedom. The moment the door of the parlor was closed after Nina, he drew a chair near to Anne, and sat down, with the unmistakable air of a man who is going into a confidential communication.

"The fact is, my dear Miss Clayton," he said, "I have something on my mind that I want to tell you; and I hope you will think my long friendship for the family a sufficient warrant for my speaking on matters which really belong chiefly to yourself. The fact is, my dear Miss Clayton, I was at a small dinner-party of gentlemen, the other day, at Colonel Grandon's. There was a little select set there, you know,—the Howards, and the Elliotts, and the Howlands, and so on,—and the conversation happened to turn upon your brother. Now, there was the very greatest respect for him; they seemed to have the highest possible regard for his motives; but still they felt that he was going on a very dangerous course."

"Dangerous?" said Anne, a little startled.

"Yes, really dangerous; and I think so myself, though I, perhaps, don't feel as strongly as some do."

"Really," said Anne, "I'm quite at a loss!"

"My dear Miss Anne, it's these improvements, you know, which you are making.—Don't misapprehend me! Admirable, very admirable, in themselves,—done from the most charming of motives, Miss Anne,—but dangerous, dangerous!"

The solemn, mysterious manner in which these last words were pronounced made Anne laugh; but when she saw the expression of real concern on the face of her good friend, she checked herself, and said,

"Pray, explain yourself. I don't understand you."

"Why, Miss Anne, it's just here. We appreciate your humanity, and your self-denial, and your indulgence to your servants. Everybody is of opinion that it's admirable. You are really quite a model for us all. But, when it comes to teaching them to read and write,

Miss Anne," he said, lowering his voice, "I think you don't consider what a dangerous weapon you are putting into their hands.
The knowledge will spread on to the other plantations; bright niggers will pick it up; for the very fellows who are most dangerous are
the very ones who will be sure to learn."

"What if they should?" said Anne.

"Why, my dear Miss Anne," said he, lowering his voice, "the facilities that it will afford them for combinations, for insurrections!
You see, Miss Anne, I read a story once of a man who made a cork
leg with such wonderful accuracy that it would walk of itself, and
when he got it on he couldn't stop its walking—it walked him to
death—actually did! Walked him up hill and down dale, till the
poor man fell down exhausted; and then it ran off with his body.
And it's running with its skeleton to this day, I believe."

And good-natured Mr. Bradshaw conceived such a ridiculous
idea, at this stage of his narrative, that he leaned back in his chair
and laughed heartily, wiping his perspiring face with a cambric
pocket-handkerchief.

"Really, Mr. Bradshaw, it's a very amusing idea, but I don't see
the analogy," said Anne.

"Why, don't you see? You begin teaching niggers, and having
reading and writing, and all these things, going on, and they begin
to open their eyes, and look round and think; and they are having
opinions of their own, they won't take yours; and they want to rise
directly. And if they can't rise, why, they are all discontented; and
there's the what's-his-name to pay with them! Then come conspiracies and insurrections, no matter how well you treat them; and,
now, we South Carolinians have had experience in this matter. You
must excuse us, but it is a terrible subject with us. Why, the leaders
of that conspiracy, all of them, were fellows who could read and
write, and who had nothing in the world to wish for, in the way of
comfort, treated with every consideration by their masters. It is a
most melancholy chapter in human nature. It shows that there is no
trust to be placed in them. And, now, the best way to get along with
negroes, in my opinion, is to make them happy; give them plenty to
eat and drink and wear, and keep them amused and excited, and
don't work them too hard. I think it's a great deal better than this
kind of exciting instruction. Mind," he said, seeing that Anne was
going to interrupt him, "mind, now, I'd have religious instruction,
of course. Now, this system of oral instruction, teaching them

hymns and passages of scripture suited to their peculiar condition, it's just the thing; it isn't so liable to these dangers. I hope you'll excuse me, Miss Anne, but the gentlemen really feel very serious about these things; they find it's affecting their own negroes. You know, somehow, everything goes round from one plantation to another; and one of them said that he had a very smart man who is married to one of your women, and he actually found him with a spelling-book, sitting out under a tree. He said if the man had had a rifle he couldn't have been more alarmed; because the man was just one of those sharp, resolute fellows, that, if he knew how to read and write, there's no knowing what he would do. Well, now, you see how it is. He takes the spelling-book away, and he tells him he will give him nine-and-thirty if he ever finds him with it again. What's the consequence? Why, the consequence is, the man sulks and gets ugly, and he has to sell him. That's the way it's operating."

"Well, then," said Anne, looking somewhat puzzled, "I will strictly forbid our people to allow spelling-books to go out of their hands, or to communicate any of these things off of the plantation."

"O, I tell you, Miss Anne, you can't do it. You don't know the passion in human nature for anything that is forbidden. Now, I believe it's more that than love of reading. You can't shut up such an experiment as you are making here. It's just like a fire. It will blaze; it will catch on all the plantations round; and I assure you it's matter of life and death with us. You smile, Miss Anne, but it's so."

"Really, my dear Mr. Bradshaw, you could not have addressed me on a more unpleasant subject. I am sorry to excite the apprehension of our neighbors; but—"

"Give me leave to remind you, also, Miss Anne, that the teaching of slaves to read and write is an offence to which a severe penalty is attached by the laws."

"I thought," said Anne, "that such barbarous laws were a dead letter in a Christian community, and that the best tribute I could pay to its Christianity was practically to disregard them."

"By no means, Miss Anne, by no means! Why, look at us here in South Carolina. The negroes are three to one over the whites now. Will it do to give them the further advantages of education and facilities of communication? You see, at once, it will not. Now, well-bred people, of course, are extremely averse to mingling in the affairs of other families; and had you merely taught a few favorites, in a private way, as I believe people now and then do, it wouldn't have seemed so bad; but to have regular provision for teaching school, and school-hours,—I think, Miss Anne, you'll find it will result in unpleasant consequences."

"Yes, I fancy," said Anne, raising herself up, and slightly coloring, "that I see myself in the penitentiary for the sin and crime of teaching children to read! I think, Mr. Bradshaw, it is time such laws were disregarded. Is not that the only way in which many laws are repealed? Society outgrows them, people disregard them, and so they fall away, like the calyx from some of my flowers. Come, now, Mr. Bradshaw, come with me to my school. I'm going to call it together," said Anne, rising, and beginning to go down the veranda steps. "Certainly, my dear friend, you ought not to judge without seeing. Wait a moment, till I call Miss Gordon."

And Anne stepped across the shady parlor, and in a few moments reäppeared with Nina, both arrayed in white cape-bonnets. They crossed to the right of the house, to a small cluster of neat cottages, each one of which had its little vegetable garden, and its plot in front carefully tended with flowers. They passed onward into a grove of magnolias which skirted the back of the house, till they came to a little building, with the external appearance of a small Grecian temple, the pillars of which were festooned with jessamine.

"Pray, what pretty little place is this?" said Mr. Bradshaw.

"This is my school-room," said Anne.

Mr. Bradshaw repressed a whistle of astonishment; but the emotion was plainly legible in his face, and Anne said, laughing,

"A lady's school-room, you know, should be lady-like. Besides, I wish to inspire ideas of taste, refinement, and self-respect, in these children. I wish learning to be associated with the idea of elegance and beauty."

They ascended the steps, and entered a large room, surrounded on three sides by black-boards. The floor was covered with white matting, and the walls hung with very pretty pictures of French lithographs, tastefully colored. In some places cards were hung up, bearing quotations of scripture. There were rows of neat desks, before each of which there was a little chair.

Anne stepped to the door and rang a bell, and in about ten minutes the patter of innumerable little feet was heard ascending the steps, and presently they came streaming in—all ages, from four or five to fifteen, and from the ebony complexion of the negro, with its closely-curling wool, to the rich brown cheek of the quadroon, with melancholy lustrous eyes, and waving hair. All were dressed alike, in a neat uniform of some kind of blue stuff, with white capes and aprons.

They filed in to the tune of one of those marked rhythmical melodies which characterize the negro music, and, moving in exact time to the singing, assumed their seats, which were arranged with regard to their age and size. As soon as they were seated, Anne, after a moment's pause, clapped her hands, and the whole school commenced a morning hymn, in four parts, which was sung so beautifully that Mr. Bradshaw, quite overpowered, stood with tears in his eyes. Anne nodded at Nina, and cast on him a satisfied glance.

After that, there was a rapid review of the classes. There was reading, spelling, writing on the black-board, and the smaller ones were formed in groups in two adjoining apartments, under the care of some of the older girls. Anne walked about superintending the whole; and Nina, who saw the scene for the first time, could not repress her exclamation of delight. The scholars were evidently animated by the presence of company, and anxious to do credit to the school and teacher, and the two hours passed rapidly away. Anne exhibited to Mr. Bradshaw specimens of the proficiency of her scholars in hand-writing, and the drawing of maps, and even the copying of small lithograph cards, which contained a series of simple drawing-patterns. Mr. Bradshaw seemed filled with astonishment.

" 'Pon my word," said he, "these are surprising! Miss Anne, you are a veritable magician—a worker of miracles! You must have found Aaron's rod,[4] again! My dear madam, you run the risk of being burned for a witch!"

"Very few, Mr. Bradshaw, know how much of beauty lies sealed up in this neglected race," said Anne, with enthusiasm.

As they were walking back to the house, Mr. Bradshaw fell a little behind, and his face wore a thoughtful and almost sad expression.

"Well," said Anne, looking round, "a penny for your thoughts!"

"O, I see, Miss Anne, you are for pursuing your advantage. I see triumph in your eyes. But yet," he added, "after all this display, the capability of your children makes me feel sad. To what end is it? What purpose will it serve, except to unfit them for their inevitable condition—to make them discontented and unhappy?"

"Well," replied Anne, "there ought to be no inevitable condition that makes it necessary to dwarf a human mind. Any condition which makes a full development of the powers that God has given us a misfortune, cannot, certainly, be a healthy one—cannot be right. If a mind will grow and rise, make way and let it. Make room for it, and cut down everything that stands in the way!"

"That's terribly levelling doctrine, Miss Anne."

"Let it level, then!" said Anne. "I don't care! I come from the old Virginia cavalier blood, and am not afraid of anything."

"But, Miss Anne, how do you account for it that the best-educated and best-treated slaves—in fact, as you say, the most perfectly-developed human beings—were those who got up the insurrection in Charleston?"[5]

"How do you account for it," said Anne, "that the best-developed and finest specimens of men have been those that have got up insurrections in Italy, Austria, and Hungary?"[6]

"Well, you admit, then," said Mr. Bradshaw, "that if you say A in this matter, you've got to say B."

"Certainly," said Anne, "and when the time comes to say B, I'm ready to say it. I admit, Mr. Bradshaw, it's a very dangerous thing to get up steam, if you don't intend to let the boat go. But when the steam is high enough, let her go, say I."

"Yes, but, Miss Anne, other people don't want to say so. The fact is, we are not all of us ready to let the boat go. It's got all our property in it—all we have to live on. If you are willing yourself, so far as your people are concerned, they'll inevitably want liberty, and you say you'll be ready to give it to them; but your fires will raise a steam on our plantations, and we must shut down these escape-valves. Don't you see? Now, for my part, I've been perfectly charmed with this school of yours; but, after all, I can't help inquiring whereto it will grow."

"Well, Mr. Bradshaw," said Anne, "I'm obliged to you for the frankness of this conversation. It's very friendly and sincere. I think, however, I shall continue to compliment the good sense and gallantry of this state, by ignoring its unworthy and unchristian laws. I will endeavor, nevertheless, to be more careful and guarded as to the manner of what I do; but, if I should be put into the penitentiary, Mr. Bradshaw, I hope you'll call on me."

"Miss Anne, I beg ten thousand pardons for that unfortunate allusion."

"I think," said Anne, "I shall impose it as a penance upon you to stay and spend the day with us, and then I'll show you my rose-garden. I have great counsel to hold with you on the training of a certain pillar-rose. You see, my design is to get you involved in my treason. You've already come into complicity with it, by visiting my school."

"Thank you, Miss Anne, I should be only too much honored to be your abettor in any treason you might meditate. But, really, I'm a most unlucky dog! Think of my having four bachelor friends engaged to dine with me, and so being obliged to decline your tempting offer! In fact, I must take horse before the sun gets any hotter."

"There he goes, for a good-hearted creature as he is!" said Anne.

"Do you know," said Nina, laughing, "that I thought that he was some poor, desperate mortal, who was on the verge of a proposal, this morning, and I ran away like a good girl, to give him a fair field?"

"Child," said Anne, "you are altogether too late in the day. Mr. Bradshaw and I walked that little figure some time ago, and now he is one of the most convenient and agreeable of friends."

"Anne, why in the world don't you get in love with somebody?" said Nina.

"My dear, I think there was something or other left out when I was made up," said Anne, laughing, "but I never had much of a fancy for the lords of creation. They do tolerably well till they come to be lovers; but then they are perfectly unbearable. Lions in love, my dear, don't appear to advantage, you know. I can't marry papa or Edward, and they have spoiled me for everybody else. Besides, I'm happy, and what do I want of any of them? Can't there be now and then a woman sufficient to herself? But, Nina, dear, I'm sorry that our affairs here are giving offence and making uneasiness."

"For my part," said Nina, "I should go right on. I have noticed that people try all they can to stop a person who is taking an unusual course; and when they are perfectly certain that they can't stop them, then they turn round and fall in with them; and I think that will be the case with you."

"They certainly will have an opportunity of trying," said Anne. "But there is Dulcimer coming up the avenue with the letter-bag. Now, child, I don't believe you appreciate half my excellence, when you consider that I used to have all these letters that fall to you every mail."

At this moment Dulcimer rode up to the veranda steps, and deposited the letter-bag in Anne's hands.

"What an odd name you have given him!" said Nina, "and what a comical-looking fellow he is! He has a sort of waggish air that reminds me of a crow."

"O, Dulcimer don't belong to our régime," said Anne. "He was the prime minister and favorite under the former reign,—a sort of licensed court jester,—and to this day he hardly knows how to do anything but sing and dance; and so brother, who is for allowing the largest liberty to everybody, imposes on him only such general and light tasks as suit his roving nature. But there!" she said, throwing a letter on Nina's lap, and at the same time breaking the seal of one directed to herself. "Ah, I thought so! You see, puss, Edward has some law business that takes him to this part of the state forthwith. Was ever such convenient law business? We may look for him to-night. Now there will be rejoicings! How now, Dulcimer? I thought you had gone," she said, looking up, and observing that personage still lingering in the shade of a tulip-tree near the veranda.

"Please, Miss Anne, is Master Clayton coming home tonight?"

"Yes, Dulcimer; so now go and spread the news; for that's what you want, I know."

And Dulcimer, needing no second suggestion, was out of sight in the shrubbery in a few moments.

"Now, I'll wager," said Anne, "that creature will get up something or other extraordinary for this evening."

"Such as what?" said Nina.

"Well, he is something of a troubadour, and I shouldn't wonder if he should be cudgelling his brain at this moment for a song. We shall have some kind of operatic performance, you may be sure."

CHAPTER VI

The Troubadour

ABOUT FIVE O'CLOCK in the evening, Nina and Anne amused themselves with setting a fancy tea-table on the veranda. Nina had gathered a quantity of the leaves of the live oak, which she possessed a
particular faculty of plaiting in long, flat wreaths, and with these she
garlanded the social round table, after it had been draped in its
snowy damask, while Anne was busy arranging fruit in dishes with
vine-leaves.

"Lettice will be in despair, to-night," said Anne, looking up, and
smiling at a neatly-dressed brown mulatto girl, who stood looking
on with large, lustrous eyes; "her occupation's gone!"

"O, Lettice must allow me to show my accomplishments," said
Nina. "There are some household arts that I have quite a talent for.
If I had lived in what's-its-name, there, that they used to tell about
in old times—Arcadia[1]—I should have made a good housekeeper;
for nothing suits me better than making wreaths, and arranging
bouquets. My nature is dressy. I want to dress everything. I want to
dress tables, and dress vases, and adorn dishes, and dress handsome
women, Anne! So look out for yourself, for when I have done
crowning the table, I shall crown you!"

As Nina talked, she was flitting hither and thither, taking up and
laying down flowers and leaves, shaking out long sprays, and fluttering from place to place, like a bird.

"It's a pity," said Anne, "that life can't be all Arcadia!"

"O, yes!" said Nina. "When I was a child, I remember there was
an old torn translation of a book called Gesner's Idyls,[2] that used to
lie about the house; and I used to read in it most charming little stories about handsome shepherds, dressed in white, playing on silver
and ivory flutes; and shepherdesses, with azure mantles and floating
hair; and people living on such delightful things as cool curds and
milk, and grapes, and strawberries, and peaches; and there was no

319

labor, and no trouble, and no dirt, and no care. Everybody lived like the flowers and the birds,—growing, and singing, and being beautiful. Ah, dear, I have never got over wanting it since! Why couldn't it be so?"

"It's a thousand pities!" said Anne. "But what constant fight we have to maintain for order and beauty!"

"Yes," said Nina; "and, what seems worse, beauty itself becomes dirt in a day. Now, these roses that we are arranging, to-morrow or next day we shall call them *litter,* and wish somebody would sweep them out of the way. But I never want to be the one to do that. I want some one to carry away the withered flowers, and wash the soiled vases; but I want to be the one to cut the fresh roses every day. If I were in an association, I should take that for my part. I'd arrange all their flowers through the establishment, but I should stipulate expressly that I should do no clearing up."

"Well," said Anne, "it's really a mystery to me what a constant downward tendency there is to everything—how everything is gravitating back, as you may say, into disorder. Now, I think a cleanly, sweet, tasteful house—and, above all, table—are among the highest works of art. And yet, how everything attacks you when you set out to attain it—flies, cockroaches, ants, mosquitos! And, then, it seems to be the fate of all human beings, that they are constantly wearing out and disarranging and destroying all that is about them."

"Yes," said Nina, "I couldn't help thinking of that when we were at the camp-meeting. The first day, I was perfectly charmed. Everything was so fresh, so cool, so dewy and sweet; but, by the end of the second day, they had thrown egg-shells, and pea-pods, and melon-rinds, and all sorts of abominations, around among the tents, and it was really shocking to contemplate."

"How disgusting!" said Anne.

"Now, I'm one of that sort," said Nina, "that love order dearly, but don't want the trouble of it myself. My prime minister, Aunt Katy, thanks to mamma, is an excellent hand to keep it, and I encourage her in it with all my heart; so that any part of the house where *I* don't go much is in beautiful order. But, bless me, I should have to be made over again before I could do like Aunt Nesbit! Did you ever see her take a pair of gloves or a collar out of a drawer? She gets up, and walks *so* moderately across the room, takes the key from under the napkin on the right-hand side of the bureau, and unlocks the drawer, as gravely as though she was going to offer a sacrifice. Then, if her gloves are the back side, underneath something else, she takes out one thing after another, so moderately; and then, when the gloves or collar are found, lays everything back exactly where it was before, locks the drawer, and puts the key back under the towel. And all this she'd do if anybody was dying, and she had to go for the doctor! The consequence is, that her room, her drawers, and everything, are a standing sermon to me. But I think I've got to be a much calmer person than I am, before this will come to pass in my case. I'm always in such a breeze and flutter! I fly to my drawer, and scatter things into little whirlwinds; ribbons, scarf, flowers—everything flies out in a perfect rainbow. It seems as if I *should die* if I didn't get the thing I wanted that minute; and, after two or three such attacks on a drawer, then comes repentance, and a long time of rolling up and arranging, and talking to little naughty Nina, who always promises herself to keep better order in future. But, my dear, she doesn't do it, I'm sorry to say, as yet, though perhaps there are hopes of her in future. Tell me, Anne,—you are not stiff and '*poky,*' and yet you seem to be endowed with the gift of order. How did it come about?"

"It was not natural to me, I assure you," said Anne. "It was a second nature, drilled into me by mamma."

"Mamma! ah, indeed!" said Nina, giving a sigh. "Then you are very happy! But, come, now, Lettice, I've done with all these; take them away. My tea-table has risen out of them like the world out of chaos," she said, as she swept together a heap of rejected vines, leaves, and flowers. "Ah! I always have a repenting turn, when I've done arranging vases, to think I've picked so many more than were necessary! The poor flowers droop their leaves, and look at me reproachfully, as if they said, 'You didn't want us—why couldn't you have left us alone?' "

"O," said Anne, "Lettice will relieve you of that. She has great talents in the floral line, and out of these she will arrange quantities of bouquets," she said, as Lettice, blushing perceptibly through her brown skin, stooped and swept up the rejected flowers into her apron.

"What have we here?" said Anne, as Dulcimer, attired with most unusual care, came bowing up the steps, presenting a note

on a waiter. "Dear me, how stylish! gilt-edged paper, smelling
of myrrh and ambergris!" she continued, as she broke the seal.
"What's this?"

" 'The Magnolia Grove troubadours request the presence of Mr.
and Miss Clayton and Miss Gordon at an operatic performance,
which will be given this evening, at eight o'clock, in the grove.'

"Very well done! I fancy some of my scholars have been busy
with the writing. Dulcimer, we shall be happy to come."

"Where upon earth did he pick up those phrases?" said Nina,
when he had departed.

"O," said Anne, "I told you that he was prime favorite of the
former proprietor, who used to take him with him wherever he
travelled, as people sometimes will a pet monkey; and, I dare say, he
has lounged round the lobbies of many an opera-house. I told you
that he was going to get up something."

"What a delightful creature he must be!" said Nina.

"Perhaps so, to you," said Anne; "but he is a troublesome person
to manage. He is as wholly destitute of any moral organs as a jack-
daw. One sometimes questions whether these creatures have any
more than a reflected mimicry of a human soul—such as the German stories imagine in Cobolds³ and water spirits. All I can see in
Dulcimer is a kind of fun-loving animal. He don't seem to have any
moral nature."

"Perhaps," said Nina, "his moral nature is something like the
cypress-vine seeds which I planted three months ago, and which
have just come up."

"Well, I believe Edward expects to see it along, one of these
days," said Anne. "His faith in human nature is unbounded. I think
it one of his foibles, for my part; but yet I try to have hopes of Dulcimer, that some day or other he will have some glimmering perceptions of the difference between a lie and the truth, and between
his own things and other people's. At present, he is the most lawless
marauder on the place. He has been so used to having his wit to
cover a multitude of sins, that it's difficult for a scolding to make
any impression on him. But, hark! isn't that a horse? Somebody is
coming up the avenue."

Both listened.

"There are two," said Nina.

Just at this instant Clayton emerged to view, accompanied by another rider, who, on nearer view, turned out to be Frank Russel. At the same instant, the sound of violins and banjos was heard, and, to Anne's surprise, a gayly-dressed procession of servants and children began to file out from the grove, headed by Dulcimer and several of his associates, playing and singing.

"There," said Anne, "didn't I tell you so? There's the beginning of Dulcimer's operations."

The air was one of those inexpressibly odd ones whose sharp, metallic accuracy of rhythm seems to mark the delight which the negro race feel in that particular element of music. The words, as usual, amounted to very little. Nina and Anne could hear,

"*O, I see de mas'r a comin' up de track,*
His horse's heels do clatter, with a clack, clack, clack!"

The idea conveyed in these lines being still further carried out by the regular clapping of hands at every accented note, while every voice joined in the chorus:

"*Sing, boys, sing; de mas'r is come!*
Give three cheers for de good man at home!
Ho! he! ho! Hurra! hurra!"

Clayton acknowledged the compliment, as he came up, by bowing from his horse; and the procession arranged itself in a kind of lane, through which he and his companion rode up to the veranda.

" 'Pon my word," said Frank Russel, "I wasn't prepared for such a demonstration. Quite a presidential reception!"

When Clayton came to the steps and dismounted, a dozen sprang eagerly forward to take his horse, and in the crowding round for a word of recognition the order of the procession was entirely broken. After many kind words, and inquiries in every direction for a few moments, the people quietly retired, leaving their master to his own enjoyments.

"You really have made quite a triumphal entry," said Nina.

"Dulcimer always exhausts himself on all such occasions," said Anne, "so that he isn't capable of any further virtue for two or three weeks."

"Well, take him while he is in flower, then!" said Russel. "But how perfectly cool and inviting you look! Really, quite idyllic! We must certainly have got into a fairy queen's castle!"

"But you must show us somewhere to shake the dust off of our feet," said Clayton.

"Yes," said Anne, "there's Aunt Praw waiting to show you your room. Go and make yourselves as fascinating as you can."

In a little while the gentlemen returned, in fresh white linen suits, and the business of the tea-table proceeded with alacrity.

"Well, now," said Anne, after tea, looking at her watch, "I must inform the company that we are all engaged to the opera this evening."

"Yes," said Nina, "the Magnolia Grove Opera House is to be opened, and the Magnolia Troubadour Troupe to appear for the first time."

At this moment they were surprised by the appearance, below the veranda, of Dulcimer, with three of his colored associates, all wearing white ribbons in their button-holes, and carrying white wands tied with satin ribbon, and gravely arranging themselves two and two on each side of the steps.

"Why, Dulcimer, what's this?" said Clayton.

Dulcimer bowed with the gravity of a raven, and announced that the committee had come to wait on the gentlemen and ladies to their seats.

"O," said Anne, "we were not prepared for our part of the play!"

"What a pity I didn't bring my opera-hat!" said Nina. "Never mind," she said, snatching a spray of multiflora rose, "this will do." And she gave it one twist round her head, and her toilet was complete.

" 'Pon my word, that's soon done!" said Frank Russel, as he watched the coronet of half-opened buds and roses.

"Yes," said Nina. "Sit down, Anne; I forgot your crown. There, wait a moment; let me turn this leaf a little, and weave these buds in here—so. Now you are a Baltimore belle, to be sure! Now for the procession."

The opera-house for the evening, was an open space in the grove behind the house. Lamps had been hung up in the trees, twinkling on the glossy foliage. A sort of booth or arbor was built of flowers and leaves at one end, to which the party were marshalled in great state. Between two magnolia-trees a white curtain was hung up; and the moment the family party made their appearance, a chorus of voices from behind the scenes began an animated song of welcome.

As soon as the party was seated, the curtain rose, and the chorus, consisting of about thirty of the best singers, males and females, came forward, dressed in their best holiday costume, singing, and keeping step as they sung, and bearing in their hands bouquets, which, as they marched round the circle, they threw at the feet of the company. A wreath of orange-blossoms was significantly directed at Nina, and fell right into her lap.

"These people seem to have had their eyes open. Coming events cast their shadows before!" said Russel.

After walking around, the chorus seated themselves at the side of the area, and the space behind was filled up with a dense sea of heads—all the servants and plantation hands.

"I declare," said Russel, looking round on the crowd of dark faces, "this sable crowd is turning a silver lining with a witness! How neat and pretty that row of children look!" And, as they spoke, a procession of the children of Anne's school came filing round in the same manner that the other had done, singing their school-songs, and casting flowers before the company. After this, they seated themselves on low seats in front of all the others.

Dulcimer and four of his companions now came into the centre.

"There," said Anne, "Dulcimer is going to be the centre piece. He is the troubadour."

Dulcimer, in fact, commenced a kind of recitative, to the tune "Mas'r's in the cold, cold ground." After singing a few lines, the quartet took up the chorus, and their voices were really magnificent.

"Why," said Nina, "it seems to me they are beginning in a very doleful way."

"O," said Anne, "wait a minute. This is the old mas'r, I fancy. We shall soon hear the tune changed."

And accordingly, Dulcimer, striking into a new tune, began to rehearse the coming in of a new master.

"There," said Anne, "now for a catalogue of Edward's virtues! They must be all got in, rhyme or no rhyme."

Dulcimer kept on rehearsing. Every four lines, the quartet struck in with the chorus, which was then repeated by the whole company, clapping their hands and stamping their feet to the time, with great vivacity.

"Now, Anne, is coming your turn," said Nina, as Dulcimer launched out, in most high-flown strains, on the beauty of Miss Anne.

"Yes," said Clayton, "the catalogue of your virtues will be somewhat extensive."

"I shall escape, at any rate," said Nina.

"Don't you be too sure," said Anne. "Dulcimer has had his eye on you ever since you've been here."

And true enough, after the next stanza, Dulcimer assumed a peculiarly meaning expression.

"There," said Anne, "do see the wretch flirting himself out like a saucy crow! It's coming! Now look out, Nina!"

With a waggish expression from the corner of his downcast eyes, he sung,

"O, mas'r is often absent—do you know where he goes?
He goes to North Carolina, for de North Carolina rose."

"There you are!" said Frank Russel. "Do you see the grin going round? What a lot of ivory! They are coming in this chorus, strong!"

And the whole assembly, with great animation, poured out on the chorus:

"O, de North Carolina rose!
O, de North Carolina rose!
We wish good luck to mas'r,
With de North Carolina rose!"

This chorus was repeated with enthusiasm, clapping of hands, and laughing.

"I think the North Carolina rose ought to rise!" said Russel.

"O, hush!" said Anne; "Dulcimer hasn't done yet."

Assuming an attitude, Dulcimer turned and sang to one of his associates in the quartet,

"O, I see two stars a rising,
Up in de shady skies!"

To which the other responded, with animation:

"No, boy, you are mistaken;
'T is de light of her fair eyes!"

"That's *thorough,* at any rate!" said Russel.
While Dulcimer went on:

"O, *I see two roses blowing,*
Togeder on one bed!"

And the other responded:

"*No, boy, you are mistaken;*
Dem are her cheeks so red!"

"And they are getting redder!" said Anne, tapping Nina with her
fan. "Dulcimer is evidently laying out his strength upon you,
Nina!"
Dulcimer went on singing:

"O, *I see a grape-vine running,*
With its curly rings, up dere!"

And the response,

"*No, boy, you are mistaken;*
'*T is her rings of curly hair!*"

And the quartet here struck up:

"*O she walks on de veranda,*
And she laughs out of de door,
And she dances like de sunshine
Across de parlor floor.
Her little feet, dey patter,
Like de rain upon de flowers;
And her laugh is like sweet waters,
Through all de summer hours!"

"Dulcimer has had help from some of the muses along there!"
said Clayton, looking at Anne.
"Hush!" said Anne; "hear the chorus."

"*O, de North Carolina rose!*
O, de North Carolina rose!
O, plant by our veranda
De North Carolina rose!"

This chorus was repeated with three times three, and the whole
assembly broke into a general laugh, when the performers bowed

and retired, and the white sheet, which was fastened by a pulley to the limb of a tree, was let down again.

"Come, now, Anne, confess that wasn't all Dulcimer's work!" said Clayton.

"Well, to tell the truth," said Anne, " 't was got up between him and Lettice, who has a natural turn for versifying, quite extraordinary. If I chose to encourage and push her on, she might turn out a second Phillis Wheatly."[4]

Dulcimer and his coadjutors now came round, bearing trays with lemonade, cake, sliced pine-apples, and some other fruits.

"Well, on my word," said Russel, "this is quite prettily got up!"

"O, I think," said Clayton, "the African race evidently are made to excel in that department which lies between the sensuous and the intellectual—what we call the elegant arts. These require rich and abundant animal nature, such as they possess; and, if ever they become highly civilized, they will excel in music, dancing, and elocution."

"I have often noticed," said Anne, "in my scholars, how readily they seize upon anything which pertains to the department of music and language. The negroes are sometimes laughed at for mispronouncing words, which they will do in a very droll manner; but it's only because they are so taken with the sounds of words that they will try to pronounce beyond the sphere of their understanding, like bright children."

"Some of these voices here are perfectly splendid," said Russel.

"Yes," said Anne, "we have one or two girls on the place who have that rich contralto voice which, I think, is oftener to be found among them than among whites."

"The Ethiopian race is a slow-growing plant, like the aloe," said Clayton; "but I hope, some of these days, they'll come into flower; and I think, if they ever do, the blossoming will be gorgeous."

"That will do for a poet's expectation," said Russel.

The performance now gave place to a regular dancing-party, which went on with great animation, yet decorum.

"Religious people," said Clayton, "who have instructed the negroes, I think have wasted a great deal of their energy in persuading them to give up dancing and singing songs. I try to regulate the propensity. There is no use in trying to make the negroes into Anglo-Saxons, any more than making a grape-vine into a pear-tree. I train the grape-vine."

"Behold," said Russel, "the successful champion of negro rights!"

"Not so very successful," said Clayton. "I suppose you've heard my case has been appealed; so that my victory isn't so certain, after all."

"O," said Nina, "yes, it must be! I'm sure no person of common sense would decide any other way; and your own father is one of the judges, too."

"That will only make him the more careful not to be influenced in my favor," said Clayton.

The dancing now broke up, and the servants dispersed in an orderly manner, and the company returned to the veranda, which lay pleasantly checkered with the light of the moon falling through trailing vines. The air was full of those occasional pulsations of fragrance which rise in the evening from flowers.

"O, how delightful," said Nina, "this fragrance of the honeysuckles! I have a perfect passion for perfumes! They seem to me like spirits in the air."

"Yes," said Clayton, "Lord Bacon says, 'that the breath of flowers comes and goes in the air, like the warbling of music.' "[5]

"Did Lord Bacon say that?" said Nina, in a tone of surprise.

"Yes; why not?" said Clayton.

"O, I thought he was one of those musty old philosophers, who never thought of anything pretty!"

"Well," said Clayton, "then to-morrow let me read you his essay on gardens, and you'll find musty old philosophers often do think of pretty things."

"It was Lord Bacon," said Anne, "who always wanted musicians playing in the next room while he was composing."

"He did?" said Nina. "Why, how delightful of him! I think I should like to hear some of his essays."

"There are some minds," said Clayton, "large enough to take in everything. Such men can talk as prettily of a ring on a lady's finger, as they can wisely on the courses of the planets. Nothing escapes them."

"That's the kind of man *you* ought to have for a lover, Anne," said Nina, laughing; "you have weight enough to risk it. I'm such a little whisk of thistle-down that it would annihilate me. Such a ponderous weight of wisdom attached to me would drag me under water, and drown me. I should let go my line, I think, if I felt such a fish bite."

"You are tolerably safe in our times," said Clayton. "Nature only sends such men once in a century or two. They are the road-makers for the rest of the world. They are quarry-masters, that quarry out marble enough for a generation to work up."

"Well," said Nina, "I shouldn't want to be a quarry-master's wife. I should be afraid that some of his blocks would fall on me."

"Why, wouldn't you like it, if he were wholly your slave?" said Frank Russel. "It would be like having the genius of the lamp at your feet."

"Ah," said Nina, "if *I* could keep him my slave; but I'm afraid he'd outwit me at last. Such a man would soon put *me* up on a shelf for a book read through. I've seen some great men,—I mean great for our times,—and they didn't seem to care half as much for their wives as they did for a newspaper."

"O," said Anne, "that's past praying for, with any husband. The newspaper is the standing rival of the American lady. It must be a warm lover that can be attracted from *that,* even before he is secure of his prize."

"You are severe, Miss Anne," said Russel.

"She only speaks the truth. You men are a bad set," said Nina. "You are a kind of necessary evil, half civilized at best. But if ever *I* set up an establishment, I shall insist upon taking precedence of the newspaper."

CHAPTER VII

Tiff's Garden

WOULD THE LIMITS of our story admit of it, we should gladly linger many days in the shady precincts of Magnolia Grove, where Clayton and Nina remained some days longer, and where the hours flew by on flowery feet; but the inevitable time and tide, which wait for no man, wait not for the narrator. We must therefore say, in brief, that when the visit was concluded, Clayton accompanied Nina once more to Canema, and returned to the circle of his own duties.

Nina returned to her own estate, with views somewhat chastened and modified by her acquaintance with Anne. As Clayton supposed, the influence of a real noble purpose in life had proved of more weight than exhortations, and she began to feel within herself positive aspirations for some more noble and worthy life than she had heretofore led. That great, absorbing feeling which determines the whole destiny of woman's existence, is in its own nature an elevating and purifying one. It is such even when placed on an unworthy object, and much more so when the object is a worthy one. Since the first of their friendship, Clayton had never officiously sought to interfere with the growth and development of Nina's moral nature. He had sufficient sagacity to perceive that, unconsciously to herself, a deeper power of feeling, and a wider range of thought, was opening within her; and he left the development of it to the same quiet forces which swell the rosebud and guide the climbing path of the vine. Simply and absolutely he lived his own life before her, and let hers alone; and the power of his life therefore became absolute.

A few mornings after her return, she thought that she would go out and inquire after the welfare of our old friend Tiff. It was a hazy, warm, bright summer morning, and all things lay in that dreamy stillness, that trance of voluptuous rest, which precedes the approach of the fiercer heats of the day. Since her absence there had been evident improvement in Tiff's affairs. The baby, a hearty, handsome little fellow, by dint of good nursing, pork-sucking, and lying out doors in the tending of breezes and zephyrs, had grown to be a creeping creature, and followed Tiff around, in his garden ministrations, with unintelligible chatterings of delight.

At the moment when Nina rode up, Tiff was busy with his morning work in the garden.

His appearance, it is to be confessed, was somewhat peculiar. He usually wore, in compliment to his nursing duties, an apron in front; but, as his various avocations pressed hard upon his time, and as his own personal outfit was ever the last to be attended to, Tiff's nether garments had shown traces of that frailty which is incident to all human things.

"Bress me," he said to himself, that morning, as he with difficulty engineered his way into them, "holes here, and holes dar! Don't want but two holes in my breeches, and I's got two dozen! Got my foot through de wrong place! Por old Tiff! Laws a massy! wish I could get hold of some of dem dar clothes dey were telling 'bout at de camp-meeting, dey wore forty years in de wilderness! 'Mazing handy dem ar times was! Well, any how, I'll tie an apron behind, and anoder in front. Bress de Lord, I's got aprons, any how! I must make up a par of breeches, some of dese yer days, when de baby's teeth is all through, and Teddy's clothes don't want no mending, and de washing is done, and dese yer weeds stops a growing in de garden. Bress if I know what de Lord want of so many weeds. 'Pears like dey comes just to plague us; but, den, we doesn't know. May be dere's some good in 'em. We doesn't know but a leetle, no way."

Tiff was sitting on the ground weeding one of his garden-beds, when he was surprised by the apparition of Nina on horseback coming up to the gate. Here was a dilemma, to be sure! No cavalier had a more absolute conception of the nature of politeness, and the claims of beauty, rank, and fashion, than Tiff. Then, to be caught sitting on the ground, with a blue apron on in front, and a red one on behind, was an appalling dilemma! However, as our readers may have discovered, Tiff had that essential requisite of good breeding, the moral courage to face an exigency; and, wisely considering that a want of cordiality is a greater deficiency than the want of costume, he rose up, without delay, and hastened to the gate to acknowledge the honor.

"Lord bress yer sweet face, Miss Nina!" he said, while the

breezes flapped and fluttered his red and blue sails, "Old Tiff's 'mazin' happy to see you. Miss Fanny's well, thank ye; and Mas'r Teddy and the baby all doing nicely. Bress de Lord, Miss Nina, be so good as to get down and come in. I's got some nice berries dat I picked in de swamp, and Miss Fanny'll be proud to have you take some. You see," he said, laughing heartily, and regarding his peculiar costume, "I wasn't looking for any quality long dis yer time o' day, so I just got on my old clothes."

"Why, Uncle Tiff, I think they become you immensely!" said Nina. "Your outfit is really original and picturesque. You're not one of the people that are ashamed of their work, are you, Uncle Tiff? So, if you just lead my horse to that stump, I'll get down."

"Laws, no, Miss Nina!" said Tiff, as with alacrity he obeyed her orders. "Spects, if Old Tiff was 'shamed of work, he'd have a heap to be 'shamed of; cause it's pretty much all work with him. 'T is so!"

"Tomtit pretended to come with me," said Nina, as she looked round; "but he lagged behind by the brook to get some of those green grapes, and I suspect it's the last I shall see of him. So, Tiff, if you please to tie Sylphine in the shade, I'll go in to see Miss Fanny."

And Nina tripped lightly up the walk, now bordered on either side by china asters and marigolds, to where Fanny was standing bashfully in the door waiting for her. In her own native woods this child was one of the boldest, freest, and happiest of romps. There was scarce an eligible tree which she could not climb, or a thicket she had not explored. She was familiar with every flower, every bird, every butterfly, of the vicinity. She knew precisely when every kind of fruit would ripen, and flower would blossom; and was so *au fait* in the language of birds and squirrels, that she might almost have been considered one of the fraternity. Her only companion and attendant, Old Tiff, had that quaint, fanciful, grotesque nature which is the furthest possible removed from vulgarity; and his frequent lectures on proprieties and conventionalities, his long and prolix narrations of her ancestral glories and distinctions, had succeeded in infusing into her a sort of childish consciousness of dignity, while at the same time it inspired her with a bashful awe of those whom she saw surrounded with the actual insignia and circumstances of position and fortune. After all, Tiff's method of education, instinctive as it was, was highly philosophical, since a certain degree of self-respect is the nurse of many virtues, and a shield from many temptations. There is also something, perhaps, in the influence of descent. Fanny certainly inherited from her mother a more delicate organization than generally attends her apparent station in life. She had, also, what perhaps belongs to the sex, a capability of receiving the mysteries and proprieties of dress; and Nina, as she stood on the threshold of the single low room, could not but be struck with the general air of refinement which characterized both it and its little mistress. There were flowers from the swamps and hedges arranged with care and taste, feathers of birds, strings of eggs of different color, dried grasses, and various little woodland curiosities, which showed a taste refined by daily intercourse with nature. Fanny herself was arrayed in a very pretty print dress, which her father had brought home in a recent visit, with a cape of white muslin. Her brown hair was brushed smoothly from her forehead, and her clear blue eyes, and fair, rosy complexion, gave her a pleasing air of intelligence and refinement.

"Thank you," said Nina, as Fanny offered her the only chair the establishment afforded; "but I'm going with Tiff out in the garden. I never can bear to be in the house such days as this. You didn't expect me over so early, Uncle Tiff; but I took a notable turn, this morning, and routed them up to an early breakfast, on purpose that I might have time to get over here before the heat came on. It's pleasant out here, now the shadow of the woods falls across the garden so. How beautifully those trees wave! Tiff, go on with your work—never mind me."

"Yes, Miss Nina, it's mighty pleasant. Why, I was out in dis yer garden at four o'clock dis morning, and 'peared like dese yer trees was waving like a psalm, so sort o' still, you know! Kind o' spreading out der hands like dey'd have prayers; and dere was a mighty handsome star a looking down. *I* spects dat ar star is one of de very oldest families up dar."

"Most likely," said Nina, cheerily. "They call it Venus, the star of love, Uncle Tiff; and I believe that is a very old family."

"Love is a mighty good ting, any how," said Tiff. "Lord bress you, Miss Nina, it makes everyting go kind o' easy. Sometimes, when I'm studding upon dese yer tings, I says to myself, 'pears like de trees in de wood, dey loves each oder. Dey stands kind o' locking arms so, and dey kind o' nod der heads, and whispers so! 'Pears like de grape-vines, and de birds, and all dem ar tings, dey lives comfortable togeder, like dey was peaceable, and liked each oder.

Now, folks is apt to get a stewin' and a frettin' round, and turning up der noses at dis yer ting, and dat ar; but 'pears like de Lord's works takes everyting mighty easy. Dey just kind o' lives along peaceable. I tink it's mighty 'structive!"

"Certainly it is," said Nina. "Old Mother Nature is an excellent manager, and always goes on making the best of everything."

"Dere's heaps done dat ar way, and no noise," said Tiff. "Why, Miss Nina, I studies upon dat ar out here in my garden. Why, look at dat ar corn, way up over your head, now! All dat are growed dis yer summer. No noise 'bout it—'pears like nobody couldn't see when 'twas done. Dey were telling us in camp-meeting how de Lord created de heaven and de earth. Now, Miss Nina, Tiff has his own thoughts, you know; and Tiff says, 'pears like de Lord is creating de heaven and de earth all de time. 'Pears like you can see Him a doing of it right afore your face; and dem growing tings are so curus! Miss Nina, 'pears for all de world like as if dey was critters! 'Pears like each of 'em has der own way, and won't go no oder! Dese yer beans, dey will come up so curus right top o' de stalks; dey will turn round de pole one way, and, if you was to tie 'em, you couldn't make 'em go round t' oder! Dey's set in der own way— dey is, for all dey's so still 'bout it! Laws, Miss Nina, dese yer tings makes Tiff laugh—does so!" he said, sitting down, and indulging in one of his fits of merriment.

"You are quite a philosopher, Tiff," said Nina.

"Laws, Miss Nina, I hopes not!" said Tiff, solemnly; " 'cause one of de preachers at de camp-meeting used up dem folk terrible, I tell you! Dat ar pretty much all I could make out of de sermon, dat people mustn't be 'losophers! Laws, Miss Nina, I hope I an't no sich!"

"O, I mean the good kind, Uncle Tiff. But how were you pleased, upon the whole, at the camp-meeting?" said Nina.

"Well," said Tiff, "Miss Nina, I hope I got something—I don't know fa'rly how much 't is. But, Miss Nina, it 'pears like as if you had come out here to instruct us 'bout dese yer tings. Miss Fanny, she don't read very well yet, and 'pears like if you could read us some out of de Bible, and teach us how to be Christians—"

"Why, Tiff, I scarcely know how myself!" said Nina. "I'll send Milly to talk to you. She is a real good Christian."

"Milly is a very nice woman," said Tiff, somewhat doubtfully; "but, Miss Nina, 'pears like I would rather have white teaching;

'pears like I would rather have you, if it wouldn't be too much trouble."

"O, no, Uncle Tiff! If you want to hear me read, I'll read to you now," said Nina. "Have you got a Bible, here? Stay; I'll sit down. I'll take the chair and sit down in the shade, and then you needn't stop your work."

Tiff hurried into the house to call Fanny; produced a copy of a Testament, which, with much coaxing, he had persuaded Cripps to bring on his last visit; and, while Fanny sat at her feet making larkspur rings, she turned over the pages, to think what to read. When she saw Tiff's earnest and eager attention, her heart smote her to think that the book, so valuable in his eyes, was to her almost an unread volume.

"What shall I read to you, Tiff? What do you want to hear?"

"Well, I wants to find out de shortest way I ken, how dese yer chil'en's to be got to heaven!" said Tiff. "Dis yer world is mighty well long as it holds out; but, den, yer see, it don't last forever! Tings is passing away!"

Nina thought a moment. The great question of questions, so earnestly proposed to her! The simple, childlike old soul hanging confidingly on her answer! At last she said, with a seriousness quite unusual with her:

"Tiff, I think the best thing I can do is to read to you about our Saviour. He came down into this world to show us the way to heaven. And I'll read you, when I come here days, all that there is about Him—all he said and did; and then, perhaps, you'll see the way yourself. Perhaps," she added, with a sigh, "I shall, too!"

As she spoke, a sudden breeze of air shook the clusters of a prairie-rose, which was climbing into the tree under which she was sitting, and a shower of rose-leaves fell around her.

"Yes," she said to herself, as the rose-leaves fell on her book, "it's quite true, what he says. Everything is passing!"

And now, amid the murmur of the pine-trees, and the rustling of the garden-vines, came on the ear of the listeners the first words of that sweet and ancient story:

"Now, when Jesus was born in Bethlehem in Judea, behold there came wise men from the East, saying, 'Where is *He* that is born King of the Jews? For we have seen his star in the East, and are come to worship Him.' "[1]

Probably more cultivated minds would have checked the progress of the legend by a thousand questions, statistical and geographical, as to where Jerusalem was, and who the wise men were, and how far the East was from Jerusalem, and whether it was probable they would travel so far. But Nina was reading to children, and to an old child-man, in whose grotesque and fanciful nature there was yet treasured a believing sweetness, like the amulets supposed to belong to the good genii of the fairy tales. The quick fancy of her auditors made reality of the story as it went along. A cloudy Jerusalem built itself up immediately in their souls, and became as well known to them as the neighboring town of E——. Herod,[2] the king, became a real walking personage in their minds, with a crown on his head. And Tiff immediately discerned a resemblance between him and a certain domineering old General Eaton, who used greatly to withstand the cause of virtue, and the Peytons, in the neighborhood where he was brought up. Tiff's indignation, when the slaughter of the innocents was narrated, was perfectly outrageous. He declared "He wouldn't have believed that of King Herod, bad as he was!" and, good-hearted and inoffensive as Tiff was in general, it really seemed to afford him comfort, "dat de debil had got dat ar man 'fore now."

"Sarves him right, too!" said Tiff, striking fiercely at a weed with his hoe. "Killing all dem por little chil'en! Why, what harm had dey done him, any way? Wonder what he thought of hisself!"

Nina found it necessary to tranquillize the good creature, to get a hearing for the rest of the story. She went on reading of the wild night-journey of the wise men, and how the star went before them till it stood over the place where the child was. How they went in, and saw the young child, and Mary his mother, and fell down before him, offering gifts of gold, frankincense, and myrrh.

"Lord bless you! I wish I'd a been dar!" said Tiff. "And dat ar chile was de Lord of glory, sure 'nough, Miss Nina! I hearn 'em sing dis yer hymn at de camp-meeting,—you know, 'bout cold on his cradle. You know it goes dis yer way." And Tiff sung, to a kind of rocking lullaby, words whose poetic imagery had hit his fancy before he knew their meaning.

"Cold on his cradle the dew-drops are shining,
    Low lies his head with the beasts of the stall;
Angels adore, in slumber reclining,
    Maker, and Saviour, and Monarch of all."[3]

Nina had never realized, till she felt it in the undoubting faith of her listeners, the wild, exquisite poetry of that legend, which, like an immortal lily, blooms in the heart of Christianity as spotless and as tender now as eighteen hundred years ago.

That child of Bethlehem, when afterwards he taught in Galilee,[4] spoke of seed which fell into a good and honest heart; and words could not have been more descriptive of the nature which was now receiving this seed of Paradise.

When Nina had finished her reading, she found her own heart touched by the effect which she had produced. The nursing, child-loving Old Tiff was ready, in a moment, to bow before his Redeemer, enshrined in the form of an infant; and it seemed as if the air around him had been made sacred by the sweetness of the story.

As Nina was mounting her horse to return, Tiff brought out a little basket full of wild raspberries.

"Tiff wants to give you something," he said.

"Thank you, Uncle Tiff. How delightful! Now, if you'll only give me a cluster of your Michigan rose!"

Proud and happy was Tiff, and, pulling down the very topmost cluster of his rose, he presented it to her. Alas! before Nina reached home, it hung drooping from the heat.

"The grass withereth, and the flower fadeth; but the word of our God shall stand forever."[5]

CHAPTER VIII

The Warning

IN LIFE ORGANIZED as it is at the South, there are two currents;—one, the current of the master's fortunes, feelings, and hopes; the other, that of the slave's. It is a melancholy fact in the history of the human race, as yet, that there have been multitudes who follow the triumphal march of life only as captives, to whom the voice of the trumpet, the waving of the banners, the shouts of the people, only add to the bitterness of enthralment.

While life to Nina was daily unfolding in brighter colors, the slave-brother at her side was destined to feel an additional burden on his already unhappy lot.

It was toward evening, after having completed his daily cares, that he went to the post-office for the family letters. Among these, one was directed to himself, and he slowly perused it as he rode home through the woods. It was as follows:

"MY DEAR BROTHER: I told you how comfortably we were living on our place—I and my children. Since then, everything has been changed. Mr. Tom Gordon came here and put in a suit for the estate, and attached me and my children as slaves. He is a dreadful man. The case has been tried and gone against us.[1] The judge said that both deeds of emancipation—both the one executed in Ohio, and the one here—were of no effect; that my boy was a slave, and could no more hold property than a mule before a plough. I had some good friends here, and people pitied me very much; but nobody could help me. Tom Gordon is a bad man—a *very* bad man. I cannot tell you all that he said to me. I only tell you that I will kill myself and my children before we will be his slaves. Harry, I have been *free*, and I know what liberty is. My children have been brought up *free*, and if I can help it they never shall know what slavery is. I have got away, and am hiding with a colored

339

family here in Natchez. I hope to get to Cincinnati, where I have friends.

"My dear brother, I did hope to do something for you. Now I cannot. Nor can you do anything for me. The law is on the side of our oppressors; but I hope God will help us. Farewell!

Your affectionate

SISTER."

It is difficult to fathom the feelings of a person brought up in a position so wholly unnatural as that of Harry. The feelings which had been cultivated in him by education, and the indulgence of his nominal possessors, were those of an honorable and gentlemanly man. His position was absolutely that of the common slave, without one legal claim to anything on earth, one legal right of protection in any relation of life. What any man of strong nature would feel on hearing such tidings from a sister, Harry felt.

In a moment there rose up before his mind the picture of Nina in all her happiness and buoyancy—in all the fortunate accessories in her lot. Had the vague thoughts which crowded on his mind been expressed in words, they might have been something like these:

"I have two sisters, daughters of one father, both beautiful, both amiable and good; but one has rank, and position, and wealth, and ease, and pleasure; the other is an outcast, unprotected, given up to the brutal violence of a vile and wicked man. She has been a good wife, and a good mother. Her husband has done all he could to save her; but the cruel hand of the law grasps her and her children, and hurls them back into the abyss from which it was his life-study to raise them. And I can do nothing! I am not even a man! And this curse is on me, and on my wife, and on my children and children's children, forever! Yes, what does the judge say, in this letter? 'He can no more own anything than the mule before his plough!' That's to be the fate of every child of mine! And yet people say, 'You have all you want; why are you not happy?' I wish they could try it! Do they think broadcloth coats and gold watches can comfort a man for all this?"

Harry rode along, with his hands clenched upon the letter, the reins drooping from the horse's neck, in the same unfrequented path where he had twice before met Dred. Looking up, he saw him the third time, standing silently, as if he had risen from the ground.

"Where did you come from?" said he. "Seems to me you are always at hand when anything is going against me!"

"Went not my spirit with thee?" said Dred. "Have I not seen it all? It is because we *will* bear this, that we have it to bear, Harry."

"But," said Harry, "what can we do?"

"Do? What does the wild horse do? Launch out our hoofs! rear up, and come down on them! What does the rattlesnake do? Lie in their path, and bite! Why did they make slaves of us? They tried the wild Indians first. Why didn't they keep to them? *They* wouldn't be slaves, and we *will!* They that *will* bear the yoke, *may* bear it!"

"But," said Harry, "Dred, this is all utterly hopeless. Without any means, or combination, or leaders, we should only rush on to our own destruction."

"Let us die, then!" said Dred. "What if we do die? What great matter is that? If they bruise our head, we can sting their heels! Nat Turner—they killed him; but the fear of him almost drove them to set free their slaves! Yes, it was argued among them. They came within two or three votes of it in their assembly.[2] A little more fear, and they would have done it. If my father had succeeded, the slaves in Carolina would be free to-day. Die?—Why not die? Christ was crucified! Has everything dropped out of you, that you can't die— that you'll crawl like worms, for the sake of living?"

"I'm not afraid of death, myself," said Harry. "God knows I wouldn't care if I did die; but—"

"Yes, I know," said Dred. "She that letteth will let, till she be taken out of the way. I tell you, Harry, there's a seal been loosed— there's a vial poured out on the air; and the destroying angel standeth over Jerusalem, with his sword drawn!"[3]

"What do you mean by that?" said Harry.

Dred stood silent, for a moment; his frame assumed the rigid tension of a cataleptic state, and his voice sounded like that of a person speaking from a distance, yet there was a strange distinctness in it.

"The words of the prophet, and the vision that he hath from the Lord, when he saw the vision, falling into a trance, and having his eyes open, and behold he saw a roll flying through the heavens, and it was written, within and without, with mourning and lamentation and woe! Behold, it cometh! Behold, the slain of the Lord shall be many! They shall fall in the house and by the way! The bride shall fall in her chamber, and the child shall die in its cradle! There shall be a cry in the land of Egypt, for there shall not be a house where there is not one dead!"[4]

"Dred! Dred! Dred!" said Harry, pushing him by the shoulder; "come out of this—come out! It's frightful!"

Dred stood looking before him, with his head inclined forward, his hand upraised, and his eyes strained, with the air of one who is trying to make out something through a thick fog.

"I see her!" he said. "Who is that by her? His back is turned. Ah! I see—it is he! And there's Harry and Milly! Try hard—try! You won't do it. No, no use sending for the doctor. There's not one to be had. They are all too busy. Rub her hands! Yes. But—it's no good. 'Whom the Lord loveth, he taketh away from the evil to come.'[5] Lay her down. Yes, it is Death! Death! Death!"

Harry had often seen the strange moods of Dred, and he shuddered now, because he partook somewhat in the common superstitions, which prevailed among the slaves, of his prophetic power. He shook and called him; but he turned slowly away, and, with eyes that seemed to see nothing, yet guiding himself with his usual dextrous agility, he plunged again into the thickness of the swamp, and was soon lost to view.

After his return home it was with the sensation of chill at his heart that he heard Aunt Nesbit reading to Nina portions of a letter, describing the march through some Northern cities of the cholera,[6] which was then making fearful havoc on our American shore.

"Nobody seems to know how to manage it," the letter said; "physicians are all at a loss. It seems to spurn all laws. It bursts upon cities like a thunderbolt, scatters desolation and death, and is gone with equal rapidity. People rise in the morning well, and are buried before evening. In one day houses are swept of a whole family."

"Ah," said Harry, to himself, "I see the meaning now, but what does it portend to us?"

How the strange foreshadowing had risen to the mind of Dred, we shall not say. Whether there be mysterious electric sympathies which, floating through the air, bear dim presentiments, on their wings, or whether some stray piece of intelligence had dropped on his ear, and been interpreted by the burning fervor of his soul, we know not. The news, however, left very little immediate impression on the daily circle at Canema. It was a dread reality in the far distance. Harry only pondered it with anxious fear.

CHAPTER IX

The Morning Star

NINA CONTINUED HER VISITS to Tiff's garden on almost every pleasant morning or evening. Tiff had always some little offering, either berries or flowers, to present, or a nice little luncheon of fish or birds, cooked in some mode of peculiar delicacy; and which, served up in sylvan style, seemed to have something of the wild relish of the woods. In return, she continued to read the story so interesting to him; and it was astonishing how little explanation it needed—how plain honesty of heart, and lovingness of nature, interpreted passages over which theologians have wrangled in vain. It was not long before Tiff had impersonated to himself each of the disciples, particularly Peter; so that, when anything was said by him, Tiff would nod his head significantly, and say, "Ah, ah! dat ar's just like him! He's allers a puttin' in; but he's a good man, arter all!"

What impression was made on the sensitive young nature, through whom, as a medium, Tiff received this fresh revelation, we may, perhaps, imagine. There are times in life when the soul, like a half-grown climbing vine, hangs wavering tremulously, stretching out its tendrils for something to ascend by. Such are generally the great transition periods of life, when we are passing from the ideas and conditions of one stage of existence to those of another. Such times are most favorable for the presentation of the higher truths of religion. In the hazy, slumberous stillness of that midsummer atmosphere, in the long, silent rides through the pines, Nina half awakened from the thoughtless dreams of childhood, yearning for something nobler than she yet had lived for, thought over, and revolved in her mind, this beautiful and spotless image of God, revealed in man, which her daily readings presented; and the world that he created seemed to whisper to her in every pulsation of its air, in every breath of its flowers, in the fanning of its winds, "He still liveth, and he loveth thee." The voice of the Good Shepherd fell on the ear of the wandering lamb, calling her to his arms; and Nina found herself one day unconsciously repeating, as she returned through the woods, words which she had often heard read at church:

"When thou saidst unto me, Seek ye my face, my heart said unto thee, Thy face, Lord, will I seek."[1]

Nina had often dreaded the idea of becoming a Christian, as one shrinks from the idea of a cold, dreary passage, which must be passed to gain a quiet home. But suddenly, as if by some gentle invisible hand, the veil seemed to be drawn which hid the face of Almighty Love from her view. She beheld the earth and the heavens transfigured in the light of his smile. A strange and unspeakable joy arose within her, as if some loving presence were always near her. It was with her when she laid down at night, and when she awoke in the morning the strange happiness had not departed. Her feelings may be best expressed by an extract from a letter which she wrote at this time to Clayton.

"It seems to me that I have felt a greater change in me within the last two months than in my whole life before. When I look back at what I was in New York, three months ago, actually I hardly know myself. It seems to me in those old days that life was only a frolic to me, as it is to the kitten. I don't really think that there was much harm in me, only the want of good. In those days, sometimes I used to have a sort of dim longing to be better, particularly when Livy Ray was at school. It seemed as if she woke up something that had been asleep in me; but she went away, and I fell asleep again, and life went on like a dream. Then I became acquainted with you and you began to rouse me again, and for some time I thought I didn't like to wake; it was just as it is when one lies asleep in the morning—it's so pleasant to sleep and dream, that one resists any one who tries to bring them back to life. I used to feel quite pettish when I first knew you, and sometimes wished you'd let me alone, because I saw that you belonged to a different kind of sphere from what I'd been living in. And I had a presentiment that, if I let you go on, life would have to be something more than a joke with me. But *you would,* like a very indiscreet man as you are, you would insist on being in sober earnest.

"I used to think that I had no heart; I begin to think I have a good deal now. Every day it seems as if I could love more and more; and a great many things are growing clear to me that I didn't use to understand, and I'm growing happier every day.

"You know my queer old protégé, Uncle Tiff, who lives in the woods here. For some time past I have been to his house every day, reading to him in the Testament, and it has had a very great effect on me. It affected me very much, in the first place, that he seemed so very earnest about religion, when I, who ought to know so much more, was so indifferent to it; and when the old creature, with tears in his eyes, actually insisted upon it that I should show his children the road to heaven, then I began to read to him the Testament, the life of Jesus. I didn't know myself how beautiful it was—how suited to all our wants. It seemed to me I never saw so much beauty in anything before; and it seems as if it had waked a new life in me. Everything is changed; and it is the beauty of Christ that has changed it. You know I always loved beauty above all things, in music, in nature, and in flowers; but it seems to me that I see something now in Jesus more beautiful than all. It seems as if all these had been shadows of beauty, but *he* is the substance. It is strange, but I have a sense of him, his living and presence, that sometimes almost overpowers me. It seems as if he had been following me always, but I had not seen him. He has been a good shepherd, seeking the thoughtless lamb. He has, all my life, been calling me child; but till lately my heart has never answered, Father! Is this religion? Is this what people mean by conversion? I tried to tell Aunt Nesbit how I felt, because now I feel kinder to everybody; and really my heart smote me to think how much fun I had made of her, and now I begin to love her very much. She was so anxious I should talk with Mr. Titmarsh, because he is a minister. Well, you know I didn't want to do it, but I thought I ought to, because poor aunty really seemed to feel anxious I should. I suppose, if I were as perfect as I ought to be, a good man's stiff ways wouldn't trouble me so. But stiff people, you know, are my particular temptation.

"He came and made a pastoral call, the other day, and talked to me. I don't think he understood me very well, and I'm sure I didn't understand him. He told me how many kinds of faith there were, and how many kinds of love. I believe there were three kinds of faith, and two kinds of love; and he thought it was important to know whether I had got the right kind. He said we ought not to love God because he loves us, but because he is holy. He wanted to know whether I had any just views of sin, as an infinite evil; and

I told him I hadn't the least idea of what infinite was; and that I hadn't any views of anything, but the beauty of Christ; that I didn't understand anything about the different sorts of faith, but that I felt perfectly sure that Jesus is so good that he would make me feel right, and give me right views, and do everything for me that I need.

"He wanted to know if I loved him because he magnified the law, and made it honorable; and I told him I didn't understand what that meant.

"I don't think, on the whole, that the talk did me much good. It only confused me, and made me very uncomfortable. But I went out to Old Tiff's in the evening, and read how Jesus received the little children. You never saw anybody so delighted as Old Tiff was. He got me to read it to him three or four times over; and now he gets me to read it every time I go there, and he says he likes it better than any other part of the Testament. Tiff and I get along very well together. He doesn't know any more about faith than I do, and hasn't any better views than I have. Aunt Nesbit is troubled about me, because I'm so happy. She says she's afraid I haven't any sense of sin. Don't you remember my telling you how happy I felt the first time I heard *real* music? I thought, before that, that I could sing pretty well; but in one hour all *my* music became trash in my eyes. And yet, I would not have missed it for the world. So it is now. That beautiful life of Jesus—so sweet, so calm, so pure, so unselfish, so perfectly *natural,* and yet so far beyond nature—has shown me what a poor, sinful, low creature I am; and yet I rejoice. I feel, sometimes, as I did when I first heard a full orchestra play some of Mozart's divine harmonies. I forgot that I was alive; I lost all thought of myself entirely; and I was perfectly happy. So it is now. This loveliness and beauty that I see makes me happy without any thought of myself. It seems to me, sometimes, that while I see it I never can suffer.

"There is another thing that is strange to me; and that is, that the Bible has grown so beautiful to me. It seems to me that it has been all my life like the transparent picture, without any light behind it; and now it is all illuminated, and its words are full of meaning to me. I am light-hearted and happy—happier than ever I was. Do you remember, the first day you came to Canema, that I told you it seemed so sad that we must die? That feeling is all gone, now. I feel that Jesus is everywhere, and that there is no such thing as dying; it is only going out of one room into another.

"Everybody wonders to see how light-hearted I am; and poor aunty says, 'she trembles for me.' I couldn't help thinking of that, the other morning I was reading to Tiff; what Jesus said when they asked him why his disciples did not fast: 'Can the children of the bride-chamber mourn while the bridegroom is with them?'[2]

"Now, my dear friend, you must tell me what you think of all this, because, you know, I always tell you everything. I have written to Livy about it, because I know it will make her so happy. Milly seems to understand it all, and what she says to me really helps me very much. I always used to think that Milly had some strange, beautiful kind of inward life, that I knew nothing of, because she would speak with so much certainty of God's love, and *act* as if it was so real to her; and she would tell me so earnestly, 'Chile, he loves you!' Now I see into it—that mystery of his love to us, and how he overcomes and subdues all things by love; and I understand how 'perfect love casteth out fear.' "[3]

To this letter Nina soon received an answer, from which also we give an extract:

"If I was so happy, my dearest one, as to be able to awaken that deeper and higher nature which I always knew was in you, I thank God. But, if I ever was in any respect your teacher, you have passed beyond my teachings now. Your childlike simplicity of nature makes you a better scholar than I in that school where the first step is to forget all our worldly wisdom, and become a little child. We men have much more to contend with, in the pride of our nature, in our habits of worldly reasoning. It takes us long to learn the lesson that faith is the highest wisdom. Don't trouble your head, dear Nina, with Aunt Nesbit or Mr. Titmarsh. *What you feel is faith.* They *define* it, and you *feel* it. And there's all the difference between the definition and the feeling, that there is between the husk and the corn.

"As for me, I am less happy than you. Religion seems to me to have two parts to it. One part is the aspiration of man's nature, and the other is God's answer to those aspirations. I have, as yet, only the first; perhaps, because I am less simple and less true; perhaps, because I am not yet become a little child. So *you* must be my guide, instead of I *yours;* for I believe it is written of the faithful, that a little child shall lead them.[4]

"I am a good deal tried now, my dear, because I am coming to a crisis in my life. I am going to take a step that will deprive me of many friends, of popularity, and that will, perhaps, alter all my course for the future. But, if I should lose friends and popularity, *you* would love me still, would you not? It is wronging you to ask such a question; but yet I should like to have you answer it. It will make me stronger for what I have to do. On Thursday of this week, my case will come on again. I am very busy just now; but the thought of you mingles with every thought."

CHAPTER X

The Legal Decision

THE TIME FOR THE SESSION of the Supreme Court had now arrived, and Clayton's cause was to be reconsidered. Judge Clayton felt exceedingly chagrined, as the time drew near. Being himself the leading judge of the Supreme Court, the declaration of the bench would necessarily be made known through him.

"It is extremely painful to me," he said, to Mrs. Clayton, "to have this case referred to me; for I shall be obliged to reverse the decision."

"Well," said Mrs. Clayton, "Edward must have fortitude to encounter the usual reverses of his profession. He made a gallant defence, and received a great deal of admiration, which will not be at all lessened by this."

"You do not understand me," said Judge Clayton. "It is not the coming out in opposition to Edward which principally annoys me. It is the nature of the decision that I am obliged to make—the doctrine that I feel myself forced to announce."

"And must you, then?" said Mrs. Clayton.

"Yes, I must," said Judge Clayton. "A judge can only perceive and declare. What I see, I must speak, though it go against all my feelings and all my sense of right."

"I don't see, for my part," said Mrs. Clayton, "how that decision can possibly be reversed, without allowing the most monstrous injustice."

"Such is the case," said Judge Clayton; "but I sit in my seat, not to make laws, nor to alter them, but simply to declare what they are. However bad the principle declared, it is not so bad as the proclamation of a falsehood would be. I have sworn truly to declare the laws, and I must keep my oath."

"And have you talked with Edward about it?"

"Not particularly. He understands, in general, the manner in which the thing lies in my mind."

This conversation took place just before it was time for Judge Clayton to go to his official duties.

The court-room, on this occasion, was somewhat crowded. Barker, being an active, resolute, and popular man, with a certain class, had talked up a considerable excitement with regard to his case. Clayton's friends were interested in it on his account; lawyers were, for the sake of the principle; so that, upon the whole, there was a good deal of attention drawn towards this decision.

Among the spectators on the morning of the court, Clayton remarked Harry. For reasons which our readers may appreciate, his presence there was a matter of interest to Clayton. He made his way toward him.

"Harry," he said, "how came you here?"

"The ladies," said Harry, "thought they would like to know how the thing went, and so I got on to my horse and came over."

As he spoke, he placed in Clayton's hand a note, and, as the paper touched his hand, a close spectator might have seen the color rise in his cheek. He made his way back to his place, and opened a law-book, which he held up before his face. Inside the law-book, however, was a little sheet of gilt-edged paper, on which were written a few words in pencil, more interesting than all the law in the world. Shall we commit the treason of reading over his shoulder? It was as follows:

"You say you may to-day be called to do something which you think right, but which will lose you many friends; which will destroy your popularity, which may alter all your prospects in life; and you ask if I can love you yet. I say, in answer, that it was not your friends that I loved, nor your popularity, nor your prospects, but *you*. I *can* love and honor a man who is not afraid nor ashamed to do what he thinks to be right; and therefore I hope ever to remain yours,   NINA.

"P. S. I only got your letter this morning, and have but just time to scribble this and send by Harry. We are all well, and shall be glad to see you as soon as the case is over."

"Clayton, my boy, you are very busy with your authorities," said Frank Russel, behind him. Clayton hastily hid the paper in his hand.

"It's charming!" said Russel, "to have little manuscript annotations on law. It lights it up, like the illuminations in old missals. But, say, Clayton, you live at the fountain-head;—how is the case going?"

"Against me!" said Clayton.

"Well, it's no great odds, after all. You have had your triumph. These after-thoughts cannot take away that. ⁕ ⁕ ⁕ ⁕ ⁕ But, hush! There's your father going to speak!"

Every eye in the court-room was turned upon Judge Clayton, who was standing with his usual self-poised composure of manner. In a clear, deliberate voice, he spoke as follows:

"A judge cannot but lament, when such cases as the present are brought into judgment. It is impossible that the reasons on which they go can be appreciated, but where institutions similar to our own exist, and are *thoroughly understood.* The struggle, too, in the judge's own breast, between the feelings of the man and the duty of the magistrate, is a severe one, presenting strong temptation to put aside such questions, if it be possible. It is useless, however, to complain of things inherent in our political state. And it is criminal in a court to avoid any responsibility which the laws impose. With whatever reluctance, therefore, it is done, the court is compelled to express an opinion upon the extent of the dominion of the master over the slave in North Carolina. The indictment charges a battery on Milly, a slave of Louisa Nesbit. ⁕ ⁕ ⁕ ⁕

"The inquiry here is, whether a cruel and unreasonable battery on a slave by the hirer is indictable. The judge below instructed the jury that it is. He seems to have put it on the ground, that the defendant had but a special property. Our laws uniformly treat the master, or other person having the possession and command of the slave, as entitled to the same extent of authority. *The object is the same, the service of the slave;* and the same powers must be confided. In a criminal proceeding, and, indeed, in reference to all other persons but the general owner, the hirer and possessor of the slave, in relation to both rights and duties, is, for the time being, the owner. ⁕ ⁕ ⁕ ⁕ But, upon the general question, whether the owner is answerable *criminaliter,*[1] for a battery upon his own slave, or other exercise of authority or force, not forbidden by statute, the court entertains but little doubt. That he is so liable, has never been decided; nor, as far as is known, been hitherto contended. There has been no prosecution of the sort. The established habits and uniform practice of the country, in this respect, is the best evidence of the portion of power deemed by the whole community requisite to the preservation of the master's dominion. If we thought differently, we could not set our notions in array against the judgment of everybody else, and say that this or that authority may be safely lopped off.

"This has indeed been assimilated at the bar to the other domestic relations: and arguments drawn from the well-established principles, which *confer* and *restrain* the authority of the parent over the child, the tutor over the pupil, the master over the apprentice, have been pressed on us.

"The court does not recognize their application. There is no likeness between the cases. They are in opposition to each other, and there is an impassable gulf between them. The difference is that which exists between freedom and slavery; and a greater cannot be imagined. In the one, the end in view is the happiness of the youth born to equal rights with that governor on whom the duty devolves of training the young to usefulness, in a station which he is afterwards to assume among freemen. To such an end, and with such a subject, moral and intellectual instruction seem the natural means; and, for the most part, they are found to suffice. Moderate force is superadded only to make the others effectual. If that fail, it is better to leave the party to his own headstrong passions, and the ultimate correction of the law, than to allow it to be immoderately inflicted by a private person. With slavery it is far otherwise. The end is the profit of the master, his security, and the public safety; the subject, one doomed, in his own person and his posterity, to live without knowledge, and without the capacity to make anything his own, and to toil that another may reap the fruits. What moral considerations shall be addressed to such a being, to convince him what it is impossible but that the most stupid must feel and know can never be true,—that he is thus to labor upon a principle of natural duty, or for the sake of his own personal happiness? Such services can only be expected from one who has no will of his own; who surrenders his will in implicit obedience to that of another. Such obedience is the consequence only of uncontrolled authority over the body. There is nothing else which can operate to produce the effect. THE POWER OF THE MASTER MUST BE ABSOLUTE, TO RENDER THE SUBMISSION OF THE SLAVE PERFECT. I most freely confess my sense of the harshness of this proposition. I feel it as deeply as any man can. And, as a principle of moral right, every person in his retirement must repudiate it. But, in the actual condition of things, it must be so. There is no remedy. This discipline belongs to the state of slavery. They cannot be disunited without abrogating at once the rights of the master, and absolving the slave from his subjection. It constitutes the curse of slavery to both the bond and the free portions of our population. But it is *inherent in the relation* of master and slave. That there may be particular instances of cruelty and deliberate barbarity, where in conscience the law might properly interfere, is most probable. The difficulty is to determine where a *court* may properly begin. Merely in the abstract, it may well be asked which power of the master accords with right. The answer will probably sweep away all of them. But we cannot look at the matter in that light. The truth is that we are forbidden to enter upon a train of general reasoning on the subject. We cannot allow the right of the master to be brought into discussion in the courts of justice. The slave, to remain a slave, must be made sensible that there is no appeal from his master; that his power is, in no instance, usurped, but is conferred by the laws of man, at least, if not by the law of God. The danger would be great, indeed, if the tribunals of justice should be called on to graduate the punishment appropriate to every temper, and every dereliction of menial duty.

"No man can anticipate the many and aggravated provocations of the master which the slave would be constantly stimulated by his own passions, or the instigation of others, to give; or the consequent wrath of the master, prompting him to bloody vengeance upon the turbulent traitor; a vengeance *generally practised with impunity, by reason of its privacy.* The court, therefore, disclaims the power of changing the relation in which these parts of our people stand to each other.[2]

*   *   *   *   *   *   *

"I repeat, that I would gladly have avoided this ungrateful question. But, being brought to it, the court is compelled to declare that while slavery exists amongst us in its present state, or until it shall seem fit to the legislature to interpose express enactments to the contrary, it will be the imperative *duty* of the judges *to recognize the full dominion of the owner over the slave,* except where the exercise of it is forbidden by statute.

"And this we do upon the ground that *this dominion is essential to the value of slaves as property, to the security of the master and the public tranquillity, greatly dependent upon their subordination;* and, in fine, as most effectually securing the general protection and comfort of the slaves themselves. Judgment below reversed; and judgment entered for the defendant."

During the delivery of the decision Clayton's eyes, by accident, became fixed upon Harry, who was standing opposite to him, and who listened through the whole with breathless attention. He observed, as it went on, that his face became pale, his brow clouded, and that a fierce and peculiar expression flashed from his dark-blue eye. Never had Clayton so forcibly realized the horrors of slavery as when he heard them thus so calmly defined in the presence of one into whose soul the iron had entered. The tones of Judge Clayton's voice, so passionless, clear, and deliberate; the solemn, calm, unflinching earnestness of his words, were more than a thousand passionate appeals. In the dead silence that followed, Clayton rose, and requested permission of the court to be allowed to say a few words in view of the decision. His father looked slightly surprised, and there was a little movement among the judges. But curiosity, perhaps, among other reasons, led the court to give consent. Clayton spoke:

"I hope it will not be considered a disrespect or impertinence for me to say that the law of slavery, and the nature of that institution, have for the first time been made known to me to-day in their true character. I had before flattered myself with the hope that it might be considered a guardian institution, by which a stronger race might assume the care and instruction of the weaker one; and I had hoped that its laws were capable of being so administered as to protect the defenceless. This illusion is destroyed. I see but too clearly now the purpose and object of the law. I cannot, therefore, as a Christian man, remain in the practice of law in a slave state. I therefore relinquish the profession, into which I have just been inducted, and retire forever from the bar of my native state."

"There!—there!—there he goes!" said Frank Russel. "The sticking-point has come at last. His conscience is up, and start him now who can!"

There was a slight motion of surprise in the court and audience. But Judge Clayton sat with unmoved serenity. The words had struck to the depth of his soul. They had struck at the root of one of his strongest hopes in life. But he had listened to them with the same calm and punctilious attention which it was his habit to give to every speaker; and, with unaltered composure, he proceeded to the next business of the court.

A step so unusual occasioned no little excitement. But Clayton was not one of the class of people to whom his associates generally felt at liberty to express their opinions of his conduct. The quiet reserve of his manners discouraged any such freedom. As usual, in cases where a person takes an uncommon course from conscientious motives, Clayton was severely criticized. The more trifling among the audience contented themselves with using the good set phrases, quixotic, absurd, ridiculous. The elder lawyers, and those friendly to Clayton, shook their heads, and said, rash, precipitate, unadvised. "There's a want of ballast about him, somewhere!" said one. "He is unsound!" said another. "Radical and impracticable!" added a third.

"Yes," said Frank Russel, who had just come up, "Clayton *is* as radical and impracticable as the sermon on the mount, and that's the most impracticable thing I know of in literature. We all *can* serve God and Mammon. We have discovered that happy medium in our day. Clayton is behind the times. He is *Jewish* in his notions. Don't you think so, Mr. Titmarsh?" addressing the Rev. Mr. Titmarsh.

"It strikes me that our young friend is extremely *ultra*," said Mr. Titmarsh. "I might feel disposed to sympathize with him in the feelings he expressed, *to some extent;* but, it having pleased the Divine Providence to establish the institution of slavery, I humbly presume it is not competent for human reason to judge of it."

"And if it had pleased the Divine Providence to have established the institution of piracy, you'd say the same thing, I suppose!" said Frank Russel.

"Certainly, my young friend," said Mr. Titmarsh. "Whatever is divinely ordered, becomes right by that fact."

"I should think," said Frank Russel, "that things were divinely ordered because they were right."

"No, my friend," replied Mr. Titmarsh, moderately; "they are right because they are ordered, however contrary they may appear to any of our poor notions of justice and humanity." And Mr. Titmarsh walked off.

"Did you hear that?" said Russel. "And they expect really to come it over us with stuff like that! Now, if a fellow don't go to church Sundays, there's a dreadful outcry against him for not being religious! And, if they get us there, that's the kind of thing they put down our throats! As if they were going to make practical men give in to such humbugs!"

And the Rev. Mr. Titmarsh went off in another direction, lamenting to a friend as follows:

"How mournfully infidelity is increasing among the young men of our day! They quote Scripture with the same freedom that they would a book of plays, and seem to treat it with no more reverence! I believe it's the want of catechetical instruction while they are children. There's been a great falling back in the teaching of the Assembly's Catechism to children when they are young! I shall get that point up at the General Assembly. If that were thoroughly committed when they are children, I think they would never doubt afterwards."

Clayton went home and told his mother what he had done, and why. His father had not spoken to him on this subject; and there was that about Judge Clayton which made it difficult to introduce a topic, unless he signified an inclination to enter upon it. He was, as usual, calm, grave, and considerate, attending to every duty with unwearying regularity.

At the end of the second day, in the evening, Judge Clayton requested his son to walk in to his study. The interview was painful on both sides.

"You are aware, my son," he said, "that the step you have taken is a very painful one to me. I hope that it was not taken precipitately, from any sudden impulse."

"You may rest assured it was not," said Clayton. "I followed the deepest and most deliberate convictions of my conscience."

"In that case, you could not do otherwise," replied Judge Clayton. "I have no criticisms to make. But will your conscience allow you to retain the position of a slave-holder?"

"I have already relinquished it," replied Clayton, "so far as my own intentions are concerned. I retain the legal relation of owner simply as a means of protecting my servants from the cruelties of the law, and of securing the opportunity to educate and elevate them."

"And suppose this course brings you into conflict with the law of the state?" said Judge Clayton.

"If there is any reasonable prospect of having the law altered, I must endeavor to do that," said Clayton.

"But," said Judge Clayton, "suppose the law is so rooted in the nature of the institution, that it cannot be repealed without uprooting the institution? What then?"

"I say repeal the law, if it do uproot the institution," said Clayton. "Fiat justitia ruat cœlum."[3]

"I supposed that would be your answer," said Judge Clayton, patiently. "That is undoubtedly the logical line of life. But you are aware that communities do not follow such lines; your course, therefore, will place you in opposition to the community in which you live. Your conscientious convictions will cross self-interest, and the community will not allow you to carry them out."

"Then," said Clayton, "I must, with myself and my servants, remove to some region where I can do this."

"That I supposed would be the result," said Judge Clayton. "And have you looked at the thing in all its relations and consequences?"

"I have," said Clayton.

"You are about to form a connection with Miss Gordon," said Judge Clayton. "Have you considered how this will affect her?"

"Yes," said Clayton. "Miss Gordon fully sustains me in the course I have taken."

"I have no more to say," said Judge Clayton. "Every man must act up to his sense of duty."

There was a pause of a few moments, and Judge Clayton added:

"You, perhaps, have seen the implication which your course throws upon us who still continue to practise the system and uphold the institution which you repudiate."

"I meant no implications," said Clayton.

"I presume not. But they result, logically, from your course," said his father. "I assure you, I have often myself pondered the question with reference to my own duties. My course is a sufficient evidence that I have not come to the same result. Human law is, at best, but an approximation, a reflection of many of the ills of our nature. Imperfect as it is, it is, on the whole, a blessing. The worst system is better than anarchy."

"But, my father, why could you not have been a reformer of the system?"

"My son, no reform is possible, unless we are prepared to give up the institution of slavery. That will be the immediate result; and this is so realized by the instinct of self-preservation, which is unfailing in its accuracy, that every such proposition will be ignored, till there is a settled conviction in the community that the institution itself is a moral evil, and a sincere determination felt to be free from it. I see no tendency of things in that direction. That body of religious men of different denominations, called, par excellence, the church, exhibit a degree of moral apathy on this subject which is to me very surprising. It is with them that the training of the community, on which any such reform could be built, must commence; and I see no symptoms of their undertaking it. The decisions and testimonies of the great religious assemblies in the land, in my youth, were frequent. They have grown every year less and less decided; and now the morality of the thing is openly defended in our pulpits, to my great disgust. I see no way but that the institution will be left to work itself out to its final result, which will, in the end, be ruinous to our country. I am not myself gifted with the talents of a reformer. My turn of mind fits me for the situation I hold. I cannot hope that I have done no harm in it; but the good, I hope, will outweigh the evil. If you feel a call to enter on this course, fully understanding the difficulties and sacrifices it would probably involve, I would be the last one to throw the influence of my private wishes and feelings into the scale. We live here but a few years. It is of more consequence that we should do right, than that we should enjoy ourselves."

Judge Clayton spoke this with more emotion than he usually exhibited, and Clayton was much touched.

"My dear father," he said, putting Nina's note into his hand, "you made allusion to Miss Gordon. This note, which I received from her on the morning of your decision, will show you what her spirit is."

Judge Clayton put on his spectacles, and read over the note deliberately, twice. He then handed it formally to his son, and remarked, with his usual brevity,

"She will do!"

CHAPTER XI

The Cloud Bursts

THE SHADOW of that awful cloud which had desolated other places now began to darken the boundaries of the plantation of Canema. No disease has ever more fully filled out the meaning of those awful words of Scripture, "The pestilence that walketh in darkness."[1] None has been more irregular, and apparently more perfectly capricious, in its movements. During the successive seasons that it has been epidemic in this country, it has seemed to have set at defiance the skill of the physicians. The system of medical tactics which has been wrought out by the painful experience of one season seems to be laughed to scorn by the varying type of the disease in the next. Certain sanitary laws and conditions would seem to be indispensable; yet those who are familiar with it have had fearful experience how like a wolf it will sometimes leap the boundaries of the best and most carefully-guarded fold, and, spite of every caution and protection, sweep all before it.

Its course through towns and villages has been equally singular. Sometimes, descending like a cloud on a neighborhood, it will leave a single village or town untouched amidst the surrounding desolations, and long after, when health is restored to the whole neighborhood, come down suddenly on the omitted towns, as a ravaging army sends back a party for prey to some place which has been overlooked or forgotten. Sometimes, entering a house, in twenty-four hours it will take all who are in it. Sometimes it will ravage all the city except some one street or locality, and then come upon that, while all else is spared. Its course, upon Southern plantations, was marked by similar capriciousness, and was made still more fatal by that peculiar nature of plantation life which withdraws the inmates so far from medical aid.

When the first letters were received describing the progress of it in northern cities, Aunt Nesbit felt much uneasiness and alarm. It is remarkable with what tenacity people often will cling to life, whose enjoyments in it are so dull and low that a bystander would scarcely think them worth the struggle of preservation. When at length the dreaded news began to be heard from one point and another in their vicinity, Aunt Nesbit said, one day, to Nina,

"Your cousins, the Gordons, in E., have written to us to leave the plantation, and come and spend some time with them, till the danger is over."

"Why," said Nina, "do they think the cholera can't come there?"

"Well," said Aunt Nesbit, "they have their family under most excellent regulations; and, living in a town so, they are within call of a doctor, if anything happens."

"Aunt," said Nina, "perhaps you had better go; but I will stay with my people."

"Why, don't you feel afraid, Nina?"

"No, aunt, I don't. Besides, I think it would be very selfish for me to live on the services of my people all my life, and then run away and leave them alone when a time of danger comes. The least I can do is to stay and take care of them."

This conversation was overheard by Harry, who was standing with his back to them, on the veranda, near the parlor door where they were sitting.

"Child," said Aunt Nesbit, "what do you suppose you can do? You haven't any experience. Harry and Milly can do a great deal better than you can. I'll leave Milly here. It's our first duty to take care of our health."

"No, aunt, I think there are some duties before that," said Nina. "It's true I haven't a great deal of strength, but I have courage; and I know my going away would discourage our people, and fill them with fear; and that, they say, predisposes to the disease. I shall get the carriage up, and go directly over to see the doctor, and get directions and medicines. I shall talk to our people, and teach them what to do, and see that it is done. And, when they see that I am calm, and not afraid, they will have courage. But, aunt, if you are afraid, I think you had better go. You are feeble; you can't make much exertion; and if you feel any safer or more comfortable, I think it would be best. I should like to have Milly stay, and she, Harry, and I, will be a board of health to the plantation."

"Harry," she said, "if you'll get up the carriage, we'll go immediately."

Again Harry felt the bitterness of his soul sweetened and tranquillized by the noble nature of her to whose hands the law had given the chain which bound him. Galling and intolerable as it would have been otherwise, he felt, when with her, that her service was perfect freedom. He had not said anything to Nina about the contents of the letter which he had received from his sister. He saw that it was an evil which she had no power over, and he shrank from annoying her with it. Nina supposed that his clouded and troubled aspect was caused wholly by the solicitude of responsibility.

In the same carriage which conveyed her to the town sat Aunt Nesbit also, and her cap-boxes, whose importance even the fear of the cholera could not lessen in her eyes. Nina found the physician quite *au fait*[2] on the subject. He had been reading about miasma and animalculæ,[3] and he entertained Nina nearly half an hour with different theories as to the cause of the disease, and with the experiments which had been made in foreign hospitals.

Among the various theories, there was one which appeared to be his particular pet; and Nina couldn't help thinking, as he stepped about so alertly, that he almost enjoyed the prospect of putting his discoveries to the test. By dint, however, of very practical and positive questions, Nina drew from him all the valuable information which he had to give her; and he wrote her a very full system of directions, and put up a case of medicines for her, assuring her that he should be happy to attend in person if he had time.

On the way home, Nina stopped at Uncle John Gordon's plantation, and there had the first experience of the difference between written directions for a supposed case, and the actual awful realities of the disease. Her Uncle John had been seized only half an hour before, in the most awful manner. The household was all in terror and confusion, and the shrieks and groans of agony which proceeded from his room were appalling. His wife, busy with the sufferer, did not perceive that the messengers who had been sent in haste for the doctor were wringing their hands in fruitless terror, running up and down the veranda, and doing nothing.

"Harry," said Nina, "take out one of the carriage-horses, and ride quick for your life, and bring the doctor over here in a minute!"

In a few moments the thing was done, and Harry was out of sight. She then walked up to the distracted servants, and commanded them, in a tone of authority, to cease their lamentations.

Her resolute manner, and the quiet tone of voice which she preserved, acted as a sedative on their excited nerves. She banished all
but two or three of the most reasonable from the house, and then
went to the assistance of her aunt.

Before long the doctor arrived. When he had been in the sick
room a few moments, he came out to make some inquiries of Nina,
and she could not help contrasting the appalled and confounded expression of his countenance with the dapper, consequential air, with
which, only two hours before, he had been holding forth to her on
animalculæ and miasma.

"The disease," he said, "presented itself in an entirely different
aspect from what he had expected. The remedies," he said, "did not
work as he anticipated; the case was a peculiar one."

Alas! before the three months were over, poor doctor, you found
many peculiar cases!

"Do you think you can save his life?" said Nina.

"Child, only God can save him!" said the physician; "nothing
works right."

But why prolong the torture of that scene, or rehearse the strug-
gles, groans, and convulsions? Nina, poor flowery child of seventeen summers, stood with the rest in mute despair. All was tried
that could be done or thought of; but the disease, like some blind,
deaf destroyer, marched on, turning neither to right nor left, till the
cries and groans grew fainter, the convulsed muscles relaxed, and
the strong, florid man lay in the last stages of that fearful collapse
which in one hour shrivels the most healthy countenance and the
firmest muscles to the shrunken and withered image of decrepid old
age. When the breath had passed, and all was over, Nina could
scarcely believe that that altered face and form, so withered and so
worn, could have been her healthy and joyous uncle, and who never
had appeared healthier or more joyous than on that morning. But,
as a person passing under the foam and spray of Niagara clings with
blind confidence to a guide whom he feels, but cannot see, Nina, in
this awful hour, felt that she was not alone. The Redeemer, all-
powerful over death and the grave, of whom she had been thinking
so much, of late, seemed to her sensibly near. And it seemed to her
as if a voice said to her, continually, "Fear not for I am with thee.
Be not dismayed, for I am thy God."4

"How calm you are, my child!" said Aunt Maria to her. "I

wouldn't have thought it was in you. I don't know what we should
do without you."

But now a frightful wail was heard.

"O, we are all dying! we are all going! O, missis, come quick!
Peter has got it! O, daddy has got it! O, my child! my child!"

And the doctor, exhausted as he was by the surprise and excitement of this case, began flying from one to another of the cabins, in
the greatest haste. Two or three of the house-servants also seemed
to be struck in the same moment, and only the calmness and
courage which Nina and her aunt maintained prevented a general
abandonment to panic. Nina possessed that fine, elastic temperament which, with the appearance of extreme delicacy, possesses
great powers of endurance. The perfect calmness which she felt enabled her to bring all her faculties to bear on the emergency.

"My good aunty, you mustn't be afraid! Bring out your religion;
trust in God," she said, to the cook, who was wringing her hands in
terror. "Remember your religion; sing some of your hymns, and do
your duty to the sick."

There is a magic power in the cheerful tone of courage, and Nina
succeeded in rallying the well ones to take care of the sick; but now
came a messenger, in hot haste, to say that the cholera had broken
out on the plantation at home.

"Well, Harry," said Nina, with a face pale, yet unmoved, "our
duty calls us away."

And, accompanied by the weary physician, they prepared to go
back to Canema. Before they had proceeded far, a man met them on
horseback.

"Is Dr. Butler with you?"

"Yes," said Nina, putting her head out of the carriage.

"O, doctor, I've been riding all over the country after you. You
must come back to town this minute! Judge Peters is dying! I'm
afraid he is dead before this time, and there's a dozen more cases
right in that street. Here, get on to my horse, and ride for your life."

The doctor hastily sprang from the carriage, and mounted the
horse; then, stopping a moment, he cast a look of good-natured pity
on the sweet, pale face that was leaning out of the carriage window.

"My poor child," he said, "I can't bear to leave you. Who will
help you?"

"God," said Nina; "I am not afraid!"

"Come, come," said the man, "do hurry!" And, with one hasty glance more, he was gone.

"Now, Harry," said Nina, "everything depends upon our keeping up our courage and our strength. We shall have no physician. We must just do the best we can. After all, it is our Lord Jesus that has the keys of death, and *he* loved us and died for us. He will certainly be with us."

"O, Miss Nina, you are an angel!" said Harry, who felt at that moment as if he could have worshipped her.

Arrived at home, Nina found a scene of terror and confusion similar to that she had already witnessed. Old Hundred lay dead in his cabin, and the lamenting crowd, gathering round, were yielding to the full tide of fear and excitement, which predisposed them to the same fate. Nina rode up immediately to the group. She spoke to them calmly; she silenced their outcries, and bade them obey her.

"If you wish, all of you, to die," she said, "this is the way towards it; but, if you'll keep quiet and calm, and do what ought to be done, your lives may be saved. Harry and I have got medicines—we understand what to do. You must follow our directions exactly."

Nina immediately went to the house, and instructed Milly, Aunt Rose, and two or three of the elderly women, in the duties to be done. Milly rose up, in this hour of terror, with all the fortitude inspired by her strong nature.

"Bress de Lord," she said, "for his grace to you, chile! De Lord is a shield. He's been wid us in six troubles, and he'll be wid us in seven. We can sing in de swellings of Jordan."

Harry, meanwhile, was associating to himself a band of the most reliable men on the place, and endeavoring in the same manner to organize them for action. A messenger was despatched immediately to the neighboring town for unlimited quantities of the most necessary medicines and stimulants. The plantation was districted off, and placed under the care of leaders, who held communication with Harry. In the course of two or three hours, the appalling scene of distress and confusion was reduced to the resolute and orderly condition of a well-managed hospital.

Milly walked the rounds in every direction, appealing to the religious sensibilities of the people, and singing hymns of trust and confidence. She possessed a peculiar voice, suited to her large development of physical frame, almost as deep as a man's bass, with the rich softness of a feminine tone; and Nina could now and then distinguish, as she was moving about the house or grounds, that triumphant tone, singing,

> *"God is my sun,*
>   *And he my shade,*
>   *To guard my head,*
> *By night or noon.*
> *Hast thou not given thy word*
>   *To save my soul from death?*
> *And I can trust my Lord,*
>   *To keep my mortal breath.*
> *I'll go and come,*
>   *Nor fear to die,*
>   *Till from on high*
> *Thou call me home."*

The house that night presented the aspect of a beleaguered garrison. Nina and Milly had thrown open all the chambers; and such as were peculiarly exposed to the disease, by delicacy of organization or tremulousness of nervous system, were allowed to take shelter there.

"Now, chile," said Milly, when all the arrangements had been made, "you jes lie down and go to sleep in yer own room. I see how 't is with you; de spirit is willing, but de flesh is weak. Chile, dere isn't much of you, but dere won't nothing go widout you. So, you take care of yerself first. Never you be 'fraid! De people's quiet now, and de sick ones is ben took care of, and de folks is all doing de best dey can. So, now, you try and get some sleep; 'cause if *you* goes we shall *all* go."

Accordingly Nina retired to her room, but before she lay down she wrote to Clayton:

"We are all in affliction here, my dear friend. Poor Uncle John died this morning of the cholera. I had been to E—— to see a doctor and provide medicines. When I came back I thought I would call a few moments at the house, and I found a perfect scene of horror. Poor uncle died, and there are a great many sick on the place now; and while I was thinking that I would stay and help aunt, a messenger came in all haste, saying that the disease had broken out on our place at home.

"We were bringing the doctor with us in our carriage, when we met a man riding full speed from E——, who told us that Judge Peters was dying, and a great many others were sick on the same street. When we came home we found the poor old coachman dead, and the people in the greatest consternation. It took us some time to tranquillize them and to produce order, but that is now done. Our house is full of the sick and the fearful ones. Milly and Harry are firm and active, and inspire the rest with courage. About twenty are taken with the disease, but not as yet in a violent way. In this awful hour I feel a strange peace, which the Bible truly says 'passeth all understanding.'[5] I see, now, that though the world and all that is in it should perish, 'Christ can give us a beautiful immortal life.'[6] I write to you because, perhaps, this may be the only opportunity. If I die, do not mourn for me, but thank God, who giveth us the victory through our Lord Jesus Christ. But, then, I trust, I shall not die. I hope to live in this world, which is more than ever beautiful to me. Life has never been so valuable and dear as since I have known you. Yet I have such trust in the love of my Redeemer, that, if *he* were to ask me to lay it down, I could do it almost without a sigh. I would follow the Lamb whithersoever he goeth. Perhaps the same dreadful evil is around you,— perhaps at Magnolia Grove. I will not be selfish in calling you here, if Anne needs you more. Perhaps she has not such reliable help as Harry and Milly are to me. So do not fear, and do not leave any duty for me. Our Father loves us, and will do nothing amiss. Milly walks about the entries singing. I love to hear her sing, she sings in such a grand, triumphant tone. Hark, I hear her now!

'*I'll go and come,*
  Nor fear to die,
  Till from on high
Thou call me home.'

"I shall write you every mail, now, till we are better.
        "Living or dying, ever your own
                                        NINA."

After writing this, Nina laid down and slept—slept all night as quietly as if death and disease were not hanging over her head. In the morning she rose and dressed herself, and Milly, with anxious care, brought to her room some warm coffee and crackers, which she insisted on her taking before she left her apartment.

"How are they all, Milly?" said Nina.

"Well, chile," said Milly, "de midnight cry has been heard among us. Aunt Rose is gone; and Big Sam, and Jack, and Sally, dey's all gone; but de people is all more quiet, love, and dey's determined to stand it out!"

"How is Harry?" said Nina, in a tremulous voice.

"He isn't sick; he has been up all night working over de sick, but he keeps up good heart. De older ones is going to have a little prayer-meeting after breakfast, as a sort of funeral to dem dat's dead; and, perhaps, Miss Nina, you'd read us a chapter."

"Certainly I will," said Nina.

It was yet an early hour, when a large circle of family and plantation hands gathered together in the pleasant, open saloon, which we have so often described. The day was a beautiful one; the leaves and shrubbery round the veranda moist and tremulous with the glittering freshness of morning dew. There was a murmur of tenderness and admiration as Nina, in a white morning-wrapper, and a cheek as white, came into the room.

"Sit down, all my friends," she said, "sit down," looking at some of the plantation-men, who seemed to be diffident about taking the sofa, which was behind them; "it's no time for ceremony now. We are standing on the brink of the grave, where all are equal. I'm glad to see you so calm and so brave. I hope your trust is in the Saviour, who gives us the victory over death. Sing," she said. Milly began the well-known hymn:

> "And must this feeble body fall,
>   And must it faint and die?
> My soul shall quit this gloomy vale,
>   And soar to realms on high;
>
> "Shall join the disembodied saints,
>   And find its long-sought rest;
> That only rest for which it pants,
>   On the Redeemer's breast."

Every voice joined, and the words rose triumphant from the very gates of the grave. When the singing was over, Nina, in a tremulous voice, which grew clearer as she went on, read the undaunted words of the ancient psalm:

"He that dwelleth in the secret place of the Most High shall abide under the shadow of the Almighty. I will say of the Lord, He is my refuge and my fortress. My God, in him will I trust. Surely he shall deliver thee from the snare of the fowler, and from the noisome pestilence. He shall cover thee with his feathers. Under his wings shalt thou trust. Thou shalt not be afraid for the terror by night, nor for the arrow that flieth by day, nor for the pestilence that walketh in darkness, nor for the destruction that wasteth at noonday. A thousand shall fall by thy side, and ten thousand at thy right hand; but it shall not come nigh thee. He shall give his angels charge over thee to keep thee in all thy ways."[7]

"It is possible," said Nina, "that we may, some of us, be called away. But, to those that love Christ, there is no fear in death. It is only going home to our Father. Keep up courage, then!"

In all cases like this, the first shock brings with it more terror than any which succeeds. The mind can become familiar with anything, even with the prospect of danger and death, so that it can appear to be an ordinary condition of existence. Everything proceeded calmly on the plantation; and all, stimulated by the example of their young mistress, seemed determined to meet the exigency firmly and faithfully. In the afternoon of the second day, as Nina was sitting in the door, she observed the wagon of Uncle Tiff making its way up the avenue; and, with her usual impulsiveness, ran down to meet her humble friend.

"O, Tiff, how do you do, in these dreadful times!"

"O, Miss Nina," said the faithful creature, removing his hat, with habitual politeness, "ef yer please, I's brought de baby here, 'cause it's dreful sick, and I's been doing all I could for him, and he don't get no better. And I's brought Miss Fanny and Teddy, 'cause I's 'fraid to leave 'em, 'cause I see a man yesterday, and he tell me dey was dying eberywhar on all de places round."

"Well," said Nina, "you have come to a sorrowful place, for they are dying here, too! But, if you feel any safer here, you and the children may stay, and we'll do for you just as we do for each other. Give me the baby, while you get out. It's asleep, isn't it?"

"Yes, Miss Nina, it's 'sleep pretty much all de time, now."

Nina carried it up the steps, and put it into the arms of Milly.

"It's sleeping nicely," she said.

"Ah, honey!" said Milly, "it'll neber wake up out of dat ar! Dat ar sleep an't de good kind!"

"Well," said Nina, "we'll help him take care of it, and we'll make room for him and the children, Milly; because we have medicines and directions, and they have nothing out there."

So Tiff and his family took shelter in the general fortress. Towards evening, the baby died. Tiff held it in his arms to the very last; and it was with difficulty that Nina and Milly could persuade him that the little flickering breath was gone forever. When forced to admit it, he seemed for a few moments perfectly inconsolable. Nina quietly opened her Testament, and read to him:

"And they brought little children unto him, that he should touch them; and his disciples rebuked those that brought them. But Jesus said, Suffer little children to come unto me, and forbid them not, for of such is the kingdom of heaven."[8]

"Bressed Lord!" said Tiff, "I'll gib him up, I will! I won't hold out no longer! I won't forbid him to go, if it does break my old heart! Laws, we's drefful selfish! But de por little ting, he was getting so pretty!"

CHAPTER XII

The Voice in the Wilderness

CLAYTON WAS QUIETLY SITTING in his law-office, looking over and arranging some papers necessary to closing his business. A colored boy brought in letters from the mail. He looked them over rapidly; and, selecting one, read it with great agitation and impatience. Immediately he started, with the open letter crushed in his hand, seized his hat, and rushed to the nearest livery-stable.

"Give me the fastest horse you have—one that can travel night and day!" he said. "I must ride for life or death!"

And half an hour more saw Clayton in full speed on the road. By the slow, uncertain, and ill-managed mail-route, it would have taken three days to reach Canema. Clayton hoped, by straining every nerve, to reach there in twenty-four hours. He pushed forward, keeping the animal at the top of his speed; and, at the first stage-stand, changed him for a fresh one. And thus proceeding along, he found himself, at three o'clock of the next morning, in the woods about fifteen miles from Canema. The strong tension of the nervous system, which had upheld him insensible to fatigue until this point, was beginning slightly to subside. All night he had ridden through the loneliness of pine-forests, with no eye looking down on him save the twinkling, mysterious stars. At the last place where he had sought to obtain horses, everything had been horror and confusion. Three were lying dead in the house, and another was dying. All along upon the route, at every stopping-place, the air had seemed to be filled with flying rumors and exaggerated reports of fear and death. As soon as he began to perceive that he was approaching the plantation, he became sensible of that shuddering dread which all of us may remember to have had, in slight degrees, in returning home after a long absence, under a vague expectation of misfortune, to which the mind can set no definite limits. When it was yet scarcely light enough to see, he passed by the cottage of Old Tiff. A strange impulse prompted him to stop and make some inquiries there, before he pushed on to the plantation. But, as he rode up, he saw the gate standing ajar, the door of the house left open; and, after repeated callings, receiving no answer, he alighted, and, leading his horse behind him, looked into the door. The gloaming starlight was just sufficient to show him that all was desolate. Somehow this seemed to him like an evil omen. As he was mounting his horse, preparing to ride away, a grand and powerful voice rose from the obscurity of the woods before him, singing, in a majestic, minor-keyed tune, these words:

> "*Throned on a cloud our God shall come,*
>   *Bright flames prepare his way;*
> *Thunder and darkness, fire and storm,*
>   *Loud on the dreadful day!*"[1]

Wearied with his night ride, his nervous system strained to the last point of tension by the fearful images which filled his mind, it is not surprising that these sounds should have thrilled through the hearer with even a superstitious power. And Clayton felt a singular excitement, as, under the dim arcade of the pine-trees, he saw a dark figure approaching. He seemed to be marching with a regular tread, keeping time to the mournful music which he sung.

"Who are you?" called Clayton, making an effort to recall his manhood.

"I?" replied the figure, "I am the voice of one crying in the wilderness! I am a sign unto this people of the judgment of the Lord!"

Our readers must remember the strange dimness of the hour, the wildness of the place and circumstances, and the singular quality of the tone in which the figure spoke. Clayton hesitated a moment, and the speaker went on:

"I saw the Lord coming with ten thousand of his saints! Before him went the pestilence, and burning coals went forth at his feet! Thy bow is made quite naked, O God, according to the oaths of the tribes! I saw the tents of Cushan in affliction, and the curtains of the land of Midian did tremble!"[2]

Pondering in his mind what this wild style of address might mean, Clayton rode slowly onward. And the man, for such he appeared to be, came out of the shadows of the wood and stood directly in his path, raising his hand with a commanding gesture.

"I know whom you seek," he said; "but it shall not be given you; for the star, which is called wormwood, hath fallen, and the time of the dead is come, that they shall be judged! Behold, there sitteth on the white cloud *one* like the Son of Man, having on his head a golden crown, and in his hand a sharp sickle!"

Then, waving his hand above his head, with a gesture of wild excitement, he shouted:

"Thrust in thy sharp sickle, and gather the clusters of the vine of the earth, for her grapes are fully ripe! Behold, the wine-press shall be trodden without the city, and there shall be blood even to the horses' bridles! Woe, woe, woe to the inhabitants of the earth, because of the trumpets of the other angels, which are yet to sound!"[3]

The fearful words pealed through the dim aisles of the forest like the curse of some destroying angel. After a pause, the speaker resumed, in a lower and more plaintive tone:

"Weep ye not for the dead! neither bewail her! Behold, the Lamb standeth on Mount Zion, and with him a hundred and forty and four thousand, having his Father's name written on their foreheads. These are they which follow the Lamb whithersoever he goeth; and in their mouth is found no guile, for they are without fault before the throne of God. Behold the angel having the seal of God is gone forth, and she shall be sealed in her forehead unto the Lamb."[4]

The figure turned away slowly, singing, as he made his way through the forest, in the same weird and funereal accents; but this time the song was a wild, plaintive sound, like the tolling of a heavy bell:

> *"Ding dong! dead and gone!*
> *Farewell, father!*
> *Bury me in Egypt's land,*
> *By my dear mother!*
> *Ding, dong! ding, dong!*
> *Dead and gone!"*

Clayton, as he slowly wound his way along the unfrequented path, felt a dim, brooding sense of mystery and terror creeping over him. The tones of the voice, and the wild style of the speaker, recalled the strange incident of the camp-meeting; and, though he endeavored strenuously to reason with himself that probably some wild and excited fanatic, made still more frantic by the presence of death and destruction all around, was the author of these fearful denunciations, still he could not help a certain weight of fearful foreboding.

This life may be truly called a haunted house, built as it is on the very confines of the land of darkness and the shadow of death. A thousand living fibres connect us with the unknown and unseen state; and the strongest hearts, which never stand still for any mortal terror, have sometimes hushed their very beating at a breath of a whisper from within the veil. Perhaps the most resolute unbeliever in spiritual things has hours of which he would be ashamed to tell, when he, too, yields to the powers of those awful affinities which bind us to that unknown realm.

It is not surprising that Clayton, in spite of himself, should have felt like one mysteriously warned. It was a relief to him when the dusky dimness of the solemn dawn was pierced by long shafts of light from the rising sun, and the day broke gladsome and jubilant, as if sorrow, sighing, and death, were a dream of the night. During the whole prevalence of this fearful curse, it was strange to witness the unaltered regularity, splendor, and beauty, with which the movements of the natural world went on. Amid fears, and dying groans, and wailings, and sobs, and broken hearts, the sun rose and set in splendor, the dews twinkled, and twilight folded her purple veil heavy with stars; birds sung, waters danced and warbled, flowers bloomed, and everything in nature was abundant, and festive, and joyous.

When Clayton entered the boundaries of the plantation, he inquired eagerly of the first person he met for the health of its mistress.

"Thank God, she is yet alive!" said he. "It was but a dream, after all!"

CHAPTER XIII

The Evening Star

THE MAILS in the State of North Carolina, like the prudential arrangements in the slave states generally, were very little to be depended upon; and therefore a week had elapsed after the mailing of Nina's first letter, describing the danger of her condition, before it was received by Clayton. During that time the fury of the shock which had struck the plantation appeared to have abated; and, while on some estates in the vicinity it was yet on the increase, the inhabitants of Canema began to hope that the awful cloud was departing from them. It was true that many were still ailing; but there were no new cases, and the disease in the case of those who were ill appeared to be yielding to nursing and remedies.

Nina had risen in the morning early, as her custom had been since the sickness, and gone the rounds, to inquire for the health of her people. Returned, a little fatigued, she was sitting in the veranda, under the shadow of one of the pillar-roses, enjoying the cool freshness of the morning. Suddenly the tramp of horse's feet was heard, and, looking, she saw Clayton coming up the avenue. There seemed but a dizzy, confused moment, before his horse's bridle was thrown to the winds, and he was up the steps, holding her in his arms.

"O, you are here yet, my rose, my bride, my lamb! God is merciful! This is too much! O, I thought you were gone!"

"No, dear, not yet," said Nina. "God has been with us. We have lost a great many; but God has spared me to you."

"Are you really well?" said Clayton, holding her off, and looking at her. "You look pale, my little rose!"

"That's not wonderful," said Nina; "I've had a great deal to make me look pale; but I am very well. I have been well through it all—never in better health—and, it seems strange to say it, but never happier. I have felt so peaceful, so sure of God's love!"

"Do you know," said Clayton, "that that peace alarms me—that strange, unearthly happiness? It seems so like what is given to dying people."

"No," said Nina, "I think that when we have no one but our Father to lean on, he comes nearer than he does any other time; and that is the secret of this happiness. But, come,—you look wofully tired; have you been riding all night?"

"Yes, ever since yesterday morning at nine o'clock. I have ridden down four horses to get to you. Only think, I didn't get your letter till a week after it was dated!"

"Well, perhaps that was the best," said Nina; "because I have heard them say that anybody coming suddenly and unprepared in the epidemic, when it is in full force, is almost sure to be taken by it immediately. But you must let me take care of you. Don't you know that I'm mistress of the fortress here—commander-in-chief and head-physician? I shall order you to your room immediately, and Milly shall bring you up some coffee, and then you must have some sleep. You can see with your eyes, now, that we are all safe, and there's nothing to hinder your resting. Come, let me lead you off, like a captive."

Released from the pressure of overwhelming fear, Clayton began now to feel the reäction of the bodily and mental straining which he had been enduring for the last twenty-four hours, and therefore he willingly yielded himself to the directions of his little sovereign. Retired to his room, after taking his coffee, which was served by Milly, he fell into a deep and tranquil sleep, which lasted till some time in the afternoon. At first, overcome by fatigue, he slept without dreaming; but, when the first weariness was past, the excitement of the nervous system, under which he had been laboring, began to color his dreams with vague and tumultuous images. He thought that he was again with Nina at Magnolia Grove, and that the servants were passing around in procession, throwing flowers at their feet; but the wreath of orange-blossoms which fell in Nina's lap was tied with black crape. But she took it up, laughing, threw the crape away, and put the wreath on her head, and he heard the chorus singing,

"O, de North Carolina rose!
O, de North Carolina rose!"

And then the sound seemed to change to one of lamentation, and the floral procession seemed to be a funeral, and a deep, melancholy voice, like the one he had heard in the woods in the morning, sang,

> *"Weep, for the rose is withered!*
> *The North Carolina rose!"*

He struggled heavily in his sleep, and, at last waking, sat up and looked about him. The rays of the evening sun were shining on the tree-tops of the distant avenue, and Nina was singing on the veranda below. He listened, and the sound floated up like a rose-leaf carried on a breeze:

> *"The summer hath its heavy cloud,*
> *The rose-leaf must fall,*
> *But in our home joy wears no shroud—*
> *Never doth it pall!*
> *Each new morning ray*
> *Leaves no sigh for yesterday—*
> *No smile passed away*
> *Would we recall!"*

The tune was a favorite melody, which has found much favor with the popular ear, and bore the title of "The Hindoo Dancing-Girl's Song;"[1] and is, perhaps, a fragment of one of those mystical songs in which oriental literature abounds, in which the joy and reünion of earthly love are told in shadowy, symbolic resemblance to the everlasting union of the blessed above. It had a wild, dreamy, soothing power, as verse after verse came floating in, like white doves from paradise, as if they had borne healing on their wings:

> *"Then haste to the happy land,*
> *Where sorrow is unknown;*
> *But first in a joyous band,*
> *I'll make thee my own.*
> *Haste, haste, fly with me*
> *Where love's banquet waits for thee;*
> *Thine all its sweets shall be,*
> *Thine, thine, alone!"*

A low tap at his door at last roused him. The door was partly opened, and a little hand threw in a half-opened spray of monthly-rosebuds.

"There's something to remind you that you are yet in the body!"

said a voice in the entry. "If you are rested, I'll let you come down, now."

And Clayton heard the light footsteps tripping down the stairs. He roused himself, and, after some little attention to his toilet, appeared on the veranda.

"Tea has been waiting for some time," said Nina. "I thought I'd give you a hint."

"I was lying very happy, hearing you sing," said Clayton. "You may sing me that song again."

"Was I singing?" said Nina; "why, I didn't know it! I believe that's my way of thinking, sometimes. I'll sing to you again, after tea. I like to sing."

After tea they were sitting again in the veranda, and the whole heavens were one rosy flush of filmy clouds.

"How beautiful!" said Nina. "It seems to me I've enjoyed these things, this summer, as I never have before. It seemed as if I felt an influence from them going through me, and filling me, as the light does those clouds."

And, as she stood looking up into the sky, she began singing again the words that Clayton had heard before:

"I am come from the happy land,
    Where sorrow is unknown;
I have parted a joyous band,
    To make thee mine own!
Haste, haste, fly with me,
Where love's banquet waits for thee;
Thine all its sweets shall be—
    Thine, thine, alone!

"The summer has its heavy cloud,
    The rose-leaf must fall—"

She stopped her singing suddenly, left the veranda, and went into the house.

"Do you want anything?" said Clayton.

"Nothing," said she, hurriedly. "I'll be back in a moment."

Clayton watched, and saw her go to a closet in which the medicines and cordials were kept, and take something from a glass. He gave a start of alarm.

"You are not ill, are you?" he said, fearfully, as she returned.

"O, no; only a little faint. We have become so prudent, you know, that if we feel the least beginning of any disagreeable sensation, we take something at once. I have felt this faintness quite often. It isn't much."

Clayton put his arm around her, and looked at her with a vague yearning of fear and admiration.

"You look so like a spirit," he said, "that I must hold you."

"Do you think I've got a pair of hidden wings?" she said, smiling, and looking gayly in his face.

"I am afraid so!" he said. "Do you feel quite well, now?"

"Yes, I believe so. Only, perhaps, we had better sit down. I think, perhaps, it is the reäction of so much excitement, makes me feel rather tired."

Clayton seated her on the settee by the door, still keeping his arm anxiously around her. In a few moments she drooped her head wearily on his shoulder.

"*You are ill!*" he said, in tones of alarm.

"No, no! I feel very well—only a little faint and tired. It seems to me it is getting a little cold here, isn't it?" she said, with a slight shiver.

Clayton took her up in his arms, without speaking, carried her in and laid her on the sofa, then rang for Harry and Milly.

"Get a horse, instantly," he said to Harry, as soon as he appeared, "and go for a doctor!"

"There's no use in sending," said Nina; "he is driven to death, and can't come. Besides, there's nothing the matter with me, only I am a little tired and cold. Shut the doors and windows, and cover me up. No, no, don't take me up stairs! I like to lie here; just put a shawl over me, that's all. I am thirsty,—give me some water!"

The fearful and mysterious disease, which was then in the ascendant, has many forms of approach and development. One, and the most deadly, is that which takes place when a person has so long and gradually imbibed the fatal poison of an infected atmosphere, that the resisting powers of nature have been insidiously and quietly subdued, so that the subject sinks under it, without any violent outward symptom, by a quiet and certain yielding of the vital powers, such as has been likened to the bleeding to death by an internal wound. In this case, before an hour had passed, though none of the violent and distressing symptoms of the disease appeared, it became evident that the seal of death was set on that fair young brow. A messenger had been despatched, riding with the desperate speed which love and fear can give, but Harry remained in attendance.

"Nothing is the matter with me—nothing is the matter," she said, "except fatigue, and this change in the weather. If I only had more over me! and, perhaps, you had better give me a little brandy, or some such thing. This is water, isn't it, that you have been giving me?"

Alas! it was the strongest brandy; but there was no taste, and the hartshorn[2] that they were holding had no smell. And there was no change in the weather; it was only the creeping deadness, affecting the whole outer and inner membrane of the system. Yet still her voice remained clear, though her mind occasionally wandered.

There is a strange impulse, which sometimes comes in the restlessness and distress of dissolving nature, *to sing;* and, as she lay with her eyes closed, apparently in a sort of trance, she would sing, over and over again, the verse of the song which she was singing when the blow of the unseen destroyer first struck her.

"The summer hath its heavy cloud,
  The rose-leaf must fall;
But in our land joy wears no shroud,
  Never doth it pall."

At last she opened her eyes, and, seeing the agony of all around, the truth seemed to come to her.

"I think I'm called!" she said. "O, I'm so sorry for you all! Don't grieve so; my Father loves me so well,—he cannot spare me any longer. He wants me to come to him. That's all—don't grieve so. It's *home* I'm going to—*home!* 'T will be only a little while, and you'll come too, all of you. You are satisfied, are you not, Edward?"

And again she relapsed into the dreamy trance, and sang, in that strange, sweet voice, so low, so weak,

"In our land joy wears no shroud,
  Never doth it pall."

Clayton,—what did he? What could he do? What have any of us done, who have sat holding in our arms a dear form, from which the soul was passing—the soul for which gladly we would have given our own in exchange! When we have felt it going with inconceivable rapidity from us; and we, ignorant and blind, vainly striving, with this and that, to arrest the inevitable doom, feeling every moment that some *other* thing might be done to save, which is not done, and that that which we are doing may be only hastening the course of the destroyer! O, those awful, agonized moments, when we watch the clock, and no physician comes, and every stroke of the pendulum is like the approaching step of death! O, is there anything in heaven or earth for the despair of such hours?

Not a moment was lost by the three around that dying bed, chafing those cold limbs, administering the stimulants which the dead, exhausted system no longer felt.

"She doesn't suffer! Thank God, at any rate, for that!" said Clayton, as he knelt over her in anguish.

A beautiful smile passed over her face, as she opened her eyes and looked on them all, and said,

"No, my poor friends, I don't suffer. I'm come to the land where they never suffer. I'm only *so* sorry for you! Edward," she said to him, "do you remember what you said to me once?—It has come now. You must bear it like a man. God calls you to some work—don't shrink from it. You are baptized with fire. It all lasts only a little while. It will be over soon, very soon! Edward, take care of my poor people. Tell Tom to be kind to them. My poor, faithful, good Harry! O! I'm going so fast!"

The voice sunk into a whispering sigh. Life now seemed to have retreated to the citadel of the brain. She lay apparently in the last sleep, when the footsteps of the doctor were heard on the veranda. There was a general spring to the door, and Dr. Butler entered, pale, haggard, and worn, from constant exertion and loss of rest.

He did not say in words that there was no hope, but his first dejected look said it but too plainly.

She moved her head a little, like one who is asleep, uneasily upon her pillow, opened her eyes once more, and said,

"Good-by! I will arise and go to my Father!"

The gentle breath gradually became fainter and fainter,—all hope was over! The night walked on with silent and solemn footsteps—soft showers fell without, murmuring upon the leaves—within, all was still as death!

"They watched her breathing through the night,
Her breathing soft and low,
As in her breast the wave of life
Kept heaving to and fro.

"So silently they seemed to speak,
So slowly moved about,
As they had lent her half their powers
To eke her living out.

"Their very hopes belied their fears,
Their fears their hopes belied—
They thought her dying when she slept,
And sleeping when she died.

"For when the morn came dim and sad,
And chill with early showers,
Her quiet eyelids closed—she had
Another morn than ours."[3]

CHAPTER XIV

The Tie Breaks

CLAYTON REMAINED at Canema several days after the funeral. He had been much affected by the last charge given him by Nina, that he should care for her people; and the scene of distress which he witnessed among them, at her death, added to the strength of his desire to be of service to them.

He spent some time in looking over and arranging Nina's papers. He sealed up the letters of her different friends, and directed them in order to be returned to the writers, causing Harry to add to each a memorandum of the time of her death. His heart sunk heavily when he reflected how little it was possible for any one to do for servants left in the uncontrolled power of a man like Tom Gordon. The awful words of his father's decision, with regard to the power of the master, never seemed so dreadful as now, when he was to see this unlimited authority passed into the hands of one whose passions were his only law. He recalled, too, what Nina had said of the special bitterness existing between Tom and Harry; and his heart almost failed him when he recollected that the very step which Nina, in her generosity, had taken to save Lisette from his lawlessness, had been the means of placing her, without remedy, under his power. Under the circumstances, he could not but admire the calmness and firmness with which Harry still continued to discharge his duties to the estate; visiting those who were still ailing, and doing his best to prevent their sinking into a panic which might predispose to another attack of disease. Recollecting that Nina had said something of some kind of a contract, by which Harry's freedom was to be secured in case of her death, he resolved to speak with him on the subject. As they were together in the library, looking over the papers, Clayton said to him:

"Harry, is there not some kind of contract, or understanding, with the guardians of the estate, by which your liberty was secured in case of the death of your mistress?"

383

"Yes," said Harry, "there is such a paper. I was to have my freedom on paying a certain sum, which is all paid into five hundred
dollars."

"I will advance you that money," said Clayton, unhesitatingly,
"if that is all that is necessary. Let me see the paper."

Harry produced it, and Clayton looked it over. It was a regular
contract, drawn in proper form, and with no circumstance wanting
to give it validity. Clayton, however, knew enough of the law
which regulates the condition in which Harry stood, to know that
it was of no more avail in his case than so much blank paper. He did
not like to speak of it, but sat reading it over, weighing every word,
and dreading the moment when he should be called upon to make
some remark concerning it; knowing, as he did, that what he had to
say must dash all Harry's hopes,—the hopes of his whole life.
While he was hesitating a servant entered and announced Mr. Jekyl;
and that gentleman, with a business-like directness which usually
characterized his movements, entered the library immediately after.

"Good-morning, Mr. Clayton," he said, and then, nodding pa-
tronizingly to Harry, he helped himself to a chair, and stated his
business, without further preamble.

"I have received orders from Mr. Gordon to come and take possession of the estate and chattels of his deceased sister, without
delay."

As Clayton sat perfectly silent, it seemed to occur to Mr. Jekyl
that a few moral reflections of a general nature would be in eti-
quette on the present occasion. He therefore added, in the tone of
voice which he reserved particularly for that style of remark:

"We have been called upon to pass through most solemn and af-
flicting dispensations of Divine Providence, lately. Mr. Clayton,
these things remind us of the shortness of life, and of the necessity
of preparation for death!"

Mr. Jekyl paused, and, as Clayton still sat silent, he went on:

"There was no will, I presume?"

"No," said Clayton, "there was not."

"Ah, so I supposed," said Mr. Jekyl, who had now recovered his
worldly tone. "In that case, of course the whole property reverts to
the heir-at-law, just as I had imagined."

"Perhaps Mr. Jekyl would look at this paper," said Harry, taking
his contract from the hand of Mr. Clayton, and passing it to Mr.

Jekyl; who took out his spectacles, placed them deliberately on his sharp nose, and read the paper through.

"Were you under the impression," said he, to Harry, "that this is a legal document?"

"Certainly," said Harry. "I can bring witnesses to prove Mr. John Gordon's signature, and Miss Nina's also."

"O, that's all evident enough," said Mr. Jekyl. "I know Mr. John Gordon's signature. But all the signatures in the world couldn't make it a valid contract. You see, my boy," he said, turning to Harry, "a slave, not being a person in the eye of the law, cannot have a contract made with him. The law, which is based on the old Roman code, holds him, *pro nullis, pro mortuis;* which means, Harry, that he's held as nothing—as dead, inert substance. That's his position in law."

"I believe," said Harry, in a strong and bitter tone, "that is what religious people call a Christian institution!"

"Hey?" said Mr. Jekyl, elevating his eyebrows, "what's that?"

Harry repeated his remark, and Mr. Jekyl replied in the most literal manner:

"Of course it is. It is a divine ordering, and ought to be met in a proper spirit. There's no use, my boy, in rebellion. Hath not the potter power over the clay, to make one lump to honor, and another to dishonor?"

"Mr. Jekyl, I think it would be expedient to confine the conversation simply to legal matters," said Clayton.

"O, certainly," said Mr. Jekyl. "And this brings me to say that I have orders from Mr. Gordon to stay till he comes, and keep order on the place. Also that none of the hands shall, at any time, leave the plantation until he arrives. I brought two or three officers with me, in case there should be any necessity for enforcing order."

"When will Mr. Gordon be here?" said Clayton.

"To-morrow, I believe," said Mr. Jekyl. "Young man," he added, turning to Harry, "you can produce the papers and books, and I can be attending to the accounts."

Clayton rose and left the room, leaving Harry with the imperturbable Mr. Jekyl, who plunged briskly into the business of the accounts, talking to Harry with as much freedom and composure as if he had not just been destroying the hopes of his whole lifetime.

If, by any kind of inward clairvoyance, or sudden clearing of his

mental vision, Mr. Jekyl could have been made to appreciate the anguish which at that moment overwhelmed the soul of the man with
whom he was dealing, we deem it quite possible that he might have
been moved to a transient emotion of pity. Even a thorough-paced
political economist may sometimes be surprised in this way, by the
near view of a case of actual irremediable distress; but he would
soon have consoled himself by a species of mental algebra, that the
greatest good of the greatest number was nevertheless secure; therefore there was no occasion to be troubled about infinitesimal
amounts of suffering. In this way people can reason away every
kind of distress but their own; for it is very remarkable that even so
slight an ailment as a moderate tooth-ache will put this kind of philosophy entirely to rout.

"It appears to me," said Mr. Jekyl, looking at Harry, after a
while, with more attention than he had yet given him, "that something is the matter with you, this morning. Aren't you well?"

"In body," said Harry, "I am well."

"Well, what is the matter, then?" said Mr. Jekyl.

"The matter is," said Harry, "that I have all my life been toiling
for my liberty, and thought I was coming nearer to it every year;
and now, at thirty-five years of age, I find myself still a slave, with
no hope of ever getting free!"

Mr. Jekyl perceived from the outside that there was something
the matter inside of his human brother; some unknown quantity in
the way of suffering, such as his algebra gave no rule for ascertain-
ing. He had a confused notion that this was an affliction, and that
when people were in affliction they must be talked to; and he proceeded accordingly to talk.

"My boy, this is a dispensation of Divine Providence!"

"I call it a dispensation of human tyranny!" said Harry.

"It pleased the Lord," continued Mr. Jekyl, "to foredoom the
race of Ham¹—"

"Mr. Jekyl, that humbug don't go down with me! I'm no more
of the race of Ham than you are! I'm Colonel Gordon's oldest
son—as white as my brother, whom you say owns me! Look at my
eyes, and my hair, and say if any of the rules about Ham pertain to
me!"

"Well," said Mr. Jekyl, "my boy, you mustn't get excited. Everything must go, you know, by general rules. We must take that
course which secures the greatest general amount of good on the

whole; and all such rules will work hard in particular cases. Slavery is a great missionary enterprise for civilizing and christianizing the degraded African."

"Wait till you see Tom Gordon's management on this plantation," said Harry, "and you'll see what sort of a christianizing institution it is! Mr. Jekyl, you *know* better! You throw such talk as that in the face of your northern visitors and you know all the while that Sodom and Gomorrah² don't equal some of these plantations, where nobody is anybody's husband or wife in particular! You know all these things, and you dare talk to me about a missionary institution! What sort of missionary institutions are the great trading-marts, where they sell men and women? What are the means of grace they use there? And the dogs, and the negro-hunters!—those are for the greatest good, too! If your soul were in our souls' stead, you'd see things differently."

Mr. Jekyl was astonished, and said so. But he found a difficulty in presenting his favorite view of the case, under the circumstances; and we believe those ministers of the Gospel, and elders, who entertain similar doctrines, would gain some new views by the effort to present them to a live man in Harry's circumstances. Mr. Jekyl never had a more realizing sense of the difference between the abstract and concrete.

Harry was now thoroughly roused. He had inherited the violent and fiery passions of his father. His usual appearance of studied calmness, and his habits of deferential address, were superinduced; they resembled the thin crust which coats over a flood of boiling lava, and which a burst of the seething mass beneath can shiver in a moment. He was now wholly desperate and reckless. He saw himself already delivered, bound hand and foot, into the hands of a master from whom he could expect neither mercy nor justice. He was like one who had hung suspended over an abyss, by grasping a wild rose; the frail and beautiful thing was broken, and he felt himself *going*, with only despair beneath him. He rose and stood the other side of the table, his hands trembling with excitement.

"Mr. Jekyl," he said, "it is all over with me! Twenty years of faithful service have gone for nothing. Myself and wife, and unborn child, are the slaves of a vile wretch! Hush, now! I will have my say for once! I've borne, and borne, and borne, and it shall come out! You men who call yourselves religious, and stand up for such tyranny,—you serpents, you generation of vipers,—how can you escape the damnation of hell? You keep the clothes of them who stone Stephen![3] You encourage theft, and robbery, and adultery, and you know it! You are worse than the villains themselves, who don't pretend to justify what they do. Now, go, tell Tom Gordon— go! I shall fight it out to the last! I've nothing to hope, and nothing to lose. Let him look out! They made sport of Samson,—they put out his eyes,—but he pulled down the temple over their heads, after all. Look out!"

There is something awful in an outburst of violent passion. The veins in Harry's forehead were swollen, his lips were livid, his eyes glittered like lightning; and Mr. Jekyl cowered before him.

"There will come a day," said Harry, "when all this shall be visited upon you! The measure you have filled to us shall be filled to you *double*—mark my words!"

Harry spoke so loudly, in his vehemence, that Clayton overheard him, and came behind him silently into the room. He was pained, shocked, and astonished; and, obeying the first instinct, he came forward and laid his hand entreatingly on Harry's shoulder.

"My good fellow, you don't know what you are saying," he said.

"Yes I do," said Harry, "and my words will be true!"

Another witness had come behind Clayton—Tom Gordon, in his travelling-dress, with pistols at his belt. He had ridden over after Jekyl, and had arrived in time to hear part of Harry's frantic ravings.

"Stop!" he said, stepping into the middle of the room; "leave that fellow to me! Now, boy," he said, fixing his dark and evil eye upon Harry, "you didn't know that your master was hearing you, did you? The last time we met, you told me I wasn't your master! *Now*, we'll see if you'll say that again! You went whimpering to your mistress, and got her to buy Lisette, so as to keep her out of *my* way! Now who owns her?—say! Do you see this?" he said, holding up a long, lithe gutta-percha cane.[4] "This is what I whip dogs with, when they don't know their place! Now, sir, down on your knees, and ask pardon for your impudence, or I'll thrash you within an inch of your life!"

"I won't kneel to my younger brother!" said Harry.

With a tremendous oath, Tom struck him; and, as if a rebound from the stroke, Harry struck back a blow so violent as to send him stumbling across the room, against the opposite wall; then turned, quick as thought, sprang through the open window, climbed down the veranda, vaulted on to Tom's horse, which stood tied at the post, and fled as rapidly as lightning to his cottage door, where Lisette stood at the ironing-table. He reached out his hand, and said, "Up, quick, Lisette! Tom Gordon's here!" And before Tom Gordon had fairly recovered from the dizziness into which the blow had thrown him, the fleet blood-horse was whirling Harry and Lisette past bush and tree, till they arrived at the place where he had twice before met Dred.

Dred was standing there. "Even so," he said, the horse stopped, and Harry and Lisette descended; "the vision is fulfilled! Behold, the Lord shall make thee a witness and commander to the people!"

"There's no time to be lost," said Harry.

"Well I know that," said Dred. "Come, follow me!"

And before sunset of that evening Harry and Lisette were tenants of the wild fastness in the centre of the swamp.

CHAPTER XV

The Purpose

IT WOULD BE scarcely possible to describe the scene which Harry left in the library. Tom Gordon was for a few moments stunned by the violence of his fall, and Clayton and Mr. Jekyl at first did not know but he had sustained some serious injury; and the latter, in his confusion, came very near attempting his recovery, by pouring in his face the contents of the large ink-stand. Certainly, quite as appropriate a method, under the circumstances, as the exhortations with which he had deluged Harry. But Clayton, with more presence of mind, held his hand, and rang for water. In a few moments, however, Tom recovered himself, and started up furiously.

"Where is he?" he shouted, with a volley of oaths; which made Mr. Jekyl pull up his shirt-collar, as became a good elderly gentleman, preparatory to a little admonition.

"My young friend—" he began.

"Blast you! None of your *young friends* to me! Where is he?"

"He has escaped," said Clayton, quietly.

"He got right out of the window," said Mr. Jekyl.

"Confound you, why didn't you stop him?" said Tom, violently.

"If that question is addressed to me," said Clayton, "I do not interfere in your family affairs."

"You *have* interfered, more than you ever shall again!" said Tom, roughly. "But, there's no use talking now; that fellow must be chased! He thinks he's got away from me—we'll see! I'll make such an example of him as shall be remembered!" He rang the bell violently. "Jim," he said, "did you see Harry go off on my horse?"

"Yes, sah!"

"Then, why in thunder didn't you stop him?"

"I tought Mas'r Tom sent him—did so!"

"You knew better, you dog! And now, I tell you, order out the best horses, and be on after him! And, if you don't catch him, it shall be the worse for you!—Stay! Get *me* a horse! I'll go myself."

Clayton saw that it was useless to remain any longer at Canema. He therefore ordered his horse, and departed. Tom Gordon cast an evil eye after him, as he rode away.

"I hate that fellow!" he said. "I'll make him mischief, one of these days, if I can!"

As to Clayton, he rode away in bitterness of spirit. There are some men so constituted that the sight of injustice, which they have no power to remedy, is perfectly maddening to them. This is a very painful and unprofitable constitution, so far as this world is concerned; but they can no more help it than they can the tooth-ache. Others may say to them, "Why, what is it to you? You can't help it, and it's none of your concern;" but still the fever burns on. Besides, Clayton had just passed through one of the great crises of life. All there is in that strange mystery of what man can feel for woman had risen like a wave within him; and, gathering into itself, for a time, the whole force of his being, had broken, with one dash, on the shore of death, and the waters had flowed helplessly backward. In the great void which follows such a crisis, the soul sets up a craving and cry for something to come in to fill the emptiness; and while the heart says no *person* can come into that desolate and sacred enclosure, it sometimes embraces a *purpose,* as in some sort a substitute.

In this manner, with solemnity and earnestness, Clayton resolved to receive as a life-purpose a struggle with this great system of injustice, which, like a parasitic weed, had struck its roots through the whole growth of society, and was sucking thence its moisture and nourishment.

As he rode through the lonely pine-woods, he felt his veins throbbing and swelling with indignation and desire. And there arose within him that sense of power which sometimes seems to come over man like an inspiration, and leads him to say, "*This* shall *not* be, and *this* shall be;" as if he possessed the ability to control the crooked course of human events. He was thankful in his heart that he had taken the first step, by entering his public protest against this injustice, in quitting the bar of his native state. What was next to be done, how the evil was to be attacked, how the vague purpose fulfilled, he could not say. Clayton was not aware, any more than others in his situation have been, of what he was undertaking. He had belonged to an old and respected family, and always, as a matter of course, been received in all circles with attention, and listened to with respect. He who glides dreamily down the glassy surface of a mighty river floats securely, making his calculations to row upward. He knows nothing what the force of that seemingly glassy current will be when his one feeble oar is set against the whole volume of its waters. Clayton did not know that he was already a marked man; that he had touched a spot, in the society where he lived, which was vital, and which that society would never suffer to be touched with impunity. It was the fault of Clayton, and is the fault of all such men, that he judged mankind by himself. He could not believe that anything, except ignorance and inattention, could make men upholders of deliberate injustice. He thought all that was necessary was the enlightening of the public mind, the direction of general attention to the subject. In his way homeward he revolved in his mind immediate measures of action. This evil should no longer be tampered with. He would take on himself the task of combining and concentrating those vague impulses towards good which he supposed were existing in the community. He would take counsel of leading minds. He would give his time to journeyings through the state; he would deliver addresses, write in the newspapers, and do what otherwise lies in the power of a free man who wishes to reach an utterly unjust law. Full of these determinations, Clayton entered again his father's house, after two days of solitary riding. He had written in advance to his parents of the death of Nina, and had begged them to spare him any conversation on that subject; and, therefore, on his first meeting with his mother and father, there was that painful blank, that heavy dulness of suffering, which comes when people meet together, feeling deeply on one absorbing subject, which must not be named. It was a greater self-denial to his impulsive, warm-hearted mother than to Clayton. She yearned to express sympathy; to throw herself upon his neck; to draw forth his feelings, and mingle them with her own. But there are some people with whom this is impossible; it seems to be their fate that they cannot speak of what they suffer. It is not pride nor coldness, but a kind of fatal necessity, as if the body were a marble prison, in which the soul were condemned to bleed and suffer alone. It is the last triumph of affection and magnanimity, when a loving heart can respect that suffering silence of its beloved, and allow that lonely liberty in which only some natures can find comfort.

Clayton's sorrow could only be measured by the eagerness and energy with which, in conversation, he pursued the object with which he endeavored to fill his mind.

"I am far from looking forward with hope to any success from your efforts," said Judge Clayton, "the evil is so radical."

"I sometimes think," said Mrs. Clayton, "that I regret that Edward began as he did. It was such a shock to the prejudices of people!"

"People have got to be shocked," said Clayton, "in order to wake them up out of old absurd routine. Use paralyzes us to almost every injustice; when people are shocked, they begin to think and to inquire."

"But would it not have been better," said Mrs. Clayton, "to have preserved your personal influence, and thus have insinuated your opinions more gradually? There is such a prejudice against abolitionists; and, when a man makes any sudden demonstration on this subject, people are apt to call him an abolitionist, and then his influence is all gone, and he can do nothing."

"I suspect," said Clayton, "there are multitudes now in every part of our state who are kept from expressing what they really think, and doing what they ought to do, by this fear. Somebody must brave this mad-dog cry; somebody must be willing to be odious; and I shall answer the purpose as well as anybody."

"Have you any definite plan of what is to be attempted?" said his father.

"Of course," said Clayton, "a man's first notions on such a subject must be crude; but it occurred to me, first, to endeavor to excite the public mind on the injustice of the present slave-law, with a view to altering it."

"And what points would you alter?" said Judge Clayton.

"I would give to the slave the right to bring suit for injury, and to be a legal witness in court. I would repeal the law forbidding their education, and I would forbid the separation of families."

Judge Clayton sat pondering. At length he said, "And how will you endeavor to excite the public mind?"

"I shall appeal first," said Clayton, "to the church and the ministry."

"You can try it," said his father.

"Why," said Mrs. Clayton, "these reforms are so evidently called for, by justice and humanity, and the spirit of the age, that I can have no doubt that there will be a general movement among all good people in their favor."

Judge Clayton made no reply. There are some cases where silence is the most disagreeable kind of dissent, because it admits of no argument in reply.

"In my view," said Clayton, "the course of legal reform, in the first place, should remove all those circumstances in the condition of the slaves which tend to keep them in ignorance and immorality, and make the cultivation of self-respect impossible; such as the want of education, protection in the family state, and the legal power of obtaining redress for injuries. After that, the next step would be to allow those masters who are so disposed to emancipate, giving proper security for the good behavior of their servants. They might then retain them as tenants. Under this system, emancipation would go on gradually; only the best masters would at first emancipate, and the example would be gradually followed. The experiment would soon demonstrate the superior cheapness and efficiency of the system of free labor; and self-interest would then come in, to complete what principle began. It is only the first step that costs. But it seems to me that in the course of my life I have met with multitudes of good people, groaning in secret under the evils and injustice of slavery, who would gladly give their influence to any reasonable effort which promises in time to ameliorate and remove them."

"The trouble is," said Judge Clayton, "that the system, though ruinous in the long run to communities, is immediately profitable to individuals. Besides this, it is a source of political influence and importance. The holders of slaves are an aristocracy supported by special constitutional privileges. They are united against the spirit of the age by a common interest and danger, and the instinct of self-preservation is infallible. No logic is so accurate.

"As a matter of personal feeling, many slaveholders would rejoice in some of the humane changes which you propose; but they see at once that any change endangers the perpetuity of the system on which their political importance depends. Therefore, they'll resist you at the very outset, not because they would not, many of them, be glad to have justice done, but because they think they cannot afford it.

"They will have great patience with you—they will even have sympathy with you—so long as you confine yourself merely to the expression of feeling; but the moment your efforts produce the slightest movement in the community, then, my son, you will see human nature in a new aspect, and know more about mankind than you know now."

"Very well," said Clayton, "the sooner the better."

"Well, Edward," said Mrs. Clayton, "if you are going to begin with the ministry, why don't you go and talk to your Uncle Cushing? He is one of the most influential among the Presbyterians in the whole state; and I have often heard him lament, in the strongest manner, the evils of slavery. He has told me some facts about its effect on the character of his church-members, both bond and free, that are terrible!"

"Yes," said Judge Clayton, "your brother will do all that. He will lament the evils of slavery in private circles, and he will furnish you any number of facts, if you will not give his authority for them."

"And don't you think that he will be willing to do something?"

"No," said Judge Clayton, "not if the cause is unpopular."

"Why," said Mrs. Clayton, "do you suppose that my brother will be deterred from doing his duty for fear of personal unpopularity?"

"No," said Judge Clayton; "but your brother has the interest of Zion on his shoulders,—by which he means the Presbyterian organization,—and he will say that he can't afford to risk his influence. And the same will be true of every leading minister of every denomination. The Episcopalians are keeping watch over Episcopacy, the Methodists over Methodism, the Baptists over Baptism. None of them dare espouse an unpopular cause, lest the others, taking advantage of it, should go beyond them in public favor. None of them will want the odium of such a reform as this."

"But I don't see any odium in it," said Mrs. Clayton. "It's one of the noblest and one of the most necessary of all possible changes."

"Nevertheless," said Judge Clayton, "it will be made to appear extremely odious. The catch-words of abolition, incendiarism, fanaticism, will fly thick as hail. And the storm will be just in proportion to the real power of the movement. It will probably end in Edward's expulsion from the state."

"My father, I should be unwilling to think," said Clayton, "that the world is quite so bad as you represent it,—particularly the religious world."

"I was not aware that I was representing it as very bad," said Judge Clayton. "I only mentioned such facts as everybody can see about them. There are undoubtedly excellent men in the church."

"But," said Clayton, "did not the church, in the primitive ages, stand against the whole world in arms? If religion be anything, must it not take the lead of society, and be its sovereign and teacher, and not its slave?"

"I don't know as to that," said Judge Clayton. "I think you'll find the facts much as I have represented them. What the church was in the primitive ages, or what it ought to be now, is not at all to our purpose, in making practical calculations. Without any disrespect, I wish to speak of things just as they are. Nothing is ever gained by false expectations."

"O," said Mrs. Clayton, "you lawyers get so uncharitable! I'm quite sure that Edward will find brother ready to go heart and hand with him."

"I'm sure I shall be glad of it, if he does," said Judge Clayton.

"I shall write to him about it, immediately," said Mrs. Clayton, "and Edward shall go and talk with him. Courage, Edward! Our woman's instincts, after all, have some prophetic power in them. At all events, we women will stand by you to the last."

Clayton sighed. He remembered the note Nina had written him on the day of the decision, and thought what a brave-hearted little creature she was; and, like the faint breath of a withered rose, the shadowy remembrance of her seemed to say to him, "Go on!"

CHAPTER XVI

The New Mother

THE CHOLERA AT LENGTH DISAPPEARED, and the establishment of our old friend Tiff proceeded as of yore. His chickens and turkeys grew to maturity, and cackled and strutted joyously. His corn waved its ripening flags in the September breezes. The grave of the baby had grown green with its first coat of grass, and Tiff was comforted for his loss, because, as he said, "he knowed he's better off." Miss Fanny grew healthy and strong, and spent many long sunny hours wandering in the woods with Teddy; or, sitting out on the bench where Nina had been wont to read to them, would spell out with difficulty, for her old friend's comfort and enlightenment, the half-familiar words of the wondrous story that Nina had brought to their knowledge.

The interior of the poor cottage bore its wonted air of quaint, sylvan refinement; and Tiff went on with his old dream of imagining it an ancestral residence, of which his young master and mistress were the head, and himself their whole retinue. He was sitting in his tent door, in the cool of the day, while Teddy and Fanny had gone for wild grapes, cheerfully examining and mending his old pantaloons, meanwhile recreating his soul with a cheerful conversation with himself.

"Now, Old Tiff," said he, "one more patch on dese yer, 'cause it an't much matter what you wars. Mas'r is allers a promising to bring home some cloth fur to make a more 'specable pair; but, laws, he never does nothing he says he will. An't no trusting in dat 'scription o' people,—jiggeting up and down de country, drinking at all de taverns, fetching disgrace on de fam'ly, spite o' all I can do! Mighty long time since he been home, any how! Shouldn't wonder if de cholera 'd cotched him! Well, de Lord's will be done! Pity to kill such critturs! Wouldn't much mind if he should die. Laws, he an't much profit to de family, coming home here wid lots o' old trash, drinking up all my chicken-money down to 'Bijah Skinflint's!

For my part, I believe dem devils, when dey went out o' de swine, went into de whiskey-bar'l. Dis yer liquor makes folks so ugly! Teddy shan't never touch none as long as dere's a drop o' Peyton blood in *my* veins! Lord, but dis yer world is full o' 'spensations! Por, dear Miss Nina, dat was a doing for de chil'en! she's gone up among de angels! Well, bress de Lord, we must do de best we can, and we'll all land on de Canaan shore at last."

And Tiff uplifted a quavering stave of a favorite melody:

"My brother, I have found
The land that doth abound
   With food as sweet as manna.
The more I eat, I find
The more I am inclined
   To shout and sing hosanna!"

"Shoo! shoo! shoo!" he said, observing certain long-legged, half-grown chickens, who were surreptitiously taking advantage of his devotional engrossments to rush past him into the kitchen.

" 'Pears like dese yer chickens never will larn nothing!" said Tiff, finding that his vigorous "shooing" only scared the whole flock in, instead of admonishing them out. So Tiff had to lay down his work; and his thimble rolled one way, and his cake of wax another, hiding themselves under the leaves; while the hens, seeing Tiff at the door, instead of accepting his polite invitation to walk out, acted in that provoking and inconsiderate way that hens generally will, running promiscuously up and down, flapping their wings, cackling, upsetting pots, kettles, and pans, in promiscuous ruin, Tiff each moment becoming more and more wrathful at their entire want of consideration.

"Bress me, if I ever did see any kind o' crittur so shaller as hens!" said Tiff, as, having finally ejected them, he was busy repairing the ruin they had wrought in Miss Fanny's fanciful floral arrangements, which were all lying in wild confusion. "I tought de Lord made room in every beast's head for some sense, but 'pears like hens an't got de leastest grain! Puts me out, seeing dem crawking and crawing on one leg, 'cause dey han't got sense 'nough to know whar to set down toder. Dey never has no idees what dey's going to do, from morning to night, I b'lieve! But, den, dere's folks dat's just like 'em, dat de Lord has gin brains to, and dey won't use 'em. Dey's always settin round, but dey never lays no eggs. So hens an't de wust crit-

turs, arter all. And I rally don' know what we'll do widout 'em!"
said Old Tiff, relentingly, as, appeased from his wrath, he took up
at once his needle and his psalm, singing lustily, and with good
courage,

"*Perhaps you'll tink me wild,*
And simple as a child,
But I'm a child of glory!"

"Laws, now," said Tiff, pursuing his reflections to himself,
"maybe he's dead now, sure 'nough! And if he is, why, I can do for
de chil'en raal powerful. I sold right smart of eggs dis yer summer,
and de sweet 'tatoes allers fetches a good price. If I could only get
de chil'en along wid der reading, and keep der manners handsome!
Why, Miss Fanny, now, she's growing up to be raal perty. She got
de raal Peyton look to her; and dere's dis yer 'bout gals and women,
dat if dey's perty, why, somebody wants to be marrying of 'em; and
so dey gets took care of. I tell you, dere shan't any of dem fellers dat
he brings home wid him have anyting to say to her! Peyton blood
an't for der money, I can tell 'em! Dem fellers allers find 'emselves
mighty onlucky as long as I's round! One ting or 'nother happens
to 'em, so dat dey don't want to come no more. Dreful por times
dey has!" And Tiff shook with a secret chuckle.

"But, now, yer see, dere's never any knowing! Dere may be
some Peyton property coming to dese yer chil'en. I's known sich
tings happen, 'fore now. Lawyers calling after de heirs; and den
here dey be a'ready fetched up. I's minding dat I'd better speak to
Miss Nina's man 'bout dese yer chil'en; 'cause he's a nice, perty
man, and nat'rally he'd take an interest; and dat ar handsome sister
of his, dat was so thick wid Miss Nina, maybe she'd be doing something for her. Any way, dese yer chil'en shall neber come to want
'long as I's above ground!"

Alas for the transitory nature of human expectations! Even our
poor little Arcadia in the wilderness, where we have had so many
hours of quaint delight, was destined to feel the mutability of all
earthly joys and prospects. Even while Tiff spoke and sung, in the
exuberance of joy and security of his soul, a disastrous phantom
was looming up from a distance—the phantom of Cripps' old
wagon. Cripps was not dead, as was to have been hoped, but returning for a more permanent residence, bringing with him a bride
of his own heart's choosing.

Tiff's dismay—his utter, speechless astonishment—may be imagined, when the ill-favored machine rumbled up to the door, and Cripps produced from it what seemed to be, at first glance, a bundle of tawdry, dirty finery; but at last it turned out to be a woman, so far gone in intoxication as scarcely to be sensible of what she was doing. Evidently, she was one of the lowest of that class of poor whites whose wretched condition is not among the least of the evils of slavery. Whatever she might have been naturally,—whatever of beauty or of good there might have been in the womanly nature within her,—lay wholly withered and eclipsed under the force of an education churchless, schoolless, with all the vices of civilization without its refinements, and all the vices of barbarism without the occasional nobility by which they are sometimes redeemed. A low and vicious connection with this woman had at last terminated in marriage—such marriages as one shudders to think of, where gross animal natures come together, without even a glimmering idea of the higher purposes of that holy relation.

"Tiff, this yer is your new mistress," said Cripps, with an idiotic laugh. "Plaguy nice girl, too! I thought I'd bring the children a mother to take care of them. Come along, girl!"

Looking closer, we recognize in the woman our old acquaintance, Polly Skinflint.

He pulled her forward; and she, coming in, seated herself on Fanny's bed. Tiff looked as if he could have struck her dead. An avalanche had fallen upon him. He stood in the door with the slack hand of utter despair; while she, swinging her heels, began leisurely spitting about her, in every direction, the juice of a quid of tobacco, which she cherished in one cheek.

"Durned if this yer an't pretty well!" she said. "Only I want the nigger to heave out that ar trash!" pointing to Fanny's flowers. "I don't want children sticking no herbs round my house! Hey, you nigger, heave out that trash!"

As Tiff stood still, not obeying this call, the woman appeared angry; and, coming up to him, struck him on the side of the head.

"O, come, come, Poll!" said Cripps, "you be still! He an't used to no such ways."

"Still!" said the amiable lady, turning round to him. "You go 'long! Didn't you tell me, if I married you, I should have a nigger to order round, just as I pleased?"

"Well, well," said Cripps, who was not by any means a cruelly-disposed man, "I didn't think you'd want to go walloping him, the first thing."

"I will, if he don't shin round," said the virago, "and you, too!"

And this vigorous profession was further carried out by a vigorous shove, which reäcted in Cripps in the form of a cuff, and in a few moments the disgraceful scuffle was at its full height. And Tiff turned in disgust and horror from the house.

"O, good Lord!" he said to himself, "we doesn't know what's 'fore us! And I's feeling so bad when de Lord took my por little man, and now I's ready to go down on my knees to thank de Lord dat he's took him away from de evil to come! To think of my por sweet lamb, Miss Fanny, as I's been bringing up so carful! Lord, dis yer's a heap worse dan de cholera!"

It was with great affliction and dismay that he saw the children coming forward in high spirits, bearing between them a basket of wild-grapes, which they had been gathering. He ran out to meet them.

"Laws, yer por lambs," he said, "yer doesn't know what's a coming on you! Yer pa's gone and married a dreful low white woman, sich as an't fit for no Christian children to speak to. And now dey's quar'ling and fighting in dere, like two heathens! And Miss Nina's dead, and dere an't no place for you to go!"

And the old man sat down and actually wept aloud, while the children, frightened, got into his arms, and nestled close to him for protection, crying too.

"What shall we do? what shall we do?" said Fanny. And Teddy, who always repeated, reverentially, all his sister's words, said, after her, in a deplorable whimper, "What shall we do?"

"I's a good mind to go off wid you in de wilderness, like de chil'en of Israel," said Tiff, "though dere an't no manna falling nowadays."

"Tiff, does marrying father make her our ma?" said Fanny.

"No 'deed, Miss Fanny, it doesn't! Yer ma was one o' de fustest old Virginny families. It was jist throwing herself 'way, marrying him! I neber said dat ar 'fore, 'cause it wan't 'spectful. But I don't care now!"

At this moment Cripps' voice was heard shouting:

"Hallo, you Tiff! Where is the durned nigger? I say, come back! Poll and I's made it up, now! Bring 'long them children, and let them get acquainted with their mammy," he said, laying hold of

Fanny's hand, and drawing her, frightened and crying, towards the house.

"Don't you be afraid, child," said Cripps; "I've brought you a new ma."

"We didn't want any new ma!" said Teddy, in a dolorous voice.

"O, yes, you do," said Cripps, coaxing him. "Come along, my little man! There's your mammy," he said, pushing him into the fat embrace of Polly.

"Fanny, go kiss your ma."

Fanny hung back and cried, and Teddy followed her example.

"Confound the durn young 'uns!" said the new-married lady. "I told you, Cripps, I didn't want no brats of t' other woman's! Be plague enough when I get some of my own!"

CHAPTER XVII

The Flight into Egypt

THE ONCE NEAT and happy cottage, of which Old Tiff was the guardian genius, soon experienced sad reverses. Polly Skinflint's violent and domineering temper made her absence from her father's establishment rather a matter of congratulation to Abijah. Her mother, one of those listless and inefficient women, whose lives flow in a calm, muddy current of stupidity and laziness, talked very little about it; but, on the whole, was perhaps better contented to be out of the range of Polly's sharp voice and long arms. It was something of a consideration, in Abijah's shrewd view of things, that Cripps owned a nigger—the first point to which the aspiration of the poor white of the South generally tends. Polly, whose love of power was a predominant element in her nature, resolutely declared, in advance, she'd make him shin round,[1] or she'd know the reason why. As to the children, she regarded them as the encumbrances of the estate, to be got over with in the best way possible; for, as she graphically remarked, "Every durned young 'un had to look out when she was 'bout!"

The bride had been endowed with a marriage-portion, by her father, of half a barrel of whiskey; and it was announced that Cripps was tired of trading round the country, and meant to set up trading at home. In short, the little cabin became a low grog-shop, a resort of the most miserable and vicious portion of the community. The violent temper of Polly soon drove Cripps upon his travels again, and his children were left unprotected to the fury of their stepmother's temper. Every vestige of whatever was decent about the house and garden was soon swept away; for the customers of the shop, in a grand Sunday drinking-bout, amused themselves with tearing down even the prairie-rose and climbing-vine that once gave a sylvan charm to the rude dwelling. Polly's course, in the absence of her husband, was one of gross, unblushing licentiousness; and the ears and eyes of the children were shocked with language and scenes too bad for repetition.

Old Tiff was almost heart-broken. He could have borne the beatings and starvings which came on himself; but the abuse which came on the children he could not bear. One night, when the drunken orgie was raging within the house, Tiff gathered courage from despair.

"Miss Fanny," he said, "jist go in de garret, and make a bundle o' sich tings as dere is, and throw 'em out o' de winder. I's been a praying night and day; and de Lord says *He*'ll open some way or oder for us! I'll keep Teddy out here under de trees, while you jist bundles up what por clothes is left, and throws 'em out o' de winder."

Silently as a ray of moonlight, the fair, delicate-looking child glided through the room where her step-mother and two or three drunken men were revelling in a loathsome debauch.

"Halloa, sis!" cried one of the men, after her, "where are you going to? Stop here, and give me a kiss!"

The unutterable look of mingled pride, and fear, and angry distress, which the child cast, as, quick as thought, she turned from them and ran up the ladder into the loft, occasioned roars of laughter.

"I say, Bill, why didn't you catch her?" said one.

"O, no matter for that," said another; "she'll come of her own accord, one of these days."

Fanny's heart beat like a frightened bird, as she made up her little bundle. Then, throwing it to Tiff, who was below in the dark, she called out, in a low, earnest whisper,

"Tiff, put up that board, and I'll climb down on it. I won't go back among those dreadful men!"

Carefully and noiselessly as possible, Tiff lifted a long, rough slab, and placed it against the side of the house. Carefully Fanny set her feet on the top of it, and, spreading her arms, came down, like a little puff of vapor, into the arms of her faithful attendant.

"Bress de Lord! Here we is, all right," said Tiff.

"O, Tiff, I'm so glad!" said Teddy, holding fast to the skirt of Tiff's apron, and jumping for joy.

"Yes," said Tiff, "all right. Now de angel of de Lord 'll go with us into de wilderness!"

"There's plenty of angels there, an't there?" said Teddy, victoriously, as he lifted the little bundle, with undoubting faith.

"Laws, yes!" said Tiff. "I don' know why dere shouldn't be in our days. Any rate, de Lord 'peared to me in a dream, and says he, 'Tiff, rise and take de chil'en and go in de land of Egypt, and be dere till de time I tell dee.' Dem is de bery words. And 't was 'tween de cockcrow and daylight dey come to me, when I'd been lying dar praying, like a hail-storm, all night, not gibing de Lord no rest! Says I to him, says I, 'Lord, I don' know nothing what to do; and now, ef you was por as I be, and I was great king, like you, I'd help you! And now, Lord,' says I, 'you *must* help us, 'cause we an't got no place else to go; 'cause, you know, Miss Nina she's dead, and Mr. John Gordon, too! And dis yer woman will ruin dese yer chil'en, ef you don't help us! And now I hope you won't be angry! But I has to be very bold, 'cause tings have got so dat we can't bar 'em no longer!' Den, yer see, I dropped 'sleep; and I hadn't no more 'n got to sleep, jist after cock-crow, when de voice come!"

"And is this the land of Egypt," said Teddy, "that we're going to?"

"I spect so," said Tiff. "Don't you know de story Miss Nina read to you, once, how de angel of de Lord 'peared to Hagar in de wilderness, when she was sitting down under de bush. Den dere was anoder one come to 'Lijah when he was under de juniper-tree, when he was wandering up and down, and got hungry, and woke up; and dere, sure 'nough, was a corn-cake baking for him on de coals![2] Don't you mind Miss Nina was reading dat ar de bery last Sunday she come to our place? Bress de Lord for sending her to us! I's got heaps o' good through dem readings."

"Do you think we really shall see any?" said Fanny, with a little shade of apprehension in her voice. "I don't know as I shall know how to speak to them."

"O, angels is pleasant-spoken, well-meaning folks, allers," said Tiff, "and don't take no 'fence at us. Of course, dey knows we an't fetched up in der ways, and dey don't spect it of us. It's my 'pinion," said Tiff, "dat when folks is honest, and does de bery best dey can, dey don't need to be 'fraid to speak to angels, nor nobody else; 'cause, you see, we speaks to de Lord hisself when we prays, and, bress de Lord, he don't take it ill of us, no ways. And now it's borne in strong on my mind, dat de Lord is going to lead us through the wilderness, and bring us to good luck. Now, you see, I's going to follow de star, like de wise men did."

While they were talking, they were making their way through dense woods in the direction of the swamp, every moment taking them deeper and deeper into the tangled brush and underwood. The children were accustomed to wander for hours through the wood; and, animated by the idea of having escaped their persecutors, followed Tiff with alacrity, as he went before them, clearing away the brambles and vines with his long arms, every once in a while wading with them across a bit of morass, or climbing his way through the branches of some uprooted tree. It was after ten o'clock at night when they started. It was now after midnight. Tiff had held on his course in the direction of the swamp, where he knew many fugitives were concealed; and he was not without hopes of coming upon some camp or settlement of them.

About one o'clock they emerged from the more tangled brushwood, and stood on a slight little clearing, where a grape-vine, depending in natural festoons from a sweet gum-tree, made a kind of arbor. The moon was shining very full and calm, and the little breeze fluttered the grape-leaves, casting the shadow of some on the transparent greenness of others. The dew had fallen so heavily in that moist region, that every once in a while, as a slight wind agitated the leaves, it might be heard pattering from one to another, like rain-drops. Teddy had long been complaining bitterly of fatigue. Tiff now sat down under this arbor, and took him fondly into his arms.

"Sit down, Miss Fanny. And is Tiff's brave little man got tired? Well, he shall go to sleep, dat he shall! We's got out a good bit now. I reckon dey won't find us. We's out here wid de good Lord's works, and dey won't none on 'em tell on us. So, now, hush, my por little man; shut up your eyes!" And Tiff quavered the immortal cradle-hymn,

> "Hush, my dear, lie still and slumber!
>   Holy angels guard thy bed;
> Heavenly blessings, without number,
>   Gently falling on thy head."[3]

In a few moments Teddy was sound asleep, and Tiff, wrapping him in his white great-coat, laid him down at the root of a tree.

"Bress de Lord, dere an't no whiskey here!" he said, "nor no drunken critturs to wake him up. And now, Miss Fanny, por chile, your eyes is a falling. Here's dis yer old shawl I put up in de pocket of my coat. Wrap it round you, whilst I scrape up a heap of dem pine-leaves, yonder. Dem is reckoned mighty good for sleeping on, 'cause dey's so healthy, kinder. Dar, you see, I's got a desput big heap of 'em."

"I'm tired, but I'm not sleepy," said Fanny. "But, Tiff, what are *you* going to do?"

"Do!" said Tiff, laughing, with somewhat of his old, joyous laugh. "Ho! ho! ho! I's going to sit up for to meditate—a 'sidering on de fowls of de air, and de lilies in de field, and all dem dar Miss Nina used to read 'bout."

For many weeks, Fanny's bed-chamber had been the hot, dusty loft of the cabin, with the heated roof just above her head, and the noise of bacchanalian revels below. Now she lay sunk down among the soft and fragrant pine-foliage, and looked up, watching the checkered roof of vine-leaves above her head, listening to the still patter of falling dew-drops, and the tremulous whirr and flutter of leaves. Sometimes the soft night-winds swayed the tops of the pines with a long swell of dashing murmurs, like the breaking of a tide on a distant beach. The moonlight, as it came sliding down through the checkered, leafy roof, threw fragments and gleams of light, which moved capriciously here and there over the ground, revealing now a great silvery fern-leaf, and then a tuft of white flowers, gilding spots on the branches and trunks of the trees; while every moment the deeper shadows were lighted up by the gleaming of fire-flies. The child would raise her head a while, and look on the still scene around, and then sink on her fragrant pillow in dreamy delight. Everything was so still, so calm, so pure, no wonder she was prepared to believe that the angels of the Lord were to be found in the wilderness. They who have walked in closest communion with nature have ever found that they have not departed thence. The wilderness and solitary places are still glad for them, and their presence makes the desert to rejoice and blossom as the rose.

When Fanny and Teddy were both asleep, Old Tiff knelt down and addressed himself to his prayers; and, though he had neither prayer-book, nor cushion, nor formula, his words went right to the mark, in the best English he could command for any occasion; and, so near as we could collect from the sound of his words, Tiff's prayer ran as follows:

"O, good Lord, now please do look down on dese yer chil'en. I started 'em out, as you told me; and now whar we is to go, and whar we is to get any breakfast, I's sure I don' know. But, O good Lord, you has got everyting in de world in yer hands, and it's mighty easy for you to be helping on us; and I has faith to believe dat you will. O, bressed Lord Jesus, dat was carried off into Egypt for fear of de King Herod, do, pray, look down on dese yer por chil'en, for I's sure dat ar woman is as bad as Herod, any day. Good Lord, you's seen how she's been treating on 'em; and now do pray open a way for us through de wilderness to de promised land. Everlasting—Amen."

The last two words Tiff always added to his prayers, from a sort of sense of propriety, feeling as if they rounded off the prayer, and made it, as he would have phrased it, more like a white prayer. We have only to say, to those who question concerning this manner of prayer, that, if they will examine the supplications of patriarchs of ancient times, they will find that, with the exception of the broken English and bad grammar, they were in substance very much like this of Tiff.

The Bible divides men into two classes: those who trust in themselves, and those who trust in God. The one class walk by their own light, trust in their own strength, fight their own battles, and have no confidence otherwise. The other, not neglecting to use the wisdom and strength which God has given them, still trust in his wisdom and his strength to carry out the weakness of theirs. The one class go through life as orphans; the other have a Father.

Tiff's prayer had at least this recommendation, that he felt perfectly sure that something was to come of it. Had he not told the Lord all about it? Certainly he had; and of course he would be helped. And this confidence Tiff took, as Jacob did a stone, for his pillow,[4] as he lay down between his children and slept soundly.

How innocent, soft, and kind, are all God's works! From the silent shadows of the forest the tender and loving presence which our sin exiled from the haunts of men hath not yet departed. Sweet fall the moonbeams through the dewy leaves; peaceful is the breeze that waves the branches of the pines; merciful and tender the little wind that shakes the small flowers and tremulous wood-grasses fluttering over the heads of the motherless children. O, thou who bearest in thee a heart hot and weary, sick and faint with the vain tumults and confusions of the haunts of men, go to the wilderness, and thou shalt find *Him* there who saith, "As one whom his mother comforteth, so will I comfort you. I will be as the dew to Israel. He shall grow as a lily, and cast forth his roots as Lebanon."[5]

Well, they slept there quietly, all night long. Between three and four o'clock, an oriole, who had his habitation in the vine above their heads, began a gentle twittering conversation with some of his neighbors; not a loud song, I would give you to understand, but a little, low inquiry as to what o'clock it was. And then, if you had been in a still room at that time, you might have heard, through all the trees of pine, beech, holly, sweet-gum, and larch, a little, tremulous stir and flutter of birds awaking and stretching their wings. Little eyes were opening in a thousand climbing vines, where soft, feathery habitants had hung, swinging breezily, all night. Low twitterings and chirpings were heard; then a loud, clear, echoing chorus of harmony answering from tree to tree, jubilant and joyous as if there never had been a morning before. The morning star had not yet gone down, nor were the purple curtains of the east undrawn: and the moon, which had been shining full all night, still stood like a patient, late-burning light in a quiet chamber. It is not everybody that wakes to hear this first chorus of the birds. They who sleep till sunrise have lost it, and with it a thousand mysterious pleasures,— strange, sweet communings,—which, like morning dew, begin to evaporate when the sun rises.

But, though Tiff and the children slept all night, we are under no obligations to keep our eyes shut to the fact that between three and four o'clock there came crackling through the swamps the dark figure of one whose journeyings were more often by night than by day. Dred had been out on one of his nightly excursions, carrying game, which he disposed of for powder and shot at one of the low stores we have alluded to. He came unexpectedly on the sleepers, while making his way back. His first movement, on seeing them, was that of surprise; then, stooping and examining the group more closely, he appeared to recognize them. Dred had known Old Tiff before; and had occasion to go to him more than once to beg supplies for fugitives in the swamps, or to get some errand performed which he could not himself venture abroad to attend to. Like others of his race, Tiff, on all such subjects, was so habitually and unfathomably secret, that the children, who knew him most intimately, had never received even a suggestion from him of the existence of any such person.

Dred, whose eyes, sharpened by habitual caution, never lost sight of any change in his vicinity, had been observant of that which had taken place in Old Tiff's affairs. When, therefore, he saw him sleeping as we have described, he understood the whole matter at once. He looked at the children, as they lay nestled at the roots of the tree, with something of a softened expression, muttering to himself, "They embrace the Rock for shelter."[6]

He opened a pouch which he wore on his side, and took from thence one or two corn-dodgers[7] and half a broiled rabbit, which his wife had put up for hunting provision, the day before; and, laying them down on the leaves, hastened on to a place where he had intended to surprise some game in the morning.

The chorus of birds we have before described awakened Old Tiff, accustomed to habits of early rising. He sat up, and began rubbing his eyes and stretching himself. He had slept well, for his habits of life had not been such as to make him at all fastidious with regard to his couch.

"Well," he said to himself, "any way, dat ar woman won't get dese yer chil'en, dis yer day!" And he gave one of his old hearty laughs, to think how nicely he had outwitted her.

"Laws," he said to himself, "don't I hear her now! 'Tiff! Tiff! Tiff!' she says. Holla away, old mist'! Tiff don't hear yer! no, nor de chil'en eider, por blessed lambs!"

Here, in turning to the children, his eye fell on the provisions. At first he stood petrified, with his hands lifted in astonishment. Had the angel been there? Sure enough, he thought.

"Well, now, bress de Lord, sure 'nough, here's de bery breakfast, I's asking for last night! Well, I knowed de Lord would do something for us; but I really didn't know as 't would come so quick! May be ravens brought it, as dey did to 'Lijah—bread and flesh in de morning, and bread and flesh at night.[8] Well, dis yer's 'couraging—'t is so. I won't wake up de por little lambs. Let 'em sleep. Dey'll be mighty tickled when dey comes fur to see de breakfast; and, den, out here it's so sweet and clean! None yer nasty 'bacca spittins of folks dat doesn't know how to be decent. Bress me, I's rather tired, myself. I spects I'd better camp down again, till de chil'en wakes. Dat ar crittur 's kep me gwine till I's got pretty stiff, wid her contrary ways. Spect she'll be as troubled as King Herod was, and all 'Rusalem wid her!"

And Tiff rolled and laughed quietly, in the security of his heart.

"I say, Tiff, where are we?" said a little voice at his side.

"Whar is we, puppit?" said Tiff, turning over; "why, bress yer sweet eyes, how does yer do, dis mornin? Stretch away, my man! Neber be 'fraid; we's in de Lord's diggins now, all safe. And de angel's got a breakfast ready for us, too!" said Tiff, displaying the provision, which he had arranged on some vine-leaves.

"O, Uncle Tiff, did the angels bring that?" said Teddy. "Why didn't you wake me up? I wanted to see them. I never saw an angel, in all my life!"

"Nor I neider, honey. Dey comes mostly when we's 'sleep. But, stay, dere's Miss Fanny, a waking up. How is ye, lamb? Is ye 'freshed?"

"O, Uncle Tiff, I've slept so sound," said Fanny; "and I dreamed such a beautiful dream!"

"Well, den, tell it right off, 'fore breakfast," said Tiff, "to make it come true."

"Well," said Fanny, "I dreamed I was in a desolate place, where I couldn't get out, all full of rocks and brambles, and Teddy was with me; and while we were trying and trying, our ma came to us. She looked like our ma, only a great deal more beautiful; and she had a strange white dress on, that shone, and hung clear to her feet; and she took hold of our hands, and the rocks opened, and we walked through a path into a beautiful green meadow, full of lilies and wild strawberries; and then she was gone."

"Well," said Teddy, "maybe 't was she who brought some breakfast to us. See here, what we've got!"

Fanny looked surprised and pleased, but, after some consideration, said,

"I don't believe mamma brought that. I don't believe they have corn-cake and roast meat in heaven. If it had been manna, now, it would have been more likely."

"Neber mind whar it comes from," said Tiff. "It's right good, and we bress de Lord for it."

And they sat down accordingly, and ate their breakfast with a good heart.

"Now," said Tiff, "somewhar roun' in dis yer swamp dere's a

camp o' de colored people; but I don' know rightly whar 't is. If we
could get dar, we could stay dar a while, till something or nuder
should turn up. Hark! what's dat ar?"

'T was the crack of a rifle reverberating through the dewy, leafy
stillness of the forest.

"Dat ar an't fur off," said Tiff.

The children looked a little terrified.

"Don't you be 'fraid," he said. "I wouldn't wonder but I
knowed who dat ar was. Hark, now! 't is somebody coming dis yer
way."

A clear, exultant voice sung, through the leafy distance,

"O, had I the wings of the morning,
I'd fly away to Canaan's shore."

"Yes," said Tiff, to himself, "dat ar's his voice. Now, chil'en," he
said, "dar's somebody coming; and you mustn't be 'fraid on him,
'cause I spects he'll get us to dat ar camp I's telling 'bout."

And Tiff, in a cracked and strained voice, which contrasted
oddly enough with the bell-like tones of the distant singer, commenced singing a part of an old song, which might, perhaps, have
been used as a signal:

"Hailing so stormily,
Cold, stormy weder;
I want my true love all de day.
Whar shall I find him? whar shall I find him?"

The distant singer stopped his song, apparently to listen, and,
while Tiff kept on singing, they could hear the crackling of approaching footsteps. At last Dred emerged to view.

"So you've fled to the wilderness?" he said.

"Yes, yes," said Tiff, with a kind of giggle, "we had to come to it,
dat ar woman was so aggravating on de chil'en. Of all de pizin critturs dat I knows on, dese yer mean white women is de pizinest!
Dey an't got no manners, and no bringing up. Dey doesn't begin to
know how tings ought fur to be done 'mong 'specable people. So
we just tuck to de bush."

"You might have taken to a worse place," said Dred. "The Lord
God giveth grace and glory to the trees of the wood. And the time
will come when the Lord will make a covenant of peace, and cause
the evil beast to cease out of the land; and they shall dwell safely in

the wilderness, and shall sleep in the woods; and the tree of the field shall yield her fruit, and they shall be safe in the land, when the Lord hath broken the bands of their yoke, and delivered them out of the hands of those that serve themselves of them."[9]

"And you tink dem good times coming, sure 'nough?" said Tiff.

"The Lord hath said it," said the other. "But first the day of vengeance must come."

"I don't want no sich," said Tiff. "I want to live peaceable."

Dred looked upon Tiff with an air of acquiescent pity, which had in it a slight shade of contempt, and said, as if in soliloquy,

"Issachar is a strong ass, couching down between two burdens; and he saw that rest was good, and the land that it was pleasant, and bowed his shoulder to bear, and became a servant unto tribute."[10]

"As to rest," said Tiff, "de Lord knows I an't had much of dat ar, if I be an ass. If I had a good, strong pack-saddle, I'd like to trot dese yer chil'en out in some good cleared place."

"Well," said Dred, "you have served him that was ready to perish, and not betrayed him who wandered; therefore the Lord will open for you a fenced city in the wilderness."[11]

"Jest so," said Tiff; "dat ar camp o' yourn is jest what I's arter. I's willin' to lend a hand to most anyting dat's good."

"Well," said Dred, "the children are too tender to walk where we must go. We must bear them as an eagle beareth her young.[12] Come, my little man!"

And, as Dred spoke, he stooped down and stretched out his hands to Teddy. His severe and gloomy countenance relaxed into a smile, and, to Tiff's surprise, the child went immediately to him, and allowed him to lift him in his arms.

"Now, I'd tought he'd been skeered o' you!" said Tiff.

"Not he! I never saw child or dog that I couldn't make come to me. Hold fast, now, my little man!" he said, seating the boy on his shoulder. "Trees have long arms; don't let them rake you off. Now, Tiff," he said, "you take the girl and come after, and when we come into the thick of the swamp, mind you step right in my tracks. Mind you don't set your foot on a tussock if I haven't set mine there before you; because the moccasons lie on the tussocks."[13]

And thus saying, Dred and his companion began making their way towards the fugitive camp.

CHAPTER XVIII

The Clerical Conference

A FEW DAYS found Clayton in the city of———, guest of the Rev. Dr. Cushing. He was a man in middle life; of fine personal presence, urbane, courtly, gentlemanly. Dr. Cushing was a popular and much-admired clergyman, standing high among his brethren in the ministry, and almost the idol of a large and flourishing church. A man of warm feelings, humane impulses, and fine social qualities, his sermons, beautifully written, and delivered with great fervor, often drew tears from the eyes of the hearers. His pastoral ministrations, whether at wedding or funeral, had a peculiar tenderness and unction. None was more capable than he of celebrating the holy fervor and self-denying sufferings of apostles and martyrs; none more easily kindled by those devout hymns which describe the patience of the saints; but, with all this, for any practical emergency, Dr. Cushing was nothing of a soldier. There was a species of moral effeminacy about him, and the very luxuriant softness and richness of his nature unfitted him to endure hardness. He was known, in all his intercourse with his brethren, as a peace-maker, a modifier, and harmonizer. Nor did he scrupulously examine how much of the credit of this was due to a fastidious softness of nature, which made controversy disagreeable and wearisome. Nevertheless, Clayton was at first charmed with the sympathetic warmth with which he and his plans were received by his relative. He seemed perfectly to agree with Clayton in all his views of the terrible evils of the slave system, and was prompt with anecdotes and instances to enforce everything that he said. "Clayton was just in time," he said; "a number of his ministerial brethren were coming to-morrow, some of them from the northern states. Clayton should present his views to them."

Dr. Cushing's establishment was conducted on the footing of the most liberal hospitality; and that very evening the domestic circle

414

was made larger by the addition of four or five ministerial brethren. Among these Clayton was glad to meet, once more, father Dickson. The serene, good man, seemed to bring the blessing of the gospel of peace with him, wherever he went.

Among others, was one whom we will more particularly introduce, as the Rev. Shubael Packthread. Dr. Shubael Packthread was a minister of a leading church, in one of the northern cities. Constitutionally, he was an amiable and kindly man, with very fair natural abilities, fairly improved by culture. Long habits, however, of theological and ecclesiastical controversy had cultivated a certain species of acuteness of mind into such disproportioned activity, that other parts of his intellectual and moral nature had been dwarfed and dwindled beside it. What might, under other circumstances, have been agreeable and useful tact, became in him a constant and lifelong *habit* of stratagem. While other people look upon words as vehicles for conveying ideas, Dr. Packthread regarded them only as mediums for concealment. His constant study, on every controverted topic, was so to adjust language that, with the appearance of the utmost precision, it should always be capable of a double interpretation. He was a cunning master of all forms of indirection; of all phrases by which people *appear* to say what they do not say, and *not* to say what they *do* say.

He was an adept also in all the mechanism of ecclesiastical debate, of the intricate labyrinths of heresy-hunting, of every scheme by which more simple and less advised brethren, speaking with ignorant sincerity, could be entrapped and deceived. He was *au fait* also in all compromise measures, in which two parties unite in one form of words, meaning by them exactly opposite ideas, and call the agreement a *union*.[1] He was also expert in all those parliamentary modes, in synod or general assembly, by which troublesome discussions could be avoided or disposed of, and credulous brethren made to believe they had gained points which they had not gained; by which discussions could be at will blinded with dusty clouds of misrepresentation, or trailed on through interminable marshes of weariness, to accomplish some manœuvre of ecclesiastical tactics.

Dr. Packthread also was master of every means by which the influence of opposing parties might be broken. He could spread a convenient report on necessary occasions, by any of those forms which do not assert, but which disseminate a slander quite as certainly as if they did. If it was necessary to create a suspicion of the orthodoxy, or of the piety, or even of the morality, of an opposing brother, Dr. Packthread understood how to do it in the neatest and most tasteful manner. He was an infallible judge whether it should be accomplished by innocent interrogations, as to whether you had heard "so and so of Mr. ———;" or, by "charitably expressed hopes that you had not heard so and so;" or, by gentle suggestions, whether it would not be as well to inquire; or, by shakes of the head, and lifts of the eyes, at proper intervals in conversation; or, lastly, by *silence* when silence became the strongest as well as safest form of assertion.

In person, he was rather tall, thin, and the lines of his face appeared, every one of them, to be engraved by caution and care. In his boyhood and youth, the man had had a trick of smiling and laughing without considering why; the grace of prudence, however, had corrected all this. He never did either, in these days, without understanding precisely what he was about. His face was a part of his stock in trade, and he understood the management of it remarkably well. He knew precisely all the gradations of smile which were useful for accomplishing different purposes. The solemn smile, the smile of inquiry, the smile affirmative, the smile suggestive, the smile of incredulity, and the smile of innocent credulity, which encouraged the simple-hearted narrator to go on unfolding himself to the brother, who sat quietly behind his face, as a spider does behind his web, waiting till his unsuspecting friend had tangled himself in incautious, impulsive, and of course contradictory meshes of statement, which were, in some future hour, in the most gentle and Christian spirit, to be tightened around the incautious captive, while as much blood was sucked as the good of the cause demanded.

It is not to be supposed that the Rev. Dr. Packthread, so skilful and adroit as we have represented him, failed in the necessary climax of such skill—that of deceiving himself. Far from it. Truly and honestly Dr. Packthread thought himself one of the hundred and forty and four thousand, who follow the Lamb whithersoever he goeth, in whose mouth is found no guile. *Prudence* he considered the chief of Christian graces. He worshipped Christian prudence, and the whole category of accomplishments which we have described he considered as the fruits of it. His prudence, in fact, served him all the purposes that the stock of the tree did to the ancient idolater. "With part thereof he eateth flesh; he roasteth roast, and is satisfied; yea, he warmeth himself, and saith, Aha, I am warm, I have seen the fire: and the residue thereof he maketh a god, even his graven image; he falleth down unto it, and worshippeth it, and prayeth unto it, and saith, Deliver me; for thou art my god."[2]

No doubt, Dr. Packthread expected to enter heaven by the same judicious arrangement by which he had lived on earth; and so he went on, from year to year, doing deeds which even a political candidate would blush at; violating the most ordinary principles of morality and honor; while he sung hymns, made prayers, and administered sacraments, expecting, no doubt, at last to enter heaven by some neat arrangement of words used in two senses.

Dr. Packthread's cautious agreeableness of manner formed a striking contrast to the innocent and almost childlike simplicity with which father Dickson, in his threadbare coat, appeared at his side. Almost as poor in this world's goods as his Master, father Dickson's dwelling had been a simple one-story cottage, in all, save thrift and neatness, very little better than those of the poorest; and it was a rare year when a hundred dollars passed through his hands. He had seen the time when he had not even wherewithal to take from the office a necessary letter. He had seen his wife suffer for medicine and comforts, in sickness. He had himself ridden without overcoat through the chill months of winter; but all these things he had borne as the traveller bears a storm on the way to his home; and it was beautiful to see the unenvying, frank, simple pleasure which he seemed to feel in the elegant and abundant home of his brother, and in the thousand appliances of hospitable comfort by which he was surrounded. The spirit within us that lusteth to envy had been chased from his bosom by the expulsive force of a higher love; and his simple and unstudied acts of constant good-will showed that simple Christianity can make the gentleman. Father Dickson was regarded by his ministerial brethren with great affection and veneration, though wholly devoid of any ecclesiastical wisdom. They were fond of using him much as they did their hymn-books and testaments, for their better hours of devotion; and equally apt to let slip his admonitions, when they came to the hard, matter-of-fact business of ecclesiastical discussion and management; yet they loved well to have him with them, as they felt that, like a psalm or a text, his presence in some sort gave sanction to what they did.

In due time there was added to the number of the circle our joyous, out-spoken friend, father Bonnie, fresh from a recent series of camp-meetings in a distant part of the state, and ready at a minute's notice for either a laugh or a prayer. Very little of the stereotype print of his profession had he; the sort of wild woodland freedom of his life giving to his manners and conversation a tone of sylvan roughness, of which Dr. Packthread evidently stood in considerable doubt. Father Bonnie's early training had been that of what is called, in common parlance, a "self-made man." He was unsophisticated by Greek or Latin, and had rather a contempt for the forms of the schools, and a joyous determination to say what he pleased on all occasions. There were also present one or two of the leading Presbyterian ministers of the North. They had, in fact, come for a private and confidential conversation with Dr. Cushing concerning the reünion of the New School Presbyterian Church with the Old.

It may be necessary to apprise some of our readers, not conversant with American ecclesiastical history, that the Presbyterian church of America is divided into two parties in relation to certain theological points, and that the adherents on either side call themselves *old* or *new* school. Some years since, these two parties divided, and each of them organized its own general assembly.

It so happened that all the slaveholding interest, with some very inconsiderable exceptions, went into the old school body. The great majority of the new school body were avowedly anti-slavery men, according to a solemn declaration, which committed the whole Presbyterian church to those sentiments, in the year eighteen hundred and eighteen.[3] And the breach between the two sections was caused quite as much by the difference of feeling between the northern and southern branches on the subject of slavery, as by any differences of doctrine.

After the first jar of separation was over, thoughts of reünion began to arise on both sides, and to be quietly discussed among leading minds.

There is a power in men of a certain class of making an organization of any kind, whether it be political or ecclesiastical, an object of absorbing and individual devotion. Most men feel empty and insufficient of themselves, and find a need to ballast their own insufficiency by attaching themselves to something of more weight than they are. They put their stock of being out at interest, and invest themselves somewhere and in something; and the love of wife or child is not more absorbing than the love of the bank where the man has invested himself. It is true, this power is a noble one; because thus a man may pass out of self, and choose God, the great good of all, for his portion. But human weakness falls below this; and, as the idolater worships the infinite and unseen under a visible symbol till it effaces the memory of what is signified, so men begin by loving institutions for God's sake, which come at last to stand with them in the place of God.

Such was the Rev. Dr. Calker. He was a man of powerful though narrow mind, of great energy and efficiency, and of that capability of abstract devotion which makes the soldier or the statesman. He was earnestly and sincerely devout, as he understood devotion. He began with loving the church for God's sake, and ended with loving her better than God. And, by the church, he meant the organization of the Presbyterian church in the United States of America. Her cause, in his eyes, was God's cause; her glory, God's glory; her success, the indispensable condition of the millennium; her defeat, the defeat of all that was good for the human race. His devotion to her was honest and unselfish.

Of course Dr. Calker estimated all interests by their influence on the Presbyterian church. He weighed every cause in the balance of her sanctuary. What promised extension and power to her, *that* he supported. What threatened defeat or impediment, *that* he was ready to sacrifice. He would, at any day, sacrifice himself and all his interests to that cause, and he felt equally willing to sacrifice others and their interests. The anti-slavery cause he regarded with a simple eye to this question. It was a disturbing force, weakening the harmony among brethren, threatening disruption and disunion. He regarded it, therefore, with distrust and aversion. He would read no facts on that side of the question. And when the discussions of zealous brethren would bring frightful and appalling statements into the general assembly, he was too busy in seeking what could be said to ward off their force, to allow them to have much influence on his own mind. Gradually he came to view the whole subject with dislike, as a pertinacious intruder in the path of the Presbyterian church. That the whole train of cars, laden with the interests of the world for all time, should be stopped by a ragged, manacled slave across the track, was to him an impertinence and absurdity. What was he, that the Presbyterian church should be divided and hin-

dered for him? So thought the exultant thousands who followed
Christ, once, when the blind beggar raised his importunate clamor,
and they bade him hold his peace. So thought not HE, who stopped
the tide of triumphant success, that he might call the neglected one
to himself, and lay his hands upon him.

Dr. Calker had from year to year opposed the agitation of the
slavery question in the general assembly of the Presbyterian church,
knowing well that it threatened disunion. When, in spite of all his
efforts, disunion came, he bent his energies to the task of reüniting;
and he was the most important character in the present caucus.

Of course a layman, and a young man also, would feel some natural hesitancy in joining at once in the conversation of those older
than himself. Clayton, therefore, sat at the hospitable breakfast-
table of Dr. Cushing rather as an auditor than as a speaker.

"Now, brother Cushing," said Dr. Calker, "the fact is, there
never was any need of this disruption. It has crippled the power of
the church, and given the enemy occasion to speak reproachfully.
Our divisions are playing right into the hands of the Methodists
and Baptists; and ground that we might hold, united, is going into
their hands every year."

"I know it," said Dr. Cushing, "and we Southern brethren
mourn over it, I assure you. The fact is, brother Calker, there's no
such doctrinal division, after all. Why, there are brethren among us
that are as new school as Dr. Draper, and we don't meddle with
them."

"Just so," replied Dr. Calker; "and we have true-blue old school
men among us."

"I think," said Dr. Packthread, "that, with suitable care, a document might be drawn up which will meet the views on both sides.
You see, we must get the extreme men on both sides to agree to
hold still. Why, now, I am called new school; but I wrote a set of
definitions once, which I showed to Dr. Pyke, who is as sharp as
anybody on the other side, and he said, 'He agreed with them entirely.' Those N—— H—— men are incautious."

"Yes," said Dr. Calker, "and it's just dividing the resources and
the influence of the church for nothing. Now, those discussions as
to the time when moral agency begins are, after all, of no great account in practical workings."

"Well," said Dr. Cushing, "it's, after all, nothing but the radical
tone of some of your abolition fanatics that stands in the way. These

slavery discussions in general assembly have been very disagreeable and painful to our people, particularly those of the Western brethren. They don't understand us, nor the delicacy of our position. They don't know that we need to be let alone in order to effect anything. Now, I am for trusting to the softening, meliorating influences of the Gospel. The kingdom of God cometh not with observation. I trust that, in his mysterious providence, the Lord will see fit, in his own good time, to remove this evil of slavery. Meanwhile, brethren ought to possess their souls in patience."

"Brother Cushing," said father Dickson, "since the assembly of eighteen hundred and eighteen, the number of slaves has increased in this country four-fold. New slave states have been added, and a great, regular system of breeding and trading organized, which is filling all our large cities with trading-houses. The ships of our ports go out as slavers, carrying loads of miserable creatures down to New Orleans; and there is a constant increase of this traffic through the country. This very summer I was at the death-bed of a poor girl, only seventeen or eighteen, who had been torn from all her friends and sent off with a coffle; and she died there in the wilderness. It does seem to me, brother Cushing, that this silent plan does not answer. We are not half as near to emancipation, apparently, as we were in eighteen hundred and eighteen."

"Has there ever been any attempt," said Clayton, "among the Christians of your denominations, to put a stop to this internal slave-trade?"

"Well," said Dr. Cushing, "I don't know that there has, any further than general preaching against injustice."

"Have you ever made any movement in the church to prevent the separation of families?" said Clayton.

"No, not exactly. We leave that thing to the conscience of individuals. The synods have always enjoined it on professors of religion to treat their servants according to the spirit of the Gospel."

"Has the church ever endeavored to influence the legislature to allow general education?" said Clayton.

"No; that subject is fraught with difficulties," said Dr. Cushing. "The fact is, if these rabid Northern abolitionists would let us alone, we might, perhaps, make a movement on some of these subjects. But they excite the minds of our people, and get them into such a state of inflammation, that we cannot do anything."

During all the time that father Dickson and Clayton had been speaking, Dr. Calker had been making minutes with a pencil on a small piece of paper, for future use. It was always disagreeable to him to hear of slave-coffles and the internal slave-trade; and, therefore, when anything was ever said on these topics, he would generally employ himself in some other way than listening. Father Dickson he had known of old as being remarkably pertinacious on those subjects; and, therefore, when he began to speak, he took the opportunity of jotting down a few ideas for a future exigency. He now looked up from his paper, and spoke:

"O, those fellows are without any reason—perfectly wild and crazy! They are monomaniacs! They cannot see but one subject anywhere. Now, there's father Ruskin, of Ohio—there's nothing can be done with that man! I have had him at my house hours and hours, talking to him, and laying it all down before him, and showing him what great interests he was compromising. But it didn't do a bit of good. He just harps on one eternal string. Now, it's all the pushing and driving of these fellows in the general assembly that made the division, in my opinion."

"We kept it off a good many years," said Dr. Packthread; "and it took all our ingenuity to do it, I assure you. Now, ever since eighteen hundred and thirty-five, these fellows have been pushing and crowding in every assembly; and we have stood faithfully in our lot, to keep the assembly from doing anything which could give offence to our Southern brethren. We have always been particular to put them forward in our public services, and to show them every imaginable deference. I think our brethren ought to consider how hard we have worked. We had to be instant in season and out of season, I can tell you. I think I may claim some little merit," continued the doctor, with a cautious smile spreading over his face; "if I have any talent, it is a capacity in the judicious use of language. Now, sometimes brethren will wrangle a whole day, till they all get tired and sick of a subject; and then just let a man who understands the use of terms step in, and sometimes, by omitting a single word, he will alter the whole face of an affair. I remember one year those fellows were driving us up to make some sort of declaration about slavery. And we really had to do it, because it wouldn't do to have the whole West split off; and there was a three days' fight, till finally we got the thing pared down to the lowest terms. We thought we would pass a resolution that slavery was a *moral evil*, if the Southern brethren like that better than the old way of calling it a sin, and we really were getting on quite harmoniously, when some of the Southern ultras took it up; and they said that moral evil meant the same as sin, and that would imply a censure on the brethren. Well, it got late, and some of the hottest ones were tired and had gone off; and I just quietly drew my pen across the word *moral*, and read the resolution, and it went unanimously. Most ministers, you see, are willing to call slavery an *evil*—the trouble lay in that word *moral*. Well, that capped the crater for that year. But, then, they were at it again the very next time they came together, for those fellows never sleep. Well, then we took a new turn. I told the brethren we had better get it on to the ground of the reserved rights of presbyteries and synods, and decline interfering. Well, then, that was going very well, but some of the brethren very injudiciously got up a resolution in the assembly recommending disciplinary measures for dancing. That was passed without much thought, because, you know, there's no great interest involved in dancing, and, of course, there's nobody to oppose such a resolution; but, then, it was very injudicious, under the circumstances; for the abolitionists made a handle of it immediately, and wanted to know why we couldn't as well recommend a discipline for slavery; because, you see, dancing isn't a sin, *per se,* any more than slavery is; and they haven't done blowing their trumpets over us to this day."

Here the company rose from breakfast, and, according to the good old devout custom, seated themselves for family worship. Two decent, well-dressed black women were called in, and also a negro man. At father Dickson's request, all united in singing the following hymn:

> "*Am I a soldier of the cross,*
> *A follower of the Lamb;*
> *And shall I fear to own his cause,*
> *Or blush to speak his name?*
> *Must I be carried to the skies*
> *On flowery beds of ease,*
> *While others fought to win the prize,*
> *And sailed through bloody seas?*
> *Sure I must fight if I would reign;*
> *Increase my courage, Lord!*
> *I'll bear the cross, endure the shame,*
> *Supported by thy word.*

The saints, in all this glorious war,
  Shall conquer, though they die;
They see the victory from afar,
  With faith's discerning eye.
When that illustrious day shall rise,
  And all thine armies shine
In robes of victory through the skies,
  The glory shall be thine."[4]

Anybody who had seen the fervor with which these brethren now united in singing these stanzas, might have supposed them a company of the primitive martyrs and confessors, who, having drawn the sword and thrown away the scabbard, were now ready for a millennial charge on the devil and all his works. None sung with more heartiness than Dr. Packthread, for his natural feelings were quick and easily excited; nor did he dream he was not a soldier of the cross, and that the species of skirmishes he had been describing were not all in accordance with the spirit of the hymn. Had you interrogated him, he would have shown you a syllogistic connection between the glory of God and the best good of the universe, and the course he had been pursuing. So that, if father Dickson had supposed the hymn would act as a gentle suggestion, he was very much mistaken. As to Dr. Calker, he joined, with enthusiasm, applying it all the while to the enemies of the Presbyterian church, in the same manner as Ignatius Loyola[5] might have sung it, applying it to Protestantism. Dr. Cushing considered the conflict described as wholly an internal one, and thus all joined alike in swelling the chorus:

"A soldier for Jesus, hallelujah!
  Love and serve the Lord."

Father Dickson read from the Bible as follows:
"Our rejoicing is this, the testimony of our consciences, that in simplicity and godly sincerity, not with fleshly wisdom, but by the grace of God, we have our conversation in the world."[6]

Father Dickson had many gentle and quiet ways, peculiar to himself, of suggesting his own views to his brethren. Therefore, having read these verses, he paused, and asked Dr. Packthread "if he did not think there was danger of departing from this spirit, and losing the simplicity of Christ, when we conduct Christian business on worldly principle."

Dr. Packthread cordially assented, and continued to the same purpose in a strain so edifying as entirely to exhaust the subject; and Dr. Calker, who was thinking of the business that was before them, giving an uneasy motion here, they immediately united in the devotional exercises, which were led with great fervor by Dr. Cushing.

CHAPTER XIX

The Result

AFTER THE DEVOTIONAL SERVICES were over, Dr. Calker proceeded immediately with the business that he had in his mind. "Now, brother Cushing," he said, "there never was any instrumentality raised up by Providence to bring in the latter day equal to the Presbyterian church in the United States of America. It is the great hope of the world; for here, in this country, we are trying the great experiment for all ages; and, undoubtedly, the Presbyterian church comes the nearest perfection of any form of organization possible to our frail humanity. It is the ark of the covenant for this nation, and for all nations. Missionary enterprises to foreign countries, tract societies, home missionary, seamen's friend societies, Bible societies, Sunday-school unions, all are embraced in its bosom; and it grows in a free country, planted by God's own right hand, with such laws and institutions as never were given to mortal man before. It is carrying us right on to the millennium; and all we want is *union.* United, we stand the most glorious, the most powerful institution in the world. Now, there was no need for you Southern brethren to be so restive as you were. We were doing all we could to keep down the fire, and keep things quiet, and you ought not to have bolted so. Since you have separated from us, what have we done? I suppose you thought we were going to blaze out in a regular abolition fury; but you see we haven't done it. We haven't done any more than when we were united. Just look at our minutes, and you'll see it. We have strong and determined abolitionists among us, and they are constantly urging and pushing. There have been great public excitements on the subject of slavery, and we have been plagued and teased to declare ourselves; but we haven't done it in a single instance—not one. You see that Ruskin and his clique have gone off from us, because we would hold still. It is true that now and then we had to let some anti-slavery man preach an opening sermon, or something of that sort; but, then, opening sermons are nothing; they don't commit anybody; they don't show the opinion of anybody but the speaker. In fact, they don't express any more than that declaration of eighteen hundred and eighteen, which stands unrepealed on *your* records, as well as on ours. Of course, we are all willing to say that slavery is an evil, 'entirely inconsistent with the spirit of the Gospel,' and all that, because that's on your own books; we only agree to say nothing about it, nowadays, in our public capacity, because what was said in eighteen hundred and eighteen is all-sufficient and prevents the odium and scandal of public controversy now. Now, for proof that what I have just said is true, look at the facts. We had three presbyteries in slaveholding states when we started, and now we have over twenty, with from fifteen to twenty thousand members. That must show you what our hearts are on this subject. And, have we not always been making overtures for reünion—really humbling ourselves to you, brethren? Now, I say you ought to take these facts into account; our slave-holding members and churches are left as perfectly undisturbed, to manage in their own way, as yours. To be sure, some of those Western men will fire off a remonstrance once a year, or something of that sort. Just let them do that; it keeps them easy and contented. And, so long as there is really no interfering in the way of discipline or control, what harm is done? You ought to bear some with the Northern brethren, unreasonable as they are; and we may well have a discussion every year, to let off the steam."

"For my part," said father Bonnie, "I want union, I'm sure. I'd tar and feather those Northern abolitionists, if I could get at them!"

"*Figuratively*, I suppose," said Dr. Packthread, with a gentle smile.

"Yes, figuratively and literally too," said father Bonnie, laughing. "Let them come down here, and see what they'll get! If they will set the country in a blaze, they ought to be the first ones to be warmed at the fire. For my part, brethren, I must say that you lose time and strength by your admissions, all of you. You don't hit the buck in the eye. I thank the Lord that I am delivered from the bondage of thinking slavery a sin, or an evil, in any sense. Our abolitionist brethren have done one good thing; they have driven us up to ex-amine the Scriptures, and there we find that slavery is not only per-mitted, but appointed, enjoined. It is a divine institution. If a

Northern abolitionist comes at me now, I shake the Bible at him, and say, 'Nay, but, O man, who art thou that repliest against God?' Hath not the potter power over the clay, to make one lump to honor, and another to dishonor?[1] I tell you brethren, it blazes from every page of the Scriptures. You'll never do anything till you get on to that ground. A man's conscience is always hanging on to his skirts; he goes on just like a bear with a trap on his legs—can't make any progress that way. You have got to get your feet on the rock of ages, I can tell you, and get the trap off your leg. There's nothing like the study of the Scriptures to clear a fellow's mind."

"Well, then," said Clayton, "would it not be well to repeal the laws which forbid the slaves to learn to read, and put the Scriptures into their hands? These laws are the cause of a great deal of misery and immorality among the slaves, and they furnish abolitionists with some of their strongest arguments."

"O," said father Bonnie, "that will never do, in the world! It will expose them to whole floods of abolition and incendiary documents, corrupt their minds, and make them discontented."

"Well," said Dr. Cushing, "I have read Dr. Carnes' book, and I must say that the scriptural argument lies, in my mind, on the other side."

"Hang Dr. Carnes' book!" said father Bonnie.

"Figuratively, I suppose," said Dr. Packthread.

"Why, Dr. Carnes' much learning has made him mad!" said father Bonnie. "I don't believe anything that can't be got out of a plain English Bible. When a fellow goes shuffling off in a Hebrew fog, in a Latin fog, in a Greek fog, I say, 'Ah, my boy, you are treed! you had better come down!' Why, is it not plain enough to any reader of the Bible, how the apostles talked to the slaves? They didn't fill their heads with stuff about the rights of man. Now, see here, just at a venture," he said, making a dive at a pocket-Bible that lay on the table,—"now, just let me read you, '*Masters, give unto your servants that which is just and equal.*' Sho! sho! that isn't the place I was thinking of. It's here, '*Servants, obey your masters!*' There's into them, you see! 'Obey your masters that are in the flesh.'[2] Now, these abolitionists won't even allow that we are masters!"

"Perhaps," said Clayton, quietly, "if the slaves could read, they'd pay more attention to the first passage that you favored us with."

"O, likely," said father Bonnie, "because, you see, their interests naturally would lead them to pervert Scripture. If it wasn't for that perverting influence of self-love, I, for my part, would be willing enough to put the Scriptures into their hands."

"I suppose," said Clayton, "there's no such danger in the case of us masters, is there?"

"I say," said father Bonnie, not noticing the interruption, "Cushing, you ought to read Fletcher's book. That book, sir, is a sweater, I can tell you; I sweat over it, I know; but it does up this Greek and Hebrew work thoroughly, I promise you. Though I can't read Greek or Hebrew, I see there's heaps of it there. Why, he takes you clear back to the creation of the world, and drags you through all the history and literature of the old botherers of all ages, and he comes down on the fathers like forty. There's Chrysostom and Tertullian,[3] and all the rest of those old cocks, and the old Greek philosophers, besides,—Plato, and Aristotle, and all the rest of them. If a fellow wants learning, there he'll get it. I declare, I'd rather cut my way through the Dismal Swamp in dog-days! But I was determined to be thorough; so I off coat, and went at it. And, there's no mistake about it, Cushing, you must get the book. You'll feel so much better, if you'll settle your mind on that point. I never allow myself to go trailing along with anything hanging by the gills. I am an out-and-outer. Walk up to the captain's office, and settle! That's what I say."

"We shall all have to do that, one of these days," said father Dickson, "and maybe we shall find it one thing to settle with the clerk, and another to settle with the captain!"

"Well, brother Dickson, you needn't look at me with any of your solemn faces! I'm settled, now."

"For my part," said Dr. Packthread, "I think, instead of condemning slavery in the abstract, we ought to direct our attention to its abuses."

"And what do you consider its abuses?" said Clayton.

"Why, the separation of families, for instance," said Dr. Packthread, "and the forbidding of education."

"You think, then," said Clayton, "that the slave ought to have a legal right to his family?"

"Yes."

"Of course, he ought to have the legal means of maintaining it?"

"Yes."

"Then, of course, he ought to be able to enter suit when this right is violated, and to bear testimony in a court of justice?"

"Yes."

"And do you think that the master ought to give him what is just and equal, in the way of wages?"

"Certainly, in one shape or another," said Dr. Packthread.

"And ought the slave to have the means of enforcing this right?"

"Certainly."

"Then the slave ought to be able to hold property?"

"Yes."

"And he should have the legal right to secure education, if he desires it?"

"Yes."

"Well," said Clayton, "when the slave has a legal existence and legal rights, can hold property and defend it, acquire education and protect his family relations, he ceases to be a slave; for, slavery consists in the fact of legal incapacity for any of these things. It consists in making a man a dead, inert substance in the hands of another, holding men *pro nullis, pro mortuis*.[4] What you call reforming abuses, is abolishing slavery. It is in this very way that I wish to seek its abolition, and I desire the aid of the church and ministry in doing it. Now, Dr. Packthread, what efforts has the church as yet made to reform these abuses of slavery?"

There was a silence of some minutes. At last Dr. Cushing replied,

"There has been a good deal of effort made in oral religious instruction."

"O, yes," said father Bonnie, "our people have been at it with great zeal in our part of the country. I have a class, myself, that I have been instructing in the Assembly's Catechism, in the oral way; and the synods have taken it up, and they are preaching the Gospel to them, and writing catechisms for them."

"But," said Clayton, "would it not be best to give them a legal ability to obey the Gospel? Is there any use in teaching the sanctity of marriage, unless you obtain for husbands and wives the legal right to live faithful to each other? It seems to me only cruelty to awaken conscience on that subject, without giving the protection and assistance of law."

"What he says is very true," said Dr. Cushing, with emphasis. "We ministers are called to feel the necessity of that with regard to

our slave church-members. You see, we are obliged to preach unlimited obedience to masters; and yet,—why, it was only last week,
a very excellent pious mulatto woman in my church came to me to
know what she should do. Her master was determined she should
live with him as a mistress; yet she has a husband on the place. How
am I to advise her? The man is a very influential man, and capable
of making a good deal of commotion; besides which, she will gain
nothing by resistance, but to be sold away to some other master,
who will do worse. Now, this is a very trying case to a minister. I'm
sure, if anything could be done, I'd be glad; but the fact is, the moment a person begins to move in the least to reform those abuses, he
is called an abolitionist, and the whole community is down on him
at once. That's the state these northern fanatics have got us into."

"O, yes," said Dr. Baskum, a leading minister, who had recently
come in. "Besides, a man can't do everything! We've got as much as
we can stagger under on our shoulders, now. We've got the building up of the church to attend to. That's the great instrumentality
which at last will set everything straight. We must do as the apostles
did,—confine ourselves to preaching the Gospel, and the Gospel
will bring everything else in its train. The world can't be made over
in a day. We must do one thing at a time. We can't afford, just at
present, to tackle in with all our other difficulties the odium and
misrepresentation of such a movement. The minute we begin to do
anything which looks like restraining the rights of masters, the cry
of church and state and abolition will be raised, and we shall be
swamped!"

"But," said father Dickson, "isn't it the right way first to find out
our duty and do it, and then leave the result with God? Ought we
to take counsel of flesh and blood in matters like these?"

"Of course not," said Dr. Packthread. "But there is a wise way
and an unwise way of doing things. We are to consider the times,
and only undertake such works as the movements of Divine Providence seem to indicate. I don't wish to judge for brethren. A time
may come when it will be their duty to show themselves openly on
this subject; but, in order to obtain a foothold for the influences of
the Gospel to work on, it may be necessary to bear and forbear
with many evils. Under the present state of things, I hope many of
the slaves are becoming hopefully pious. Brethren seem to feel that
education will be attended with dangers. Probably it might. It
would seem desirable to secure the family relations of the slaves, if

it could be done without too much sacrifice of more important things. After all, the kingdom of our Lord Jesus Christ is not of this world. The apostles entered no public protest against the abuses of slavery, that we read of."

"It strikes me," said Clayton, "that there is a difference between our position under a republican government,—in which we vote for our legislators, and, in fact, make the laws ourselves, and have the admitted right to seek their repeal,—and that of the apostles, who were themselves slaves, and could do nothing about the laws. We make our own laws, and every one of us is responsible for any unjust law which we do not do our best to alter. We have the right to agitate, write, print, and speak, and bring up the public mind to the point of reform; and, therefore, we are responsible if unjust laws are not repealed."

"Well," said father Dickson, "God forgive me that I have been so remiss in times past! Henceforth, whatever others may do, I will not confer with flesh and blood; but I will go forth and declare the word of the Lord plainly to this people, and show unto the house of Judah[5] their transgressions. And now I have one thing to say to our dear Northern brethren. I mourn over the undecided course which they take. Brethren in slave states are beset with many temptations. The whole course of public opinion is against them. They need that their Northern brethren should stand firm, and hold up their hands. Alas! how different has been their course! Their apologies for this mighty sin have weakened us more than all things put together. Public opinion is going back. The church is becoming corrupted. Ministers are drawn into connivance with deadly sin. Children and youth are being ruined by habits of early tyranny. Our land is full of slave-prisons; and the poor trader—no man careth for his soul! Our poor whites are given up to ignorance and licentiousness; and our ministers, like our brother Bonnie, here, begin to defend this evil from the Bible. Brother Calker, here, talks of the Presbyterian church. Alas! in her skirts is found the blood of poor innocents, and she is willing, for the sake of union, to destroy them for whom Christ died. Brethren, you know not what you do. You enjoy the blessing of living in a land uncursed by any such evils. Your churches, your schools, and all your industrial institutions, are going forward, while ours are going backward; and you do not feel it, because you do not live among us. But take care! One part of the country cannot become demoralized, without, at last, affecting the other. The sin you cherish and strengthen by your indifference, may at last come back in judgments that may visit even you. I pray God to avert it! But, as God is just, I tremble for you and for us! Well, good-by, brethren; I must be on my way. You will not listen to me, and my soul cannot come into your counsels."

And father Dickson rose to depart.

"O, come, come, now, brother, don't take it so seriously!" said Dr. Cushing. "Stay, at least, and spend the day with us, and let us have a little Christian talk."

"I must go," said father Dickson. "I have an appointment to preach, which I must keep, for this evening, and so I must bid you farewell. I hoped to do something by coming here; but I see that it is all in vain. Farewell, brethren; I shall pray for you."

"Well, father Dickson, I should like to talk more with you on this subject," said Dr. Cushing. "Do come again. It is very difficult to see the path of duty in these matters."

Poor Dr. Cushing was one of those who are destined, like stationary ships, forever to float up and down in one spot, only useful in marking the ebb and flood of the tide. Affection, generosity, devotion, he had—everything but the power to move on.

Clayton, who had seen at once that nothing was to be done or gained, rose, and said that his business was also pressing, and that he would accompany father Dickson on his way.

"What a good fellow Dickson is!" said Cushing, after he returned to the room.

"He exhibits a very excellent spirit," said Dr. Packthread.

"O, Dickson would do well enough," said Dr. Calker, "if he wasn't a monomaniac. That's what's the matter with him! But when he gets to going on this subject, I never hear what he says. I know it's no use to reason with him—entirely time lost. I have heard all these things over and over again."

"But I wish," said Dr. Cushing, "something could be done."

"Well, who doesn't?" said Dr. Calker. "We all wish something could be done; but, if it can't, it can't; there's the end of it. So now let us proceed, and look into business a little more particularly."

"After all," said Dr. Packthread, "you old school brethren have greatly the advantage of us. Although you have a few poor good souls, like this Dickson, they are in so insignificant a minority that they can do nothing—can't even get into the general assembly, or send in a remonstrance, or petition, or anything else; so that you are never plagued as we are. We cannot even choose a moderator from the slaveholding states, for fear of an explosion; but you can have slaveholding moderators, or anything else that will promote harmony and union."

CHAPTER XX

The Slave's Argument

ON HIS RETURN HOME, Clayton took from the post-office a letter, which we will give to our readers.

"MR. CLAYTON: I am now an outcast. I cannot show my face in the world, I cannot go abroad by daylight; for no crime, as I can see, except resisting oppression. Mr. Clayton, if it were proper for your fathers to fight and shed blood for the oppression that came upon them, why isn't it right for us? They had not half the provocation that we have. Their wives and families were never touched. They were not bought, and sold, and traded, like cattle in the market, as we are. In fact, when I was reading that history, I could hardly understand what provocation they did have. They had everything easy and comfortable about them. They were able to support their families, even in luxury. And yet they were willing to plunge into war, and shed blood. I have studied the Declaration of Independence. The things mentioned there were bad and uncomfortable, to be sure; but, after all, look at the laws which are put over *us!* Now, if they had forbidden them to teach their children to read,—if they had divided them all out among masters, and declared them incapable of holding property as the mule before the plough,—there would have been some sense in that revolution.

"Well, how was it with our people in South Carolina? Denmark Vesey was a *man!* His history is just what George Washington's would have been, if you had failed. What set him in his course? The Bible and your Declaration of Independence. What does your Declaration say? 'We hold these truths to be self-evident, that *all men are created equal;* that they are endowed by their Creator with certain *inalienable* rights: that among these are life, liberty, and the pursuit of happiness. That *to secure these rights* governments are instituted among men. That *whenever any form of government becomes destructive of any of these ends, it is the right of the people to*

alter or to abolish it.' Now, what do you make of that? This is read
to us, every Fourth of July. It was read to Denmark Vesey and Peter Poyes, and all those other brave, good men, who dared to follow your example and your precepts. Well, they failed, and your
people hung them. And they said they couldn't conceive what
motive could have induced them to make the effort. They had food
enough, and clothes enough, and were kept very comfortable. Well,
had not your people clothes enough, and food enough? and
wouldn't you still have had enough, even if you had remained a
province of England to this day,—much better living, much better
clothes, and much better laws, than we have to-day? I heard your
father's interpretation of the law; I heard Mr. Jekyl's; and yet, when
men rise up against such laws, you wonder what in the world could
have induced them! That's perfectly astonishing!

"But, of all the injuries and insults that are heaped upon us, there
is nothing to me so perfectly maddening as the assumption of your
religious men, who maintain and defend this enormous injustice by
the Bible. We have all the right to rise against them that they had to
rise against England. They tell us the Bible says, 'Servants, obey
your masters.' Well, the Bible says, also, 'The powers that be are ordained of God, and whoso resisteth the power, resisteth the ordinance of God.'[1] If it was right for them to resist the ordinance of
God, it is right for us. If the Bible does justify slavery, why don't
they teach the slave to read it? And what's the reason that two of
the greatest insurrections came from men who read scarcely anything else but the Bible? No, the fact is, they don't believe this
themselves. If they did, they would try the experiment fairly of giving the Bible to their slaves. I can assure you the Bible looks as different to a slave from what it does to a master, as everything else in
the world does.

"Now, Mr. Clayton, you understand that when I say *you*, along
here, I do not mean you personally, but the generality of the community of which you are one. I want you to think these things over,
and, whatever my future course may be, remember my excuse for it
is the same as that on which your government is built.

"I am very grateful to you for all your kindness. Perhaps the
time may come when I shall be able to show my gratitude. Meanwhile, I must ask one favor of you, which I think you will grant for
the sake of that angel who is gone. I have a sister, who, as well as
myself, is the child of Tom Gordon's father. She was beautiful and

good, and her owner, who had a large estate in Mississippi, took her to Ohio, emancipated and married her. She has two children by him, a son and a daughter. He died, and left his estate to her and her children. Tom Gordon is the heir-at-law. He has sued for the property, and obtained it. The act of emancipation has been declared null and void, and my sister and her children are in the hands of that man, with all that absolute power; and they have no appeal from him for any evil whatever. She has escaped his hands, so she wrote me once; but I have heard a report that he has taken her again. The pious Mr. Jekyl will know all about it. Now, may I ask you to go to him, and make inquiries, and let me know? A letter sent to Mr. James Twitchel, at the post-office near Canema, where our letters used to be taken, will get to me. By doing this favor, you will secure my eternal gratitude. HARRY GORDON."

Clayton read this letter with some surprise, and a good deal of attention. It was written on very coarse paper, such as is commonly sold at the low shops. Where Harry was, and how concealed, was to him only a matter of conjecture. But the call to render him any assistance was a sacred one, and he determined on a horseback excursion to E., the town where Mr. Jekyl resided.

He found that gentleman very busy in looking over and arranging papers in relation to that large property which had just come into Tom Gordon's hands. He began by stating that the former owner of the servants at Canema had requested him, on her deathbed, to take an interest in her servants. He had therefore called to ascertain if anything had been heard from Harry.

"Not yet," said Mr. Jekyl, pulling up his shirt-collar. "Our plantations in this vicinity are very unfortunate in their proximity to the swamp. It's a great expense of time and money. Why, sir, it's inconceivable, the amount of property that's lost in that swamp! I have heard it estimated at something like three millions of dollars! We follow them up with laws, you see. They are outlawed regularly, after a certain time, and then the hunters go in and chase them down; sometimes kill two or three a day, or something like that. But, on the whole, they don't effect much."

"Well," said Clayton, who felt no disposition to enter into any discussion with Mr. Jekyl, "so you think he is there?"

"Yes, I have no doubt of it. The fact is, there's a fellow that's been seen lurking about this swamp, off and on, for years and years.

Sometimes he isn't to be seen for months; and then again he is seen or heard of, but never so that anybody can get hold of him. I have no doubt the niggers on the plantation know him; but, then, you can never get anything out of them. O, they are deep! They are a dreadfully corrupt set!"

"Mr. Gordon has, I think, a sister of Harry's, who came in with this new estate," said Mr. Clayton.

"Yes, yes," said Mr. Jekyl. "She has given us a good deal of trouble, too. She got away, and went off to Cincinnati, and I had to go up and hunt her out. It was really a great deal of trouble and expense. If I hadn't been assisted by the politeness and kindness of the marshal and brother officers, it would have been very bad. There is a good deal of religious society, too, in Cincinnati; and so, while I was waiting, I attended anniversary meetings."

"Then you did succeed," said Clayton. "I came to see whether Mr. Gordon would listen to a proposition for selling her."

"O, he has sold her!" said Mr. Jekyl. "She is at Alexandria,[2] now, in Beaton & Burns' establishment."

"And her children, too?"

"Yes, the lot. I claim some little merit for that, myself. Tom is a fellow of rather strong passions, and he was terribly angry for the trouble she had made. I don't know what he would have done to her, if I hadn't talked to him. But I showed him some debts that couldn't be put off any longer without too much of a sacrifice; and, on the whole, I persuaded him to let her be sold. I have tried to exert a good influence over him, in a quiet way," said Mr. Jekyl. "Now, if you want to get the woman, like enough she may not be sold, as yet."

Clayton, having thus ascertained the points which he wished to know, proceeded immediately to Alexandria. When he was there, he found a considerable excitement.

"A slave-woman," it was said, "who was to have been sent off in a coffle the next day, had murdered her two children."[3]

The moment that Clayton heard the news, he felt an instinctive certainty that this woman was Cora Gordon. He went to the magistrate's court, where the investigation was being held, and found it surrounded by a crowd so dense that it was with difficulty he forced his way in. At the bar he saw seated a woman dressed in black, whose face, haggard and wan, showed yet traces of former beauty. The splendid dark eyes had a peculiar and fierce expression. The thin lines of the face were settled into an immovable fixedness of calm determination. There was even an air of grave, solemn triumph on her countenance. She appeared to regard the formalities of the court with the utmost indifference. At last she spoke, in a clear, thrilling, distinct voice:

"If gentlemen will allow me to speak, I'll save them the trouble of that examination of witnesses. It's going a long way round to find out a very little thing."

There was an immediate movement of curiosity in the whole throng, and the officer said,

"You are permitted to speak."

She rose deliberately, untied her bonnet-strings, looked round the whole court, with a peculiar but calm expression of mingled triumph and power.

"You want to know," she said, "who killed those children! Well, I will tell you;" and again her eyes travelled round the house, with that same strong, defiant expression; "I killed them!"

There was a pause, and a general movement through the house.

"Yes," she said, again, "I killed them! And, O, how glad I am that I have done it! Do you want to know what I killed them for? Because I loved them!—loved them so well that I was willing to give up my soul to save theirs! I have heard some persons say that I was in a frenzy, excited, and didn't know what I was doing. They are mistaken. I was not in a frenzy; I was not excited; and I did know what I was doing! and I bless God that it is done! I was born the slave of my own father. Your old proud Virginia blood is in my veins, as it is in half of those you whip and sell. I was the lawful wife of a man of honor, who did what he could to evade your cruel laws, and set me free. My children were born to liberty; they were brought up to liberty, till my father's son entered a suit for us, and made us *slaves*. Judge and jury helped him—all your laws and your officers helped him—to take away the rights of the widow and the fatherless! The judge said that my son, being a slave, could no more hold property than the mule before his plough; and we were delivered into Tom Gordon's hands. I shall not say what he is. It is not fit to be said. God will show at the judgment-day. But I escaped, with my children, to Cincinnati. He followed me there, and the laws of your country gave me back to him. To-morrow I was to have gone in a coffle and leave these children—my son a slave for life—my daughter—" She looked round the court-room with an expression which said more than words could have spoken. "So I heard them say their prayers and sing their hymns, and then, while they were asleep and didn't know it, I sent them to lie down in green pastures with the Lord. They say this is a dreadful sin. It may be so. I am willing to lose my soul to have *theirs saved*. I have no more to hope or fear. It's all nothing, now, where I go or what becomes of me. But, at any rate, they are safe. And, now, if any of you mothers, in my place, wouldn't have done the same, you either don't know what slavery is, or you don't love your children as I have loved mine. This is all."

She sat down, folded her arms, fixed her eyes on the floor, and seemed like a person entirely indifferent to the further opinions and proceedings of the court.

She was remanded to jail for trial. Clayton determined, in his own mind, to do what he could for her. Her own declaration seemed to make the form of a trial unnecessary. He resolved, however, to do what he could to enlist for her the sympathy of some friends of his in the city.

The next day he called, with a clergyman, and requested permission to see her. When they entered her cell, she rose to receive them with the most perfect composure, as if they had called upon her in a drawing-room. Clayton introduced his companion as the Rev. Mr. Denton. There was an excited flash in her eyes, but she said, calmly,

"Have the gentlemen business with me?"

"We called," said the clergyman, "to see if we could render you any assistance."

"No, sir, you cannot!" was the prompt reply.

"My dear friend," said the clergyman, in a very kind tone, "I wish it were in my power to administer to you the consolations of the Gospel."

"I have nothing to do," she answered, firmly, "with ministers who pretend to preach the Gospel, and support oppression and robbery! Your hands are defiled with blood!—so don't come to me! I am a prisoner, here, and cannot resist. But, when I tell you that I prefer to be left alone, perhaps it may have some effect, even if I am a slave!"

Clayton took out Harry's letter, handed it to her, and said:

"After you have read this, you will, perhaps, receive me, if I should call again to-morrow, at this hour."

The next day, when Clayton called, he was conducted by the jailer to the door of the cell.

"There is a lady with her now, reading to her."

"Then I ought not to interrupt her," said Clayton, hesitating.

"O, I suspect it would make no odds," said the jailer.

Clayton laid his hand on his to stop him. The sound that came indistinctly through the door was the voice of prayer. Some woman was interceding, in the presence of eternal pity, for an oppressed and broken-hearted sister. After a few moments the door was partly opened, and he heard a sweet voice, saying:

"Let me come to you every day, may I? I know what it is to suffer."

A smothered sob was the only answer; and then followed words, imperfectly distinguished, which seemed to be those of consolation. In a moment the door was opened, and Clayton found himself suddenly face to face with a lady in deep mourning. She was tall, and largely proportioned; the outlines of her face strong, yet beautiful, and now wearing the expression which comes from communion with the highest and serenest nature. Both were embarrassed, and made a momentary pause. In the start she dropped one of her gloves. Clayton picked it up, handed it to her, bowed, and she passed on. By some singular association, this stranger, with a serious, radiant face, suggested to him the sparkling, glittering beauty of Nina; and it seemed, for a moment, as if Nina was fluttering by him in the air, and passing away after her. When he examined the emotion more minutely afterwards, he thought, perhaps, it might have been suggested by the perception, as he lifted the glove, of a peculiar and delicate perfume, which Nina was fond of using. So strange and shadowy are the influences which touch the dark, electric chain of our existence.

When Clayton went into the cell, he found its inmate in a softened mood. There were traces of tears on her cheek, and an open Bible on the bed; but her appearance was calm and self-possessed, as usual. She said:

"Excuse my rudeness, Mr. Clayton, at your last visit. We cannot always command ourselves to do exactly what we should. I thank you very much for your kindness to us. There are many who are kindly disposed towards us; but it's very little that they can do."

"Can I be of any assistance in securing counsel for you?" said Clayton.

"I don't need any counsel. I don't wish any," said she. "I shall make no effort. Let the law take its course. If you ever should see Harry, give my love to him—that's all! And, if you can help him, pray do! If you have time, influence, or money to spare, and can get him to any country where he will have the common rights of a human being, pray do, and the blessing of the poor will come on you! That's all I have to ask."

Clayton rose to depart. He had fulfilled the object of his mission. He had gained all the information, and more than all, that he wished. He queried with himself whether it were best to write to Harry at all. The facts that he had to relate were such as were calculated to kindle to a fiercer flame the excitement which was now consuming him. He trembled, when he thought of it, lest that excitement should blaze out in forms which should array against him, with still more force, that society with which he was already at war. Thinking, however, that Harry, perhaps, might obtain the information in some less guarded form, he sat down and wrote him the following letter:

"I have received your letter. I need not say that I am sorry for all that has taken place—sorry for your sake, and for the sake of one very dear both to me and to you. Harry, I freely admit that you live in a state of society which exercises a great injustice. I admit your right, and that of all men, to life, liberty, and the pursuit of happiness. I admit the right of an oppressed people to change their form of government, *if they can.* I admit that your people suffer under greater oppression than ever our fathers suffered. And, if I believed that they were capable of obtaining and supporting a government, I should believe in their right to take the same means to gain it. But I do not, at present; and I think, if you will reflect on the subject, you will agree with me. I do not think that, should they make an effort, they would succeed. They would only embitter the white race against them, and destroy that sympathy which many are beginning to feel for their oppressed condition. I know it seems a very unfeeling thing for a man who is at ease to tell one, who is oppressed and suffering, to be patient; and yet I must even say it. It is my place, and our place, to seek repeal of the unjust laws which oppress you. I see no reason why the relation of master and servants may not be continued through our states, and the servants yet be free men. I am satisfied that it would be for the best interests of master as well as slave. If this is the truth, time will make it apparent, and the change will come. With regard to you, the best counsel I can give is, that you try to escape to some of the northern states; and I will furnish you with means to begin life there under better auspices. I am very sorry that I have to tell you something very painful about your sister. She was sold to a trading-house in Alexandria, and, in desperation, has killed both her children! For this she is now in prison, awaiting her trial! I have been to see her, and offered every assistance in my power. She declines all. She does not wish to live, and has already avowed the fact; making no defence, and wishing none to be made for her. Another of the bitter fruits of this most unrighteous system! She desired her love and kind wishes to you. Whatever more is to be known, I will tell you at some future time.

"After all that I have said to you in this letter, I cannot help feeling, for myself, how hard, and cold, and insufficient, it must seem to you! If I had such a sister as yours, and her life had been so wrecked, I feel that I might not have patience to consider any of these things; and I am afraid you will not. Yet I feel this injustice to my heart. I feel it like a personal affliction; and, God helping me, I will make it the object of my life to remedy it! Your sister's trial will not take place for some time; and she has friends who do all that can be done for her."

Clayton returned to his father's house, and related the result of his first experiment with the clergy.

"Well, now," said Mrs. Clayton, "I must confess I was not prepared for this."

"I was," said Judge Clayton. "It's precisely what I expected. You have tried the Presbyterians, with whom our family are connected; and now you may go successively to the Episcopalians, the Methodists, the Baptists, and you will hear the same story from them all. About half of them defend the thing from the Bible, in the most unblushing, disgusting manner. The other half acknowledge and lament it as an evil; but they are cowed and timid, and can do nothing."

"Well," said Clayton, "the greatest evidence to my mind of the inspiration of the Scriptures is, that they are yet afloat, when every new absurdity has been successively tacked to them."

"But," said Mrs. Clayton, "are there no people that are faithful?"

"None in this matter that I know of," said Judge Clayton, "except the Covenanters and the Quakers among us, and the Free-will Baptists[4] and a few others at the North. And their number and influence is so small, that there can be no great calculation made on them for assistance. Of individuals, there are not a few who earnestly desire to do something; but they are mostly without faith or hope, like me. And, from the communities—from the great organizations in society—no help whatever is to be expected."

CHAPTER XXI

The Desert

THERE IS NO STUDY in human nature more interesting than the aspects of the same subject seen in the points of view of different characters. One might almost imagine that there were no such thing as absolute truth, since a change of situation or temperament is capable of changing the whole force of an argument. We have been accustomed, even those of us who feel most, to look on the arguments for and against the system of slavery with the eyes of those who are at ease. We do not even know how fair is freedom, for we were always free. We shall never have all the materials for absolute truth on this subject, till we take into account, with our own views and reasonings, the views and reasonings of those who have bowed down to the yoke, and felt the iron enter into their souls. We all console ourselves too easily for the sorrows of others. We talk and reason coolly of that which, did we feel it ourselves, would take away all power of composure and self-control. We have seen how the masters feel and reason; how good men feel and reason, whose public opinion and Christian fellowship support the master, and give him confidence in his position. We must add, also, to our estimate, the feelings and reasonings of the slave; and, therefore, the reader must follow us again to the fastness in the Dismal Swamp.

It is a calm, still, Indian-summer afternoon. The whole air is flooded with a golden haze, in which the tree-tops move dreamily to and fro, as if in a whispering revery. The wild climbing grape-vines, which hang in thousand-fold festoons round the enclosure, are purpling with grapes. The little settlement now has among its inmates Old Tiff and his children, and Harry and his wife. The children and Tiff had been received in the house of the widow whose husband had fallen a victim to the hunters, as we mentioned in one of our former chapters. All had united in building for Harry and Lisette a cabin contiguous to the other.

Old Tiff, with his habitual industry, might now be seen hoeing

445

in the sweet-potato patch, which belonged to the common settlement. The children were roaming up and down, looking after autumn flowers and grapes.

Dred, who had been out all the night before, was now lying on the ground on the shady side of the clearing, with an old, much-worn, much-thumbed copy of the Bible by his side. It was the Bible of Denmark Vesey, and in many a secret meeting its wild, inspiring poetry had sounded like a trumpet in his youthful ear.

He lay with his elbow resting on the ground, his hands supporting his massive head, and his large, gloomy, dark eyes fixed in revery on the moving tree-tops as they waved in the golden blue. Now his eye followed sailing islands of white cloud, drifting to and fro above them. There were elements in him which might, under other circumstances, have made him a poet.

His frame, capacious and energetic as it was, had yet that keenness of excitability which places the soul en rapport with all the great forces of nature. The only book which he had been much in the habit of reading—the book, in fact, which had been the nurse and forming power of his soul—was the Bible, distinguished above all other literature for its intense sympathy with nature. Dred, indeed, resembled in organization and tone of mind some of those men of old who were dwellers in the wilderness, and drew their inspirations from the desert.

It is remarkable that, in all ages, communities and individuals who have suffered under oppression have always fled for refuge to the Old Testament, and to the book of Revelation in the New. Even if not definitely understood, these magnificent compositions have a wild, inspiring power, like a wordless yet impassioned symphony played by a sublime orchestra, in which deep and awful sub-bass instruments mingle with those of ethereal softness, and wild minors twine and interlace with marches of battles and bursts of victorious harmony.

They are much mistaken who say that nothing is efficient as a motive that is not definitely understood. Who ever thought of understanding the mingled wail and roar of the Marseillaise?[1] Just this kind of indefinite stimulating power has the Bible to the souls of the oppressed. There is also a disposition, which has manifested itself since the primitive times, by which the human soul, bowed down beneath the weight of mighty oppressions, and despairing, in its own weakness, seizes with avidity the intimations of a coming judgment, in which the Son of Man, appearing in his glory, and all his holy angels with him, shall right earth's mighty wrongs.

In Dred's mind this thought had acquired an absolute ascendency. All things in nature and in revelation he interpreted by this key.

During the prevalence of the cholera, he had been pervaded by a wild and solemn excitement. To him it was the opening of a seal— the sounding of the trumpet of the first angel. And other woes were yet to come.

He was not a man of personal malignity to any human being. When he contemplated schemes of insurrection and bloodshed, he contemplated them with the calm, immovable firmness of one who felt himself an instrument of doom in a mightier hand. In fact, although seldom called into exercise by the incidents of his wild and solitary life, there was in him a vein of that gentleness which softens the heart towards children and the inferior animals. The amusement of his vacant hours was sometimes to exercise his peculiar gifts over the animal creation, by drawing towards him the birds and squirrels from the coverts of the forest, and giving them food. Indeed, he commonly carried corn in the hunting-dress which he wore, to use for this purpose. Just at this moment, as he lay absorbed in revery, he heard Teddy, who was near him, calling to his sister.

"O, Fanny, do come and see this squirrel, he is so pretty!"

Fanny came running, eagerly. "Where is he?" she said.

"O, he is gone; he just went behind that tree."

The children, in their eagerness, had not perceived how near they were to Dred. He had turned his face towards them, and was looking at them with a pleased expression, approaching to a smile.

"Do you want to see him?" he said. "Stop a few minutes."

He rose and scattered a train of corn between him and the thicket, and, sitting down on the ground, began making a low sound, resembling the call of the squirrel to its young. In a few moments Teddy and Fanny were in a tremor of eager excitement, as a pair of little bright eyes appeared among the leaves, and gradually their owner, a brisk little squirrel, came out and began rapidly filling its chops with the corn. Dred still continued, with his eyes fixed on the animal, to make the same noise. Very soon two others were seen following their comrade. The children laughed when they saw the headmost squirrel walk into Dred's hand, which he had laid upon the ground, the others soon following his example. Dred took them up, and, softly stroking them, they seemed to become entirely amenable to his will; and, to amuse the children, he let them go into his hunting-pouch to eat the corn that was there. After this, they seemed to make a rambling expedition over his whole person, investigating his pockets, hiding themselves in the bosom of his shirt, and seeming apparently perfectly fearless, and at home.

Fanny reached out her hand, timidly. "Won't they come to me?" she said.

"No, daughter," said Dred, with a smile, "they don't know you. In the new earth the enmity will be taken away, and then they'll come."

"I wonder what he means by the new earth!" said Fanny.

Dred seemed to feel a kind of pleasure in the admiration of the children, to which, perhaps, no one is wholly insensible. He proceeded, therefore, to show them some other of his accomplishments. The wood was resounding with the afternoon song of birds, and Dred suddenly began answering one of the songsters with an exact imitation of his note. The bird evidently heard it, and answered back with still more spirit; and thus an animated conversation was kept up for some time.

"You see," he said, "that I understand the speech of birds. After the great judgment, the elect shall talk with the birds and the beasts in the new earth. Every kind of bird has a different language, in which they show why men should magnify the Lord, and turn from their wickedness. But the sinners cannot hear it, because their ear is waxed gross."

"I didn't know," said Fanny, hesitatingly, "as that was so. How did you find it out?"

"The Spirit of the Lord revealed it unto me, child."

"What is the Spirit?" said Fanny, who felt more encouraged, as she saw Dred stroking a squirrel.

"It's the Spirit that spoke in the old prophets," he said.

"Did it tell you what the birds say?"

"I am not perfected in holiness yet, and cannot receive it. But the birds fly up near the heavens, wherefore they learn droppings of the speech of angels. I never kill the birds, because the Lord hath set them between us and the angels for a sign."

"What else did the Spirit tell you?" said Teddy.

"He showed me that there was a language in the leaves," said Dred. "For I rose and looked, and, behold, there were signs drawn on the leaves, and forms of every living thing, with strange words, which the wicked understand not, but the elect shall read them. And, behold, the signs are in blood, which is the blood of the Lamb, that descendeth like dew from heaven."

Fanny looked puzzled. "Who are the elect?" she said.

"They?" said Dred. "They are the hundred and forty and four thousand, that follow the Lamb whithersoever he goeth. And the angels have charge, saying, 'Hurt not the earth till these are sealed in their forehead.' "[2]

Fanny instinctively put her hand to her forehead. "Do you think they'll seal me?" she said.

"Yes," said Dred; "such as you are of the kingdom."

"Did the Spirit tell you that?" said Fanny, who felt some considerable anxiety.

"Yea, the Spirit hath shown me many such things," said Dred. "It hath also revealed to me the knowledge of the elements, the revolutions of the planets, the operations of the tide, and changes of the seasons."

Fanny looked doubtfully, and, taking up her basket of wild grapes, slowly moved off, thinking that she would ask Tiff about it.

At this moment there was a rustling in the branches of the oaktree which overhung a part of the clearing near where Dred was lying, and Harry soon dropped from the branches on to the ground. Dred started up to receive him.

"How is it?" said he. "Will they come?"

"Yes; by midnight to-night they will be here. See here," he added, taking a letter from his pocket, "what I have received."

It was the letter which Clayton had written to Harry. It was remarkable, as Dred received it, how the wandering mystical expression of his face immediately gave place to one of shrewd and practical earnestness. He sat down on the ground, laid it on his knee, and followed the lines with his finger. Some passages he seemed to read over two or three times with the greatest attention, and he would pause, after reading them, and sat with his eyes fixed gloomily on the ground. The last part seemed to agitate him strongly. He gave a sort of suppressed groan.

"Harry," he said, turning to him, at last, "behold the day shall come when the Lord shall take out of our hand the cup of trembling, and put it into the hand of those that oppress us. Our soul is exceedingly filled now with the scorning of them that are at ease, and with the contempt of the proud. The prophets prophesy falsely, the rulers bear rule by their means, and the people love to have it so. But what will it be in the end thereof? Their own wickedness shall reprove them, and their backsliding shall correct them. Listen to me, Harry," he said, taking up his Bible, "and see what the Lord saith unto thee. 'Thus saith the Lord my God, Feed the flock of the slaughter; whose possessors slay them, and hold themselves not guilty, and they that sell them say, blessed be the Lord, for I am rich. And their own shepherds pity them not. For I will no more pity the inhabitants of the land, saith the Lord. But, lo, I will deliver the men, every one into his neighbor's hand, and into the hand of his king. And they shall smite the land, and out of their hand I will not deliver them. And I will feed the flock of slaughter, even you, O ye poor of the flock. And I took unto me two staves: the one I called beauty, and the other I called bands. And I fed the flock. And I took my staff, even beauty, and cut it asunder, that I might break my covenant which I had made with all the people. And it was broken in that day, so the poor of the flock that waited on me knew it was the word of the Lord. Then I cut asunder mine other stave, even bands, that I might break the brotherhood between Judah and Israel. The burden of the word of the Lord for Israel, saith the Lord, which stretcheth forth the heavens, and layeth the foundations of the earth, and formeth the spirit of man within him. Behold, I will make Jerusalem a cup of trembling to all the people round about. Also in that day I will make Jerusalem a burdensome stone for all people. All that burthen themselves with it shall be cut to pieces. In that day, saith the Lord, I will smite every horse with astonishment, and every rider with madness. And I will open mine eyes on the house of Judah, and will smite every horse of the people with blindness. In that day I will make the governors of Judah like a hearth of fire among the wood, and like a torch of fire in a sheaf, and they shall devour all the people on the right and the left.'³

"Harry," said he, "these things are written for our learning. We will go up and take away her battlements, for they are not the Lord's!"

The gloomy fervor with which Dred read these words of Scripture, selecting, as his eye glanced down the prophetic pages, passages whose images most affected his own mind, carried with it an overpowering mesmeric force.

Who shall say that, in this world, where all things are symbolic, bound together by mystical resemblances, and where one event is the archetype of thousands, that there is not an eternal significance in these old prophecies? Do they not bring with them "*springing and germinant* fulfilments" wherever there is a haughty and oppressive nation, and a "flock of the slaughter"?[4]

"Harry," said Dred, "I have fasted and prayed before the Lord, lying all night on my face, yet the token cometh not! Behold, there are prayers that resist me! The Lamb yet beareth, and the opening of the second seal delayeth! Yet the Lord had shown unto me that we should be up and doing, to prepare the way for the coming of the Lord! The Lord hath said unto me, 'Speak to the elders, and to the prudent men, and prepare their hearts.' "[5]

"One thing," said Harry, "fills me with apprehension. Hark, that brought me this letter, was delayed in getting back; and I'm afraid that he'll get into trouble. Tom Gordon is raging like a fury over the people of our plantation. They have always been held under a very mild rule; and every one knows that a plantation so managed is not so immediately profitable as it can be made for a short time by forcing everything up to the highest notch. He has got a man, there, for overseer—Old Hokum—that has been famous for his hardness and meanness; and he has delivered the people, unreservedly, into his hands. He drinks, and frolics, and has his oyster-suppers, and swears he'll shoot any one that brings him a complaint. Hokum is to pay him so much yearly, and have to himself all that he makes over. Tom Gordon keeps two girls, there, that he bought for himself and his fellows, just as he wanted to keep my wife!"

"Be patient, Harry! This is a great christianizing institution!" said Dred, with a tone of grave irony.

"I am afraid for Hark," said Harry. "He is the bravest of brave fellows. He is ready to do anything for us. But, if he is taken, there will be no mercy."

Dred looked on the ground, gloomily. "Hark was to be here to-night," he said.

"Yes," said Harry, "I wish we may see him."

"Harry," said Dred, "when they come, to-night, read them the Declaration of Independence of these United States, and then let each one judge of our afflictions, and the afflictions of their fathers, and the Lord shall be judge between us. I must go and seek counsel of the Lord."

Dred rose, and, giving a leap from the ground, caught on the branch of the oak, which overhung their head, and, swinging himself on the limb, climbed in the thickness of the branches, and disappeared from view. Harry walked to the other side of the clearing, where his lodge had been erected. He found Lisette busy within. She ran to meet him, and threw her arms around his neck.

"I am so glad you've come back, Harry! It is so dreadful to think what may happen to you while you are gone! Harry, I think we could be very happy here. See what a nice bed I have made in this corner, out of leaves and moss! The women are both very kind, and I am glad we have got Old Tiff and the children here. It makes it seem more natural. See, I went out with them, this afternoon, and how many grapes I have got! What have you been talking to that dreadful man about? Do you know, Harry, he makes me afraid? They say he is a prophet. Do you think he is?"

"I don't know, child," said Harry, abstractedly.

"Don't stay with him too much!" said Lisette. "He'll make you as gloomy as he is."

"Do I need any one to make me gloomy?" said Harry. "Am I not gloomy enough? Am I not an outcast? And you, too, Lisette?"

"It isn't so very dreadful to be an outcast," said Lisette. "God makes wild grapes for us, if we are outcasts."

"Yes, child," said Harry, "you are right."

"And the sun shines so pleasant, this afternoon!" said Lisette.

"Yes," said Harry; "but by and by cold storms and rain will come, and frosty weather!"

"Well," said Lisette, "then we will think what to do next. But don't let us lose this afternoon, and these grapes, at any rate."

CHAPTER XXII

Jegar Sahadutha[1]

AT TWELVE O'CLOCK, that night, Harry rose from the side of his sleeping wife, and looked out into the darkness. The belt of forest which surrounded them seemed a girdle of impenetrable blackness. But above, where the tree-tops fringed out against the sky, the heavens were seen of a deep, transparent violet, blazing with stars. He opened the door, and came out. All was so intensely still that even the rustle of a leaf could be heard. He stood listening. A low whistle seemed to come from a distant part of the underwood. He answered it. Soon a crackling was heard, and a sound of cautious, suppressed conversation. In a few moments a rustling was heard in the boughs overhead. Harry stepped under.

"Who is there?" he said.

"The camp of the Lord's judgment!" was the answer, and a dark form dropped on the ground.

"Hannibal?" said Harry.

"Yes, Hannibal!" said the voice.

"Thank God!" said Harry.

But now the boughs of the tree were continually rùstling, and one after another sprang down to the ground, each one of whom pronounced his name, as he came.

"Where is the prophet?" said one.

"He is not here," said Harry. "Fear not, he will be with us."

The party now proceeded to walk, talking in low voices.

"There's nobody from the Gordon place, yet!" said Harry, uneasily.

"They'll be along," said one of them. "Perhaps Hokum was wakeful, to-night. They'll give him the slip, though."

The company had now arrived at the lower portion of the clearing, where stood the blasted tree, which we formerly described, with its funeral-wreaths of moss. Over the grave which had recently been formed there Dred had piled a rude and ragged monument of stumps of trees, and tufts of moss, and leaves. In the top of one of the highest stumps was stuck a pine-knot, to which Harry now applied a light. It kindled, and rose with a broad, red, fuliginous glare, casting a sombre light on the circle of dark faces around. There were a dozen men, mulatto, quadroon, and negro. Their countenances all wore an expression of stern gravity and considerate solemnity.

Their first act was to clasp their hands in a circle, and join in a solemn oath never to betray each other. The moment this was done, Dred emerged mysteriously from the darkness, and stood among them.

"Brethren," he said, "this is the grave of your brother, whose wife they would take for a prey! Therefore he fled to the wilderness. But the assembly of the wicked compassed him about, and the dogs tore him, and licked up his blood, and here I buried him! Wherefore, this heap is called JEGAR SAHADUTHA! For the God of Abraham and Nahor,[2] the God of their fathers, shall judge betwixt us. He that regardeth not the oath of brethren, and betrayeth counsel, let his arm fall from his shoulder-blade! Let his arm be broken from the bone! Behold, this heap shall be a witness unto you; for it hath heard all the words that ye have spoken!"

A deep-murmured "Amen" rose solemnly among them.

"Brethren," said Dred, laying his hand upon Harry, "the Lord caused Moses to become the son of Pharaoh's daughter, that he might become learned in the wisdom of the Egyptians, to lead forth his people from the house of bondage. And, when he slew an Egyptian, he fled into the wilderness, where he abode certain days, till the time of the Lord was come. In like manner hath the Lord dealt with our brother. He shall expound unto you the laws of the Egyptians; and for me, I will show unto you what I have received from the Lord."

The circle now sat down on the graves which were scattered around, and Harry thus spoke:

"Brothers, how many of you have been at Fourth of July celebrations?"

"I have! I have! All of us!" was the deep response, uttered not eagerly, but in low and earnest tones.

"Brethren, I wish to explain to you to-night the story that they celebrate. It was years ago that this people was small, and poor, and despised, and governed by men sent by the King of England, who, they say, oppressed them. Then they resolved that they would be free, and govern themselves in their own way, and make their own laws. For this they were called rebels and conspirators; and, if they had failed, every one of their leaders would have been hung, and nothing more said about it. When they were agreeing to do this, they met together and signed a paper, which was to show to all the world the reason why. You have heard this read by them when the drums were beating and the banners flying. Now hear it here, while you sit on the graves of men they have murdered!"

And, standing by the light of the flaring torch, Harry read that document which has been fraught with so much seed for all time. What words were those to fall on the ears of thoughtful bondmen!

"Governments derive their just power from the consent of the governed." "When a long train of abuses and usurpations, pursuing invariably the same object, evinces a determination to reduce them under absolute despotism, it is their *right* and their *duty* to throw off such government."

"Brothers," said Harry, "you have heard the grievances which our masters thought sufficient to make it right for them to shed blood. They rose up against their king, and when he sent his armies into the country, they fired at them from the windows of the houses, and from behind the barns, and from out of the trees, and wherever they passed, till they were strong enough to get together an army, and fight them openly."

"Yes," said Hannibal, "I heard my master's father tell of it. He was one of them."

"Now," said Harry, "the Lord judge between us and them, if the laws that they put upon us be not worse than any that lay upon them. They complained that they could not get justice done to them in the courts. But how stands it with us, who cannot even come into a court to plead?"

Harry then, in earnest and vehement language, narrated the abuse which had been inflicted upon Milly; and then recited, in a clear and solemn voice, that judicial decision which had burned itself into his memory, and which had confirmed and given full license to that despotic power. He related the fate of his own contract—of his services for years to the family for which he had labored, all ending in worse than nothing. And then he told his sister's history, till his voice was broken by sobs. The audience who sat around were profoundly solemn; only occasionally a deep, smothered groan seemed to rise from them involuntarily.

Hannibal rose. "I had a master in Virginny. He was a Methodist preacher. He sold my wife and two children to Orleans, and then sold me. My next wife was took for debt, and she's gone."

A quadroon young man rose. "My mother was held by a minister in Kentucky. My father was a good, hard-working man. There was a man set his eye on her, and wanted her; but she wouldn't have anything to do with him. Then she told her master, and begged him to protect her; but he sold her. Her hair turned all white in that year, and she went crazy. She was crazy till she died!"

"I's got a story to tell, on that," said a middle-aged negro man, of low stature, broad shoulders, and a countenance indicative of great resolution, who now rose. "I's got a story to tell."

"Go on, Monday," said Harry.

"You spoke 'bout de laws. I's seen 'bout dem ar. Now, my brother Sam, he worked with me on de great Morton place, in Virginny. And dere was going to be a wedding dere, and dey wanted money, and so some of de colored people was sold to Tom Parker, 'cause Tom Parker he was a buying up round, dat ar fall; and he sold him to Souther, and he was one o' yer drefful mean white trash, dat lived down to de bush. Well, Sam was nigh 'bout starved, and so he had to help hisself de best way he could; and he used fur to trade off one ting and 'nother fur meal to Stone's store, and Souther he told him 'dat he'd give him hell if he caught him.' So, one day, when he missed something off de place, he come home and he brought Stone with him, and a man named Hearvy. He told him dat he was going to cotch it. I reckon dey was all three drunk. Any how, dey tied him up, and Souther he never stopped to cut him, and to slash him, and to hack him; and dey burned him with chunks from de fire, and dey scalded him with boiling water. He was strong man, but dey worked on him dat way all day, and at last he died. Dey hearn his screeches on all de places round. Now, brethren, you jest see what was done 'bout it. Why, mas'r and some of de gen'lemen round said dat Souther 'wasn't fit to live,' and it should be brought in de courts; and sure 'nough it was; and, 'cause he is my own brother, I listened for what dey would say. Well, fust dey begun with saying dat it wan't no murder at all, 'cause slaves, dey said, wan't people, and dey couldn't be murdered. But den de man on t' oder side he read heaps o' tings to show dat dey *was* people—dat dey *was* human critturs. Den de lawyer said dat dere wan't no evidence dat Souther meant fur to kill him, any how. Dat it was de right of de master to punish his slave any way he thought fit. And how was he going to know dat it would kill him? Well, so dey had it back and forth, and finally de jury said 'it was murder in de second degree.' Lor! if dat ar's being murdered in de second degree, I like to know what de fust is! You see, dey said he must go to de penitentiary for five years. But, laws, he didn't, 'cause dere's ways enough o' getting out of dese yer tings; 'cause he took it up to de upper court, and dey said 'dat it had been settled dat dere couldn't be noting done agin a mas'r fur no kind of beating or 'busing of der own slaves. Dat de master must be protected, even if 't was ever so cruel.'*

"So, now, brethren, what do you think of dat ar?"

At this moment another person entered the circle. There was a general start of surprise and apprehension, which immediately gave place to a movement of satisfaction and congratulation.

"You have come, have you, Henry?" said Harry.

But at this moment the other turned his face full to the torchlight, and Harry was struck with its ghastly expression.

"For God's sake, what's the matter, Henry? Where's Hark?"

"Dead!" said the other.

As one struck with a pistol-shot leaps in the air, Harry bounded, with a cry, from the ground.

"Dead?" he echoed.

"Yes, dead, at last! Dey's all last night a killing of him."

"I thought so! O, I was afraid of it!" said Harry. "O, Hark! Hark! Hark! God do so to me, and more also, if I forget this!"

---

*Lest any of our readers should think the dark witness who is speaking mistaken in his hearing, we will quote here the words which stand on the Virginia law records, in reference to this very case.

"It has been decided by this court, in Turner's case, that the owner of a slave, for the *malicious, cruel, and excessive beating of his own slave, cannot be indicted.* * * It is the policy of the law in respect to the relation of master and slave, and for the sake of securing proper subordination and obedience on the part of the slave, to *protect the master from prosecution, even if the whipping and punishment be malicious, cruel, and excessive.*"—7 Grattan, 673, 1851, *Souther vs. Commonwealth.*

Any one who has sufficiently strong nerves to peruse the records of this trial will see the effect of the slave system on the moral sensibilities of educated men.

The thrill of a present interest drew every one around the narrator, who proceeded to tell how "Hark, having been too late on his return to the plantation, had incurred the suspicion of being in communication with Harry. How Hokum, Tom Gordon, and two of his drunken associates, had gathered together to examine him by scourging.[3] How his shrieks the night before had chased sleep from every hut of the plantation. How he died, and gave no sign." When he was through, there was dead and awful silence.

Dred, who had been sitting during most of these narrations, bowed, with his head between his knees, groaning within himself, like one who is wrestling with repressed feeling, now rose, and, solemnly laying his hand on the mound, said:

"*Jegar Sahadutha!* The God of their fathers judge between us! If they had a right to rise up for their oppressions, shall they condemn us? For judgment is turned away backward, and justice standeth afar off! Truth is fallen in the street, and equity cannot enter! Yea, truth faileth, and he that departeth from evil maketh himself a prey! They are not ashamed, neither can they blush! They declare their sin as Sodom, and hide it not! The mean man boweth down, and the great man humbleth himself! Therefore, forgive them not, saith the Lord!"

Dred paused a moment, and stood with his hands uplifted. As a thunder-cloud trembles and rolls, shaking with gathering electric fire, so his dark figure seemed to dilate and quiver with the force of mighty emotions. He seemed, at the moment, some awful form, framed to symbolize to human eye the energy of that avenging justice which all nature shudderingly declares.

He trembled, his hands quivered, drops of perspiration rolled down his face, his gloomy eyes dilated with an unutterable volume of emotion. At last the words heaved themselves up in deep chesttones, resembling the wild, hollow wail of a wounded lion, finding vent in language to him so familiar, that it rolled from his tongue in a spontaneous torrent, as if he had received their first inspiration.

"Hear ye the word of the Lord against this people! The harvest groweth ripe! The press is full! The vats overflow! Behold, saith the Lord—behold, saith the Lord, I will gather all nations, and bring them down to the valley of Jehoshaphat, and will plead with them for my people, whom they have scattered among the nations! Woe unto them, for they have cast lots for my people, and given a boy for a harlot, and sold a girl for wine, that they may drink! For three transgressions of Israel, and for four, I will not turn away the punishment thereof, saith the Lord! Because they sold the righteous for silver, and the needy for a pair of shoes! They pant after the dust on the head of the poor, and turn aside the way of the meek! And a man and his father will go in unto the same maid, to profane my holy name! Behold, saith the Lord, I am pressed under you, as a cart is pressed full of sheaves!

"The burden of the beasts of the South! The land of trouble and anguish, from whence cometh the young and old lion, the viper, and fiery, flying serpent! Go write it upon a table, and note it in a book, that it may be for time to come, for ever and ever, that this is a rebellious people, lying children—children that will not hear the law of the Lord! Which say to the seers, See not! Prophesy not unto us right things! Speak unto us smooth things! Prophesy deceits! Wherefore, thus saith the Holy One of Israel, Because ye despise his word, and trust in oppression, and perverseness, and stay thereon; therefore, this iniquity shall be to you as a breach ready to fall, swelling out in a high wall, whose breaking cometh suddenly in an instant! And he shall break it as the breaking of a potter's vessel!"[4]

Pausing for a moment, he stood with his hands tightly clasped before him, leaning forward, looking into the distance. At last, with the action and energy of one who beholds a triumphant reality, he broke forth:

"Who is this that cometh from Edom, with dyed garments, from Bozrah? This, that is glorious in his apparel, travelling in the greatness of his strength?"[5]

He seemed to listen, and, as if he had caught an answer, he repeated:

"I that speak in righteousness, mighty to save!"[6]

"Wherefore art thou red in thine apparel, and thy garments like him that treadeth in the wine-press? I have trodden the wine-press alone, and of the people there was none with me; for I will tread them in my anger, and trample them in my fury, and their blood shall be sprinkled on my garments, and I will stain all my raiment! For the day of vengeance is in my heart, and the year of my redeemed is come! And I looked, and there was none to help! And I wondered that there was none to uphold! Therefore mine own arm brought salvation, and my fury it upheld me! For I will tread down the people in mine anger, and make them drunk in my fury!"[7]

Gradually the light faded from his face. His arms fell. He stood a few moments with his head bowed down on his breast. Yet the spell of his emotion held every one silent. At last, stretching out his hand, he broke forth in passionate prayer:

"How long, O Lord, how long? Awake! Why sleepest thou, O Lord? Why withdrawest thou thy hand? Pluck it out of thy bosom! We see not the sign! There is no more any prophet, neither any among us, that knoweth how long! Wilt thou hold thy peace forever? Behold the blood of the poor crieth unto thee! Behold how they hunt for our lives! Behold how they pervert justice, and take away the key of knowledge! They enter not in themselves, and those that are entering in they hinder! Behold our wives taken for a prey! Behold our daughters sold to be harlots! Art thou a God that judgest on the earth? Wilt thou not avenge thine own elect, that cry unto thee day and night? Behold the scorning of them that are at ease, and the contempt of the proud! Behold how they speak wickedly concerning oppression! They set their mouth against the heavens, and their tongue walketh through the earth! Wilt thou hold thy peace for all these things, and afflict us very sore?"

The energy of the emotion which had sustained him appeared gradually to have exhausted itself. And, after standing silent for a few moments, he seemed to gather himself together as a man awaking out of a trance, and, turning to the excited circle around him, he motioned them to sit down. When he spoke to them in his ordinary tone:

"Brethren," he said, "the vision is sealed up, and the token is not yet come! The Lamb still beareth the yoke of their iniquities; there be prayers in the golden censers which go up like a cloud! And there is silence in heaven for the space of half an hour! But hold yourselves in waiting, for the day cometh! And what shall be the end thereof?"[8]

A deep voice answered Dred. It was that of Hannibal.

"We will reward them as they have rewarded us! In the cup that they have filled to us we will measure to them again!"

"God forbid," said Dred, "that the elect of the Lord should do that! When the Lord saith unto us, Smite, then will we smite! We will not torment them with the scourge and fire, nor defile their women, as they have done with ours! But we will slay them utterly, and consume them from off the face of the earth!"

At this moment the whole circle were startled by the sound of a voice which seemed to proceed deep in from among the trees, singing, in a wild and mournful tone, the familiar words of a hymn:

"Alas! and did my Saviour bleed,
And did my Sovereign die?
Would he devote that sacred head
For such a wretch as I?"[9]

There was a dead silence as the voice approached still nearer, and the chorus was borne upon the night air:

"O, the Lamb, the loving Lamb,
The Lamb of Calvary!
The Lamb that was slain, but liveth again,
To intercede for me!"

And, as the last two lines were sung, Milly emerged and stood in the centre of the group. When Dred saw her, he gave a kind of groan, and said, putting his hand out before his face:

"Woman, thy prayers withstand me!"

"O, brethren," said Milly, "I mistrusted of yer councils, and I's been praying de Lord for you. O, brethren, behold de Lamb of God! If dere must come a day of vengeance, pray not to be in it! It's de Lord's strange work. O, brethren, is we de fust dat's been took to de judgment-seat? dat's been scourged, and died in torments? O, brethren, who did it afore us? Didn't He hang bleeding three hours, when dey mocked Him, and gave Him vinegar? Didn't He sweat great drops o' blood in de garden?"

And Milly sang again, words so familiar to many of them that, involuntarily, several voices joined her:

"Agonizing in the garden,
On the ground your Maker lies;
On the bloody tree behold Him,
Hear Him cry, before He dies,
It is finished! Sinners, will not this suffice?"[10]

"O, won't it suffice, brethren!" she said. "If de Lord could bear all dat, and love us yet, shan't we? O, brethren, dere's a better way. I's been whar you be. I's been in de wilderness! Yes, I's heard de sound of dat ar trumpet! O, brethren! brethren! dere was blackness and darkness dere! But I's come to Jesus, de Mediator of de new covenant, and de blood of sprinkling, which speaketh better tings

than dat of Abel. Hasn't *I* suffered? My heart has been broke over
and over for every child de Lord give me! And, when dey sold my
poor Alfred, and shot him, and buried him like a dog, O, but didn't
my heart burn? O, how I hated her dat sold him! I felt like I'd kill
her! I felt like I'd be glad to see mischief come on her children! But,
brethren, de Lord turned and looked upon me like he done on Peter.[11] I saw him with de crown o' thorns on his head, bleeding,
bleeding, and I broke down and forgave her. And de Lord turned
her heart, and he was our peace. He broke down de middle wall
'tween us, and we come together, two poor sinners, to de foot of de
cross. De Lord he judged her poor soul! She wan't let off from her
sins. Her chil'en growed up to be a plague and a curse to her! Dey
broke her heart! O, she was saved by fire—but, bress de Lord, she
was saved! She died with her poor head on my arm—she dat had
broke my heart! Wan't dat better dan if I'd killed her? O, brethren,
pray de Lord to give 'em repentance! Leave de vengeance to him.
Vengeance is mine—I will repay, saith de Lord.[12] Like he loved us
when we was enemies, love yer enemies!"

A dead silence followed this appeal. The key-note of another
harmony had been struck. At last Dred rose up solemnly:

"Woman, thy prayers have prevailed for this time!" he said. "The
hour is not yet come!"

CHAPTER XXIII

Frank Russel's Opinions

CLAYTON WAS STILL pursuing the object which he had undertaken. He determined to petition the legislature to grant to the slave the right of seeking legal redress in cases of injury; and, as a necessary step to this, the right of bearing testimony in legal action. As Frank Russel was candidate for the next state legislature, he visited him for the purpose of getting him to present such a petition.

Our readers will look in on the scene, in a small retired back room of Frank's office, where his bachelor establishment as yet was kept. Clayton had been giving him an earnest account of his plans and designs.

"The only safe way of gradual emancipation," said Clayton, "is the reforming of law; and the beginning of all legal reform must of course be giving the slave legal personality. It's of no use to enact laws for his protection in his family state, or in any other condition, till we open to him an avenue through which, if they are violated, his grievances can be heard, and can be proved. A thousand laws for his comfort, without this, are only a dead letter."

"I know it," said Frank Russel; "there never was anything under heaven so atrocious as our slave-code. It's a bottomless pit of oppression. Nobody knows it so well as we lawyers. But, then, Clayton, it's quite another thing what's to be done about it."

"Why, I think it's very plain what's to be done," said Clayton. "Go right forward and enlighten the community. Get the law reformed. That's what I have taken for my work; and, Frank, you must help me."

"Hum!" said Frank. "Now, the fact is Clayton, if I were a stiff white neckcloth, and had a *D.D.*[1] to my name, I should tell you that the interests of Zion stood in the way, and that it was my duty to preserve my influence, for the sake of being able to take care of the Lord's affairs. But, as I am not so fortunate, I must just say, without further preface, that it won't do for me to compromise Frank Russel's interests. Clayton, I can't afford it—that's just it. It won't do. You see, our party can't take up that kind of thing. It would be just setting up a fort from which our enemies could fire on us at their leisure. If I go in to the legislature, I have to go in by my party. I have to represent my party, and, of course, I can't afford to do anything that will compromise them."

"Well, now, Frank," said Clayton, seriously and soberly, "are you going to put your neck into such a noose as this, to be led about all your life long—the bond-slave of a party?"

"Not I, by a good deal!" said Russel. "The noose will change ends, one of these days, and I'll drag the party. But we must all stoop to conquer, at first."

"And do you really propose nothing more to yourself than how to rise in the world?" said Clayton. "Isn't there any great and good work that has beauty for you? Isn't there anything in heroism and self-sacrifice?"

"Well," said Russel, after a short pause, "may be there is; but, after all, Clayton, *is* there? The world looks to me like a confounded humbug, a great hoax; and everybody is going in for grub; and, I say, hang it all, why shouldn't I have some of the grub, as well as the rest?"

"Man shall not live by bread alone!" said Clayton.

"Bread's a pretty good thing, though, after all," said Frank, shrugging his shoulders.

"But," said Clayton, "Frank, I am in earnest, and you've got to be. I want you to go with me down to the depths of your soul, where the water is still, and talk to me on honor. This kind of half-joking way that you have isn't a good sign, Frank; it's too old for you. A man that makes a joke of everything at your age, what will he do before he is fifty? Now, Frank, you do know that this system of slavery, if we don't reform it, will eat out this country like a cancer."

"I know it," said Frank. "For that matter, it has eaten into us pretty well."

"Now," said Clayton, "if for nothing else, if we had no feeling of humanity for the slave, we must do something for the sake of the whites, for this is carrying us back into barbarism, as fast as we can go. Virginia has been ruined by it—run all down. North Carolina, I believe, has the enviable notoriety of being the most ignorant and poorest state in the Union. I don't believe there's any country in old, despotic Europe where the poor are more miserable, vicious, and degraded, than they are in our slave states. And it's depopulating us; our men of ability, in the lower classes, who want to be respectable, won't stand it. They will go off to some state where things *move on.* Hundreds and hundreds move out of North Carolina, every year, to the Western States. And it's all this unnatural organization of society that does it. We have got to contemplate some mode of abolishing this evil. We have got to take the first step towards progress, some time, or we ourselves are all undone."

"Clayton," said Frank, in a tone now quite as serious as his own, "I tell you, as a solemn fact, that we can't do it. Those among us who have got the power in their hands are determined to keep it, and they are wide awake. They don't mean to let the *first* step be taken, because they don't mean to lay down their power. The three fifths vote[2] that they get by it is a thing they won't part with. They'll die first. Why, just look at it! There is at least twenty-four millions of property held in this way. What do you suppose these men care about the poor whites, and the ruin of the state, and all that? The poor whites may go to the devil, for all them; and as for the ruin of the state, it won't come in *their* day; and 'after us the deluge,' you know. That's the talk! These men are our masters; they are yours; they are mine; they are masters of everybody in these United States. They can crack their whips over the head of any statesman or clergyman, from Maine to New Orleans, that disputes their will. They govern the country. Army, navy, treasury, church, state, everything is theirs; and whoever is going to get up must go up on their ladder. There isn't any other ladder. There isn't an interest, not a body of men, in these whole United States, that they can't control; and I tell you, Clayton, you might as well throw ashes into the teeth of the north wind, as undertake to fight their influence. Now, if there was any hope of doing any good by this, if there was the least prospect of succeeding, why, I'd join in with you; but there isn't. The thing is a fixed fact, and why shouldn't I climb up on it, as well as everybody else?"

"Nothing is fixed," said Clayton, "that isn't fixed in right. God and nature fight against evil."

"They do, I suppose; but it's a long campaign," said Frank, "and I must be on the side that will win while I'm alive. Now, Clayton, to you I always speak the truth; I won't humbug you. I worship *success.* I am of Frederick the Great's creed, 'that Providence goes with the strongest battalions.'³

"I wasn't made for defeat. I must have power. The preservation of this system, whole and entire, is to be the policy of the leaders of this generation. The fact is, they stand where it *must* be their policy. They *must* spread it over the whole territory. They *must* get the balance of power in the country, to build themselves up against the public opinion of mankind.

"Why, Clayton, moral sentiment, as you call it, is a humbug! The whole world acquiesces in *what goes*—they always have. There is a great outcry about slavery now; but let it *succeed,* and there won't be. When they can out-vote the Northern States, they'll put *them* down. They have kept them subservient by intrigue so far, and by and by they'll have the strength to put them down by force. England makes a fuss now; but let them only succeed, and she'll be civil as a sheep. Of course, men always make a fuss about injustice, when they have nothing to gain by holding their tongues; but England's mouth will be stopped with cotton—you'll see it. They love trade, and hate war. And so the fuss of anti-slavery will die out in the world. Now, when you see what a poor hoax human nature is, what's the use of bothering? The whole race together aren't worth a button, Clayton, and self-sacrifice for such fools is a humbug. That's my programme!"

"Well, Frank, you have made a clean breast; so will I. The human race, as you say, may be a humbug, but it's every man's duty to know for himself that *he* isn't one. *I* am not. I do *not* worship success, and *will* not. And if a cause is a right and honorable one, I will labor in it till I die, whether there is any chance of succeeding or not."

"Well, now," said Frank Russel, "I dare say it's so. I respect your sort of folks; you form an agreeable heroic poem, with which one can amuse the tediousness of life. I suppose it won't do you any good to tell you that you are getting immensely unpopular, with what you are doing."

"No," said Clayton, "it won't."

"I am really afraid," said Russel, "that they'll mob you, some of these bright days."

"Very well," said Clayton.

"O, of course, I knew it would be very well; but, say, Clayton, what do you want to get up a petition on *that* point for? Why don't you get up one to prevent the separation of families? There's been such a muss made about that in Europe, and all around the world, that it's rather the fashion to move about that a little. Politicians like to appear to intend to begin to do something about it. It has a pleasing effect, and gives the Northern editors and ministers something to say, as an apology for our sins. Besides, there are a good many simple-hearted folks, who don't see very deep into things, that really think it possible to do something effective on this subject. If you get up a petition for that, you might take the tide with you; and I'd do something about it, myself."

"You know very well, Frank, for I told you, that it's no use to pass laws for that, without giving the slaves power to sue or give evidence, in case of violation. The improvement I propose touches the root of the matter."

"That's the fact—it surely does!" said Russel. "And, for that very reason, you'll never carry it. Now, Clayton, I just want to ask you one question. Can you fight? *Will* you fight? Will you wear a bowie-knife and pistol, and shoot every fellow down that comes at you?"

"Why, no, of course, Frank. You know that I never was a fighting man. Such brute ways are not to my taste."

"Then, my dear sir, you shouldn't set up for a reformer in Southern states. Now, I'll tell you one thing, Clayton, that I've heard. You made some remarks at a public meeting, up at E., that have started a mad-dog cry, which I suppose came from Tom Gordon. See here; have you noticed this article in the *Trumpet of Liberty?*"[4] said he, looking over a confused stack of papers on his table. "Where's the article? O, here it is."

At the same time he handed Clayton a sheet bearing the motto "Liberty and union, now and forever, one and inseparable,"[5] and pointed to an article headed

"COVERT ABOLITIONISM! CITIZENS, BEWARE!

"We were present, a few evenings ago, at the closing speech delivered before the Washington Agricultural Society, in the course of which the speaker, Mr. Edward Clayton, gratuitously wandered away from his subject to make inflammatory and seditious comments on the state of the laws which regulate our negro population. It is time for the friends of our institutions to be awake. Such remarks, dropped in the ear of a restless and ignorant population, will be a fruitful source of sedition and insurrection. This young man is supposed to be infected with the virus of Northern abolitionists. We cannot too narrowly watch the course of such individuals; for the only price at which we can maintain liberty is eternal vigilance. Mr. Clayton belongs to one of our oldest and most respected families, which makes his conduct the more inexcusable."

Clayton perused this with a quiet smile, which was usual with him.

"The hand of Joab[6] is in that thing," said Frank Russel.

"I'm sure I said very little," said Clayton. "I was only showing the advantage to our agriculture of a higher tone of moral feeling among our laborers, which, of course, led me to speak of the state of the law regulating them. I said nothing but what everybody knows."

"But, don't you know, Clayton," said Russel, "that if a fellow has an enemy—anybody bearing him the least ill-will—that he puts a tremendous power in his hands by making such remarks? Why, our common people are so ignorant that they are in the hands of anybody who wants to use them. They are just like a swarm of bees; you can manage them by beating on a tin pan. And Tom Gordon has got the tin pan now, I fancy. Tom intends to be a swell. He is a born bully, and he'll lead a rabble. And so you must take care. Your family is considerable for you; but, after all, it won't stand you in stead for everything. Who have you got to back you? Who have you talked with?"

"Well," said Clayton, "I have talked with some of the ministry—"

"And, of course," said Frank, "you found that the leadings of Providence didn't indicate that *they* are to be martyrs! You have their prayers *in secret*, I presume; and if you ever get the cause on the upper hill-side, they'll come out and preach a sermon for you. Now, Clayton, I'll tell you what I'll do. If Tom Gordon attacks you, I'll pick a quarrel with him, and shoot him right off the reel. My stomach isn't nice about those matters, and that sort of thing won't compromise me with my party."

"Thank you," said Clayton, "I shall not trouble you."

"My dear fellow," said Russel, "you philosophers are very much mistaken about the use of carnal weapons. As long as you wrestle with flesh and blood, you had better use fleshly means. At any rate, a gentlemanly brace of pistols won't hurt you; and, in fact, Clayton,

I am serious. You *must* wear pistols,—there are no two ways about it. Because, if these fellows know that a man wears pistols and will use them, it keeps them off. They have an objection to being shot, as this is all the world they are likely to have. And I think, Clayton, you can fire off a pistol in as edifying and dignified a manner, as you can say a grace on proper occasions. The fact is, before long there will be a row kicked up. I'm pretty sure of it. Tom Gordon is a deeper fellow than you'd think, and he has booked himself for Congress; and he means to go in on the thunder-and-blazes principle, which will give him the vote of all the rabble. He'll go into Congress to do the fighting and slashing. There always must be a bully or two there, you know, to knock down fellows that you can't settle any other way. And nothing would suit him better, to get his name up, than heading a crusade against an abolitionist."

"Well," said Clayton, "if it's come to that, that we can't speak and discuss freely in our own state, where are we?"

"Where are we, my dear fellow? Why, I know where we are; and if you don't, it's time you did. Discuss freely? Certainly we can, on *one* side of the question; or on both sides of any other question than this. But this you can't discuss freely, and they can't afford to let you, as long as they mean to keep their power. Do you suppose they are going to let these poor devils, whites, get their bandages off their eyes, that make them so easy to lead now? There would be a pretty bill to pay, if they did! Just now, these fellows are in as safe and comfortable a condition for use as a party could desire; because they have got votes, and we have the guiding of them. And they rage, and swear, and tear, for our institutions, because they are fools, and don't know what hurts them. Then, there's the niggers. Those fellows are deep. They have as long ears as little pitchers, and they are such a sort of fussy set, that whatever is going on in the community is always in their mouths, and so comes up that old fear of insurrection. That's the awful word, Clayton! *That* lies at the bottom of a good many things in our state, more than we choose to let on. These negroes are a black well; you never know what's at the bottom."

"Well," said Clayton, "the only way, the only safeguard to prevent this is reform. They are a patient set, and will bear a great while; and if they only see that anything is being done, it will be an effectual prevention. If you want insurrection, the only way is to shut down the escape-valve; for, will ye nill ye, the steam must rise.

You see, in this day, minds *will grow.* They *are* growing. There's no help for it, and there's no force like the force of growth. I have seen a rock split in two by the growing of an elm-tree that wanted light and air, and would make its way up through it. Look at all the aristocracies of Europe. They have gone down under this force. Only one has stood—that of England. And how came that to stand? Because it knew when to *yield;* because it never confined discussion; because it gave way gracefully before the growing force of the people. That's the reason it stands to-day, while the aristocracy of France has been blown to atoms."

"My dear fellow," said Russel, "this is all very true and convincing, no doubt; but you won't make *our* aristocracy believe it. They have mounted the lightning, and they are going to ride it whip and spur. They are going to annex Cuba and the Sandwich Islands,[7] and the Lord knows what, and have a great and splendid slaveholding empire. And the North is going to be what Greece was to Rome. We shall govern it, and it will attend to the arts of life for us. The South understands governing. We are trained to rule from the cradle. We have leisure to rule. We have nothing else to do. The free states have their factories, and their warehouses, and their schools, and their internal improvements, to take up their minds; and, if we are careful, and don't tell them too plain where we are taking them, they'll never know it till they get there."

"Well," said Clayton, "there's one element of force that you've left out in your calculation."

"And what's that?" said Russel.

"God," said Clayton.

"I don't know anything about him," said Russel.

"You may have occasion to learn, one of these days," said Clayton. "I believe he is alive yet."

CHAPTER XXIV

Tom Gordon's Plans

TOM GORDON, in the mean while, had commenced ruling his paternal plantation in a manner very different from the former indulgent system. His habits of reckless and boundless extravagance, and utter heedlessness, caused his cravings for money to be absolutely insatiable; and, within legal limits, he had as little care how it was come by, as a highway robber. It is to be remarked that Tom Gordon was a worse slaveholder and master from the very facts of certain desirable qualities in his mental constitution; for, as good wine makes the strongest vinegar, so fine natures perverted make the worse vice. Tom had naturally a perfectly clear, perceptive mind, and an energetic, prompt temperament. It was impossible for him, as many do, to sophisticate and delude himself with false views. He marched up to evil boldly, and with his eyes open. He had very little regard for public opinion, particularly the opinion of conscientious and scrupulous people. So he carried his purposes, it was very little matter to him what any one thought of them or him; they might complain till they were tired.

After Clayton had left the place, he often pondered the dying words of Nina, "that he should care for her people; that he should tell Tom to be kind to them." There was such an impassable gulf between the two characters, that it seemed impossible that any peaceable communication should pass between them. Clayton thought within himself that it was utterly hopeless to expect any good arising from the sending of Nina's last message. But the subject haunted him. Had he any right to withhold it? Was it not his duty to try every measure, however apparently hopeless?

Under the impulse of this feeling, he one day sat down and wrote to Tom Gordon an account, worded with the utmost simplicity, of the last hours of his sister's life, hoping that he might read it, and thus, if nothing more, his own conscience be absolved.

Death and the grave, it is true, have sacred prerogatives, and it is

often in their power to awaken a love which did not appear in life.
There are few so hard as not to be touched by the record of the last
hours of those with whom they have stood in intimate relations. A
great moralist says, "There are few things not purely evil of which
we can say, without emotion, this is the last."

The letter was brought to Tom Gordon one evening when, for a
wonder, he was by himself; his associates being off on an excursion,
while he was detained at home by a temporary illness. He read it
over, therefore, with some attention. He was of too positive a character, however, too keenly percipient, not to feel immediate pain in
view of it. A man of another nature might have melted in tears over
it, indulged in the luxury of sentimental grief, and derived some
comfort, from the exercise, to go on in ways of sin. Not so with
Tom Gordon. He could not afford to indulge in anything that
roused his moral nature. He was doing wrong of set purpose, with
defiant energy; and his only way of keeping his conscience quiet
was to maintain about him such a constant tumult of excitement as
should drown reflection. He could not afford a tête-à-tête conversation with his conscience;—having resolved, once for all, to go on
in his own wicked way, serving the flesh and the devil, he had to
watch against anything that might occasion uncomfortable conflict
in his mind. He knew very well, lost man as he was, that there was
something sweet and pure, high and noble, against which he was
contending; and the letter was only like a torch, which a fair angel
might hold up, shining into the filthy lair of a demon. He could not
bear the light; and he had no sooner read the note, than he cast it
into the fire, and rang violently for a hot brandy-toddy, and a fresh
case of cigars. The devil's last, best artifice to rivet the fetters of his
captives is the opportunity which these stimulants give them to
command insanity at will.

Tom Gordon was taken to bed drunk; and, if a sorrowful
guardian spirit hovered over him as he read the letter, he did not
hear the dejected rustle of its retreating wings. The next day nothing
was left, only a more decided antipathy to Clayton, for having occasioned him so disagreeable a sensation.

Tom Gordon, on the whole, was not unpopular in his vicinity.
He determined to rule them all, and he did. All that uncertain, uninstructed, vagrant population, which abound in slave states, were at
his nod and beck. They were his tools—prompt to aid him in any of
his purposes, and convenient to execute vengeance on his adver-

saries. Tom was a determined slaveholder. He had ability enough to see the whole bearings of that subject, from the beginning to the end; and he was determined that, while he lived, the first stone should never be pulled from the edifice in his state. He was a formidable adversary, because what he wanted in cultivation he made up in unscrupulous energy; and, where he might have failed in argument, he could conquer by the cudgel and the bludgeon. He was, as Frank Russel had supposed, the author of the paragraph which had appeared in the *Trumpet of Freedom,* which had already had its effect in awakening public suspicion.

But what stung him to frenzy, when he thought of it, was, that every effort which he had hitherto made to recover possession of Harry had failed. In vain he had sent out hunters and dogs. The swamp had been tracked in vain. He boiled and burned with fierce tides of passion, as he thought of him in his security defying his power.

Some vague rumors had fallen upon his ear of the existence, in the swamp, of a negro conspirator, of great energy and power, whose lair had never yet been discovered; and he determined that he would raise heaven and earth to find him. He began to suspect that there was, somehow, understanding and communication between Harry and those who were left on the plantation, and he determined to detect it. This led to the scene of cruelty and tyranny to which we made allusion in a former chapter. The mangled body was buried, and Tom felt neither remorse nor shame. Why should he, protected by the express words of legal decision? He had only met with an accident in the exercise of his lawful power on a slave in the act of rebellion.

"The fact is, Kite," he said, to his boon-companion, Theophilus Kite, as they were one day sitting together, "I'm bound to have that fellow. I'm going to publish a proclamation of outlawry, and offer a reward for his head. That will bring it in, I'm thinking. I'll put it up to a handsome figure, for that will be better than nothing."

"Pity you couldn't catch him alive," said Kite, "and make an example of him!"

"I know it," said Tom. "I'd take him the long way round, that I would! That fellow has been an eye-sore to me ever since I was a boy. I believe all the devils that are in me are up about him."

"Tom," said Kite, "you've got the devil in you—no mistake!"

"To be sure I have," said Tom. "I only want a chance to express him. I wish I could get hold of the fellow's wife! I could make him wince there, I guess. I'll get her, too, one of these days! But, now, Kite, I'll tell you, the fact is, somebody round here is in league with him. They know about him, I know they do. There's that squeaky, leathery, long-nosed Skinflint, trades with the niggers in the swamp—I know he does! But he is a double-and-twisted liar, and you can't get anything out of him. One of these days I'll burn up that old den of his, and shoot him, if he don't look out! Jim Stokes told me that he slept down there, one night, when he was tracking, and that he heard Skinflint talking with somebody between twelve and one o'clock; and he looked out, and saw him selling powder to a nigger."

"O, that couldn't be Harry," said Kite.

"No, but it's one of the gang that he is in with. And, then, there's that Hark. Jim says that he saw him talking,—giving a letter, that he got out of the post-office, to a man that rode off towards the woods. I thought we'd have the truth out of his old hide! But he didn't hold out as I thought he would."

"Hokum don't understand his business," said Kite. "He shouldn't have used him up so fast."

"Hokum is a bother," said Tom, "like all the rest of those fellows! Hark was a desperately-resolute fellow, and it's well enough he is dead, because he was getting sullen, and making the others rebellious. Hokum, you see, had taken a fancy to his wife, and Hark was jealous."

"Quite a romance!" said Kite, laughing.

"And now I'll tell you another thing," said Tom, "that I'm bound to reform. There's a canting, sneaking, dribbling, whining old priest, that's ravaging these parts, and getting up a muss among people about the abuses of the slaves; and I'm not going to have it. I'm going to shut up his mouth. I shall inform him, pretty succinctly, that, if he does much more in this region, he'll be illustrated with a coat of tar-and-feathers."

"Good for you!" said Kite.

"Now," said Tom, "I understand that to-night he is going to have a general snivelling season in the old log church, out on the cross run, and they are going to form a church on anti-slavery principles. Contemptible whelps! Not a copper to bless themselves with! Dirty, sweaty, greasy mechanics, with their spawn of children! Think of the impudence of their getting together and passing anti-slavery resolutions, and resolving they won't admit slave-holders to the communion! I have a great mind to let them try the dodge, once! By George, if I wouldn't walk up and take their bread and wine, and pitch it to thunder!"

"Are they really going to form such a church?"

"That's the talk," said Tom. "But they'll find they have reckoned without their host, I fancy! You see, I just tipped Jim Stokes the wink. Says I, Jim, don't you think they'll want you to help the music there, to-night? Jim took at once; and he said he would be on the ground with a dog or two, and some old tin pans. O, we shall get them up an orchestra, I promise you! And some of our set are going over to see the fun. There's Bill Akers, and Bob Story, and Sim Dexter, will be over here to dinner, and towards evening we'll ride over."

CHAPTER XXV

Lynch Law

THE RAYS OF THE AFTERNOON SUN were shining through the fringy needles of the pines. The sound of the woodpecker reverberated through the stillness of the forest, answering to thousand woodland notes. Suddenly, along the distant path, a voice is heard singing, and the sound comes strangely on the ear through the dreamy stillness:

"Jesus Christ has lived and died—
What is all the world beside?
This to know is all I need,
This to know is life indeed.
Other wisdom seek I none—
Teach me this, and this alone:
Christ for me has lived and died,
Christ for me was crucified."

And, as the last lines fall upon the ear, a figure, riding slowly on horseback, comes round the bend of the forest path. It is father Dickson. It was the habit of this good man, much of whose life was spent in solitary journeyings, to use the forest arches for that purpose for which they seemed so well designed, as a great cathedral of prayer and praise. He was riding with the reins loose over the horse's neck, and a pocket-Bible in his hand. Occasionally he broke out into snatches of song, like the one which we heard him singing a few moments ago. As he rides along now, he seems absorbed in mental prayer. Father Dickson, in truth, had cause to pray. The plainness of speech which he felt bound to use had drawn upon him opposition and opprobrium, and alienated some of his best friends. The support which many had been willing to contribute to his poverty was entirely withdrawn. His wife, in feeble health, was toiling daily beyond her strength; and hunger had looked in at the door, but each day prayer had driven it away. The petition, "Give us this day our daily bread," had not yet failed to bring an answer;

but there was no bread for to-morrow. Many friendly advisers had told him that, if he would relinquish a futile and useless undertaking, he should have enough and to spare. He had been conferred with by the elders in a vacant church, in the town of E., who said to him, "We enjoy your preaching when you let alone controverted topics; and if you'll agree to confine yourself solely to the Gospel, and say nothing on any of the delicate and exciting subjects of the day, we shall rejoice in your ministrations." They pleaded with him his poverty, and the poor health of his wife, and the necessities of his children; but he answered, " 'Man shall not live by bread alone.'[1] God is able to feed me, and he will do it." They went away, saying that he was a fool, that he was crazy. He was not the first whose brethren had said, "He is beside himself."[2]

As he rode along through the forest paths, he talked of his wants to his Master. "Thou knowest," he said, "how I suffer. Thou knowest how feeble my poor wife is, and how it distresses us both to have our children grow up without education. We cast ourselves on thee. Let us not deny thee; let us not betray thee. Thou hadst not where to lay thy head; let us not murmur. The disciple is not above his master, nor the servant above his lord." And then he sang:

"Jesus, I my cross have taken,
    All to leave and follow thee;
Naked, poor, despised, forsaken,
    Thou my all henceforth shalt be!
Let the world despise and leave me—
    They have left my Saviour too;
Human looks and words deceive me—
    Thou art not, like them, untrue!
And, while thou shalt smile upon me,
    God of wisdom, power, and might,
Foes may hate, and friends disown me,
    Show thy face and all is bright!"

And, as he sang and prayed, that strange joy arose within him which, like the sweetness of night flowers, is born of darkness and tribulation. The soul hath in it somewhat of the divine, in that it can have joy in endurance beyond the joy of indulgence.

They mistake who suppose that the highest happiness lies in wishes accomplished—in prosperity, wealth, favor, and success. There has been a joy in dungeons and on racks passing the joy of harvest. A joy strange and solemn, mysterious even to its possessor. A white stone dropped from that signet-ring, peace, which a dying Saviour took from his own bosom, and bequeathed to those who endure the cross, despising the shame.

As father Dickson rode on, he lifted his voice, in solemn exultation:

> "*Soul, then know thy full salvation;*
>   *Rise o'er fear, doubt, and care;*
> *Joy to find, in every station,*
>   *Something still to do or bear.*
> *Think what spirit dwells within thee;*
>   *Think what Father's smiles are thine;*
> *Think that Jesus died to win thee;*
>   *Child of heaven, wilt thou repine?*"[3]

At this moment Dr. Cushing, in the abundant comforts of his home, might have envied father Dickson in his desertion and poverty. For that peace seldom visited him. He struggled wearily along the ways of duty, never fulfilling his highest ideal; wearied by confusing accusations of conscience, and deeming himself happy only because, having never lived in any other state, he knew not what happiness was like. He alternately condemned his brother's rashness, and sighed as he thought of his uncompromising spirituality; and once or twice he had written him a friendly letter of caution, enclosing him a five-dollar bill, wishing that he might succeed, begging that he would be careful, and ending with the pious wish that we might all be guided aright; which supplication, in many cases, answers the purpose, in a man's inner legislation, of laying troublesome propositions on the table. Meanwhile the shades of evening drew on, and father Dickson approached the rude church which stood deep in the shadow of the woods. In external appearance it had not the pretensions even of a New England barn, but still it had echoed prayers and praises from humble, sincere worshippers. As father Dickson rode up to the door, he was surprised to find quite a throng of men, armed with bludgeons and pistols, waiting before it. One of these now stepped forward, and, handing him a letter, said,

"Here, I have a letter for you to read!"

Father Dickson put it calmly in his pocket. "I will read it after service," said he.

The man then laid hold of his bridle. "Come out here!" he said; "I want to talk to you."

"Thank you, friend, I will talk with you after meeting," said he. "It's time for me to begin service."

"The fact is," said a surly, wolfish-looking fellow, who came behind the first speaker, "the fact is, we an't going to have any of your d——d abolition meetings here! If he can't get it out, I can!"

"Friends," said father Dickson, mildly, "by what right do you presume to stop me?"

"We think," said the first man, "that you are doing harm, violating the laws—"

"Have you any warrant from the civil authorities to stop me?"

"No, sir," said the first speaker; but the second one, ejecting a large quid of tobacco from his mouth, took up the explanation in a style and taste peculiarly his own.

"Now, old cock, you may as well know fust as last, that we don't care a cuss for the civil authorities, as you call them, 'cause we's going to do what we darn please; and we don't please have you yowping abolishionism round here, and putting deviltry in the heads of our niggers! Now, that ar's plain talk!"

This speech was chorused by a group of men on the steps, who now began to gather round and shout,

"Give it to him! That's into him! make the wool fly!"

Father Dickson, who was perfectly calm, now remarked in the shadow of the wood, at no great distance, three or four young men mounted on horses, who laughed brutally, and called out to the speaker,

"Give him some more!"

"My friends," said father Dickson, "I came here to perform a duty, at the call of my heavenly Master, and you have no right to stop me."

"Well, how will you help yourself, old bird? Supposing we haven't?"

"Remember, my friends, that we shall all stand side by side at the judgment seat to give an account for this night's transactions. How will you answer for it to God?"

A loud, sneering laugh came from the group under the trees, and a voice, which we recognize as Tom Gordon's, calls out,

"He is coming the solemn dodge on you, boys! Get on your long faces!"

"Come," said the roughest of the speakers, "this here don't go down with us! We don't know nothing about no judgments; and as to God, we an't none of us seen him, lately. We 'spect he don't travel round these parts."

"The eyes of the Lord are in every place, beholding the evil and the good," said father Dickson.

Here one in the mob mewed like a cat, another barked like a dog, and the spectators under the tree laughed more loudly than ever.

"I say," said the first speaker, "you shan't go to getting up rat-traps and calling 'em meetings! This yer preaching o' yourn is a cussed sell, and we won't stand it no longer! We shall have an insurrection among our niggers. Pretty business, getting up churches where you won't have slaveholders commune! I's got niggers my-self, and I know I's bigger slave than they be, and I wished I was shet of them! But I an't going to have no d——d old parson dictat-ing to me about my affairs! And we won't, none of the rest of us, will we? 'Cause them that an't got niggers now means to have. Don't we, boys?"

"Ay, ay, that we do! Give it to him!" was shouted from the party.

"It's our right to have niggers, and we will have them, if we can get them," continued the speaker.

"Who gave you the right?" said father Dickson.

"Who gave it? Why, the constitution of the United States, to be sure, man! Who did you suppose? An't we got the freest govern-ment in the world? Is we going to be shut out of communion, 'cause we holds niggers? Don't care a cuss for your old commu-nion, but it's the *principle* I's going for! Now, I tell you what, old fellow, we've got you; and you have got to promise, right off the reel, that you won't say another word on this yer subject."

"Friend, I shall make no such promise," said father Dickson, in a tone so mild and steadfast that there was a momentary pause.

"You'd better," said a man in the crowd, "if you know what's good for you!"

A voice now spoke from the circle of the young men,

"Never cave in, boys!"

"No fear of us!" responded the man who had taken the most prominent part in the dialogue hitherto. "We'll serve it out to him! Now, ye see, old feller, ye're treed, and may as well come down, as the coon said to Davy. You can't help yourself, 'cause we are ten to one; and if you don't promise peaceable, we'll make you!"

"My friends," said father Dickson, "I want you to think what you are doing. Your good sense must teach you the impropriety of your course. You know that you are doing wrong. You know that it isn't right to trample on all law, both human and divine, out of professed love to it. You must see that your course will lead to perfect anarchy and confusion. The time may come when your opinions will be as unpopular as mine."

"Well, what then?"

"Why, if your course prevails, you must be lynched, stoned, tarred and feathered. This is a two-edged sword you are using, and some day you may find the edge turned towards you. You may be seized, just as you are seizing me. You know the men that threw Daniel into the den got thrown in themselves."[4]

"Daniel who?" shouted one of the company; and the young men under the tree laughed insultingly.

"Why are you afraid to let me preach, this evening?" said father Dickson. "Why can't you hear me, and, if I say anything false, why can't you show me the falsehood of it? It seems to me it's a weak cause that can only get along by stopping men's mouths."

"No, no—we an't going to have it!" said the man who had taken the most active part. "And now you've got to sign a solemn promise, this night, that you won't ever open your mouth again about this yer subject, or we'll make it worse for you!"

"I shall never make such a promise. You need not think to terrify me into it, for I am not afraid. You must kill me before you can stop me."

"D——n you, then, old man," said one of the young men, riding up by the side of him, "I'll tell you what you shall do! You shall sign a pledge to leave North Carolina in three days, and never come back again, and take your whole spawn and litter with you, or you shall be chastised for your impudence! Now, look out, sir, for you are speaking to your betters! Your insolence is intolerable! What business have you passing strictures reflecting on the conduct of gentlemen of family? Think yourself happy that we let you go out of the state without the punishment that your impudence deserves!"

"Mr. Gordon, I am sorry to hear you speaking in that way," said father Dickson, composedly. "By right of your family, you certainly ought to know how to speak as a gentleman. You are holding language to me that you have no right to hold, and uttering threats that you have no means of enforcing."

"You'll see if I haven't!" replied the other, with an oath. "Here, boys!"

He beckoned one or two of the leaders to his side, and spoke with them in a low voice. One of them seemed inclined to remonstrate.

"No, no—it's too bad!" he said.

But the others said,

"Yes, it serves him right! We'll do it! Hurra, boys! We'll help on the parson home, and help him kindle his fire!"

There was a general shout, as the whole party, striking up a ribald song, seized father Dickson's horse, turned him round, and began marching in the direction of his cabin in the woods.

Tom Gordon and his companions, who rode foremost, filled the air with blasphemous and obscene songs, which entirely drowned the voice of father Dickson whenever he attempted to make himself heard. Before they started, Tom Gordon had distributed freely of whiskey among them, so that what little manliness there might have been within seemed to be "set on fire of hell."[5] It was one of those moments that try men's souls.

Father Dickson, as he was hurried along, thought of that other *one*, who was led by an infuriate mob through the streets of Jerusalem, and he lifted his heart in prayer to the Apostle and High Priest of his profession, the God in Jesus. When they arrived before his little cabin, he made one more effort to arrest their attention.

"My brethren," he said.

"None of your brethren! Stop that cant!" said Tom Gordon.

"Hear me one word," said father Dickson. "My wife is quite feeble. I'm sure you wouldn't wish to hurt a sick woman, who never did harm to any mortal creature."

"Well, then," said Tom Gordon, facing round to him, "if you care so very much about your wife, you can very easily save her any further trouble. Just give us the promise we want, and we'll go away peaceably, and leave you. But, if you won't, as true as there is a God in heaven, we'll pull down every stick of timber in your old kennel! I'll tell you what, old man, you've got a master to deal with, now!"

"I cannot promise not to preach upon this subject."

"Well, then, you must promise to take yourself out of the state. You can go among your Northern brethren, and howl and mawl round there; but we are not going to have you here. I have as much respect for respectable ministers of the Gospel as any one, when they confine themselves to the duties of their calling; but, when they come down to be intriguing in our worldly affairs, they must expect to be treated as we treat other folks that do that. Their black coats shan't protect them! We are not going to be priest-ridden, are we, boys?"

A loud whoop of inflamed and drunken merriment chorused this question. Just at this moment the door of the cottage was opened, and a pale, sickly-looking woman came gliding out to the gate.

"My dear," she said, and her voice was perfectly calm, "don't yield a hair's breadth, on my account. I can bear as well as you. I am not afraid. I am ready to die for conscience' sake. Gentlemen," she said, "there is not much in this house of any value, except two sick children. If it is agreeable to you to pull it down, you can do it. Our goods are hardly worth spoiling, but you can spoil them. My husband, be firm; don't yield an inch!"

It is one of the worst curses of slavery that it effaces from the breast all manly feeling with regard to woman. Every one remembers the story how the frail and delicate wife of Lovejoy[6] placed her weakness as a shield before the chamber door where her husband was secreted, and was fought with brutal oaths and abuse by the drunken gang, who were determined to pass over her body, if necessary, to his heart! They who are trained to whip women in a servile position, of course can have none of the respect which a free man feels for woman as woman. They respect the sex when they see it enshrined by fashion, wealth, and power; but they tread it in the dust when in poverty and helplessness it stands in the path of their purposes.

"Woman," said Tom Gordon, "you are a fool! You needn't think to come it round us with any of that talk! You needn't think we are going to stop on your account, for we shan't! We know what we are about."

"So does God!" said the woman, fixing her eye on him with one of those sudden looks of power with which a noble sentiment sometimes lights up for a moment the weakest form.

There was a momentary pause, and then Tom broke out into oaths and curses.

"I'll tell you what, boys," he said, "we had better bring matters to a point! Here, tie him up to this tree, and give him six-and-thirty! He is so dreadful fond of the niggers, let him fare with them! We know how to get a promise out of him!"

The tiger was now fully awake in the crowd. Wild oaths and cries of "Give it to him! Give it to him, G——d d——n him!" arose.

Father Dickson stood calm; and, beholding him, they saw his face as if it had been that of an angel, and they gnashed on him with their teeth. A few moments more, and he was divested of his outer garments, and bound to a tree.

"Now will you promise?" said Tom Gordon, taking out his watch. "I give you five minutes."

The children, now aroused, were looking out, crying, from the door. His wife walked out and took her place before him.

"Stand out of the way, old woman!" said Tom Gordon.

"I will not stand out of the way!" she said, throwing her arms round her husband. "You shall not get to him but over my body!"

"Ben Hyatt, take her away!" said Tom Gordon. "Treat her decently, as long as she behaves herself."

A man forced her away. She fell fainting on his shoulder.

"Lay her down," said Tom Gordon. "Now, sir, your five minutes are up. What have you got to say?"

"I have to say that I shall not comply with your demands."

"Very well," said Tom, "it's best to be explicit."

He drew his horse a little back, and said to a man who was holding a slave-whip behind,

"Give it to him!"

The blows descended. He uttered no sound. The mob, meanwhile, tauntingly insulted him.

"How do you like it? What do you think of it? Preach us a sermon, now, can't you? Come, where's your text?"

"He is getting stars and stripes, now!" said one.

"I reckon he'll see stars!" said another.

"Stop," said Tom Gordon. "Well, my friend," he said, "you see we are in earnest, and we shall carry this through to the bitter end, you may rely on it. You won't get any sympathy; you won't get any support. There an't a minister in the state that will stand by you. They all have sense enough to let our affairs alone. They'd any of them hold a candle here, as the good elder did when they thrashed Dresser,[7] down at Nashville. Come, now, will you cave in?"

But at this moment the conversation was interrupted by the riding up of four or five gentlemen on horseback, the headmost of whom was Clayton.

"What's this?" he exclaimed, hurriedly. "What, Mr. Gordon—father Dickson! What—what am I to understand by this?"

"Who the devil cares what you understand? It's no business of yours," said Tom Gordon; "so stand out of my way!"

"I shall make it some of my business," said Clayton, turning round to one of his companions. "Mr. Brown, you are a magistrate?"

Mr. Brown, a florid, puffy-looking old gentleman, now rode forward.

"Bless my soul, but this is shocking! Mr. Gordon, don't! how can you? My boys, you ought to consider!"

Clayton, meanwhile, had thrown himself off his horse, and cut the cords which bound father Dickson to the tree. The sudden reäction of feeling overcame him. He fell, fainting.

"Are you not ashamed of yourselves?" said Clayton, indignantly glancing round. "Isn't this pretty business for great, strong men like you, abusing ministers that you know won't fight, and women and children that you know can't!"

"Do you mean to apply that language to me?" said Tom Gordon.

"Yes, sir, I do mean just that!" said Clayton, looking at him, while he stretched his tall figure to its utmost height.

"Sir, that remark demands satisfaction."

"You are welcome to all the satisfaction you can get," said Clayton, coolly.

"You shall meet me," said Tom Gordon, "where you shall answer for that remark!"

"I am not a fighting man," said Clayton; "but, if I were, I should never consent to meet any one but my equals. When a man stoops to do the work of a rowdy and a bully, he falls out of the sphere of gentlemen. As for you," said Clayton, turning to the rest of the company, "there's more apology for you. You have not been brought up to know better. Take my advice; disperse yourselves now, or I shall take means to have this outrage brought to justice."

There is often a magnetic force in the appearance, amid an excited mob, of a man of commanding presence, who seems perfectly calm and decided. The mob stood irresolute.

"Come, Tom," said Kite, pulling him by the sleeve, "we've given him enough, at any rate."

"Yes, yes," said Mr. Brown, "Mr. Gordon, I advise you to go home. We must all keep the peace, you know. Come, boys, you've done enough for one night, I should hope! Go home, now, and let the old man be; and there's something to buy you a treat, down at Skinflint's. Come, do the handsome, now!"

Tom Gordon sullenly rode away, with his two associates each side; but, before he went, he said to Clayton,

"You shall hear of me again, one of these days!"

"As you please," said Clayton.

The party now set themselves about recovering and comforting the frightened family. The wife was carried in and laid down on the bed. Father Dickson was soon restored so as to be able to sit up, and, being generally known and respected by the company, received many expressions of sympathy and condolence. One of the men was an elder in the church which had desired his ministerial services. He thought this a good opportunity of enforcing some of his formerly expressed opinions.

"Now, father Dickson," he said, "this just shows you the truth of what I was telling you. This course of yours won't do; you see it won't, now. Now, if you'd agree not to say anything of these troublesome matters, and just confine yourself to the preaching of the Gospel, you see you wouldn't get into any more trouble; and, after all, it's the Gospel that's the root of the matter. The Gospel will gradually correct all these evils, if you don't say anything about them. You see, the state of the community is peculiar. They won't bear it. We feel the evils of slavery just as much as you do. Our souls are burdened under it," he said, complacently wiping his face with his handkerchief. "But Providence doesn't appear to open any door here for us to do anything. I think we ought to abide on the patient waiting on the Lord, who, in his own good time, will bring light out of darkness, and order out of confusion."

This last phrase being a part of a stereotyped exhortation with which the good elder was wont to indulge his brethren in church prayer-meetings, he delivered it in the sleepy drawl which he reserved for such occasions.

"Well," said father Dickson, "I must say that I don't see that the preaching of the Gospel, in the way we have preached it hitherto, has done anything to rectify the evil. It's a bad sign if our preaching doesn't make a conflict. When the apostles came to a place, they said, 'These men that turn the world upside down are come hither.' "[8]

"But," said Mr. Brown, "you must consider our institutions are peculiar; our negroes are ignorant and inflammable, easily wrought upon, and the most frightful consequences may result. That's the reason why there is so much sensation when any discussion is begun which relates to them. Now, I was in Nashville when that Dresser affair took place. He hadn't said a word—he hadn't opened his mouth, even—but he was known to be an abolitionist; and so they searched his trunks and papers, and there they found documents expressing abolition sentiments, sure enough. Well, everybody, ministers and elders, joined in that affair, and stood by to see him whipped. I thought, myself, they went too far. But there is just where it is. People are not reasonable, and they won't be reasonable, in such cases. It's too much to ask of them; and so everybody ought to be cautious. Now, I wish, for my part, that ministers would confine themselves to their appropriate duties. 'Christ's kingdom is not of this world.'[9] And, then, you don't know Tom Gordon. He is a terrible fellow! I never want to come in conflict with him. I thought I'd put the best face on it, and persuade him away. I didn't want to make Tom Gordon my enemy. And I think, Mr. Dickson, if you must preach these doctrines, I think it would be best for you to leave the state. Of course, we don't want to restrict any man's conscience; but when any kind of preaching excites brawls and confusion, and inflames the public mind, it seems to be a duty to give it up."

"Yes," said Mr. Cornet, the elder, "we ought to follow the things which make for peace—such things whereby one may edify another."

"Don't you see, gentlemen," said Mr. Clayton, "that such a course is surrendering our liberty of free speech into the hands of a mob? If Tom Gordon may dictate what is to be said on one subject, he may on another; and the rod which has been held over our friend's head to-night may be held over ours. Independent of the right or wrong of father Dickson's principles, he ought to maintain his position, for the sake of maintaining the right of free opinion in the state."

"Why," said Mr. Cornet, "the Scripture saith, 'If they persecute you into one city, flee ye into another.' "[10]

"That was said," said Clayton, "to a people that lived under despotism, and had no rights of liberty given them to maintain. But, if we give way before mob law, we make ourselves slaves of the worst despotism on earth."

But Clayton spoke to men whose ears were stopped by the cotton of slothfulness and love of ease. They rose up, and said,

"It was time for them to be going."

Clayton expressed his intention of remaining over the night, to afford encouragement and assistance to his friends, in case of any further emergency.

CHAPTER XXVI

More Violence

CLAYTON ROSE THE NEXT MORNING, and found his friends much better than he had expected after the agitation and abuse of the night before. They seemed composed and cheerful.

"I am surprised," he said, "to see that your wife is able to be up this morning."

"They that wait on the Lord shall renew their strength,"[1] said father Dickson. "How often I have found it so! We have seen times when I and my wife have both been so ill that we scarcely thought we had strength to help ourselves; and a child has been taken ill, or some other emergency has occurred that called for immediate exertion, and we have been to the Lord and found strength. Our way has been hedged up many a time—the sea before us and the Egyptians behind us; but the sea has always opened when we have stretched our hands to the Lord. I have never sought the Lord in vain. He has allowed great troubles to come upon us; but he always delivers us."

Clayton recalled the sneering, faithless, brilliant Frank Russel, and compared him, in his own mind, with the simple, honest man before him.

"No," he said, to himself, "human nature is not a humbug, after all. There are some real men—some who will not acquiesce in what is successful, if it be wrong."

Clayton was in need of such living examples; for, in regard to religion, he was in that position which is occupied by too many young men of high moral sentiment in this country. What he had seen of the worldly policy and time-serving spirit of most of the organized bodies professing to represent the Christian faith and life, had deepened the shadow of doubt and distrust which persons of strong individuality and discriminating minds are apt to feel in certain stages of their spiritual development. Great afflictions—those which tear up the roots of the soul—are often succeeded, in the course of the man's history, by a period of scepticism. The fact is, such afflictions are disenchanting powers; they give to the soul an earnestness and a power of discrimination which no illusion can withstand. They teach us what we need, what we must have to rest upon; and, in consequence, thousands of little formalities, and empty shows, and dry religious conventionalities, are scattered by it like chaff. The soul rejects them, in her indignant anguish; and, finding so much that is insincere, and untrue, and unreliable, she has sometimes hours of doubting all things.

Clayton saw again in the minister what he had seen in Nina—a soul swayed by an attachment to an invisible person, whose power over it was the power of a personal attachment, and who swayed it, not by dogmas or commands, merely, but by the force of a sympathetic emotion. Beholding, as in a glass, the divine image of his heavenly friend, insensibly to himself the minister was changing into the same image. The good and the beautiful to him was an embodied person,—even Jesus his Lord.

"What may be your future course?" said Clayton, with anxiety. "Will you discontinue your labors in this state?"

"I may do so, if I find positively that there is no gaining a hearing," said father Dickson. "I think we owe it to our state not to give up the point without a trial. There are those who are willing to hear me—willing to make a beginning with me. It is true they are poor and unfashionable; but still it is my duty not to desert them till I have tried, at least, whether the laws can't protect me in the exercise of my duty. The hearts of all men are in the hands of the Lord. He turneth them as the rivers of water are turned. This evil is a great and a trying one. It is gradually lowering the standard of morals in our churches, till men know not what spirit they are of. I held it my duty not to yield to the violence of the tyrant, and bind myself to a promise to leave, till I had considered what the will of my Master would be."

"I should be sorry," said Clayton, "to think that North Carolina couldn't protect you. I am sure, when the particulars of this are known, there will be a general reprobation from all parts of the country. You might remove to some other part of the state, not cursed by the residence of a man like Tom Gordon. I will confer with my uncle, your friend Dr. Cushing, and see if some more eligible situation cannot be found, where you can prosecute your labors. He is at this very time visiting his wife's father, in E., and I will ride over and talk with him to-day. Meanwhile," said Clayton, as he rose to depart, "allow me to leave with you a little contribution to help the cause of religious freedom in which you are engaged."

And Clayton, as he shook hands with his friend and his wife, left an amount of money with them such as had not crossed their palms for many a day. Bidding them adieu, a ride of a few hours carried him to E., where he communicated to Dr. Cushing the incidents of the night before.

"Why, it's perfectly shocking—abominable!" said Dr. Cushing. "Why, what are we coming to? My dear young friend, this shows the necessity of prayer. 'When the enemy cometh in like a flood, the Spirit of the Lord must lift up a standard against him.' "[2]

"My dear uncle," said Clayton, rather impatiently, "it seems to me the Lord has lifted up a standard in the person of this very man, and people are too cowardly to rally around it."

"Well, my dear nephew, it strikes me you are rather excited," said Dr. Cushing, good-naturedly.

"Excited?" said Clayton. "I ought to be excited! You ought to be excited, too! Here's a good man beginning what you think a necessary reform, and who does it in a way perfectly peaceable and lawful, who is cloven down under the hoof of a mob, and all you can think of doing is to pray to *the Lord* to raise up a standard! What would you think, if a man's house were on fire, and he should sit praying the Lord that in his mysterious providence he would put it out?"

"O, the cases are not parallel," said Dr. Cushing.

"I think they are," said Clayton. "Our house is the state, and our house is on fire by mob law; and, instead of praying the Lord to put it out, you ought to go to work and put it out yourself. If all you ministers would make a stand against this, uncle, and do all you can to influence those to whom you are preaching, it wouldn't be done again."

"I am sure I should be glad to do something. Poor father Dickson! such a good man as he is! But, then, I think, Clayton, he was rather imprudent. It don't do, this unadvised way of proceeding. We ought to watch against rashness, I think. We are too apt to be precipitate, and not await the leadings of Providence. Poor Dickson! I tried to caution him, the last time I wrote to him. To be sure, it's no excuse for them; but, then, I'll write to brother Barker on the subject, and we'll see if we can't get an article in the *Christian Witness*. I don't think it would be best to allude to these particular circumstances, or to mention any names; but there might be a general article on the importance of maintaining the right of free speech, and of course people can apply it for themselves."

"You remind me," said Clayton, "of a man who proposed commencing an attack on a shark by throwing a sponge at him. But, now, really, uncle, I am concerned for the safety of this good man. Isn't there any church near you to which he can be called? I heard him at the camp-meeting, and I think he is an excellent preacher."

"There are a good many churches," said Dr. Cushing, "which would be glad of him, if it were not for the course he pursues on that subject; and I really can't feel that he does right to throw away his influence so. He might be the means of converting souls, if he would only be quiet about this."

"Be quiet about fashionable sins," said Clayton, "in order to get a chance to convert souls! What sort of converts are those who are not willing to hear the truth on every subject? I should doubt conversions that can only be accomplished by silence on great practical immoralities."

"But," said Dr. Cushing, "Christ and the apostles didn't preach on the abuses of slavery, and they alluded to it as an existing institution."

"Nor did they preach on the gladiatorial shows," said Clayton; "and Paul draws many illustrations from them. Will you take the principle that everything is to be let alone now about which the apostles didn't preach directly?"

"I don't want to enter into that discussion now," said Dr. Cushing. "I believe I'll ride over and see brother Dickson. After all, he is a dear, good man, and I love him. I'd like to do something for him, if I were not afraid it might be misunderstood."

Toward evening, however, Clayton, becoming uneasy at the lonely situation of his clerical friend, resolved to ride over and pass the night with him, for the sake of protecting him; and, arming himself with a brace of pistols, he proceeded on his ride. As the day had been warm, he put off his purpose rather late, and darkness overtook him before he had quite accomplished his journey.

Riding deliberately through the woodland path in the vicinity of the swamp, he was startled by hearing the tramp of horses' hoofs behind him. Three men, mounted on horseback, were coming up, the headmost of whom, riding up quickly behind, struck him so heavy a blow with a gutta percha cane, as to fell him to the earth. In an instant, however, he was on his feet again, and had seized the bridle of his horse.

"Who are you?" said he; for, by the dim light that remained of the twilight, he could perceive that they all wore masks.

"We are men," said one of them, whose voice Clayton did not recognize, "that know how to deal with fellows who insult gentlemen, and then refuse to give them honorable satisfaction."

"And," said the second speaker, "we know how to deal with renegade abolitionists, who are covertly undermining our institutions."

"And," said Clayton, coolly, "you understand how to be cowards; for none but cowards would come three to one, and strike a man from behind! Shame on you! Well, gentlemen, act your pleasure. Your first blow has disabled my right arm. If you wish my watch and my purse, you may help yourselves, as cut-throats generally do!"

The stinging contempt which was expressed in these last words seemed to enrage the third man, who had not spoken. With a brutal oath, he raised his cane again, and struck at him.

"Strike a wounded man, who cannot help himself—do!" said Clayton. "Show yourself the coward you are! You are brave in attacking defenceless women and children, and ministers of the Gospel!"

This time the blow felled Clayton to the earth, and Tom Gordon, precipitating himself from his saddle, proved his eligibility for Congress by beating his defenceless acquaintance on the head, after the fashion of the chivalry of South Carolina.[3] But, at this moment, a violent blow from an unseen hand struck his right arm, and it fell, broken, at his side. Mad with pain, he poured forth volumes of oaths, such as our readers have never heard, and the paper refuses to receive. And a deep voice said from the woods,

"Woe to the bloody and deceitful man!"[4]

"Look for the fellow! where is he?" said Tom Gordon.

The crack of a rifle, and a bullet which passed right over his head, answered from the swamp, and the voice, which he knew was Harry's, called from within the thicket,

"Tom Gordon, beware! Remember Hark!" At the same time another rifle-shot came over their heads.

"Come, come," said the other two, "there's a gang of them. We had better be off. You can't do anything with that broken arm, there." And, helping Tom into the saddle, the three rode away precipitately.

As soon as they were gone, Harry and Dred emerged from the thicket. The latter was reported among his people to have some medical and surgical skill. He raised Clayton up, and examined him carefully.

"He is not dead," he said.

"What shall we do for him?" said Harry. "Shall we take him along to the minister's cabin?"

"No, no," said Dred; "that would only bring the Philistines[5] upon him!"

"It's full three miles to E.," said Harry. "It wouldn't do to risk going there."

"No, indeed," said Dred. "We must take him to our stronghold of Engedi, even as Samson bore the gates of Gaza.[6] Our women shall attend him, and when he is recovered we will set him on his journey."

CHAPTER XXVII

Engedi

THE QUESTION MAY OCCUR to our readers, why a retreat which appeared so easily accessible to the negroes of the vicinity in which our story is laid, should escape the vigilance of hunters.

In all despotic countries, however, it will be found that the oppressed party become expert in the means of secrecy. It is also a fact that the portion of the community who are trained to labor enjoy all that advantage over the more indolent portion of it which can be given by a vigorous physical system, and great capabilities of endurance. Without a doubt, the balance of the physical strength of the South now lies in the subject race. Usage familiarizes the dwellers of the swamp with the peculiarities of their location, and gives them the advantage in it that a mountaineer has in his own mountains. Besides, they who take their life in their hand exercise their faculties with more vigor and clearness than they who have only money at stake; and this advantage the negroes had over the hunters.

Dred's "strong hold of Engedi," as we have said, was isolated from the rest of the swamp by some twenty yards of deep morass, in which it was necessary to wade almost to the waist. The shore presented to the eye only the appearance of an impervious jungle of cat-brier and grape-vine rising out of the water. There was but one spot on which there was a clear space to set foot on, and that was the place where Dred crept up on the night when we first introduced the locality to our readers' attention.

The hunters generally satisfied themselves with exploring more apparently accessible portions; and, unless betrayed by those to whom Dred had communicated the clue, there was very little chance that any accident would ever disclose the retreat.

Dred himself appeared to be gifted with that peculiar faculty of discernment of spirits which belonged to his father, Denmark Vesey, sharpened into a preternatural intensity by the habits of his wild and dangerous life. The men he selected for trust were men as impenetrable as himself, the most vigorous in mind and body on all the plantations.

The perfectness of his own religious enthusiasm, his absolute certainty that he was inspired of God, as a leader and deliverer, gave him an ascendency over the minds of those who followed him, which nothing but religious enthusiasm ever can give. And this was further confirmed by the rigid austerity of his life. For all animal comforts he appeared to entertain a profound contempt. He never tasted strong liquors in any form, and was extremely sparing in his eating; often fasting for days in succession, particularly when he had any movement of importance in contemplation.

It is difficult to fathom the dark recesses of a mind so powerful and active as his, placed under a pressure of ignorance and social disability so tremendous. In those desolate regions which he made his habitation, it is said that trees often, from the singularly unnatural and wildly stimulating properties of the slimy depths from which they spring, assume a goblin growth, entirely different from their normal habit. All sorts of vegetable monsters stretch their weird, fantastic forms among its shadows. There is no principle so awful through all nature as the principle of *growth*. It is a mysterious and dread condition of existence, which, place it under what impediment or disadvantage you will, is constantly forcing on; and when unnatural pressure hinders it, develops in forms portentous and astonishing. The wild, dreary belt of swamp-land which girds in those states scathed by the fires of despotism is an apt emblem, in its rampant and we might say delirious exuberance of vegetation, of that darkly struggling, wildly vegetating swamp of human souls, cut off, like it, from the usages and improvements of cultivated life.

Beneath that fearful pressure, souls whose energy, well-directed, might have blessed mankind, start out in preternatural and fearful developments, whose strength is only a portent of dread.

The night after the meeting which we have described was one, to this singular being, of agonizing conflict. His psychological condition, as near as we can define it, seemed to be that of a human being who had been seized and possessed, after the manner related in ancient fables, by the wrath of an avenging God. That part of the moral constitution, which exists in some degree in us all, which leads us to feel pain at the sight of injustice, and to desire retribu-

tion for cruelty and crime, seemed in him to have become an absorbing sentiment, as if he had been chosen by some higher power
as the instrument of doom. At some moments the idea of the crimes
and oppressions which had overwhelmed his race rolled in upon
him with a burning pain, which caused him to cry out, like the fated
and enslaved Cassandra,[1] at the threshold of the dark house of
tyranny and blood.

This sentiment of justice, this agony in view of cruelty and
crime, is in men a strong attribute of the highest natures; for he who
is destitute of the element of moral indignation is effeminate and
tame. But there is in nature and in the human heart a pleading, interceding element, which comes in constantly to temper and soften
this spirit and this element in the divine mind, which the Scriptures
represent by the sublime image of an eternally interceding high
priest, who, having experienced every temptation of humanity, constantly urges all that can be thought in mitigation of justice. As a
spotless and high-toned mother bears in her bosom the anguish of
the impurity and vileness of her child, so the eternally suffering,
eternally interceding love of Christ bears the sins of our race. But
the Scriptures tell us that the mysterious *person*, who thus stands
before all worlds as the image and impersonation of divine tenderness, has yet in reserve this awful energy of wrath. The oppressors,
in the last dread day, are represented as calling to the mountains and
rocks to fall on them, and hide them from the wrath of the LAMB.
This idea had dimly loomed up before the mind of Dred, as he read
and pondered the mysteries of the sacred oracles; and was expressed
by him in the form of language so frequent in his mouth, that "the
Lamb was bearing the yoke of the sins of men." He had been
deeply affected by the presentation which Milly had made in their
night meeting of the eternal principle of intercession and atonement. The sense of it was blindly struggling with the habitual and
overmastering sense of oppression and wrong.

When his associates had all dispersed to their dwellings, he threw
himself on his face, and prayed, "O, Lamb of God, that bearest the
yoke, why hast thou filled me with wrath? Behold these graves! Behold the graves of my brothers, slain without mercy, and, Lord,
they do not repent! Thou art of purer eyes than to behold evil, and
canst not look on iniquity. Wherefore lookest thou upon them that
deal treacherously, and holdest thy tongue when the wicked de-

voureth the man that is more righteous than he? They make men as
fishes in the sea, as creeping things that have no ruler over them.
They take them up with the angle. They catch them in their net, and
gather them in their drag. Therefore they rejoice and are glad.
Therefore they sacrifice unto their net, and burn incense unto their
drag, because by them their portion is fat, and their meat plenteous.
Shall they, therefore, empty their net, and not spare continually to
slay the nations? Did not he that made them in the womb make us?
Did not the same God fashion us in the womb? Doubtless thou art
our Father, though Abraham be ignorant of us, and Israel acknowl-
edgeth us not. Thou, O God, art our Father, our Redeemer. Wherefore forgettest thou us forever, and forsakest us so long a time? Wilt
thou not judge between us and our enemies? Behold, there is none
among them that stirreth himself up to call upon thee, and he that
departeth from evil maketh himself a prey. They lie in wait, they set
traps, they catch men, they are waxen fat, they shine, they overpass
the deeds of the wicked, they judge not the cause of the fatherless;
yet they prosper, and the right of the needy do they not judge. Wilt
thou not visit for these things, O Lord? Shall not thy soul be
avenged on such a nation as this? How long wilt thou endure? Behold under the altar the souls of those they have slain! They cry
unto thee continually. How long, O Lord, dost thou not judge and
avenge? Is there any that stirreth himself up for justice? Is there any
that regardeth our blood? We are sold for silver; the price of our
blood is in thy treasury; the price of our blood is on thine altars!
Behold, they build their churches with the price of our hire! Behold, the stone doth cry out of the wall, and the timber doth answer
it. Because they build their towns with blood, and establish their
cities by iniquity. They have all gone one way. There is none that
careth for the spoilings of the poor. Art thou a just God? When wilt
thou arise to shake terribly the earth, that the desire of all nations
may come? Overturn, overturn, and overturn, till *he* whose right it
is shall come!"[2]

Such were the words, not uttered continuously, but poured forth
at intervals, with sobbings, groanings, and moanings, from the recesses of that wild fortress. It was but a part of that incessant prayer
with which oppressed humanity has besieged the throne of justice
in all ages. We who live in ceiled houses would do well to give heed
to that sound, lest it be to us that inarticulate moaning which goes
before the earthquake. If we would estimate the force of almighty

justice, let us ask ourselves what a mother might feel for the abuse of her helpless child, and multiply that by infinity.

But the night wore on, and the stars looked down serene and solemn, as if no prayer had gone through the calm, eternal gloom; and the morning broke in the east resplendent.

Harry, too, had passed a sleepless night. The death of Hark weighed like a mountain upon his heart. He had known him for a whole-souled, true-hearted fellow. He had been his counsellor and friend for many years, and he had died in silent torture for him. How stinging is it at such a moment to view the whole respectability of civilized society upholding and glorifying the murderer; calling his sin by soft names, and using for his defence every artifice of legal injustice! Some in our own nation have had bitter occasion to know this, for we have begun to drink the cup of trembling which for so many ages has been drank alone by the slave. Let the associates of Brown[3] ask themselves if they cannot understand the midnight anguish of Harry!

His own impulses would have urged to an immediate insurrection, in which he was careless about his own life, so the fearful craving of his soul for justice was assuaged. To him the morning seemed to break red with the blood of his friend. He would have urged to immediate and precipitate action. But Dred, true to the enthusiastic impulses which guided him, persisted in waiting for that sign from heaven which was to indicate when the day of grace was closed, and the day of judgment to begin. This expectation he founded on his own version of certain passages in the prophets, such as these:

"I will show wonders in heaven above, and signs in the earth beneath; blood, and fire, and vapor of smoke! The sun shall be turned into darkness, and the moon into blood, before that great and notable day of the Lord shall come!"[4]

Meanwhile, his associates were to be preparing the minds of the people, and he was traversing the swamps in different directions, holding nightly meetings, in which he read and expounded the prophecies to excited ears. The laborious arguments, by which Northern and Southern doctors of divinity have deduced from the Old Testament the divine institution of slavery, were too subtle and fine-spun to reach his ear amid the denunciations of prophecies, all turning on the sin of oppression. His instinctive understanding of the spirit of the Bible justified the sagacity which makes the supporter of slavery, to this day, careful not to allow the slave the

power of judging it for himself; and we leave it to any modern proslavery divine whether, in Dred's circumstances, his own judgment
might not have been the same.

After daylight, Harry saw Dred standing, with a dejected countenance, outside of his hut.

"I have wrestled," he said, "for thee; but the time is not yet! Let
us abide certain days, for the thing is secret unto me; and I cannot
do less nor more till the Lord giveth commandment. When the
Lord delivereth them into our hands, one shall chase a thousand,
and two put ten thousand to flight!"[5]

"After all," said Harry, "our case is utterly hopeless! A few poor,
outcast wretches, without a place to lay our heads, and they all revelling in their splendor and their power! Who is there in this great
nation that is not pledged against us? Who would not cry *Amen*, if
we were dragged out and hung like dogs? The North is as bad as the
South! They kill us, and the North consents and justifies! And all
their wealth, power, and religion, are used against us. We are the
ones that all sides are willing to give up. Any party in church or of
state will throw in our blood and bones as a make-weight, and
think nothing of it. And, when I see them riding out in their splendid equipages, their houses full of everything that is elegant, they so
cultivated and refined, and our people so miserable, poor, and
down-trodden, I haven't any faith that there is a God!"

"Stop!" said Dred, laying his hand on his arm. "Hear what the
prophet saith. 'Their land, also, is full of silver and gold; neither is
there any end of their treasures. Their land, also, is full of horses;
neither is there any end of their chariots. Their land also is full of
idols. They worship the work of their own hands. Enter into the
rock, and hide thee in the dust, for fear of the Lord, and for the
glory of His majesty. The lofty looks of man shall be humbled, and
the haughtiness of man shall be bowed down, and the Lord alone
shall be exalted in that day. For the day of the Lord of Hosts shall
be on every one that is proud and lofty, and upon every one that is
lifted up; and he shall be brought low! And upon all the cedars of
Lebanon that are high and lifted up, and upon all the oaks of
Bashan, and upon all the high mountains, and upon all the hills that
are lifted up, and upon every high tower, and upon every fenced
wall, and upon all the ships of Tarshish, and upon all pleasant pictures! And the loftiness of man shall be bowed down, the haughtiness of man shall be made low! And they shall go in the holes of the

rocks, and in the caves of the earth, for fear of the Lord, and for his majesty, when he ariseth to shake terribly the earth!' "[6]

The tall pines, and whispering oaks, as they stood waving in purple freshness at the dawn, seemed like broad-winged attesting angels, bearing witness, in their serene and solemn majesty, to the sublime words, "Heaven and earth shall not pass away till these words have been fulfilled!"[7]

After a few moments a troubled expression came over the face of Dred.

"Harry," he said, "verily, he is a God that hideth himself! He giveth none account to any of these matters. It may be that I shall not lead the tribes over this Jordan; but that I shall lay my bones in the wilderness! But the day shall surely come, and the sign of the Son of Man shall appear in the air, and all tribes of the earth shall wail, because of him! Behold, I saw white spirits and black spirits, that contended in the air; and the thunder rolled, and the blood flowed, and the voice said, 'Come rough, come smooth! Such is the decree. Ye must surely bear it!' But, as yet, the prayers of the saints have power; for there be angels, having golden censers, which be the prayers of saints. And the Lord, by reason thereof, delayeth. Behold I have borne the burden of the Lord even for many years. He hath covered me with a cloud in the day of his anger, and filled me with his wrath; and his word has been like a consuming fire shut in my bones! He hath held mine eyes waking, and my bones have waxed old with my roarings all the day long! Then I have said, 'O, that thou wouldst hide me in the dust! That thou wouldst keep me secret till thy wrath be past!' "[8]

At this moment, soaring upward through the blue sky, rose the fair form of a wood-pigeon, wheeling and curving in the morning sunlight, cutting the ether with airy flight, so smooth, even, and clear, as if it had learnt motion from the music of angels.

Dred's eye, faded and haggard with his long night-watchings, followed it for a moment with an air of softened pleasure, in which was blent somewhat of weariness and longing.

"O, that I had wings like a dove!" he said. "Then would I flee away and be at rest! I would hasten from the windy storm and tempest! Lo, then I would wander far off, and remain in the wilderness!"[9]

There was something peculiar in the power and energy which this man's nature had of drawing others into the tide of its own sympathies, as a strong ship, walking through the water, draws all the smaller craft into its current.

Harry, melancholy and disheartened as he was, felt himself borne out with him in that impassioned prayer.

"I know," said Dred, "that the new heavens and the new earth shall come, and the redeemed of the Lord shall walk in it. But, as for me, I am a man of unclean lips, and the Lord hath laid on me the oppressions of the people![10] But, though the violent man prevail against me, it shall surely come to pass!"

Harry turned away, and walked slowly to the other side of the clearing, where Old Tiff, with Fanny, Teddy, and Lisette, having kindled a fire on the ground, was busy in preparing their breakfast. Dred, instead of going into his house, disappeared in the thicket. Milly had gone home with the man who came from Canema. The next day, as Harry and Dred made a hunting excursion through the swamp, returning home in the edge of the evening, they happened to be passing near the scene of lawless violence which we have already described.

CHAPTER XXVIII

The Slave Hunt

TOM GORDON, for the next two or three days after his injury, was about as comfortable to manage as a wounded hyena. He had a thousand varying caprices every hour and moment; and now one and now another prevailed. The miserable girls who were held by him as his particular attendants were tormented by every species of annoyance which a restless and passionate man, in his impatience, could devise.

The recent death of Milly's mistress by the cholera had reduced her under Tom's authority; and she was summoned now from her work every hour to give directions and advice, which, the minute they were given, were repudiated with curses.

"I declare," said Aunt Katy, the housekeeper, "if Mas'r Tom isn't 'nough to use a body off o' der feet. It's jist four times I's got gruel ready for him dis last two hours—doing all I could to suit him; and he swars at it, and flings it round real undecent. Why, he's got fever, and does he spect to make things taste good to him, when he's got fever! Why, course I can't, and no need of him calling me a devil, and all that! That ar's very unnecessary, I think. I don't believe in no such! The Gordons allers used to have some sense to 'em, even if they was cross; but he an't got a grain. I should think he was 'sessed wid Old Sam,[1] for my part. Bringing 'sgrace on us all, the way he cuts up! We really don' know how to hold up our head, none of us. The Gordons have allers been sich a genteel family! Laws, we didn't know what privileges we had when we had Miss Nina! Them new girls, dressed up in all their flounces and ferbuloes! Guess they has to take it!"

In time, however, even in spite of his chafing, and fretfulness, and contempt of physicians' prescriptions, Tom seemed to recover, by the same kind of fatality which makes ill-weeds thrive apace. Meanwhile he employed his leisure hours in laying plans of revenge, to be executed as soon as he should be able to take to his horse again. Among other things, he vowed deep vengeance on Abijah Skinflint, who, he said, he knew *must* have sold the powder and ammunition to the negroes in the swamp. This may have been true, or may not; but, in cases of lynch-law, such questions are indifferent matter. A man is accused, condemned, and judged, at the will of his more powerful neighbor. It was sufficient to Tom that *he thought so;* and, being sick and cross, thought so just now with more particular intensity.

Jim Stokes, he knew, cherished an animosity of long standing towards Abijah, which he could make use of in enlisting him in the cause. One of the first uses, therefore, which Tom made of his recovered liberty, after he was able to ride out, was to head a raid on Abijah's shop. The shop was without ceremony dismantled and plundered; and the mob, having helped themselves to his whiskey, next amused themselves by tarring and feathering him; and, having insulted and abused him to their satisfaction, and exacted a promise from him to leave the state within three days, they returned home glorious in their own eyes. And the next week a brilliant account of the affair appeared in the *Trumpet of Liberty,* headed

"Summary Justice."

Nobody pitied Abijah, of course; and, as he would probably have been quite willing to join in the same sort of treatment for any one else, we know not that we are particularly concerned for his doom. The respectable people in the neighborhood first remarked that they didn't approve of mobs in general, and then dilated, with visible satisfaction, on this in particular, after a fashion of that stupid class that are called respectable people, generally. The foolish mob gloried and exulted, not considering that any day the same weapons might be turned against them. The mob being now somewhat drilled and animated, Tom proposed, while their spirit was up, to get up a hunting in the swamp, which should more fully satisfy his own private vengeance. There is a sleeping tiger in the human breast that delights in violence and blood; and this tiger Tom resolved to unchain.

The act of outlawry had already publicly set up Harry as a mark for whatever cruelty drunken ingenuity might choose to perpetrate. As our readers may have a curiosity in this kind of literature, we will indulge them with a copy of this:

"State of North Carolina, Chowan County.
"Whereas, complaint upon oath hath this day been made to us, two of the Justices of the Peace for the said county and state aforesaid, by Thomas Gordon, that a certain male slave belonging to him, named Harry, a carpenter by trade, about thirty-five years old, five feet four inches high, or thereabouts; dark complexion, stout built, blue eyes, deep sunk in his head, forehead very square, tolerably loud voice; hath absented himself from his master's service, and is supposed to be lurking about in the swamp, committing acts of felony or other misdeeds. These are, therefore, in the name of the state aforesaid, to command said slave forthwith to surrender himself, and return home to his said master. And we do hereby, by virtue of the act of assembly, in such case made and provided, intimate and declare that, if the said slave Harry doth not surrender himself, and return home immediately after the publication of these presents, that any person or persons may kill and destroy the said slave by such means as he or they may think fit, without accusation or impeachment of any crime or offence for so doing, and without incurring any penalty or forfeiture thereby.   Given under our hands and seal,

JAMES T. MULLER,   { SEAL }
T. BUTTERCOURT."* { SEAL }

One can scarcely contemplate without pity the condition of a population which grows up under the influence of such laws and customs as these. That the lowest brutality and the most fiendish cruelty should be remorselessly practised by those whose ferocity thus receives the sanction of the law, cannot be wondered at. Tom Gordon convened at his house an assemblage of those whom he used as the tools and ministers of his vengeance. Harry had been secretly hated by them all in his prosperous days, because, though a slave, he was better dressed, better educated, and, on the whole, treated with more consideration by the Gordon family and their guests, than they were; and, at times, he had had occasion to rebuke some of them for receiving from the slaves goods taken from the plantation. To be sure, while he was prosperous they were outwardly subservient to him, as the great man of a great family; but

---

*The original document from which this is taken can be seen in the appendix. It appeared in the *Wilmington Journal*, December 18, 1850.

now he was *down,* as the amiable fashion of the world generally is, they resolved to make up for their former subservience by redoubled insolence.

Jim Stokes, in particular, bore Harry a grudge, for having once expressed himself with indignation concerning the meanness and brutality of his calling; and he was therefore the more willing to be made use of on the present occasion. Accordingly, on the morning we speak of, there was gathered before the door of the mansion at Canema a confused mélange of men, of that general style of appearance which, in our times, we call "Border Ruffians,"[2]—half-drunken, profane, obscene as the harpies which descended on the feast of Æneas.[3] Tom Gordon had only this advantage among them, that superior education and position had given him the power, when he chose, of assuming the appearance and using the language of a gentleman. But he had enough of grossness within, to enable him at will to become as one of them. Tom's arm was still worn in a sling, but, as lack of energy never was one of his faults, he was about to take the saddle with his troop. At present they were drawn up before the door, laughing, swearing, and drinking whiskey, which flowed in abundance. The dogs—the better-mannered brutes of the two, by all odds—were struggling in their leashes with impatience and excitement. Tom Gordon stood forth on the veranda, after the fashion of great generals of old, who harangued their troops on the eve of battle. Any one who has read the speeches of the leaders who presided over the sacking of Lawrence[4] will get an idea of some features in this style of eloquence, which our pen cannot represent.

"Now, boys," said Tom, "you are getting your names up. You've done some good work already. You've given that old, snivelling priest a taste of true orthodox doctrine, that will enlighten him for the future. You've given that long-nosed Skinflint light enough to see the error of *his* ways."

A general laugh here arose, and voices repeated,

"Ah, ah, that we did! Didn't we, though?"

"I reckon you did!" said Tom Gordon. "I reckon he didn't need candles to see his sins by, that night! Didn't we make a candle of his old dog-kennel? Didn't he have light to see his way out of the state by? and didn't we give him a suit to keep him warm on the road? Ah, boys, that was a warm suit—no mistake! It was a suit that will stick to him, too! He won't trade that off for rum, in a hurry, I'm thinking! Will he, boys?"

Bursts of crazy, half-drunken applause here interrupted the orator.

"Pity we hadn't put a match to it!" shouted one.

"Ah, well, boys, you did enough for that time! Wait till you catch these sneaking varmins in the swamp, you shall do what you like with them. Nobody shall hinder you, that's law and order. These foxes have troubled us long enough, stealing at our hen-roosts while we were asleep. We shall make it hot for them, if we catch them; and we are going to catch them. There are no two ways about it. This old swamp is like Davy's coon—it's got *to come down!* And it will come down, boys, when it sees *us* coming. No mistake about that! Now, boys, mind, catch him alive, if you can; but shoot him, if you can't. Remember, I'll give a hundred and fifty dollars for his head!"

A loud shout chorused this last announcement, and Tom descended in glory to take his place in his saddle.

Once, we suppose, this history would not have been believed, had it been told; but of late our own sons and brothers have been hounded and hunted by just such men, with such means.

The fire which began in the dry tree has spread to the green!

Long live the *great Christianizing Institution!!!*

CHAPTER XXIX

"All Over"

CLAYTON, at the time of the violent assault which we have described, received an injury upon the head which rendered him insensible.

When he came to himself, he was conscious at first only of a fanning of summer breezes. He opened his eyes, and looked listlessly up into the blue sky, that appeared through the thousand leafy hollows of waving boughs. Voices of birds warbling and calling, like answering echoes, to each other, fell dreamily on his ear. Some gentle hand was placing bandages about his head; and figures of women, he did not recognize, moved whisperingly around him, tending and watching.

He dropped asleep again, and thus for many hours lay in a kind of heavy trance.

Harry and Lisette had vacated, for his use, their hut; but, as it was now the splendid weather of October, when earth and sky become a temple of beauty and serenity, they tended him during the hours of the day in the open air, and it would seem as if there were no art of healing like to this. As air and heat and water all have a benevolent tendency to enter and fill up a vacuum, so we might fancy the failing vitality of the human system to receive accessions of vigor by being placed in the vicinity of the healthful growths of nature. All the trees which John saw around the river of life[1] and heaven bore healing leaves; and there may be a sense in which the trees of our world bear leaves that are healing both to body and soul. He who hath gone out of the city, sick, disgusted, and wearied, and lain himself down in the forest, under the fatherly shadow of an oak, may have heard this whispered to him in the leafy rustlings of a thousand tongues.

* * * * * * *

"See," said Dred to Harry, as they were watching over the yet insensible form of Clayton, "how the word of the Lord is fulfilled on this people. He shall deliver them, every man, into the hand of his neighbor; and he that departeth from evil maketh himself a prey!"

"Yes," said Harry; "but this is a good man; he stands up for our rights. If he had his way, we should soon have justice done us."

"Yes," said Dred, "but it is even as it was of old; 'behold I send unto you prophets and wise men, and some of them shall ye slay. For this people's heart is waxed gross, and their ears have they closed. Therefore, the Lord shall bring upon this generation the blood of all the slain, from the blood of righteous Abel to the blood of Zacharias, the son of Barachias, whom they slew between the temple and the altar.' "[2]

        *   *   *   *   *   *   *

After a day or two spent in a kind of listless dreaming, Clayton was so far recovered as to be able to sit up and look about him. The serene tranquillity of the lovely October skies seemed to fall like a spell upon his soul.

Amidst the wild and desolate swamp, here was an island of security, where nature took men to her sheltering bosom. A thousand birds, speaking with thousand airy voices, were calling from breezy tree-tops, and from swinging cradles of vine-leaves; white clouds sailed, in changing and varying islands, over the heavy green battlements of the woods. The wavering slumberous sound of thousand leaves, through which the autumn air walked to and fro, consoled him. Life began to look to him like a troubled dream, forever past. His own sufferings, the hours of agony and death which he had never dared to remember, seemed now to wear a new and glorified form. Such is the divine power in which God still reveals himself through the lovely and incorruptible forms of nature.

Clayton became interested in Dred, as a psychological study. At first he was silent and reserved, but attended to the wants of his guest with evident respect and kindness. Gradually, however, the love of expression, which lies hidden in almost every soul, began to unfold itself in him, and he seemed to find pleasure in a sympathetic listener. His wild jargon of hebraistic phrases, names, and allusions, had for Clayton, in his enfeebled state, a quaint and poetic interest. He compared him, in his own mind, to one of those old rude Gothic doorways, so frequent in European cathedrals, where scriptural images, carved in rough granite, mingle themselves with a

thousand wayward, fantastic freaks of architecture; and sometimes
he thought, with a sigh, how much might have been accomplished
by a soul so ardent and a frame so energetic, had they been enlightened and guided.

Dred would sometimes come, in the shady part of the afternoon,
and lie on the grass beside him, and talk for hours in a quaint, rambling, dreamy style, through which there were occasional flashes of
practical ability and shrewdness.

He had been a great traveller—a traveller through regions generally held inaccessible to human foot and eye. He had explored not
only the vast swamp-girdle of the Atlantic, but the everglades of
Florida, with all their strange and tropical luxuriance of growth; he
had wandered along the dreary and perilous belt of sand which
skirts the southern Atlantic shores, full of quicksands and of dangers, and there he had mused of the eternal secret of the tides, with
whose restless, never-ceasing rise and fall the soul of man has a
mysterious sympathy. Destitute of the light of philosophy and science, he had revolved in the twilight of his ardent and struggling
thoughts the causes of natural phenomena, and settled those questions for himself by theories of his own. Sometimes his residence
for weeks had been a stranded hulk, cast on one of these inhos-
pitable shores, where he fasted and prayed, and fancied that answering voices came to him in the moaning of the wind and the sullen
swell of the sea.

Our readers behold him now, stretched on the grass beside the
hut of Harry and Lisette, in one of his calmest and most commu-
nicative moods.

The children, with Lisette and the women, were searching for
grapes in a distant part of the enclosure; and Harry, with the other
fugitive man, had gone to bring in certain provisions which were to
have been deposited for them in a distant part of the swamp by
some of their confederates on one of the plantations. Old Tiff was
hoeing potatoes diligently in a spot not very far distant, and evidently listening to the conversation with an ear of shrewd attention.

"Yes," said Dred, with that misty light in his eye which one may
often have remarked in the eye of enthusiasts, "the glory holds off,
but it is coming! Now is the groaning time! *That* was revealed to
me when I was down at Okerecoke,[3] when I slept three weeks in
the hulk of a ship out of which all souls had perished."

"Rather a dismal abode, my friend," said Clayton, by way of drawing him on to conversation.

"The Spirit drove me there," said Dred, "for I had besought the Lord to show unto me the knowledge of things to come; and the Lord bade me to go from the habitations of men, and to seek out the desolate places of the sea, and dwell in the wreck of a ship that was forsaken for a sign of desolation unto this people. So I went and dwelt there, and the Lord called me Amraphal,[4] because hidden things of judgment were made known unto me. And the Lord showed unto me that even as a ship which is forsaken of the waters, wherein all flesh have died, so shall it be with the nation of the oppressor."

"How did the Lord show you this?" said Clayton, bent upon pursuing his inquiry.

"Mine ear received it in the night season," said Dred, "and I heard how the whole creation groaneth and travaileth,[5] waiting for the adoption; and because of this he hath appointed the tide."

"I don't see the connection," said Clayton. "Why because of this?"

"Because," said Dred, "every day is full of labor, but the labor goeth back again into the seas. So that travail of all generations hath gone back, till the desire of all nations shall come, and He shall come with burning and with judgment, and with great shakings; but in the end thereof shall be peace. Wherefore, it is written that in the new heavens and the new earth there shall be no more sea."[6]

These words were uttered with an air of solemn, assured confidence, that impressed Clayton strangely. Something in his inner nature seemed to recognize in them a shadow of things hoped for. He was in that mood into which the mind of him who strives with the evils of this world must often fall—a mood of weariness and longing; and heard within him the cry of the human soul, tempest-tossed and not comforted, for rest and assurance of the state where there shall be no more sea.

"So, then," he said unto Dred, "so, then, you believe that these heavens and earth shall be made new."

"Assuredly," said Dred. "And the King shall reign in righteousness. He shall deliver the needy when he crieth,—the poor and him that hath no helper. He shall redeem their souls from deceit and violence. He shall sit upon a white cloud, and the rainbow shall be round about his head.[7] And the elect of the Lord shall be kings and priests on the earth."

"And do you think you shall be one of them?" said Clayton.

Dred gave a kind of inward groan.

"Not every one that prophesieth in his name shall be found worthy!" he said. "I have prayed the Lord, but he hath not granted me the assurance. I am the rod of his wrath, to execute vengeance on his enemies. Shall the axe magnify itself against him that lifteth it?"[8]

The conversation was here interrupted by Harry, who, suddenly springing from the tree, came up, in a hurried and agitated manner.

"The devil is broke loose!" he said. "Tom Gordon is out, with his whole crew at his heels, beating the swamp! A more drunken, swearing, ferocious set I never saw! They have got on to the trail of poor Jim, and are tracking him without mercy!"

A dark light flashed from Dred's eye, as he sprang upon his feet.

"The voice of the Lord shaketh the wilderness; yea, the wilderness of Kadesh.[9] I will go forth and deliver him!"

He seized his rifle and shot-bag, and in a few moments was gone. It was Harry's instinct to have followed him; but Lisette threw herself, weeping, on his neck.

"Don't go—don't!" she said. "What shall we all do without you? Stay with us! You'll certainly be killed, and you can do no good!"

"Consider," said Clayton, "that you have not the familiarity with these swamps, nor the wonderful physical power of this man. It would only be throwing away your life."

The hours of that day passed gloomily. Sometimes the brutal sound of the hunt seemed to sweep near them,—the crack of rifles, the baying of dogs, the sound of oaths,—and then again all went off into silence, and nothing was heard but the innocent patter of leaf upon leaf, and the warbling of the birds, singing cheerily, ignorant of the abyss of cruelty and crime over which they sang.

Towards sunset a rustling was heard in the branches of the oak, and Dred dropped down into the enclosure, wet, and soiled, and wearied. All gathered round him, in a moment.

"Where is Jim?" asked Harry.

"Slain!" said Dred. "The archers pressed him sore, and he hath fallen in the wilderness!"

There was a general exclamation of horror. Dred made a movement to sit down on the earth. He lost his balance, and fell; and they all saw now, what at first they had not noticed, a wound in his breast, from which the blood was welling. His wife fell by his side, with wild moans of sorrow. He lifted his hand, and motioned her from him.

"Peace," he said, "peace! It is enough! Behold, I go unto the witnesses who cry day and night!"[10]

The circle stood around him in mute horror and surprise. Clayton was the first who had presence of mind to kneel and stanch the blood. Dred looked at him; his calm, large eyes filled with supernatural light.

"All over!" he said.

He put his hand calmly to his side, and felt the gushing blood. He took some in his hand and threw it upward, crying out, with wild energy, in the words of an ancient prophet,

"O, earth, earth, earth! Cover thou not my blood!"[11]

Behind the dark barrier of the woods the sun was setting gloriously. Piles of loose, floating clouds, which all day long had been moving through the sky in white and silvery stillness, now one after another took up the rosy flush, and became each one a light-bearer, filled with ethereal radiance. And the birds sang on as they ever sing, unterrified by the great wail of human sorrow.

It was evident to the little circle that He who is mightier than the kings of the earth was there, and that that splendid frame, which had so long rejoiced in the exuberance of health and strength, was now to be resolved again into the eternal elements.

"Harry," he said, "lay me beneath the heap of witness. Let the God of their fathers judge between us!"

CHAPTER XXX

The Burial

THE DEATH OF DRED fell like a night of despair on the hearts of the little fugitive circle in the swamps—on the hearts of multitudes in the surrounding plantations, who had regarded him as a prophet and a deliverer. He in whom they trusted was dead! The splendid, athletic form, so full of wild vitality, the powerful arm, the trained and keen-seeing eye, all struck down at once! The grand and solemn voice hushed, and all the splendid poetry of olden time, the inspiring symbols and prophetic dreams, which had so wrought upon his own soul, and with which he had wrought upon the souls of others, seemed to pass away with him, and to recede into the distance and become unsubstantial, like the remembered sounds of mighty winds, or solemn visions of evening clouds, in times long departed.

On that night, when the woods had ceased to reverberate the brutal sounds of baying dogs, and the more brutal profanity of drunken men; when the leaves stood still on the trees, and the forest lay piled up in the darkness like black clouds, and the morning star was standing like a calm angelic presence above them, there might have been heard in the little clearing a muffled sound of footsteps, treading heavily, and voices of those that wept with a repressed and quiet weeping, as they bore the wild chieftain to his grave beneath the blasted tree. Of the undaunted circle who had met there at the same hour many evenings before, some had dared to be present to-night; for, hearing the report of the hunt, they had left their huts on the plantations by stealth, when all were asleep, and, eluding the vigilance of the patrols, the night watch which commonly guards plantations, had come to the forest to learn the fate of their friends; and bitter was the dismay and anguish which filled their souls when they learned the result. It is melancholy to reflect, that among the children of one Father an event which excites in one class bitterness

and lamentation should in another be cause of exultation and triumph. But the world has been thousands of years and not yet
learned the first two words of the Lord's prayer; and not until all
tribes and nations have learned these will his kingdom come, and
his will be done, on earth, as it is in heaven.

Among those who stood around the grave, none seemed more
bowed down and despairing than one whom we have before introduced to the reader, under the name of Hannibal. He was a tall and
splendidly formed negro, whose large head, high forehead, and
marked features, indicated resolution and intellectual ability. He
had been all his life held as the property of an uneducated man, of
very mean and parsimonious character, who was singularly divided
in his treatment of him, by a desire to make the most of his energies
and capabilities as a slave, and a fear lest they should develop so fast
as to render him unfit for the condition of slavery.

Hannibal had taught himself to read and write, but the secret of
the acquisition was guarded in his own bosom, as vigilantly as the
traveller among thieves would conceal in his breast an inestimable
diamond; for he well knew that, were these acquisitions discovered,
his master's fears would be so excited as to lead him to realize at
once a present sum upon him, by selling him to the more hopeless
prison-house of the far South, thus separating him from his wife
and family.

Hannibal was generally employed as the keeper of a ferry-boat
by his master, and during the hours when he was waiting for passengers found many opportunities for gratifying, in an imperfect
manner, his thirst for knowledge.

Those who have always had books about them more than they
could or would read know nothing of the passionate eagerness with
which a repressed and starved intellect devours in secret its stolen
food.

In a little chink between the logs of his ferry-house there was secreted a Bible, a copy of Robinson Crusoe, and an odd number of a
Northern newspaper which had been dropped from the pocket of a
passenger; and when the door was shut and barred at night, and his
bit of pine knot lighted, he would take these out and read them
hour by hour. There he yearned after the wild freedom of the desolate island. He placed his wife and children, in imagination, in the
little barricaded abode of Robinson. He hunted and made coats of

skin, and gathered strange fruits from trees with unknown names, and felt himself a free man.

Over a soul so strong and so repressed it is not to be wondered at that Dred should have acquired a peculiar power. The study of the Bible had awakened in his mind that vague tumult of aspirations and hopes which it ever excites in the human breast; and he was prompt to believe that the Lord who visited Israel in Egypt had listened to the sighings of their captivity, and sent a prophet and a deliverer to his people.

Like a torch carried in a stormy night, this hope had blazed up within him; but the cold blast of death had whistled by, and it was extinguished forever.

Among the small band that stood around the dead, on the edge of the grave, he stood, looking fixedly on the face of the departed. In the quaint and shaggy mound to which Dred had attached that strange, rugged, oriental appellation, *Jegar Sahadutha,* or the "heap of witness," there was wildly flaring a huge pine-knot torch, whose light fell with a red, distinct glare on the prostrate form that lay there like a kingly cedar uprooted, no more to wave its branches in air, yet mighty in its fall, with all the shaggy majesty of its branches around. Whatever might have been the strife and struggle of the soul once imprisoned in that form, there was stamped upon the sombre face an expression of majestic and mournful tranquillity, as if that long-suffering and gracious God, to whose judgment he had made his last appeal, had rendered that judgment in mercy. When the statesmen and mighty men of *our* race die, though they had the weaknesses and sins of humanity, they want not orators in the church to draw the veil gently, to speak softly of their errors and loudly of their good, and to predict for them, if not an abundant entrance, yet at least a safe asylum among the blessed; and something not to be rebuked in our common nature inclines to join in a hopeful amen. It is not easy for us to believe that a great and powerful soul can be lost to God and itself forever.

But he who lies here so still and mournfully in this flickering torch-light had struggling within him the energies which make the patriot and the prophet. Crushed beneath a mountain of ignorance, they rose blind and distorted; yet had knowledge enlightened and success crowned them, his name might have been, with that of Toussaint,[1] celebrated in mournful sonnet by the deepest thinking poet of the age.

"Thou hast left behind
Powers that will work for thee; air, earth, and skies;
There's not a breathing of the common wind
That will forget thee; thou hast great allies;
Thy friends are exaltations, agonies,
And love, and man's unconquerable mind."[2]

The weight of so great an affliction seemed to have repressed the usual vivacity with which the negro is wont to indulge the expression of grief. When the body was laid down by the side of the grave, there was for a time a silence so deep that the rustling of the leaves, and the wild, doleful clamor of the frogs and turtles in the swamps, and the surge of the winds in the pine-tree tops, were all that met the ear. Even the wife of the dead stood with her shawl wrapped tightly about her, rocking to and fro, as if in the extremity of grief.

An old man in the company, who had officiated sometimes as preacher among the negroes, began to sing a well-known hymn very commonly used at negro funerals, possibly because its wild and gloomy imagery has something exciting to their quick imaginations. The words rose on the night air:

"Hark, from the tombs a doleful sound,
My ears attend the cry;
Ye living men, come view the ground
Where you must shortly lie."

During the singing of this verse Hannibal stood silent, with his arms gloomily folded, his eyes fixed on the lifeless face. Gradually the sentiment seemed to inspire his soul with a kind of serene triumph; he lifted his head, and joined his deep bass voice in the singing of the second verse:

"Princes, this clay must be your bed,
In spite of all your towers;
The tall, the wise, the reverend head,
Must lie as low as ours."

"Yes," he said, "brethren, that will be the way of it. They triumph and lord it over us now, but their pomp will be brought down to the grave, and the noise of their viols. The worm shall be spread under them, and the worm shall cover them; and when we come to stand together at the judgment seat, our testimony will be took there if it never was afore; and the Lord will judge atween us and our oppressors,—that's one comfort. Now, brethren, let's jest lay him in the grave, and he that's a better man, or would have done better in his place, let him judge him if he dares."

They lifted him up and laid him into the grave; and in a few moments all the mortal signs by which that soul had been known on earth had vanished, to appear no more till the great day of judgment and decision.

CHAPTER XXXI

The Escape

CLAYTON HAD NOT BEEN an unsympathizing or inattentive witness of these scenes.

It is true that he knew not the whole depth of the affair; but Harry's letter and his own observations had led him, without explanation, to feel that there was a perilous degree of excitement in some of the actors in the scene before him, which, unless some escape-valve were opened, might lead to most fatal results.

The day after the funeral, he talked with Harry, wisely and kindly, assuming nothing to himself on the ground either of birth or position; showing to him the undesirableness and hopelessness, under present circumstances, of any attempt to right by force the wrongs under which his class were suffering, and opening to him and his associates a prospect of a safer way by flight to the Free States.

One can scarcely appreciate the moral resolution and force of character which could make a person in Clayton's position in society—himself sustaining, in the eye of the law, the legal relation of a slaveholder—give advice of this kind. No crime is visited with more unsparing rigor by the régime of Southern society than the aiding or abetting the escape of a slave. He who does it is tried as a negro-stealer; and in some states death, in others a long and disgraceful imprisonment in the penitentiary, is the award.

For granting the slightest assistance and succor, in cases like these,—for harboring the fugitive for even a night,—for giving him the meanest shelter and food,—persons have been stripped of their whole property, and turned out destitute upon the world. Others, for no other crime, have languished years in unhealthy dungeons, and coming out at last with broken health and wasted energies; nor has the most saintly patience and purity of character in the victim been able to lessen or mitigate the penalty.

It was therefore only by the discerning power of a mind sufficiently clear and strong to see its way through the mists of educational association, that Clayton could feel himself to be doing right in thus violating the laws and customs of the social state under which he was born. But, in addition to his belief in the inalienable right of every man to liberty, he had at this time a firm conviction that nothing but the removal of some of these minds from the oppressions which were goading them could prevent a development of bloody insurrection.

It is probable that nothing has awakened more bitterly the animosity of the slaveholding community than the existence in the Northern States of an indefinite yet very energetic institution, known as *the underground railroad;*[1] and yet, would they but reflect wisely on the things that belong to their peace, they would know that this has removed many a danger from their dwellings. One has only to become well acquainted with some of those fearless and energetic men who have found their way to freedom by its means, to feel certain that such minds and hearts would have proved, in time, an incendiary magazine under the scorching reign of slavery. But, by means of this, men of that class who cannot be kept in slavery have found a road to liberty which endangered the shedding of no blood but their own; and the record of the strange and perilous means by which these escapes have been accomplished sufficiently shows the resolute nature of the men by whom they were undertaken.

It was soon agreed that a large party of fugitives should in concert effect their escape. Harry, being so white as easily to escape detection out of the immediate vicinity where he was known, assumed the task of making arrangements, for which he was amply supplied with money by Clayton.

It is well known that there are, during the greater part of the year, lumberers engaged in the cutting and making of shingles, who have extensive camps in the swamp, and live there for months at a time. These camps are made by laying foundations of logs on the spongy soil, thus forming platforms on which rude cabins are erected. In the same manner roads are constructed into distant parts of the swamp, by means of which transportation is carried on. There is also a canal cut through the middle of the swamp, on which small sailing craft pass backwards and forwards with shingles and produce.

In the employ of these lumberers are multitudes of slaves hired from surrounding proprietors. They live here in a situation of comparative freedom, being only obliged to make a certain number of staves or shingles within a stipulated time, and being furnished with very comfortable provision. Living thus somewhat in the condition of freemen, they are said to be more intelligent, energetic, and self-respecting, than the generality of slaves. The camp of the fugitives had not been without intercourse with the camp of lumberers, some five miles distant. In cases of straits they had received secret supplies from them, and one or two of the more daring and intelligent of the slave lumberers had attended some of Dred's midnight meetings. It was determined, therefore, to negotiate with one of the slaves who commanded a lighter, or small vessel, in which lumber was conveyed to Norfolk,[2] to assist their escape.

On some consultation, however, it was found that the numbers wanting to escape were so large as not to be able, without exciting suspicion, to travel together, and it was therefore decided to make two detachments. Milly had determined to cast in her lot with the fugitives, out of regard to her grandchild, poor little Tomtit, whose utter and merry thoughtlessness formed a touching contrast to the gravity and earnestness of her affections and desires for him. He was to her the only remaining memorial of a large family, which had been torn from her by the ordinary reverses and chances of slavery; and she clung to him, therefore, with the undivided energy of her great heart. As far as her own rights were concerned, she would have made a willing surrender of them, remaining patiently in the condition wherein she was called, and bearing injustice and oppression as a means of spiritual improvement, and seeking to do what good lay in her power.

Every individual has an undoubted right, if he chooses, thus to resign the rights and privileges of his earthly birthright; but the question is a very different one when it involves the improvement and the immortal interests of those for whom the ties of blood oblige him to have care.

Milly, who viewed everything with the eye of a Christian, was far less impressed by the rigor and severity of Tom Gordon's administration than by the dreadful demoralization of character which he brought upon the plantation.

Tomtit being a bright, handsome child, his master had taken a particular fancy to him. He would have him always about his person, and treated him with the same mixture of indulgence and caprice which one would bestow upon a spaniel. He took particular pleasure in teaching him to drink and to swear, apparently for nothing else than the idle amusement it afforded him to witness the exhibition of such accomplishments in so young a child.

In vain Milly, who dared use more freedom with him than any other servant, expostulated. He laughed or swore at her, according to the state in which he happened to be. Milly, therefore, determined at once to join the flying party, and take her darling with her. Perhaps she would not have been able to accomplish this, had not what she considered a rather fortunate reverse, about this time, brought Tomtit into disgrace with his master. Owing to some piece of careless mischief which he had committed, he had been beaten with a severity as thoughtless as the indulgence he at other times received, and, while bruised and trembling from this infliction, he was fully ready to fly anywhere.

Quite unexpectedly to all parties, it was discovered that Tom Gordon's confidential servant and valet, Jim, was one of the most forward to escape. This man from that peculiar mixture of boldness, adroitness, cunning, and drollery, which often exists among negroes, had stood for years as prime and undisputed favorite with his master; he had never wanted for money, or for anything that money could purchase; and he had had an almost unreproved liberty of saying, in an odd fashion, what he pleased, with the licensed audacity of a court buffoon.

One of the slaves expressed astonishment that he, in his favored position, should think of such a thing. Jim gave a knowing inclination of his head to one side, and said:

"Fac' is, bredren, dis chile is jest tired of dese yer partnership concerns. I and mas'r, we has all tings in common, sure 'nough; but den I'd rather have less of 'em, and have something dat's *mine;* 'sides which, I never's going to have a wife till I can get one dat'll belong to myself; dat ar's a ting I's 'ticular 'bout."

The conspirators were wont to hold their meetings nightly in the woods, near the swamp, for purposes of concert and arrangement.

Jim had been trusted so much to come and go at his own pleasure, that he felt little fear of detection, always having some plausible excuse on hand, if inquiries were made.

It is to be confessed that he had been a very profane and irreverent fellow, often attending prayer-meetings, and other religious exercises of the negroes, for no other apparent purpose than to be able

to give burlesque imitations of all the proceedings, for the amusement of his master and his master's vile associates. Whenever, therefore, he was missed, he would, upon inquiry, assert, with a knowing
wink, that "he had been out to de prayer-meetin'."

"Seems to me, Jim," says Tom, one morning, when he felt peculiarly ill-natured, "seems to me you are doing nothing but go to
meeting, lately. I don't like it, and I'm not going to have it. Some
deviltry or other you are up to, and I'm going to put a stop to it.
Now, mind yourself; don't you go any more, or I'll give you—"

We shall not mention particularly what Tom was in the habit of
threatening to give.

Here was a dilemma. One attendance more in the woods this
very night was necessary,—was, indeed, indispensable. Jim put all
his powers of pleasing into requisition. Never had he made such
desperate efforts to be entertaining. He sang, he danced, he mim-
icked sermons, carried on mock meetings, and seemed to whip all
things sacred and profane together, in one great syllabub of uproarious merriment; and this to an idle man, with a whole day upon his
hands, and an urgent necessity for never having time to think, was
no small affair.

Tom mentally reflected in the evening, as he lay stretched out in
the veranda, smoking his cigar, what in the world he should do
without Jim, to keep him in spirits; and Jim, under cover of the
day's glory, had ventured to request of his master the liberty of an
hour, which he employed in going to his tryst in the woods. This
was a bold step, considering how positively he had been forbidden
to do it in the morning; but Jim heartily prayed to his own wits, the
only god he had been taught to worship, to help him out once
more. He was returning home, hastening, in order to be in season
for his master's bed-time, hoping to escape unquestioned as to
where he had been.

The appointments had all been made, and, between two and
three o'clock that night, the whole party were to strike out upon
their course, and ere morning to have travelled the first stage of
their pilgrimage towards freedom.

Already the sense of a new nature was beginning to dawn on
Jim's mind—a sense of something graver, steadier, and more manly,
than the wild, frolicksome life he had been leading; and his bosom
throbbed with a strange, new, unknown hope.

Suddenly, on the very boundary of the spot where the wood

joins the plantation, who should he meet but Tom Gordon, sent there as if he had been warned by his evil stars.

"Now, Lord help me! if dere is any Lord," said Jim. "Well, I's got to blaze it out now de best way I ken."

He walked directly up to his master, with his usual air of saucy assurance.

"Why, Jim," said Tom, "where have you been? I've been looking for you."

"Why, bless you, mas'r, honey, I's been out to de meetin'."

"Didn't I tell you, you dog," said Tom, with an oath, "that you were not to go to any more of those meetings?"

"Why, laws, mas'r, honey, chile, 'fore my heavenly mas'r, I done forgot every word you said!" said Jim. "I's so kind o' tumbled up and down this day, and things has been so cur'us!"

The ludicrous grimace and tone, and attitude of affected contrition, with which all this was said, rather amused Tom; and, though he still maintained an air of sternness, the subtle negro saw at once his advantage, and added, " 'Clare if I isn't most dead! Ole Pomp, he preached, and he gets me so full o' grace I's fit to bust. Has to do something wicked, else I'll get translated one dese yer days, like 'Lijah, and den who'd mas'r have fur to wait on him?"

"I don't believe you've been to meeting," said Tom, eying him with affected suspicion. "You've been out on some spree."

"Why, laws, mas'r, honey, you hurts my feelings! Why, now, I's in hopes you'd say you see de grace a shining out all over me. Why, I's been in a clar state of glorrufication all dis evening. Dat ar old Pomp, dar's no mistake, he does lift a body up powerful!"

"You don't remember a word he said, now, I'll bet," said Tom. "Where was the text?"

"Text!" said Jim, with assurance; " 't was in the twenty-fourth chapter of Jerusalem, sixteenth verse."

"Well," said Tom, "what was it? I should like to know."

"Laws, mas'r, I b'lieve I can 'peat it," said Jim, with an indescribable air of waggish satisfaction. " 'T was dis yer: 'Ye shall sarch fur me in de mornin' and ye won't find me.' Dat ar's a mighty solemn text, mas'r, and ye ought to be 'flecting on 't."

And Tom had occasion to reflect upon it, the next morning, when, having stormed, and swore, and pulled until he broke the bell-wire, no Jim appeared. It was some time before he could actually realize or believe he was gone.

"The ungrateful dog! The impudent puppy, who had had all his life everything he wanted, to run away from him!"

Tom aroused the whole country in pursuit; and, as servants were found missing in many other plantations, there was a general excitement through the community. The *Trumpet of Liberty* began to blow dolorous notes, and articles headed, "The results of Abolitionist teaching, and covert incendiarism," began to appear. It was recommended that a general search should be made through the country for all persons tinctured with abolitionist sentiments, and immediate measures pursued to oblige them to leave the state forthwith.

One or two respectable gentlemen, who were in the habit of taking the *National Era*,[3] were visited by members of a vigilance committee, and informed that they must immediately drop the paper or leave the state; and when one of them talked of his rights as a free citizen, and inquired how they would enforce their requisitions, supposing he determined to stand for his liberty, the party informed him succinctly to the following purport: "If you do not comply, your corn, grain, and fodder, will be burned; your cattle driven off; and, if you still persist, your house will be set on fire and consumed, and you will never know who does it."

When the good gentleman inquired if this was freedom, his instructors informed him that freedom consisted in their right and power to make their neighbors submit to their own will and dictation; and he would find himself in a free country so far as this, that every one would feel at liberty to annoy and maltreat him so long as he opposed the popular will.

This modern doctrine of liberty has of late been strikingly and edifyingly enforced on the minds of some of our brethren and sisters in the new states, to whom the offer of relinquishing their principles or their property and lives has been tendered with the same admirable explicitness.

It is scarcely necessary to remark that both these worthy gentlemen, to use the language of their conquerors, "caved in," and thus escaped with no other disadvantage than a general plundering of their smoke-houses, the hams in which were thought a desirable addition to a triumphal entertainment proposed to be given in honor of law and order by THE ASSOCIATE BANDS of the GLORIOUS IMMORTAL COONS, the body-guard which was Tom Gordon's instrument in all these exploits.

In fact, this association, although wanting the advantage of an ordaining prayer and a distribution of Bibles, as has been the case with some more recently sent from Southern states, to beat the missionary drum of state rights and the principles of law and order on our frontiers, yet conducted themselves in a manner which might have won them approbation even in Col. Buford's regiment,[4] giving such exhibitions of liberty as were sufficient to justify all despots for putting it down by force for centuries to come.

Tom Gordon was the great organizer and leader of all these operations; his suspicions had connected Clayton with the disappearance of his slaves, and he followed upon his track with the sagacity of a bloodhound.

The outrage which he had perpetrated upon him in the forest, so far from being a matter of sham or concealment, was paraded as a cause for open boast and triumph. Tom rode about with his arm in a sling as a wounded hero, and received touching testimonials and demonstrations from sundry ladies of his acquaintance for his gallantry and spirit. When on the present occasion he found the pursuit of his slaves hopeless, his wrath and malice knew no bounds, and he determined to stir up and enkindle against Clayton to the utmost degree the animosities of the planters around his estate of Magnolia Grove.

This it was not difficult to do. We have already shown how much latent discontent and heart-burning had been excited by the course which Clayton and his sister had pursued on their estate.

Tom Gordon had a college acquaintance with the eldest son of one of the neighboring families, a young man of as reckless and dissipated habits as his own.

Hearing, therefore, that Clayton had retired to Magnolia Grove, he accepted an invitation of this young man to make him a visit, principally, as it would appear, for the purpose of instigating some mischief.

CHAPTER XXXII

Lynch Law Again

THE READER NEXT beholds Clayton at Magnolia Grove, whither he had fled to recruit his exhausted health and spirits. He had been accompanied there by Frank Russel.

Our readers may often have observed how long habits of intimacy may survive between two persons who have embarked in moral courses, which, if pursued, must eventually separate them forever.

For such is the force of moral elements, that the ambitious and self-seeking cannot *always* walk with those who love good for its own sake. In this world, however, where all these things are imperfectly developed, habits of intimacy often subsist a long time between the most opposing affinities.

The fact was that Russel would not give up the society of Clayton. He admired the very thing in him which he wanted himself; and he comforted himself for not listening to his admonitions by the tolerance and good-nature with which he had always heard them. When he heard that he was ill, he came to him and insisted upon travelling with him, attending him with the utmost fidelity and kindness.

Clayton had not seen Anne before since his affliction—both because his time had been very much engaged, and because they who cannot speak of their sorrows often shrink from the society of those whose habits of intimacy and affection might lead them to desire such confidence. But he was not destined in his new retreat to find the peace he desired. Our readers may remember that there were intimations conveyed through his sister some time since of discontent arising in the neighborhood.

The presence of Tom Gordon soon began to make itself felt. As a conductor introduced into an electric atmosphere will draw to itself the fluid, so he became an organizing point for the prevailing dissatisfaction.

He went to dinner-parties and talked; he wrote in the nearest paper; he excited the inflammable and inconsiderate; and, before he had been there many weeks, a vigilance association was formed among the younger and more hot-headed of his associates, to search out and extirpate covert abolitionism. Anne and her brother first became sensible of an entire cessation of all those neighborly acts of kindness and hospitality, in which Southern people, when in a good humor, are so abundant.

At last, one day Clayton was informed that three or four gentlemen of his acquaintance were wishing to see him in the parlor below.

On descending, he was received first by his nearest neighbor, Judge Oliver, a fine-looking elderly gentleman, of influential family connection.

He was attended by Mr. Bradshaw, whom we have already introduced to our readers, and by a Mr. Knapp, who was a very wealthy planter, a man of great energy and ability, who had for some years figured as the representative of his native state in Congress.

It was evident, by the embarrassed air of the party, that they had come on business of no pleasing character.

It is not easy for persons, however much excited they may be, to enter at once upon offensive communications to persons who receive them with calm and gentlemanly civility; therefore, after being seated, and having discussed the ordinary topics of the weather and the crops, the party looked one upon another, in a little uncertainty which should begin the real business of the interview.

"Mr. Clayton," at length said Judge Oliver, "we are really sorry to be obliged to make disagreeable communications to you. We have all of us had the sincerest respect for your family, and for yourself. I have known and honored your father many years, Mr. Clayton; and, for my own part, I must say I anticipated much pleasure from your residence in our neighborhood. I am really concerned to be obliged to say anything unpleasant; but I am under the necessity of telling you that the course you have been pursuing with regard to your servants, being contrary to the laws and usages of our social institutions, can no longer be permitted among us. You are aware that the teaching of slaves to read and write is forbidden by the law, under severe penalties. We have always been liberal in the interpretation of this law. Exceptional violations, conducted with privacy and discretion, in the case of favored servants, whose general good conduct seems to merit such confidence, have from time to time existed, and passed among us without notice or opposition; but the instituting of a regular system of instruction, to the extent and degree which exists upon your plantation, is a thing so directly in the face of the law, that we can no longer tolerate it; and we have determined, unless this course is dropped, to take measures to put the law into execution."

"I had paid my adopted state the compliment," said Clayton, "to suppose such laws to be a mere relic of barbarous ages, which the practical Christianity of our times would treat as a dead letter. I began my arrangements in all good faith, not dreaming that there could be found those who would oppose a course so evidently called for by the spirit of the Gospel, and the spirit of the age."

"You are entirely mistaken, sir," said Mr. Knapp, in a tone of great decision, "if you suppose these laws are, or can ever be, a matter of indifference to us, or can be suffered to become a dead letter. Sir, they are founded in the very nature of our institutions. They are indispensable to the preservation of our property, and the safety of our families. Once educate the negro population, and the whole system of our domestic institutions is at an end. Our negroes have acquired already, by living among us, a degree of sagacity and intelligence which makes it difficult to hold an even rein over them; and, once open the flood-gates of education, and there is no saying where they and we might be carried. I, for my part, do not approve of these exceptional instances Judge Oliver mentioned. Generally speaking, those negroes whose intelligence and good conduct would make them the natural recipients of such favors are precisely the ones who ought not to be trusted with them. It ruins them. Why, just look at the history of the insurrection that very nearly cut off the whole city of Charleston: what sort of men were those who got it up? They were just your steady, thoughtful, well-conducted men,—just the kind of men that people are teaching to read, because they think they are so good it can do no harm. Sir, my father was one of the magistrates on the trial of those men, and I have heard him say often there was not one man of bad character among them. They had all been *remarkable* for their good character. Why, there was that Denmark Vesey, who was the head of it: for twenty years he served his master, and was the most faithful creature that ever breathed; and after he got his liberty, everybody respected him, and liked him. Why, at first, my father said the magistrates could not be brought to arrest him, they were so sure that he could not have been engaged in such an affair. Now, all the leaders in that affair could read and write. They kept their lists of names; and nobody knows, or ever will know, how many were down on them, for those fellows were deep as the grave, and you could not get a word out of them. Sir, they died and made no sign; but all this is a warning to us."

"And do you think," said Clayton, "that if men of that degree of energy and intelligence are refused instruction, they will not find means to get knowledge for themselves? And if they do get it themselves, in spite of your precautions, they will assuredly use it against you.

"The fact is, gentlemen, it is inevitable that a certain degree of culture must come from their intercourse with us, and minds of a certain class *will* be stimulated to desire more; and all the barriers we put up will only serve to inflame curiosity, and will make them feel a perfect liberty to use the knowledge they conquer from us against us. In my opinion, the only sure defence against insurrection is systematic education, by which we shall acquire that influence over their minds which our superior cultivation will enable us to hold. Then, as fast as they become fitted to enjoy rights, we must grant them."

"Not we, indeed!" said Mr. Knapp, striking his cane upon the floor. "We are not going to lay down our power in that way. We will not allow any such beginning. We must hold them down firmly and consistently. For my part, I dislike even the system of oral religious instruction. It starts their minds, and leads them to want something more. It's indiscreet, and I always said so. As for teaching them out of the Bible,—why, the Bible is the most exciting book that ever was put together! It always starts up the mind, and it's unsafe."

"Don't you see," said Clayton, "what an admission you are making? What sort of a system must this be, that requires such a course to sustain it?"

"I can't help that," said Mr. Knapp. "There's millions and millions invested in it, and we can't afford to risk such an amount of property for mere abstract speculation. The system is as good as forty other systems that have prevailed, and will prevail. We can't take the frame-work of society to pieces. We must proceed with things as they are. And now, Mr. Clayton, another thing I have to say to you," said he, looking excited, and getting up and walking the floor. "It has been discovered that you receive incendiary documents through the post-office; and this cannot be permitted, sir."

The color flushed into Clayton's face, and his eye kindled as he braced himself in his chair. "By what right," he said, "does any one pry into what I receive through the post-office? Am I not a free man?"

"No, sir, you are not," said Mr. Knapp,—"not free to receive that which may imperil a whole neighborhood. You are not free to store barrels of gunpowder on your premises, when they may blow up ours. Sir, we are obliged to hold the mail under supervision in this state; and suspected persons will not be allowed to receive communications without oversight. Don't you remember that the general post-office was broken open in Charleston,[1] and all the abolition documents taken out of the mail-bags and consumed, and a general meeting of all the most respectable citizens, headed by the clergy in their robes of office, solemnly confirmed the deed?"

"I think, Mr. Knapp," said Judge Oliver, interposing in a milder tone, "that your excitement is carrying you further than you are aware. I should rather hope that Mr. Clayton would perceive the reasonableness of our demand, and of himself forego the taking of these incendiary documents."

"I take no incendiary documents," said Clayton, warmly. "It is true I take an anti-slavery paper, edited at Washington,[2] in which the subject is fairly and coolly discussed. I hold it no more than every man's duty to see both sides of a question."

"Well, there, now," said Mr. Knapp, "you see the disadvantage of having your slaves taught to read. If they could not read your papers, it would be no matter what you took; but to have them get to reasoning on these subjects, and spread their reasonings through our plantations,—why, there'll be the devil to pay, at once."

"You must be sensible," said Judge Oliver, "that there must be some individual rights which we resign for the public good. I have looked over the paper you speak of, and I acknowledge it seems to me very fair; but, then, in our peculiar and critical position, it might prove dangerous to have such reading about my house, and I never have it."

"In that case," said Clayton, "I wonder you don't suppress your own newspapers; for as long as there is a congressional discussion, or a Fourth of July oration or senatorial speech in them, so long they are full of incendiary excitement. Our history is full of it, our state bills of rights are full of it, the lives of our fathers are full of it; we must suppress our whole literature, if we would avoid it."

"Now, don't you see," said Mr. Knapp, "you have stated just so many reasons why slaves must not learn to read?"

"To be sure I do," said Clayton, "if they are always to remain slaves, if we are never to have any views of emancipation for them."

"Well, they *are* to remain slaves," said Mr. Knapp, speaking with excitement. "Their condition is a finality; we will not allow the subject of emancipation to be discussed, even."

"Then, God have mercy on you!" said Clayton, solemnly; "for it is my firm belief that, in resisting the progress of human freedom, you will be found fighting against God."

"It isn't the cause of human freedom," said Mr. Knapp, hastily. "They are not human; they are an inferior race, made expressly for subjection and servitude. The Bible teaches this plainly."

"Why don't you teach them to read it, then?" said Clayton, coolly.

"The long and the short of the matter is, Mr. Clayton," said Mr. Knapp, walking nervously up and down the room, "you'll find this is not a matter to be trifled with. We come, as your friends, to warn you; and, if you don't listen to our warnings, we shall not hold ourselves responsible for what may follow. You ought to have some consideration for your sister, if not for yourself."

"I confess," said Clayton, "I had done the chivalry of South Carolina the honor to think that a lady could have nothing to fear."

"It is so generally," said Judge Oliver, "but on this subject there is such a dreadful excitability in the public mind, that we cannot control it. You remember, when the commissioner was sent by the Legislature of Massachusetts to Charleston,[3] he came with his daughter, a very cultivated and elegant young lady; but the mob was rising, and we could not control it, and we had to go and beg them to leave the city. I, for one, wouldn't have been at all answerable for the consequences, if they had remained."

"I must confess, Judge Oliver," said Clayton, "that I have been surprised, this morning, to hear South Carolinians palliating two such events in your history, resulting from mob violence, as the breaking open of the post-office, and the insult to the representative of a sister state, who came in the most peaceable and friendly spirit, and to womanhood in the person of an accomplished lady. Is this hydra-headed monster, the mob, to be our governor?"

"O, it is only upon this subject," said all three of the gentlemen, at once; "this subject is exceptional."

"And do you think," said Clayton, "that

'—you can set the land on fire,
To burn just so high, and no higher'?

You may depend upon it you will find that you cannot. The mob that you smile on and encourage when it does work that suits you, will one day prove itself your master in a manner that you will not like."

"Well, now, Mr. Clayton," said Mr. Bradshaw, who had not hitherto spoken, "you see this is a very disagreeable subject; but the fact is, we came in a friendly way to you. We all appreciate, personally, the merits of your character, and the excellence of your motives; but, really sir, there is an excitement rising, there is a state of the public mind which is getting every day more and more inflammable. I talked with Miss Anne on this subject, some months ago, and expressed my feelings very fully; and now, if you will only give us a pledge that you will pursue a different course, we shall have something to take hold of to quiet the popular mind. If you will just write and stop your paper for the present, and let it be understood that your plantation system is to be stopped, the thing will gradually cool itself off."

"Gentlemen," said Clayton, "you are asking a very serious thing from me, and one which requires reflection. If I am violating the direct laws of the state, and these laws are to be considered as still in vital force, there is certainly some question with regard to my course; but still I have responsibilities for the moral and religious improvement of those under my care, which are equally binding. I see no course but removal from the state."

"Of course, we should be sorry," said Judge Oliver, "you should be obliged to do that; still we trust you will see the necessity, and our motives."

"Necessity is the tyrant's plea, I believe," said Clayton, smiling.

"At all events, it is a strong one," replied Judge Oliver, smiling also. "But I am glad we have had this conversation; I think it will enable me to pacify the minds of some of our hot-headed young neighbors, and prevent threatened mischief."

After a little general conversation, the party separated on apparently friendly terms, and Clayton went to seek counsel with his sister and Frank Russel.

Anne was indignant, with that straight-out and generous indignation which belongs to women, who, generally speaking, are ready to follow their principles to any result with more inconsiderate fearlessness than men. She had none of the anxieties for herself which Clayton had for her. Having once been witness of the brutalities of a slave-mob, Clayton could not, without a shudder, connect any such possibilities with his sister.

"I think," said Anne, "we had better give up this miserable sham of a free government, of freedom of speech, freedom of conscience, and all that, if things must go on in this way."

"O," said Frank Russel, "the fact is that our republic, in these states, is like that of Venice; it's not a democracy, but an oligarchy, and the mob is its standing army. We are, all of us, under the 'Council of Ten,'[4] which has its eyes everywhere. We are free enough as long as our actions please them; when they don't, we shall find their noose around our necks. It's very edifying, certainly, to have these gentlemen call on you to tell you that they will not be answerable for consequences of excitement which they are all the time stirring up; for, after all, who cares what you do, if they don't? The large proprietors are the ones interested. The rabble are their hands, and this warning about popular excitement just means, 'Sir, if you don't take care, I shall let out my dogs, and then I won't be answerable for consequences.' "

"And you call this liberty!" said Anne, indignantly.

"O, well," said Russel, "this is a world of humbugs. We call it liberty because it's an agreeable name. After all, what is liberty, that people make such a breeze about? We are all slaves to one thing or another. Nobody is absolutely free, except Robinson Crusoe, in the desolate island; and he tears all his shirts to pieces and hangs them up as signals of distress, that he may get back into slavery again."

"For all that," said Anne, warming, "I know there is such a thing as liberty. All that nobleness and enthusiasm which has animated people in all ages for liberty cannot be in vain. Who does not thrill at those words of the Marsellaise:

'O, *Liberty, can men resign thee,*
Once having felt thy generous flame?
Can dungeons, bolts, or bars, confine thee,
Or whips thy noble spirit tame?' "

"These are certainly agreeable myths," said Russel, "but these things will not bear any close looking into. Liberty has generally meant the liberty of me and my nation and my class to do what we please; which is a very pleasant thing, certainly, to those who are on the upper side of the wheel, and probably involving much that's disagreeable to those who are under."

"That is a heartless, unbelieving way of talking," said Anne, with tears in her eyes. "I know there have been some right true, noble souls, in whom the love of liberty has meant the love of right, and the desire that every human brother should have what rightly belongs to him. It is not *my* liberty, nor *our* liberty, but the *principle* of liberty itself, that they strove for."

"Such a principle, carried out logically, would make smashing work in this world," said Russel. "In this sense, where is there a free government on earth? What nation ever does or ever did respect the right of the weaker, or ever will, till the millennium comes?—and that's too far off to be of much use in practical calculations; so don't let's break our hearts about a name. For my part, I am more concerned about these implied threats. As I said before, 'the hand of Joab is in this thing.'[5] Tom Gordon is visiting in this neighborhood, and you may depend upon it that this, in some way, comes from him. He is a perfectly reckless fellow, and I am afraid of some act of violence. If he should bring up a mob, whatever they do, there will be no redress for you. These respectable gentlemen, your best friends, will fold their hands, and say, 'Ah, poor fellow! we told him so!' while others will put their hands complacently in their pockets, and say, 'Served him right!' "

"I think," said Clayton, "there will be no immediate violence. I understood that they pledged as much when they departed."

"If Tom Gordon is in the camp," said Russel, "they may find that they have reckoned without their host in promising that. There are two or three young fellows in this vicinity who, with his energy to direct them, are reckless enough for anything; and there is always an abundance of excitable rabble to be got for a drink of whiskey."

The event proved that Russel was right. Anne's bedroom was in the back part of the cottage, opposite the little grove where stood her school-room.

She was awakened, about one o'clock, that night, by a broad, ruddy glare of light, which caused her at first to start from her bed, with the impression that the house was on fire.

At the same instant she perceived that the air was full of barbarous and dissonant sounds, such as the beating of tin pans, the braying of horns, and shouts of savage merriment, intermingled with slang oaths and curses.

In a moment, recovering herself, she perceived that it was her school-house which was in a blaze, crisping and shrivelling the foliage of the beautiful trees by which it was surrounded, and filling the air with a lurid light.

She hastily dressed, and in a few moments Clayton and Russel knocked at her door. Both were looking very pale.

"Don't be alarmed," said Clayton, putting his arm around her with that manner which shows that there is everything to fear; "I am going out to speak to them."

"Indeed, you are going to do no such thing," said Frank Russel, decidedly. "This is no time for any extra displays of heroism. These men are insane with whiskey and excitement. They have probably been especially inflamed against you, and your presence would irritate them still more. Let me go out: I understand the *ignobile vulgus*[6] better than you do; besides which, providentially, I haven't any conscience to prevent my saying and doing what is necessary for an emergency. You shall see me lead off this whole yelling pack at my heels in triumph. And now, Clayton, you take care of Anne, like a good fellow, till I come back, which may be about four or five o'clock to-morrow morning. I shall toll all these fellows down to Muggins', and leave them so drunk they cannot stand for one three hours."

So saying, Frank proceeded hastily to disguise himself in a shaggy old great coat, and to tie around his throat a red bandanna silk handkerchief, with a very fiery and dashing tie, and surmounting these equipments by an old hat which had belonged to one of the servants, he stole out of the front door, and, passing around through the shrubbery, was very soon lost in the throng who sur-

rounded the burning building. He soon satisfied himself that Tom
Gordon was not personally among them,—that they consisted entirely of the lower class of whites.

"So far, so good," he said to himself, and, springing on to the
stump of a tree, he commenced a speech in that peculiar slang dialect which was vernacular with them, and of which he perfectly
well understood the use.

With his quick and ready talent for drollery, he soon had them
around him in paroxysms of laughter; and, complimenting their
bravery, flattering and cajoling their vanity, he soon got them completely in his power, and they assented, with a triumphant shout, to
the proposition that they should go down and celebrate their victory at Muggins' grocery, a low haunt about a mile distant, whither,
as he predicted, they all followed him. And he was as good as his
word in not leaving them till all were so completely under the
power of liquor as to be incapable of mischief for the time being.

About nine o'clock the next day he returned, finding Clayton
and Anne seated together at breakfast.

"Now, Clayton," he said, seating himself, "I am going to talk to
you in good, solemn earnest, for once. The fact is, you are check-
mated. Your plans for gradual emancipation, or reform, or anything
tending in that direction, are utterly hopeless; and, if you want to
pursue them with your own people, you must either send them to
Liberia,[7] or to the Northern States. There was a time, fifty years
ago, when such things were contemplated with some degree of sincerity by all the leading minds at the South. That time is over. From
the very day that they began to open new territories to slavery, the
value of this kind of property mounted up, so as to make emancipation a moral impossibility. It is, as they told you, a *finality;* and
don't you see how they make everything in the Union bend to it?
Why, these men are only about three tenths of the population of
our Southern States, and yet the other seven tenths virtually have
no existence. All they do is to vote as they are told—as they know
they must, being too ignorant to know any better.

"The mouth of the North is stuffed with cotton, and will be kept
full as long as it suits us. Good, easy gentlemen, they are so satisfied
with their pillows, and other accommodations inside of the car, that
they don't trouble themselves to reflect that we are the engineers,
nor to ask where we are going. And, when any one does wake up
and pipe out in melancholy inquiry, we slam the door in his face,

and tell him 'Mind your own business, sir,' and he leans back on his cotton pillow, and goes to sleep again, only whimpering a little, that 'we might be more polite.'

"They have their fanatics up there. We don't trouble ourselves to put them down; we make them do it. They get up mobs on our account, to hoot troublesome ministers and editors out of their cities; and their men that they send to Congress invariably do all our dirty work. There's now and then an exception, it is true; but they only prove the rule.

"If there was any public sentiment at the North for you reformers to fall back upon, you might, in spite of your difficulties, do something; but there is not. They are all implicated with us, except the class of born fanatics, like you, who are walking in that very unfashionable narrow way we've heard of."

"Well," said Anne, "let us go out of the state, then. I will go anywhere; but I will not stop the work that I have begun."

CHAPTER XXXIII

Flight

THE PARTY OF FUGITIVES, which started for the North, was divided into two bands. Harry, Lisette, Tiff, and his two children, assumed the character of a family, of whom Harry took the part of father, Lisette the nurse, and Tiff the manservant.

The money which Clayton had given them enabling them to furnish a respectable outfit, they found no difficulty in taking passage under this character, at Norfolk, on board a small coasting-vessel bound to New York.

Never had Harry known a moment so full of joyous security as that which found him out at sea in a white-winged vessel, flying with all speed toward the distant port of safety.

Before they neared the coast of New York, however, there was a change in their prospects. The blue sky became darkened, and the sea, before so treacherously smooth, began to rise in furious waves. The little vessel was tossed baffling about by contrary and tumultuous winds.

When she began to pitch and roll, in all the violence of a decided storm, Lisette and the children cried for fear. Old Tiff exerted himself for their comfort to the best of his ability. Seated on the cabin-floor, with his feet firmly braced, he would hold the children in his arms, and remind them of what Miss Nina had read to them of the storm that came down on the Lake of Gennesareth, and how Jesus was in the hinder part of the boat, asleep on a pillow.[1] "And he's dar yet," Tiff would say.

"I wish they'd wake him up, then," said Teddy, disconsolately; "I don't like this dreadful noise! What does he let it be so for?"

Before the close of that day the fury of the storm increased; and the horrors of that night can only be told by those who have felt the like. The plunging of the vessel, the creaking and straining of the timbers, the hollow and sepulchral sound of waves striking against the hull, and the shiver with which, like a living creature, she seemed to tremble at every shock, were things frightful even to the experienced sailor; much more so to our trembling refugees.

The morning dawned only to show the sailors their bark drifting helplessly toward a fatal shore, whose name is a sound of evil omen to seamen.

It was not long before the final crash came, and the ship was wedged among rugged rocks, washed over every moment by the fury of the waves.

All hands came now on deck for the last chance of life. One boat after another was attempted to be launched, but was swamped by the furious waters. When the last boat was essayed, there was a general rush of all on board. It was the last chance for life. In such hours the instinctive fear of death often overbears every other consideration; and the boat was rapidly filled by the hands of the ship, who, being strongest and most accustomed to such situations, were more able to effect this than the passengers. The captain alone remained standing on the wreck, and with him Harry, Lisette, Tiff, and the children.

"Pass along," said the captain, hastily pressing Lisette on board, simply because she was the first that came to hand.

"For de good Lord's sake," said Tiff, "put de chil'en on board; dere won't be no room for me, and 't an't no matter! You go 'board and take care of 'em," he said, pushing Harry along.

Harry mechanically sprang into the boat, and the captain after him. The boat was full.

"O, do take poor Tiff—do!" said the children, stretching their hands after their old friend.

"Clear away, boys,—the boat's full!" shouted a dozen voices; and the boat parted from the wreck, and sunk in eddies and whirls of boiling waves, foam, and spray, and went, rising and sinking, onward driven toward the shore.

A few, looking backwards, saw a mighty green wave come roaring and shaking its crested head, lift the hull as if it had been an eggshell, then dash it in fragments upon the rocks. This was all they knew, till they were themselves cast, wet and dripping, but still living, upon the sands.

A crowd of people were gathered upon the shore, who, with the natural kindness of humanity on such occasions, gathered the drenched and sea-beaten wanderers into neighboring cottages, where food and fire, and changes of dry clothing, awaited them.

The children excited universal sympathy and attention, and so many mothers of the neighborhood came bringing offerings of clothing, that their lost wardrobe was soon very tolerably replaced. But nothing could comfort them for the loss of their old friend. In vain the "little dears" were tempted with offers of cake and custard, and every imaginable eatable. They sat with their arms around each other, quietly weeping.

No matter how unsightly the casket may be which holds all the love there is on earth for us, be that love lodged in the heart of the poorest and most uneducated, the whole world can offer no exchange for the loss of it.

Tiff's devotion to these children had been so constant, so provident, so absolute, that it did not seem to them possible they could live a day without him; and the desolation of their lot seemed to grow upon them every hour. Nothing would restrain them. They would go out and look up and down, if, perhaps, they might meet him; but they searched in vain. And Harry, who had attended them, led them back again, disconsolate.

"I say, Fanny," said Teddy, after they had said their prayers, and laid down in their little bed, "has Tiff gone to heaven?"

"Certainly he has," said Fanny, "if ever anybody went there."

"Won't he come and bring us pretty soon?" said Teddy. "He won't want to be there without us, will he?"

"O, I don't know," said Fanny. "I wish we could go; the world is so lonesome!"

And, thus talking, the children fell asleep. But it is written in an ancient record, "Weeping may endure for a night, but joy cometh in the morning;"[2] and, verily, the next morning Teddy started up in bed, and awakened his sister with a cry of joy.

"O, Fanny! Fanny! Tiff isn't dead! I heard him laughing."

Fanny started up, and, sure enough, there came through the partition which separated their little sleeping-room from the kitchen a sound very much like Tiff's old, unctuous laugh.

One would have thought no other pair of lungs could have rolled out the jolly Ho, ho, ho, with such a joyous fulness of intonation.

The children hastily put on their clothes, and opened the door.

"Why, bress de Lord! poppets, here dey is, sure 'nough! Ho! ho! ho!" said Tiff, stretching out his arms, while both the children ran and hung upon him.

"O, Tiff, we are so glad! O, we thought you was drowned; we've been thinking so all night."

"No, no, no, bress de Lord! You don't get shet of Ole Tiff dat ar way! Won't get shet him till ye's fetched up, and able to do for yerselves."

"O, Tiff, how did you get away?"

"Laws! why, chil'ens, 't was a very strait way. I told de Lord 'bout it. Says I, 'Good Lord, you knows I don't car nothing 'bout it on my own 'count; but 'pears like dese chil'en is so young and tender, I couldn't leave dem, no way;' and so I axed him if he wouldn't jest please to help me, 'cause I knowed he had de power of de winds and de sea. Well, sure 'nough, dat ar big wave toted me clar up right on de sho'; but it tuk my breff and my senses so I didn't farly know whar I was. And de peoples dat foun' me took me a good bit 'way to a house down here, and dey was 'mazing good to me, and rubbed me wid de hot flannels, and giv me one ting and anoder, so 't I woke up quite peart dis mornin', and came out to look up my poppets; 'cause, yer see, it was kinder borne in on my mind dat I should find you. And now yer see, chil'en, you mark my words, de Lord ben wid us in six troubles, and in seven, and he'll bring us to good luck yet. Tell ye, de sea han't washed dat ar out o' me, for all its banging and bruising." And Tiff chuckled in the fulness of his heart, and made a joyful noise.

His words were so far accomplished that, before many days, the little party, rested and refreshed, and with the losses of their wardrobe made up by friendly contributions, found themselves under the roof of some benevolent friends in New York.

Thither, in due time, the other detachment of their party arrived, which had come forward under the guidance of Hannibal, by ways and means which, as they may be wanted for others in like circumstances, we shall not further particularize.

Harry, by the kind patronage of friends, soon obtained employment, which placed him and his wife in a situation of comfort.

Milly and her grandson, and Old Tiff and his children, were enabled to hire a humble tenement together; and she, finding employment as a pastry-cook in a confectioner's establishment, was able to provide a very comfortable support, while Tiff presided in the housekeeping department.

After a year or two an event occurred of so romantic a nature, that, had we not ascertained it as a positive fact, we should hesitate to insert it in our veracious narrative.

Fanny's mother had an aunt in the Peyton family, a maiden lady of very singular character, who, by habits of great penuriousness, had amassed a large fortune, apparently for no other purpose than that it should, some day, fall into the hands of somebody who would know how to enjoy it.

Having quarrelled, shortly before her death, with all her other relatives, she cast about in her mind for ways and means to revenge herself on them, by placing her property out of their disposal.

She accordingly made a will, bequeathing it to the heirs of her niece Susan, if any such heirs existed; and if not, the property was to go to an orphan asylum.

By chance, the lawyer's letter of inquiry was addressed to Clayton, who immediately took the necessary measures to identify the children, and put them in possession of the property.

Tiff now was glorious. "He always knowed it," he said, "dat Miss Sue's chil'en would come to luck, and dat de Lord would open a door for them, and he had."

Fanny, who was now a well-grown girl of twelve years, chose Clayton as her guardian; and, by his care, she was placed at one of the best New England schools, where her mind and her person developed rapidly.

Her brother was placed at school in the same town.

As for Clayton, after some inquiry and consideration, he bought a large and valuable tract of land in that portion of Canada where the climate is least severe, and the land the most valuable for culture.

To this place he removed his slaves, and formed there a township, which is now one of the richest and finest in the region.

Here he built for himself a beautiful residence, where he and his sister live happily together, finding their enjoyment in the improvement of those by whom they are surrounded.

It is a striking comment on the success of Clayton's enterprise, that the neighboring white settlers, who at first looked coldly upon him, fearing he would be the means of introducing a thriftless population among them, have been entirely won over, and that the value of the improvements which Clayton and his tenants have made has nearly doubled the price of real estate in the vicinity.

So high a character have his schools borne, that the white settlers in the vicinity have discontinued their own, preferring to have their children enjoy the advantages of those under his and his sister's patronage and care.★

Harry is one of the head men of the settlement, and is rapidly acquiring property and consideration in the community.[3]

A large farm, waving with some acres of fine wheat, with its fences and out-houses in excellent condition, marks the energy and thrift of Hannibal, who, instead of slaying men, is great in felling trees and clearing forests.

He finds time, winter evenings, to read, with "none to molest or make afraid."[4] His oldest son is construing Cæsar's Commentaries[5] at school, and often reads his lesson of an evening to his delighted father, who willingly resigns the palm of scholarship into his hands.

As to our merry friend Jim, he is the life of the settlement. Liberty, it is true, has made him a little more sober; and a very energetic and capable wife, soberer still; but yet Jim has enough and to spare of drollery, which makes him an indispensable requisite in all social gatherings.

He works on his farm with energy, and repels with indignation any suggestion that he was happier in the old times, when he had abundance of money, and very little to do.

One suggestion more we almost hesitate to make, lest it should give rise to unfounded reports; but we are obliged to speak the truth.

Anne Clayton, on a visit to a friend's family in New Hampshire, met with Livy Ray, of whom she had heard Nina speak so much, and very naturally the two ladies fell into a most intimate friendship; visits were exchanged between them, and Clayton, on first introduction, discovered the lady he had met in the prison in Alexandria.

The most intimate friendship exists between the three, and, of course, in such cases reports will arise; but we assure our readers we

★These statements are all true of the Elgin settlement, founded by Mr. King, a gentleman who removed and settled his slaves in the south of Canada.

have never heard of any authentic foundation for them; so that, in this matter, we can clearly leave every one to predict a result according to their own fancies.

We have now two sketches, with which the scenery of our book must close.

CHAPTER XXXIV

Clear Shining After Rain

CLAYTON HAD OCCASION to visit New York on business.

He never went without carrying some token of remembrance from the friends in his settlement to Milly, now indeed far advanced in years, while yet, in the expressive words of Scripture, "her eye was not dim, nor her natural force abated."[1]

He found her in a neat little tenement in one of the outer streets of New York, surrounded by about a dozen children, among whom were blacks, whites, and foreigners. These she had rescued from utter destitution in the streets, and was giving to them all the attention and affection of a mother.

"Why, bless you, sir," she said to him, pleasantly, as he opened the door, "it's good to see you once more! How is Miss Anne?"

"Very well, Milly. She sent you this little packet; and you will find something from Harry and Lisette, and all the rest of your friends in our settlement.—Ah! are these all your children, Milly?"

"Yes, honey; mine and de Lord's. Dis yer's my second dozen. De fust is all in good places, and doing well. I keeps my eye on 'em, and goes round to see after 'em a little, now and then."

"And how is Tomtit?"

"O, Tomtit's doing beautiful, thank 'e, sir. He's 'come a Christian, and jined the church; and they has him to wait and tend at the anti-slavery office, and he does *well.*"

"I see you have black and white here," said Clayton, glancing around the circle. "Laws, yes," said Milly, looking complacently around; "I don't make no distinctions of color,—I don't believe in them. White chil'en, when they 'haves themselves, is jest as good as black, and I loves 'em jest as well."

"Don't you sometimes think it a little hard you should have to work so in your old age?"

"Why, bress you, honey, no! I takes comfort of my money as I goes along. Dere's a heap in me yet," she said, laughing. "I's hoping to get dis yer batch put out and take in anoder afore I die. You see," she said, "dis yer's de way I took to get my heart whole. I found it was getting so sore for my chil'en I'd had took from me, 'pears like the older I grow'd the more I thought about 'em; but long 's I keeps doing for chil'en it kinder eases it. I calls 'em all mine; so I's got good many chil'en now."

We will inform our reader, in passing, that Milly, in the course of her life, on the humble wages of a laboring woman, took from the streets, brought up, and placed in reputable situations, no less than *forty* destitute children.*

When Clayton returned to Boston, he received a note written in a graceful female hand, from Fanny, expressing her gratitude for his kindness to her and her brother, and begging that he would come and spend a day with them at their cottage in the vicinity of the city. Accordingly, eight o'clock the next morning found him whirling in the cars through green fields and pleasant meadows, garlanded with flowers and draped with bending elms, to one of those peaceful villages which lie like pearls on the bosom of our fair old mother, Massachusetts.

Stopping at ——— station, he inquired his way up to a little eminence which commanded a view of one of those charming lakes which open their blue eyes everywhere through the New England landscape. Here, embowered in blossoming trees, stood a little Gothic cottage, a perfect gem of rural irregularity and fanciful beauty. A porch in the front of it was supported on pillars of cedar, with the rough bark still on, around which were trained multitudes of climbing roses, now in full flower. From the porch a rustic bridge led across a little ravine into a summer-house, which was built like a nest into the branches of a great oak which grew up from the hollow below the knoll on which the house stood.

A light form, dressed in a pretty white wrapper, came fluttering across the bridge, as Clayton ascended the steps of the porch. Perhaps our readers may recognize in the smoothly-parted brown hair, the large blue eyes, and the bashful earnestness of the face, our sometime little friend Fanny; if they do not, we think they'll be fa-

---

*These circumstances are true of an old colored woman in New York, known by the name of Aunt Katy, who in her youth was a slave, and who is said to have established among these destitute children the first Sunday-school in the city of New York.

miliar with the cheery "ho, ho, ho," which comes from the porch, as our old friend Tiff, dressed in a respectable suit of black, comes bowing forward. "Bress de Lord, Mas'r Clayton,—it's good for de eyes to look at you! So, you's come to see Miss Fanny, now she's come to her property, and has got de place she ought for to have. Ah, ah!—Old Tiff allers know'd it! He seed it—he know'd de Lord would bring her out right, and he did. Ho! ho! ho!"

"Yes," said Fanny, "and I sometimes think I don't enjoy it half as well as Uncle Tiff. I'm sure he ought to have some comfort of us, for he worked hard enough for us,—didn't you, Uncle Tiff?"

"Work! bress your soul, didn't I?" said Tiff, giggling all over in cheerful undulations. "Reckon I has worked, though I doesn't have much of it to do now; but I sees good of my work now'days,—does so. Mas'r Teddy, he's grow'd up tall, han'some young gen'leman, and he's in college,—only tink of dat! Laws! he can make de Latin fly! Dis yer's pretty good country, too. Dere's families round here dat's e'enamost up to old Virginny; and she goes with de best on 'em—dat she does."

Fanny now led Clayton into the house, and, while she tripped up stairs to change her morning dress, Tiff busied himself in arranging cake and fruit on a silver salver, as an apology for remaining in the room.

He seemed to consider the interval as an appropriate one for making some confidential communications on a subject that lay very near his heart. So, after looking out of the door with an air of great mystery, to ascertain that Miss Fanny was really gone, he returned to Clayton, and touched him on the elbow with an air of infinite secrecy and precaution.

"Dis yer an't to be spoke of out loud," he said. "I's ben mighty anxious; but, bress de Lord, I's come safely through; 'cause, yer see, I's found out he's a right likely man, beside being one of de very fustest old families in de state; and dese yer old families here 'bout as good as dey was in Virginny; and, when all's said and done, it's de men dat's de ting, after all; 'cause a gal can't marry all de generations back, if dey's ever so nice. But he's one of your likeliest men."

"What's his name?" said Clayton.

"Russel," said Tiff, lifting up his hand apprehensively to his mouth, and shouting out the name in a loud whisper. "I reckon he'll be here to-day, 'cause Mas'r Teddy's coming home, and going to bring him wid him; so please, Mas'r Clayton, you won't notice nothing; 'cause Miss Fanny, she's jest like her ma,—she'll turn red clar up to her har, if a body only looks at her. See here," said Tiff, fumbling in his pocket, and producing a spectacle-case, out of which he extracted a portentous pair of gold-mounted spectacles; "see what he give me, de last time he's here. I puts dese yer on of a Sundays, when I sets down to read my Bible."

"Indeed," said Clayton; "have you learned, then, to read?"

"Why, no, honey, I don'no as I can rightly say dat I's larn'd to read, 'cause I's 'mazing slow at dat ar; but, den, I's larn'd all de best words, like Christ, Lord, and God, and dem ar; and whar dey's pretty thick, I makes out quite comfortable."

We shall not detain our readers with minute descriptions of how the day was spent: how Teddy came home from college a tall, handsome fellow, and rattled over Latin and Greek sentences in Tiff's delighted ears, who considered his learning as, without doubt, the eighth wonder of the world; nor how George Russel came with him, a handsome senior, just graduated; nor how Fanny blushed and trembled when she told her guardian her little secret, and, like other ladies, asked advice after she had made up her mind.

Nor shall we dilate on the yet brighter glories of the cottage three months after, when Clayton, and Anne, and Livy Ray, were all at the wedding, and Tiff became three and four times blessed in this brilliant consummation of his hopes. The last time we saw him he was walking forth in magnificence, his gold spectacles set conspicuously astride of his nose, trundling a little wicker wagon, which cradled a fair, pearly little Miss Fanny, whom he informed all beholders was "de very sperit of de Peytons."

APPENDIX I

Nat Turner's Confessions

As an illustration of the character and views ascribed to Dred, we make a few extracts from the Confessions of Nat Turner, as published by T. R. Gray, Esq., of Southampton, Virginia, in November, 1831. One of the principal conspirators in this affair was named Dred.

We will first give the certificate of the court, and a few sentences from Mr. Gray's introductory remarks, and then proceed with Turner's own narrative.

"We, the undersigned, members of the court convened at Jerusalem, on Saturday, the fifth day of November, 1831, for the trial of Nat, *alias* Nat Turner, a negro slave, late the property of Putnam Moore, deceased, do hereby certify, that the confession of Nat, to Thomas R. Gray, was read to him in our presence, and that Nat acknowledged the same to be full, free, and voluntary; and that furthermore, when called upon by the presiding magistrate of the court to state if he had anything to say why sentence of death should not be passed upon him, replied he had nothing further than he had communicated to Mr. Gray. Given under our hands and seals at Jerusalem, this fifth day of November, 1831.

JEREMIAH COBB, *(Seal.)* THOMAS PRETLOW, *(Seal.)*
JAMES W. PARKER, *(Seal.)* CARR BOWERS, *(Seal.)*
SAMUEL B. HINES, *(Seal.)* ORRIS A. BROWNE, *(Seal.)*"

"*State of Virginia, Southampton County, to wit:*
"I, James Rochelle, Clerk of the County Court of Southampton, in the State of Virginia, do hereby certify, that Jeremiah Cobb, Thomas Pretlow, James W. Parker, Carr Bowers, Samuel B. Hines, and Orris A. Browne, Esqrs., are acting justices of the peace in and for the county aforesaid; and were members of the court which convened at Jerusalem, on Saturday, the fifth day of November,

1831, for the trial of Nat, *alias* Nat Turner, a negro slave, late the property of Putnam Moore, deceased, who was tried and convicted, as an insurgent in the late insurrection in the County of Southampton aforesaid, and that full faith and credit are due and ought to be given to their acts as justices of the peace aforesaid.

(*Seal.*)   In testimony whereof, I have hereunto set my hand, and caused the seal of the court aforesaid to be affixed, this fifth day of November, 1831.

JAMES ROCHELLE, C. S. C. C."

"Everything connected with this sad affair was wrapt in mystery, until NAT TURNER, the leader of this ferocious band, whose name has resounded throughout our widely-extended empire, was captured.

"Since his confinement, by permission of the jailer, I have had ready access to him; and, finding that he was willing to make a full and free confession of the origin, progress, and consummation, of the insurrectory movements of the slaves, of which he was the contriver and head, I determined, for the gratification of public curiosity, to commit his statements to writing, and publish them, with little or no variation, from his own words.

"He was not only the contriver of the conspiracy, but gave the first blow towards its execution.

"It will thus appear, that whilst everything upon the surface of society wore a calm and peaceful aspect, whilst not one note of preparation was heard to warn the devoted inhabitants of woe and death, a gloomy fanatic was revolving in the recesses of his own dark, bewildered, and overwrought mind, schemes of indiscriminate massacre to the whites. Schemes too fearfully executed, as far as his fiendish band proceeded in their desolating march. No cry for mercy penetrated their flinty bosoms. No acts of remembered kindness made the least impression upon these remorseless murderers. Men, women, and children, from hoary age to helpless infancy, were involved in the same cruel fate. Never did a band of savages do their work of death more unsparingly.

"Nat has survived all his followers, and the gallows will speedily close his career. His own account of the conspiracy is submitted to the public, without comment. It reads an awful, and, it is hoped, a useful lesson, as to the operations of a mind like his, endeavoring to grapple with things beyond its reach. How it first became bewildered and confounded, and finally corrupted and led to the conception and perpetration of the most atrocious and heartrending deeds.

"If Nat's statements can be relied on, the insurrection in this county was entirely local, and his designs confided but to a few, and these in his immediate vicinity. It was not instigated by motives of revenge or sudden anger; but the result of long deliberation, and a settled purpose of mind—the offspring of gloomy fanaticism acting upon materials but too well prepared for such impressions."

"I was thirty-one years of age the second of October last, and born the property of Benjamin Turner, of this county. In my childhood a circumstance occurred which made an indelible impression on my mind, and laid the groundwork of that enthusiasm which has terminated so fatally to many, both white and black, and for which I am about to atone at the gallows. It is here necessary to relate this circumstance. Trifling as it may seem, it was the commencement of that belief which has grown with time; and even now, sir, in this dungeon, helpless and forsaken as I am, I cannot divest myself of. Being at play with other children, when three or four years old, I was telling them something, which my mother, overhearing, said it had happened before I was born. I stuck to my story, however, and related some things which went, in her opinion, to confirm it. Others being called on, were greatly astonished, knowing that these things had happened, and caused them to say, in my hearing, I surely would be a prophet, as the Lord had shown me things that had happened before my birth. And my father and mother strengthened me in this my first impression, saying, in my presence, I was intended for some great purpose, which they had always thought from certain marks on my head and breast. (A parcel of excrescences, which, I believe, are not at all uncommon, particularly among negroes, as I have seen several with the same. In this case he has either cut them off, or they have nearly disappeared.)

"My grandmother, who was very religious, and to whom I was much attached—my master, who belonged to the church, and other religious persons who visited the house, and whom I often saw at prayers, noticing the singularity of my manners, I suppose, and my uncommon intelligence for a child, remarked I had too much sense to be raised, and, if I was, I would never be of any service to any one as a slave. To a mind like mine, restless, inquisitive, and observant of everything that was passing, it is easy to suppose that religion was the subject to which it would be directed; and, although this subject principally occupied my thoughts, there was nothing that I saw or heard of to which my attention was not directed. The manner in which I learned to read and write, not only had great influence on my own mind, as I acquired it with the most perfect ease,—so much so, that I have no recollection whatever of learning the alphabet; but, to the astonishment of the family, one day, when a book was shown me, to keep me from crying, I began spelling the names of different objects. This was a source of wonder to all in the neighborhood, particularly the blacks—and this learning was constantly improved at all opportunities. When I got large enough to go to work, while employed I was reflecting on many things that would present themselves to my imagination; and whenever an opportunity occurred of looking at a book, when the school-children were getting their lessons, I would find many things that the fertility of my own imagination had depicted to me before. All my time, not devoted to my master's service, was spent either in prayer, or in making experiments in casting different things in moulds made of earth, in attempting to make paper, gunpowder, and many other experiments, that, although I could not perfect, yet convinced me of its practicability if I had the means.*

"I was not addicted to stealing in my youth, nor have ever been; yet such was the confidence of the negroes in the neighborhood, even at this early period of my life, in my superior judgment, that they would often carry me with them when they were going on any roguery, to plan for them. Growing up among them with this confidence in my superior judgment, and when this, in their opinions, was perfected by Divine inspiration, from the circumstances already alluded to in my infancy, and which belief was ever afterwards zealously inculcated by the austerity of my life and manners, which became the subject of remark by white and black; having soon discovered to be great, I must appear so, and therefore studiously avoided mixing in society, and wrapped myself in mystery, devoting my time to fasting and prayer.

"By this time, having arrived to man's estate, and hearing the Scriptures commented on at meetings, I was struck with that particular passage which says, 'Seek ye the kingdom of heaven, and all

*When questioned as to the manner of manufacturing those different articles, he was found well informed.

things shall be added unto you.' I reflected much on this passage, and prayed daily for light on this subject. As I was praying one day at my plough, the Spirit spoke to me, saying, 'Seek ye the kingdom of heaven, and all things shall be added unto you.' *Question.* 'What do you mean by the Spirit?' *Answer.* 'The Spirit that spoke to the prophets in former days,'—and I was greatly astonished, and for two years prayed continually, whenever my duty would permit; and then again I had the same revelation, which fully confirmed me in the impression that I was ordained for some great purpose in the hands of the Almighty. Several years rolled round, in which many events occurred to strengthen me in this my belief. At this time I reverted in my mind to the remarks made of me in my childhood, and the things that had been shown me; and as it had been said of me in my childhood, by those by whom I had been taught to pray, both white and black, and in whom I had the greatest confidence, that I had too much sense to be raised, and if I was I would never be of any use to any one as a slave; now, finding I had arrived to man's estate, and was a slave, and these revelations being made known to me, I began to direct my attention to this great object, to fulfil the purpose for which, by this time, I felt assured I was intended. Knowing the influence I had obtained over the minds of my fellow-servants—(not by the means of conjuring and such-like tricks—for to them I always spoke of such things with contempt), but by the communion of the Spirit, whose revelations I often communicated to them, and they believed and said my wisdom came from God,— I now began to prepare them for my purpose, by telling them something was about to happen that would terminate in fulfilling the great promise that had been made to me.

"About this time I was placed under an overseer, from whom I ran away, and, after remaining in the woods thirty days, I returned, to the astonishment of the negroes on the plantation, who thought I had made my escape to some other part of the country, as my father had done before. But the reason of my return was, that the Spirit appeared to me and said I had my wishes directed to the things of this world, and not to the kingdom of heaven, and that I should return to the service of my earthly master—'For he who knoweth his Master's will, and doeth it not, shall be beaten with many stripes, and thus have I chastened you.' And the negroes found fault, and murmured against me, saying that if they had my sense they would not serve any master in the world. And about this time I had a vision—and I saw white spirits and black spirits engaged in battle, and the sun was darkened—the thunder rolled in the heavens, and blood flowed in streams—and I heard a voice saying, 'Such is your luck, such you are called to see; and let it come rough or smooth, you must surely bear it.'

"I now withdrew myself as much as my situation would permit from the intercourse of my fellow-servants, for the avowed purpose of serving the Spirit more fully; and it appeared to me, and reminded me of the things it had already shown me, and that it would then reveal to me the knowledge of the elements, the revolution of the planets, the operation of tides, and changes of the seasons. After this revelation in the year 1825, and the knowledge of the elements being made known to me, I sought more than ever to obtain true holiness before the great day of judgment should appear, and then I began to receive the true knowledge of faith. And from the first steps of righteousness until the last, was I made perfect; and the Holy Ghost was with me, and said, 'Behold me as I stand in the heavens.' And I looked and saw the forms of men in different attitudes; and there were lights in the sky, to which the children of darkness gave other names than what they really were; for they were the lights of the Saviour's hands, stretched forth from east to west, even as they were extended on the cross on Calvary for the redemption of sinners. And I wondered greatly at these miracles, and prayed to be informed of a certainty of the meaning thereof; and shortly afterwards, while laboring in the field, I discovered drops of blood on the corn, as though it were dew from heaven; and I communicated it to many, both white and black, in the neighborhood—and I then found on the leaves in the woods hieroglyphic characters and numbers, with the forms of men in different attitudes, portrayed in blood, and representing the figures I had seen before in the heavens. And now the Holy Ghost had revealed itself to me, and made plain the miracles it had shown me; for as the blood of Christ had been shed on this earth, and had ascended to heaven for the salvation of sinners, and was now returning to earth again in the form of dew,—and as the leaves on the trees bore the impression of the figures I had seen in the heavens,—it was plain to me that the Saviour was about to lay down the yoke he had borne for the sins of men, and the great day of judgment was at hand.

"About this time I told these things to a white man (Etheldred T. Brantley), on whom it had a wonderful effect; and he ceased from his wickedness, and was attacked immediately with a cutaneous eruption, and blood oozed from the pores of his skin, and after praying and fasting nine days he was healed. And the Spirit appeared to me again, and said, as the Saviour had been baptized, so should we be also; and when the white people would not let us be baptized by the church, we went down into the water together, in the sight of many who reviled us, and were baptized by the Spirit. After this I rejoiced greatly, and gave thanks to God. And on the 12th of May, 1828, I heard a loud noise in the heavens, and the Spirit instantly appeared to me and said the Serpent was loosened, and Christ had laid down the yoke he had borne for the sins of men, and that I should take it on and fight against the Serpent, for the time was fast approaching when the first should be last and the last should be first. *Ques.* 'Do you not find yourself mistaken now?'—*Ans.* 'Was not Christ crucified?' And by signs in the heavens that it would make known to me when I should commence the great work, and until the first sign appeared I should conceal it from the knowledge of men; and on the appearance of the sign (the eclipse of the sun, last February), I should arise and prepare myself, and slay my enemies with their own weapons. And immediately on the sign appearing in the heavens, the seal was removed from my lips, and I communicated the great work laid out for me to do, to four in whom I had the greatest confidence (Henry, Hark, Nelson, and Sam). It was intended by us to have begun the work of death on the 4th of July last. Many were the plans formed and rejected by us, and it affected my mind to such a degree that I fell sick, and the time passed without our coming to any determination how to commence—still forming new schemes and rejecting them, when the sign appeared again, which determined me not to wait longer.

"Since the commencement of 1830 I had been living with Mr. Joseph Travis, who was to me a kind master, and placed the greatest confidence in me; in fact, I had no cause to complain of his treatment to me. On Saturday evening, the 20th of August, it was agreed between Henry, Hark, and myself, to prepare a dinner the next day for the men we expected, and then to concert a plan, as we had not yet determined on any. Hark, on the following morning, brought a pig, and Henry brandy; and being joined by Sam, Nelson, Will, and Jack, they prepared in the woods a dinner, where, about three o'clock, I joined them."

"Q. Why were you so backward in joining them?"

"*A.* The same reason that had caused me not to mix with them for years before.

"I saluted them on coming up, and asked Will how came he there. He answered, his life was worth no more than others, and his liberty as dear to him. I asked him if he thought to obtain it. He said he would, or lose his life. This was enough to put him in full confidence. Jack, I knew, was only a tool in the hands of Hark. It was quickly agreed we should commence a home (Mr. J. Travis') on that night; and until we had armed and equipped ourselves, and gathered sufficient force, neither age nor sex was to be spared—which was invariably adhered to. We remained at the feast until about two hours in the night, when we went to the house and found Austin."

We will not go into the horrible details of the various massacres, but only make one or two extracts, to show the spirit and feelings of Turner:

"I then went to Mr. John T. Harrow's; they had been here and murdered him. I pursued on their track to Capt. Newit Harris', where I found the greater part mounted and ready to start. The men, now amounting to about forty, shouted and hurraed as I rode up. Some were in the yard, loading their guns; others drinking. They said Captain Harris and his family had escaped; the property in the house they destroyed, robbing him of money and other valuables. I ordered them to mount and march instantly; this was about nine or ten o'clock, Monday morning. I proceeded to Mr. Levi Waller's, two or three miles distant. I took my station in the rear, and, as it was my object to carry terror and devastation wherever we went, I placed fifteen or twenty of the best armed and most to be relied on in front, who generally approached the houses as fast as their horses could run. This was for two purposes—to prevent their escape, and strike terror to the inhabitants; on this account I never got to the houses, after leaving Mrs. Whitehead's, until the murders were committed, except in one case. I sometimes got in sight in time to see the work of death completed; viewed the mangled bodies as they lay, in silent satisfaction, and immediately started in quest of other victims. Having murdered Mrs. Waller and ten children, we started for Mr. Wm. Williams',—having killed him and two little boys that were there; while engaged in this, Mrs. Williams fled and got some distance from the house, but she was pursued, overtaken, and compelled to get up behind one of the company, who brought her back, and, after showing her the mangled body of her lifeless husband, she was told to get down and lay by his side, where she was shot dead.

"The white men pursued and fired on us several times. Hark had his horse shot under him, and I caught another for him as it was running by me; five or six of my men were wounded, but none left on the field. Finding myself defeated here, I instantly determined to go through a private way, and cross the Nottoway River at the Cypress Bridge, three miles below Jerusalem, and attack that place in the rear, as I expected they would look for me on the other road, and I had a great desire to get there to procure arms and ammunition. After going a short distance in this private way, accompanied by about twenty men, I overtook two or three, who told me the others were dispersed in every direction.

"On this, I gave up all hope for the present; and on Thursday night, after having supplied myself with provisions from Mr. Travis', I scratched a hole under a pile of fence-rails in a field, where I concealed myself for six weeks, never leaving my hiding-place but for a few minutes in the dead of the night to get water, which was very near. Thinking by this time I could venture out, I began to go about in the night, and eavesdrop the houses in the neighborhood; pursuing this course for about a fortnight, and gathering little or no intelligence, afraid of speaking to any human being, and returning every morning to my cave before the dawn of day. I know not how long I might have led this life, if accident had not betrayed me. A dog in the neighborhood passing by my hiding-place one night while I was out, was attracted by some meat I had in my cave, and crawled in and stole it, and was coming out just as I returned. A few nights after, two negroes having started to go hunting with the same dog, and passed that way, the dog came again to the place, and having just gone out to walk about, discovered me and barked; on which, thinking myself discovered, I spoke to them to beg concealment. On making myself known, they fled from me. Knowing then they would betray me, I immediately left my hiding-place, and was pursued almost incessantly, until I was taken, a fortnight afterwards, by Mr. Benjamin Phipps, in a little hole I had dug out with my sword, for the purpose of concealment, under the top of a fallen tree.

"During the time I was pursued, I had many hair-breadth escapes, which your time will not permit you to relate. I am here loaded with chains, and willing to suffer the fate that awaits me."

Mr. Gray asked him if he knew of any extensive or concerted plan. His answer was, I do not. When I questioned him as to the insurrection in North Carolina happening about the same time, he denied any knowledge of it; and when I looked him in the face, as though I would search his inmost thoughts, he replied, "I see, sir, you doubt my word; but can you not think the same ideas, and strange appearances about this time in the heavens, might prompt others, as well as myself, to this undertaking?" I now had much conversation with and asked him many questions, having forborne to do so previously, except in the cases noted in parenthesis; but during his statement, I had, unnoticed by him, taken notes as to some particular circumstances, and, having the advantage of his statement before me in writing, on the evening of the third day that I had been with him, I began a cross-examination, and found his statement corroborated by every circumstance coming within my own knowledge, or the confessions of others who had been either killed or executed, and whom he had not seen or had any knowledge of since the 22d of August last. He expressed himself fully satisfied as to the impracticability of his attempt. It has been said he was ignorant and cowardly, and that his object was to murder and rob for the purpose of obtaining money to make his escape. It is notorious that he was never known to have a dollar in his life, to swear an oath, or drink a drop of spirits. As to his ignorance, he certainly never had the advantages of education, but he can read and write (it was taught him by his parents), and for natural intelligence and quickness of apprehension is surpassed by few men I have ever seen. As to his being a coward, his reason as given for not resisting Mr. Phipps shows the decision of his character. When he saw Mr. Phipps present his gun, he said he knew it was impossible for him to escape, as the woods were full of men; he therefore thought it was better to surrender, and trust to fortune for his escape. He is a complete fanatic, or plays his part most admirably. On other subjects he possesses an uncommon share of intelligence, with a mind capable of attaining anything, but warped and perverted by the influence of early impressions. He is below the ordinary stature, though strong and active, having the true negro face, every feature of which is strongly marked. I shall not attempt to describe the effect of his narrative, as told and commented on by himself, in the condemned hole of the prison. The calm, deliberate composure with which he spoke of his late deeds and intentions; the expression of his fiend-like face when excited by enthusiasm, still bearing the stains of the blood of helpless innocence about him; clothed with rags and covered with chains, yet daring to raise his manacled hands to heaven, with a spirit soaring above the attributes of man. I looked on him, and my blood curdled in my veins.

THE CHAPTER HEADED *Jegar Sahadutha* contains some terrible stories. It is to be said, they are all facts on judicial record, of the most fiend-like cruelty, terminating in the death of the victim, where the affair has been judicially examined, and the perpetrator escaped death, and in most cases *any* punishment for his crime.

1. Case of Souther.

"SOUTHER V. THE COMMONWEALTH. 7 GRATTAN, 673, 1851.

"The killing of a slave by his master and owner, by wilful and excessive whipping, is murder in the first degree: though it may not have been the purpose and intention of the master and owner to kill the slave.

"Simon Souther was indicted at the October term, 1850, of the Circuit Court for the County of Hanover, for the murder of his own slave. The indictment contained fifteen counts, in which the various modes of punishment and torture by which the homicide was charged to have been committed were stated singly, and in various combinations. The fifteenth count unites them all: and, as the court certifies that the *indictment was sustained by the evidence,* the giving the facts stated in that count will show what was the charge against the prisoner, and what was the proof to sustain it.

"The count charged that on the 1st day of September, 1849, the prisoner tied his negro slave, Sam, with ropes about his wrists, neck, body, legs, and ankles, to a tree. That whilst so tied, the prisoner first whipped the slave with switches. That he next beat and cobbed the slave with a shingle, and compelled two of his slaves, a man and a woman, also to cob the deceased with the shingle. That whilst the deceased was so tied to the tree, the prisoner did strike, knock, kick, stamp, and bent him upon various parts of his head, face, and body; that he applied fire to his body; * * * * that he then washed his body with warm water, in which pods of red pepper had been put and steeped; and he compelled his two slaves aforesaid also to wash him with this same preparation of warm water and red pepper. That after the tying, whipping, cobbing, striking, beating, knocking, kicking, stamping, wounding, bruising, lacerating, burning, washing, and torturing, as aforesaid, the prisoner untied the deceased from the tree in such a way as to throw him with violence to the ground; and he then and there did knock, kick, stamp, and beat the deceased upon his head, temples, and various parts of his body. That the prisoner then had the deceased carried into a shed-room of his house, and there he compelled one of his slaves, in his presence, to confine the deceased's feet in stocks, by making his legs fast to a piece of timber, and to tie a rope about the neck of the deceased, and fasten it to a bed-post in the room, thereby strangling, choking, and suffocating, the deceased. And that whilst the deceased was thus made fast in stocks, as aforesaid, the prisoner did kick, knock, stamp, and beat him upon his head, face, breast, belly, sides, back, and body; and he again compelled his two slaves to apply fire to the body of the deceased, whilst he was so made fast as aforesaid. And the count charged that from these various modes of punishment and torture, the slave Sam then and there died. It appeared that the prisoner commenced the punishment of the deceased in the morning, and that it was continued throughout the day; and that the deceased died in the presence of the prisoner, and one of his slaves, and one of the witnesses, whilst the punishment was still progressing.

"Field J. delivered the opinion of the court.

"The prisoner was indicted and convicted of *murder in the second degree*, in the Circuit Court of Hanover, at its April term last past, and was sentenced to the *penitentiary for five years*, the period of time ascertained by the jury. The murder consisted in the killing of a negro man-slave by the name of Sam, the property of the prisoner, by cruel and excessive whipping and torture, inflicted by Souther, aided by two of his other slaves, on the 1st day of September, 1849. The prisoner moved for a new trial, upon the ground that the offence, *if any*, amounted only to manslaughter. The motion for a new trial was overruled, and a bill of exceptions taken to the opinion of the court, setting forth the facts proved, or as many of them as were deemed material for the consideration of the application for a new trial. The bill of exception states: That the slave Sam, in the indictment mentioned, was the slave and property of the prisoner. That for the purpose of chastising the slave for the offence of getting drunk, and dealing, as the slave confessed and alleged, with Henry and Stone, two of the witnesses for the Commonwealth, he caused him to be tied and punished in the presence of the said witnesses, with the exception of slight whipping with peach or apple tree switches, before the said witnesses arrived at the scene after they were sent for by the prisoner (who were present by request from the defendant), and of several slaves of the prisoner, in the manner and by the means charged in the indictment; and the said slave died under and from the infliction of the said punishment, in the presence of the prisoner, one of his slaves, and of one of the witnesses for the Commonwealth. But it did not appear that it was the design of the prisoner to kill the said slave, unless such design be properly inferable from the manner, means, and duration, of the punishment. And, on the contrary, it did appear that the prisoner frequently declared, while the said slave was undergoing the punishment, that he believed the said slave was feigning, and pretending to be suffering and injured when he was not. The judge certifies that the slave was punished in the *manner and by the means charged in the indictment*. The indictment contains fifteen counts, and sets forth a case of the most cruel and excessive whipping and torture. ✳ ✳ ✳ ✳

"It is believed that the records of criminal jurisprudence do not contain a case of more atrocious and wicked cruelty than was presented upon the trial of Souther; and yet it has been gravely and earnestly contended here by his counsel that his offence amounts to manslaughter only.

"It has been contended by the counsel of the prisoner that a man cannot be indicted and prosecuted for the cruel and excessive whipping of his own slave. That it is lawful for the master to chastise his slave, and that if death ensues from such chastisement, unless it was intended to produce death, it is like the case of homicide which is committed by a man in the performance of a lawful act, which is manslaughter only. It has been decided by this court in Turner's

case, 5 Rand, that the owner of a slave, for the malicious, cruel, and
excessive beating of his own slave, cannot be indicted; yet it by no
means follows, when such malicious, cruel, and excessive beating
results in death, though not intended and premeditated, that the
beating is to be regarded as lawful for the purpose of reducing the
crime to manslaughter, when the whipping is inflicted for the sole
purpose of chastisement. *It is the policy of the law, in respect to the
relation of master and slave, and for the sake of securing proper subordination and obedience on the part of the slave, to protect the
master from prosecution in all such cases, even if the whipping and
punishment be malicious, cruel, and excessive.* But in so inflicting
punishment for the sake of punishment, the owner of the slave acts
at his peril; and if death ensues in consequence of such punishment,
the relation of master and slave affords no ground of excuse or pal-
liation. The principles of the common law, in relation to homicide,
apply to his case without qualification or exception; and, according
to those principles, the act of the prisoner, in the case under consideration, amounted to murder. ✻ ✻ ✻ The crime of the prisoner is
not manslaughter, but murder in the first degree."

2. Death of Hark

*The master is, as we have asserted, protected from prosecution by
express enactment, if the victim dies in the act of resistance to his
will, or under moderate correction.*

"Whereas by another Act of the Assembly, passed in 1774, the
killing of a slave, however wanton, cruel, and deliberate, is only
punishable in the first instance by imprisonment and paying the
value thereof to the owner, which *distinction of criminality between
the murder of a white person and one who is equally a human creature, but merely of a different complexion, is* DISGRACEFUL TO HU-
MANITY, AND DEGRADING IN THE HIGHEST DEGREE TO THE LAWS
AND PRINCIPLES OF A FREE, CHRISTIAN, AND ENLIGHTENED COUN-
TRY, Be it enacted, &c., That if any person shall hereafter be guilty
of wilfully and maliciously killing a slave, such offender shall, upon
the first conviction thereof, be adjudged guilty of murder, and shall
suffer the same punishment as if he had killed a free man: *Provided
always, this act shall not extend to the person killing a slave* OUT-
LAWED BY VIRTUE OF ANY ACT OF ASSEMBLY OF THIS STATE, *or to*

any slave in the act of resistance to his lawful owner or master, or to any slave dying under moderate correction."

Instance in point;—

"FROM THE 'NATIONAL ERA,' WASHINGTON, NOVEMBER 6, 1851.

"HOMICIDE CASE IN CLARKE COUNTY, VIRGINIA.

"Some time since, the newspapers of Virginia contained an account of a horrible tragedy, enacted in Clarke County, of that state. A slave of Colonel James Castleman, it was stated, had been chained by the neck, and whipped to death by his master, on the charge of stealing. The whole neighborhood in which the transaction occurred was incensed; the Virginia papers abounded in denunciations of the cruel act; and the people of the North were called upon to bear witness to the justice which would surely be meted out in a slave state to the master of a slave. We did not publish the account. The case was horrible; it was, we were confident, exceptional. It should not be taken as evidence of the general treatment of slaves. We chose to delay any notice of it till the courts should pronounce their judgment, and we could announce at once the crime and its punishment, so that the state might stand acquitted of the foul deed.

"Those who were so shocked at the transaction will be surprised and mortified to hear that the actors in it have been tried and *acquitted!* and when they read the following account of the trial and verdict, published at the instance of the friends of the accused, their mortification will deepen into bitter indignation.

"FROM THE 'SPIRIT OF JEFFERSON.'

" 'COLONEL JAMES CASTLEMAN.—The following statement, understood to have been drawn up by counsel, since the trial, has been placed by the friends of this gentleman in our hands for publication:

" 'At the Circuit Superior Court of Clarke County, commencing on the 13th of October, Judge Samuels presiding, James Castleman and his son Stephen D. Castleman were indicted jointly for the murder of negro Lewis, property of the latter. By advice of their counsel, the parties elected to be tried separately, and the attorney for the Commonwealth directed that James Castleman should be tried first.

" 'It was proved, on this trial, that for many months previous to the occurrence the money-drawer of the tavern kept by Stephen D. Castleman, and the liquors kept in large quantities in his cellar, had been pillaged from time to time, until the thefts had attained to a considerable amount. Suspicion had, from various causes, been directed to Lewis, and another negro, named Reuben (a blacksmith), the property of James Castleman; but, by the aid of two of the house-servants, they had eluded the most vigilant watch.

" 'On the 20th of August last, in the afternoon, S. D. Castleman accidentally discovered a clue, by means of which, and through one of the house-servants implicated, he was enabled fully to detect the depredators, and to ascertain the manner in which the theft had been committed. He immediately sent for his father, living near him, and, after communicating what he had discovered, it was determined that the offenders should be punished at once, and before they should know of the discovery that had been made.

" 'Lewis was punished first; and in a manner, as was fully shown, to preclude all risk of injury to his person, by stripes with a broad leathern strap. He was punished severely, but to an extent by no means disproportionate to his offence; nor was it pretended, in any quarter, that this punishment implicated either his life or health. He confessed the offence, and admitted that it had been effected by false keys, furnished by the blacksmith, Reuben.

" 'The latter servant was punished immediately afterwards. It was believed that he was the principal offender, and he was found to be more obdurate and contumacious than Lewis had been in reference to the offence. Thus it was proved, both by the prosecution and the defence, that he was punished with greater severity than his accomplice. It resulted in a like confession on his part, and he produced the false key, one fashioned by himself, by which the theft had been effected.

" 'It was further shown, on the trial, that Lewis was whipped in the upper room of a warehouse, connected with Stephen Castleman's store, and near the public road, where he was at work at the time; that after he had been flogged, to secure his person, whilst they went after Reuben, he was confined by a chain around his neck, which was attached to a joist above his head. The length of this chain, the breadth and thickness of the joist, its height from the floor, and the circlet of chain on the neck, were accurately measured; and it was thus shown that the chain unoccupied by the circlet and the joist was a foot and a half longer than the space between the shoulders of the man and the joist above, or to that extent the chain hung loose above him; that the circlet (which was fastened so as to prevent its contraction) rested on the shoulders and breast, the chain being sufficiently drawn only to prevent being slipped over his head, and that there was no other place in the room to which he could be fastened except to one of the joists above. His hands were tied in front; a white man, who had been at work with Lewis during the day, was left with him by the Messrs. Castleman, the better to insure his detention, whilst they were absent after Reuben. It was proved by this man (who was a witness for the prosecution) that Lewis asked for a box to stand on, or for something that he could jump off from; that after the Castlemans had left him he expressed a fear that when they came back he would be whipped again; and said, if he had a knife, and could get one hand loose, he would cut his throat. The witness stated that the negro "stood firm on his feet," that he could turn freely in whatever direction he wished, and that he made no complaint of the mode of his confinement. This man stated that he remained with Lewis about half an hour, and then left there to go home.

" 'After punishing Reuben, the Castlemans returned to the warehouse, bringing him with them; their object being to confront the two men, in the hope that by further examination of them jointly all their accomplices might be detected.

" 'They were not absent more than half an hour. When they entered the room above, Lewis was found hanging by the neck, his feet thrown behind him, his knees a few inches from the floor, and his head thrown forward,—the body warm and supple (or relaxed), but life was extinct.

" 'It was proved by the surgeons who made a post-mortem examination before the coroner's inquest that the death was caused by strangulation by hanging; and other eminent surgeons were examined to show, from the appearance of the brain and its blood-vessels after death (as exhibited at the post-mortem examination), that the subject could not have fainted before strangulation.

" 'After the evidence was finished on both sides, the jury, from their box, and of their own motion, without a word from counsel on either side, informed the court that they had agreed upon their verdict. The counsel assented to its being thus received, and a verdict of "*Not guilty*" was immediately rendered. The attorney for the commonwealth then informed the court that all the evidence for the prosecution had been laid before the jury; and, as no new evidence could be offered on the trial of Stephen D. Castleman, he submitted to the court the propriety of entering a *nolle prosequi*. The judge replied that the case had been fully and fairly laid before the jury upon the evidence; that the court was not only satisfied with the verdict, but, if any other had been rendered, it must have been set aside; and that, if no further evidence was to be adduced on the trial of Stephen, the attorney for the commonwealth would exercise a proper discretion in entering a *nolle prosequi* as to him, and the court would approve its being done. A *nolle prosequi* was entered accordingly, and both gentlemen discharged.

" 'It may be added that two days were consumed in exhibiting the evidence, and that the trial was by a jury of Clark County. Both the parties had been on bail from the time of their arrest, and were continued on bail whilst the trial was depending.'

"Let us admit that the evidence does not prove the legal crime of homicide: what candid man can doubt, after reading this *ex parte* version of it, that the slave died in consequence of the punishment inflicted upon him?

"In criminal prosecutions the federal constitution guarantees to the accused the right to a public trial by an impartial jury; the right to be informed of the nature and cause of the accusation; to be confronted with the witnesses against him; to have compulsory process for obtaining witness in his favor; and to have the assistance of counsel; guarantees necessary to secure innocence against hasty or vindictive judgment,—absolutely necessary to prevent injustice. Grant that they were not intended for slaves; every master of a slave must feel that they are still morally binding upon him. He is the sole judge; he alone determines the offence, the proof requisite to establish it, and the amount of the punishment. The slave, then, has a peculiar claim upon him for justice. When charged with a crime, common humanity requires that he should be informed of it, that he should be confronted with the witnesses against him, that he should be permitted to show evidence in favor of his innocence.

"But how was poor Lewis treated? The son of Castleman said he had discovered who stole the money; and it was forthwith 'determined that the offenders should be punished at once, and *before they should know of the discovery that had been made.*' Punished without a hearing! Punished on the testimony of a house-servant, the nature of which does not appear to have been inquired into by the court! Not a word is said which authorizes the belief that any careful examination was made, as it respects their guilt. Lewis and Reuben were assumed, on loose evidence, without deliberate investigation, to be guilty; and then, without allowing them to attempt to show their evidence, they were whipped until a confession of guilt was extorted by bodily pain.

"Is this Virginia justice?"

" '*To the Editor of the Era:*

" 'I see that Castleman, who lately had a trial for whipping a slave to death in Virginia, was "*triumphantly acquitted,*"—as many expected. There are three persons in this city, with whom I am acquainted, who staid at Castleman's the same night in which this awful tragedy was enacted. They heard the dreadful lashing, and the heartrending screams and entreaties of the sufferer. They implored the only white man they could find on the premises, not engaged in the bloody work, to interpose, but for a long time he refused, on the ground that he was a dependant, and was afraid to give offence; and that, moreover, they had been drinking, and he was in fear for his own life, should he say a word that would be displeasing to them. He did, however, venture, and returned and reported the cruel manner in which the slaves were chained, and lashed, and secured in a blacksmith's vice. In the morning, when they ascertained that one of the slaves was dead, they were so shocked and indignant that they refused to eat in the house, and reproached Castleman with his cruelty. He expressed his regret that the slave had died, and especially as he had ascertained that he *was innocent* of the accusation for which he had suffered. The idea was that he had fainted from exhaustion; and, the chain being round his neck, he was strangled. The persons I refer to are themselves slaveholders; but their feelings were so harrowed and lacerated that they could not sleep (two of them are ladies), and for many nights afterwards their rest was disturbed, and their dreams made frightful, by the appalling recollection.

" 'These persons would have been material witnesses, and would have willingly attended on the part of the prosecution. The knowledge they had of the case was communicated to the proper authorities, yet their attendance was not required. The only witness was that dependent who considered his own life in danger.

Yours, &c.,   J. F.' "

THE LAW OF OUTLAWRY.

Revised Statutes of North Carolina, chap. cxi., sect. 22:

" 'Whereas, MANY TIMES *slaves run away and lie out, hid and lurking in swamps, woods, and other obscure places,* killing cattle and hogs, and committing other injuries to the inhabitants of this state; in all such cases, upon intelligence of any slave or slaves lying out as aforesaid, any two justices of the peace for the county wherein such slave or slaves is or are supposed to lurk or do mischief, shall, and they are hereby empowered and required to issue proclamation against such slave or slaves (reciting his or their names, and the name or names of the owner or owners, if known), thereby requiring him or them, and every of them, forthwith to surrender him or themselves; and also to empower and require the sheriff of the said county to take such power with him as he shall think fit and necessary for going in search and pursuit of, and effectually apprehending, such outlying slave or slaves; which proclamation shall be published at the door of the court-house, and at such other places as said justices shall direct. And if any slave or slaves, against whom proclamation hath been thus issued, stay out, and do not immediately return home, it shall be lawful for any person or persons whatsoever to kill and destroy such slave or slaves by *such ways and means as he shall think fit,* without accusation or impeachment of any crime for the same.'

" 'STATE OF NORTH CAROLINA, LENOIR COUNTY.—Whereas complaint hath been this day made to us, two of the justices of the peace for the said county, by William D. Cobb, of Jones County, that two negro slaves belonging to him, named Ben (commonly known by the name of Ben Fox) and Rigdon, have absented themselves from their said master's service, and are lurking about in the Counties of Lenoir and Jones, committing acts of felony; these are, in the name of the state, to command the said slaves forthwith to surrender themselves, and turn home to their said master. And we do hereby also require the sheriff of said County of Lenoir to make diligent search and pursuit after the above-mentioned slaves. . . . And we do hereby, by virtue of an act of assembly of this state concerning servants and slaves, intimate and declare, if the said slaves do not surrender themselves and return home to their master immediately after the publication of these presents, that any person may kill or destroy said slaves by such means as he or they think fit, without accusation or impeachment of any crime or offence for so doing, or without incurring any penalty of forfeiture thereby.

" 'Given under our hands and seals, this 12th of November, 1836.

B. COLEMAN J. P. [Seal.]

JAS. JONES, J. P.'   [Seal.]

" '$200 REWARD.—Ran away from the subscriber, about three years ago, a certain negro man, named Ben, commonly known by the name of Ben Fox; also one other negro, by the name of Rigdon, who ran away on the eighth of this month.

" 'I will give the reward of one hundred dollars for each of the above negroes, to be delivered to me, or confined in the jail of Lenoir or Jones Country, *or for the killing of them, so that I can see them.*

" '*November* 12, 1836,   W. D. COBB.'

"That this act was *not* a dead letter, also, was plainly implied in the protective act first quoted. If slaves were not, as a matter of fact, ever outlawed, why does the act formally recognize such a class?— 'provided that this act shall not extend to the killing of any slave *outlawed* by any act of the assembly.' This language sufficiently indicates the existence of the custom.

"Further than this, the statute-book of 1821 contained two acts: the first of which provides that all masters, in certain counties, who have had slaves killed in consequence of outlawry, shall have a claim on the treasury of the state for their value, unless cruel treatment of the slave be proved on the part of the master; the second act extends the benefits of the latter provision to all the counties in the state.

"Finally there is evidence that this act of outlawry was executed so recently as the year 1850,—the year in which 'Uncle Tom's Cabin' was written. See the following from the *Wilmington Journal* of December 13, 1850.

" 'STATE OF NORTH CAROLINA, NEW HANOVER COUNTY.— Whereas complaint, upon oath, hath this day been made to us, two of the justices of the peace for the said state and county aforesaid, by Guilford Horn, of Edgecombe County, that a certain male slave belonging to him, named Harry, a carpenter by trade, about forty years old, five feet five inches high, or thereabouts; yellow complexion; stout built; with a scar on his left leg (from the cut of an axe); has very thick lips; eyes deep sunk in his head; forehead very square; tolerably loud voice; has lost one or two of his upper teeth; and has a very dark spot on his jaw, supposed to be a mark,—hath absented himself from his master's service, and is supposed to be lurking about in this county, committing acts of felony or other misdeeds; these are, therefore, in the name of state aforesaid, to command the said slave forthwith to surrender himself and return home to his said master; and we do hereby, by virtue of the act of assembly in such cases made and provided, intimate and declare that if the said slave Harry doth not surrender himself and return home immediately after the publication of these presents, that any person or persons may KILL and DESTROY the said slave by such means as he or they may think fit, without accusation or impeachment of any crime or offence in so doing, and without incurring any penalty or forfeiture thereby.

" 'Given under our hands and seals, this 20th day of June, 1850.
JAMES T. MILLER, J. P.   [*Seal.*]
W. C. BETTENCOURT, J. P.' [*Seal.*]

" 'ONE HUNDRED AND TWENTY-FIVE DOLLARS REWARD will be paid for the delivery of the said Harry to me at Tosnott Depot, Edgecombe County, or for his confinement in any jail in the state, so that I can get him; or *One Hundred and Fifty Dollars will be given for his head.*

" 'He was lately heard from in Newbern, where he called himself Henry Barnes (or Burns), and will be likely to continue the same name, or assume that of Copage or Farmer. He has a free mulatto woman for a wife, by the name of Sally Bozeman, who has lately removed to Wilmington, and lives in that part of the town called Texas, where he will likely be lurking.

" 'Masters of vessels are particularly cautioned against harboring or concealing the said negro on board their vessels, as the full penalty of the law will be rigorously enforced.   GUILFORD HORN.

" '*June 29th*, 1850.' "

This last advertisement was cut by the author from the *Wilmington Journal*, December 18th, 1850, a paper published in Wilmington, North Carolina.

APPENDIX III

Church Action on Slavery

IN REFERENCE to this important subject, we present a few extracts from the first and second chapters of the fourth part of the "Key to Uncle Tom's Cabin:"

Let us review the declarations that have been made in the Southern church, and see what principles have been established by them:

1. That slavery is an innocent and lawful relation, as much as that of parent and child, husband and wife, or any other lawful relation of society. (Harmony Pres., S. C.)

2. That it is consistent with the most fraternal regard for the good of the slave. (Charleston Union Pres., S. C.)

3. That masters ought not to be disciplined for selling slaves without their consent. (New School Pres. Church, Petersburg, Va.)

4. That the right to buy, sell, and hold men for purposes of gain, was given by express permission of God. (James Smylie and his Presbyteries.)

5. That the laws which forbid the education of the slave are right, and meet the approbation of the reflecting part of the Christian community. (Ibid.)

6. That the fact of slavery is not a question of morals at all, but is purely one of political economy. (Charleston Baptist Association.)

7. The right of masters to dispose of the time of their slaves has been distinctly recognized by the Creator of all things. (Ibid.)

8. That slavery, as it exists in these United States, is not a moral evil. (Georgia Conference, Methodist.)

9. That, without a new revelation from heaven, no man is entitled to pronounce slavery wrong.

10. That the separation of slaves by sale should be regarded as separation by death, and the parties allowed to marry again. (Shiloh Baptist Ass., and Savannah River Ass.)

11. That the testimony of colored members of the churches shall not be taken against a white person. (Methodist Church.)

In addition, it has been plainly avowed, by the expressed principles and practice of Christians of various denominations, that they regard it right and proper to put down all inquiry upon this subject by Lynch law.

The Old School Presbyterian Church, in whose communion the greater part of the slaveholding Presbyterians of the South are found, has never felt called upon to discipline its members for upholding a system which denies legal marriage to all slaves. Yet this church was agitated to its very foundation by the discussion of a question of morals which an impartial observer would probably consider of far less magnitude, namely, whether a man might lawfully marry his deceased wife's sister. For the time, all the strength and attention of the church seemed concentrated upon this important subject. The trial went from Presbytery to Synod, and from Synod to General Assembly; and ended with deposing a very respectable minister for this crime.

Rev. Robert J. Breckenridge, D.D., a member of the Old School Assembly, has thus described the state of the slave population as to their marriage relations:

"The system of slavery denies to a whole class of human beings the sacredness of marriage and of home, compelling them to live in a state of concubinage; for, in the eye of the law, no colored slave-man is the husband of any wife in particular, nor any slave-woman the wife of any husband in particular; no slave-man is the father of any child in particular, and no slave-child is the child of any parent in particular."

Now, had this church considered the fact that three millions of men and women were, by the laws of the land, obliged to live in this manner, as of equally serious consequence, it is evident, from the ingenuity, argument, vehemence, Biblical research, and untiring zeal, which they bestowed on Mr. McQueen's trial, that they could have made a very strong case with regard to this also.

The history of the united action of denominations which included churches both in the slave and free states is a melancholy exemplification, to a reflecting mind, of that gradual deterioration of the moral sense which results from admitting any compromise, however slight, with an acknowledged sin. The best minds in the world cannot bear such a familiarity without injury to the moral sense. The facts of the slave system and of the slave laws, when presented to disinterested judges in Europe, have excited a universal outburst of horror; yet, in assemblies composed of the wisest and best clergymen of America, these things have been discussed from year to year, and yet brought no results that have, in the slightest degree, lessened the evil. The reason is this. A portion of the members of these bodies had pledged themselves to sustain the system, and peremptorily to refuse and put down all discussion of it; and the other part of the body did not consider this stand so taken as being of sufficiently vital consequence to authorize separation.

Nobody will doubt that, had the Southern members taken such a stand against the divinity of our Lord, the division would have been immediate and unanimous; but yet the Southern members do maintain the right to buy and sell, lease, hire, and mortgage, multitudes of men and women, whom, with the same breath, they declare to be members of their churches, and true Christians. The Bible declares of all such that they are the temples of the Holy Ghost; that they are the members of Christ's body, of his flesh and bones. Is not the doctrine that men may lawfully sell the members of Christ, his body, his flesh and bones, for purposes of gain, as really a heresy as the denial of the divinity of Christ? and is it not a dishonor to Him who is over all, God blessed forever, to tolerate this dreadful opinion, with its more dreadful consequences, while the smallest heresies concerning the imputation of Adam's sin are pursued with eager vehemence? If the history of the action of all the bodies thus united can be traced downwards, we shall find that, by reason of this tolerance of an admitted sin, the anti-slavery testimony has every year grown weaker and weaker. If we look over the history of all denominations, we shall see that at first they used very stringent language with relation to slavery. This is particularly the case with the Methodist and Presbyterian bodies, and for that reason we select these two as examples. The Methodist Society, especially, as organized by John Wesley, was an anti-slavery society, and the Book of Discipline contained the most positive statutes against slaveholding. The history of the successive resolutions of the Conference of this church is very striking. In 1780, before the church was regularly organized in the United States, they resolved as follows:

"The conference acknowledges that slavery is contrary to the laws of God, man, and nature, and hurtful to society; contrary to the dictates of conscience and true religion; and doing what we would not others should do unto us."

In 1784, when the church was fully organized, rules were adopted prescribing the times at which members who were already slaveholders should emancipate their slaves. These rules were succeeded by the following:

"Every person concerned, who will not comply with these rules, shall have liberty quietly to withdraw from our Society within the twelve months following the notice being given him, as aforesaid; otherwise the assistants shall exclude him from the Society.

"No person holding slaves shall in future be admitted into the Society, or to the Lord's Supper, till he previously comply with these rules concerning slavery.

"Those who buy, sell, or give slaves away, unless on purpose to free them, shall be expelled immediately."

In 1801:

"We declare that we are more than ever convinced of the great evil of African slavery, which still exists in these United States.

"Every member of the Society who sells a slave shall immediately, after full proof, be excluded from the Society, etc.

"The Annual Conferences are directed to draw up addresses for the gradual emancipation of the slaves, to the legislature. Proper committees shall be appointed by the Annual Conference, out of the most respectable of our friends, for the conducting of the business; and the presiding elders, deacons, and travelling preachers, shall procure as many proper signatures as possible to the addresses, and give all the assistance in their power, in every respect, to aid the committees, and to further the blessed undertaking. Let this be continued from year to year, till the desired end be accomplished."

In 1836, let us notice the change. The General Conference held its annual session in Cincinnati, and resolved as follows:

"Resolved, by the delegates of the Annual Conferences in General Conference assembled, that they are decidedly opposed to modern abolitionism, and wholly disclaim any right, wish, or intention, to interfere in the civil and political relation between master and slave, as it exists in the slaveholding States of this Union."

These resolutions were passed by a very large majority. An address was received from the Wesleyan Methodist Conference in

England, affectionately remonstrating on the subject of slavery. The Conference refused to publish it. In the pastoral address to the churches are these passages:

"It cannot be unknown to you that the question of slavery in the United States, by the constitutional compact which binds us together as a nation, is left to be regulated by the several State Legislatures themselves; and thereby is put beyond the control of the general government, as well as that of all ecclesiastical bodies, it being manifest that in the slaveholding States themselves the entire responsibility of its existence, or non-existence, rests with those State Legislatures. * * * * These facts, which are only mentioned here as a reason for the friendly admonition which we wish to give you, constrain us, as your pastors, who are called to watch over your souls, as they must give account, to exhort you to abstain from all abolition movements and associations, and to refrain from patronizing any of their publications," etc. * * * * * * * * *

The subordinate conferences showed the same spirit.

In 1836, the New York Annual Conference resolved that no one should be elected a deacon or elder in the church unless he would give a pledge to the church that he would refrain from discussing this subject.★

In 1838, the Conference resolved—

"As the sense of this Conference, that any of its members, or probationers, who shall patronize *Zion's Watchman,* either by writing in commendation of its character, by circulating it, recommending it to our people, or procuring subscribers, or by collecting or remitting moneys, shall be deemed guilty of indiscretion, and dealt with accordingly."

It will be recollected that *Zion's Watchman* was edited by Le Roy Sunderland, for whose abduction the State of Alabama had offered fifty thousand dollars.

In 1840, the General Conference at Baltimore passed the resolution that we have already quoted, forbidding preachers to allow colored persons to give testimony in their churches. It has been computed that about eighty thousand people were deprived of the right of testimony by this Act. This Methodist Church subsequently broke into a Northern and Southern Conference. The

★ This resolution is given in Birney's pamphlet.

Southern Conference is avowedly all pro-slavery, and the Northern Conference has still in its communion slaveholding conferences and members.

Of the Northern Conferences, one of the largest, the Baltimore, passed the following:

"*Resolved,* That this Conference disclaims having any fellowship with abolitionism. On the contrary, while it is determined to maintain its well-known and long-established position, by keeping the travelling preachers composing its own body free from slavery, it is also determined not to hold connection with any ecclesiastical body that shall make non-slaveholding a condition of membership in the church, but to stand by and maintain the discipline as it is."

The following extract is made from an address of the Philadelphia Annual Conference to the Societies under its care, dated Wilmington, Delaware, April 7, 1847:

"If the plan of separation gives us the pastoral care of you, it remains to inquire whether we have done anything, as a conference, or as men, to forfeit your confidence and affection. We are not advised that even in the great excitement which has distressed you for some months past, any one has impeached our moral conduct, or charged us with unsoundness in doctrine, or corruption or tyranny in the administration of discipline. But we learn that the simple cause of the unhappy excitement among you is, that some suspect us, or affect to suspect us, of being abolitionists. Yet no particular act of the Conference, or any particular member thereof, is adduced as the ground of the erroneous and injurious suspicion. We would ask you, brethren, whether the conduct of our ministry among you for sixty years past ought not to be sufficient to protect us from this charge. Whether the question we have been accustomed, for a few years past, to put to candidates for admission among us, namely, Are you an abolitionist? and, without each one answered in the negative, he was not received, ought not to protect us from the charge. Whether the action of the last Conference on this particular matter ought not to satisfy any fair and candid mind that we are not, and do not desire to be, abolitionists. * * * *. We cannot see how we can be regarded as abolitionists, without the ministers of the Methodist Episcopal Church South being considered in the same light. * * *

"Wishing you all heavenly benedictions, we are, dear brethren, yours, in Christ Jesus,

J. P. Durbin,
J. Kennaday,
Ignatius T. Cooper, } *Committee.*"
William H. Gilder,
Joseph Castle,

These facts sufficiently define the position of the Methodist church. The history is melancholy, but instructive. The history of the Presbyterian church is also of interest.

In 1793, the following note to the eighth commandment was inserted in the Book of Discipline, as expressing the doctrine of the church upon slave-holding:

"1 Tim. 1:10.—The law is made for MAN-STEALERS. This crime among the Jews exposed the perpetrators of it to capital punishment (Exodus 21:15); and the apostle here classes them with sinners of the first rank. The word he uses, in its original import, comprehends all who are concerned in bringing any of the human race into slavery, or in retaining them in it. *Hominum fures, qui servos vel liberos, abducunt, retinent, vendunt, vel emunt.* Stealers of men are all these who bring off slaves or freemen, and KEEP, SELL, or BUY THEM. To steal a free man, says Grotius, is the highest kind of theft. In other instances, we only steal human property; but when we steal or retain men in slavery, we seize those who, in common with ourselves, are constituted by the original grant lords of the earth."

No rules of church discipline were enforced, and members whom this passage declared guilty of this crime remained undisturbed in its communion, as ministers and elders. This inconsistency was obviated in 1816 by expunging the passage from the Book of Discipline. In 1818 it adopted an expression of its views on slavery. This document is a long one, conceived and written in a very Christian spirit. The Assembly's Digest says, page 341, that it was *unanimously* adopted. The following is its testimony as to the nature of slavery:

"We consider the voluntary enslaving of one part of the human race by another as a gross violation of the most precious and sacred rights of human nature, as utterly inconsistent with the law of God which requires us to love our neighbor as ourselves, and as totally irreconcilable with the spirit and principles of the Gospel of Christ, which enjoin that 'all things whatsoever ye would that men should do to you, do ye even so to them.' Slavery creates a paradox in the moral system. It exhibits rational, accountable, and immortal beings in such circumstances as scarcely to leave them the power of moral action. It exhibits them as dependent on the will of others whether they shall receive religious instruction; whether they shall know and worship the true God; whether they shall enjoy the ordinances of the Gospel; whether they shall perform the duties and cherish the endearments of husbands and wives, parents and children, neighbors and friends; whether they shall preserve their chastity and purity, or regard the dictates of justice and humanity. Such are some of the consequences of slavery,—consequences not imaginary, but which connect themselves with its very existence. The evils to which the slave is always exposed often take place in fact, and in their very worst degree and form; and where all of them do not take place,—as we rejoice to say that in many instances, through the influence of the principles of humanity and religion on the minds of masters, they do not,—still the slave is deprived of his natural right, degraded as a human being, and exposed to the danger of passing into the hands of a master who may inflict upon him all the hardships and injuries which inhumanity and avarice may suggest."

This language was surely decided, and it was *unanimously* adopted by slaveholders and non-slaveholders. Certainly one might think the time of redemption was drawing nigh. The declaration goes on to say:

"It is manifestly the duty of all Christians who enjoy the light of the present day, when the inconsistency of slavery both with the dictates of humanity and religion has been demonstrated, and is generally seen and acknowledged, to use honest, earnest, unwearied endeavors to correct the errors of former times, and as speedily as possible to efface this blot on our holy religion, and to OBTAIN THE COMPLETE ABOLITION of slavery throughout Christendom and throughout the world."

Here we have the Presbyterian Church, slaveholding and non-slaveholding, virtually formed into one great *abolition society,* as we have seen the Methodist was.

The Assembly then goes on to state that the slaves are not *at present* prepared to be free,—that they tenderly sympathize with the portion of the church and country that has had this evil entailed upon them, where, as they say, "a great and the most virtuous part of the community ABHOR SLAVERY, and wish ITS EXTERMINATION."

But they exhort them to commence immediately the work of instructing slaves, with a view to preparing them for freedom, and to let no greater delay take place than "a regard to public welfare *indispensably* demands;" "to be governed by no other considerations than an *honest and impartial regard to the happiness of the injured party, uninfluenced by the expense and inconvenience* which such regard may involve." It warns against "*unduly extending this plea of necessity,*"—against making it a cover for the *love and practice of slavery*. It ends by recommending that any one who shall sell a fellow-Christian without his consent be immediately disciplined and suspended.

If we consider that this was *unanimously* adopted by slaveholders and all, and grant, as we certainly do, that it was adopted in all honesty and good faith, we shall surely expect something from it. We should expect forthwith the organizing of a set of common schools for the slave children; for an efficient religious ministration; for an entire discontinuance of trading in Christian slaves; for laws which make the family relations sacred. Was any such thing done or attempted? Alas! Two years after this, came the ADMISSION OF MISSOURI, and the increase of demand in the Southern slave-market, and the internal slave-trade. Instead of school-teachers, they had slave-traders; instead of gathering *schools,* they gathered *slave-coffles.* Instead of building school-houses, they built slave-pens and slave-prisons, jails, barracoons, factories, or whatever the trade pleases to term them; and so went the plan of gradual emancipation.

In 1834, sixteen years after, a committee of the Synod of Kentucky, in which state slavery is generally said to exist in its mildest form, appointed to make a report on the condition of the slaves, gave the following picture of their condition. First, as to their spiritual condition, they say:

"After making all reasonable allowances, our colored population can be considered, at the most, but semi-heathen.

"Brutal stripes, and all the various kinds of personal indignities, are not the only species of cruelty which slavery licenses. The law does not recognize the family relations of the slave, and extends to him no protection in the enjoyment of domestic endearments. The members of a slave-family may be forcibly separated, so that they shall never more meet until the final judgment. And cupidity often induces the masters to practise what the law allows. Brothers and sisters, parents and children, husbands and wives, are torn asunder, and permitted to see each other no more. These acts are daily occuring in the midst of us. The shrieks and the agony often witnessed on such occasions proclaim with a trumpet-tongue the iniquity and cruelty of our system. The cries of these sufferers go up to the ears of the Lord of Sabaoth. There is not a neighborhood where these heartrending scenes are not displayed. There is not a village or road that does not behold the sad procession of manacled outcasts, whose chains and mournful countenances tell that they are exiled by force from all that their hearts hold dear. Our church, years ago, raised its voice of solemn warning against this flagrant violation of every principle of mercy, justice, and humanity. Yet we blush to announce to you and to the world, that this warning has been often disregarded, even by those who hold to our communion. Cases have occurred, in our own denomination, where professors of the religion of mercy have torn the mother from her children, and sent her into a merciless and returnless exile. Yet acts of discipline have rarely followed such conduct."

Hon. James G. Birney, for years a resident of Kentucky, in his pamphlet, amends the word *rarely* by substituting *never*. What could show more plainly the utter inefficiency of the past act of the Assembly, and the necessity of adopting some measures more efficient? In 1835, therefore, the subject was urged upon the General Assembly, entreating them to carry out the principles and designs they had avowed in 1818.

Mr. Stuart, of Illinois, in a speech he made upon the subject, said:

"I hope this Assembly are prepared to come out fully and declare their sentiments, that slaveholding is a most flagrant and heinous SIN. Let us not pass it by in this indirect way, while so many thousands and tens of thousands of our fellow-creatures are writhing under the lash, often inflicted, too, by ministers and elders of the Presbyterian church.

* * * * * * * *

"In this church a man may take a free-born child, force it away from its parents, to whom God gave it in charge, saying, 'Bring it up for me,' and sell it as a beast, or hold it in perpetual bondage, and not only escape corporeal punishment, but really be esteemed an excellent Christian. Nay, even ministers of the Gospel and doctors of divinity may engage in this unholy traffic, and yet sustain their high and holy calling.

*   *   *   *   *   *   *   *

"Elders, ministers, and doctors of divinity, are, with both hands, engaged in the practice."

One would have thought facts like these, stated in a body of Christians, were enough to wake the dead; but, alas! we can become accustomed to very awful things. No action was taken upon these remonstrances except to refer them to a committee, to be reported on at the next session, in 1836.

The moderator of the Assembly in 1836 was a slaveholder, Dr. T. S. Witherspoon, the same who said to the editor of the *Emancipator,* "I draw my warrant from the scriptures of the Old and New Testament to hold my slaves in bondage. The principle of holding the heathen in bondage is recognized by God. When the tardy process of the law is too long in redressing our grievances, we at the South have adopted the summary process of Judge Lynch."

The majority of the committee appointed made a report as follows:

"Whereas the subject of slavery is inseparably connected with the laws of many of the states in this Union, with which it is by no means proper for an ecclesiastical judicature to interfere, and involves many considerations in regard to which great diversity of opinion and intensity of feeling are known to exist in the churches represented in this Assembly; and whereas there is great reason to believe that any action on the part of this Assembly, in reference to this subject, would tend to distract and divide our churches, and would probably in no wise promote the benefit of those whose welfare is immediately contemplated in the memorials in question:

"Therefore, Resolved,

"1. That it is not expedient for the Assembly to take any further order in relation to this subject.

"2. That as the notes which have been expunged from our public formularies, and which some of the memorials referred to the committee request to have restored, were introduced irregularly, never had the sanction of the church, and, therefore, never possessed any authority, the General Assembly has no power, nor would they think it expedient, to assign them a place in the authorized standards of the church."

The minority of the committee, the Rev. Messrs. Dickey and Beman, reported as follows:

"*Resolved*, 1. That the buying, selling, or holding a human being as property, is in the sight of God a heinous sin, and ought to subject the doer of it to the censures of the church.

"2. That it is the duty of every one, and especially of every Christian, who may be involved in this sin, to free himself from its entanglement without delay.

"3. That it is the duty of every one, especially of every Christian, in the meekness and firmness of the Gospel, to plead the cause of the poor and needy, by testifying against the principle and practice of slaveholding, and to use his best endeavors to deliver the church of God from the evil, and to bring about the emancipation of the slaves in these United States, and throughout the world."

The slaveholding delegates, to the number of forty-eight, met *apart*, and *Resolved*,

"That if the General Assembly shall undertake to exercise authority on the subject of slavery, so as to make it an immorality, or shall in any way declare that Christians are criminal in holding slaves, that a declaration shall be presented by the Southern delegation declining their jurisdiction in the case, and our determination not to submit to such decision."

In view of these conflicting reports, the Assembly resolved as follows:

"Inasmuch as the constitution of the Presbyterian church, in its preliminary and fundamental principles, declares that no church judicatories ought to pretend to make laws to bind the conscience in virtue of their own authority; and as the urgency of the business of the Assembly, and the shortness of the time during which they can continue in session, render it impossible to deliberate and decide judiciously on the subject of slavery in its relation to the church, therefore, Resolved, that this whole subject be indefinitely postponed."

The amount of the slave-trade at the time when the General Assembly refused to act upon the subject of slavery at all may be inferred from the following items. The *Virginia Times,* in an article published in this very year of 1836, estimated the number of slaves exported for sale from that state alone, during the twelve months preceding, at forty thousand. The *Natchez* (Miss.) *Courier* says that in the same year the States of Alabama, Missouri, and Arkansas, imported two hundred and fifty thousand slaves from the more northern states. If we deduct from these all who may be supposed to have emigrated with their masters, still what an immense trade is here indicated!

Two years after, the General Assembly, by a sudden and very unexpected movement, passed a vote exscinding, without trial, from the communion of the church, four synods, comprising the most active and decided anti-slavery portions of the church. The reasons alleged were, doctrinal differences and ecclesiastical practices inconsistent with Presbyterianism. By this act about five hundred ministers and sixty thousand members were cut off from the Presbyterian church.

That portion of the Presbyterian church called New School, considering this act unjust, refused to assent to it, joined the exscinded synods, and formed themselves into the New School General Assembly. In this communion only three slaveholding presbyteries remained; in the old there were between thirty and forty.

The course of the Old School Assembly, after the separation, in relation to the subject of slavery, may be best expressed by quoting one of their resolutions, passed in 1845. Having some decided anti-slavery members in its body, and being, moreover, addressed on the subject of slavery by associated bodies, they presented, in this year, the following deliberate statement of their policy. (Minutes for 1845, p. 18.)

"*Resolved,* 1. That the General Assembly of the Presbyterian Church in the United States was originally organized, and has since continued the bond of union in the church, upon the conceded principle that the existence of domestic slavery, under the circumstances in which it is found in the Southern portion of the country, is no bar to Christian communion.

"2. That the petitions that ask the Assembly to make the holding of slaves in itself a matter of discipline do virtually require this judicatory to dissolve itself, and abandon the organization under which, by the Divine blessing, it has so long prospered. The tendency is evidently to separate the Northern from the Southern portion of the church—a result which every good Christian must deplore, as tending to the dissolution of the Union of our beloved country, and which every enlightened Christian will oppose, as bringing about a ruinous and unnecessary schism between brethren who maintain a common faith.

"Yeas, Ministers and Elders, 168.

"Nays, " " " 13."

It is scarcely necessary to add a comment to this very explicit declaration. It is the plainest possible disclaimer of any protest against slavery; the plainest possible statement that the existence of the ecclesiastical organization is of more importance than all the moral and social considerations which are involved in a full defence and practice of American slavery.

The next year a large number of petitions and remonstrances were presented, requesting the Assembly to utter additional testimony against slavery.

In reply to the petitions, the General Assembly reäffirmed all their former testimonies on the subject of slavery for sixty years back, and also affirmed that the previous year's declaration must not be understood as a retraction of that testimony; in other words, they expressed it as their opinion, in the words of 1818, that slavery is *"wholly opposed to the law of God,"* and *"totally irreconcilable with the precepts of the Gospel of Christ;"* and yet that they "had formed their church organization upon the conceded principle that the existence of it, under the circumstances in which it is found in the Southern States of the Union, is no bar to Christian communion."

Some members protested against this action. (Minutes, 1846. Overture No. 17.)

Great hopes were at first entertained of the New School body. As a body, it was composed mostly of anti-slavery men. It had in it those synods whose anti-slavery opinions and actions had been, to say the least, one very efficient cause for their excision from the Church. It had only three slaveholding Presbyteries. The power was all in its own hands. Now, if ever, was their time to cut this loathsome encumbrance wholly adrift, and stand up, in this age of concession and conformity to the world, a purely protesting church, free from all complicity with this most dreadful national immorality.

On the first session of the General Assembly this course was most vehemently urged, by many petitions and memorials. These memorials were referred to a committee of decided anti-slavery men. The argument on one side was, that the time was now come to take decided measures to cut free wholly from all pro-slavery complicity, and avow their principles with decision, even though it should repel all such churches from their communion as were not prepared for immediate emancipation.

On the other hand, the majority of the committee were urged by opposing considerations. The brethren from slave states made to them representations somewhat alike to these: "Brethren, our hearts are with you. We are with you in faith, in charity, in prayer. We sympathized in the injury that had been done you by excision. We stood by you then, and are ready to stand by you still. We have no sympathy with the party that have expelled you, and we do not wish to go back to them. As to this matter of slavery, we do not differ from you. We consider it an evil. We mourn and lament over it. We are trying, by gradual and peaceable means, to exclude it from our churches. We are going as far in advance of the sentiment of our churches as we consistently can. We cannot come up to more decided action without losing our hold over them, and, as we think, throwing back the cause of emancipation. If you begin in this decided manner, we cannot hold our churches in the union; they will divide, and go to the Old School."

Here was a very strong plea, made by good and sincere men. It was an appeal, too, to the most generous feelings of the heart. It was, in effect, saying, "Brothers, we stood by you, and fought your battles, when everything was going against you; and, now that you have the power in your hands, are you going to use it so as to cast us out?"

Those men, strong anti-slavery men as they were, were affected. One member of the committee foresaw and feared the result. He felt and suggested that the course proposed conceded the whole question. The majority thought, on the whole, that it was best to postpone the subject. The committee reported that the applicants, for reasons satisfactory to themselves, had withdrawn their papers.

The next year, in 1839, the subject was resumed; and it was again urged that the Assembly should take high, and decided, and unmistakable ground; and certainly, if we consider that all this time not a single church had emancipated its slaves, and that the power of the institution was everywhere stretching and growing and increasing, it would certainly seem that something more efficient was necessary than a general understanding that the church agreed with the testimony delivered in 1818. It was strongly represented that it was time something was done. This year the Assembly decided to refer the subject to Presbyteries, to do what they deemed advisable. The words employed were these: "Solemnly referring the whole subject to the lower judicatories, to take such action as in their judgment is most judicious, and adapted to remove the evil." The Rev. George Beecher moved to insert the word moral before evil; they declined.*

This brought, in 1840, a much larger number of memorials and petitions; and very strong attempts were made by the abolitionists to obtain some decided action.

The committee this year referred to what had been done last year, and declared it inexpedient to do anything further. The subject was indefinitely postponed. At this time it was resolved that the Assembly should meet only once in three years. Accordingly, it did not meet till 1843. In 1843, several memorials were again presented, and some resolutions offered to the Assembly, of which this was one (Minutes of the General Assembly for 1843, p. 15):

"Resolved, That we affectionately and earnestly urge upon the Ministers, Sessions, Presbyteries, and Synods, connected with this Assembly, that they treat this as all other sins of great magnitude; and by a diligent, kind, and faithful application of the means which God has given them, by instruction, remonstrance, reproof, and effective discipline, seek to purify the church of this great iniquity."

This resolution they declined. They passed the following:

"Whereas there is in this Assembly great diversity of opinion as to the proper and best mode of action on the subject of slavery; and whereas, in such circumstances, any expression of sentiment would carry with it but little weight, as it would be passed by a small majority, and must operate to produce alienation and division; and whereas the Assembly of 1839, with great unanimity, referred this whole subject to the lower judicatories, to take such order as in their judgment might be adapted to remove the evil;—Resolved, That the Assembly do not think it for the edification of the church for this body to take any action on the subject."

They, however, passed the following:

"Resolved, That the fashionable amusement of promiscuous dancing is so entirely unscriptural, and eminently and exclusively that of 'the world which lieth in wickedness,' and so wholly inconsistent with the spirit of Christ, and with that propriety of Christian deport-

*Goodell's History of the Great Struggle between Freedom and Slavery.

ment and that purity of heart which his followers are bound to maintain, as to render it not only improper and injurious for professing Christians either to partake in it, or to qualify their children for it, by teaching them the 'art,' but also to call for the faithful and judicious exercise of discipline on the part of Church Sessions, when any of the members of their churches have been guilty."

Thus has the matter gone on from year to year, ever since.

In 1856 we are sorry to say that we can report no improvement in the action of the great ecclesiastical bodies on the subject of slavery, but rather deterioration. Notwithstanding all the aggressions of slavery, and notwithstanding the constant developments of its horrible influence in corrupting and degrading the character of the nation, as seen in the mean, vulgar, assassin-like outrages in our national Congress, and the brutal, blood-thirsty, fiend-like proceedings in Kansas, connived at and protected, if not directly sanctioned and in part instigated, by our national government;—notwithstanding all this, the great ecclesiastical organizations seem less disposed than ever before to take any efficient action on the subject. This was manifest in the General Conference of the Methodist Episcopal Church North, held at Indianapolis during the spring of the present year, and in the General Assemblies of the Presbyterian Church, held at New York at about the same time.

True, a very large minority in the Methodist Conference resisted with great energy the action, or rather no action, of the majority, and gave fearless utterance to the most noble sentiments; but in the final result the numbers were against them.

The same thing was true to some extent in the New School Presbyterian General Assembly, though here the anti-slavery utterances were, on the whole, inferior to those in the Methodist Conference. In both bodies the Packthreads, and Cushings, and Calkers, and Bonnies, are numerous, and have the predominant influence, while the Dicksons and the Ruskins are fewer, and have far less power. The representations, therefore, in the body of the work, though very painful, are strictly just. Individuals, everywhere in the free states, and in some of the slave states, are most earnestly struggling against the prevailing corruption; but the churches, as such, are, for the most part, still on the wrong side. There are churches free from this stain, but they are neither numerous nor popular.

For an illustration of the lynching of Father Dickson, see "Key to Uncle Tom's Cabin," Part III., Chapter VIII.

EXPLANATORY NOTES

1. *"Away ... dew":* From Thomas Moore (1779–1852), "A Ballad. The Lake of the Dismal Swamp" (1806).

PREFACE

1. *broad regions ... forbidden it to enter:* The Kansas–Nebraska Bill of 1854 repealed the Missouri Compromise of 1820–1821, which prohibited the spread of slavery into the unsettled portions of the Louisiana Purchase north of latitude 36° 30'.
2. *Judge Ruffin:* Judge Thomas Ruffin (1787–1870) of North Carolina issued a famous ruling in the 1829 North Carolina case of *State* v. *Mann* that "the power of the master must be absolute to render the submission of the slave perfect." That decision is "placed in the mouth" of Judge Clayton; see volume II, chapter X.

VOLUME I

CHAPTER I
The Mistress of Canema

1. *Venus:* Roman and Greek goddess of love and beauty; and probably a more specific reference to the Greek statue *Venus de Milo* in the Louvre in Paris.
2. *Byronic:* A reference to the Romantic poet Lord George Gordon Byron (1788–1824). The Byronic hero was known for his dark, brooding rejection of conventional society. Stowe admired Byron, though when she learned of his supposed incestuous relationship with his half-sister Augusta, she published a notorious attack, *Lady Byron Vindicated* (1870).
3. *cachucha:* A Spanish dance resembling the bolero.
4. *billets-doux:* Love letters.

5. *curl-papers:* Papers that fix locks of hair into curls.
6. *Don Juan:* Legendary seducer and social rebel; see Lord Byron's *Don Juan* (1818–1820).
7. *sack pattern:* A pattern for a loose, unbelted dress.

CHAPTER II
Clayton

1. *dramatis personæ:* The characters in a play.
2. *marooning party:* A pleasure party or outing, usually lasting several days.
3. *'Law . . . world':* From Richard Hooker (1554–1600), *Ecclesiastical Polity* (1594–1597), Book I. A clergyman of the Church of England, Hooker argued for the central place of reason in the Church's civil and ecclesiastical policies.
4. *Viri Romæ:* Men of Rome.
5. *Regulus, or Quintus Curtius, or Mucius Scævola:* Famous patriot-martyrs: the Roman general Marcus Atilius Regulus (who died circa 250 B.C.) was tortured to death by the Carthaginians after advising the Romans to reject their conditions for ending the First Punic War; Quintus Curtius voluntarily plunged into a crevice in the floor of the Roman forum in order to fulfill an ancient prophecy that a sacrificial victim was needed to preserve the forum; and Quintus Mucius Scævola was a Roman soldier of the sixth century B.C. who heroically demonstrated his resistance to his captors by placing his hand in flames and refusing to speak.
6. *quadroon:* A term used in the nineteenth century (and less often in the twentieth century) to refer to people who were thought to be one-fourth "black"; more generally, the term referred to light-skinned peoples of mixed racial ancestry.
7. *Mahomet's paradise:* A reference to Muhammed (570–632), founder of Islam.
8. *'What . . . soul?':* Mark 8:36.
9. *'All . . . me':* Matthew 4:9.
10. *Liberator:* Founded in 1831 in Boston by William Lloyd Garrison (1805–1879), the *Liberator* was the best-known and most influential antislavery newspaper of the antebellum period.
11. *'a light . . . gentiles':* Luke 2:32.
12. *Selah:* In Psalms, an instruction to raise the voice, as when praising God.
13. *Ophir:* A region rich in gold and sandalwood trees; see 1 Kings 9:28, 10:11–12.

CHAPTER III
The Clayton Family and Sister Anne

1. *Thaddeus of Warsaw, and William Wallace:* Heroes of the popular novels *Thaddeus of Warsaw* (1803) and *The Scottish Chiefs* (1810) by the Scottish novelist Jane Porter (1776–1850).
2. *'If . . . all':* From Alexander Pope (1688–1744), "The Rape of the Lock" (1712).
3. *White Mountains:* Mountain range in New Hampshire.
4. *Hannah More:* An English author and social reformer, Hannah More (1745–1833) was best known for her religious and philanthropic writings, such as *Thoughts on the Importance of Manners of the Great to General Society* (1788).

CHAPTER IV
The Gordon Family

1. *Eboe:* Ibo—a people of the area around the lower Niger Valley in Africa.
2. *colporteur:* Traveling peddler of Bibles and religious tracts.
3. *rusticated:* Suspended.
4. *Law's Serious Call:* A reference to the British clergyman William Law's (1686–1761) *A Serious Call to a Devout and Holy Life* (1728), a classic of Christian devotional literature.
5. *Owen on the One Hundred and Nineteenth Psalm:* In his writings, the English Puritan John Owen (1616–1683) emphasized Psalm 119 as a particularly resonant devotional text.
6. *somerset:* Somersault.
7. *"We's . . . on us!":* Derived from Luke 17:10.
8. *"upright as the palm-tree":* Jeremiah 10:5. In her 1863 essay, "Sojourner Truth, the Libyan Sibyl," Stowe describes Truth in similar terms.
9. *Madras:* Brightly colored fabric.

CHAPTER V
Harry and His Wife

1. *basque:* Close-fitting woman's garment covering the body from the neckline to the waistline.
2. *les tableaux vivans:* Staged performances of scenes; literally, living pictures.

CHAPTER VI
The Dilemma

1. *Lacedemonians:* Inhabitants of ancient Sparta.

CHAPTER VII
Consultation

1. *Undine:* A popular fairy tale published in 1811 by the German novel-ist and playwright Friedrich de La Motte-Fouqué (1777–1843).
2. *Knight Heldebound:* The knight who marries the water sprite Undine, who seeks to become human through the marriage.

CHAPTER VIII
Old Tiff

1. *gander-pullings:* Southern "sport" in which men compete to pull the heads off ganders.
2. *Governor Berkley:* A passionate Royalist and authoritarian ruler, Sir William Berkeley (1606–1677), colonial governor of Virginia, regularly punished Protestant dissenters and was eventually sent to England and discredited.
3. *'Come . . . rest':* Matthew 11:28.

CHAPTER XI
The Lovers

1. *Xerxes:* King of ancient Persia, Xerxes (486–465 B.C.) led armies against Athens and other Greek cities and was eventually killed by the captain of his own bodyguard unit. The incident mentioned by Clay-ton can be found in the Greek historian Herodotus's chronicles of the Persian wars.
2. *Alexander:* The legendary military and political leader Alexander the Great (356–323 B.C.), king of Macedon, conquered much of Asia be-fore dying of a fever at age thirty-three.
3. *caricoling:* Caracoling; skipping about in a sprightly manner.
4. *Copley and Stuart:* References to the American portrait painters John Singleton Copley (1738–1815) and Gilbert Stuart (1755–1828).
5. *Favorita:* An opera of 1840 by the Italian composer Gaetano Doni-zetti (1797–1848).
6. *Gibbon's . . . Empire:* A reference to Edward Gibbon's (1737–1794) *The History of the Decline and Fall of the Roman Empire*

(1776–88). Gibbon strongly opposed the American Revolution and was criticized by clerics for the historical criticism of Christianity in his famous *History.*

7. *compends:* Compendiums.

8. *Walter Scott's novels:* Among the most widely read novels of the popular British novelist Sir Walter Scott (1771–1832) were the historical romances *Waverley* (1814) and *Ivanhoe* (1819).

9. *Napoleon Bonaparte:* The French general Napoleon Bonaparte (1769–1821), emperor of France from 1804 to 1815, waged intermittent wars against England, Prussia, and other countries beginning around 1796, and was defeated by British forces at Waterloo in 1815.

10. *Presbyterian church:* Protestant Christian denomination that works with a pyramidical structure composed of clerics and lay people. Such a church organization was seen by some antebellum Protestants as more "democratic" than Episcopalianism, which placed a greater emphasis on the role of the bishops and had closer ties to the Anglican church.

CHAPTER XII
Explanations

1. *'cracker funeral':* Derogatory reference to a funeral for a poor white person.

2. *'Our . . . Heaven':* Matthew 6:9.

CHAPTER XIII
Tom Gordon

1. *at sixes and sevens:* In disorder and confusion.

2. *creole:* In Louisiana, usually a reference to a person of Spanish or French ancestry.

3. *tow-string order of women:* "Tow" is a fiber of flax or hemp; the expression suggests parsimony, disorder, and lack of style.

4. *'ravis de vous voir':* Ravished to see you.

5. *'enfant mignon':* Darling child.

6. *Candace queen of Ethiopia:* See Acts 8:27.

CHAPTER XIV
Aunt Nesbit's Loss

1. *hire out:* "Hiring out" was the practice in which a slave was sent to work for someone else for pay. Usually most or all of the money went to the slave's owner.

2. *'See there . . . is'*: 1 Timothy 4:8.
3. *Jesuits . . . Japan:* Under the leadership of Saint Francis Xavier (1506–1552), the Jesuits, a religious order of the Roman Catholic Church, attempted to convert the Japanese; the mission was persecuted and wiped out during the early seventeenth century.
4. *Nat Turner:* In August 1831, the slave Nat Turner (1800–1831) led a slave rebellion in Southampton County, Virginia, which resulted in over two hundred white and black deaths. Southern whites blamed abolitionist meddling for the rebellion, and subsequently strengthened the slave codes. Many Northern blacks regarded Turner as a hero.
5. *Denmark Vesey:* During the early months of 1822, Denmark Vesey (1767?–1822), a free black Charleston carpenter, recruited numerous Charleston blacks to join him in a plot to rise up against the whites at an agreed-upon time and take the city. In June, nervous house servants exposed the plot to white authorities, and Vesey and many of his compatriots were executed.

CHAPTER XV
Mr. Jekyl's Opinions

1. *a curse upon Canaan:* When Noah's son Ham viewed him naked and drunk, Noah cursed Ham's son Canaan, declaring that he would henceforth be regarded as a servant; see Genesis 9:20–28. Proslavery writers often cited this moment as providing biblical justification for slavery.

CHAPTER XVI
Milly's Story

1. *'De Lord . . . want':* Psalms 23:1.
2. *Since Missouri came in:* The Missouri Compromise of 1820–1821 admitted Missouri to the Union as a slave state.
3. *chincapins:* Chinquapins; shrubby chestnuts.
4. *'render unto her double!':* The phrase has its source in Zechariah 9:12. In the *Narrative of Sojourner Truth* (1850), Truth makes a similar curse on her slave mistress.
5. *Nemesis:* Greek goddess of divine retribution.
6. *Sinai:* When the Israelites escaped from Egypt, they entered the wilderness of Sinai; see Exodus 19.
7. *"Lord . . . threshing-floor":* See 1 Chronicles 21:18–29.
8. *'O . . . arguments':* Job 23:3–4.
9. *'He . . . all things':* Romans 8:32.

10. *Calvary:* The place where Jesus was crucified; see Luke 23:33.
11. *"blood . . . Lamb":* See Revelation 7:14, 12:11; the passage refers to Christ's sacrifice.

CHAPTER XVII
Uncle John

1. *Hesperides:* In Greek mythology, Hesperides were clear-voiced maidens who watched over the tree bearing golden apples that Gaea gave to Hera at her marriage to Zeus.
2. *delirium tremens:* Trembling and anxiety brought on by an excessive consumption of alcohol.

CHAPTER XVIII
Dred

1. *Dismal:* A massive, densely forested and tangled swamp located in southeast Virginia and northeast North Carolina, the Dismal Swamp acquired a reputation during the antebellum period as an area of hiding for fugitive slaves.
2. *Parthian:* A reference to Parthia, an ancient country in west Asia conquered by the Iranians in A.D. 226. The Parthians were known as legendary archers.
3. *phrenologists:* Practitioners of phrenology, a popular pseudoscience of the antebellum period. Phrenologists believed that an individual's mental and moral traits could be determined by studying the shape of his or her skull.
4. *naphtha:* A volatile fuel.
5. *. . . 'it shall':* As is true for many of his speeches, Dred's fundamental biblical source is Exodus's account of Moses leading the Israelites from Egyptian bondage.
6. *Meroz:* See Judges 5:23; Meroz was cursed by an angel of the Lord for not helping the covenanted people.
7. *". . . for a prey!":* Dred's speech draws on Jeremiah 12:3; Lamentations 3:30; and Judges 5:23.
8. *kiss the rod:* To accept punishment submissively as the working of God.
9. *fip:* Short for fippenny piece, a Spanish silver coin worth about six cents.
10. *'Servants . . . masters':* Ephesians 6:5.
11. *Abel:* The son of Adam and Eve, Abel was killed by his brother Cain; see Genesis 4:1–8. In Matthew 23:35, Abel is described as the first martyr.

CHAPTER XIX
The Conspirators

1. *"Resistance . . . God":* A passage found in the papers of Thomas Jefferson (1743–1826) after his death.
2. *an account of the insurrection:* A reference to *An Official Report of the Trials of Sundry Negroes, Charged with an Attempt to Raise an Insurrection in the State of South Carolina* (Charleston, 1822), which Stowe draws on for her account of Denmark Vesey's trial. On Denmark Vesey, see also note 5, chapter XIV.
3. *"Hercules and the Wagoner":* Fable told by Aesop (circa sixth century B.C.) and retold by Babrius (circa second century A.D.); the moral in Aesop is that self-help is the best help.
4. *Mandingo:* A people of West Africa living in the area of the upper Niger Valley.
5. *Vaudois:* French for Waldenses, a Protestant religious sect organized in the twelfth century by Peter Waldo that preached the value of apostolic poverty as the path to perfection. The group participated in the Protestant Reformation and was persecuted in Switzerland during the seventeenth century.
6. *nail of Jael . . . with himself:* Refers to heroic Israelites of Judges who used violence to defeat their enemies: Jael, the wife of Heber, drove a nail through the head of the defeated commander of Canaan's army while he slept (Judges 4:17–22); Shamgar killed 600 Philistines with an ox goad (Judges 3:31, 5:6); Gideon helped the Israelites defeat the Midianites during a battle in which he and his men blew trumpets in the name of the Lord (Judges 7); and Samson destroyed his Philistine enemies and himself when he pulled down the Philistines' temple with his bare hands (Judges 16).
7. *Elijah . . . honey:* The Hebrew prophet Elijah survived forty days and nights on the mountain of God (Horeb) with the help of a meal sent by an angel of God; see 1 Kings 19:8. On John the Baptist's preaching in the wilderness, see Matthew 3.
8. *strange hieroglyphics . . . upon the leaves:* In *The Confessions of Nat Turner* (1831), Turner described how he "found in the leaves in the woods hieroglyphic characters."

CHAPTER XX
Summer Talk at Canema

1. *Pharaoh's lean kine:* See Genesis 41; "kine" is an archaic word for cows.

2. *Norma:* A popular opera by Vincenzo Bellini (1801–1835), first performed in 1831.
3. *'diggings':* Living quarters.
4. *camp-meeting:* Outdoor religious gathering, sometimes lasting several days.

CHAPTER XXI
Tiff's Preparations

1. *Grace Church:* One of New York City's more fashionable churches.
2. *Canaan:* The Promised Land of the Israelites.
3. *Methodists:* Protestant Christian denomination inspired by the teachings of John Wesley (1703–1791), who emphasized rule and method in religious conduct.
4. *Baptists:* Protestant Christian denomination that emphasizes the importance of baptism—a rite of purification by water that symbolizes God's grace in freeing individuals from sin.
5. *fatted calf:* Sacrificial calf in Luke 15:23–30.

CHAPTER XXII
The Worshippers

1. *the five points of Calvinism:* Doctrines central to Lyman Beecher's beliefs: total depravity (the idea that all humans are sinful); unconditional election (God decides whom to save as an expression of His will, and salvation is not based on anything outside of or beyond His will); limited atonement (Jesus Christ died only for the elect); irresistible grace (those of the elect called into salvation cannot resist His call); perseverance of the Saints (those who are saved are eternally secure in Christ). Stowe came to believe that Christ offered salvation to the converted.
2. *helot:* Slave.
3. *vocation:* A reference to the Compromise of 1850's Fugitive Slave Law, which mandated that all U.S. citizens were legally obligated to return runaway slaves to their masters.
4. *"Am I . . . Lamb":* From a hymn by Isaac Watts (1674–1748), in Henry Ward Beecher's *Plymouth Collection of Hymns and Times* (New York: A. S. Barnes, 1855), p. 178. Beecher's hymnbook was a source for many of the hymns in the novel.
5. *Revised Statutes of North Carolina:* In response to the circulation of David Walker's *Appeal* (1829), which called on slaves to kill their mas-

ters, and to the Nat Turner rebellion of 1831, North Carolina, like other Southern states, revised its slave codes during 1830–1832.

6. *curse of Cain:* Angered by Cain's killing of his brother· Abel, God placed a mark on Cain as a sign of His curse; see Genesis 4:15.

CHAPTER XXIII
The Camp-Meeting

1. *thunders of Sinai:* According to some accounts, Moses received the Ten Commandments on Mount Sinai in northeast Egypt.
2. *'Isn't . . . fruit':* 2 Timothy 2:6.
3. *"In journeyings . . . burn not?":* 2 Corinthians 11:26–29.
4. *'Ye . . . you':* Leviticus 25:44–46.
5. *Mount Zion:* Emblematic of Jerusalem, the Promised Land.
6. *Emanuel's chariot-wheels:* Reference to Jesus Christ in His role as messiah; see Isaiah 7:14, 8:8, and Matthew 1:23.
7. *free grace:* As opposed to the Calvinistic doctrine that God offered salvation only to the elect, many evangelical Protestants preached the doctrine of free grace—that Christ offered salvation to believers.
8. *John Wesley:* The founder of Methodism, the English evangelical John Wesley (1703–1791) preached the importance of methodically undertaking religious duties; he also championed the concept of free grace.
9. *pro tem.:* For the time being.
10. *"The heavens . . . knowledge":* Psalms 19:1–2.
11. *"Woe unto you . . . surely visit you!":* Dred's sermonic speech draws on the following biblical passages: Joel 2:1–2; Amos 5:18, 21–22, 8:4–7; Exodus 13:19.
12. *"Hear . . . desolate!":* The remainder of Dred's sermon draws on the following biblical passages: Isaiah 14:13, 19; Amos 8:9; Joel 3:15; Nahum 3:1–5.
13. *". . . thou me?":* The four stanzas of Dickson's hymn are from William Cowper's (1731–1800) "Hyacinth," in Beecher, *Plymouth Collection*, p. 268.
14. *"what . . . soul?":* See Mark 8:36.
15. *slave-coffle:* Slaves tied together to form a train.
16. *'He . . . hand?':* Isaiah 44:20.
17. *"Cursed be Canaan":* From Genesis 9:25; see also chapter XV, note 1.
18. *"He . . . lose it":* See John 12:25.
19. *" 'What have I done?' The temple . . . are we!":* See Jeremiah 7:4.
20. *"Then . . . broken":* See Ecclesiastes 12:6.
21. *"I must . . . outcasts!":* Dred's remarks to Harry draw on Matthew 8:20 and Isaiah 35:7.

VOLUME II

CHAPTER I
Life in the Swamps

1. *en rapport:* In relation.
2. *mesmerists:* Practitioners of the forms of hypnosis championed by the French revolutionary utopianist Franz Anton Mesmer (1734–1815). Mesmerism was in vogue in the United States during the 1840s and 1850s.
3. *Highland seers:* Reference to the prophets, visionaries, and rebels of the mountainous region in northern Scotland (the Highlands) who had traditionally rejected the authority of the Scottish monarchy.
4. *demoniac of Gadara:* See Matthew 8:28; a reference to two possessed men of an ancient town near the Sea of Galilee.
5. *"Wake . . . fire!":* See Isaiah 51:9, Psalms 29:4–8. Kadesh was an oasis in the desert south of Palestine.
6. *"Rend . . . them!":* See Psalms 144:5–6.
7. *opening of the seals:* Drawn from Revelation 6:1; reference to the events leading to the millennial coming of the Kingdom of God on earth.
8. *Arcturus and Orion:* According to Greek mythology, the giant-sized hunter Orion was slain by Artemis and placed in the sky as a constellation; the Greeks regarded the bright star Arcturus as the guardian of the bear.
9. *"He . . . lies":* See Isaiah 28:17.

CHAPTER II
More Summer Talk

1. *Five Points:* A slum in Manhattan's Sixth Ward notorious during the nineteenth century as a center of vice and debauchery.
2. *'The earth . . . mine':* From a hymn by John Newton (1725–1807), in Beecher, *Plymouth Collection*, p. 180.
3. *'Let . . . laws':* From Andrew Fletcher of Saltoun's (1653–1716) *Political Works* (1703). Fletcher fought for Scottish independence.
4. *Caliban:* The misshapen "evil" character of Shakespeare's *The Tempest* (c. 1611).
5. *anathema maranatha:* See 1 Corinthians 16:22; a reference to those who do not love Jesus Christ.
6. *Jenny Lind:* A phenomenally popular singer of the time, Jenny Lind (1820–1887) was known as the "Swedish Nightingale."

CHAPTER V
Magnolia Grove

1. *water-cure:* Popular during the nineteenth century, particularly among middle- and upper-class women, hydropathy (or water cure) emphasized bathing and filling the body with water as a way of restoring health. Stowe herself took the water cure at a resort in Brattleboro, Vermont, in 1846.
2. *against the law to do it:* In North Carolina and other Southern states, it was illegal to teach slaves how to read or write; many of these laws were instituted (or more strictly enforced) after the 1831 slave rebellion led by Nat Turner.
3. *serfs were in England:* The practice of serfdom, a form of semi-bondage, disappeared in England in the late Middle Ages.
4. *Aaron's rod:* Aaron was the brother of Moses and first high priest of the Hebrews; Jehovah worked miracles on his rod, changing it into a serpent and causing it to bear almonds. See Exodus 7.
5. *the insurrection in Charleston:* Denmark Vesey's conspiracy.
6. *insurrections in Italy, Austria, and Hungary:* A reference to the European revolutions of 1848, which were generally regarded in the U.S. as republican revolutions against aristocratic and despotic powers.

CHAPTER VI
The Troubadour

1. *Arcadia:* A relatively isolated area of ancient Greece traditionally celebrated as a paradise.
2. *Gesner's Idyls:* Reference to the Swiss poet and artist Salomon Gesner (1730–1788), whose pastoral poems *Idyllen* (1756) were popular in English translations.
3. *Cobolds:* Kobolds; in German folklore, spirits who haunt houses and perform useful services.
4. *Phillis Wheatly:* The African-American poet Phillis Wheatley (1753–1784) was the author of *Poems* (1773), which were popular in England in the late eighteenth century. Her work was republished and widely disseminated by antebellum abolitionists.
5. *'that . . . music':* From Francis Bacon's (1561–1626) "Of Gardens" (1625).

CHAPTER VII
Tiff's Garden

1. *'Where . . . worship Him':* Matthew 2:1–2.
2. *Herod:* A ruler of Palestine at the time of Jesus' birth, Herod was subject to fits of insanity and, as described in Matthew 2, executed all of the children of Bethlehem (the "slaughter of the innocents") in the hope of killing the child Jesus.
3. *"Cold . . . all":* From a hymn by Reginald Heber (1783–1826), in Beecher, *Plymouth Collection,* p. 90.
4. *Galilee:* A region in northern Israel and the chief locale of the ministry of Jesus, the "child of Bethlehem."
5. *"The grass . . . forever":* Isaiah 40:8.

CHAPTER VIII
The Warning

1. *"The case . . . gone against us":* For a discussion of similar cases, see Stowe, *A Key to Uncle Tom's Cabin,* part 2, chapter 13.
2. *"within two or three votes . . . assembly":* In the aftermath of Nat Turner's slave rebellion of 1831, the Virginia legislature met in 1832 to debate the future of slavery in the state. A proposition supporting gradual emancipation of the slaves was defeated by a margin of fifteen votes (73 to 58).
3. *"the destroying angel . . . drawn!":* See Numbers 22:23, 31.
4. *"The words . . . dead!":* See Ezekiel 2:9–10, Exodus 12:30.
5. *'Whom . . . come':* Isaiah 57:1.
6. *cholera:* There were major cholera epidemics in the North and South in 1832 and 1849.

CHAPTER IX
The Morning Star

1. *"When . . . seek":* Psalms 27:8.
2. *'Can . . . them?':* Matthew 9:15.
3. *'perfect . . . fear':* 1 John 4:18.
4. *"a little child shall lead them":* See Isaiah 11:6.

CHAPTER X
The Legal Decision

1. *criminaliter:* Criminally.
2. *". . . each other":* See the discussion of Judge Ruffin's 1829 decision on

State v. *Mann* (1829) in Stowe, *A Key to Uncle Tom's Cabin*, part 2, chapter 2. Stowe appropriates the language of that decision for Judge Clayton's decision.

3. *"Fiat justitia ruat cœlum":* Let there be justice, even if the heavens crumble; see William Watson's (1559?–1603) *A Decacordon of Ten Quodlibeticall Questions Concerning Religion and State* (1602) for the first known citing of this maxim in an English work.

CHAPTER XI
The Cloud Bursts

1. *"The . . . darkness":* Psalms 91:6.
2. *au fait:* Qualified.
3. *miasma and animalculæ:* Noxious germs and microorganisms.
4. *"Fear not . . . thy God":* Isaiah 41:10.
5. *'passeth all understanding':* Philippians 4:7.
6. *'Christ . . . life':* See 1 John 5:11, 13.
7. *"He that dwelleth . . . thy ways":* Psalms 91:1–7, 11.
8. *"And they brought . . . heaven":* Mark 10:14.

CHAPTER XII
The Voice in the Wilderness

1. *"Throned . . . day!":* From a hymn by Isaac Watts, in Beecher, *Plymouth Collection*, p. 106.
2. *"O God . . . tremble!":* See Habakkuk 3:5–9. Midian, or Midianites, were a nomadic people of east Palestine; Cushan is obscure, though some identify the name with the African Cush.
3. *"I know whom . . . sound!":* See Revelation 8:10–13; 14:14–20.
4. *"Weep . . . Lamb":* See Jeremiah 22:10; Revelation 14:1, 14:5.

CHAPTER XIII
The Evening Star

1. *"The Hindoo Dancing-Girl's Song":* Stowe probably had in mind one of these two popular antebellum songs: Howard Z. Crosby's "The Hindoo Girl's Song" (1843), published by G. Willis in Philadelphia; Alfred H. Coon's "The Hindoo Girl's Song" (1846), published by Benteen in Baltimore.
2. *hartshorn:* The antler of a male deer.
3. *"They watched . . . ours":* From Thomas Hood (1799–1845), "The Death Bed" (1825).

CHAPTER XIV
The Tie Breaks

1. *the race of Ham:* In Genesis, when Noah's son Ham viewed him lying naked in a drunken stupor, Noah cursed Ham's descendants. See Genesis 9:20–28. Oral traditions collected in the Talmud claimed that the curse resulted in Ham having black descendants; this interpretation was echoed by racists in the eighteenth and nineteenth century.
2. *Sodom and Gomorrah:* The proverbially evil Cities of the Plain destroyed by Jehovah; see Genesis 18–19.
3. *"them who stone Stephen!":* Stephen was one of the seven chosen men of the Holy Spirit; his miracles were greeted with scorn (see Acts 6).
4. *gutta-percha cane:* A cane made from the gum of a sap tree. In May 1856, South Carolina congressman Preston Brooks attacked Massachusetts senator Charles Sumner with a gutta-percha cane.

CHAPTER XVII
The Flight into Egypt

1. *shin round:* To walk fast, move to obey an order quickly.
2. *". . . de coals!":* Tiff's remarks draw on Genesis 16:7, 1 Kings 19:5–6. Hagar was the handmaid, or slave, of Abraham's wife, Sarah, and mother of Abraham's eldest son, Ishmael. As a result of Sarah's jealous rage, Hagar and Ishmael were sent out into the wilderness.
3. *"Hush . . . head":* From Isaac Watts's "Cradle Hymn," in Beecher, *Plymouth Collection*, p. 441.
4. *"Jacob . . . pillow":* In Genesis 28, Jacob takes a stone for a pillow and dreams of beholding a ladder to heaven. Upon awakening, he makes the stone into a consecrated pillar named Beth-el (house of God).
5. *"As one . . . Lebanon":* See Isaiah 66:13, Hosea 14:5.
6. *"They . . . shelter":* An ironic reworking of Job 24:8, which presents God as concerned that the unholy "embrace the Rock for want of a shelter."
7. *corn-dodgers:* Bread made of fried or baked corn meal.
8. *"May . . . night":* A reference to 1 Kings 17:6.
9. *"The Lord God . . . them":* See Ezekiel 34:25, 27.
10. *"Issachar . . . tribute":* Genesis 49:14–15. Issachar was the son of Jacob and Leah and ancestor of one of the twelve tribes of Israel.
11. *"you . . . wilderness":* See Isaiah 16:3, Jeremiah 15:20, 2 Samuel 20:6.
12. *"We . . . young":* Dred's words draw on God's urging of Moses to watch over the children of Israel; see Deuteronomy 32:11.
13. *"moccasons lie on the tussocks":* Water moccasins are poisonous snakes; tussocks are clumps of grass in thickets.

CHAPTER XVIII
The Clerical Conference

1. *compromise . . . a union:* The wording suggests parallels between clerical compromises and the Compromise of 1850, which Stowe ab-
horred.
2. *"With . . . god":* Isaiah 44:16–17.
3. *eighteen hundred and eighteen:* In 1818, a general assembly of the
Presbyterian church voted to affirm that slavery was inconsistent with
the law of God. But the same assembly also adopted the position that
immediate emancipation posed grave threats to the nation.
4. *"Am I . . . be thine":* From a hymn by Isaac Watts, in Beecher, *Plymouth Collection*, p. 178.
5. *Ignatius Loyola:* The Spanish churchman Ignatius of Loyola (1491–
1556) was the founder of the Jesuits, a religious order of the Roman
Catholic Church.
6. *"Our . . . world":* 2 Corinthians 1:12.

CHAPTER XIX
The Result

1. *'Nay . . . dishonor?:* See Romans 9:20–21.
2. *'Masters . . . flesh.'* See Colossians 4:1, Ephesians 6:5.
3. *Chrysostom and Tertullian:* Saint John Chrysostom (c. 347–407)
worked to advance Christianity in Greece and Rome and was eventually banished, dying in exile at an isolated spot near the Black Sea; Tertullian (Quintus Septimus Florens Tertullianus, c. 160–c. 230) was a
Roman theologian and defender of Christianity who established his
own sect circa 213.
4. *pro nullis, pro mortuis:* As nothing, as dead.
5. *Judah:* The fourth son of Jacob and Leah and ancestor of one of the
twelve tribes of Israel.

CHAPTER XX
The Slave's Argument

1. *'The powers . . . God':* Romans 13:1–2.
2. *Alexandria:* A city in northeast Virginia.
3. *"murdered her two children":* In a sensational case of 1856, the fugitive slave Margaret Garner attempted to kill her four children rather
than have them reenslaved; one of the children died.
4. *"Covenantors and the Quakers . . . and the Free-will Baptists":* Christian groups committed to antislavery. Founded by George Fox

(1624–1691), the Quakers, or Society of Friends, were especially well known for their commitment to nonviolence and abolitionism. See the chapter "The Quaker Settlement" in Stowe's *Uncle Tom's Cabin.* Most Freewill Baptists were based in New England; Covenanters had roots in Scottish Presbyterianism.

CHAPTER XXI
The Desert

1. *the Marseillaise:* The French national anthem, based on a revolutionary battle song composed in 1792.
2. *"They are the hundred... their forehead' ":* Revelation 7:3–4.
3. '*. . . and the left':* Dred's speech draws on Isaiah 51:22, Zechariah 11:4–14, 12:1–6.
4. *"flock of the slaughter":* Zechariah 11:4.
5. *'Speak . . . hearts':* See Isaiah 29:14.

CHAPTER XXII
Jegar Sahadutha

1. *Jegar Sahadutha:* Heap of witness, or cairn, raised by Jacob and his uncle Laban as a mark of their covenant; see Genesis 31:47.
2. *Nahor:* Abraham's brother (Genesis 22:20–23, Joshua 24:2).
3. *scourging:* Whipping with a lash.
4. *". . . potter's vessel":* Dred's speech draws on Joel 3:13, 3:2–3; Amos 2:6–7, 2:13; Isaiah 30:6, 8–14. Jehoshaphat was a king of Judah during the ninth century B.C.; see 1 Kings 22.
5. *"Who . . . strength?":* See Isaiah 63:1. Edom was another name for Esau, the brother of Jacob, and for the land given to him and his descendants; Bozrah was an important city of Edom.
6. *"I that . . . to save!":* See Isaiah 63:1.
7. *"Wherefore . . . fury!":* See Isaiah 63:2–6.
8. *"the vision . . . thereof?":* See Revelation 8:1–3.
9. *"Alas . . . I?":* From a hymn by Isaac Watts, in Beecher, *Plymouth Collection,* p. 144.
10. *"Agonizing . . . suffice?":* From a hymn by an unidentified author, in Beecher, *Plymouth Collection,* p. 118.
11. *Peter:* St. Peter was one of Christ's apostles.
12. *"Vengeance . . . Lord":* See Romans 12:19.

CHAPTER XXIII
Frank Russel's Opinions

1. *D.D:* Doctor of Divinity.
2. *three fifths vote:* As established by the U.S. Constitution, each slave counted for three-fifths of a person in determining a state's congressional representation. Thus, antislavery writers asserted, there was actually incentive for Southern states to increase the number of their slaves.
3. *'that . . . battalions':* Frederick the Great (1712–1786) was king of Prussia. In the *Decline and Fall of the Roman Empire* (1776), Edward Gibbon ascribes the quote to Voltaire.
4. *Trumpet of Liberty:* Probably an invented title, though an obscure newspaper with that title was printed in Tennessee in the late 1830s.
5. *"Liberty and union . . . inseparable":* Daniel Webster (1782–1852) in his "Second Speech on Foot's Resolution" (1830). Delivered during his congressional debates with South Carolinian Robert Hayne (1791–1839) on the tariff, nullification, and states' rights, the speech was one of Webster's most impassioned in favor of nationalistic unification. The Foot Resolution, sponsored by Samuel Foot (1780–1846) of Connecticut, sought to limit the sale of public lands and was opposed by Southern states' rights advocates and those who championed western expansionism.
6. *Joab:* Violent and vindictive commander of David's army; see 2 Samuel 3, 18, 20.
7. *annex Cuba and the Sandwich Islands:* Central to antebellum U.S. expansionism were efforts to take control of Cuba and the Hawaiian islands. Because slavery was legal in Cuba, antislavery writers were especially resistant to plans to purchase or invade the Spanish-controlled island.

CHAPTER XXV
Lynch Law

1. *'Man . . . alone':* Matthew 4:4, Luke 4:4.
2. *"He is beside himself":* Mark 3:21.
3. *"Jesus, I my cross have taken . . . wilt thou repine?":* A hymn by "Miss Grant," in Beecher, *Plymouth Collection,* p. 274.
4. *"You know . . . themselves?":* See Daniel 6:24.
5. *"set on fire of hell":* James 3:6.
6. *Lovejoy:* In 1837, the abolitionist editor Elijah Lovejoy (1802–1837) was killed in Alton, Illinois, by a proslavery mob that stormed the press of his *Observer.*

7. *Dresser:* An abolitionist and peace advocate, Amos Dresser (1812–1904), in the summer of 1835, attempted to distribute antislavery literature in the South. In a highly publicized incident, a vigilance committee in Tennessee subjected him to a public whipping.
8. *'These . . . hither':* Acts 17:6.
9. *'Christ's . . . world':* John 18:36.
10. *'If . . . another':* Matthew 10:23.

CHAPTER XXVI
More Violence

1. *"They . . . strength":* See Isaiah 40:31.
2. *'When . . . him':* Isaiah 59:19.
3. *the chivalry of South Carolina:* An ironic reference to South Carolina congressman Preston Brooks's vicious caning of Massachusetts senator Charles Sumner in May 1856.
4. *"Woe . . . man!":* See Psalms 5:6, 55:23.
5. *Philistines:* Non-Semitic peoples who inhabited Palestine, the Philistines, according to the Hebrew Bible, were for centuries the enemies of the Israelites.
6. *Engedi . . . Gaza:* An oasis on the west shore of the Dead Sea, Engedi was where David hid from Saul (Joshua 15:62, 1 Samuel 24:1–4). Gaza was the principal city of the Philistines. Among Samson's heroic actions was his lifting of the gates of Gaza (Judges 16:1–3).

CHAPTER XXVII
Engedi

1. *Cassandra:* According to Greek legend, Cassandra was a Trojan princess with the power of prophecy. After she spurned Apollo's advances, he made her prophetic powers a curse by ensuring that no one would believe her prophecies. She eventually became the slave of Agamemnon and was killed by his wife, Clytemnestra.
2. *"O, Lamb of God . . . shall come!":* Dred's speech draws on Revelations 6:16, Habakkuk 1:13–17, Haggai 2:7.
3. *Brown:* In direct response to proslavery attacks on antislavery groups in Kansas, the militant antislavery crusader John Brown (1800–1859) led a raid on proslavery groups at Pottawatomie Creek, killing five settlers. Brown became best known for his effort to spark a slave insurrection by taking the federal arsenal at Harpers Ferry. He was captured and hanged in December 1859.
4. *"I . . . come!":* Acts 2:19–20.

5. *"When . . . flight!"*: An allusion to Deuteronomy 32:30.
6. *'Their land . . . earth!'*: Isaiah 2:7–19. Bashan was a region east of Jordan conquered by the Israelites, and Tarshish was a country distant from Palestine, traditionally identified with Spain.
7. *"Heaven . . . fulfilled!"*: See Matthew 24:34–35.
8. *'O . . . past!'*: Job 40:13.
9. *"O . . . wilderness!"*: Psalms 55:6–7.
10. *"I know . . . people!"*: See Isaiah 66:22, 6:5.

CHAPTER XXVIII
The Slave Hunt

1. *Old Sam:* The devil.
2. *"Border Ruffians"*: Term used by antislavery Northerners to describe the militant proslavery forces attempting to intimidate Kansas into adopting a proslavery state constitution.
3. *Æneas:* According to classical legend, the founder of Rome. His heroic deeds are at the center of Virgil's *Aeneid*.
4. *the sacking of Lawrence:* In May 1856 proslavery forces attacked the free-state town of Lawrence, Kansas.

CHAPTER XXIX
"All Over"

1. *John saw around the river of life:* A reference to John the Baptist; see Mark 1:5.
2. *'behold . . . altar'*: Matthew 23:34–35. "Zacharias" is probably a reference to the prophet Zechariah, son of Barachias (Berechiah).
3. *Okerecoke:* Ocracoke Island and adjoining inlet off the North Carolina coast.
4. *Amraphal:* King of Shinar, who warred against the kings of Sodom and Gomorrah; see Genesis 14.
5. *"the whole . . . travaileth"*: See Romans 8:22.
6. *" . . . no more sea"*: See Revelation 21:1.
7. *"He shall sit . . . head"*: See Revelation 10:1.
8. *"Shall the axe magnify . . . it?"*: See Isaiah 10:15.
9. *"the wilderness of Kadesh"*: See Deuteronomy 1:19.
10. *"Behold . . . night!"*: Dred's remark draws on Luke 18:7.
11. *"O . . . blood!"*: See Job 16:18.

CHAPTER XXX
The Burial

1. *Toussaint:* A self-educated former slave, Toussaint L'Ouverture (c. 1744–1803) was one of the leaders of the late eighteenth-century Haitian uprising against French colonial rule. The slave uprising resulted in the deaths of tens of thousands of blacks and whites between 1791 and 1804, and ultimately led to the emergence of Haiti as an independent black nation in the Americas. Toussaint became the governor of San Domingo in 1801. In 1802 Napoleon sent troops in a last-gasp effort to regain control of the region. Toussaint was arrested and deported to France, where he died in prison a martyr to the principles of liberty in an age of revolution.
2. *"Thou . . . mind":* From William Wordsworth (1770–1850), "To Toussaint L'Ouverture" (1803).

CHAPTER XXXI
The Escape

1. *underground railroad:* The name for the network of antislavery workers and sympathizers who helped slaves escape from slavery to freedom by hiding them in homes and other places of refuge.
2. *Norfolk:* A seaport in southeast Virginia.
3. *National Era:* Antislavery newspaper published in Washington, D.C., from 1847 to 1860. *Uncle Tom's Cabin* was serialized in the paper from June 1851 to April 1852.
4. *Col. Buford's regiment:* In 1856, a certain Colonel Jefferson Buford of Alabama, who spent around $20,000 of his own money, led a proslavery contingent of over 300 men into Kansas.

CHAPTER XXXII
Lynch Law Again

1. *general post-office . . . Charleston:* On the evening of July 29, 1835, Charleston citizens broke into the local post office, seized abolitionist publications, and ignited them in a public bonfire. Around this time there were increasing calls in Southern states for the suppression of "incendiary" abolitionist materials.
2. *anti-slavery paper, edited at Washington:* The *National Era.* (In theory, then, Clayton could have read *Uncle Tom's Cabin*!)
3. *commissioner . . . to Charleston:* In an effort to keep free Northern blacks from interacting with the free and enslaved blacks of the South, Southern officials, in the wake of Nat Turner's rebellion, imposed laws

requiring that free black sailors be imprisoned while their ships made stops in Southern ports. These acts outraged abolitionists, and in 1844 Massachusetts sent Samuel Hoar (1778–1856) as a commissioner to South Carolina to lodge a formal protest. He was greeted by angry mobs and quickly returned to Massachusetts.

4. *'Council of Ten':* Secretive ruling body of republican Venice.
5. *'the hand of Joab is in this thing':* See 2 Samuel 14:19.
6. *ignobile vulgus:* Vulgar or common people of low character; a derogatory reference to the masses.
7. *Liberia:* The American Colonization Society founded this East African colony in the early 1820s as the appropriate "home" for the free blacks.

CHAPTER XXXIII
Flight

1. *Lake . . . pillow:* See Mark 4:37–38; Lake Gennesareth was another name for the Sea of Galilee.
2. *"Weeping . . . morning":* Psalms 30:5.
3. *the community:* Founded around 1850 in southwestern Canada West by William King (1812–1895), a Presbyterian minister, the Elgin community overcame initial white resistance to emerge as a model black agricultural community. By 1861 approximately 300 families lived on its 10,000-acre grounds.
4. *"none to molest or make afraid":* Zechariah 3:10.
5. *Cæsar's Commentaries:* Caius Julius Caesar (102?–44 B.C.), *Commentaries on the Gallic War* and *Commentaries on the Civil War.*

CHAPTER XXXIV
Clear Shining After Rain

1. *"her eye . . . abated":* In Deuteronomy 34:7 (with "his eye" instead of "her eye") a reference to Moses.